Leah

W9-BRV-515

Crossing California

Crossing California

ADAM LANGER

RIVERHEAD BOOKS

a member of Penguin Group (USA) Inc.

New York

2004

This is a work of fiction. Names, characters, places, and incidents either are the product of the author's imagination or are used fictitiously, and any resemblance to actual persons, living or dead, businesses, companies, events, or locales is entirely coincidental.

Riverhead Books
a member of
Penguin Group (USA) Inc.
375 Hudson Street
New York, NY 10014

Copyright © 2004 by Adam Langer
All rights reserved. No part of this book may be reproduced, scanned, or distributed in any printed or electronic form without permission. Please do not participate in or encourage piracy of copyrighted materials in violation of the author's rights. Purchase only authorized editions.
Published simultaneously in Canada

Library of Congress Cataloging-in-Publication Data

Langer, Adam.
Crossing California / Adam Langer.
p.   cm.
ISBN 1-57322-274-7
1. Jews—Illinois—Chicago—Fiction.   2. Jewish families—Fiction.
3. Chicago (Ill.)—Fiction.   I. Title.
PS3612.A57C76   2004   2003066719
813'.6—dc22

Printed in the United States of America
1   3   5   7   9   10   8   6   4   2

This book is printed on acid-free paper. ∞

Book design by Stephanie Huntwork
Map by Jeffrey L. Ward

To my parents, Esther and Seymour Langer.

And, of course, to Beate.

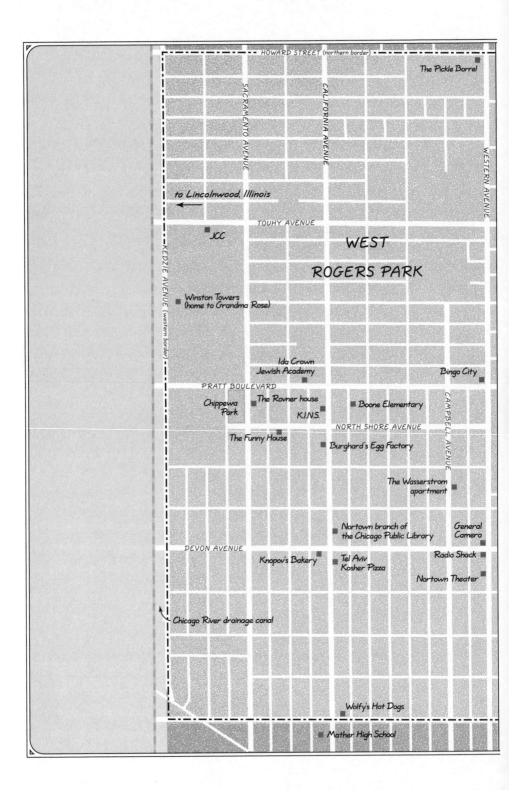

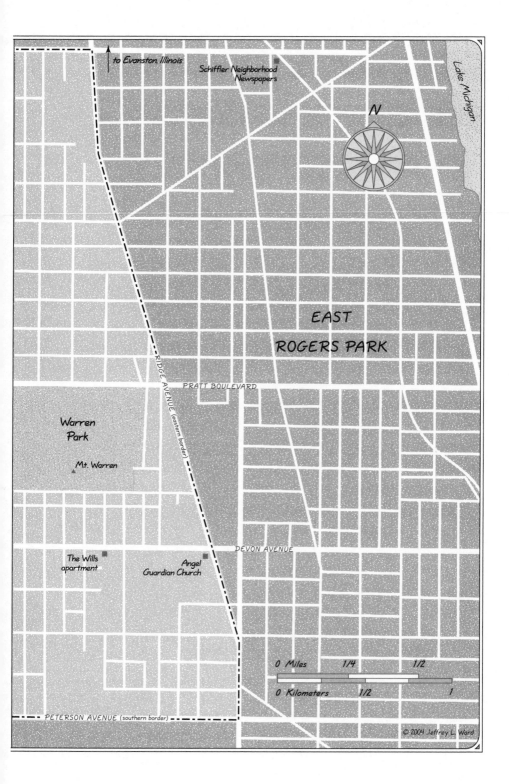

to Evanston, Illinois

Schiffler Neighborhood
Newspapers

Lake Michigan

N

EAST

ROGERS PARK

PRATT BOULEVARD

Warren
Park

Mt. Warren

RIDGE AVENUE (eastern border)

DEVON AVENUE

The Wills
apartment

Angel
Guardian Church

0 Miles   1/4   1/2

0 Kilometers   1/2   1

PETERSON AVENUE (southern border)

© 2004 Jeffrey L. Ward

"We are at a turning point in our history. There are two paths to choose."

—JIMMY CARTER, 1979

"Those who say that we are in a time when there are no heroes just don't know where to look."

—RONALD REAGAN, 1981

"If the real thing don't do the trick, you better make up something quick."

—"BARRACUDA," HEART
(A. WILSON, N. WILSON, R. FISHER, M. DeROSIER)

November/December 1979

— — — —

"Grave problems confront us. The challenges they present are of sobering magnitude. They cry out for solution. So, with the help of God, let us begin."

—JANE M. BYRNE, MAYOR OF CHICAGO

Jill

The day after an estimated seventy Americans were taken hostage at the U.S. Embassy in Tehran, Jill Wasserstrom paused on the corner of North Shore and California Avenues to contemplate the accuracy of what she had proudly declared to Lana Rovner during recess at K.I.N.S. Hebrew School. What she had told Lana hadn't been quite true. She hadn't given Muley Scott Wills a big old hickey after eighth-grade phys ed at Boone Elementary School. She hadn't given Muley Scott Wills any sort of hickey at all. What had happened was that Muley Scott Wills had asked her if she wanted to go with him to Sun Drugs to pick up some items for his mother. She'd said sure, she had time before she had to go to Hebrew school, so she'd gone with him to buy a heating pad, a bottle of aspirin, two blocks of Neapolitan ice cream, three packs of Now and Later's, and a bag of Warner's spice drops, which they consumed before he said good-bye to her in front of K.I.N.S. But, Jill realized as she continued walking south on California, Muley Wills was unlikely to deny any story that made it seem as if their relationship was more profound than it actually was, which was why it had been a safe bet to tell Lana Rovner she'd given Muley the hickey: If Lana— who was always asking intrusive questions about Jill and Muley's relationship— actually went up to Muley some day in the future and asked if Jill had given him said hickey, no doubt Muley either would say nothing or would immediately confirm the story to conceal the fact that Jill had never given him a hickey. Or anything else for that matter.

At the corner of Albion and California, Jill Wasserstrom turned east and crossed the street. California Avenue was the first of two east-west dividing lines in West Rogers Park. It was one of the only two-way streets in the neighborhood and one of the only commercial ones. On California, there were service stations, synagogues, and small grocery stores, a firehouse, a diner, and a funeral home, the Shang Chai Kosher Restaurant and Tel Aviv Kosher Pizza, Burghard's Egg Factory and the Nortown branch of the Chicago Public Library. West of California were the parks and the single-family houses, the houses with evergreen bushes, maple trees, and underground sprinklers out front, the houses with banisters, stoops, and steps carpeted with Astroturf, the houses whose doors were rarely locked. Here and there were apartment buildings—grim white or sky-blue brick edifices that smelled of senior citizens and their warm lunches—but they were the exceptions. Doctors lived west of California. Lawyers, too. Not the top-of-the-line doctors or lawyers; they mostly lived downtown or in the northern suburbs. The doctors here mostly worked for the county and the lawyers generally worked for the city. Still, for the most part, everything west of California was pristine and white-collar and Jewish, or Indian, Italian, Filipino, or Korean, all of which amounted to essentially the same thing. Lana Rovner lived west of California, on Sacramento Avenue across the street from Chippewa Park, where she sometimes sat on the benches and watched her brother Larry play two-on-two with his musician buddies from the Ida Crown Jewish Academy.

East of California, there was a discernible change in the light. Here, the red-brick apartment buildings and smoke-gray bungalows soaked up the sun, and the streets seemed just a bit narrower. East of California, there was precious little greenery or open space, save for the playground of the Boone Elementary School and the front lawns of churches. Here, the houses were the exceptions. Jill Wasserstrom lived next to one on Campbell Avenue, on the second floor of a four-story walk-up. She, her sister Michelle, and their father, Charlie Wasserstrom—manager of the newly opened It's in the Pot! restaurant in a shopping mall in nearby Lincolnwood—lived in a one-bedroom apartment; Michelle, a junior at Mather High School, and Jill shared a room.

The landscape changed once again at Western Avenue, a sprawling four-lane street that spanned the entire city of Chicago. On Western, there was Bingo City, Fluky's Hot Dogs, the Nortown Theater, and more car dealerships than on any other street in the city. There were no houses on Western, only apartments above diners, pet stores, restaurants, and taverns. East of Western was Warren Park. Once an exclusive country club, it was now a vast expanse of overgrown grass, of cracked tennis courts, muddy soccer fields, rusted charcoal grills, and one toboggan hill, a former garbage heap now known to the kids in the neighborhood as Mt. Warren. The cozy shops of Devon Avenue—with its bakeries, record stores, and Judaica emporiums—stopped at the Western intersection. East of Western were grimy grocery stores, five-and-ten shops, liquor stores, restaurants with their neon lights flickering, bars with Old Milwaukee signs in their windows, the Seconds to Go Thrift Shop, Burger King, and the dingy Laundrytown above which Muley Wills lived with his mother, who shelved books at the Nortown Library and supplemented her measly income by cleaning houses.

Jill had just finished Hebrew school and it was already dark outside, which meant that maybe somebody would be home when she got there, but come to think of it, probably not. Her father had recently started taking extra shifts at the restaurant to pay for the Bat Mitzvah she had already told him she didn't want, *really* didn't want, and Michelle was probably still at the high school, rehearsing for the winter musical: *H.M.S. Pinafore.* The echoing loneliness of the apartment, which had once struck Jill as a symbol of her utter abandonment, was now little more than simple fact—something she dealt with every day, like spending the last thirty minutes of Math class waiting for Mrs. Cardash to inspect her homework just because her name came near the end of the alphabet, or going to bed with a pillow over her head to block out the detailed discussions in which Michelle attempted to engage their father about the kinds of boys she liked, the kinds of boys who worked on cars, the kinds of boys who called up WLS and dedicated Boston songs to her, the kinds of boys who played street hockey and ogled her at Blackhawks games.

When she got to the apartment, Jill picked up the mail lying on the tan carpet outside their door—mostly her father's magazines that were too big to fit into the box. She entered the apartment, deposited the mail on the kitchen counter, and walked down the hallway to her room. She dumped her book bag on her bed, hung her coat in the closet, then returned to her desk and picked up the battered copy of *Romeo and Juliet* she was supposed to finish for Reading the next morning. Actually, she had read it two weeks earlier—the date that Mrs. Korab, who had organized the semester around "Conflicts and Resolutions," had originally indicated on the homework sheet. But by now, Jill had forgotten so much of it that she figured she'd have to start over. She went to the kitchen, looked briefly in the refrigerator—her father's leftovers from the restaurant made her shudder and slam the door shut—then took a breakfast bar out of the cabinet and walked into the living room. She turned on a lamp and sat on the couch, which doubled as her father's bed.

Before opening her book, she briefly considered going to the kitchen and taking one of her father's Millers out of the fridge. She further considered rummaging through Michelle's dresser drawers and finding the green Cricket lighter, the water pipe, and one of those mysterious foil packets her sister hoarded. But Jill quickly rejected both options—not because she'd be caught; rather, because she wouldn't. And then she'd just have to remain there in the apartment all night, drunk or stoned with her dad and her sister, and, really, what was the point of that? She was twelve years old and already her sister had ruined practically every vice for her—braying after coming home drunk from theater parties with a "Don't tell Dad" wink; vacantly amazed by the stupidest TV cop shows after having smoked hash in the alley with Gareth Overgaard and Myra Tuchbaum; chattering nonstop about this guy's hands or that guy's car, when it was patently clear to Jill that all of those "gorgeous" guys would wind up just squeaking by at community college; blasting Eric Clapton and stinking up the record collection with her Merits ("All the cool girls smoke Merits; all the burnouts smoke Marlboros," Michelle once informed her). Jill couldn't smoke, she couldn't drink, she couldn't listen to her sister's albums, she couldn't put anything up on the wall—the entire room, even her side, was plastered with Michelle's posters of Pink Floyd and Lynyrd Skynyrd and The Who and Led Zeppelin—it seemed nearly impossible to rebel in any way that wasn't somehow secondhand.

It was November 1979 and, to Jill Wasserstrom, time was trudging by so slowly that it seemed as if it would take five decades to get through the next five years. Five years from now, she would have just entered college, and her father would have the whole apartment to himself; he could convert her and Michelle's room into a workshop—not that he knew how to fix anything. She, meanwhile, would be long gone—taking courses in Art History to nourish her soul, and in Law or Medicine so that she'd be able to make enough money to send Michelle anonymous monthly payments to support her drug habit or pay her shrink or bail her boyfriends out of Cook County before they stood trial for grand theft auto.

The only difficulty was getting through those next five years, or more precisely, those next four years and ten months. Four years and ten months ago, she hadn't even started Hebrew school; she hadn't even heard of crazy old Rabbi Einstein or Rabbi Meltzer or, Lord help her, Rabbi Shmulevits. Four years and ten months ago, she had just skipped from second to third grade at Boone Elementary. Four years and ten months ago, her sister had seemed perfectly smart. Four years and ten months ago, her mother had seemed perfectly healthy. Four years and ten months ago, they had been talking about moving into a house west of California.

Jill heard keys jingling outside the door—her father. It always took twenty seconds for him to find the right key. He'd try one, then another, then get the right one but turn it the wrong way, lock the door instead of open it, take two shoves to open the door because he couldn't do it in one try. Charlie Wasserstrom asked if anybody was home. Jill closed her eyes and pretended to sleep. "Oh," Charlie said, loudly shutting the door. "I didn't think you'd be asleep." Jill kept her eyes shut and listened to him tiptoe, hang up his raincoat in the closet, apologize for the clatter of keys when the coat fell to the floor ("Sorry, sorry"), open the refrigerator door, take out a beer, set it down just a bit too hard on the kitchen counter ("Sorry, sorry"), go to the bathroom, shut the door, urinate loudly, flush, then jiggle the toilet handle, stop to hear the coughing and swirling of the bowl attempting to refill itself, jiggle the handle again, then tiptoe back to the living room. He told Jill he was sorry to wake her but he had good news.

Charlie Wasserstrom's good news was never the sort of good news worth waiting up to hear; what tended to excite him seemed so utterly trivial that his happiness usually depressed Jill. Like the time he arrived home, beaming, turning up WDHF-FM loud, and shh-ing her and Michelle each time they asked what was so exciting, finally punching his fist in the air when some guffawing deejay called Captain Whammo ("You're listening to 95-and-a-half, *the Whammo line!*") announced that "Charlie Wasserstrom of North Campbell Avenue has won two tickets to see the Electric Light Orchestra at the Aragon Ballroom!"—even though Charlie had never heard of E.L.O. and gave the tickets to Michelle, whom he'd dropped off at the concert with some flat-skulled water polo player who pawed her all through the car ride home while Charlie said nothing, except when Michelle confronted him afterward and his only response had been, "I didn't want to interrupt; I thought you kids were having a good time."

Charlie Wasserstrom enjoyed getting things for free—or for half-off—even if he had never really wanted those things in the first place. He would come home with armloads of off-brand cereal, LPs from the cutout bin, liver sausage and Tater Tots, discontinued board games like Numble, Coup D'Etat, and Situation-Four. All this filled Jill with such dread that whenever her father said, "I have some good news," the only thing she could associate it with was the time he returned with her mother from the "routine doctor's appointment" and said they had "something serious to discuss."

Jill assumed the "good news" would concern the Bat Mitzvah, most likely something she'd heard before—Charlie often presented old news as revelation— something about how Mr. Alan Farbman from the restaurant would be donating a deli tray, something about how her rich great-aunt Beileh would not only match the most expensive gift but beat it by at least $10. But Charlie didn't mention any of that; instead, he said, "I bet you can't guess who came into the restaurant tonight." Jill said he was right, she couldn't guess. She asked who had come into It's in the Pot!, knowing full well that the restaurant's clientele was culled from a mere two groups—people who chain-smoked and people on respirators.

"Gail Schiffler-Bass," he said. The name made no impression and the additional information her father offered—"the gal from the paper"—didn't illuminate matters but did make Jill just a touch more intrigued until Charlie explained, "you know, from the *Nortown Leader,*" at which point Jill regretted whatever enthusiasm she might have briefly displayed. The *Nortown Leader,* part of the chain of Schiffler Neighborhood Newspapers, was little more than a series of coupons—two-for-one dining at the Yenching Chinese restaurant; one free appetizer at Sally's Stage (featuring roller-skating waitresses); a free car wash with a fill-up at the Nortown Standard station—and advertisements ("Devon Bank Salutes Its Loyal Customers," "Rosel Hair Designers: A Cut Above The Rest"), occasionally interrupted by tepid articles about charity fund-raisers and community events ("New Basketball Courts at Lerner Park; Seniors Say It's No Slam-Dunk"), followed by pages of classifieds, display ads, and announcements: Las Vegas Night at K.I.N.S. Synagogue, a screening of *The Canterville Ghost* at the Nortown Library, free blood pressure testing, a JCC singles disco dance night led by Sandi Hirsch. There was a Lifestyle section with community theater and restaurant reviews, but the only part of the paper Jill ever read was the police blotter, and even it was unimpressive; the only crimes of note took place east of Western and they never involved anyone she knew.

"She's gonna give us a write-up," Charlie continued, then repeated her name for emphasis. "Gail Schiffler-Bass is gonna do a write-up. She talked to me for maybe fifteen minutes. She wanted to know everything I knew. Mr. Farbman said it was okay. So I told her everything I knew."

Jill wasn't certain why her father was so excited; he'd only been at It's in the Pot! for three weeks, and though managing that restaurant was a step up from his previous position (counterman at Fannie's Deli on Touhy: "We Specialize In Lox!"), until today Jill had not heard him say anything positive about it ("They water down the matzo ball soup; you're not gonna attract repeat customers that way," "They don't keep the chopped liver covered, and they come to me, angry 'cause there's flies," "Mr. Farbman said he doesn't believe in overtime; the hours are the hours"). The worst of it all was his obsequious tone whenever he referred to Mr. Farbman, as if Farbman were worthy of this sort of respect, as if he weren't ten years younger than her father, as if he didn't have a bad mustache, slick, black hair parted down the middle, a thick gold bracelet, and a gargantuan high school ring, as if he hadn't completely humiliated her father the one time she'd met him at the restaurant, calling him "Hey, Charlie," as if her father were retarded—"Hey, Charlie, where does toothpicks go?" "Hey, Charlie, where's the ashtrays?"—all the while, her father with that same obsequious tone: "Yes, Mr. Farbman; sorry, Mr. Farbman; I'll get right to that, Mr. Farbman; right away, sir, right away."

No doubt her father's excitement derived from some twisted idea that once the restaurant got reviewed it would attract more customers, then maybe "Mr. Farbman" would credit the restaurant's success to his loyal employee. Or maybe her father just wanted to see his name in print: "'We also serve an excellent variety of soups,' effused Charlie Wasserstrom, manager of It's in the Pot! and noted Thousand Island dressing enthusiast." "'We really hope to give Lincolnwood an eatery they can be proud of,' thundered the bumbling Wasserstrom, manager of It's in the Pot! and owner of Chicago's largest collection of Frank Sinatra records." It was all too grim to consider further. Jill told her father she had homework and went off to her bedroom, taking *Romeo and Juliet* with her, leaving her father to the couch, his beer, his leftover brisket, and his dreams of fame.

Jill was sitting at her desk and just about ready for bed when her sister Michelle burst breathlessly through the doorway, her oversized red-and-white plaid flannel shirt reeking of cigarette smoke, her blond hair stiff, brittle, and tousled. "Stay there. Don't move. I've got a bulletin," Michelle said. She dashed out of the bedroom, shutting the door behind her.

Jill hadn't done much work before her sister's arrival. She'd breezed through *Romeo and Juliet,* her lab book was in acceptable shape, her Latin vocabulary was memorized. She had exited the bedroom once, only to find her father still in his black pants, white shirt, and clip-on black necktie, snoring on the couch with the TV still on—the sports reporter on the Channel 9 News yammering about Walter Payton and the Chicago Bears' 35–7 trouncing of the Detroit Lions. The rest of the time she had spent thinking about nuclear war and the end of the universe. There had been a field trip to the Adler Planetarium the previous week, and she and Muley Wills had spent most of the time making fun of the Sky Show narrator, who imbued every syllable he uttered with great importance: "Perhaps [pause] there will come [pause] a new [deep breath] Ice [pause] AGE. Perhaps [pause] the Earth's [pause] gravitational PULL [pause] will draw the moon IT-SELF [pause] to its SURFACE."

She hadn't listened carefully to the narration, only enough to mock it with Muley at lunch in the cafeteria, which may have been immature but seemed far more civil than Connie Sherman's approach. She'd spent the whole Sky Show passing a joint back and forth with Dvorah Kerbis and saying "Decent." At any rate, any deep meaning in the Sky Show eluded her as she and Muley entertained each other at their own lunch table: "Perhaps [pause] this sloppy [pause] JOE is [pause] the most REPULSIVE [pause] thing the UNIVERSE [pause] has ever KNOWN." Until Shmuel Weinberg asked their Science teacher, Dr. Bender, something no one else had considered.

What did it mean about the moon being pulled down by the Earth's gravity, Shmuel wanted to know. Dr. Bender said it was a good question. He said it meant that one day, "a long time from now," the Earth would pull the moon down to its surface and there would be a gigantic explosion. Then the Earth would get its very own set of rings, "just like Saturn."

Shmuel contemplated Dr. Bender's response. "Wouldn't that destroy things?" he asked.

"Oh, don't worry," said Dr. Bender. "We'll all be dead by then."

"That's right," Connie Sherman blurted out cheerfully. "From nuclear war."

Jill had rolled her eyes during the exchange. But ever since, whenever her thoughts wandered, invariably they settled on these two images: the destruction of the Earth by a crash-landing Moon; the destruction of the Earth by nuclear war. And then an image of her mother would come to her, an image of the con-

versation they'd had after the first week of *Aleph* at Hebrew school. Rabbi Einstein had discussed an old Jewish legend about the end of the world—he said it
was referenced obliquely in the *Adon Olam,* the prayer that terrified Jill because
of the one line of it she remembered, *"And in the end, when all will cease to be,
he will remain the eternal king,"* and didn't that seem odd, that God, or G-D, or
Hashem, as they were supposed to refer to him, would want to remain the eternal king after all would "cease to be"? Wouldn't that just be devastatingly lonely,
wouldn't God just want to start the world over and eliminate some of the mistakes he'd made in the first go-round? Death, for example? Or evil? Rabbi Einstein said that Jewish legend held that at the end of the world, all the dead would
rise and celebrate together. The story had seemed incomplete, unsatisfying—if
they were supposed to celebrate, what would they be celebrating? The end of the
world? And did this mean all the dead or just the dead Jews? And if it meant just
the Jews, then what would happen to everyone else? Would they have a party
too? And what would happen after the party, Jill wanted to know. Would
everybody just go back to being dead? Would the party go on eternally? And if
so, wouldn't it just be better to end the world now, so everybody could come
back? What was G-D waiting for exactly? Was any of this true, she asked her
mother, that at the end of the world, everyone would come back?

"I hope so," her mother said. "There are some people I'd sure like to see."

Which was the phrase that was jackhammering Jill Wasserstrom's skull when
her sister returned to their bedroom and told her she had misspoken. She didn't
have a "bulletin"; she had a "news flash." Michelle flopped down, then bounced
briefly on Jill's bed—a girlish habit that seemed rehearsed to appear sisterly but
to Jill seemed simply patronizing. Michelle jumped off the bed and sat on the
desk. "Maybe it's not a news flash either," Michelle said. "Maybe it's really a
white paper." Finally, she decided: "No, it's not that either. Actually, it's an edict."

Issuing an edict was as serious as it got. Michelle reserved the issuing of edicts
for life-altering decisions. Breaking off relations with boys—or inviting them to
"taste the salty brine in Davy Jones's locker," as Michelle referred to it—was
rarely accorded edict status. When she relayed that sort of information, it only received the label of "bulletin." The last *edict* Jill recalled Michelle issuing concerned vowing to lose her virginity to the unfortunately named Eddie Pinkstaff.
More recently, in a fit of rage, Michelle had issued another edict, declaring she
would refuse to take the PSAT practice college entrance exam since she wasn't

planning to go to college at all. Later, Michelle retracted that edict, declaring it, in the words of a Watergate-era White House press secretary, "inoperative."

"And you will *witness* this," Michelle said. "I am hereby resigning from all extracurricular drama activities. I am quitting the show and the club—I don't care if it *sabotages* them. That is *it*. Edict declared. Edict witnessed. Edict issued."

If this turned out to be true, it would doubtless prove to be the defining edict of Michelle's high school career. She had been involved with every Mather High production since she had arrived two years earlier, scoring the part of Anne Frank as a freshman, then nabbing virtually every lead role thereafter, except in *Rosencrantz and Guildenstern Are Dead*, for which the director—a former TV actor now serving a jail sentence—insisted on an all-male cast and required each actor to slowdance with him during their audition. Michelle had played Eileen in *Wonderful Town*, Portia in *Julius Caesar*, and Emily in *Our Town*. This year, as a junior, she had served on the executive drama board for *Coolshow!*, the annual student-written musical variety show. And now she was just three weeks away from opening night for *H.M.S. Pinafore*. She was to play Buttercup. She had been offered the role of the Captain's daughter Josephine, but gracefully stepped aside so that her friend Myra Tuchbaum—a senior who had never been in a musical despite having auditioned for every single one, and who provided her and their mutual friend Gareth Overgaard, also a senior, with free pot—could play the part. As Buttercup, Michelle would sing a duet with the ladykilling Millard Schwartz, who had allegedly never been turned down for a date; Michelle's intent had been to provide him with his first *no*—a task she, no doubt, could have performed had she not wandered in late one Saturday night to Eastern Style Pizza right when Millard was getting off work and happened to have a jug of apple wine in the trunk of his rusted, olive-green Opel Manta, which, for once, wasn't in the shop.

Jill asked why Michelle was quitting. Everything had been cruising along just fine, Michelle said. Even Millard had been taking a surprisingly professional approach to rehearsals; he had vowed not to get high until the first cast party. Today had been the first rehearsal with orchestra, and Michelle had been eagerly anticipating working with the conductor, Douglas Sternberg. Sternberg was a Mather legend. He had graduated in 1972, and seven years later his pictures still adorned the walls outside of the auditorium. He had founded *Coolshow!* He had gone to state four straight years with the speech team, taking top honors at the state tournament in Normal, Illinois, in 1971 in Humorous Interpretation (inhabiting twelve characters in his edit of *The Comedy of Errors*). Little had been known about what had become of him. There were rumors he'd gone to Hollywood, that he was writing nudie musicals off-Broadway, that he'd written the original score to *The Way We Were* but had argued with Barbra Streisand, who insisted all his music be removed. Whatever the truth was, now he was back—subbing for Milner Geist, who had conducted every Mather musical since 1954 and, now that he was at home recovering from cracked ribs, had called upon one of his most celebrated students to replace him for *Pinafore,* after which Geist promised to return for *Coolshow 1980!*

At rehearsal, Sternberg had seemed brusque, standoffish, but that had been his reputation. And Michelle had rather enjoyed the way he'd dressed down the orchestra, which had gotten used to taking advantage of hapless Mr. Geist. She particularly enjoyed how Sternberg ended every sentence with "shall we?": "Let's take that from the top, shall we?" "Let's try that the exact same way, but this time in tune, shall we?"

"But *then,*" Michelle said, rummaging through her dresser drawer and pulling out a pack of Merits. "But *then,*" she said, flicking her lighter, holding the cigarette between her thumb and forefinger and inhaling ("I'm sorry," she said. "I know you don't like it when it stinks up your clothes, but sometimes you just need it—it's like having an orgasm"). "But *then,*" she said, opening the window, letting a gust of autumn air whoosh into the bedroom, "he starts in on *me.*" She was standing with her back to the window, cigarette hand against the ledge, smoke drifting outside. What had happened, she explained, was that they had been rehearsing Act I. She'd memorized the entire operetta weeks earlier, but she was smart enough not to show that off immediately; that only made people think she was "superconceited." So when she rehearsed, she'd always say, "Let me try that off book," and make a couple of mistakes and laugh about it and say, "Sorry, I screwed up, can you hand me the script?" just so people would know that she was human and not some nutcase with a photographic memory, even though she did have one. So Myra Tuchbaum had assayed "Refrain, Audacious Tar!" and it had been a really "strong effort." Michelle was proud of her, even though she had been slightly off-key.

"Then comes me," Michelle said. She explained that she had no intention of showing off all the work she had done prior to rehearsal. She wasn't going to do that whole juggling trick again. There had been the time when Myra wanted to be a juggling serving wench at King Richard's Faire, had made a big deal about how tough juggling was, and she had made everyone in *Anne Frank* gather around her as she took three tennis balls and juggled them, woofing with each throw—*woof woof woof.* The spectacle had infuriated Michelle, so she went up to Myra right in front of everybody and said, "That doesn't look hard, let me try that," and juggled flawlessly for five minutes straight while Myra stood gaping at her until Michelle handed the balls back saying, "Nah, that's not that tough," whereupon Myra called her a bitch, then Michelle called Myra a whore, and soon they were best friends. So anyway, Michelle sang "Buttercup's Song," but didn't attempt the working-class British accent she'd perfected, didn't belt, didn't embellish with any tremolos. The only flourish she added was a wink on the line "Sailors should never be shy," which was just a private joke between her and Millard—something he'd said to her when they had been "finger-fucking" ("Oh, I'm sorry: virgin ears," she said to Jill) one night in Warren Park.

After she was done and she knew she'd nailed it ("It's an instinct," she said. "You know when you've nailed something"), Sternberg approached Mr. Linton, the pudgy, snowy-haired director who'd cast her in every show he'd directed, and all Sternberg said was, "I thought you said you had people who knew how to sing, Hank." The two of them had gone out into the hall while the cast sat silently, straining to hear Sternberg's voice. Michelle stood up in front of the cast and said that this was "bullshit." If this guy was such "hot shit," what was he doing here? What they should do was walk out in protest when Sternberg returned. Everyone said yeah, they'd do it. But when Sternberg and Linton returned, she was the only one who stood, and when she walked to the door, nobody joined her, so she kept walking right out of the auditorium, out the front door of the school. She briefly considered going back, but she had her pride, and besides, the door had locked behind her.

"So," Michelle said, flicking her cigarette butt out the window, "there's the edict."

Jill was never really sure if Michelle wanted her to interject or if she just wanted her to listen, because whenever she agreed, Michelle invariably contradicted her and said Jill didn't really understand the complex predicament she was discussing ("But I kind of led him on," she would say whenever Jill would say Michelle was right, the guy she was talking about sure was a jerk, "But you have to see it from his point of view," "But I was being kind of a bitch, too," "But you've never really been in that situation, Jill, no offense"). Disagreeing with Michelle was even worse; she'd lash out furiously, apologize later, then hold a grudge for days. And if Jill remained silent, Michelle would say, "Well, what do *you* think? Why aren't you saying anything?" Therefore, Jill was more than a little relieved when the telephone's ring filled the silence. Michelle leapt up, saying, "I'll get rid of whoever it is; I want to finish this conversation." But an hour later, she was still talking to Millard, saying, "I'll think about it; that's all I can promise. I made a vow to the show, but I made a vow to myself, too." And as that phone conversation droned on into the early morning, Jill Wasserstrom lay wide awake in bed, trying to think about anything aside from her mother, the end of the world, and the *Adon Olam.*

 R O V N E R

Lana

By the time she reached Sacramento Avenue, Lana Rovner had almost forgotten, though not completely, Jill Wasserstrom's remark about giving Muley Wills a big hickey after eighth-grade PE at Boone. Lana had no idea why Jill resented her so much, how she could say something so vulgar, whether she was trying to corrupt her because she had a sense of decency—or whether Jill had really given a big, disgusting hickey to the strange, brainy black kid whose mother cleaned the Rovners' house. Lana ultimately attributed Jill's statement to jealousy. The Rovners lived across from the park; her father, Michael, was a radiologist specializing in diseases of the chest; her mother, Ellen, was a psychologist; her brother, Larry, had already gotten into Brandeis early decision; and Lana herself attended the Baker Demonstration School in the northern suburb of Evanston, and though she was in the seventh grade there, the school was so progressive that the grade was referred to as the "seventh pod"; the Wasserstroms, on the other hand, lived in a walk-up east of California, Jill attended eighth grade, but at *Boone,* which Lana had transferred out of when she was seven, Jill's sister was a burnout, her dad slung pastrami. Enough said. The rest was not something polite people discussed, so Lana decided not to think about whether Jill was turning into a skanky slut like her sister. Instead, she'd think about how she would get a 20 on her creative report, and what gift she would demand when she got it.

The second of Lana Rovner's creative reports was approaching and she'd been reasonably satisfied with the 17.5 she'd scored for her report, "Diseases of the Chest." No one had scored higher in the first round. Almost everyone had gotten 12s and 13s: Edgar Barnes, the one black boy in Lana's class, who had read from note cards for his stultifying presentation about cells; Jonathan Wolk, who wore his Little League uniform and discussed the rules of baseball; Mary Beth Wales, whose report on jockey Steve Cauthen ended after three minutes; Jamie Henderson, who made up his report about Kiss as he went along—"Uh, Kiss, uh, is basically Gene Simmons and Peter Criss and Paul Stanley, and uh, Ace Frehley." But now it was Round 2 and Steve Orenstein had scored a 19 with his report on UFOs—never mind that Steve's dad had been college buddies with J. Allen Hynek, a Northwestern professor who ran a UFO studies center and had access to slides. She had to get that 20.

Lana walked west on Pratt. It wasn't the quickest way back from K.I.N.S., but she preferred to take the busiest street, because even though she lived on the safest block in the safest neighborhood in Chicago, she still didn't like walking down dark streets. The lights were on in the Chippewa Park Fieldhouse, proba- bly for a Girl Scout meeting. Lana had been a Brownie for two weeks, but she had quit after her Grandma Rose had told her it was *"goyishe nachas."* Lana didn't like being the only Jew anywhere. It was strange enough being the only Jew at Baker; Steve Orenstein's father was Jewish, but his parents celebrated Christ- mas, which made Lana the only semi-practicing member of the faith in school, a fact that asserted itself with remarkable regularity, such as when the Music teacher, Mrs. Reay, asked her to play the role of the dreidel in a school assembly or when Jamie Henderson remarked that he hated all Jews, "but I guess you're okay." Lana's status as sole Baker Jew left her spending a goodly amount of time sticking up for members of her religion, insisting to Mary Beth Wales that Barbra Streisand was *not* ugly, that Woody Allen's films were, in fact, funny, and no, just because Chanukah was eight days long that didn't mean she got eight gifts.

As she approached her house, Lana swelled with pride at the fact that it was the only one on the block without Astroturf carpeting on its steps and, consequently, the only one that didn't look "Polish." It was Grandma Rose's phrase, one her mother warned her never to use outside the house, that was the way Rose's generation talked, that's why Grandma Rose said she wouldn't shop on State Street with all the *"tinkle,"* that she knew a great "Chinaman tailor," that she had gone with a tour group to Cave-In-The-Rock and they had turned right back because it was "black as the ace of spades." But even so, Lana knew what her grandmother meant and it would hit her every time she saw the iridescent green Astroturf on the front stairways of the Smalls and the Sternbergs, every time she collected the mail that had arrived mistakenly in the Mazers' mailbox and saw the plastic on the couches and the armchairs. Grandma Rose was right. It was Polish. There was no other word for it.

Lana entered the house—the door was nearly always unlocked—and inhaled the aromas of Lemon Pledge and Jubilee. Deirdre Wills had already cleaned up and left, and even though she did a mediocre job and had, so went the story, more than once helped herself to the Rovners' Kahlúa, continuing to employ her was easier than finding someone else. And since Deirdre hadn't really helped herself to the liquor while each Rovner family member had, at one time or another, secretly guzzled from the cabinet, keeping Deirdre around provided all the Rovners with a handy alibi for their drinking. From the kitchen counter, Lana picked up a note from her mother—she had just run out to pick up dinner and would be back by six. Lana set the table for four, then took her homework and went downstairs to Larry's room, which, she had to admit, was the best room in the house.

Lana liked her own room well enough; she liked that it let out onto a little private porch. It certainly smelled better than Larry's. But though she had picked out everything in the room—the rose red walls, the lavender canopy over the bed, the framed Johnny Hallyday posters—something about the room had saddened her ever since her parents had started talking about moving out. The move was at least a year away—there was no point in going anywhere until Larry was at Brandeis—and there was strong disagreement between Ellen and Michael about where they would go. Michael favored a condominium on Michigan Avenue, while Ellen—who found condominiums oppressive, and the majority of whose clients lived in the north suburbs—preferred a house in Evanston, where the public schools were better. And now, even though Lana hoped this fundamental disagreement would prevent her parents from ever moving anywhere, sleeping in her room no longer filled her with the sense of security it once had; instead, it filled her with a feeling of loss.

"Lana?" Larry asked when she knocked on the door.

"Yeah," Lana said.

Larry told her to give him a second.

About four years earlier, Larry Rovner had relocated from the bedroom next to Lana's room to the basement storage room, where there was space for his Nerf basketball net and his drum kit. In the meantime, their mother had redecorated Larry's room and converted it into her office. Thus, "Larry Rovner's Space-Age Bachelor Pad," as the stenciled sign on the door read, was born. There were four things Larry loved equally, and each was represented in the room: basketball, rock 'n' roll, Israel, and girls. There was a basketball autographed by Pete Maravich, posters of Artis Gilmore and John Havlicek. There was the drum kit, a stereo, record albums piled high against the wall, a guitar he was teaching himself to play. There were posters of Jerusalem, books by Philip Roth, Mordecai Richler, and Isaac Bashevis Singer. And right above his bed, flanked by posters of Jaclyn Smith and Bo Derek, was the model Cheryl Tiegs in a white fishnet bathing suit.

Larry unlatched the door. There were sweat stains under the arms of his red T-shirt, which spelled out Coca-Cola in Hebrew. He said he'd been drumming. He had a new song and had finally gotten the rhythm part right. He asked Lana if she wanted to hear it and she said sure. It didn't matter to her whether he played or not; what was important was that Larry was allowing her access to his intriguing and adult-like existence. And whether he was shooting baskets, staying up all night typing up another paper about the raid on Entebbe for Social Studies, calling up one of the girls who were part of what he referred to as his "harem," or drumming until Ellen told him to stop, the Sternbergs had called to complain, Lana felt privileged doing her homework in his room.

Larry's song was called "Six Days," and he played it with great conviction and a palpable rage, which he accentuated by sneering and rotating his right shoulder forward on every other beat. And every time he kicked the bass drum, his yarmulke—the only one worn in the Rovner family—bobbed up and down on his newly trimmed Isro. It was a riff on the Bob Dylan song "Seven Days," the only tune Larry could tolerate on Rolling Stones guitarist Ron Wood's solo album

Gimme Some Neck. Larry had thrown out most of his Dylan records after the artist's 1978 conversion to Christianity, and the one he hadn't thrown out—*Street Legal*—he had slammed hard and broken against his Air Hockey table. He had a similar aversion to Bruce Springsteen, whose work he had admired until he became convinced Springsteen was denying his Jewish heritage. "Six Days" was both a hard slap in the face of Dylan's Christianity (instead of "Seven more days and she'll be coming," Larry sang, "Six more days and you'll be running") and a tribute to the soldiers who fought in Israel's Six-Day War.

Larry hoped to premiere the song at the first public performance of the band he'd assembled from his fellow seniors at the Ida Crown Jewish Academy. The band was called, simply, Rovner! and they were scheduled to play in the basement of K.I.N.S. during the final weekend of the annual, month-long Purim Carnival. And if that went well, Rabbi Meltzer said, he would ask them back for the Passover after-seder party. Meltzer might have been a member of the clergy and a graduate of Yeshiva University, waiting desperately for Rabbi Shmulevits to retire, but he was a rock 'n' roller at heart, and at every school assembly he brought out his doubleneck acoustic guitar and played "Runaround Sue." And even if he didn't understand Larry's passion for Led Zeppelin, Larry knew he would understand the integrity and power that Rovner! brought to their music.

Larry asked Lana to listen carefully to the lyrics he was howling over the beat he thumped out, but after the opening line ("Egypt released me, but you're still in chains"), she opened her Weather book to prep for the next day's cloud test. She had no idea how to complete her homework; in addition to the cloud test, she had thirty pages of reading, a metric conversion table to fill out, a list of state capitals to memorize, plus a page-long poetry interpretation report analyzing the lyrics of the Paul Simon songs "Some Folks' Lives Roll Easy" and "Learn How to Fall." But her attention kept veering from the picture of cirrocumulus clouds in her Weather book, because all she could think of was the creative report she was to deliver the next Friday. The report had been the suggestion of both of her parents. The topic: Marie Curie. What Lana liked best about it was the fact that, like Lana's grandfather on her father's side, Marie Curie had been born in Poland— Lana made no connection between having Polish ancestors and decorating one's house in a "Polish" fashion—but had married a Frenchman. Lana adored France and hoped to live there someday. Plus, Curie's discoveries had led the way for modern radiology, her father's profession.

Larry finished his song. Lana said she liked it, though she preferred show tunes to rock music and had memorized the soundtracks to *Pippin, Bye Bye Birdie,* and *Annie,* all of which she'd seen either in touring productions at the Shubert or in New York with her family when the four of them used to take vacations together. With the exception of the increasingly rare overnight at their house in Lake Geneva, they had not gone out of town since their 1977 trip two and a half years ago to Williamsburg, Virginia, which had sounded as if it would be boring, and was. Michael Rovner had vowed that the next time they took a trip, they would spend it in style—they'd go to Paris and stay in the Lutetia, as he and Ellen had on their honeymoon. But now every time Lana mentioned it, her father told her to discuss it with her mother and her mother told her they'd discuss it later.

Larry told Lana he was really proud of his song but thought it "might not be right for radio." It was definitely an album cut, not a single. But he and Rovner! now had eight album-ready songs, and there were already two maybe three hit singles in there ("My Milk, Your Honey," "[I'm a] Man of Faith," and possibly "Ain't God a Trip?"), plus one ballad that might work for a movie soundtrack ("Take Me to Your Promised Land"). He had remembered his mother once saying that Deirdre Wills's ex-boyfriend was a hotshot in the record industry; he would try to get him a copy of the forthcoming, self-titled Rovner! cassette. The only problem was trying to figure out what would happen if he managed to attract a record label right before he was supposed to move to Waltham, Mass. Wouldn't that be the most ironic thing? Lana said hopefully that if that were the case, maybe he'd have to stick around Chicago for another year to see what would happen with the band. Larry agreed. "Music is what moves me," he said.

Larry liked talking to Lana; she was the one girl who didn't seem to question the possibility that he could do it all, not like the girls at the Academy—the ones with whom he'd gone out on first dates (he didn't tend to go out on many second dates), who'd glaze over whenever he discussed how he'd conduct Rovner!'s world tours: no Friday night concerts no matter how much that would cost his tour promoters, just like Sandy Koufax, who wouldn't pitch for the Dodgers on the High Holidays.

Though Lana could not know this, the one thing Larry feared more than anything was that one day she would see through him, that one day he would forget to latch his door and she, in turn, would forget to knock, and she'd find him naked and hunched over in his bed, perched on his knees, left hand propping up his body, right hand on his penis, rubbing furiously while shooting his come onto a picture of one of those high-heeled girls he liked staring at in *Oui* magazine. And then Lana would no longer see him as the "Jerusarock-jock" he fancied himself. Rather, she would see him as a lonely, pathetic, masturbating dreamer who would have immediately traded rock 'n' roll stardom for a steady girlfriend, one who'd open her mouth and use her tongue while kissing, like that rich New York girl Hannah Goodman, whom he'd met a year and a half earlier on the Young Israel youth tour and who had only sent him two bland postcards since that last night in the hotel room her parents had rented for her, where she had taken his virginity, leaving him to wonder even now whether it mattered that he had sex in Israel since he was still a virgin as far as America was concerned.

"Dinnertime!" Ellen Rovner shouted. Larry put down his drumsticks and followed his sister upstairs.

Dinner at the Rovners was the culinary equivalent of speed-reading, and the ritual had become even speedier ever since the stove had exploded and Michael and Ellen had decided to replace home-cooked meals with takeout food. The stove had been repaired, but now was used primarily for warming up leftovers or for the rare birthdays and holidays when Ellen cooked. On the table, there were slabs of ribs, still in the cardboard box, a quartered barbecued chicken in an aluminum tray, Styrofoam containers of coleslaw and barbecue sauce, dinner rolls and pads of butter in wax bags. At each place setting there was a bottle of pop— three Cokes, and a Diet-Rite for Lana. No napkins, just a roll of paper towels at the center of the table. Larry said he wouldn't be having ribs, but insisted that anyone eating them had to say the *bracha,* which nobody did since Ellen was an atheist, Michael had never learned the prayer, and Lana never ate ribs because they were gross.

Putting out all the takeout food at once and eliminating first, second, and third courses—a ritual that had made dinner at least a forty-minute affair in more leisurely days—had cut that time in half. And keeping the food in its aluminum and Styrofoam containers replaced the arduous task of dishwashing with the time-saving measure of dumping everything into a trash bag at meal's end. The result was that dinner rarely exceeded the time it did on this particular night— from Larry's 6:01 *bracha* to Ellen Rovner's 6:19 "So, is everybody through? Do you want to start dumping?" The *pas de quatre* that occurred during the intervening eighteen minutes consisted of four monologues delivered in the descending order of their orators' ages.

Michael Rovner, who removed the flesh from each of his barbecued ribs by means of fork and knife before consuming them, told a story about how he had presented his first-year residents with an X-ray that showed something lodged below the rib cage of a male patient. One of the Iranian gals, the one with the thick ankles, had theorized that it was a recurrence of old TB; the lone Pakistani had guessed a bullet fragment; Laura Kim had come closest—she thought she saw a ring or a piece of jewelry. In fact, according to Michael, there had been a ring on the X-ray, but also something puffy the Iranian had mistaken for TB. It turned out that during surgery, someone had been eating Cracker Jack, and a piece of caramel corn and the toy surprise had fallen into the wound. Though there was little give-and-take among the Rovners, Lana sensed that nodding, commenting, and laughing at the ends of stories was how adults acted. So throughout her father's story, she listened intently, hmming and ahhing at appropriate points, then remarking finally, "That is hilarious."

Ellen Rovner, who only managed to eat a chicken drumstick—a *pullki,* as she called it—and some coleslaw, made a cutting remark about the declining quality of medical residents, then proceeded to talk about one of her patients. Since she knew that discussing her patients' cases was unethical, she never referred to them by name, identifying them only by age, occupation, and location, such as a thirty-nine-year-old neurotic parakeet trainer from West Rogers Park or a suicidal seventeen-year-old from Mather High. In this case, the story concerned a "forty-one-year-old spinster from Milwaukee." The woman was "frustrated in multifarious ways," and exhibited "multifarious, libidinous tendencies," none of which made much sense to Lana, though she was certain the story dealt with either sex or death, since those were the only two topics her mother discussed using vocabulary words she couldn't understand. Lana had had to consult the dictionary to learn that her grandfather on her father's side had died, since all her mother would say on the topic of Grandpa Al was "There's nothing more we can do for him; he met his demise." The multifariously libidinous woman had sought treatment because she'd become obsessed with watching her neighbors across the alley. Ever since she'd noticed her libidinous neighbors, she'd become strangely interested in "relating to herself," and dreamed frequently about "relating" to the libidinous couple. And what she wanted Ellen to help her with was learning how to ignore that couple. At the end of their fifty-minute session, Ellen had advised, "Why don't you just pull down your damn shades?" The woman said thanks, she hadn't thought of that.

"That's funny," Lana said, then repeated what her mother had said: "Why don't you just pull down your damn shades?"

Larry was next to speak and by now almost everyone was done eating save for Lana, who took small forkfuls of her chicken, just as she had been taught, chewing each forkful between twenty-five and thirty times before swallowing. Larry discussed a girl he'd met at the most recent Ida Crown basketball game, a girl named Randi Nathan from Von Steuben High. She had come with her friends, but there hadn't been enough room on the Von Steuben side, so she was sitting behind the Ida Crown bench during the pregame shoot-around. She and Larry started talking and somehow they had gotten onto the topic of movies and she had said that she wanted to go to the Nortown to see *French Postcards.* He had told her that he had really wanted to see it too, but that none of his friends wanted to go see some "dorky French love movie"—a comment that irked Lana because she'd mentioned *French Postcards* to Larry at least ten times, hoping he would offer to take her, since Mary Beth Wales had never stopped bragging to their French teacher about how great it was.

Larry said that Randi had given him her number and he had called her up and said, "How about going to see the movie Saturday night?" and she'd said sure, how about the 7 o'clock show? and Larry said that they'd better see the 9 o'clock because it was "a little too close to the end of the Sabbath"—a remark he made challengingly since he was the only member of the Rovner family who occasionally observed it—so Randi had said sure, they could see the 9 o'clock, but if it was going to be that late, she'd definitely be hungry afterward and could they go to the Jerusalem for pizza? So, would it be okay, Larry wanted to know, if he took the Volvo on Saturday so he could pick Randi up? Ellen Rovner said that was fine with her; she had no plans for Saturday night—Michael was on call and he'd have the gold Avanti with his new, personalized RENVOR license plates—of course Larry could have her Volvo—even though she was the only person at the dinner table who suspected correctly that every last detail of the story, save for the fact that the Nortown was showing *French Postcards* at 9, had been invented. The truth of the matter was that there was a 33⅓ percent chance Larry would hang out with his band after practice and take turns at the batting cages, another 33⅓ percent chance he would condescend to accept Missy Eisenstadt's invitation to watch her younger sister Bibi dance in the Arie Crown Day School production of *Petrouchka,* and a final 33⅓ percent chance he would spend the night driving up and down Western Avenue contemplating whether it was worth taking the one-in-two-zillion chance that one of his teachers, friends, or relatives might recognize his mother's car parked in front of the Oak Theater's All-Nude Revue. But there was further a 100 percent chance that no matter which of those three options he chose, he would wind up telling his mother that he had spent the evening with the mythical Randi Nathan, if only to stop her incessant questions that could with one key inflection make a top high school scholar and musician feel like an incontrovertibly ugly and pathetic, sweaty masturbator.

"That sounds like a good movie," Lana said, thoughtful and mature. "I hope you enjoy it."

Michael Rovner made a motion to get up from the table, but before he could, Lana piped up and asked if anyone knew how to make her clothes phosphorescent; she asked if spraying her clothes with white phosphorescent paint might work. Her father allowed that it might and asked why she wanted to know. She said that it might be the way she would introduce her creative report on Marie Curie. The first thing Ms. Powis would grade her on was an "attention getter," which was worth two out of twenty points. And though some of her fellow students had managed to get the other students' attention—Matt Swannee had jumped up and down on a box of exploding snap-n-pops; Tom Bain had belched; and she herself had played the *1812 Overture* loud for her chest X-ray report—Ms. Powis was a tough grader. No one had gotten two out of two, because Ms. Powis had said that all the aforementioned attention-getting devices were "out of context"—she had written that phrase on the board. Lana theorized that if she entered in darkness, her entire outfit glowing while a voice she recorded on tape said first in French and then in English, "Marie Sklodowska Curie saw the world from inside as no one before," she would not only get the class's attention, she would be able to do so fully "in context." Her father said it sounded like a good idea. He said he would drive her to the hardware store to get the paint.

"Great," she said. "Then I'll get a 20. I know it."

Lana's father asked what she wanted as a gift if she got the 20. Ellen Rovner looked at him sternly—she disapproved of reward-based systems, but said nothing. Lana had anticipated her father's question. She had even presented her statement—"Then I'll get a 20. I know it"—in such a way that it presupposed Michael's question. She had hoped the question would come, hoped that it would come at the table—in front of witnesses. Calmly, politely, unassumingly, she requested the one thing she had wanted on her Bat Mitzvah and did not receive, the one thing she now wanted above all else.

"I want us all to take a trip to Paris for my winter break," she said.

"All right," her father said slowly. He swallowed. "All right, if it's affordable."

Ellen Rovner stood up. "So," she said, "is everybody through? Should we start dumping?"

WILLS / SILVERMAN

Muley

After Muley Wills had left Jill Wasserstrom at the back entrance of K.I.N.S., where Lana Rovner had loudly demanded to know what Jill had been doing with him, Muley walked in the direction of his apartment. But he didn't go straight there. Instead, he sauntered through the alleys between Devon and Arthur Avenues looking in trash cans for things to take or to sell. Jill's remark to Lana about the hickey had perplexed him when he overheard it—not because he thought that it hinted at any secret infatuation. He had all but given up that hope, especially after his one attempted kiss on the cheek while they were climbing the jungle gym during recess in sixth grade wound up missing its mark and smacking right into her chin; her braces had collided with her lower lip, giving her a mouth full of blood. Rather, what perplexed him about the hickey remark was Jill's snide, knowing tone, the one he'd only heard her employ when she was making fun of their teachers, particularly recess monitor Aviva Bernstein, hawk of the playground, perched on her lifeguard's chair, whistle around her neck, always ready to swoop down from her post, point a talon down at an errantly thrown ball, and gleefully snap, "Give me that ball; it's not yours anymore." Today it seemed that Jill was making fun of *him,* and furthermore, she was doing it in front of that opinionated, malevolent Francophile girl he recalled from Boone before she had transferred to a private school in Evanston.

Standing in the alley behind the telephone shop on California and Devon, where he found a spool of copper wire, Muley decided to write Jill's remark off to her moodiness. After her mother died, she had become increasingly sarcastic and short-tempered and he had made allowances. It was easier to do that than to call into question the motives of the one person in his eighth-grade class whom he could call a true friend. Muley put the wire in a pocket of his army jacket. Maybe, he thought, he could find another miniature speaker behind Radio Shack and complete one more crystal radio. They were certainly among his least creative projects. Most of the time, they only tuned in a couple of AM stations, sometimes only country tunes on WMAQ. But since they were mounted on squares of discarded wood from cracked two-by-fours Muley had salvaged from a construction site by the Chicago River drainage canal where Orthodox Jews emptied their pockets of sins for Tashlich, they had an illicit, underground air. There was always a kid from the neighborhood, some burnout down at Mather, or a retiree out for a bargain who would buy one for five bucks.

Muley walked through the alley carrying a Sun Drugs shopping bag. The errand he had run for his mother had thrown off his timing. Not only was the Neapolitan ice cream sure to melt if he dawdled as much as he liked to, he was also about twenty minutes behind his usual schedule, which meant that he would miss out on both dinner and some key alley finds. With his tall, gangly build, his loping gait, and his fraying army jacket, Muley was well known to the shop owners in the neighborhood; between 4:30 and 5, a number of them would emerge from the backs of their stores, shout "Hey, Muley," and present him with food. Bess Vaysberg from Knopov's Bakery would offer jam-filled *delcos* or *kichels* coated with granules of sugar; Ravi Khan from the Family Pizzeria provided tomatoes, green peppers, and cheese; Tommy Ho from the Shikdang Restaurant had hot and spicy bean curd at the ready; and Boaz at Nagilah Israel offered burnt falafel balls. Muley Wills had an insatiable appetite and an unvanquishable constitution, but food, though certainly welcome, was not the true purpose of his alley strolls. Food fueled him with enough energy so that he generally only needed four hours of sleep per night. Food was good to keep in the refrigerator on the off chance that his mother would eat some of it instead of the sweets she favored. But food would not make Muley money. For that, he turned to the alley behind Crawford's department store, where flawed pants or shirts could be turned into material for reupholstering jobs; Cut-Rate toys and Hobby Models, which stacked up discontinued and damaged kits for model cars and ships that Muley could strip down for parts; General Camera, which tossed out faulty flash-bulbs and cracked lenses; and Radio Shack, where most days at 4:55, Ajay Patel would take his cigarette break and load Muley up with batteries, cable, wire, and transformers.

But now it was past 5:00, Ajay's break was over—Muley could see the still-smoking butt of a cigarette on the asphalt beneath an orangey-pink alley light. Therefore, Muley would return to his apartment to pursue one of many unfin-ished projects, none of which seemed likely to generate the sort of income he sought. The way he figured it, he would need an additional $17,000 before his mother would be able to quit her jobs, go to school full-time, complete her final year and a half, and receive her long-sought degree in English Literature. Over the course of the last three years, some combination of ingenuity, perseverance, and all-too-sporadic luck had allowed him to put approximately $3,500 in his Lincoln Federal account. But at that rate, he wouldn't even have half the amount he needed before he'd have college bills of his own.

Everything would have been easier if Deirdre Wills had finally allowed him to take money from his father, or at least to convert his father's annual birthday gifts into cash. But Deirdre was adamant on this topic. She didn't want payments; she didn't want child support. If Carl Slappit Silverman wanted to give Muley some overpriced gift once a year on his birthday, that was fine, but no money would change hands. Working for the library and cleaning houses west of California was not the future she had envisioned for herself, but it was far better than taking money from him.

As Muley had heard the story, his mother had met Carl Silverman in 1966 while still a freshman at the Circle campus of the University of Illinois. Carl had been born on the old West Side and lived in Hyde Park. He had majored in Phi-losophy at the University of Chicago but had dropped out three years earlier when he discovered the blues.

It had happened one September night when he had taken his bone-white 1957 Thunderbird convertible out for a drive. He'd been working on a paper about Immanuel Kant and the Sublime but had been unable to connect Kant's theories to his own everyday existence. Suddenly, he realized he was lost on Indiana Avenue—every time he turned, he found a dead end. He got out of the car to ask for directions and found himself inside a crowded club called Theresa's where Muddy Waters was on stage singing "Sail on, my little honeybee, sail on," and it was at that precise moment that Carl discovered the meaning of the Sublime. He stayed until closing time and wound up giving Waters's pianist a ride home.

He came back the next eight nights, and each time he was thrilled to be the only white dude in the club. Nobody knew his name at Theresa's, but soon everyone started calling him Slappit because of how he slapped his hands against the tables when the music played. On the eighth night, he approached Waters and asked if he'd ever thought about cutting a record. Waters responded that he had, in fact, cut a number of records. Nevertheless, the next day Carl quit college, went to a music studio, and reserved ten hours for the following Sunday night in the hopes that Waters would record with him. Waters never showed, but some other musicians did, including Walter "Big Man" Wallace. They recorded ten songs, enough for an album Silverman called "Big Man Blues," Slappit Records' first release. Silverman took half his life savings, pressed five hundred copies, piled them in the back of his T-Bird, and drove from college campus to college campus, selling records for $1 each. When the first five hundred sold out, he printed another thousand. And when those thousand sold out, he had enough money to return to the studio.

By the time he met Deirdre, Carl had a small office and recording studio on North Avenue, above the Old Town Alehouse. He had already made eight records, and was about to make his ninth, this time with blues harpist Jimmy Wills, Deirdre's father. The album, *Wills's Ways,* would feature seven original Wills compositions, Waters's "Long Distance Call," and one tune Silverman himself had written: "Feelin' Lowdown But I Ain't Feelin' Too Bad." Deirdre first met Carl at her home, where her father had invited him—or maybe, upon further reflection, where Carl had invited himself. Jimmy Wills had never talked much, but now he was also suffering from cirrhosis of the liver. After consuming his dinner, he said he was ready for bed, and she was left to entertain Carl for the remainder of the evening, which was fairly easy, given that it only took one question to start Carl off on an hour-long soliloquy on any of his favorite topics, which included—but were not limited to—black music, Southern food, civil rights, and

Vietnam. He'd been kept out of the service by his extremely flat feet. At one point, he took off his shoes and socks and walked around barefoot to demonstrate just how flat they were.

Deirdre didn't find him attractive—he was unkempt, his features were harsh, he was at least three inches shorter than she was, and something about him smelled, if not outright bad then certainly stale—but she found his attention flattering and his knowledge impressive. And mainly because saying no to Carl didn't seem to be something anyone could do particularly well, she found herself going out with him practically every night—gamely attempting to enjoy the Steak Diane he insisted on ordering for her at Fritzel's, where he mistook her distaste for red meat for embarrassment at having so much money and attention lavished upon her—ultimately ending up in his bed down the hall from Slappit Studios while he played Muddy Waters records loud. It hadn't been her first time—that honor had come at the age of fifteen courtesy of Nolan Walsh, a church friend of her older brother Victor. But she wouldn't have been all that surprised if it was Carl's first time. It seemed more likely that he had just recently invented his swiveling and side-to-side thrashing technique accompanied by his deep moaning of "rock baby rock, now roll, roll; rock baby rock, now roll, roll" than learned it, as he asserted, from "the best goddamn hooker on Lake Street."

Though their nighttime encounters became more frequent, the man's technique did not improve. Nevertheless, three months after their first night together, Deirdre became pregnant. When he learned of the pregnancy, Carl became elated and insisted they name the child—boy or girl—"Muley," because the first time they made love, he had ejaculated just at the moment Muddy Waters sang "another mule kickin' in your stall." Deirdre consented but added the middle name Scott for her favorite author, F. Scott Fitzgerald. Shortly after Muley was born, Deirdre's father wound up in County Hospital. A private hospice was suggested, where Jimmy Wills's needs could be better attended to and where he might enjoy a greater degree of comfort. But it was expensive. Carl, who had moved into the Wills's house, suggested instead that they spend as much time as possible with Jimmy, invite his old friends over, allow him to play with his grandson, keep his mind occupied and his spirits up. This made good sense to Deirdre, who took a leave of absence from her studies and followed Carl's plan, even as her father's health declined markedly—until one day when she had the radio tuned to a rock station. Muley Scott was asleep in her bedroom and Jimmy Wills was sitting at the kitchen table, apparently cheerful, even though his breaths sounded wheezy and labored. At some point, Deirdre noticed the station was playing one of her father's songs—"Don't You Do That Thang"—only it wasn't him singing it.

"Daddy," she said. "Isn't that one of yours?"

"Don't sound like it," he muttered, coughed, then cleared his throat.

But she was certain of it, and after Carl came home that night, she asked him about it in the kitchen while her father and Muley were asleep. Carl beamed. He'd heard it, too. The manager for an English white-boy blues band had paid for the rights to cover two of Jimmy Wills's tunes. "Don't You Do That Thang" was already a hit in the UK and was now getting U.S. airplay. Deirdre asked if that meant a good deal of money was involved; Carl said of course, that was the point, but when she asked what percentage her father would see, Carl's mood soured. He told her he had taken a risk when he had purchased Jimmy Wills's tunes, that he hadn't coerced him, he hadn't put a gun to his head, and now that he was just beginning to see some return on his investment, damned if he was going to start renegotiating the deal. The money "Don't You Do That Thang" was generating wasn't just sitting around waiting for somebody to spend it; it was already being invested in both of their futures, in Muley's future, too. Deirdre asked how much her father had sold his song for. Carl said he didn't want to get into the particulars of the deal. Deirdre asked him again how much he had paid; if he didn't tell her how much, she would have to ask him to leave. Carl told her to "cool out" and said they'd discuss it later. Deirdre said she wasn't going to "cool out," nor was she going to "discuss it later." She asked him once more how much he had paid for "Don't You Do That Thang." Carl finally said he hadn't bought that song, in particular; he had bought her father's "catalog," which consisted of about sixty songs, and he had paid good money for it. Deirdre asked him what "good money" meant. Carl told her he'd spent nearly $1,000, and when she asked what "nearly $1,000" meant, he told her $800. Deirdre did some quick math. That meant, she said, that the song she had heard on the radio had been purchased for $13.33. Carl said obviously it wasn't that simple as they both heard Muley start to cry.

"Get out of our house," Deirdre told him. She went to get Muley and lifted him onto her shoulder.

Carl stormed out, taking a suitcase with him, saying that was fine with him, if that was her attitude, he was gonna leave, and he wasn't gonna come back either, that was final. Carl gave her a few days to simmer down, but the next time he tried calling, the phone had already been disconnected. Deirdre had borrowed money from her brother and moved in with him and they had brought their father to the hospice. Carl managed to track her down there one day. She was calmer, but also resolute. She told him their relationship was through. She didn't want money; if he tried to give her any, she'd just return it. If he wanted, he could send Muley gifts on his birthday, but she would refuse anything beyond that. Not only that, she would spread word throughout her father's network of musicians that Silverman was a crook. It was an idle threat—Jimmy Wills didn't have much of a network, unless you counted the guys he used to get drunk and shoot the shit with at Gerri's Palm Tavern. But it achieved the desired effect; Carl left her alone. Soon, he got out of the blues business, turned his attention to rock, and moved to LA. By 1974, Slappit Records was a multimillion-dollar record company, three months before Carl's thirtieth birthday.

Deirdre did not fare quite so well. After her father died in 1967—Muley was six months old at the time—she worked a series of jobs that declined in prestige each time she was fired, which was what inevitably happened between one hour and one year after she took a new one. She waited tables downtown at Charmets; she worked the soda fountain in the basement of Marshall Field's. She had trouble moving upward in any particular field because it was exceedingly rare to find anyone she had previously worked with to recommend her to any prospective employer. At nearly every job, she seemed to be sleepwalking, her eyes glazed, her mind oceans away. People would ask her questions and she'd take so long to answer that she wouldn't notice that her interlocutors had already started walking away. The job at the library had lasted as long as it had (eleven months) because she could get by with speaking no more than seven sentences per day. And, cleaning houses—though certainly demeaning and frustrating—was perfect too, since she could begin working when her employers left their houses and finish before they returned.

All this did not provide much for her and Muley to live on, though, nor did it allow her to save anything toward the college degree Muley knew she wanted. But the $3,500 he had earned had been incredibly labor-intensive, like trying to come up with $100 with only nickels, pennies, and dimes. At his age, he wasn't allowed to work an after-school job. And since Deirdre had forbidden him from making money by doing anything with even a hint of illegality about it, he was left to piece together whatever he could making electronic devices, entering photography contests, and working for $50 on weekends cutting up interview tape at WBOE, the local affiliate of National Public Radio.

Muley had swung that radio gig through Ajay Patel at Radio Shack. One of Ajay's regular customers, Mel Coleman, a weekend producer at WBOE and a frustrated writer, sought to hire a cheap intern so that he could work on novels and scripts after everyone else had gone home. Mel had authored a slim, ribald paperback advice book about women, grooming, and dating entitled *Mel's Manual for Men*. During the three months Muley had been working at WBOE, Mel had supposedly been refining a Chicago mob novel called *Godfathers of Soul*, but more often passed time eating health food, watching Muley work, and lecturing him about what constituted good writing: "Don't waste your time with description; nobody can see what you're talking about anyway"; "Don't write art shit; nobody wants to read it"; and "Make sure every chapter you write's got either a weapon, a fight, or a girl. And make sure your last chapter's got all three." Muley listened politely while editing interview tapes as Mel razzed him about girls and belittled Muley's chances at ever finding gainful employment. Not a day would go by when Mel wouldn't tell Muley, "Bet you wish you could do something with a network, make yourself some real money."

In the "editing suite"—suite was a generous description—there was a crude, dittoed flier advertising for correspondents for *Young Town,* a new WBOE program featuring "Real Kids from Real Places with REAL STORIES to Tell." Muley had surreptitiously copied the information and kept it taped to the wall above his desk at home, but it was only one of the moneymaking opportunities he was considering. There was a monthly trick photography contest in a photo magazine that seemed promising—top prize $50 plus five free issues—but Muley had already taken the $15 third prize the previous month for a photo of Jill Wasserstrom standing in midair and he had to wait sixty days before he entered another contest at that magazine. National Geographic's *World Magazine* was offering $100 for sandwich recipes; Muley had invented a "Chicken Cruncher" that used crumbled barbecued potato chips for texture and cream of chicken soup as a condiment, but even he hadn't been able to finish eating it. He had gotten encouraging rejection letters from the Milton Bradley game company for his Metric Hockey game; the letter was signed by the chief games designer, who termed Muley a "young man of no small talent." The *Chicago Tribune* want ads had advertised cash payments for inventions, and Muley had already created a working model for a miniature radar scope that could determine the speed of passing objects.

The *Young Town* tryout required entrants to produce a "five-minute recorded segment" about "a person who has profoundly influenced your life," which sounded easy enough except that there were few individuals who he could legitimately say had influenced him. Muley's life rarely seemed either noteworthy or dramatic enough to reflect upon, and those parts that might have qualified weren't those that Muley preferred to consider. He did quite well in school with personal essays, in which he both invented and overdramatized his life to such an extent that his teachers tended to pity his plight and admire his courage. His 700-word effort, "Nikki's Last Trip," about his fictional brother's overdose, was a third-prize winner in an All-City Essay Contest, which netted him a signed statement of congratulations from then-mayor Michael Bilandic. And Boone principal Loretta Wharram invented a new "Right Path" Award shortly after reading Muley's poem "Why I Won't Do It," in which he discussed how he had attempted suicide and snorting cocaine: "But I have heard old reason's voice /And it calls me to a brave new shore / For now I know I have a choice /And I won't do those things no more."

When Muley walked into his apartment, his mother was sitting and reading in a burnt-orange beanbag chair on the living room floor, a precarious stack of library books beside her. With the exception of Muley's bedroom, which was overstocked with gifts from Carl Slappit Silverman, the Wills's apartment, though large—it took up half the third floor of the building—was sparse, monastic. There were three mismatched wooden chairs, two floor lamps, a clock radio, and the beanbag chair in the living room. The kitchen was a counter, two wooden stools, a refrigerator, and a stove with one working burner. Deirdre's bedroom contained a cracked white dresser and a mattress on the floor. The bathroom had a stained mirror, a ratty shower curtain, and a toilet that gurgled throughout the night.

Seeing that his mother was reading, Muley did not interrupt her, for he knew that it was one of her few pleasures. Instead, he went to the kitchen and cut off a slice of Neapolitan ice cream and brought it to her on a plate with a spoon. Deirdre thanked him, and touched his hand briefly when he handed her the ice cream. But she didn't look up, just kept reading, swatting pages every time she finished one. A few days after she had taken the job at the library, Deirdre told Muley that her goal was to read every book in the literature section that she hadn't read before. It was not a large library, nor was it particularly well stocked; if it had been possible to read every book in any library, Nortown's would have been the one. But if Deirdre's goal seemed quixotic, Muley never would have said so. He never doubted anyone's ambitions—above his bed, there was a Ferrari ad clipped out of *Omni Magazine;* that ad read, "What Can Be Conceived Can Be Created." But more important, whenever Deirdre finished the book she'd been reading, she would come into his room to tell him the story. And though the stories she told may not have been as captivating as the ones Deirdre had told him many years before—his favorites had always been adventures that involved some amount of fantasy: *The Adventures of Baron Munchausen,* G. K. Chesterton's *The Man Who Was Thursday,* and Dr. Lewis Ridle's *The Talented Assistant*—and, though he might have preferred to talk to his mother about school or his projects or even girls, still, he would stay up feverishly doing homework, entering contests, devising inventions until she was done with her book.

On Muley Wills's desk was the gift he'd received from his father that September for his thirteenth birthday: A Radio Shack TRS-80 computer. As stipulated by Deirdre Wills, whose address and phone number were unlisted, the computer had been sent to Deirdre's brother Victor, who now lived in Atlanta, and Victor had forwarded it to Muley. The TRS-80 already had a thin layer of dust on its keyboard. In the first week he'd had it, Muley had taught it to play a very rudimentary game of chess. The machine could also draw stick figures and graphs and play Hang the Butcher, but it lacked the satisfying, tactile quality of pen and paper, of screws, wire, nail, and wood, and like practically every other expensive gift Muley had received from his father—from the Pong video game to the Weather Forecaster to the simulation game World War III—it fell into disuse almost immediately.

Against a wall in Muley's bedroom stood a lacquered, wooden bookcase Muley had built to house the books that Deirdre occasionally bought for him. He had always told her that those books meant more to him than anything his father had ever sent him. But she always regarded him dubiously when he said it, thought it odd that a thirteen-year-old boy would feel such a need to comfort an adult by saying such a thing, thought it somehow shameful that an adult would need so badly to be comforted by a child.

Still, what he told her was true; the only gift from his father that Muley used with any regularity was an NHL Pro Street Hockey set with a Stan Mikita stick, a net, and an orange plastic puck, all of which had helped make him—despite his negligible athletic skill—the most feared floor hockey player in all of Boone Elementary. He had become fascinated by the game when he was five and felt somewhat responsible that the Blackhawks hadn't won a Stanley Cup in his lifetime. He was six when the Blackhawks made the finals, and during the last game against the Montreal Canadiens, he was listening to Lloyd Pettit's radio broadcast and playing with a roll of masking tape. He noticed that when he ripped a piece of tape, goaltender Tony Esposito would come up with a key save. Henri Richard would fire a shot from center ice, Muley would rip off a piece of tape, and Esposito would make the save. It worked all through the third period with the score tied 4–4, but for just the minute, not even a minute, that he was going to be in the bathroom, he had handed the roll of tape to his mother and told her that if the Blackhawks were being threatened she should rip a piece of tape. And in that minute, that less than a minute, Yvan "The Roadrunner" Cournoyer shot what would prove to be the game-winning goal. It didn't matter that his mother had ripped the tape for him; he had known perfectly well that he had been the only one who could control the Blackhawks' destiny. And now, anytime he felt angry or frustrated, or whenever he just needed to brainstorm, he'd bring the net to the alley, pretend he was Stan Mikita, and slap goal after goal after goal.

That night, as he sat up in bed trying to think of someone who had profoundly influenced his life for the five-minute *Young Town* tape, he thought he might write something about Yvan Cournoyer. But after his mother came to tell him the story of Charles Dickens's *Dombey and Son,* he decided that a Canadiens right winger wasn't nearly significant enough. So he decided to make something up instead.

Michelle

O n the day she was to confront interim music director Douglas Sternberg, quit *H.M.S. Pinafore,* and resign from the Mather High drama club, Michelle Wasserstrom left her tough-girl outfit at home. She put her hair up in a bun and, instead of ripped jeans, a flannel shirt over a faded REO Speedwagon jersey, and dark blue sneakers, she wore a velour, sky-blue sweater with a high neck, a denim skirt with a slit up the right side, cowboy boots, and two dabs of Magie Noir perfume that she had received from some guy she couldn't re- member. Well, actually she *could* remember: some twerp named Arik who'd at- tempted to woo her in eighth grade with gifts that were as sad as they were sincere—a coleus plant, a picture book about Nadia Comaneci, unlistenable al- bums by Wings and David Crosby, a crystal radio purchased from some black kid far cooler than Arik could ever dream of being, and when all that failed, a stack of Bicentennial quarters, which she had returned to him. "If I wanted to be a hooker, it'd have to be for a lot more than quarters," she'd said. But that morn- ing when Jill Wasserstrom asked her where she had gotten the perfume, she said she couldn't remember. "All those guys run into one," Michelle said.

As was their ritual, the two of them walked west on Albion until they got to California. Normally, Michelle talked the whole way, but today she spent most of the walk deep in thought while Jill discussed Mrs. Korab's "Conflicts and Reso- lutions" projects; today, they would be picking countries and opposition groups in preparation for debates. Most of the kids were hoping to get either Israel or the PLO, and a few wanted to be Poland or the Solidarity trade union. But Jill, bored and aggravated by Mrs. Korab, hoped to challenge her, as well as herself. Korab had failed her and given her a "Do Over" on the first assigned essay— "The Greatest Country in the World." Jill had chosen the Soviet Union. When Mrs. Korab returned the paper, she wrote on it, "No, America is the greatest country in the world. DO OVER." Jill next wrote about Sweden. Once again she received a "D.O." Finally, after Jill rewrote the paper, declaring that it was an inane question and that almost every country was the greatest to those living there, Mrs. Korab declared a truce and gave her an "F" for Fair.

Now, for the debates, Jill sought to defend the least popular cause imaginable. The other morning, her father had, as always, left the radio on, tuned yet again to WBBM Newsradio 78, a station that literally made Jill nauseous as it reminded her of long Sunday Drives in her father's maroon Ford Granada to and from her uncle Dave's house in Elmhurst on "Parmesan Sundays," when Aunt Peppy would serve chicken, veal, or eggplant "Parmesan," riding with the windows fogged up, the windshield wipers, the defrost, and the floor heat going, and someone on the radio talking in a nasal voice about lines of cars waiting at gas stations. The WBBM report had discussed the dim prospects for the release of the American hostages in Tehran, which, Jill told Michelle, had given her direction for her assignment; she would ask Muley Wills if he would take the deposed Shah of Iran and she would take the side of the followers of the Ayatollah Khomeini.

"Really? Ayatollah Khomeini?" said Michelle, who wasn't listening carefully. "That sounds interesting."

At the corner of California and Albion, Michelle gave Jill a soul handshake and Jill headed north to Boone Elementary, while Michelle walked south on California. Most days, she hitched a ride to Mather, but today she walked the whole way. On her walk, she rehearsed her speech, particularly the tone of it—defiant yet forgiving, open yet resolved. "I am addressing you," she would begin, "as an officer in full standing of the Mather High School drama club." What made Michelle successful as an actress—her dedication to getting every line and gesture just right, her inability to put down a script until she had memorized all her lines and all her cues—thwarted her in other aspects of her life. When she focused on one thing—like, say, resigning from the drama club—she could no longer give her attention to anything else.

She had done no homework, hadn't even checked her assignment sheets to see if there were any quizzes she'd have to sneak out of. But Michelle had a strategy that served her well in classes in which she'd done no work. At the very beginning of class, she'd raise her hand and, when called upon, ask a question about the final exam. Then she'd sit back with an interested but not overly interested expression on her face; she'd learned to not appear too captivated by a lecture, or else a teacher, frustrated by an unresponsive class, would see her hand upon her chin, her head bobbing thoughtfully, and immediately call on her. And when it came time for an opinion question, anything that might draw on knowledge outside of the day's assignment, she'd lazily flop her arm back and opine at length when it was her turn to do so, making sure what she said was just a little too long-winded, a little too repetitive, so that a teacher would be less inclined to bring her into the discussion again. This approach had proved flawless in all classes except Trig. But Michelle was well aware that her Trig teacher, Mr. Hull, was obsessed by her body—sniffed the air when she walked by, had even told her once that she had good legs, just up and *said* that: "Michelle, you have reeeally gooood legs." So she'd routinely come into Hull's class late, smile, ask if he needed anyone to write on the board, then, when he said no, take a long time walking to her desk—let him look at her ass if he was that hard up—after which he'd be too embarrassed to even glance in her direction. After class, she'd rocket out of the room so he wouldn't have time to say anything disgusting to her.

The day went according to plan. After asking her English teacher, Mrs. Magnuson, when she would hand out topic sheets for final papers, she could think about how she would berate Douglas Sternberg in a quiet, understated way that would leave him utterly devastated. There was an outside chance he might even quit, rendering her resignation unnecessary. And then, after weighing in with an opinion that had some tangential relationship to William Faulkner's *As I Lay Dying*, she envisioned her tearful farewell to the drama director, Mr. Linton.

History class had gone even better. What sometimes was even more effective than loudly announcing random opinions was disagreeing strongly with the smartest, most talkative students. Not only did this tactic suffice as her contribution for the day, it won her respect as a courageous, independent thinker. In this case, she differed violently with Matthias Kimmel, who had come out in strong support of the internment of Japanese-Americans during WWII. "I so totally disagree with that," Michelle said. "That's just pigheaded and barbaric." And when Matthias asked for clarification, she repeated that what Matthias had said was "pigheaded and barbaric." Mr. Pitlock finally cut off discussion with, "Come on, come on, can't we hear from some other people today," after which Michelle could think for the rest of the period about Douglas Sternberg and *H.M.S. Pinafore*. She thought about them all through study hall, all through her hot-dog-and-fries lunch at Wolfy's, all through Trig, where Mr. Hull told her no, he didn't need anything written on the board, and all through PE, which she sat out, claiming to be suffering from "a woman thing; you know what I mean."

The only time her mind drifted was during Health, which was essentially Sex Ed taught with filmstrips about drugs, cigarettes, alcohol, and "Avoiding Stress in Your Daily Life." Technically, Michelle had already taken Health, but there had been a scandal when it was discovered that Bill Baumgarten—who had coached swimming at Mather since the late 1940s and still, for "hygiene purposes" insisted all boys' swim classes be conducted in the nude—hadn't been teaching anything at all. Instead, he'd been taking movies from the low shelves in the A/V room and letting his students watch Charlie Chaplin shorts, wrestling matches, travelogues, and, over the course of three consecutive sessions, his favorite film, *I Am a Fugitive from a Chain Gang,* while he sat in the back row and slept. Baumgarten had been relieved of his duties and all students who had taken Health with him in previous years were required to retake it with the new swimming coach, Rob "Straight Arrow" Farrow.

Straight Arrow, as he welcomed students to call him, was a onetime all-state swimmer from downstate Bourbonnais, and though only twenty-four, he was generally considered Mather's most talented coach. But in Health class, he seemed to know far less about drugs or sex than any of his students, never mind that he was already father to three young boys. With his innocent country boy's smile and his collection of inspirational T-shirts ("We've Got God," "Find God Now; Ask Me How," and "Have God, Will Travel"), he was a never-ending source of amazement and amusement to a class replete with pot-smoking, Cheap Trick–listening, fornicating and/or masturbating Jews and Catholics. Thus, his students constantly sought out new schemes to either embarrass or corrupt him, all of which inevitably failed and wound up only shaming their perpetrators, as in the time after Michelle, Myra Tuchbaum, and portly philosopher and former stage crew captain Gareth Overgaard had spent the night in Myra's basement and whipped up three batches of hash brownies in an Easy-Bake oven. Michelle had suggested they bake another batch and present it to Straight Arrow the next day. Which they did, whereupon Farrow told the trio, "Well, that sure is awful considerate of you. I don't touch chocolate myself, but my boys sure love it and they'll be awful thankful if I can slip them past their mother." That class concluded on a note of unconvincing slapstick comedy when Michelle approached

Straight Arrow's desk, told him "I don't feel so good," put a hand to her head, swooned, and collapsed, knocking the brownies to the floor. And the next day, consumed by guilt, Myra and Michelle brought a pan of nonspiked brownies to class. But Farrow refused them, saying, "My boys and I thought it was wonderful you brought those brownies, but when I told my wife, she said I better not take anything from anybody in case there was 'funny stuff' in them. Now, I know there's not, but just to keep my wife happy, I'm gonná have to say no."

Today, the futile effort to corrupt Straight Arrow had more modest aims. Before class, Myra had suggested a game of Twenty-five. The game began at the start of class. Everyone who wanted to play put a quarter in Myra's beat-up leather pencil case. The object was to get Straight Arrow to use one word in class twenty-five times and whoever asked the question that resulted in the twenty-fifth utterance of the agreed-upon word would win the contents of Myra's case. The pot had grown to $16.50 since Straight Arrow had not said either of the previous words (*homosexual* and *nocturnal emission*) as many as twenty times. Today's word, *condom* (Farrow pronounced it "con-DOME"), seemed far more likely to yield a winner. Practically all twenty-two students had their notebooks open and their pencils ready to keep score.

Michelle had begun the scoring early by asking if she could get pregnant through her jeans ("Not if your partner's using a con-DOME," Straight Arrow replied). Myra wanted to know which was a better method of birth control: coitus interruptus or a "con-DOME." ("A con-DOME," Farrow said.) Even the least talkative students became avid players. Ed Ruggierio, who normally spent the class carving images of marijuana paraphernalia into his desk with the words "Do Bongs" beside them, raised his hand for the first time all semester and scored two points by asking what somebody should do if he had an abnormally large penis and usually ripped his condom before ejaculating. "You can try a large con-DOME," Straight Arrow said. "Or you can try wearing two con-DOMES."

By the time a half hour had passed, the score was up to twenty-one and Michelle had all but forgotten about *H.M.S. Pinafore*. The entire class held its breath as Ed asked a question that seemed likely to push the score over twenty-five with fifteen minutes to spare. He asked Coach Farrow if he could enumerate all the different brands of condoms on the market and which provided the best value. But all Straight Arrow offered was "Well, there's all kinds of brands; there's Trojans, there's Ramses, you got all different kinds." Twenty-one Health students exhaled. But then Straight Arrow called on Myra, who asked, "Now I usually pronounce it 'condom,' but you keep saying 'con-DOME.' Which one is it?" To Michelle, this seemed a clear violation of some rule, but there was no way to challenge the question when Farrow responded, "Well, some people say condom, some people say con-DOME. Me, I say con-DOME." The score was up to twenty-four, and now almost every student had his or her hand up.

"This is real good," Straight Arrow said. "This is a real good topic."

Desperately, Michelle blurted out, "Which did you say? Condom? Con-DOME?"

But Farrow shook his head. "No, no," he said. "You know the rules—someone who's got their hand up. Who's got their hand up?" Michelle shot her hand up in the air as the coach surveyed the class, his eyes sweeping from left to right, looking now here, now there. "All right," he said, his gaze settling upon Ed Ruggierio. "I'm glad to see you participating today, Ed. What's on your mind?"

"Well, here's what I'm wondering," Ed said, sweeping his hair out of his eyes, but he was interrupted by a knock on the door.

"One second." Farrow held up a finger and walked to the door. He opened it to reveal Douglas Sternberg standing in the hall in a wrinkled white shirt with the sleeves rolled up, a thin, black leather tie with a white treble clef at the bottom, faded Levi's, and Hush Puppies. Sternberg whispered something to Farrow, who turned to Myra and Michelle. "Mr. Sternberg wants to borrow you gals," he said.

As they approached Sternberg, Michelle and Myra shared uneasy glances. Sternberg muttered "My office" to them, then slouched down the hallway, his head fixed on the ground as the girls tried to keep up, Myra wondering if she had left her pipe at rehearsal, Michelle hoping Douglas would issue a heartfelt apology for his behavior the previous night, which she could promptly reject, and neither of them thinking about the game of Twenty-five Ed Ruggierio had just won by asking, "I know what condoms are, but what are rubbers and shakers?" "Those are just other words for con-DOMES," Coach Farrow had said. Soon after, the coach asked why everyone had stopped participating.

Once Michelle and Myra had made their way down the hall to the drama office, Sternberg gruffly told Michelle to wait outside while he talked to Myra. There was no place to sit, so she paced the hallway for what seemed like an hour, pausing a moment to open the backstage door to the auditorium and gaze out nostalgically upon the vast stage and the empty seats before it. She feared the reason Sternberg was keeping Myra in there was that she was feebly arguing to keep her part, that he was planning to remove her from the role for which Michelle had so vociferously argued her case. But when Myra emerged, she was grinning elatedly. Michelle didn't have a chance to ask why, because just a moment later Sternberg was standing in the doorway muttering, "Miss Wasserstrom?"

Michelle strode quickly into the office. "I'll wait for you," Myra said as the door closed.

Sternberg sat on the desk and focused on a point in space behind Michelle's head. She waited for him to ask her if she wanted to sit down so she could refuse, but he didn't say anything, so she uttered one of her prepared lines: "What I have to say won't take long."

"Good. Because what I have to say won't take long either," Sternberg said, still not looking her in the eye. He said he knew it was still early in the rehearsal process and he appreciated the efforts she'd put into the production, but after the previous day's rehearsal, it seemed clear to him that he would need "a higher caliber of performer in the role of Buttercup." He wasn't asking her to leave the show—for the chorus, he'd need as many voices as he could find—but he'd talked to Henry Linton and they both felt it necessary to "go in a different direction."

Michelle's mind reeled. In the space of mere seconds, nearly a dozen responses swirled through her brain. She thought that Sternberg's beard was unkempt and looked rather pubic. She also thought that what Sternberg had said was perhaps the most offensive thing anyone had ever said to her, including the time that Eddie Pinkstaff had said he'd bet that in five years, she'd have a big ass. She also thought that Sternberg was right, that she had no talent, that she was just fooling herself, that in ten years, she'd be all washed up, lucky to get a job waitressing and making balloon animals at the Pickle Barrel restaurant, like that creep who appeared there on weekends. She also thought that if she had a gun, she might kill him. She also thought she might cry. But when Sternberg told her that the decision was hers—she could either keep the role and embarrass herself or make "the honorable choice" and "step down"—the only thing she said to him as she stormed for the door, her eyes blazing with a wounded but murderous rage, was "See you in rehearsal, Sternberg."

Myra was waiting impatiently outside, thumbs tucked in the front pocket of her overalls. Michelle asked her what the fuck she was grinning about.

"What'd he say?" Myra wanted to know.

"Just bullshit," Michelle said. She asked if they could "grab a quick square" before last period. Myra said she was out of cigarettes, but maybe they could bum one from some burnout in the smoking area. Nobody was out there, though. It was nearly 2:45 and most of the smokers had cut out; they were over in the Wolfy's parking lot eating french fries, sneaking bong hits by the tennis courts, lurking around the Driver's Ed range discussing the finer points of hot-wiring muscle cars. Michelle and Myra just stood in the cold mist, hands in their pockets, Michelle bitching that it was too cold to be wearing a skirt, Myra bitching that it was too cold to be wearing clogs and no socks.

"Fucking asshole," Michelle said, blowing on her hands and rubbing them against each other.

"Who?"

"Sterndick."

"Really?" Myra asked. "I think he's kind of cute."

"You're fucking high," Michelle said.

"Wish I were," said Myra. "You know what he told me?"

Michelle shook her head.

"He told me that my singing voice was 'gentle and undulating' and he'd never heard anyone 'do justice' to 'Refrain, Audacious Tar' like I did."

Michelle felt her cheeks flush and her stomach drop like a floor suddenly opening up beneath her. It was so absurd that it was almost funny—for him to say that about Myra, Myra Tuchbaum, who, though fun to party and swap sex stories with, had no musical theater experience, wore the same nasty faded overalls and blue bandanna every day, was only really convincing on stage playing fifty-year-old Jewish or Italian mothers, had a scratchy voice that sounded like cigarettes, and—this was mean but had to be acknowledged, Michelle thought—was really quite *heavy* to be playing a love interest.

And then it dawned on her. Jesus Christ, she should have seen through it immediately. This was some asshole director's technique, some supposedly subtle means of *motivating* her. How old did he think she was? Thirteen? That tactic worked when she was performing in fables for the JCC Footlighters Troupe, when old Morrie Weiss threw his annual tantrum one week before opening day and threatened to cancel the show, screaming, "You're dreck, I've never seen such dreck," then stormed out the door with his fat high school lackey Hippo trailing behind him. He'd return ten minutes later muttering Yiddish epithets, swigging from a flask of Canadian Club, and threatening to quit and leave Hippo in charge, while all the terrified adolescents scrambled around, saying, "We're gonna do the best job we've ever done" and "Yeah, let's do it for Morrie" and "Get it right so we don't have to work with Hippo." And then on the night before the show, Morrie would come in drunk, tears in his eyes, and say this was the best cast he'd ever worked with, the best show he'd ever directed. But she was a junior now; did Douglas Sternberg really think she would fall for that crap?

Armed with this knowledge, feeling exasperated yet also exhilarated for having figured it out so quickly, Michelle could dismiss Sternberg from those whose opinions were worthy of consideration, reestablish solidarity with Myra ("He's right; it's about time someone recognized how hard you're working"), and spend Debate class thinking not about *H.M.S. Pinafore* but about whether to break up with Millard Schwartz, even though Schwartz's uncle was friends with a scalper who'd promised tenth-row seats for the December Who concert at the Amphitheater. While Barry Tewlow and Ed Ruggierio delivered their "persuasive speeches," Barry's about why *Playboy* should be read for its editorial content, Ed's about marijuana legalization, Michelle determined that since the Who concert was sold out, there was really no reason to send Millard to Davy Jones's locker, since he was no more or less irritating, clingy, or expectant than any of her previous three boyfriends. Plus, he had a car.

At that night's rehearsal, after Mr. Linton had assured her that, no matter what Douglas Sternberg said, she was his only choice to play Buttercup, Michelle felt completely at ease. What Sternberg had said to her earlier was better than a compliment; it was an insult uttered by someone she didn't respect, serving only to prove its opposite. When Buttercup was supposed to be off stage, Michelle sat in the auditorium in the second row, chewing sour apple gum, her boots wedged in the space between the two seats in front of her, smiling approvingly at the rehearsal, applauding after Myra Tuchbaum and Dean Poulos's duet, rolling her eyes and smirking when Sternberg railed against the chorus. When Mr. Linton's cheeks turned red because Millard Schwartz could not follow the steps of the sailors' dance, she offered to go out and get coffee. And when it was her turn to go on stage, despite the fact that she had blown off vocal warm-ups to go smoke with Myra and Ed Ruggierio, who made them pay him a quarter for cigarettes even though he'd won $16.50 during Twenty-five, she felt so in control of her

body and her voice that it barely even bothered her that Sternberg would probably take credit for her performance. When it came time to plant a kiss on Millard,
it felt a million times better than it ever had in his ridiculous Opel with its selection of three already-antique 8-track tapes. "What's up with you, Shelly?" Myra
asked her during a break. "You get laid last night or what?"

During rehearsal, she was well aware that Sternberg was intentionally ignoring her. He told the chorus they sounded like "a bunch of raving ninnies," and if
they didn't come in with "and a right good captain, too!" on beat, he'd have them
replaced by a group of "retards" from a nearby school for students with behav-
ioral problems. But whenever Michelle finished a number, he just said, "All right,
let's move on, shall we?" and flipped ahead in the score.

Rehearsal ended at 9:03 P.M. Sternberg tried intimidating the custodian who
wanted to close up the school on time by telling him, "As long as we work, you
work," but when the lights went out three minutes later, Mr. Linton said that
everybody had done a good job and he'd see them all on Monday. A group of ju-
niors and seniors told Michelle that they were going for pizza at Gulliver's, which
would necessarily lead to a trip to get stoned atop Mt. Warren and, ultimately, sex
with Millard Schwartz. But appealing as this sounded, it also seemed both immature and overly familiar. And since Michelle was feeling particularly pleased
with herself, she turned down the opportunity. She said she'd promised to treat
her little sister to a night out.

This wasn't true, not even remotely, but as she walked north on California
past the tennis courts, the pink neon Wolfy's sign before her, she did feel as if
she'd been neglecting Jill lately, spending too much time complaining to her, not
giving her enough good, solid advice; if she'd known as much on her Bat Mitzvah
as she did now, she wouldn't have made as many mistakes, Michelle thought.
Then she tried to think of any mistakes she'd really made but couldn't recall any
that weren't funny in retrospect. This train of thought was promptly derailed by
the sound of a honking car horn.

A sleek, black Jaguar XJ-S was driving slowly up California, approaching Peterson; out of the driver's-side window, a hand was motioning to her. Michelle
had made a habit of getting into strange cars ever since she had been a freshman
and, during homeroom orientation, had seen a film entitled *Stranger Danger,* in
which some pervert whose voice echoed ominously enticed teens, asking them to
"Come get in my *car car car;* come take some *candy candy candy.*" It was one of

many films she had found insulting to her intelligence and that inspired her to act counter to its advice. Had it not been for filmstrips, educational movies, and Rabbi Shmulevits's sermons, she might never have smoked pot, had unprotected sex, or contemplated getting into the Jaguar. In fact, the only thing that made her hesitate was how clean and expensive the car looked. She would have favored catching a ride in a beat-up Dodge Demon, its tailpipe dragging against the asphalt, kicking up sparks. She liked cars with mufflers that rumbled, cars with flames painted on the side, cars from which the stereo had been stolen, replaced by a $9.95 tape recorder playing snatches of Deep Purple and Yes songs taped off the radio. She liked cars with glove compartments filled with tapes, crumpled cigarette packages, condoms, and owner's manuals charred by battery acid.

The Jaguar, on the other hand, looked like the car of someone "respectable," someone who lived west of California, someone in his forties with a wife and family, someone who coached Little League on weekends but harbored strange, inner demons whose cravings were satisfied by clandestine hand jobs in parking lots behind abandoned breweries, someone far creepier than the driver of any $50 beater. Nevertheless, Michelle walked toward the car. It was only when she had reached the yellow center line that she recognized Douglas Sternberg.

"Miss Wasserstrom?" he said.

She said nothing.

"You heading north?"

She nodded.

"I'll give you a lift." And before she could come up with a quick, plausible excuse, Sternberg repeated himself. "Come on, get in, I'll give you a lift."

It all happened too quickly—the honking, the wave, the walk to the car—for Michelle to gauge her true emotional reaction; before she had figured out whether she was really still upset with Sternberg, she was sitting in his passenger seat, adjusting the seatback, kicking her right boot up on the dashboard, and telling him he could drop her off on Campbell. The scene unfolded before her as if it weren't really happening, part of a dream in which someone acted like one person but looked like another—it was Richard Nixon, *but it was really my father;* it was some creep in a Jaguar, *but then he was Douglas Sternberg.* And since it all did feel like a dream, it didn't seem to matter what she did. The radio was tuned to WFMT, a classical music station, but without asking, she leaned over and turned the knob one station over to The Loop, which was playing Molly

Hatchet. She turned up the volume. And when Sternberg started speaking, she yawned loudly without covering her mouth.

Sternberg said he had a confession to make. Michelle opened the window halfway and dangled her boot outside. "I didn't mean what I said this afternoon," he said. "It's obvious how good you are. You know that."

Michelle shrugged as Sternberg turned the station back to WFMT, which was broadcasting news headlines: In Iran, ten hostages had been released but more than fifty remained imprisoned. At the corner of California and Rosemont, Sternberg stopped at a red light and stared blankly out the window in the direction of the Ner Tamid Synagogue; on the wall in raised metal letters, a passage from the Talmud was written—"And Thou Shalt Teach Them Diligently Unto Thy Children." Sternberg said that in part he'd been testing Michelle, seeing if she was as resilient as she seemed. That was part of it, he said. Michelle turned the radio dial back to The Loop. She cranked up "Flirting with Disaster."

The other part of it was more complicated, he said. When he looked at her, he saw a lot of what he'd been like in high school. He'd been the star of every show. He'd been voted "Most Likely to Go to Hollywood" his junior year and "Most Likely to Go to Broadway" his senior. Now he'd been to both places and wished that somebody had told him how hard it would be, how both cities were strewn with Most Likely To's, how being a star at Mather meant nothing outside of West Rogers Park.

As he signaled a right turn onto Devon, Sternberg said he'd been up since six working on a musical—something big, something exciting, something that hadn't been tried before—but now he was exhausted and needed some coffee, did she know any place where he might get some? Michelle told him he could probably get a cup at Gigio's. Douglas asked if she'd mind if they stopped for a quick cup. Michelle said sure, she didn't mind, but she'd stay in the car. While he was gone, she blasted the radio, cranking "Fly by Night," the first of two Rush songs The Loop was playing for Doubleshot Night. The car sucked, she thought; the leather smell was asphyxiating and, she noted, there was nothing interesting in the glove compartment.

When Sternberg returned, he turned down the volume of the radio. He drove east slowly, catching every light. The neighborhood brought back memories, he said. He used to live just a bit west of here, and now everything was different. The businesses were getting more diverse; there were Indians here now and Pakistanis and even some Arabs east of California. And the West Side was getting increasingly Orthodox. But he didn't mind any of it. He said he found it interesting. Then he asked Michelle if she liked any music besides rock 'n' roll and if she'd ever been to the opera. Michelle said she had been to the Lyric Opera to see *La Bohème* and enjoyed it, omitting that the reason she'd enjoyed it was that it had been part of a drama club field trip and not only had she and Myra snuck a pipe into the bathroom during intermission, they had managed to trick Barry Tewlow into thinking they were having an orgasm contest; whoever got his girlfriend off first, they told him, would win Myra's dime bag. During the moment when the actress playing Mimi was singing one of her consumptive arias, Tewlow's mousy, beak-nosed girlfriend Debbie Posner moaned, "Ohhhh, ohhhh, Barry!" Michelle and Myra laughed so hard that an usher booted them out; they smoked in the back of the school bus until the opera was over.

Douglas said he didn't care much for *Bohème.* There was very little opera he liked; most of it was "kitsch." But this season, the Lyric was premiering *Einstein on the Beach,* by Philip Glass. He had an extra ticket; he asked if Michelle might be interested in joining him.

"It's about Einstein?" Michelle asked, dubious. An image popped into her head of Rabbi Einstein, her *Aleph* teacher, skulking about Lunt Avenue Beach in a pair of saggy, pee-stained trunks.

"It's contemporary," Douglas told her. "You might find it interesting. You wouldn't have to say you were going with me."

There were few things Michelle would pass up if they would make for good stories afterward, though accompanying Douglas Sternberg came awfully close to crossing the border between what was either beyond consideration or worth it for the hilarity it would later provide.

"When?" she asked. They were stalled at the corner of Devon and Western. Michelle said he could drop her off here, but Sternberg said he didn't mind driving a few blocks out of his way. It was late, he said; it wasn't a good time to be walking.

"December eighth," he said.

They were crossing Western now, luggage, electronics, and T-shirt importers to the north of them, a tavern, an empty Cantonese restaurant, Laundrytown, and the Willses' apartment to the south.

Michelle shook her head. "Can't do it," she said. "There's a Who concert."

Sternberg reminded her that there was a technical rehearsal for *Pinafore* scheduled for that day and his invitation was based only on condition that it be replaced by something of equal educational value. A Who concert didn't qualify. Michelle said that she and Millard had already cleared the date with Mr. Linton. Douglas asked what Millard had to do with it, was he her boyfriend? Michelle said she wasn't technically dating him, they just screwed from time to time and would continue to do so until she had money to buy concert tickets.

Sternberg stopped his car in the Burger King parking lot. Attendance at the December 8 rehearsal was mandatory, he said; those who missed it would be replaced by their understudy for the run of the show. Michelle snorted at this assertion. She suggested to Sternberg that he sell his ticket to "Rabbi Einstein Goes to the Beach" and buy a ticket to the Who concert; maybe that way he might scare up a date instead of threatening people who didn't want to go with him to the opera.

Douglas Sternberg suddenly got quiet. The radio was playing "Working Man." Michelle was tapping her boot against the windshield in time with the cymbal. Fiercely, he twisted the volume knob all the way to the right. It was a good radio. Even with the volume turned all the way up, the sound didn't lose any of its fidelity. Michelle kept tapping her boot. Sternberg stared straight ahead, bit his lip. Then, furiously, he threw his arm across Michelle's lap and flung open the door with such force that it slammed back shut. He threw it open again, then stared straight at her. Michelle knew the best way to leave a car was to do it slowly. She smirked briefly, swiveled to her right, placed her feet on the parking lot asphalt, stood up, and rested one hand on top of the car door.

"See you at rehearsal, Sternberg," she said as he slammed the accelerator, the car door swinging shut on its own as the Jaguar completed a loop in the parking lot. Sternberg sped west on Devon, Rush blaring out of his speakers as Muley Wills, pointing his radar scope out his front window, clocked him at 52 miles an hour.

Burger King was closed, but Michelle had a taste for french fries. It was crisp outside and clear, a nice night for a walk. She figured she'd stop by the apartment and pick up Jill, and maybe they could take a walk to Lippy's Red Hot Ranch before it closed at ten. Michelle liked Devon this far east. The farther west she walked, the more bored she became. The more sleazy import-export shops and the fewer Judaica bookstores the better. Living west of Western was fine; it was safer for Jill, safer for her father. But if she ever had to live west of California, she just might have to kill herself.

When Michelle got home, her father was on the couch snoring, a copy of the *Nortown Leader* beside him. He sprang up when she arrived. He said he'd just been reading the *Leader* and must have dozed for a second. He was reading Gail Schiffler-Bass's review of the House of Canton; she was a good writer, he said— smart. "She's the gal that talked to me a good while," he explained.

Michelle walked over to him and kissed his sandpapery cheek; he hadn't shaved since the morning, but he still smelled faintly of lime.

"I'm gonna go get some fries," she said. "I'm gonna see if Jill wants to come."

Charlie made as if to stand. "I can give you kids a ride," he said.

"No, Dad, go to sleep," Michelle said. "We've got to talk: girl stuff."

"Oh," Charlie said, and he slumped back down. "Girl stuff."

When Michelle walked into her bedroom, she knew something had changed since she had left that morning but couldn't immediately identify what it was. Jill was at the desk sitting cross-legged on her chair, a stack of *Time* and *Newsweek* magazines and an opened copy of the Inter–Jericho volume of *Encyclopaedia Britannica* in front of her. She was writing feverishly in a notebook.

"Hey, Jilly-Jill," Michelle said. Jill looked up, said hi, and went back to her work. Michelle asked if she felt like going to Lippy's for fries. Jill said no, she was too busy. Michelle knew there was really no purpose to doing homework in grammar school, but she didn't push it. Somehow, the concept of being rejected by her little sister made her feel old, clumsy, unattractive.

"What are you working on?" Michelle asked, peering over Jill's shoulder.

"The report about Iran," Jill said without looking up.

Michelle nodded, pretended that she was interested, that she thought school mattered. And then, as she walked to the door saying she'd be back within the hour, it struck her: what was different about the room. She stared at the wall above Jill's bed. Jill had taken down all the posters from her side of the room. Gone were Led Zeppelin, Pink Floyd, and Mick Jagger. In their place, a picture clipped out of *Newsweek* of Ayatollah Khomeini.

Michelle took a long look at the back of her sister's head as she wrote at her desk. "I'm getting fries," she said.

Larry

I n 1970, when the Beatles officially announced their breakup, Larry Rovner was only eight, and he didn't understand why they couldn't just work out their differences. But now, as he sat in his basement bedroom and practice facility with his bass player, Arik Levine, waiting vainly for the other members of Rovner! to arrive, it all made sense. It was true that at their last practice, Ben Jacobs had said there was a fifty-fifty chance he'd make it and a fifty-fifty chance he'd have to go with his parents for kosher Chinese. And Randy Weinstock had said they should start without him and if his family wasn't going to St. Joe for the weekend, he'd let them know. The simple fact that Randy and Ben hadn't arrived wasn't what troubled Larry as much as what that fact clearly symbolized: that he was the only band member fully committed to the music. The argument they had had the previous week was typical. Ben had said he didn't mind calling the band Rovner! but wondered if it wasn't sending the wrong message; there were four band members and the name could just as easily have been anybody's surname. Larry, not wanting to bring up the obvious fact that, no, it couldn't just as easily be anyone else's surname, since he'd started the band and had written all of the songs except two, reminded Ben that they had agreed the name should be one of the band members' surnames and, quite simply, his was the coolest. You couldn't call a band Jacobs!, you couldn't call a band Levine!, and you certainly couldn't call one Weinstock! Arik said that Weinstock! would be funny, because everyone would think it was a joke about Woodstock. Yes, Larry said, it was a good joke, but this was a serious band.

The conversation had ended there and practice had gone well until Randy's mom came by to pick him up and Arik invited her down to listen and she had told Larry to enunciate more when he sang because she couldn't hear the words. It had taken all of Larry's inner fortitude to keep from kicking her out of the basement. But now Larry wondered if they all weren't holding some sort of grudge. Maybe that's why no one was here. Yes, Arik Levine was here, but he was the most expendable member of the band and he made Larry uncomfortable, sitting there with his bass on his lap, reading a creased copy of Ray Bradbury's *The Martian Chronicles.* Larry didn't know how long he could sit in silence at his drum kit, pretending to revise the lyrics to his song "(My Lovin' Ain't) Always Orthodox" in his spiral notebook, wishing he knew how to play guitar well enough so that he could play the Purim show solo and acoustic. So after a half hour of Arik reading and Larry crossing out and rewriting the same words, Larry said it didn't seem like the other guys were going to show, and maybe he should just give Arik a ride home. Arik said okay, but he had to call his dad first and tell him not to pick him up. Larry said he had to get something from upstairs before they left anyway.

The Rovner house was empty. Larry's father had phoned to say he'd been called in to work that night at Chicago Lutheran. And his mother and Lana had walked over to the Nortown Library to check out books about Marie Curie, after which they would try to see the 7:00 show of *French Postcards* at the Nortown Theater. Once Larry had gotten rid of Arik and returned home, the time would have seemed optimal to try to decode the scrambled images of X-rated movies broadcast on Channel 46 via a new, experimental pay-per-view service called YOUR-TV—available only in a few Chicago area zip codes. But when Larry flipped the TV in his father's bedroom to Channel 46, the only image he could make out after staring at the rainbow swirls on the screen was Julie Andrews in a nun's outfit. A quick glance at the *TV Prevue* confirmed his worst suspicions: YOUR-TV's adult broadcasting service did not begin until 10:00 P.M., at which point he'd have to wait for everyone to go to sleep before he could slip into the living room to watch the last scrambled minutes of *Sex Patrol.*

Lately, for Larry Rovner, life seemed to be little more than a series of detours on the road to calm, unhurried masturbation. YOUR-TV was just the most acute symptom of a greater problem. For even when everybody was asleep, he could never be fully certain that Lana would not come downstairs for a glass of milk, that his mother would not come downstairs to fetch a glass of Kahlúa, that his father would not come downstairs to ask what he was watching. Usually, he could pull his hand out of his shorts and flip the channel in time to some old movie or community affairs broadcast, and tell his father or his mother or his sister, "There's nothing good on; I'm going back downstairs to sleep." But that didn't alleviate the stress he experienced from the chance that he *might* be discovered, which was compounded by the fact that YOUR-TV scrambled not only its image to nonpaying households but the audio as well, and he had to turn the volume up all the way so that he could hear the dialogue. He knew no one upstairs could hear the sound he had to strain to make out while standing and jerking himself off in front of the TV. The problem was that every ten minutes or so, Channel 46 provided a station ID, which was *not* scrambled, so that more than once, near the point of some porn star's climax, the TV would scream out at parent- and sister-waking volume, "YOU'RE WATCHING YOUR-TV. SUBSCRIBE NOW!"

A phone number Ben Jacobs had given him—976-GOOP—had proved equally, if not more, problematic. Larry had mistakenly thought that it would cost the same as calling sports results to find out basketball scores, and phoned "Inge" from *Swank* magazine about a dozen times to listen to her recorded voice tell him, "*Ach!* You have caught me right in *zee* middle of my exercises." Larry knew the phone bill was wrong when it displayed thirty-five calls totaling $105, but he also knew that his explanation ("Actually, there's a girl from K.I.N.S. who ran away to California and got a job working for the phone sex line and me and Ben kept calling up because we thought we could convince her to move back to Chicago") was not credible. He never stopped to consider why the number of calls had trebled, attributing it to either an accounting error or an unscrupulous billing department.

One might have thought that Larry's father, a rabid pornophile himself, would have been slightly more open-minded about his son's interest in "girlie mags." But the one time he noticed that Larry had pilfered a magazine from the meticulously organized collection he kept by the toilet in his bathroom, he knocked on Larry's door, and when Larry answered, he had extended his hand and demanded "*Penthouse,* April 1976 edition, please?" adding superfluously, "Whenever you're done with it."

Everything, it seemed, was conspiring to rob Larry of his privacy. He always had the sensation that he was being judged, watched both up close and from a distance, that someone was always just around the corner waiting to catch him in some lewd act. Which was why he knew that after he had dropped Arik off, even though he would spend part of his night in the Volvo cruising up and down Western Avenue, there was no chance in hell he would have the courage to buy a ticket at the Oak Theater for the All-Nude Revue ("Bring Your Cameras!" the ad in the *Tribune* said). But just on the outside chance that he might happen to drive by right after a fire had emptied the theater, allowing him a private show, he took a $20 bill from his father's sock drawer. If nothing else, that action allowed Larry to consider the possibility that the evening's highlight might not be one that would be shattered by a voice bellowing, "YOU'RE WATCHING YOUR-TV!"

After an uncomfortable drive, in which a grand total of forty-three words were exchanged, Larry told Arik he'd see him at the next band practice, after which Larry turned on the radio and was thrilled to hear "Sultans of Swing," by Dire Straits, a band fronted by Jewish guitarist Mark Knopfler. Larry turned it up loud, slammed on the gas, and swerved onto Western heading south to Peterson. There were few things more enjoyable than driving his mother's car with a breeze going and the radio on; when he was driving, every song sounded good, and every song sounded easy. The Oak Theater was only a few miles ahead on Western, but he wasn't quite ready to go there, so he turned west and challenged himself to drive by as many girls' houses as possible before he got to California. Sometimes Larry stayed up late at night reading the phone book, memorizing the addresses of girls he considered "north of decent-looking." But even though he spent countless hours planning this or that date, washing and conditioning his hair with Agree, fluffing it up with an Afro pick until it sat just right, picking the least-messy item on the menu at Nagilah Israel, holding in his piss so his date wouldn't picture him going to the bathroom, practicing the end-of-the-evening-in-the-Volvo dialogue, he was certain that the best relationships were the ones that started by accident. That's how it had happened with Hannah Goodman; they'd sat next to each other on the motor coach on the way back from the Wailing Wall; they were both leaving the next day, her parents had already left, she was lonely, she said, and invited him up to her room to watch TV. Two Maccabee beers and three bags of peanuts later, his virginity was gone. And six hours later, so was Hannah. It was the best night of his life and none of it had been planned; therefore, at every opportunity, Larry sought to create scenarios in which more accidents of this sort might be possible.

True, it was unlikely he'd find Allie Shapiro walking home on Artesian Street at precisely 7:45 P.M., but if he went right then left then right then left from Artesian to Granville to Campbell to Rosemont to Maplewood to Devon, chances were better that if he couldn't find Allie, he might run into Shirley Patinkin or Sandy Strimling or Debbie Posner or any of the other girls whose addresses lay between Western and California. He made sure not to go any farther west, fearing that he might encounter Missy Eisenstaedt and her family en route to *Petrouchka* (Larry had declined that invitation, citing band practice and a cold). But Larry didn't find anyone, so he drove back north to Peterson to get a hot dog at Wolfy's instead.

Wolfy's hot dogs weren't kosher, especially not when slathered with cheese, but the temptation of a double cheese dog with everything and a large fries was too great to let Jewish doctrine interfere. And rather than be ashamed by his purchase, Larry approached it with a "What's it to you?" attitude, adjusting his yarmulke clip as he bellowed, "Double cheese the works!" The idea was to consume the frankfurter en route to the Oak Theater, ripped Wolfy's bag spread out on his lap to prevent cheese from dripping on his pants. But this plan was altered slightly when someone came up from behind him and poked him in the shoulder.

"Hey, yeshiva boy," Michelle Wasserstrom said.

Larry recognized her immediately. In fact, he wondered briefly why her apartment on Campbell hadn't been one of the stops he usually included on his driving tours of the Cute Girls' Homes of West Rogers Park. He remembered her most clearly from grade *Dalet* at K.I.N.S., where in the space of the 1975–76 school year she had transformed from a fairly demure girl who obediently recited the *Ashrai* to a sullen, sarcastic underachiever unable to remember any words at all to the kaddish, the Jewish prayer for the dead. And then there had been the grotesque spectacle of her Bat Mitzvah; he remembered the reception, held in some basement that had an aspect of horror movie about it; at any moment, it looked as if the walls would bleed. He remembered asking Chaya Wasserstrom— for that had been her Hebrew name—why her mother wasn't there, and she had stormed right past him. He remembered the champagne snowball, the way Chaya would drape herself over whatever boy she was dancing with, kissing him long, deep, and hard every time the bandleader said "champagne snowball," while her eight-year-old sister stared down at the ground and her father kept grinning artificially and forcing laughs. He remembered finding that scene appalling, but he also wondered why she hadn't chosen him for the snowball.

He hadn't seen much of her after that; she rarely showed up to *Heh* the following year, and when she did, she sat in the back with Avi Sherman and mocked Rabbi Meltzer, intentionally screwing up the songs he led on guitar. And now she was standing before him in blue jeans and a faded denim jacket over a black

T-shirt on which was written in white script, "Disco Sucks!" Larry pretended to take a moment to place her, fearing that if he identified her right off, she'd immediately deduce he was the sort of person who knew the addresses and a good percentage of the phone numbers of almost every girl he'd known since second grade. "Don't I know you from somewhere?" he asked. Larry stopped for a moment and pretended to finally recognize her. "Chaya," he said, snapping his fingers and pointing at her.

"Ye-*HOO*-da," she said.

"Larry's okay," he said as they shook hands. "I don't use Yehuda when I'm out of school."

"Ida Crown?" she asked.

He nodded. "Yeah."

"Come on," she said and motioned to him.

"What's going on?" he asked.

"You're buying us beer."

She led him to a back table that looked out onto Peterson Avenue. She introduced him to Myra Tuchbaum, whom Larry also pretended not to recognize at first, even though they had all gone to Hebrew school together and he distinctly recalled conversations that he and Ben, then Binyamin, Jacobs had had about Myra's chest. For a time, they had referred to breasts as "Tuchbaums."

"You might recall her better as Shiffra," Michelle said.

"Oh, that's right, that's right," Larry said. "I knew you looked familiar."

Myra assessed him dubiously and looked back down, hoping Larry didn't know that his mother was her psychologist. Meanwhile, Michelle introduced Larry to Gareth Overgaard, a hefty, bearded fellow in a green revolutionary army cap. Gareth, Michelle explained, was confused about his sexuality and was beset by a high voice that usually gave him away to liquor store checkout workers who carded him the moment they heard him speak.

"Yehuda's our secret weapon," Michelle said as Gareth gave her the finger. "They're not gonna card some yeshiva boy."

Larry reminded her that he wasn't at the yeshiva; he was "up at the academy," and it wasn't Orthodox Judaism there, it was Conservative. He said that ever since Bob Dylan's conversion he'd made an effort to seem more Orthodox in his appearance, but he still had some "significant reservations" about some aspects of Jewish doctrine. But Michelle continued undaunted. She asked him to say a *bracha* over her french fries. After a bit more time teasing Larry, she returned to her conversation with Myra and Gareth, most of which was conducted in a sort of code where words like "Sternberg," "Straight Arrow," and "ConDOME" made Myra and Michelle ripple with laughter. The one time Larry tried to insinuate himself into the discussion by asking, "So, what do you and Shiffra do for fun?" Michelle and Myra turned on him and simultaneously burst into a song from *H.M.S. Pinafore:* "Refrain, audacious tar / Your suit from pressing, / Remember what you are, / And whom addressing!" before ignoring him completely.

Larry just sat there enjoying his hot dog, in part happy to be in the company of two cool, experienced girls, in part chagrined by how inconsequential his presence seemed. He wondered whether they would even notice if he got up and left; he also wondered what might happen if he wound up at Michelle's apartment and they'd both had too much beer, if there were truly girls outside of Israeli hotel rooms who made the first move. In a way, his experience with Hannah Goodman had proved to be a curse. His virginity gone, he now had little patience for all the steps that led up to coital bliss, if that was even a possibility with any Ida Crown girls, most of whom said they were saving themselves for marriage, while the others, the rabid Zionists, may have slept around, but only with members of the Israeli Army, whose jackets they wore to and from school as proof of their conquests and their dedication to the cause. On the other hand, though, he was not sexually experienced enough to fool any potential partner into thinking he wasn't a virgin.

Once Larry polished off his hot dog, Michelle said it was time to get beer. They packed into Gareth's chocolate police cruiser and drove over to Armanetti's Liquors on Western with Gareth's Modern Lovers tape playing loud, Michelle at the wheel. "Ass, gas, or grass," Myra cackled as Larry sat next to her in the backseat. "No one rides for free." Larry spent most of the drive drumming in pantomime, really getting into it, hoping someone would ask if he played drums in a band, but nobody did. Gareth lit a joint, inhaled, and passed it to Myra, who took a small hit; she passed it back to Michelle, who took a big one. Michelle glanced back at Larry and offered him the joint. But he shook his head. "I don't like mixing pot and beer," he said, hoping he sounded convincing.

In the Armanetti's parking lot, Larry collected $5 each from Myra and Gareth—Michelle said she'd owe them—then got out of the car and bought five racks of Hamm's. "Jesus Christ, Rovner. Hamm's?" Gareth asked when Larry got back in the car, which was enveloped in a fog of pot smoke. "We said cheap beer; we didn't say expensive piss." Myra laughed hysterically at Larry's choice of beer. "Expensive piss," she repeated. Consistently surrounded by boys who desired Michelle and either ignored her or used her as a way to get to Michelle, she took on the role of her friend's surly bouncer, only allowing a choice few beyond the red velvet rope, ignoring or ridiculing the rest. Michelle thanked "Yehuda" for the beer, then she asked if he wanted to hang out with them. Myra gave a look of mild disbelief, which she soon replaced with one of charity, as if he were a retarded boy getting a chance to throw a high hard one to Dave Kingman during Chicago Cubs batting practice.

"Where're you guys going?" Larry asked.

"Mt. Warren," Michelle said. "Until Millard gets off work."

Larry hoped that she didn't mean Millard Schwartz, a kid he remembered from Hebrew school and JCC basketball camp, one who had single-handedly changed Larry's long-held assertion that there was no such thing as a dumb Jew. Millard, blond-haired and blue-eyed, but neither adopted nor the child of converts, was all sharp elbows and hard fouls, full of admonitions for his teammates. He would fire passes past outstretched arms, then snarl, "It was *there,* man!"

"Sure, I guess," Larry said. "I was gonna meet some people, but not till later."

Michelle parked the car on Western by Warren Park across from the Hank Schiffler Ford dealership. As they walked toward Mt. Warren, Michelle said she was hungry. "Doughnuts, Wasserstrom. Definitely doughnuts," Gareth said. Larry offered to go to Dunkin' Donuts. Gareth shrugged and said okay. "Yeah," Myra snorted. "He did such a great job getting the beer."

"I better come, make sure you get the right ones," Michelle said.

"All right," Larry said. "Let's go."

"Gimme cigarettes," Michelle said.

Myra threw her a pack of Merits and said, "Don't bogart all my squares, wench."

Michelle caught the pack. "Then don't bogart all our beer, bitch," she said.

"You drivin' my car, Wasserstrom?" asked Gareth, who was cool about letting other people drive his car, but not when he wasn't in it.

"We can walk," Larry said. "It's a nice night."

Actually, it wasn't a particularly nice night. It was cold and windy, and though it wasn't raining, the mist seemed to dampen the body from the inside out. Still, Larry was happy to walk. Walking south on Western meant they would pass the Nortown Theater, and there was a chance that, if the timing was right, they would walk by right when *French Postcards* was letting out, at which point, if he ran into his mother and sister, he could corroborate his fictional tale about taking Randi Nathan to the movie, the only question being whether to (a) introduce Michelle as Randi, or (b) invent some breakup story: "Nah, I got tired of Randi; Mom, this is Michelle." Larry asked Michelle for a cigarette and sucked on it cautiously.

Michelle was cold and harried, but Larry walked slowly, gesturing effusively with his cigarette hand, stopping to make points. He talked a lot about Rovner! They had enough material for an album, and even though his mom wanted him to go to college, he said, he wasn't sure he was gonna; he wasn't sure he had the grades for it anyway, he boasted—he might have to go to community college, work a night job until the band caught on. He left out the part about the solid-A average and the early admission into Brandeis, whose rigorous academic program, he was certain, would prepare him for medicine, law, or rabbinical school if the rock 'n' roll lifestyle ever got too shallow for him. Instead, he talked about how he and his mom really got into it sometimes, how she said if he blasted *Zeppelin Four* one more time, she was gonna kick him out of the house. He said fine, he didn't give a shit, he was gonna leave anyway, get his own apartment. They worked it out, he said, but he was paying rent now, just so she wouldn't have anything to hold over him; now he could play his music as long and loud as he wanted. Michelle asked what kind of music he played.

"I listen to a lot of Nazareth and a lot of Zeppelin," he said. "It's got a lotta anger in it, a lotta rage. There're some times when I wanna beat the shit outta somebody, but I don't do it for real; I do it with my music."

"Yeah," Michelle said, not buying any of it. "I've dated guys like that, but sometimes I think I'm getting too old and I just wonder if the right sensitive Orthodox guy came around, maybe I'd give it all up to be with him."

"I've got a sensitive side, too," Larry said quickly as they approached the Nortown Theater. "That's why I like movies like this. I've seen it five times, but I'd see it again if you wanted to." Michelle responded with a noncommittal grunt. They were standing in front of the Nortown and Larry was hoping Lana and his mom would be coming out, just so he could snub them. But there was only so long he could stand in front of the *French Postcards* poster, so they kept walking south, past the "Coming Next Week" sign for *In Search of Historic Jesus,* until they got to Dunkin' Donuts.

While Larry and Michelle were in the doughnut shop, taking an extra-long time as Michelle talked the counterman into giving them free Munchkins, Lana and Ellen Rovner walked north on Western in the opposite direction of Dunkin' Donuts. Lana had loved the movie; she said she was sorry her father had had to work that night and couldn't make it. Her mother said maybe when her father got a free moment, he could see the movie with her since she wouldn't see it again; romance bored her silly. By the time Michelle and Larry emerged from the doughnut shop, the 7 o'clock crowd was already gone and there was a line for the 9. Figuring they had just missed his mother and sister, Larry walked fast, nearly sprinting past Dewitt's Shoes and Woolworth's. But when they reached Devon, he still couldn't see any sign of them.

Myra and Gareth were drinking beers atop Mt. Warren when Larry and Michelle returned with the doughnuts. Gareth was fiddling with a pocketknife and talking about becoming an anarchist. He'd attended some meetings; the only problem was that he didn't like the people involved, and what was the point of being an anarchist if you had to associate with people, shouldn't everyone be an anarchist on their own time, wasn't that kind of the point? He studiously carved a small A in the ground.

"Jesus," Myra exclaimed. "How many fucking doughnuts did you get, Shelley?"

"Two dozen plus Munchkins," Michelle said. "What can I say? The guy liked me."

"Munchkins suck, but I'll eat 'em, Wasserstrom," said Gareth. He put away his pocketknife and opened the Munchkin box.

Larry took another beer and guzzled it. Then he picked up a chocolate-glazed Munchkin and took a small bite. What he needed was a quick exit. He had already asked Michelle to see *French Postcards* and she hadn't definitely said no. In his experience, the more you asked a girl to go out with you, the more opportunities she had to reject you.

From the top of Mt. Warren, you could see just about all, or at least three-quarters, of West Rogers Park. To the north were the gas stations, the car and motorcycle dealerships, Fluky's Hot Dogs, and Baskin-Robbins Ice Cream, all visible on Western Avenue, a long pathway of pink lights leading to the dim white suburb of Evanston. To the west were the apartments and bungalows located between Western and California Avenues and the houses between California and Kedzie, and the Chicago River drainage canal at the border of West Rogers Park and the suburb of Lincolnwood. Behind the four teenagers sitting, drinking beer, smoking, and eating doughnuts lay the dark expanse of Warren Park, which ended at the neighborhood's eastern border; beyond it, the hippies and street gangs of East Rogers Park. East of them, Lake Michigan. The view to the south was obscured by blocks of brownstones, their backs forming a sort of barricade. In the distance, you could see the peak of the Angel Guardian Church steeple on Ridge, and past it, the tops of downtown skyscrapers—the John Hancock, the Sears Tower—but nothing in between. At his twelfth birthday party, Larry had dubbed Mt. Warren "the Golan Heights" for its strategic location and panoramic view. The apartments to the south were the fortified border against Syria, but to the north and east were Evanston, Kenilworth, and Glencoe, the lakefront suburbs with mansions that dotted the coast along "the Sea of Galilee."

Larry considered his Dunkin' Munchkin. He looked out onto Western Avenue. A white Cadillac DeVille was driving slowly north, and out of the vehicle's moon roof, emerging as if from the hatch of a submarine, a drunk couple, perhaps en route to a homecoming dance—he in a powder-blue tuxedo and a white, ruffled shirt, she in a matching, filmy dress, her head garlanded by forget-me-nots—were taking in the night air. From the car radio came the muffled sounds of Al Jolson singing "California, Here I Come." Suddenly, the young man threw his fists straight up and punched the air three times. "Reagan for President," he shouted. "Reagan for President!" He grabbed his girlfriend, kissed her, and shouted, "Hey HEY hey," as they celebrated the California governor's long-anticipated, official announcement of his candidacy for the presidential nomination.

Larry let the Dunkin' Munchkin fly. It sailed through the air and exploded against the side of the Cadillac with a brown chocolate *thuk*. The Cadillac slowed, but did not stop.

"Fucking *goys*," Larry shouted.

"Hey," said Gareth. Larry expected an argument and was all too prepared to leave after a bitter exchange. But instead, what Gareth said was "Give me one of those shits." He picked up a Munchkin, stood up, and whipped it across Western. It smacked against the window of the Hank Schiffler Ford showroom.

"Yeah," Gareth bellowed. "Gimme two, gimme two!" Larry took three, handed the two jam-filled ones to Gareth, and kept the chocolate for himself. "Bus!" Gareth shouted as a green CTA bus motored north on Western. He kicked his leg high and fired the doughnut hole into the side of the bus, squirting jam upon impact. Michelle and Myra stood up to investigate. "Doughnut wars!" Gareth explained. He ate half of a jelly doughnut hole. "Grab a Munchkin, ladies!"

"This is the stupidest thing ever," Myra said as Michelle grabbed a Munchkin.

"This is excellent," Michelle corrected. Myra quickly relented and took a Munchkin. "Whoever thought of this is a genius," Michelle said.

Larry smiled. For the first time all night, it felt as if there were four people standing up there, not one standing in the background of the other three—four musketeers side by side atop Mt. Warren, doughnut holes at the ready to defend their turf. On the sidewalk below, two tough kids on tiny Huffy bicycles were cruising the boulevard.

"Look at those assholes," Gareth said. "Anyone that big riding a bike that small's a fucking asshole!" Four doughnut holes zoomed down like miniature thunderbolts from Mt. Olympus—two hit the bikers, one skipped through the spokes of the front bike, and the other skittered onto the street, sending a short plume of cinnamon dust up into the air. The bikers swore and kept riding.

"Dude!" Michelle looked at Larry, impressed. "I didn't know you had it in you."

"He doesn't," said Myra. "He's just drunk."

"Did somebody say joint?" asked Gareth. He pulled a small plastic bag of joints out of his jeans pocket and lit one. He passed it to Larry; this time Larry took a hit, pretended to savor the taste, and passed it to Michelle, then went to get another beer. They started to strategize, to conserve Munchkins. They'd only target expensive cars—especially Jaguars, if they saw any, Michelle said—and when it came to targeting people, they'd only throw at individuals they knew for sure were assholes.

Muley Wills was loping south on Western, carrying a book bag over his shoulder, clanking a shopping cart filled with wire and gadgetry. Myra aimed a doughnut at him, but Gareth grabbed her arm before she could throw it. "What the hell are you doing, Tuchbaum?" he asked. "That kid's cool."

"He's just some kid," Myra said.

"No, he's cool," Gareth repeated. Michelle nodded, confirming Gareth's assertion. Myra picked up a white frosted doughnut and threw it down to the street, where it smacked against the front passenger-side window of Gareth's car.

"That's not cool," Gareth grumbled.

The last Munchkin of the evening, white frosted and filled with strawberry jam, belonged to Larry Rovner, who held it as if it were the last snowball of winter. His head reeling from the four beers he'd already quaffed, he circled the top of Mt. Warren, considering targets. He walked a few paces north, unzipped his jeans, and urinated grandiosely.

"Yeshiva boy!" Michelle shouted. "Yeshiva boy!"

Larry grinned broadly and walked back to the group. "We've got to do this every Saturday night," he said. He zipped up his jeans, tucked in his shirt, and put a hand on Gareth's shoulder. "We could come back here with slingshots and see how far the Munchkins can really go. If we gave them just enough propulsion, we could probably go all the way to Devon. Or we could set up from different locations, make it kind of like a weekend club."

Silence ensued.

Then Gareth spoke. "I don't know about that, Rovner," he said, squirming free of Larry's grip. And in that moment, Larry felt a profound sense of deflation. The last Munchkin should have been a culmination; instead it felt like an anticlimax. The doughnuts would be gone and then the friendship. He felt puky now. He didn't aim the Munchkin; he just flung it as if he were throwing a stone into a choppy ocean where it would have no chance of skipping. He turned away as he threw it, not even caring where it landed. But the moment he turned, Gareth looked up.

"Rollers!" Gareth shouted, indicating a passing squad car. "Rollers! Rollers! Rollers!"

Larry's Munchkin skipped off the hood of the squad car. The car screeched to a halt as Gareth grabbed a six-pack in one hand and rumbled down the other side of the hill, Myra and Michelle running behind him. Larry froze for a moment as two cops sprang from their car and ran toward Mt. Warren. Then he motored down the hill, unable to gauge how far the others had gotten, the ground before him just a vast inkblot. His right foot hit something hard, a brick, a stone, or a wooden slat. He stumbled face-forward, not quite falling yet but his head and torso now nearly parallel to the steep slope of the hill, his legs and feet kicking up speed in spite of themselves, then finally giving way, his stomach crashing into the mud, his jaw hitting the earth hard, then his body rolling downward, rolling into something heavy as Gareth yelled "Fuck!," the two of them rolling now, kicking Michelle's legs out from under her, in Larry's mouth the taste of mud, hair, shampoo, his own blood, and Michelle's Magie Noir perfume. Then the three of them landed at the bottom of the hill, Gareth flat on his back grunting, Michelle on top of Larry, nearly straddling him as the two of them gasped, then laughed. Michelle brushed grass and mud out of her eyes. Larry looked up at the night sky, strands of Michelle's hair still in his mouth.

Myra was standing above them. "We've gotta get Millard," she said. "We're late."

"Who?" Larry asked.

"Her boyfriend," Myra snapped. "Millard Schwartz."

"He can wait," Michelle said; then she stopped, feeling the others' eyes upon her. She stood slowly. "All right," she said. She glanced down at Larry lying below her. "Yeah, let's get out of here."

"I'm not moving," Gareth said, still on his back. A police siren was heard. "Okay, I'm moving." Larry stumbled behind them, something pounding inside his head, the slight taste of perfume—acidic, vaguely poisonous—in his mouth.

Two police officers swept Mt. Warren with their flashlights, and another squad car was approaching. Near the southern edge of the park, Gareth, Michelle, Myra, and Larry, ready at a moment's notice to scale the fence and escape into the alley, watched the police officers walk back toward the sidewalk. One walked over to the window of the other squad car. They conferred for about a minute. Then the second car drove off and the two officers got back into their car. Once the coast was clear, the four teenagers walked toward Gareth's car. Then they remembered the beer; there was another six-pack on Mt. Warren. Larry said he'd wait for them and keep watch over the beer until they returned with Millard. "Keep watch over it? You mean drink it, Rovner," Gareth said. No, Larry said, he'd just drink one more and watch the rest until they came back.

"Better keep your word, Yehuda," Michelle said, putting a finger to his lips, but what she said sounded false to him now. He didn't know if she would even go with him to see *French Postcards*. He didn't know if he even wanted to go with her anyhow. Well, sure he did, he decided quickly. He could discuss it with her the next day when he called to apologize for drinking all of their beer and leaving before they came back.

Larry stood alone atop Mt. Warren, drinking cans of Hamm's until the pink lights of Western began to shimmer as if he were seeing them through a trail of smoke. At some point, he had lost his yarmulke, but it still felt as if it were resting atop his head, making an ever-so-slight indentation in his mound of curls. He was staring west, well past the roof of his house on Sacramento, well past the condo complex of Winston Towers on Kedzie, where Grandma Rose lived, well past the city's western border and out toward O'Hare Airport, where the red and white lights of jets taking off and landing dotted the sky. There was a song in this, he thought, a truly great song—not the sort of hard-driving rock 'n' roll song that Rovner! would become known for. A ballad, something that could be played solo and acoustic, with maybe a drum kicking in during the second verse, no electric guitar at all. Something about love, longing, and loss. All the great rock bands had one great ballad—"Free Bird" or "Dream On" or "Soar"—that's what he'd call it, a song about looking out to the western horizon, wanting so bad to soar but feeling so sore.

By the time he'd finished all the beer, he had the chorus figured out: "Soar / I wanna soar / But I feel so sore / I know you're sure / You heard it all before / And it SHAKES you to the core / And you just gotta SOAR!" He could see Gareth parking his car on Western and all of them getting out—Myra and Gareth and Michelle and Millard Schwartz, Michelle and Millard Schwartz with their hands in each other's back blue jeans pockets, Michelle and Millard Schwartz making out as they neared the foot of Mt. Warren. Larry turned and quickly made his way down the other side of the hill.

Larry thought the others might follow him to demand payment for the beer he'd drunk, so he walked back toward Wolfy's via side streets, cutting south on Campbell, stopping briefly in front of the Wasserstroms' apartment building, where a picture of someone that looked like, but couldn't possibly be, Ayatollah Khomeini gazed out of an upstairs window. By the time he got back to his car, he had a version of "Soar" that he knew was rock-solid, and as he started up the motor, he sang it. When he opened the windows and jammed down on the accelerator, he sang even louder, hitting the gas every time he sang the word "soar." He sang it all the way down Western, past the Rosehill Cemetery and the pale green corroded bronze statue of Abraham Lincoln, under the viaducts, past the super-market where the glorious Riverview Amusement Park once stood, until he saw Armitage Avenue and the marquee of the Oak Theater advertising its "LIVE ALL-NUDE REVUE." And as he felt a surge of excitement course through his groin, he no longer cared that someone might see him parking his car in front of Arturo's Tacos and walking across the street toward the theater. He had the taste of liquor and dope and Michelle Wasserstrom's shampoo and perfume, now just a bit stale in his mouth, and the number-one single from Rovner!'s self-titled de-but album still ringing in his head, sounding better every time he heard the cho-rus. It was when he got to the middle of Western that he noticed the gold Avanti parked right out front of the Oak Theater, and though he checked to make sure, he didn't really need to look at the RENVOR license plate to figure out to whom it belonged. Larry walked back across the street and got into his mother's Volvo, started it up, and drove back north with the windows shut, the radio off, and something that felt like a meat tenderizer slamming up against the inside of his skull. When he got home, Lana was sitting on the couch in her pajamas watching the film *Funny Girl.*

Larry did not so much as greet her, just gruffly asked, "Dad home?" and when Lana said, "He's on call," he snorted dubiously and walked upstairs to his father's bathroom. He elbowed open the door; he didn't need to turn on the light to find the magazines. They were in four neat piles—the *Playboy*s and *Penthouse*s to the left of the toilet; the *Hustler*s and the *Oui*s to the right. Larry combined them into two stacks, crouched down, and picked them up. His muscles quiv-ered with the weight of the fifty-odd periodicals as he walked back downstairs.

"You need help with the door, Larr?" Lana asked. He shook his head, then squeezed the magazines together between his arms and his thighs, and used his thumb and forefinger to twist the doorknob and pull open the door. He bumped open the screen door with his behind, and pulled the front door shut. He had first thought he would just dump the magazines in the alley, but his father might find them there. So instead, he dropped them in the trunk of his mother's car, got in the driver's seat, and drove west. Once he reached the Chicago River drainage canal, he got into the right lane, turned on the flashers, and popped the trunk.

The last time he'd stood over the canal was for Tashlich, symbolically expiat-ing his sins by emptying the lint from his pockets into the water below. Now he stood there with a stack of his father's magazines, which he tossed down one by one into the water as he solemnly uttered the Hebrew prayer recited at the beginning of all joyous occasions: *"Baruch atoh adonay, elohaynu melech haolam, shehecheyanu v'kiy'manu v'higyanu lazman hazeh."*

Blessed are you, Lord our God, King of the Universe, for granting us life, for sustaining us, and for helping us to reach this day.

Amen.

WILLS / SILVERMAN

Peachy Moskowitz

Though she was born in Russia, Muley Scott Wills's cousin, Peachy Moskowitz, had not seen her homeland since 1974, when, at the age of fourteen, she escaped from the Toronto dressing room of her father, Alexander, staff doctor for the Kirov Ballet. In the melee that followed a performance of *Don Quixote* when Mikhail Baryshnikov leapt offstage into a crowd of adoring fans, then into a car that spirited him to asylum, Peachy slipped out a back door of the Toronto Opera House to freedom, unnoticed.

As various government agencies debated whether to return her to Moscow or to find her a permanent home, she spent months being shuttled from home to home, including a five-week stint on Deirdre and Muley Wills's living room couch. She was a distant cousin of Muley's father, Carl Silverman, who, despite his wealth, said he didn't have room for her. For Deirdre and Muley, though, Peachy was a perfect houseguest, willing to do anything to repay the inconvenience of her presence. She had a rare generosity of spirit, which tended to bring out the best in whomever she came in contact with. When Peachy was in the house, Deirdre Wills's depression ebbed, her fury dissipated, and she magically became warmer; she was easy to laugh and easy to cry, the mother Muley always knew she could be if circumstances had been slightly different for her. On one memorably odd evening, Muley came home from second grade and was thrilled to see Peachy teaching his mother how to dance the Funky Chicken.

But Peachy spoke hardly any English; what little she knew was a discomfiting amalgam of phrases learned from American films and pop songs, most of which were twenty years out of date. It would have been almost easier if she'd known no English at all, for Muley Wills's charge—as his mother instructed him—was not only to teach her his language but also to help her unlearn all her outdated slang, the sort that had made people call her by her favorite word, "Peachy," instead of her birth name Clara.

What was wonderful for Muley about Peachy, aside from her radiance, was how much teaching her taught him. Only in teaching her English did he come to understand how lazy his language had become. At seven, he had already developed bad habits. He was already saying "ain't" and "damn" and "hell" and all the other words that the bad kids on the playground used. But that was before he stopped hanging out with them and started teaching Peachy English; that was before Peachy started teaching Muley about life. During the first six days of the week, Muley would teach Peachy basic grammar. But on the seventh day, Peachy would teach him in her rapidly improving English one of "Peachy's Lessons from Life."

The lesson of the week would appear written at the bottom of a single sheet of paper beneath an elaborate watercolor drawing, which would depict a story from Peachy's life. The first lesson was "If you tell them where you're going, they'll follow you there." It was accompanied by a drawing of a young, pony-tailed girl peering out from behind a brick wall while a phalanx of torchbearing men ran the other way through driving snow. It referred to an evening when she had told her father she was going down to the river to feed ducks. In fact, she was sneaking off to the Moscow Circus to watch the workmen load in the brown bears. But Peachy never made it to the circus. While running to the Kropotinskya Metro stop via a shortcut where she was certain she would not be discovered, she slipped on a patch of ice, twisted her ankle, hit her head on the ground, and lost consciousness. Hours later, she awoke to see her father and a group of his colleagues dashing toward the river to try to find her while her voice, straining to reach them, was lost to the wind and snow. She made her way back home, but by then it was nearly morning and her father—drunk and despondent—had already given up hope of ever finding her. If she had told her father where she had been going, Peachy explained to Muley, he would have been able to find her; he would have taken her to the hospital immediately and the damage done to her ankle by hobbling home could have been averted; she could have danced with the Kirov just as her father had always wished.

Luckily for Muley, Peachy's lessons did not end when she found a permanent home, even when she had mastered English. For even though she saw Muley less and less as time went on, even though her vocabulary soon exceeded his and she found work as an interpreter, still every week there would be a lesson. It would come in the mail from Washington or Skokie or Bonn—one single sheet with a watercolor illustration and one of Peachy's "Lessons from Life." By now, there were nearly 250 of them and Muley tried to live his life by every single one. For with every lesson he received, he felt himself grow just a bit older and just a bit wiser.

Or at least, that's what Muley Scott Wills said in his *Young Town* audition tape. In reality, there was no such person as Peachy Moskowitz—at least as far as he knew. And as for Peachy's "Lessons from Life," they had been quickly adapted from *Mel's Manual for Men,* the paperback volume that Mel Coleman, Muley's supervisor at WBOE Radio, had written. Only in Mel's book—available for forty-five cents in the remainder bin at Kroch's and Brentano's—the advice was intended to teach playboys how to treat ladies. Among Mel's other words of wisdom: "Always bring a raincoat; you never know when it's gonna pour," "If the lady don't know, the lady don't *gotta* know," and "The more you wash it, the more you can use it."

Muley had arrived early on a Saturday at WBOE, bringing Jill Wasserstrom along with him, partly because he liked the company on the el ride downtown and partly because he correctly suspected that Jill could occupy Mel in conversation while he worked on the *Young Town* tape. On the B train, Muley and Jill spent most of their time discussing boyfriends and girlfriends and what it might be like to have one. Neither mentioned the other during the entirety of their conversation, Jill merely suggesting that it would be refreshing to find a cute guy who was nice and liked her, Muley opining that though he wouldn't necessarily want to be tied down to a girlfriend just for the sake of having one, he might be willing to make that concession if just the right girl came along. Muley told Jill that he didn't care if a girl was good- or bad-looking, just so long as she was smart—a statement that seemed insulting to Jill on multiple levels of possible interpretation, so she didn't respond, just stared out the window as the el train descended from the Fullerton stop down into the subway.

Muley and Jill had been friends all through Boone Elementary, yet none of their peers ever thought of them as a couple. They seemed asexual, too smart and too peculiar to become creatures with any potential for reproduction; they were aberrations that would either be improved upon or eliminated completely in future genetic cycles, their jokes, their ambitions, and their interests representative of a generation not their own. They watched black-and-white movies and listened to Thelonious Monk records, and on Saturday afternoons, they sat in Jill's bedroom and listened to WXFM, which broadcast old radio programs, such as *Suspense* and Orson Welles's Mercury Theatre. There was an unspoken agreement between them that neither would seek to address the status of their relationship for fear of jeopardizing it. All of which made it uncomfortable for both of them when Mel Coleman insisted on referring to Jill as "Muley's old lady."

Though Muley had feared that Mel, dressed in white linen slacks and a maroon silk shirt open halfway down, might regale Jill with his usual repertoire of bawdy tales, the weekend producer promised he would say nothing ungentlemanly. He promised Muley in front of Jill that he would "make up a whole lotta bull" to make the lad seem like a real catch. And true to his word, while Muley worked fast in Studio B cutting up interview tape of Mayor Byrne on her plans for the following summer's Chicagofest, Mel sat in the cafeteria eating a soy burger and speaking glowingly of Muley. He told Jill that Muley did more work around WBOE than he did, that Muley was a better editor than anyone who worked the weekend, himself included, that he himself had a bit of talent, but Muley was someone to watch out for. But after Jill asked him when he would stop telling the truth and, as promised, "make up a whole lotta bull," Mel's mood switched markedly. He groused briefly about the injustices exacted upon him by station management, then quickly excused himself to work on his novel. Jill joined Muley in Studio B where he was taping Peachy Moskowitz's story.

Muley imbued every second of his five-minute tape with great attention to detail, inserting thematically appropriate music beneath his own narration, interspersed with sound effects: wind and rain for the alleyways of Moscow, dancing feet for the Kirov Ballet, a cacophony of foreign voices to suggest the Babel of tongues Peachy encountered upon her arrival in America. He opened with one of his favorite pieces of music, Zoltán Kodály's *Háry János Suite,* in which the title character's outlandish, entirely invented exploits are introduced by a sneeze. Muley was not much of a performer, but he used his liabilities as an actor to give his narration the illusion of plainspoken honesty. At the conclusion, he pretended to stumble over the phrase "So long" while describing the day Peachy left his home and said, "No, do not say 'So long.' Say 'See you soon.'"

"It was the first phrase I ever taught her," Muley read over the exultant *Troika* from Prokofiev's *Lieutenant Kije* suite. "But I guess until I met her, I never knew what it meant. Like so many other things." The music reached a crescendo, then faded out: "This story has been written, produced, and edited for radio by Muley Scott Wills."

Muley dumped his recording onto a cassette, placed it in an envelope with the entry form, and slid it into the mailbox of Donna Mayne, who coordinated the station's children's programming. Then he brought Mel the interview carts he had cut up and collected $40—Mel said he'd pay him the remaining $10 the next week. Muley had considered playing the tape for Mel before he and Jill left, but Mel started off on one of his tirades about management, how they never let folks like him and Muley rise to the higher echelons, never let them work as on-air talent—"Muley and I both know what we're talking about here; your old lady don't have to know about this." The best chance Muley had to work for the station, Mel told him, was as night watchman once old Lloyd Cubbins retired.

After they left the station, Muley asked Jill if she wanted to come back to his apartment and listen to the *Best of Groucho* album he'd checked out of the library. But Jill said she had too much homework to do; maybe they could work together at her house on their Shah-Ayatollah project once she was done with Hebrew school on Sunday. Sundays were the worst, she said, because not only did she have to withstand four hours of filmstrips, touch football, and prayers, she also had to go to Bat Mitzvah practice. There she would sit in Rabbi Shmulevits's dark-brown office that smelled of mothballs and old socks while he continuously corrected her Hebrew pronunciation in her *haftorah* passage without ever telling her what any of the words meant. Then, the singing with Cantor Fishman, who couldn't keep a tune, and, finally, the speech—God, the speech—the speech she would have to deliver before the entire congregation.

Muley said he was busy on Sunday. Working on the Shah-Ayatollah project was just about the last thing he wanted to do, with or without Jill, and he found the passion she brought to it frustrating. Ever since the second-grade mock election in which students were asked to cast ballots in the election for Illinois governor and sheriff, Jill had been on the losing side of issues. At first, it was just because she was siding with the politics of her mother, who tended to support the underdog, but later it became her own passion. She wore a Bill Singer button the day that lakefront liberal was trounced by Richard J. Daley's Chicago machine; in fifth-grade debates, she spoke passionately for the independent candidacy of Eugene McCarthy. The only time she'd supported a winning candidate was when Jane Byrne upset Mayor Michael Bilandic to claim the Chicago mayoralty in 1979. There was an initial thrill to the victory, but the euphoria soon wore off and was replaced by an indefinable sense of helplessness, as if the world were over, nothing were worth fighting for anymore, victory had been achieved, and nothing felt different at all. Jill resolved never to back another winning cause.

Muley was impressed by her political passions but couldn't work up much enthusiasm for the Shah-Ayatollah debate. Politics was a great deal less compelling than more tangible concerns, like radios or hockey or Marx Brothers movies or cheering up his mother. He tried so hard to be interested in everything around him, to find a puzzle or a challenge everywhere he looked, but he found politics soporific. The Ayatollah project had no bearing on reality, would never help him make the money he needed, would never amount to anything other than a letter grade and a piece of paper that would stay in a drawer until it became yellow and brittle.

It wasn't until the next Saturday at his apartment that Muley even bothered to look at the news clippings Jill had assembled regarding the Iranian hostage crisis, and that was only because the Sherlock Holmes movie he had wanted to watch had been interrupted by technical difficulties. He was staring at an article about the legacy of Mohammad Reza Pahlavi when the phone rang. Relieved, he put the offending article back in Jill's clear binder, then picked up the phone. On the other end of the line was Donna Mayne from WBOE; she had listened to his tape and wanted to know if he could make a callback the following Saturday evening.

"Anytime," Muley said.

The callback was held at the Bismarck Hotel, a once-grand, now-decaying establishment in the Chicago Loop. About forty overdressed boys and girls between the ages of twelve and fourteen, most of them with their parents, milled about the dim hall in front of the hotel's once-opulent Walnut Ballroom.

Lana Rovner—in a tan pantsuit, her hair bobbed just that morning—was seated on a black metal folding chair beside her mother, studying the scripts stacked up on a coffee table in front of the ballroom door. Lana wasn't sure if she would be asked to recite the monologue she'd had her father rent time at Universal Studios to record, but she had memorized it just in case. She hoped her mother wasn't offended that she had chosen her father as the person who had most profoundly influenced her life. It wasn't that one parent had really been more influential, she explained. But she had been allowed to choose only one person—the rules had specified that. She sincerely hoped, she said, that her mother wasn't mad, although the only thing Ellen Rovner was mad about was that her husband had said he'd be working that day, which meant she had to drive Lana to the callback herself.

Lana surveyed the crowd outside the ballroom. She recognized a few faces, particularly that of P.C. Pendleton, who had already worked as a news anchor on a local TV show entitled *Just Kiddin'* before it was canceled to make way for *Pink Panther* cartoons. Lana had auditioned for that show and had made it to the second round of callbacks, where she had read opposite Pendleton, who'd seemed a gentleman throughout. But the moment before the cameraman cued her, he hissed, *"Fuck up, fuck up, fuck up, you're gonna fuck up"* to her, which totally broke her concentration and she had blown the audition. Her concentration was better now; she could approach P.C., there in his navy blue three-piece suit, shake his hand firmly, and tell him good luck, though he seemed to have no memory of her whatsoever. And when she saw Muley Wills and Jill Wasserstrom, him in that shabby army jacket and ripped blue jeans, her in overalls and her sister's old sneakers, she could shake Jill's hand too and tell her she was glad to see she had made it through the first round. It didn't enter Lana's mind that Muley might have been there to audition. She was unable to think of him as anyone other than the son of the woman who worked at the library and cleaned her house. "Good luck, Jill," Lana said. She shook Jill's hand again and went back to sit by her mother. Mel Coleman, in an open white silk shirt and custard-yellow pants, opened the doors to the ballroom. "They got us opening doors for them now, brother," he told Muley. "Get out while you've got a chance."

After the kids and their parents filed into the ballroom and sat in the folding chairs assembled in front of a stage, Donna Mayne, a serious woman in a lime-green suit, a cream blouse, and a thick gold necklace, explained the callback process. First, she said, holding a clipboard, she was going to do an "appearance check." The cast of *Young Town* would be making many personal appearances, where they would be representing both the station and the city, and she wanted to make sure that everyone in the cast "looked like Chicago." During the appearance check, she would eliminate twenty of the forty people who had been called back. After the appearance check, everyone would wait in the hall and study the scripts—she called them "sides"—that were out on the coffee tables. She would ask people in two at a time and listen to them read. Through that process, she would "cut loose" ten more people. Once these ten were left, she and the host of *Young Town,* Lennie Kidd, would interview each remaining candidate. Afterward, the five cast members would be announced; those not lucky enough to make the final cast would be declared honorary *Young Town* clubhouse members, entitling them to a *Young Town* button and a yearlong subscription to the *Young Town* newsletter. She told everyone to relax; this was supposed to be fun. Then she introduced Lennie Kidd.

Kidd, whose real name was Lennie Bass, was a fixture on the Chicago entertainment scene. He wore a vampire costume to introduce horror movies on a local UHF station where he played "Dr. Frankenfear, The Count of Terror." He created balloon animals in front of the Pickle Barrel restaurant. He was a stand-up comedian and the emcee of his own trained parakeet circus. Occasionally, he appeared on radio shows, where he sang folk-song spoofs, such as his Clancy Brothers riff, "Miss Riordan's on the Rag"—*"Miss Riordan's on the rag, my boy, Miss Riordan's on the rag / You can hear the sound in Dublin Town / Miss Riordan's on the rag."* He was also a patient of Ellen Rovner's, which was why she excused herself and went into the hallway when he was introduced. Lennie and Donna had revamped WBOE's moribund children's programming and had won several Jack Benny radio awards for shows, such as *It's Not Easy Being Purple,* in which a world full of green people shun a purple person within their midst. In that show, Lennie played all of the characters, but *Young Town* would be different—a newsmagazine completely written and reported by kids. The program had received more development grant money than any other in the station's history.

Kidd, his beard neatly trimmed, strutted onto the stage, affecting a pimp walk. He wore a train engineer's cap, overalls with narrow black-and-white vertical stripes, and black hi-tops. He carried a boom box. Blasting out of it was the sound of a group clapping in 4/4 rhythm. Lennie put the boom box down and, with his hands up in the air, clapped along with the tape. "C'mon!" he shouted. "C'mon!" Donna, standing off to the left side of the stage, clapped unenthusiastically, and though Muley only clapped inaudibly and Jill didn't clap at all, almost every child and his or her parents clapped effusively with Lennie. "C'mon!" Lennie said, clapping with his hands way out in front of his chest. "C'mon!" Then, in a high, cartoonish voice, Lennie chanted the *Young Town* theme—"The *Young Town* Kids are on the air / It's the show that kids and grown-ups can share / We travel around from town to town / We're all Lennie Kidd's friends so come on down / Come on down to *Youuuung Towwwwwn*."

Lennie led a chant of "*Young Town* Kids are number one," after which he walked offstage, and Donna asked parents and friends to wait in the hall. Then she asked the forty children to stand in a line. She said she would tell everybody one of two things—either "Please stay," after which they would sit down and await further instructions. Or she would tell them "thank you for coming." If she told them that, they would exit out the back of the ballroom, where Mel Coleman was stationed. Mel would give them a special "thank-you" pack on their way out.

Donna walked back and forth in front of the children, back and forth. And again. And again. Her demeanor suggested a drill sergeant inspecting troop uniforms. A minute passed, and then another. Donna stared down at a short boy in a navy blue golf shirt, tan slacks, and penny loafers. His eyes were big, unblinking. Finally, unable to stand the tension, the boy asked her, "What am I supposed to do? Do you want me to do something?"

"Thank you for coming," Donna said, and paced the stage, making quicker work of the rest. "Please stay, please stay," she said. "Thank you for coming. Please stay. Thank you for coming."

Lana tried not to look at Donna; she focused on what would happen if she got cast in the show and P.C. Pendleton didn't. But it was obvious P.C. would get cast, he'd already done a TV show, and now she'd have to deal with him all the time if she got cast. Well, maybe he was more mature now and wouldn't tell her to "*foul up, foul up, you're gonna foul up,*" or whatever it was he had said.

"Please stay," Donna said to Lana, then told another half dozen to "please stay" and another half dozen "thank you for coming." She told P.C. to "please stay" and when she got to Muley, she said, "Please stay, Muley." When there were twenty kids left in the ballroom, Donna said she would divide everyone into pairs. The pairs would go out to the hallway to rehearse and then be called in one at a time to read. Then Donna would tell them either "Please stay" or "Thank you for coming." Muley would read with P.C. Pendleton and Lana was to read with Julie Ying.

Julie Ying was so intimidating that Lana immediately wanted her as a friend. Julie was a seventh-grader at Francis Parker, the private school where the wealthiest Jewish families sent their children. Parker kids were on commercials and in movies, and for their eighth-grade trip, they didn't go to Washington, D.C., they went to Katmandu. Julie herself not only played three instruments (violin, piano, and ukulele), she was also an extra in the annual Ruth Page production of *The Nutcracker.* After high school, she said, she would give up performing and go to Stanford, where she would study to become a chemical engineer. But the amazing thing was how nice Julie was: After they had rehearsed their "sides," she insisted they exchange phone numbers and invited her to see *Ice Follies,* starring former Olympic skater Peggy Fleming, then sleep over at her house.

Muley's discussion with P.C. Pendleton was considerably more formal. Pendleton did most of the talking. He said they shouldn't bother rehearsing—what mattered was not getting the lines exactly as written; what Donna Mayne was looking for was camaraderie and give-and-take. He spoke with an air that suggested he'd been born to aristocracy, though his father had actually founded the Pendleton Demolition Company and was married to Weezie Berkman of Berkman Containers. P.C. talked to Muley about the artists he admired—Ray Charles, Richard Pryor, and Aretha Franklin. He asked whether Muley was a fan of the Chicago Bulls and what he thought of Operation PUSH. Muley told P.C. that he had to go talk to his friend Jill, who was sitting by herself on a nearby folding chair, reading a book: Saul Alinsky's *Reveille for Radicals.*

"How's the Imperial Wizard?" Jill asked Muley when he came over to her.

"He's okay," said Muley, who disliked few people and couldn't really think of anyone he truly despised. He told Jill the audition might take a while longer. Jill said she might stick around or she might take a walk; either way, why didn't they meet back at the hotel at nine.

Two children—a miserable, red-nosed girl in a polka-dotted dress and a gleeful boy in a cowboy shirt and boots—emerged from the ballroom accompanied by Mel Coleman, who called out, "Lana Rovner and Julie Ying—your dime, your dance floor, ladies." The two girls sprang up and followed him in.

Up on the ballroom's stage, there was a long, flimsy desk with two microphones on it. This would be a blind test, Donna said over a public address system. She told Lana and Julie to sit at the desk; she and Lennie would be listening offstage.

"Can we hear a ten-count from both of them?" Donna asked over the PA.

"Give us a count from one to ten," Mel said. One after the other, the girls counted into the mike. "All right," Mel said. "When I do this"—he snapped a finger at them—"that's showtime. You ready?"

The girls nodded.

"You'll be great," Julie said, beaming. She lightly rubbed Lana's shoulder.

Mel said, "In three . . . two . . . one," flipped the mike switch, and snapped his finger down hard.

"Hi," Julie said. "This is Julie Ying."

"And this is Lana Rovner."

Their voices boomed over the PA.

"And we would like to welcome you to *Young Town.*"

"The only show written, produced, and directed by kids and for kids."

"And we're gonna have a great show today. We're gonna take a trip to the Lincoln Park Zoo and talk to a real, live zookeeper who keeps real, live lions."

"And then we'll check out the coal mine at the Museum of Science and Industry."

"It's gonna be so neat, Lana."

"Neat?"

"Yeah, Lana. It's gonna be really neat."

"No, Julie; we don't say *'neat'* anymore; that's what kids used to say. We say *'cool.'*"

"Cool?"

"That's right, Julie."

"Then this is gonna be the *coolest* show ever."

"That's right."

"So stay tuned for *Cool Town.*"

"No, Julie. *Young Town.*"

"Right, *Young Town.*"

The two of them said the last line in unison: "On WBOE Radio Chicago."

Lana Rovner's heart plummeted. She hadn't stumbled over a single line, but it certainly hadn't been the best she'd ever done it. The fact that Julie was patting her shoulder now, telling her she'd done a great job, only made her feel worse. There was no way she would get cast; she wasn't as smart as Julie, she wasn't as pretty, and she wasn't Japanese or Chinese.

Donna emerged from behind the screen, stood in the aisle, and studied the girls. She took a long time before she spoke. She looked at Julie. "Please stay," she said. She turned to Lana.

"Please stay," she said. Lana let out a huge sigh, felt her eyes tear up; she embraced Julie as Donna told Mel to show the girls out and bring in P.C. and Muley.

Jill Wasserstrom had left her book at the Bismarck and gone for a walk in the Chicago Loop, which was almost deserted now. But even so, as she walked east on Randolph in the direction of once-regal movie palaces that were now either shuttered or showing horror and kung fu triple features for $2, she was not frightened. She only got scared when she was with other people or at home, lying in bed in the dark, thinking over and over of that one line she remembered from the *Adon Olam: "And in the end, when all will cease to be, he will remain the eternal king."*

With no one else walking on Randolph Street, Jill passed the Greyhound bus station and contemplated what it would be like to get on a bus and go from one end of the country to the other. Her mother had done that once, taken a bus from New York City to L.A., where she thought she would be in movies, then headed back east two weeks later and got off in Chicago. Jill walked toward the Woods Theater, which was showing *School of Terror* and *The Tongfather,* then turned north on Dearborn, where men in overcoats were waiting in front of Michael Todd's Cinestage, which played X-rated movies all night long. She turned east and walked down Lake Street underneath the elevated train tracks, passing dimly lit diners, twenty-four-hour parking lots, and a haberdashery, the whine and rumble of trains overhead.

The bell on the Liberty Federal Savings sign was shining dark blue; that meant it would get colder that night. In the summer, the sign was usually bright red. The bank was closed. So were most of the restaurants. There were lights on in the windows of the office buildings, the Borg-Warner and the Prudential—once the tallest building in the city—but if anything, the lights made the buildings seem more alienated.

Jill wanted to get to the lake. She walked south awhile before she found a street that led her over the rail lines of the Illinois Central Railroad. Occasionally, a bum would walk by, muttering to himself or asking her for a quarter she didn't have. She walked past Grant Park, which was alive every summer with the sounds of symphony concerts. Empty now. Four square blocks of black-green grass. Empty chairs in front of a shuttered band shell. She cut diagonally across the park, a slight crunch of frost under her sneakers. When she got to Lake Shore Drive, she stopped at the light and waited for traffic to pass—cars sped past at 45 miles per hour, south to Hyde Park and Indiana, north to Rogers Park and the suburbs—the lake before her growing nearer when the lights switched from red to green, and she crossed the Drive.

Jill stood before Lake Michigan. Her mother had wanted her ashes to be scattered in this lake. Charlie Wasserstrom had given her his word on that, but when the day came, he couldn't do it. He hadn't known before that Jewish law forbade it. The lake was black and wild now as Jill stood beneath a bright streetlamp, staring out to the horizon, feeling a light, cold spray against her cheeks. To her left, Navy Pier, and beyond it, the lights of Lincoln Park and Evanston. To her right, the dome of the planetarium. When she looked at it, she thought of the Sky Show she had seen there, the narrator's voice talking about a new Ice Age, Dr. Bender saying, "Don't worry, we'll all be dead by then." When he had said it, it had scared her. Now, if anything, it was funny. Even the fact that it had frightened her seemed funny—funny that it mattered at all, funny that she had ever thought that anything did.

"And in the end," she said out loud, "when all will cease to be, he will remain the eternal king." She hoped those words would sound funny to her now, just as the others did. But they didn't. Not at all. And in that instant Jill spoke them, she felt suddenly cold, suddenly afraid, suddenly alone. She saw that there was no one to the left of her, no one to the right, only cars and skyscrapers behind her, only the cold, black lake in front. She felt her heart thumping hard and fast against her chest. But she didn't start running until she had crossed Lake Shore Drive.

— — — —

Muley and P.C. were in the Bismarck ballroom now, preparing to read the side about the Lincoln Park Zoo and the difference between "neat" and "cool." P.C. had an eerie calm about him, a cockiness he was trying hard to conceal, like a man about to place a bet on a horse race he's fixed. After Mel Coleman led P.C. and Muley onstage—Mel had said to Muley, "If you don't waste this smart-ass white boy, you're gonna have *me* to contend with"—P.C. said he felt bad that he'd already had so much TV and radio experience; that kind of made it unfair for everyone.

Mel flipped the mike switch and gave Muley and P.C. a count of five, during which P.C., all smiles and sympathetic eyes, leaned over to Muley and whispered to him. As he whispered, the PA system kicked in and Donna Mayne, Lennie Kidd, Mel Coleman, and perhaps even some people out in the hallway could hear P.C. begin to tell Muley *"Fuck up, fuck up, you're gonna fuck up"* before he stopped, realizing his voice was being broadcast. The only person for whom Pendleton's words didn't completely register was Muley, who, of course, had heard what had been said but didn't think P.C. was actually trying to break his concentration, just thought he was having some fun. In the moment before Mel cued them, he laughed and said, "No, man, it's gonna be you."

P.C. never recovered his concentration. He spoke too fast, garbled his lines, and at the end of the reading, didn't even bother to deliver the line he was supposed to say simultaneously with Muley: "On WBOE Radio Chicago." Once Donna emerged to tell P.C. "Thank you for coming" and Muley "Please stay, Muley," P.C. was already halfway to the door, but not before Mel could tell him, "Better luck next time, bitch."

Then there were ten left, five boys and five girls. There was Muley Wills, Lana Rovner, Julie Ying, and the gleeful boy in the cowboy outfit, whose name was Pablo De La Fuente. Debbie Diaz and Brian Chi—who attended the Walt Disney Magnet School—were the only ones aside from Muley who attended public school. The others consisted of Nick Oliopoulos, whose father was an alderman and whose mother sat on the women's board of the Chicago Symphony Orchestra; Vicky Blackwell, who modeled Healthtex clothes for kids and whose mother was a voice-over for potato chips, automobiles, and YOUR-TV; Jonathan Greenberg, whose family owned the largest fabric wholesaler in the city; and

Lisa-Anne Williams, whose father had played for the Chicago Bears and retired early to start the New Centurions Christian youth camp.

Mel called Lana in from the hallway for her one-on-one. "I hope you get it," Julie said. "I hope you get it more than me." Lana said thanks, but the remark perplexed her; she understood Julie's wanting her to get cast—she wanted Julie to get cast too—but more than her? That was weird; she wondered if Julie was one of those weird Christian people. Sometimes Orientals turned out to be weird Christian people; she was excited to see *Ice Follies* with her but was having second thoughts about sleeping over.

The stage was set up as before, and now Lennie Kidd was sitting at the desk. The unnerving thing about Lennie was the fact that when he prepped Lana for her interview, he was completely devoid of humor. But the moment Mel cued him, his eyes flashed with excitement, his posture perked up, and he spoke one octave higher than before. "Hey, *Young Town* Kids," he effused ecstatically into the microphone. "We have a very special guest with us in our studio today. This is a very talented young lady. Let's give her a big hand, huh? Can we give a big hand for Lana Rovner, ladies and gentleman?" Mel Coleman applauded halfheartedly. "Hey, great," Lennie continued. "Now, we're gonna ask our very special guest some very special questions, and the first question I'd like to ask you, Lana, is: What is your favorite color?"

"Blue," Lana said instantly—she was not going to hem or haw over a single question. She had told herself that she was going to do the same thing great Olympic gymnasts said they did when they wanted to get a perfect ten: She was going to "stick it."

"Wow," Lennie said. "Blue, that's a great color, Lana. Why blue?"

"Because I love water," Lana lied. "I love the ocean. I love going to the beach, and I love the Seine River. That's the best river; it's in France."

"Golly, France, huh?" Lennie said. "That's pretty cool. Have you ever been to France, Lana?"

"Yes, I have, Lennie," Lana lied confidently. "And it's the best country with the best food and the best people and the best museums."

"Wow," Lennie said. "That's pretty cool, huh?"

Lennie asked Lana ten more questions and she nailed every single one, from "Who are your heroes?" to which Lana replied, "My mom, my dad, Marie Curie, and Nadia Comaneci" to "What do you want to be when you grow up?" Lana responded that she wanted to be a radiologist or a psychologist; either way, she'd see through people and help them.

"Wow, cool!" Lennie shouted. "Well, we've really enjoyed having you on our show. That's all for me. I'm Lennnnniiiiee Kidd for WBO-EEEEE." Then Lennie grunted thanks and told her to wait in the hallway until they were done with the other interviews. Lana wasn't sure why he was so surly but was certain it had nothing to do with her performance: She had "stuck it."

Muley was a considerably less confident interviewee. He didn't like talking about himself or answering questions. He never was terribly sure of his own opinions; he almost always saw both points of view. So when a guffawing Lennie Kidd asked him, "Hey, Muley, tell the folks out in Radioland what your favorite color is," the only response he could come up with was, "Well, I don't really have any favorite. I like them all okay. Sometimes I like purple, I guess." And even when Lennie was almost feeding him answers, begging him to be more enthusiastic—"Come on, Muley, you mean you really don't have a favorite musical instrument?"—all Muley said was "I just don't; I wish I had something better to tell you." Lennie rushed through his script, exasperated. His second-to-last question was a throwaway, one Lana had tackled in a single sentence: "What lessons do you have for the kids out there?" Lana had simply said, "Listen to your parents and don't grow up too fast; there's lots of cool stuff you'll miss if you do." But Muley's response was considerably more cryptic. "Sometimes even when you don't wanna, you gotta look where the sun ain't shining," he said.

Mel Coleman looked up. He knew this phrase; it had appeared in his book, *Mel's Manual for Men,* but when Lennie asked Muley about the phrase, Muley said it was one of Peachy Moskowitz's "Lessons from Life." He said that Peachy had been living in Moscow with her father in a one-room apartment, making dinners out of whatever they could scavenge from garbage drums. For years, Peachy's father had told her that though they were poor, at one time they had been rich. But her mother had died before she could tell them where she had hidden her jewelry; every night they had searched for it, but they had run out of hiding places, and after a while, Peachy didn't believe the jewels ever existed. Then, one day, she came home to find her father slumped on the bathroom floor, drunk and passed out again, bottle of vodka still in his hand. She grabbed the vodka, poured it down the toilet, and flushed. But the toilet wouldn't flush. She took the cover off the tank to try and fix it, and there they were—her mother's jewels—in the one place they hadn't thought to look, in a place where the sun didn't shine. The truth was, Peachy explained to Muley, to find what you're looking for, you have to look in places you never thought of looking.

Lennie Kidd's voice descended an octave and became the voice he used when dealing with adults—wooing women at discos or explaining to his ex-wife why he couldn't perform sexually.

"Who's this Peachy Moskowitz?" he asked.

"She's the reason I'm here," Muley said. He made a circling gesture with his hands that suggested both the entire world and his small place in it. And then Muley told him about Peachy Moskowitz, perhaps the smartest and most beautiful woman he had ever laid eyes upon, a woman who would have put Natalia Makarova to shame, had she not injured her ankle on a windy Moscow night. And as he spoke, he could almost feel himself falling in love with Peachy Moskowitz—not realizing Lennie Kidd was doing the same.

"Golly," Lennie said, "I bet the kids in Radioland would love to meet your cousin, huh? Well, that's all the time we have. We sure do thank you for coming on our show. This has been Lennie Kidd for *Young Town* and WBOEEEEEE."

Jill Wasserstrom had returned to the Bismarck lobby, and now Muley and all the other finalists were sitting there, waiting for Donna Mayne to ask them back in and announce the final cast. Julie Ying was demonstrating to Lana how she did cartwheels, while her parents, dressed in prim business attire, looked on disapprovingly. Pablo De La Fuente had challenged Brian Chi to a game of pantomime tennis and declared with every serve that he had delivered an ace and that he was "killing" Brian Chi—"I'm killing you in Wimbledon and I'm killing you in the U.S. Open," Pablo cried. Debbie Diaz was sitting cross-legged on the floor doing a Word Search; Jonathan Greenberg's mother was quizzing him on square roots; P.C. Pendleton was swearing at somebody on a pay phone; Lisa-Anne Williams was listening to her father tell a story about faith and the power to dream; Vicky Blackwell and her mother were both putting on makeup; Jill Wasserstrom was asking Muley if he wanted to come over and read about the Ayatollah or listen to records. Muley thought he noticed something different about Jill. But before he could ask her if something was wrong, Mel Coleman poked his head out of the doorway and asked everyone to return to the ballroom.

Donna Mayne asked the finalists to stand in a line. This wouldn't take long, she promised. First, she wanted to say how thrilled she was with the candidates—

she hadn't imagined they would be able to find so many talented actors. Brian Chi asked if there was a possibility that people who didn't get cast might be used as understudies. Donna told him it wasn't very likely. She told him it was very late, that everyone wanted to go home, that everyone should hold their questions. Then she told him "Thank you for coming."

That was good, Lana Rovner thought. She figured they'd only take one Oriental and it would be Julie. Sure enough, when Donna got to Julie, she told her "Please stay." Yes, Lana thought, Julie deserved it. People who were nice to her deserved to be rewarded. Debbie Diaz was told "Thank you for coming," and that chafesome little brat Pablo De La Fuente ran a lap around the auditorium with his arms outstretched, making airplane noises, when Donna told him "Please stay." Nick Oliopoulos was told "Thank you for coming," as was Jonathan Greenberg. Out of the remaining four—Muley Wills, Lisa-Anne Williams, Vicky Blackwell, and Lana Rovner—three still had to be chosen. She had a 75 percent chance. There would be one black, Lana was certain of it, so when Donna told Lisa-Anne Williams "Please stay," she wasn't surprised. But when Donna told Muley "Please stay, Muley," Lana felt her entire world suddenly spinning out of its orbit, hurtling off somewhere she had never dreamed it could travel. And by the time Donna had said to Vicky Blackwell "Please stay," and to Lana "Thank you for coming," Lana could barely process what had happened. When she walked out into the lobby, dazed, she was clutching a *Young Town* thank-you pack and she didn't even know who had given it to her. All she knew was that she didn't want it, so she dropped it on the floor.

Ellen Rovner had been paging through the paperback copy of *Reveille for Radicals* that Jill had left behind when Lana emerged from the ballroom.

"What happened?" Ellen Rovner asked her daughter.

"It was completely rigged," Lana said as she steamed down the hallway and out the front door of the hotel, exiting onto Randolph Street. "I don't even know why you made me come to this thing. You knew it would be like this. This was all part of your plot." Ellen Rovner asked her what plot she was referring to. Lana was about to elaborate, but then changed her mind when she noticed P.C. Pendleton standing on Dearborn Street looking up and down the block.

Lana's first inclination was to confront P.C. and declare that she held him personally responsible for having missed out on making the *Just Kiddin'* TV series two years earlier. But she decided she was more mature than that. So instead, she walked up to P.C. and told him she had always admired him on *Just Kiddin'* and was sorry things hadn't worked out better for either of them. P.C. shook her hand and asked her name—he said he hadn't remembered her from the callback. Lana introduced herself again and asked if he needed a ride. "You're too kind," P.C. said.

In Ellen Rovner's Volvo, Lana and P.C. discussed just about everything except *Young Town.* Lana had brought it up, but P.C. had dismissed the topic curtly, saying, "Let's not talk about injustice." Instead, they talked about movies, Olympic skating, gymnastics, and ballet. And then P.C. asked Lana to tell him what she enjoyed eating. Lana said it was a toss-up between the barbecued ribs at Ruthie's (her father's favorite) and the crab rangoon at the Blue Peacock (her mother's). P.C. said he didn't know the restaurants to which she referred; normally, his family dined at the Cape Cod Room or Avenue One at the Drake.

"Oh," Lana exclaimed. "The Drake! That's where my Bat Mitzvah was." She felt sorry immediately after she'd said it, as if by admitting her Judaism she would seem somehow less worthy to participate in the high-society discussions of the old-money Gold Coast Pendletons, never mind that she was proud of being Jewish and tried to trumpet that fact in front of as many goyim at Baker as possible ("No, I can't go to that party," she would say. "It's Rosh Hashanah." "No, I can't eat Wonder Bread on Passover; it's *chametz.*" "No, I can't even drink a pop; it's Yom Kippur—I'm fasting!"), never mind that P.C. Pendleton's mother's name was Weezie Berkman.

Before P.C. exited the car in front of his family's mansion on Burton Place, he told Lana he would be having a New Year's Eve party; he wondered if she would be his guest. It would be "somewhat dressy," he said, though "not formal." Lana beamed and said she'd love to. After P.C. had shut the door to the car, Lana asked her mother if she thought P.C. had asked her out on a date. Ellen said she sincerely hoped not, because until she was a sophomore in high school, Lana wasn't allowed to go on dates; she was only allowed to go to parties. Not that Ellen Rovner was really that dogmatic on the topic; she had a generally negative view of her children's intelligence and attractiveness and thought it was healthier for them to blame her than themselves for their inability to find significant others. To her, the idea that anyone would date either her sweaty, neurotic son or her nasty, competitive daughter was fantastical; P.C.'s offer had been an act of charity, or worse.

Lana still thought it might have been a date, but decided to keep it to herself; her mother had a way of deflating her fantasies with a mere word. In truth, she had never been out on a date. Never even kissed a boy. Well, almost never. There had been a champagne snowball at her Bat Mitzvah, but that didn't count—her parents had been right there. Also, there had been that wretched party at Mary Beth Wales's house where all the boys had demanded a game of Spin the Bottle and practically every time she spun, her bottle had pointed at Jamie Henderson, whose idea of a good time was hanging out on the mats before school, trying futilely to set world records for the *Guinness Book* ("I bet I can set the record for most times in a row anyone's ever played 'Slow Ride,' " he'd said once). One time, she got to school early and saw him standing on the radiator with the window open and his pants around his ankles, trying to set the world record for peeing distance. "I bet if I get a boner, I can set it," he'd said. And at Mary Beth's party, every time the bottle pointed at Jamie, they would go behind the trees and she'd say, "Let's just shake hands." The third time, though, Jamie moaned, "But she's just gonna say, 'Let's shake hands.'" At which point, Mary Beth informed her that was against the rules. You couldn't "just shake hands." So Lana went behind the trees with Jamie and let him kiss her on the cheek. But the next day at school, she walked in and everybody started giggling and she couldn't figure out why—until PE when she was getting undressed for swimming and Mary Beth said, "God, we just said you had to kiss; you didn't have to let him go up your shirt." That lie even got as far as the PE teacher, Ms. Russell, who took Lana aside, asked if she had been "sexually acting out," if she had let boys start "exploring," and if she "had sexual problems."

By the time she got home, Lana was no longer feeling completely resentful about not having made *Young Town*. She was going to see *Ice Follies* with her new friend Julie Ying and she was going to go on a date with P.C. Pendleton, even though he wasn't Jewish, which could pose some problems if they were ever going to have kids. She would happily marry a gentile but he'd have to convert, because no way could she bring a gentile boy to meet Grandma Rose, who would look him over and say, "What're you doin' bringin' home goyim?" And by the way, what was Jill Wasserstrom doing with that black kid Muley—didn't she have a grandmother who told her he was *tinkle*? Well, maybe if she didn't have a mother, she didn't have a grandmother—that was sad, actually—but even so, it was weird. Still, as for Lana herself, she decided as she walked up the stairs to her house, things were definitely looking up—even though no one was home on Sacramento, even though her father had said he'd be there when they got back.

What Muley and Jill were doing, as it turned out, was sitting in Mel Coleman's powder-blue 1974 Chevy Nova driving north. As he drove, Mel advised Muley to avoid taking guff from station management; he was convinced that Muley had been cast only so Donna and Lennie could have somebody to boss around. "Don't let them make you play any butlers," Mel told Muley. "Don't let them make you play any pimps. Don't let them make you play any kinda Kunta Kinte. If they make you play a Pullman porter, you're gonna walk and Mel's gonna walk right along with you."

Muley was only half paying attention; he had already started thinking about his other projects. For a moment in the Bismarck, when he realized he had made the cast, he had been proud. For another moment, when he heard he would be paid $150 per episode, he was happy. But after those moments had passed and Lennie Kidd had waved good-bye and screamed, "See ya in *Young Town,* smart kids!" Muley had already begun thinking about what he could do to augment his income; $150 was certainly more than he usually made from his projects, and now it seemed as though he could have the money he needed in a little more than a year and a half. But still that seemed a lifetime away. And still a part of him thought that the longer he took to get his mother the money she never asked for but he knew she needed, the less chance there was that she'd take it from him, and he wanted so badly for her to have it.

Mel dropped Jill off at her apartment on Campbell, and as she was getting out of the car, he leaned over to Muley and said, "How 'bout some beers, son, you and me?" But then Jill said, "I thought we were going to do some work."

"Seems like your old lady's got other plans for you," Mel said.

As soon as Jill and Muley entered the empty apartment, the phone rang. Jill picked it up—as usual, a guy for Michelle. "Tell her Larry called," the voice said. "She's got the number."

Muley was standing dumbly in the front hallway, searching his mind for an excuse for why he couldn't stick around to discuss the Shah and the Ayatollah. But the moment he said, "Well, I guess I'll leave you to Iran," Jill asked him if he wanted to listen to records. Muley thought she meant comedy records. But then she took off her shoes and walked in her socks back to her bedroom, extracted one of the albums from Michelle's "unlistenable pile"—Billy Joel's *The Stranger*—

turned up the volume, and asked if he remembered the slowdance they'd learned in Disco in seventh grade. For years at Boone, in the spring, Rita Weinbaum from the Weinbaum Dance Studio would teach the kids square dancing, and every year she would play the same scratchy 78 rpm square dance record, slap her hands, and chant, "First couple, sashay up! First couple, sashay down!" But after Rita Weinbaum retired and moved to Las Vegas, she was replaced by the vivacious Sandi Hirsch, who taught the kids disco dancing. Sandi Hirsch wore cowboy jackets and light-blue eye shadow, and told the kids about the guys she met when she was dancing at Faces on Rush Street. Under Sandi's tutelage, they learned the Bump, the Hustle, the Bus Stop, the Chicago Walk, and the slow-dance that Jill eased Muley Wills into as Billy Joel sang, "A bottle of white, a bottle of red."

They stood there like that for some time, Muley Wills's uncertain hands just touching the waist of Jill Wasserstrom's jeans, Jill's hands just grazing Muley's shoulders. Muley remembered that when Sandi Hirsch had taught them this dance, he had called it the Rocking Boat, because it seemed that all they did was rock back and forth. As Muley and Jill rocked back and forth, Muley's mind occasionally drifted to the beautiful, brilliant Peachy Moskowitz, whom he wished somehow was real, while Jill tried to avoid thinking about the moment tonight when she'd felt afraid, truly afraid. But now Jill was smiling, nearly giggling, until Muley asked her why; she said it was because she almost felt like she was inside of a movie. Muley smiled as they continued rocking until the record ended. Then Jill put the needle back at the beginning of the LP. She kissed Muley lightly on the cheek during the first song and he kissed her on the cheek during the second one, but didn't dare kiss her cheek again until the third time the album side played. They continued in this manner for some time, until Michelle Wasserstrom, still wearing her *H.M.S. Pinafore* makeup, burst into the room and demanded, "Who the hell put on Billy Joel?"

Charlie

The day Charlie Wasserstrom was fired from It's in the Pot!, he was taken aback by his daughter Jill's cheerful reaction: "Well, I guess that means the Bat Mitzvah's off. Oh well, too bad." He quickly assured her that was not the case, of course they'd still have the Bat Mitzvah, although he wasn't sure how he'd pay for it now.

Charlie had been waiting patiently for Gail Schiffler-Bass's review of the restaurant in the *Nortown Leader.* The review had been delayed for a month, pre-empted by reviews of restaurants that had purchased larger display ads. It was finally published in December under the headline, "New Lincolnwood Restaurant Goes to *Pot.*" Bass took a creative approach to her reviews. Her review of the Bialy Boy Restaurant, which had come out during Passover, used parodies of the Haggadah's four questions to introduce sections: "Why on this night of all other nights would we want to eat here?" "Why on this night of all other nights would we want to have soggy chicken?" "Why on this night of all other nights would noodle kugel be gray?" And finally: "Why on this night of all other nights wouldn't we have stayed in Egypt if we knew we'd wind up here?"

In the case of It's in the Pot! she introduced each paragraph with what she termed "Wasserstrom's Theses." Having extensively interviewed Charlie, who spoke highly of the restaurant, she used his quotes, then viciously refuted them. As in:

Wasserstrom Thesis #3: "We have a wide selection of appetizers here."

Schiffler-Bass's Refutation: Actually, there are four on the menu and only one—pickled herring—that any sane person would ever consider consuming.

Or:

Wasserstrom Thesis #6: "It's conveniently located and the parking couldn't be better."

Schiffler-Bass's Refutation: Technically, this is correct, but how many of us enjoy eating with a view of the Datsuns in the shopping mall?

And finally:

Wasserstrom Thesis #20: "It's a great value for the money."

Schiffler-Bass's Refutation: Not as great as staying home.

Bass closed her review by saying that Wasserstrom was immensely talented at spouting the party line and suggested he find work in Jimmy Carter's reelection campaign. When Charlie walked into work that day, hostess Carla Tannenbaum told him, "The boss wants to see you, doll," and Charlie huffed his way through the restaurant to the closet-sized room off the kitchen where Alan Farbman maintained his office. To Farbman, the fact that Charlie had done nothing but compliment his restaurant was irrelevant; all that mattered as he shoved the article in Charlie's direction was the fact that his establishment had been eviscerated and his manager was responsible.

"I don't care who said what to who," he said. "All I know is, that's your name down there, and bottom line"—he said "bottom line" whenever he made a point—"that's all I *need* to know."

Charlie desperately pleaded his case, apologized for having spoken to Schiffler-Bass, said he knew he had "overstepped his bounds." Farbman said he understood, "But the bottom line's the bottom line and there's not a lot I can do about that." He added that he was sorry he wouldn't be able to follow through on his offer to donate a deli tray to Jill's Bat Mitzvah.

Though he had worked numerous jobs over the course of his forty-six years, Charlie Wasserstrom had never been unemployed for more than a week. Growing up on the West Side of Chicago, where the city's poor, immigrant Jews had been concentrated until a great Diaspora sent them radiating across the city—the poorest ones to Albany Park, the somewhat more successful ones to West Rogers Park, and the ones who had truly arrived to the lakefront and the northern suburbs—Charlie had started working when he was eleven. After school at Sumner Elementary, he would ride the Garfield Park subway downtown, then head south to his father Jacob Wasserstrom's soda pop factory at 45th and Lenox, on the South Side. He worked there after school and on weekends, and all through high school at Manley, loading crates onto the backs of Wasserstrom Beverage Company trucks, along with his twin brother Dave.

The idea was that he and Dave would eventually take over the business, but it never fully recovered from the hit it took in WWII, when sugar became scarce. Business got worse with each passing year until, in 1956, the Wasserstrom Beverage Company went bankrupt. Afterward, Dave joined the army and was stationed at Camp Pendleton, where he found a buddy in his barracks—Artie Schumer—and a girl, Peppy Stein, while he was on leave in Las Vegas. Within six months of his return to Chicago, Dave was married to Peppy, living west of the city in a small house in Elmhurst, running a five-and-dime shop with Artie, and telling his parents he was too busy to visit them more than once a month; shortly thereafter, he became father to Arthur David Wasserstrom, the first of two boys. Charlie, on the other hand, kept out of the service because he was overweight and had high blood pressure, lived at home until he was twenty-seven, and worked deli jobs to help support his mother Molly, who kept the books at the Romanian Sausage Factory, and his father, who suffered a heart attack after the pop factory closed and never completely regained his health.

After Jacob Wasserstrom died in 1960, Charlie's mother moved into an apartment Dave rented for her. The apartment was about twenty miles northeast of Dave and Peppy's house, but only a five-minute walk from the studio Charlie found for himself on Touhy not far from the Pinewood Restaurant, where he got his first job managing a sit-down restaurant. It was at the Pinewood where he met Rita Shore, whose name was really Becky Schulman; she had changed it when she left home at the age of seventeen to pursue an acting career, first in New York, then in L.A. She had found chorus girl gigs on Broadway, but L.A. had been a complete bust. The girl she moved with found a husband less than two weeks after they arrived there, leaving Becky with the full rent for their apartment, at which point she decided she was done with the whole racket and got on an eastbound bus. But rather than just switch buses in Chicago and head back to Manhattan or to her parents' apartment in Poughkeepsie, she'd stayed and worked as a waitress while she tried to figure out what to do with her life.

She had planned to become an acting teacher. Instead, she married Charlie Wasserstrom and changed her name back to Becky within four months of his arrival at the Pinewood, where she served as a dinner hostess. He may not have been the brightest man she'd ever met—Max Goodman, the composer of the revue *Girls-A-Million!,* her first singing-and-dancing gig in New York, had taken those honors. And he certainly wasn't the most attractive. But if anything, rotund, frequently breathless Charlie Wasserstrom's lack of magnetism and savoir-faire made him even more appealing. His childish earnestness was endearing; his adoration flattering. He was honest, devoted, quick to please, and easy to satisfy. If they received more than a few glances from passersby on her beloved Lunt Avenue Beach, wondering what she might be doing with that galoot, she reveled in the implicit compliment those glances gave her and pitied and loved him all the more for them.

After they were married in a small ceremony at B'nai Reuven and had moved into East Rogers Park, they journeyed from restaurant to restaurant, generally working as a manager-and-hostess team. After the Pinewood, they worked at Elliott's Pine Log, Grassfields, and the Candlelight Restaurant. In 1962, when Michelle was born, the Candlelight's marquee read "It's a Girl!" By then, they had moved west, still in East Rogers Park though, to an apartment on Coyle. When Jill was born in 1967, they moved into an apartment on Fairfield, in West Rogers Park, just one block east of California. Charlie and Becky talked frequently about moving into a house, and had their sights set on one particular dwelling they called the "Funny House" just west of California on North Shore. It was a low house with a long, flat, black roof that sat on top of it like a cap on the head of a graduating senior. There was ivy outside the house and ginkgo trees out front. One day in 1975, when they were walking hand in hand, they noticed a moving truck out front, but that was more than two weeks after they had gone together to the doctor and learned the cause of Becky's blurred vision and her increasingly frequent, painful headaches.

After Becky died, the Wasserstroms moved back east, to Campbell Avenue. Charlie worked a series of subsistence jobs—deliveryman for Lasser's Beverages, counterman at New York Bagels and Bialys on Touhy, then next door at Fannie's Deli. With It's in the Pot!, it seemed as if he had finally turned a corner. But now his own naïveté and enthusiasm had sidetracked him once again. He had been so enthralled with the idea of being interviewed and quoted in a newspaper that he hadn't stopped to think how his quotes might be used or that Gail Schiffler-Bass seemed to detest every restaurant she encountered, even the ones that took out half-page ads in the *Nortown Leader.*

Which was why, instead of immediately going out and looking for work, checking if that "Experienced Counterman Needed" sign was still in the window of Little Louie's Diner, he found himself driving north to the offices of the Schiffler Newspapers just off of Howard Street. Howard was the northern border between Chicago and Evanston, the city's one dry suburb, still under the influence of the Women's Christian Temperance Union. And though the south side of Howard might not have had quite as many of the shot-and-a-beer taverns, liquor stores, and B-girl joints that had predominated during the 1940s and '50s, it was still the first stop for Northwestern students to get off the el to shoot pool, buy beer, or find a cheap bag of reefer.

Schiffler Newspapers was located just east of the elevated train tracks. It was a one-story, windowless, chocolate-brown brick building with a poorly paved parking lot in the back. The editorial, advertising, and publishing offices and the printing facilities were all located here, and not only those of the *Nortown Leader,* but also the *Portage Leader,* the *Andersonville Leader,* the *Edgewater Leader,* and the *Budlong Beacon.* The newspapers came out once a week and the same Gail Schiffler-Bass community theater and restaurant reviews ran in each issue, as did the Letter from the Publisher, Howard Schiffler—Gail's father—whose booster-ish column dealt with one of four topics: "Let's Applaud a Business That Helps the Community," "Let's Applaud the Diversity of Our Community," "Let's Applaud Our Community Leaders," and "Let's Applaud Our High School Sports Teams." In the first instance, Howard Schiffler would hit up local businesses to buy advertising; in the second, he would lean on ethnic stores and shops; in the third, he'd get local politicians to take out ads; and in the final case, he'd get all three to buy: "DeWitt's Shoes Salutes the Mather Rangers' Winning Season."

The paper's ambitions were modest, its prose was frequently execrable, but Schiffler ran it like an old-time daily. The women wore skirts and made coffee, and the men wore flimsy white shirts and fat red neckties. The editorial staff was almost exclusively male—Jack Slutsky, copy chief; Ted Keegan, city reporter; J. Leslie Peterson, society columnist. The one exception to the old boys' network was Gail, who, when she arrived at the papers in 1962 after graduating with a journalism B.A. from the University of Illinois, was viewed skeptically and commented upon derisively at the Coke machine. The thought was that she was another one of Howard's nepotistic hires, like his nephew Gary, who was once given the prep sports beat and whose illiterate, mindless copy ("Then Taft got a goal, then Senn got a goal, then Taft got a goal, then Taft got a goal") was invariably rewritten. But shortly after she took over the lifestyle beat, Gail proved the sharpest and quickest reporter and the liveliest writer on staff. She had been wooed by the *Tribune* to write for their "Feminique" section, but she was content to remain at Schiffler, where it was understood that she would take over as publisher once Howard retired.

The newsroom was a Babel of typing, ringing phones, wire machines, and conversations shouted over the din. The wire machines may have been useless for weekly community newspapers, but they gave the place the gravity Howard Schiffler sought. Metal desks—three per island—were set off from one another at diagonals. The men's desks were chaotic heaps of paper—wirebound reporters' notebooks stained with coffee and mustard, crumpled-up sheets of yellow paper with phone numbers scrawled on them, typed article drafts smudged with red and black typewriter ribbon, dank paperback style manuals and dictionaries, all of which looked and smelled as if they'd been salvaged from basement floods. Gail's desk, however, was immaculate. There was one stack of typing paper and one stack of carbon paper to the left of her IBM Selectric—she was the only one in the office who didn't work on a manual typewriter, and the only one who had paid for her own. To the right of the typewriter was a telephone and a full ashtray. Everything else was filed away in gray metal drawers.

Gail was rummaging through a file drawer, smoking a Virginia Slim, when Charlie walked right past the receptionist to her desk; in his cheap white shirt, navy blue necktie, and black trousers underneath a worn gray raincoat, he looked so much like a Schiffler Newspapers reporter that the receptionist just nodded as he passed. And now, as he watched Gail pull a file, toss it down on her desk, and slam the drawer shut, he had no idea why he had come, what he intended to say. She couldn't give him his job back. He turned to go, but as he did, Gail snapped toward him.

"Wasserstrom," she said in a manner that suggested rudeness born of familiarity. It was as if she had not only known he'd been standing there but he had developed a habit of doing it and it had begun to grate on her.

"Ms. Bass," he said uncertainly.

"So what did he do?" she asked. "Fire you?"

Charlie stared at her.

"It's what always happens," she explained. Whenever her reviews came out, restaurants would try to find someone to blame. Usually, it was a manager, she said, but one time, all the roller-skating waitresses from Sally's Stage had come in to confront her.

"I'm not the first?" Charlie asked.

"Not the first to see me. Not the first one to ask that," Gail said. "So what do you want me to do? Get your job back?" Charlie said nothing. "All right," she said. "Let's get your job back." She walked briskly toward the front of the newsroom, grabbed a fake mink overcoat from a rack, punched a fist into a sleeve without slowing her pace, and put her other hand through the other sleeve when she was out in the parking lot, Charlie panting to keep up.

"Do you want your job back or not?" she asked.

Charlie said of course he wanted his job back, but he didn't understand what she could do about it. She said she did it all the time; she had done it the previous month with Morrie Weiss, who had been fired for stealing from the House of Canton, even though the guilty party had been the owner's son. She had told the owner if he didn't rehire Morrie, she would write an article about the vermin in the restaurant's kitchens as part of her series "The Rogers Park Rats." Gail opened the passenger door to her white Mercedes and told Charlie to get in.

During the drive, Gail quizzed Charlie about his job. Frankly, she said, she didn't know why he wanted it back, the food was awful, the owner was a schmuck, and the only people who went to It's in the Pot! were senior citizens from Winston Towers who came there with their respirators. Charlie said yes, his youngest daughter had said the same thing, at which point Gail began quizzing him about his family. She'd always wanted kids, she said, but was glad she had never had any with her ex-husband, who was completely unreliable. She had met him downstate at the U of I when she was working at the *Daily Illini* and he was doing magic shows at frat parties. They had been deeply in love all through their twenties, but she hadn't seen him in years; the last time she'd run into him, she'd been assigned to review the Pickle Barrel restaurant, and he was there making balloon animals.

Charlie usually enjoyed the company of talkative people, because it meant he didn't have to talk much himself. But what was odd about being with Gail was that although she was one of the most talkative women he'd ever met, he found himself talking more to her than he ever did to anyone else. He told her about his children, about his late wife, about his successful brother, about his late mother, about growing up on the old West Side, about baseball, about how much he had wanted to play for the Sox when he was growing up—he hadn't remembered that until that very minute, and wondered if he had ever told his wife about it; it seemed as if he hadn't thought about it in forty years. And then, as Gail pulled the car into the It's in the Pot! parking lot, partly because he feared confrontation and partly because he didn't want to stop the conversation he was enjoying, he said, "You know what; you're right. I really don't want this job back."

Charlie thought Gail would be angry. But instead of yelling, sighing, or whining at him—which was what his daughters did whenever he changed his mind—Gail said, "Well, we've got to find you a job. Where are we going to find you one?" She began listing restaurants and he kept vetoing them. He didn't want another counter job—there was no way to make a living at it. He didn't want to work in a chain; he wanted to work for a person, not a corporation. And then it hit him—but the moment it hit him, it hit Gail too. "You don't want to work in a restaurant at all, do you, Charlie?" she asked. That was right, he said, surprised. Gail asked if he wanted to discuss it over lunch.

They went to Myron and Phil's on Devon Avenue, where Gail ordered a Manhattan and Charlie ordered the Pritikin Chicken, because he said he was watching his weight, though he managed to make up for the calories he was watching with several lumps of chopped liver from the relish tray. Ostensibly, they were dining together so that Gail could figure out where Charlie might best find employment. But more often, they found themselves veering off onto the topic of Gail's difficulty in finding suitable men to date. She was through with the discos, she said; she was through with being fixed up with friends' least attractive relatives; she wouldn't date any of the men at work; she didn't like the Jewish men who went to singles events at the JCC. All through the conversation, it failed to strike Charlie that Gail had any deep reason for telling him of her dating woes. He was a good listener. People talked to him; they told him their problems, he looked like he cared, and generally he did. And it didn't occur to Gail that she was telling him her life story for any other reason than that he was, in fact, a good listener, that he seemed to care.

When the check came and Gail put down a twenty and stood, Charlie was rather dismayed that they were no longer discussing his job search, but he didn't want to bring it up for fear of seeming as though he had only been humoring her so she could help him find work. As they drove east on Devon, passing Levinson's Bakery and Minky's Bicycle Shop, then crossing California, he kept hoping that she would return to the job topic. But when she talked about jobs, she talked about her own, how she enjoyed it, but that it wasn't particularly taxing. Back at the U of I, she had written poetry. Now the only time she used that skill was in her restaurant reviews, as in the limerick she penned for a review of O'Hara's Grill ("There once was a gal named Siobhan / Who sold bathroom fixtures just north of Devon / But now she serves food / and this may sound rude / But the place still smells like a john").

When Gail turned left on Western and started heading north, Charlie assumed she was driving back to the Schiffler offices, but she slowed down when they reached Warren Park. She signaled for a turn, then parked across the street from the Hank Schiffler Ford dealership. Charlie asked what was going on. "I thought you wanted a job, Charlie," Gail said.

Hank Schiffler, Howard Schiffler's younger brother, was known in West Rogers Park as Hank Shiva, because of his propensity for cutting deals on new cars with people whose relatives had just recently died. He read the obituaries religiously and was a fixture at memorial services at Piser-Weinstein chapel, where he helped himself to sheetcake, cold cuts, and Canadian Club, and then, if invited, visited the family's house to pay his respects while they were sitting *shiva*. He was generally not seen as an ambulance-chasing vulture—he was usually more welcome than the gaggle of relatives who often came only out of obligation; at least everyone knew that when there was a funeral, Hank truly wanted to be there. There was something comforting about his presence, a sign that life was going on. And the truth was, he did offer better values than any other Ford dealer on Western.

The only time Charlie had met Hank had been at Becky's funeral. Hank had told him that Charlie's loss was a loss not only for his family but for the whole community. Then he asked him if the maroon Granada out front was his. Charlie said it was. Hank said he hadn't remembered selling him the car; he remembered all of his customers. Charlie said he had bought it from his cousin, who ran Irv Stein Ford. Hank said Irv was a good man, then asked Charlie how much he had spent. Charlie told him and Hank said Irv had given him a good price, but not quite as good a price as he would have given him. He told him the next time he needed a new car, he'd give him a good deal. Hank gave Charlie his card, then went to talk to the rabbi—he asked him how he liked his LTD.

Charlie told Gail he had never thought of selling cars, but he liked Fords and it might be worth a try. He sat in the waiting room of the dealership while Gail went in to talk to Hank. A Muzak version of Chuck Mangione's "Feels So Good" was playing, and the place smelled of leather interior and lemon disinfectant.

When he got tired of leafing through car brochures, Charlie strolled around the showroom. Two salesmen in gray suits—a tall bald man and a shorter, gray-haired man with a salt-and-pepper mustache—were gazing out the window at the traffic on Western. The shorter man smoked a cigarette. When Charlie peered through the driver-side window of a Fairmont, the taller man approached him and said, "Good time to be looking." Charlie nodded.

"For a car, I mean," the man said, somewhat louder. His name tag read Dave Sherman.

The man said the car Charlie was looking at was a good family car and asked if Charlie had kids. Charlie said he did—two girls. The man said he had a girl, Connie, who was thirteen—she was getting to be the age where she started acting like a woman, but he still thought of her as a little girl. Charlie nodded. The man asked if Charlie was looking to buy for himself or his wife. Charlie said he wasn't looking to buy; he was just killing time. The man said he could go right ahead, take as much time as he wanted. Then he went back to the shorter man and they both looked out the window. The taller man bummed a cigarette from the shorter man.

At that moment, Charlie realized he could be good at this job. The way the taller man had treated him, that hadn't been the right way to sell a car. He immediately tried to make the sale, and when he found out he wasn't buying, he left. He never asked Charlie his name or what he did for a living. True, he wasn't buying now, but if they had struck up a nice conversation, he might have come back. As it stood, the man had given him no reason to stop going to Irv Stein.

This was what he explained to Hank Shiva when Gail asked Charlie back to his office. Shiva, who looked younger than Wasserstrom remembered—he was very tan—listened, impressed. Gail said see, she knew what she was talking about—the guy was a natural. Hank told Charlie he wanted to "level" with him. He said he could use a new salesman. The guys he had were okay; they were fine for selling cars to people who had already decided they wanted to buy, but they couldn't convert anybody. He liked Charlie's face, he said; there was nothing intimidating about it. He filled up a white plastic Ford bag with literature about new car models. He told Charlie to study the cars, learn them inside and out, then come back the next day and they could talk more.

At home that night, neither Jill nor Michelle expressed much enthusiasm for Charlie's potential new career. "You're gonna sell cars?" Michelle asked as she was walking out the door wearing a denim jacket with The Who written on it in black marker—an arrow was shooting off the "O." "That's fine, Dad," she said. "Just so long as you don't work for Hank Shiva." She kissed him on the cheek, then told him that if anyone called asking where she was, he should say she was at dress rehearsal for *H.M.S. Pinafore.* A car horn honked and she said she had to go; Millard was waiting.

Jill, who was prepping for her Shah-Ayatollah debate, reacted with relative indifference. "If that's what you want to do, you should do it," she said. Charlie told her a good car salesman could make $40,000 a year. If he made that kind of dough, he said, then they might be able to move out of the Campbell apartment, maybe even move west to a house, not the Funny House they used to talk about but at least a nice small one on Francisco or Mozart. Jill regarded her father frostily. She remembered discussions like this from when she was much younger and didn't relish the memories. She told him to be realistic, then went to her room to work.

When Charlie returned to Hank Shiva's office the next morning, Hank shook his hand warmly and asked if he was ready to sell cars. Charlie said he thought so. Hank offered him a doughnut and asked Charlie if he had read over the Ford brochures. Charlie said he didn't need a doughnut, but he said he had read the material and was impressed. Before, he had been fairly sure that Ford made the best cars in America; now he was certain of it.

Hank said they should "take a little spin" around the showroom and he'd explain how he liked "to do business." He liked his salesmen to look sharp. If they didn't come in looking sharp, they didn't work that day. Mustaches were okay; beards were out. They stopped at a Fairmont, the one Charlie had been looking at the other day. There was an itemized price list affixed to a window. The first thing Charlie had to know, Hank said, was that wasn't what the customer would pay anyway. If a car was a "hot car," one that had to be back-ordered, like the Mustangs, the customer would pay above-list. If a car was a dud, like the Fairmont, the customer would pay below. He told Charlie that pricing could go up or down depending on whether or not the customer seemed like "a real schmuck." Financing was another thing Charlie would learn about. If a customer took the list price on a Fairmont, Charlie could give them a standard financing deal; if they worked it down $1,000, Charlie could jack it up 3 percent. If a "load of coal" came into the dealership, that was a whole different deal. In the case of a "load of coal," the best approach was to make a yellow checkmark on their financing deal to identify them as such. And in that case, you could work the rate all the way up to 25 percent. If they wanted to complain, that was fine. More often than not, they wouldn't complain at all—there weren't a lot of dealerships that gave any financing deal to a "load of coal."

Charlie asked what a "load of coal" meant. Hank told him it meant blacks. He didn't want to give the wrong impression—he wasn't against blacks—there were people in the South who had gone around lynching people; that was crazy. But there were two kinds of black people; there were blacks and there were *schwarzers.* Blacks he had no trouble with. There was one black kid he knew named Jimmy—a black kid about sixty years old who washed the dealership's windows, had to get a whole lot of custard and jam off just a couple weeks before, didn't even gripe. But then there were *schwarzers;* he didn't want to go into detail. He said he felt that Charlie knew what he meant.

Each time he heard Hank use the word *schwarzer,* Charlie felt his stomach constrict and his heart pound fast. He had heard the word all the time at the pop factory from his father and every "Parmesan Sunday" from his brother Dave and his wife Peppy—how once you got on the Eisenhower Expressway, the neighborhood started getting *schwarz,* how Peppy didn't like taking the Douglas el downtown because it was too *schwarz,* how Dave and Peppy's son Manny had a poster of former White Sox star Richie Allen in his bedroom and they had laughed uproariously when Artie Schumer ran downstairs shouting, "Hey, somebody call the cops quick! There's a big *schwarzer* on Manny's wall!" Charlie was secretly proud that after Parmesan Sundays, Jill and Michelle would mock Dave and Peppy's racism as they drove home. "Oy, I can't take it," Michelle would say as they drove past the Hillside Theater. "It's too *schwarz.*" "Do you want to stop at Kiddieland?" Jill would ask. "Oy, please," Michelle would respond. "Too *schwarz,* too *schwarz.*"

The only black friend Charlie had ever had was Lloyd from his father's factory—they had played catch in Washington Park together from time to time. But after the factory had closed, he had lost track of Lloyd. And now, even though he abhorred the word *schwarz,* he was still leery of his daughter's friendship with that boy Muley Wills. He liked Muley; he was a sharp kid. He just feared what others would say. Things were tough enough for Jews, but they were tougher for blacks, and he would prefer for Jill's sake that things be easier for her. His kids had had enough hardship already.

But Charlie didn't broach any of these issues with Hank Shiva. Instead he told him he knew what he meant. And when Hank told Charlie he was a good man, and he was sure he'd be top earner on the floor within six months, Charlie said he'd be in before nine on Monday, ready to start his training, even though as he walked out, he felt a strong and surprising urge to grab the doughnuts on Hank Shiva's desk and hurl them one by one at the showroom window.

What had kept Charlie from speaking up during his interview with Hank was not only his fear of conflict. And it was not just the money that would have allayed his fears about the Bat Mitzvah bills. What kept him nodding his way through Hank Shiva's patter was Gail Schiffler-Bass, the thought that refusing the job would upset her. She had gone out of her way to find him work and it seemed insulting and thankless to let her down. Nevertheless, as he drove up Western, wasting gasoline he really couldn't afford to burn, he grew more and more certain that he could not take the job and that he would have to give Gail an excuse for why he couldn't take it. When he got to the Schiffler Newspapers office, Gail was seated at her desk, cigarette smoldering in her ashtray, tarantula fingers skittering madly over the keys of her typewriter.

"Wasserstrom," she said. He had no idea how she had sensed his presence. She asked if he'd seen Hank but didn't stop typing, just kept focused on her article and occasionally threw looks back at him. "He liked you," she said.

"You talked with him?" Charlie asked.

Gail shook her head. "Why wouldn't he like you?" she asked. "When do you start?"

Charlie said nothing.

She repeated the question: "When do you start?"

Charlie shrugged, then shook his head.

"Aren't you taking it?" Gail asked.

"No," Charlie said. It was a word he rarely uttered. It felt oddly powerful saying it.

Gail stopped typing and turned around. She studied Charlie closely. "You're not taking it," she said.

"No," Charlie Wasserstrom said. "I don't think I am."

A smile began to form on Gail's face, a smile with just a hint of pride about it. "What did it?" she asked. "Was it the 'load of coal'?"

"Yeah. That," Charlie said. "That and other things."

"Charlie Wasserstrom," she said. "You're a rare thing in this world."

"What's that?" he asked.

"A decent man," she said. Then she asked if he'd be interested in a job selling ads for the Schiffler Newspapers. And when he said he might be, depending on what the job entailed, she asked if he wanted to have dinner on Friday. He said he would like to, but he had to see his daughter in *H.M.S. Pinafore.* Gail asked if she could come with him. Charlie said he saw no reason why not.

When Charlie met Gail at the Mather High auditorium for the opening night of *H.M.S. Pinafore,* the seats were already three-quarters full; the stragglers were still outside—the guys in lettermen's jackets with girlfriends in the chorus, the impatient wives eyeing their watches, waiting for their husbands to park the car, the alums walking down the hallway with an air of nostalgia and ownership, grandmas and grandpas walking in slowly, very slowly.

Muley and Jill were already sitting near the back of the auditorium, still appearing very much like a couple, even if Muley had just that day defeated her in the Shah-Ayatollah debate. Somehow, word had spread among the students that Jill would only feel victorious if she was unanimously defeated, but the students—led by Shmuel Weinberg—had voted Jill the winner 22–0, a result that was overturned by Mrs. Korab, who sought to punish Jill for her "negative attitude." "How can anyone support the Ayatollah with the hostages still there?" she demanded.

Charlie waved to Muley and Jill but sat far away from them; he knew they wanted their privacy. He wondered if Jill would be angry he was here with Gail, but Jill had no reaction. She figured Gail was someone from the PTA, someone from It's in the Pot!, someone from the synagogue, someone uninteresting at any rate. That her father was on a date never entered her mind.

Gail was telling Charlie how much she liked high school theater, that she was tired of seeing traveling road shows at the Shubert or the Studebaker, where you could tell the performers were just in it for the paycheck. Charlie said he didn't get to see much theater. He was about to tell her about the first high school show he'd seen Michelle in, the one where she played Anne Frank, but when he began discussing it, a voice behind him said, "Mr. Wasserstrom?" As he turned around, Charlie searched his memory for any trace of the young man with the yarmulke, the unbuttoned blue oxford over a Led Zeppelin "Zoso" shirt, leaning over and extending his hand.

"Larry Rovner," the young man said, shaking Charlie's hand effusively. "Yehuda," he added, as if that would explain everything. "I was in Hebrew School with Chaya."

Charlie said sure, he remembered. He asked Larry how he'd been. Larry said he was doing really well; he was looking forward to Chanukah break. It would be his last Chanukah break before Brandeis. Charlie asked what he was doing for Chanukah. Larry said he didn't know. His family had discussed going to Paris, but he wasn't sure he could go; he was completing a record album. He also said that Chanukah break might be his last chance to hang out with Michelle. They'd talked about getting together, maybe seeing *French Postcards,* but he'd been busy with his band and she'd been busy with the show. Just then, Douglas Sternberg entered with the orchestra and tapped his baton against his music stand, and the lights went down.

From the moment the curtain opened to reveal the deck of the H.M.S. *Pinafore,* sailors scrubbing the deck, cleaning the brass, and singing, "We sail the ocean blue, and our saucy ship's a beauty," to the end of the first act, with the whole cast extolling the virtues of a British sailor, "His eyes should flash and his breast protrude, and this should be his customary Atti-TUDE," stamping their feet on the stage and saluting with that last syllable, Charlie Wasserstrom thought the production, with the exception of Myra Tuchbaum's matronly performance as the leading lady, was really top-notch. And as for Michelle, he didn't know when he'd ever seen her play this sort of character. She was truly another person onstage. She had always been a star to him but now he really thought that everyone around him was thinking that too. Maybe she was right, maybe she could make a living at this. That's what he would tell her after the show, he decided, as he furiously applauded the first act.

But he wouldn't have to wait until the end of the show, because once the first act was over, he saw Michelle walking up the aisle toward him. She was wearing her blue jeans and a denim jacket over a black T-shirt that said, "The Loop: Where Chicago Rocks!" He didn't understand how she had changed her costume so quickly.

"I'm not in the show," she explained, wondering aloud why the hell Charlie and Jill hadn't picked up the phone any of the "gajillion times" she'd called to tell them she wasn't going to be in tonight's performance. "You can go home and come back tomorrow because I'm not in the show," she said. "Never mind the why and wherefore; Sterndick wouldn't let me do it."

Charlie asked what had happened. The whole thing had been an "utter fiasco," Michelle said. Months ago she had cleared December 8 with Mr. Linton so she and Millard could go to the Who concert at the Amphitheater with the seats his uncle had secured for them. Douglas Sterndick had asked her to go to some opera about Rabbi Einstein's pee-stained trunks, but when she said she was seeing The Who instead, he'd gone apeshit and told her she'd be out of the show if she didn't show up for tech. She hadn't believed his bluff for an instant. She could go to a fricking Who concert; it was not that big of a scandal.

But the Who concert had turned into a fiasco. Millard had picked her up at seven. Just a minute or two later, though, he started looking for parking on Western. She thought he wanted to get doughnuts or pick up cigarettes. Then she saw the sign on the Nortown Theater: "Who Concert on Closed Circuit TV." Michelle just about exploded. Millard was not seriously going to take her to see the Who video simulcast on-screen in a movie theater, was he? Millard tried to explain that his uncle had made a mistake—he had promised concert tickets but had gotten tickets for the simulcast instead. Michelle asked how long he'd known. Millard said just for a couple of days; he'd wanted to tell her, but thought she'd get mad. Michelle said that was right, which was why she was mad right now. Millard said he was as disappointed as she was and they should just try to have a good time. They could sit in the balcony and party the whole time. Michelle said to just give her the fucking ticket and leave her alone. She didn't buy his story; he had just strung her along. She snatched the ticket, and Millard, pissed off, went to rehearsal. And when Sternberg asked Millard why he was late and where Michelle was, Millard said she was at the Who concert. Sternberg called Sarah Silver out of her chorus warm-up. He told her to get into Buttercup's costume; she was taking Miss Wasserstrom's part.

Michelle, as it turned out, didn't enjoy the Who concert at all. All the rock-star antics she had once thought looked so cool looked totally absurd on a big screen—Pete Townshend's windmilling guitar style was totally gay; Roger Daltrey's twirling microphone act was stupid; John Entwistle's three-piece suit looked retarded; Kenny Jones couldn't drum worth shit. "Baba O'Riley" was a dumb song. "Music Must Change" was dumber. "Sister Disco" was just about the dumbest song ever; rock concerts, come to think of it, were totally stupid, totally dumb, totally gay. She left with a headache long before the encore, right when Daltrey was caterwauling "Won't Get Fooled Again."

All during dress rehearsals, Sternberg said nothing to her. But then came opening night, and there was twerpy Sarah Silver in her costume. When she approached Sterndick and asked him what the deal was, he told her to talk to Mr. Linton, who informed her that she had violated drama club policy and would have to sit out opening night. Sternberg had wanted her to sit out the entire run of the show, but they had agreed she would only miss this opening performance. Michelle didn't want to give Sterndick the perverse satisfaction of having her lash out at him, so after a few outbursts of "That is so unprofessional," and "That is just so fucking retarded," she kept quiet. She would sit right in the front row, watch the show, and see that little sexless bitch Sarah Silver—who had had the nerve to tell her, "It's really not right to miss tech"—make an ass of herself. She sat there expressionless, watching the final warm-ups—though she did burst out laughing when Millard looked at her and glared, then asked Sarah if they could practice their kiss one more time.

Larry Rovner opined that this was total bullshit, then said "Excuse me" to Charlie and Gail, then said that he was sorry, but it was, in fact, "total bullshit." Michelle agreed, then asked him wasn't it Shabbos, and "shouldn't you be in shul, yeshiva boy?" Larry told Michelle he'd made an exception because he hadn't wanted to miss the show. He said that he was going to the refreshment stand to get some M&M's and a noncarbonated orange pop and asked if anyone else wanted anything. Charlie said he didn't want anything and neither did Gail—which seemed somewhat odd to Michelle. She hadn't registered that her father even knew Gail. She suddenly felt out of place, vaguely unclean. She told Larry no, she didn't want anything from the concession stands; everything there was totally nasty. Larry asked what she was doing after the show. She said there was a cast party at Sarah Silver's, but she wasn't going. Larry asked what she was going to do instead.

"Sleep, yeshiva boy," she said, then pulled out a pack of Merits from her jacket and told her father she was leaving; she'd see him whenever. Larry followed behind but lost sight of her when he got to the refreshment stand. After Michelle had left, Gail told Charlie that his daughter had a lot of "spunk." She wondered what Charlie and his family were doing the first night of Chanukah. If they weren't busy, she could make brisket and latkes and then they could light candles. Charlie said yes, he'd like to, but he'd have to check with his daughters first. Then the lights flashed on and off, signaling the end of intermission. Larry returned carrying three orange pops and three bags of M&M's. "I thought you and Mrs. Wasserstrom might like some anyway," he said.

The next night in the Mather lobby after the show, after Charlie had congratulated Michelle on her performance, told her that although he didn't approve of her calling Sarah Silver a "sexless Minnie Mouse twerp" that she was still clearly the better performer, and that he really enjoyed that energetic new conductor Mr. Sternberg, he broached the subject of Chanukah dinner over at his friend Gail's house. Jill had already declined, citing a paper she was writing on Julius Nyerere and Tanzania. Michelle, caught up in the thrill of her performance, did not immediately recall who Gail was, and said it sounded like fun. "I just hope that's not the same night I promised Myra I'd do something with her," she said.

Unfortunately, Michelle *had*, she informed her father on the day before Chanukah, promised to meet Myra at the JCC pool to "do laps"—Myra had a part-time job working for the JCC senior activities director and had copied the key to the pool. If Michelle had substituted the word "bongs" for "laps," the story would have been a good deal more accurate, although the full truth would have included a game of Strip Pinafore. This was a game in which every member of the cast—with the exception of Millard Schwartz and Sarah Silver—would recite their lines from the show at top speed. Every time you got a line right, you got a bong hit. Every time you got one wrong, you took off an item of clothing. Sex was forbidden by Strip Pinafore rules—fornicating in the water just hours after the last geriatric rehabilitation session seemed ghastly to both Michelle and Myra. The only potential wild card was that Myra had invited Douglas Sternberg as a joke and he hadn't said no. The idea of Sterndick blowing a line, then removing either his brown socks or his suede Hush Puppies was even more unappetizing to Michelle than senior swim, although Myra promised that, given the right attitude, "it could be hysterical."

B efore they left their apartment on the first evening of Chanukah—Michelle for the JCC, Jill for Muley's apartment, Charlie for Gail's house—the Wasserstroms exchanged Chanukah gifts. Charlie gave Michelle a stack of record albums he'd purchased at Dog Ear Records on Devon, each more appalling than the other—among them, Jethro Tull's *Stormwatch* and a Steve Martin comedy album. Michelle said they were "awesome, thanks," before relegating them to her "unlistenable pile." Charlie got Jill a Polaroid camera, which instantly developed out-of-focus pictures that were too dark. He said he would have gotten her something more, but the Bat Mitzvah was forthcoming. This was supposed to comfort Jill, but it just made her feel guilty, thinking of all the money he was spending. For Charlie, Michelle purchased and Jill chipped in $5 for a BEST DAD T-shirt and a pair of headphones so he could listen to the nasal news announcers on Newsradio 78 without disturbing his daughters. Charlie thought the T-shirt was the best Chanukah gift anyone had ever given to him. Jill and Michelle had agreed to not get anything for each other, though Michelle promised Jill she'd treat her to a Girls' Day Out sometime soon. They all rapidly said the three blessings over the Chanukah candles and let them burn for a minute or two. Then Michelle lost patience and blew them out.

Meanwhile, on North Shore Avenue, Gail Schiffler-Bass was cooking dinner for the first time in more than four years. A brisket was in the oven, a bowl full of latke batter was on the kitchen counter, and her Cuisinart was full of pureed beets for borscht. She had wiped the dust off her rusty menorah and placed it in the window, put candles and a blue linen tablecloth on the dining room table, and opened up a bottle of Kedem wine. But when Charlie Wasserstrom arrived, he barely noticed any of that. He didn't register the smell of brisket cooking with carrots and onions, didn't notice the candles or the wineglasses, didn't see that Gail had put on a new blue dress that matched her tablecloth or that she had taken off her glasses and put in contacts. The only thing that caught his attention was this—Gail Schiffler-Bass lived in the Funny House.

Ellen & Michael

I n her ten-odd years as a clinical psychologist, Ellen Rovner had developed a negative view of human behavior and humans in general, and that view tended to encompass her children as well as her husband. She generally saw humans as sexually frustrated, self-deluded liars; they were jealous, competitive, petty, uncharitable, suspicious, and rarely worthy of pity, since they were so often reprehensible. But in the private practice she opened in 1971 in the medical building at the Old Orchard Shopping Mall in Skokie, those opinions had won her a devoted following, mostly among women who found her opinions frank, honest, and refreshing, even at their most hostile.

As for her children, she considered Larry a young man of high achievement but low potential. That he managed to get into Brandeis and pull A's at Ida Crown—which she had allowed him to attend, thinking that deep immersion in religion was the quickest way to get him to renounce it, thus ending this troublesome teenage phase—was less a statement of his qualities than of the overall mediocrity of his generation. At Brandeis, he would continue his high school practice of pulling all-nighters to get good grades, then boasting that he hadn't studied at all. Afterward, he would emerge at the top of the pack of a bottom-of-the-pack law school and get a middle-of-the-pack job working for the State's Attorney's office. He would marry a dumpy Jewish-American Princess—maybe a special ed teacher with low SAT scores who couldn't get into a decent state school. They would move into a modest house in a low-rent suburb and have two or three children who would continue along the inevitable downward march of intellectual history. Larry was harmless, somewhat pathetic but inoffensive—in many ways, the best one could have hoped for, given his father.

In Ellen's estimation, Lana was infinitely more devious than her brother. Though she had never been as good a student as Larry, Lana—Ellen was convinced—was destined for a promising future. She would secure one of those jobs for which American society puzzlingly reserved its admiration—radio news announcer, perhaps. Ellen could just hear Lana's voice waking her up in the morning: "It's Day 57 of the hostage crisis and I'm Lana Rovner with the day's traffic, weather, and sports." She would marry above her station; she would make certain her children would get their educations at Francis Parker, since she hadn't been able to get in there herself. She would appear at charity functions that would raise less money than they'd cost to throw. Above all, she would achieve success, no matter how much she lied and schemed to get there.

A prime example was the 20 Lana received for her creative report on Marie Curie. Although Ellen was unaware of the circumstances under which Lana had unconvincingly forged the number 20 on her Creative Report on her evaluation sheet, it would have been obvious to any observant adult that she had done it. Ellen had no idea what injustices had been visited upon Lana, what misdeeds Ms. Powis had performed in order to give Lana that vexing 19.5, causing her to stoop to subterfuge, thus allowing her to secure the trip to Paris her father had promised her. Ellen could not have known that Lana had done absolutely everything required of her, fulfilled beyond question every two-point category Ms. Powis had graded on the evaluation sheet.

As promised, Lana had slathered a white blouse with phosphorescent paint and entered in darkness while Edith Piaf sang, *"Non, je ne regrette rien."* It was a good attention getter. Ms. Powis gave her two out of two points for it. She got two points for the "Memorized—notecards OK" category. She got two points for "Clear Organizational Style," starting with Curie's birth, ending with her death, and ticking off "Major Accomplishments" one through five. She got two "Interaction" points by leading her fellow students in a game of Radium Charades. She got two points for "Clear Concise Speaking Style," two points for "Accurate and Detailed Research," two points for "Use of Audio-Visual Aids," two points for "Knows Her Topic and Demonstrates Enthusiasm for It," and two points for "Responds Well to Questions," for there had really been only one question. Ms. Powis had asked it and it was the same one she asked everybody—"Lana, who do you think would play Marie Curie if they were making a movie of her life?" Lana had answered, "Since Marie Curie was so talented and discovered so much, there's really only one actress smart enough to play her and that's Meryl Streep."

But then came the final category, the one Ms. Powis called "Intangibles," and though Ms. Powis wrote on the score sheet, "Beautiful job, Lana," she only gave her a 1.5.

"But if I'd given you a 20," Ms. Powis said over and over after school while Ellen Rovner waited in the car, "then you'd have nothing to work for on your next project." That was it, then; Lana had been working for a 20 she could never have received. Thus, knowing that her father had only agreed to sponsor the France trip if she'd gotten the 20 and knowing that Ms. Powis's scoring system was rigged, she used a scissors and the office Xerox machine to create a new score sheet, one that had "20—Great Job, Lana" written on the top. And during the whole ride home from Baker to K.I.N.S., she explained everything she had done to get two points in each category, adding embellishments every time her mother said "Mmn" or "Really" or "Is that right?"

Which was how Ellen had gotten into trouble with the whole Paris trip. Keeping outwardly neutral and hoping others would eventually come to the right conclusions on their own might have been effective in psychoanalysis, but she did not use that technique in her sessions; she was confrontational in therapy but passive-aggressive at home. She never actually told Michael that she disapproved of the idea of motivating scholastic performance through rewards. She thought that saying "Do you think that's the best idea?" was sufficient to get her point across. Thus, Michael had allowed the Getting-a-20-Gets-a-Trip-to-Paris theory to become indisputable fact, and Ellen could not tell her daughter the trip was canceled even after he had said that he and Larry were too busy to go and why didn't "the gals" just go by themselves. She would have thought it unfair to punish a child—even this child—for the sins of her father.

Michael Rovner's main problem, Ellen was convinced, was that he was gay. And not only was he gay, Ellen thought, he would never admit it to himself or to anyone else, which made him useless to anyone of either sex. Of course it may have been true that Michael Rovner's most satisfying sexual experience had involved being orally serviced through the so-called glory hole by a marine in the next booth at Little Bo's Peep Show; he nevertheless found himself attracted to scores of women on a daily basis—nurses, waitresses, women walking on the sidewalk, crossing the street, ladling out matzo balls at It's in the Pot! Which was why he had suggested Ellen and Lana's Paris trip in the first place—to give himself two weeks to discover whether he could find a relationship more satisfying than the one he had with his wife. If he couldn't, then he would try to romance Ellen once again with flowers and dance clubs and prime rib dinners. If he could, that would just speed up plans for the separation Ellen had just begun discussing with him, the one Ellen said could take place once Lana was in high school and Larry was at Brandeis.

The concept of separating from or, worse, divorcing his wife was terrifying to Michael Rovner—less so when he was flirting with Laura Kim, his favorite X-ray resident, who brought him and his radiologist buddy Steve Ross macaroons every Monday, but terrifying nonetheless. His love for Ellen ebbed and flowed according to her proximity. At home on Sacramento, he could not bear to be apart from her, ached when she slept in the bedroom down the hall, was too petrified to confront her even when he'd been certain she'd tossed out his pornography collection. At a distance, though, when he was at the hospital or a strip club, he dreaded returning home to a cold, loveless marriage, occasionally wished that a bus might strike Ellen so that he could guiltlessly pursue a relationship with Laura Kim, who frequently hugged him and caressed his shoulders. Often, Michael thought about how different his life might have been if he had impregnated Ellen's roommate instead of her.

For the main reason that he had begun sleeping—first only sleeping—with Ellen Leventhal was that he was desperately in love with Patricia Rota, Ellen's roommate at the University of Chicago. Patricia was a whip-smart History major who was rumored to be "easy" but ended every one of their dates with a peck on the cheek, after which she would see him to the door and duck out of the way of his patented, swooping kiss. Michael would saunter into the adjoining room and ask Ellen if she was still awake and if there was room for him in her bed. After a while, he began visiting Ellen's room when he knew Patricia wasn't there, and they would drink the scotch she kept stashed under her bed and have sex. There was never any great romance between them. Ellen saw Michael as little more than the next in the ongoing series of lovers she had taken after she had broken free of her father's oppressive household. Until Ellen got pregnant, both she and Michael had other plans: his to seduce Patricia after her choir practice; hers to live in Paris and study at the Sorbonne. The only difference was that Ellen frankly discussed her plans, while Michael merely told Ellen how much he loved her, how he longed to live with her and marry her.

Michael's vision for the future, uncertain as he might have been about it in his own mind, was the one that prevailed. It was realized in an outdoor ceremony on the Midway Plaisance just south of the U of C campus. Neither's parents attended, Michael's because his father—who hailed from Poland and worked as a suit salesman on Roosevelt Road—strongly disapproved of marriages of convenience, while his mother Rose disapproved of just about everything and everyone except her immediate family. Ellen's widowed father, Dr. Max Leventhal—director of the Leventhal Hospital and a prominent member of a small Hyde Park Jewish aristocracy—objected for reasons relating to status, and it was his violent objections that had, in part, led Ellen to marry Michael and forgo the abortion her father had said he could arrange. Both Max Leventhal and the Rovners came to grudgingly accept their new in-laws, though it was money from Michael's parents that helped put the down payment on the Sacramento home, while Max—who believed in children making their own way in the world—sent measly cash gifts to the Rovners on birthdays and Chanukah.

Ellen's approach to marriage and parenthood was one of dour professionalism. Michael may have played catch with Larry and bought Lana surprises from Marshall Field's, but Ellen was the one who dropped Lana off and picked her up at school and attended parent-teacher conferences. Michael may have hugged his children more, given them more compliments and presents, but she felt that she was clearly the better parent and it irked her when he said things like "I know you're busy, but you should really spend more time with the kids; they don't think you like them," as if his method of parenting—arriving home late with armloads of expensive, irrelevant gifts on holidays and birthdays, which completely eclipsed her own sensible, useful presents, then grinning proudly at her—was likely to win him the BEST DAD shirt she'd glimpsed some plump man wearing proudly under his navy blue parka one recent morning.

But Ellen could see the end of her sentence coming and it seemed better to just serve it as painlessly and nonconfrontationally as possible. Though she was appalled by Michael's endorsement of Lana's winter-break Paris plan and aghast when he had said he was too busy to go, none of it surprised her. She quietly consented, knowing full well that some pathetic Michael Rovner scheme was lurking behind it.

Had she been pressed, Ellen would have predicted that Michael's scheme would involve two weeks of homoerotic carousing with Steve Ross, with whom he attended White Sox and Blackhawk games and played tennis at the JCC,

where she imagined them taking extralong showers. As for herself, she was looking forward to the Paris trip as an opportunity to get up early, take long walks,
and read Virginia Woolf over coffee and croissants. Two weeks one-on-one with
Lana was hardly the fantasy journey to Paris she'd been imagining ever since college, but she became somewhat more enthusiastic about the trip's prospects after
signing Lana up for a series of day trips sponsored by a youth-oriented travel organization.

The journey began promisingly. The flight had been oversold, but the ticket
agent had told them they could move up to first class. This excited, then terrified
Lana, who poked her mother in the ribs and told her no, no, they couldn't do
that, because P.C. Pendleton had said there was a dress code in first class and
they had worn the wrong outfits and wouldn't be allowed to fly. Ellen ignored her
class-obsessed daughter, who was beginning to remind her of her own father and
evil stepmother; she took the upgrade, and walked proudly into first class in
jeans, while her embarrassed daughter sunk miserably into a window seat. Lana's
mood improved after she took a sip of her mother's champagne, but then turned
again to trepidation when a black man in a navy blue pin-striped suit settled in
across the aisle. Lana wondered if he might be carrying a gun; black men in
movies and on the news frequently carried guns, and whenever she rode through
black neighborhoods, she would crouch low in her seat and hope none of the
black people they passed would shoot them. The first time Lana had watched the
Academy Awards, she had seen Isaac Hayes wearing thick gold chains and performing the theme to *Shaft,* and that memory still insinuated itself into her night-
mares.

Lana's heart leapt into her throat as she saw the man in the pin-striped suit
flip open a black leather attaché case and remove—no, not a gun, thank *Hashem,*
she thanked *Hashem* for he had answered her prayers, had heard her reciting the
first lines of the *Ashrai* over and over, but a paperback book: *Le Procès,* by Franz
Kafka. The man, who had noticed her gazing in his direction, thought she might
have been looking at his strawberries and said perhaps she might desire one.
Lana shook her head, grimaced, and grabbed the travel guide she had stuffed
into the seat pocket in front of her. She pretended to study it.

Ellen Rovner said that her daughter was shy and had never sat in first class before. The man said that he understood and hoped the flight would prove "en-
riching for the mind as well as the soul." His voice was rich, mellifluous, and

slightly accented; as she pretended to read, Lana wondered if he might be some-body famous, perhaps Sidney Poitier or Harry Belafonte. Ellen asked if he was French; he said no, he had lived in France for a time, but he was born in the Ivory Coast, where he was now returning. Ellen had recalled years ago reading about the end of the colonial era there in the early 1960s. That was right, the man said, 1960 exactly, but she couldn't have been reading newspapers in 1960, he said; she was too young. Ellen laughed at that; she said he probably hadn't even been born in 1960.

Even during the most turbulent moments of the 747's initial ascent, the con-versation between Ellen Rovner and Julius Bernard, as he introduced himself, did not wane. Julius said he had grown up in Grand Lahou on the Atlantic coast, and had attended college in Paris. His father had owned a cocoa plantation and was now serving in the cabinet of Felix Houphouet-Boigny. Julius had just re-cently finished his Ph.D. at the University of Chicago in Political Science—Ellen liked how he said "political science," the way it rolled off his tongue and sounded like "Mmm-boleeteecal science"—the topic of which had been, he said, "in a very general sort of way," the "myths of institutional solidity and the permanence of porousness." He would soon be returning, after a week of "eating well and re-laxing" in his family's Paris apartment, to take a position at the Economic Com-munity for West Africa. Julius asked what she did for a living. Ellen said she took shallow, middle-aged women's money and helped them rationalize having wasted years of their lives in unfulfilling relationships with shallow, middle-aged men.

"She's a psychologist," Lana said.

When the movie began, Julius asked if Lana wanted to trade seats with him—he said he had a better view of the screen. Lana said no, thanks, she had seen *The China Syndrome* before. By the time the film was over, Ellen expected she was through with her interaction with Julius Bernard. But once they began their de-scent into Paris, Julius asked if they might grace him with their presence for din-ner the following evening. Lana, who now wondered if Julius might be a terrorist, one of those Ugandan followers of Idi Amin who took Jews hostage, requiring the Israeli army to rescue them, reminded her mother that they had tickets for *Don Quixote* starring Rudolf Nureyev. Julius said that he, too, would be attend-ing the ballet and was inviting them for dinner following the performance. Ellen told Julius they would love to. Lana wondered why her mother seemed so happy—she was only this happy when she was drunk.

It was true that Ellen Rovner was happy and this was not only the result of a handsome man ten years her junior flirting with her. It was also the idea of Paris itself. She had only been to the city once before—on her honeymoon, a poorly planned trip that neither she nor Michael could afford, particularly since her father had refused to contribute. There had, in theory, been something wonderfully improvisational about the honeymoon, though Michael had consistently tried to ruin it, refusing to let the trip take its natural course and attempting to infuse every moment with hackneyed notions of romance. It was not enough to walk along the banks of the Seine; he had to read Baudelaire while they did it. They couldn't merely enjoy the view from the prow of the *bateau-mouche;* Michael had to paw her every time they passed under a bridge and saw couples kissing above them. When she said she wanted to take a bath in their hotel room, Michael did not understand that was all she meant, that though the idea of him in there in the bath with her with Jacques Brel playing on the radio might have seemed romantic, it was in fact claustrophobic, oppressive, and, frankly, cold. When they made love, several times she had to fake *not* having an orgasm, because his narcissistic delight in her pleasure was hard to stomach. She had told him before the honeymoon that going to Paris had been her dream, but she had not told him that in the dream she was single and free, not three months pregnant and married to Michael Rovner. That she was now traveling to Paris without her husband told half the story of her marriage. That she was happy about it told the other.

Michael Rovner's own euphoria at having the house to himself, or almost to himself, quickly transformed itself into panic when he realized that two weeks was hardly sufficient time to find a brand-new relationship that would allow him to ease out of one marriage and, soon enough, into another. He felt like the hero of a silent comedy in which some poor schnook has to find a wife by midnight or else lose the family inheritance. He'd always thought that his wife had undervalued him sexually, and this was his opportunity to discover his true worth. The last time he had been out on a date, he'd been twenty years old, a poor college student, a virgin; now he was successful, experienced—he could have so many opportunities. True, it would be sad for the kids to see their parents split up, but that had been Ellen's idea, and both kids would surely benefit from seeing their father happy with a new wife, one more indulgent and openly affectionate. Laura Kim, for example.

Laura Kim was not only the sharpest resident in Michael's radiology depart-ment, she had also won the Hot Legs contest two years in a row at the Thirsty Whale nightclub in her hometown of River Grove, a fact that she had mentioned in the "Additional Activities" section of her résumé and one that Michael Rovner and Steve Ross took note of while making their final hiring decisions. Laura Kim was cool. Laura Kim was a free spirit. Laura Kim wore boots. Laura Kim called Michael "Doc" and once told him he had good shoulders. Laura Kim went to Rush Street nightclubs, collected guys' phone numbers, then flung them out her car window when she drove home down Lake Shore Drive. The only question was how to get her alone for one evening; once that was accomplished, every-thing else would be easy. She might even take a shower with him. He liked the idea of girls taking showers with him. He and Steve Ross talked about it at length—well, mostly Steve talked about it, said one time in reference to Laura, "Now there's a girl who'd take a shower with you," while Michael had smiled em-barrassedly and said, "I don't know about that," then went home and mastur-bated. The next morning before work, Ellen was getting dressed and listening to the news on WBOE, and Michael said, "Feel like taking a shower?" and she'd just laughed. On their honeymoon, she'd loved when he jumped into the tub with her, but there was nothing spontaneous about her anymore.

One time Michael had walked by Larry's room and heard Larry say over the telephone to some girl, "Hey, do you want to spend some time together one-on-one?" He'd been impressed by how mature his son sounded. He wished he'd been as self-assured as Larry when he'd been his age, always going out with this or that girl, sometimes two at the same time, and not just the quiet girls he'd pur-sued in high school, the tough, aggressive ones, too—Randi Nathan, the girl Hannah he'd met in Israel—the kinds of girls Steve Ross would have dated. Not him. Not Michael Rovner, who had lost his virginity to the woman who would be-come his wife and even now hadn't told her for fear she would divorce him if he actually came out and said it—though every time they had sex, he was certain she knew. He resolved that the next day at lunch in the hospital cafeteria he would say to Laura, "Hey, do you want to spend some time together one-on-one?"

And when he did just that, repeated that exact phrase, he was stunned by her reply. "Sure, Doc," she cackled. "Your place or mine?" Laura said she had some white wine chilling in her fridge and had planned to drink it herself, so maybe they could go there after work, drink the wine, then head to Chinatown, pick up dinner, and bring it back, eat it, watch TV, and "talk." Michael had hoped to be able to go home, change, and shower beforehand; Ellen had told him that his crotch tended to smell funny after a day at work. But he wasn't about to revise the schedule, fearing that Laura might change her mind and opt out entirely. He hoped she wouldn't try to go down on him; he could go down on her and then suggest a romantic shower afterward.

But the drive from work to Laura's apartment in Andersonville proved surprisingly stiff. As they had walked to his car from work, there had been an effervescent energy emanating from both of them, nervous chatter, laughter, sly innuendoes. But the moment they shut the car doors, the mood shifted abruptly. Laura would say something, then Michael would say something, then the conversation would stop. Then Michael would make a joke and Laura wouldn't laugh, she would just say "That's a fucking riot," and then the conversation would stop again. It was as if they both realized the gravity of what they were about to do, the sound of the doors signifying a shift from flirtatious fantasy into something messy and real.

"Can I ask you a question, Doc?" Laura asked as she poured Michael a glass of wine and sat down beside him on her pink living room couch that Michael hoped could pull out into a bed. Michael said sure, she could ask him anything. He quickly prepared responses to questions she might ask: "No, I don't go to the gym much; I've just always been pretty fit"; "Yes, of course I brought some, but I figured you'd be on the pill." He didn't have time to prepare for the question she did ask, but it would have been the next one he'd have thought of.

"What would you do," she asked, "if you really liked a guy, but you knew he was married?"

Michael felt a gulp in his groin. He asked if she really liked the guy. She said she wasn't sure, she thought she did, but they hadn't spent that much time together and she really couldn't live with herself if she broke up a marriage. Michael said that if the man wanted to be with her, that meant the marriage was already rocky; he was just waiting for the right gal to come along. Laura asked if he was just saying that to make her feel better. Michael said no, that's what he believed—besides, he couldn't imagine anyone who wouldn't leave his wife for someone like her. Laura smiled and told him he said the sweetest things. Michael asked if he knew the guy. Laura said she was embarrassed to say. Michael said she shouldn't be embarrassed, she could trust him, he cared about her. Laura said again that he was sweet. Then she asked him if Steve Ross was the kind of guy who bragged about girls or if he kept things to himself. Michael asked what sorts of things she meant. Laura said things like taking showers with her. Michael said no, he hadn't heard anything about that.

The fact that Steve Ross was having an affair with Laura Kim was absolutely appalling to Michael. True, he had been contemplating something similar for weeks, but his situation was different. Steve had two kids but they were two and four; Michael's were practically grown. And Steve's wife Mandy was the sweetest woman he'd ever met, she cooked six days a week, always made lunch for Steve, and not just sandwiches, sometimes fried chicken or barbecued beef. The heart-breaking thing was that Mandy would be completely devastated if she ever found out that her husband had been showering with Laura Kim, but she'd eventually forgive him. As for Ellen, she probably wouldn't care much if Michael cheated on her, but she'd divorce him anyway.

All through the evening, Michael attempted to sabotage Laura and Steve's relationship by administering what Steve usually referred to as a "cockblock." He talked at length about Steve's children—they were "great kids, really terrific." Nina was the prettiest little girl and Steve Junior was such a little troublemaker, yet so sweet to his little sister. At one point, Laura started to cry. "You're making me feel like such a little slut," she said. Michael said he didn't understand why; that was ridiculous—of course she wasn't a slut.

At the end of the evening, Laura implored Michael not to tell anyone of their conversation. Michael said her secret was safe with him. Laura hugged him and apologized for getting so emotional. Michael said he hoped he had been helpful and that everything would work out. Laura said she hoped so too; she said that once she and Steve had spent a weekend together, things would seem a lot clearer. She asked Michael if he wanted a nightcap; he said he'd like to, but he was worn out. She kissed him lightly on the lips before he walked out, then slammed the door shut hard after him.

Things were somewhat more civilized in Paris. In her first two days with her mother, Lana saw the Eiffel Tower, the Louvre, the Jeu De Paume, and the Orangerie, though not Notre Dame or the Sainte-Chapelle cathedral, because Larry had warned her in advance that it was sacrilegious to go into places

of Christian worship. She had ordered breakfast from room service and purchased a red beret from Printemps all by herself and all in French. Her mother
had read two books by Virginia Woolf. On the night of the ballet, Lana had asked
her mother if they were "still going to meet that African guy." Ellen told her yes
they were and to stop referring to Julius as "that African guy"—if she was so opposed to the dinner, Lana could stay at the hotel and Ellen would meet Julius herself. But Lana didn't like that idea either. Ellen, who generally wasn't directly
hostile toward her children, saw little choice in this case. She suggested that the
real reason Lana didn't want to go was that she was self-conscious about her
French and was worried that Julius would reveal that it wasn't as fluent as she
thought it was, at which point Lana said fine, she'd have dinner with the African
guy, but they'd have to be back by midnight.

Yet when the clock struck one at Julius Bernard's apartment, it was Ellen
Rovner who was apologizing because she could no longer keep her eyes open,
while Lana, who had become completely enchanted with Julius, was pleading to
stay a few minutes longer. Not only had Julius brought Lana and her mother
backstage at the Paris Opéra, not only had he taken them up to his apartment on
the Rue du Faubourg St.-Honoré, not only had he cooked them a scrumptious
dinner followed by a plate of cheeses and pear sorbet, he had spoken almost the
entire time to Lana in French and she had understood every word. They had discussed ballet, museums, and restaurants, in particular the Tour D'Argent, which
P.C. Pendleton had insisted was the best restaurant in Paris. "Yes, yes, maybe in
1963, but the world moves on," Julius had said, in English. She would write that
in her postcard to P.C., Lana thought—"Yes, but the world moves on."

As Julius walked them to his door, he said he hoped that he would see them
again before he left Paris. Ellen said she hoped so too, and Lana said, *"Sans doute,
sans doute."* But as he helped Ellen put on her coat, he suddenly whispered to
her, "When you get outside, say you have forgotten something and ring the doorbell. I have to ask you something in private." The statement was so surprisingly
forward that Ellen saw no choice but to comply. When she and Lana had left the
building and were approaching a taxi waiting out front, Ellen nervously rubbed
her ear and said, "Oh my dear, I think I left my earring. Tell the taxi driver to
wait." Ellen dashed back to the front door of the building and rang the bell and
as she heard a click and pushed open the door, her mind raced with possibilities
of what would happen when she got to Julius's floor, whether he would attempt

to sweep her into a kiss, how long would they be able to have sex, Ellen wondered, before Lana would suspect something was amiss.

Julius was waiting in front of his door as Ellen reached the top of the stairs, panting yet suffused with almost giddy energy as he reached out his hands, clasped hers, pulled her gently toward him, and said that it was good of her, so good of her to come. He said he was normally not so indiscreet, but there was so little time—would there be any chance, he asked, to see each other again? Ellen felt appalled. Ellen felt thrilled. Ellen felt miraculously transported into one of her patients' monologues, the sort that made her glower and flutter her eyes wearily, for she suspected the stories were never more than half-true. Ellen said that the day after tomorrow, Lana would be taking a day trip to Versailles—could they see each other in the afternoon? Julius said he would be honored.

When she returned to the taxi, Ellen noticed that Lana's mood had changed. Ellen apologized for keeping Lana waiting—she must have had too much wine, she said, she had thought she was missing an earring, but it turned out she hadn't worn any after all. She didn't know why she had been so silly, she said. It was time for bed; she was exhausted. Maybe the next morning when they woke up, they could have crêpes for breakfast—crêpes with a little bit of sugar and Grand Marnier. Didn't that sound yummy? she asked. She attempted uncharacteristically to embrace her daughter, but then felt Lana's body stiffen. It occurred to her that Lana remembered that she hadn't been wearing earrings at all, recalled that Lana had berated her for going to the opera without earrings, and said they wouldn't be let into the box seats dressed all schlumpy.

"Mom," Lana Rovner said curtly as she shook free of her mother's embrace, "why do you always have to drink so much?"

It was amazing how one short sentence spoken by such a small person could radically change the mood of another, could instantly turn the warm backseat of a taxi into a cold, sepulchral chamber. One moment earlier, Ellen had felt carefree and happy, willing to treat her daughter more as a friend and less as a patient or employee. Now she once again saw her daughter as a great weight pressing down upon her, an eternal cloud hovering just above her head. And though part of her wanted to retract her response the moment after she'd made it, it did reflect exactly how she felt.

"Because I have children," she said.

— — — —

The moment Michael Rovner had learned of Steve Ross's dalliance with Laura Kim, two weeks shifted from being a brief period of bliss to an endless passage of solitude. And though the appeal of infidelity had not passed with his first failed attempt, it was no longer accompanied by the hope of a future of infinite happiness and fulfillment as much as it was by the desire to stave off two weeks of loneliness. He stayed late in the radiology department every night until he ran out of X-rays and then drove home slowly, taking Western all the way north. The strip clubs and X-rated movie houses he favored when Ellen was in town no longer held the same appeal. Under normal circumstances, he felt daring inside them; not the last time, though, when he sat in the audience of the Oak Theater watching a girl dressed up as Dorothy from *The Wizard of Oz* stripping as she sang "Follow the Yellow Dick Road." Now he felt like someone who actually frequented these places. The bouncers knew him—"Nice seeing you again, buddy," they said. They couldn't have been much older than Larry, they might even have been at Larry's Bar Mitzvah, he might have played touch football with them at one of Larry's birthday parties. They might come up to Larry, say, "Hey, saw your dad; you'll never guess where." The dancers might know Larry—he might be dating one of them. He couldn't go there anymore. They would tell Larry; Larry would be disgusted—he would tell Ellen; Ellen would divorce him.

He tried the Division Street dance clubs, where he felt like the only person old enough to get in. At The Snuggery, a cute girl named Deb gave him her phone number, but when he tried calling it later that night, he got a recorded message for Lincoln Carpeting, which advertised on late-night TV. When Monday arrived, Michael had all but given up the idea that anyone but his wife would ever find him sexually attractive; even her once-a-month regimen seemed generous now, more than he was entitled to. He avoided lunch with Laura Kim and Steve Ross, went home early, leaving a pile of X-rays for the next morning, picked up shrimp toast and sweet and sour chicken from Hong Min, and proceeded to eat what he hadn't consumed in the car on the living room couch straight out of the boxes.

"Good thing Deirdre's coming tomorrow," Larry said, eyeing Michael's mess as he and Arik Levine wrestled Larry's drum kit out the door for the Rovner! rehearsal, where they were planning to record "Soar."

Deirdre. The name didn't register immediately.

"Cleaning lady, Dad," Larry explained.

Michael asked what time she usually arrived. Larry said Mom usually let her in at around 7:30 and she stayed until one. Michael asked if Larry would be able to let Deirdre in. Larry said no, he would be sleeping over at Ben's. He didn't like being in the house when she was cleaning; he didn't like using the bathroom, knowing the cleaning woman might barge in on him. Michael said that was okay, he'd leave the door open for Deirdre, not to worry.

Michael was intrigued. He'd seen a movie like this once. In the middle of the night, unable to sleep, he had gone down to the living room to watch television and found the channel tuned to UHF-46, which was now a pay TV station called YOUR-TV. Channel 46's image was scrambled, but every so often it would descramble itself for a few seconds and reveal an unbroken image—in this case, a woman in a French maid's outfit vacuuming as a man lay naked in bed. The moment she began slipping off the maid's outfit, though, the image was scrambled again and all he could see were jittery, flesh-colored shapes. He turned the volume all the way up and listened to the grunting and the music and the moaning, and then, suddenly, the sultry PA announcer's voice shouted out the Station ID: "YOU'RE WATCHING YOUR-TV! SUBSCRIBE NOW!" The voice was so loud that Lana came down bleary-eyed, closely followed by Ellen; both asked what the noise was. Michael quickly turned down the volume, flipped off the TV, and told them that he'd been wondering that too, and had come downstairs to find out why the TV was still on. Maybe Larry had forgotten to shut it off, he suggested. "Really, you think Larry? Hmn," Ellen said, but didn't pursue it further.

On the morning that Deirdre was coming, Michael took the day off from work. He left a note on the door—"It's Open. Come On In!"—and sprawled out on his bed in what he determined to be a provocative pose. Deirdre Wills arrived at 7:30 and let herself in. Michael could hear her as she worked downstairs. He heard her fill a pail with water. He heard mopping. He heard footsteps going down into the basement. He heard the washing machine sloshing around, the whooshing of the vacuum cleaner, the sink being twisted on, then off, then on, then off. He regretted there were no books to read, other than Samuel Eliot Morison's *European Discovery of America*.

It was nearly eleven when he finally heard footsteps coming upstairs. He sat up in bed, one leg crossed over the other. He heard the vacuum start up, heard it rolling over the carpet in the hallway, in Lana's bedroom, in Ellen's office—he didn't refer to it as her bedroom, even though she slept in it practically every night. And then he heard a hand on his bedroom doorknob, saw it twist, saw the door open, saw Deirdre Wills in a blue denim shirt and black jeans pushing the vacuum forward, saw sheets and pillowcases in a laundry hamper in the hallway behind her, felt his penis grow stiff. Deirdre barely looked up to see him, just nodded in his direction as she vacuumed the carpet around the bed, as if she were the servant to a very rich but eccentric family of whose antics it was considered impolite to take note. Whatever seductive lines Michael had been planning would not have sounded particularly suave shouted over the whirring and wheezing of the vacuum cleaner. He had to wait until she had exited the bedroom, gone downstairs with the laundry hamper, and returned twenty minutes later with a couple of rags and a peach-colored pail filled with household cleansers. She was spritzing Windex on the mirror above the dresser when Michael said hello. Eyes still on the mirror, Deirdre grunted hello back. Then Michael asked if she wanted to "hop in." There was plenty of room, he said. Deirdre Wills stopped spritzing and looked at him lying there in his Jockey shorts.

"What?" she asked.

"Do you want to hop in?" he asked, slipping under the quilt cover. "It's nice and toasty."

Deirdre stared darkly at Michael Rovner. Then she asked if he wanted to die. Michael smiled, somewhat nervously, and made as if to speak again, but Deirdre told him to keep his mouth shut, otherwise she'd kill him that very minute. She finished wiping the mirror, then placed the rag and the bottle of Windex down on the dresser. She walked out of the bedroom and down the stairs. Then she grabbed her coat and walked out of the house.

On the day Ellen was to meet Julius Bernard, the bus for Versailles was scheduled to leave at eleven, but she and Lana awoke early. After hot chocolate at the Café De La Paix, they returned to the hotel, where Lana changed into a blazer she deemed suitable for a trip to a château. Ellen told Lana she would walk her downstairs and see her off. She said she'd been to Versailles before and wanted to use the day to go to the Bibliothèque Nationale to peruse the psychology literature. It wasn't an inconceivable assertion—she'd even mentioned she'd be interested in doing that while they had been planning the trip, but also thought such an arcane field trip would give Lana little motivation to accompany her. Not that that seemed terribly likely; Lana had consistently given the impression that she thought she was traveling in the company of somebody particularly boorish, Midwestern, and slow. But infidelity was new to Ellen and she sought to take as many precautions as possible.

Though she had never been a strong believer in marriage, in sessions with her patients Ellen Rovner had always found infidelity particularly tawdry, distasteful, low-class, and distinctly non-Jewish. When one of the Northbrook women who paid for the privilege of spending fifty minutes in her company told her about taking up with the piano tuner or the landscaper or the TV repairman, she found the whole scenario depressing and lonely. Still, that aside, Ellen was fairly certain she would be having sex with Julius Bernard that afternoon and she was excited about the prospect. Though she, technically, would be cheating on her husband, to her it didn't feel like unfaithfulness. The fact that she was in Paris made her marriage seem irrelevant; the fact that Julius would be leaving for the Ivory Coast eliminated the possibility of any long-term commitment; the fact that Julius was African—no matter how many times she had taken her children along to civil rights protests and checked Pete Seeger and Weavers albums out of the Nortown Library, never mind that she had protested against state's attorney Ed Hanrahan following the assassination of Black Panther leader Fred Hampton—still made what she was preparing to do that afternoon feel like something altogether different from infidelity.

Ellen told Lana that they wouldn't have time to eat before the tour bus left; she'd run out and get her a ham and cheese so she'd have something for lunch, didn't that sound yummy? Lana said no, it didn't sound all that yummy, frankly. Ham wasn't kosher first of all, plus Ellen was mixing it with dairy—hadn't Larry taught her anything? Ellen said she'd get her a different sort of sandwich. Lana said no, thanks, she wasn't hungry. Ellen said she had to eat something and went to the bakery across the street from the hotel.

Ellen was fairly convinced that her daughter was anorexic but had never mentioned it to Lana for a variety of reasons, chief among them being the paradox inherent in accusing someone of having an eating disorder: If one of the chief triggers for anorexia was a feeling of loss of control, the accusation could itself seem like a controlling act. Furthermore, if Ellen admitted that Lana actually had a serious medical condition, that could impinge upon her plans to separate from her husband. Thus, she paid close attention to her daughter's diet and tried to make sure she didn't skip meals.

Ellen bought a cheese sandwich and brought it back to the hotel room. At the bakery, she had noticed that a 100-franc note was missing from her wallet. This was not remarkable; Lana often burrowed in her mother's wallet, though she usually only took about $5 at any given time. Ellen asked Lana if she'd seen a 100-franc note anywhere. No, said Lana, who was scribbling something at the desk, another missive to P.C. Pendleton, Ellen presumed. Lana said maybe her mother was getting absentminded in her old age; she kept writing her letter, which she took special pains to hunch over and conceal whenever Ellen approached the desk. Ellen told her daughter that she had bought her a sandwich. Lana asked her what kind. Ellen said cheese. Lana sneered, said "Eew," told her mother to put it down on her desk, and continued writing. Ellen said she'd better get moving, the bus would be leaving any minute. Lana asked if Ellen thought she wasn't smart enough to figure out how to get downstairs by herself; she wasn't a baby. Ellen said fine, they'd meet back at the hotel at six and decide where to have dinner. Lana asked why every statement her mother made revolved around food. Ellen said fine, she was going to take a shower; Lana could catch the tour bus by herself.

When Ellen emerged from the bathroom, she was relieved to find the hotel room empty. She wished she could have sex with Julius immediately, skip the preliminaries, just jump into bed and fuck, not even return to the hotel, just fuck until the day of the flight home and either take the plane and divorce her husband the minute she saw him standing outside customs with a bouquet of roses—Michael never missed an opportunity for an easy cliché—or not go home at all. The hell with her job and her family; she could work here and screw random strangers whenever she got the urge.

Consumed by this fantasy, Ellen then suddenly noticed the cheese baguette still on the desk. She could have left it there, but she didn't want to contribute to her daughter's starvation. She grabbed the sandwich and took the elevator down to the lobby. The tour bus was just pulling away when Ellen stepped outside. She jogged briefly after the bus, waved the sandwich, then put it down at her side, certain Lana would tell her how embarrassing she was. She turned back toward the hotel, then noticed her daughter a half block away, walking briskly in the direction of the Rue de Rivoli.

Ellen started to shout after Lana but stopped. She thought she might go back inside the hotel, but she didn't do that either. Instead, she followed her daughter at a comfortable distance as Lana turned the corner. Ellen had constantly suspected her daughter of lying and scheming, but was never 100 percent sure, and so she kept up the pretense of believing Lana's absurd tales of getting twenties on her creative reports or being Ms. Powis's favorite student. Yet, here was physical, incontrovertible proof. Lana had said she was going to get on the Versailles bus, but nevertheless she was now ambling down the Rue de Rivoli, entering some tourist-trap gift shop, then, soon after, exiting and walking into the bookshop next door, then out of that shop and into a tobacconist's. It was no better but also no worse than expected; Lana was a liar, that much had been confirmed, but the worst she could plot was going shopping with money that was not hers. Satisfied with her discovery and convinced that her daughter would get along just fine, Ellen returned to her hotel room, took a bite out of Lana's sandwich, dumped the rest into the trash, got undressed, masturbated, changed into a brown leather skirt and a black leotard top, and went out for a leisurely walk before her scheduled tryst with Julius.

By the time she got to Julius's door, she had imagined what sex with him would be like in so many different permutations that there was something almost regrettable about having to perform the act, to reduce a myriad of fantasies into one singular truth. Imagining it happening and walking to his apartment now was almost enough. Almost. She rang the bell, the door clicked open, and she walked up to the top floor. She hoped they could dispense with niceties, with forced conversation. She wished she would walk in and find him naked on his bed; she had glimpsed a scene like that once when she'd been flipping channels and YOUR-TV had forgotten to scramble its signal. She didn't really expect to find Julius in that state, however; he was too much of a gentleman for that.

The other thing she didn't expect as Julius Bernard—dressed in a sleeveless argyle sweater over a white shirt and a stretchy maroon tie, and smoking a pipe—opened the door was to see Lana sitting on his couch, sipping hot chocolate, a China plate of croissants on the low glass table in front of her. Julius explained that Lana had arrived twenty minutes earlier and had been kind enough to bring him a card and a going-away gift: the pipe he was smoking. Ellen's mind raced wildly. She didn't know whether to insist that her daughter leave immediately—she and Julius had adult things to do—or to come right out and admit her infidelity, just say, "I'm divorcing your father and I'll be fucking this man as my first act of independence." Luckily, Lana provided her with the cover she needed.

"I can't believe you followed me here," she said.

"Believe it," Ellen said. She *had* followed her, she said. She had gone down to give her her sandwich, noticed she hadn't gotten on the bus, then followed her here. And now, she apologized to Julius, she was taking Lana back to the hotel, because clearly she couldn't be trusted on her own. Julius pleaded Lana's case, saying that she had "only the most honorable of intentions," and that if anyone was to blame it was him; he hadn't scheduled a proper good-bye. He had had plans for the afternoon, he said, "a rendezvous with a lady friend," but he trusted that lady friend would understand if he canceled their appointment—he gazed sternly at Ellen, then invited the two of them to join him for an afternoon drive to Versailles. Lana said they'd love to.

On the drive to and from Versailles, Ellen sat in the backseat and listened to her daughter and Julius discuss restaurants and clothes; Julius would politely correct her grammar and told her several times in English, "Yes, I believe some people from your country would feel as you do." Afterward, Julius dropped them back at their hotel. He thanked Lana once again for the pipe and tobacco and both of them for their company. Ellen kissed him on the cheek and thanked him for "babysitting" her daughter. She said she was sorry that he had canceled his plans with his lady friend; she hoped the lady friend might be able to meet him for lunch sometime later in the week. Julius told her that seemed unlikely; that rendezvous would have to wait either for "another time or another life."

The rest of Ellen and Lana's time together in Paris proceeded crisply; after breakfast, Lana would take walks while Ellen read Virginia Woolf in the hotel. Then Lana would return, show off what she had purchased—for her father, a bottle of aftershave; for her brother, LPs by Yves Simon and Gérard Lenorman; for herself, souvenirs and clothes—after which, Ellen would take a walk and Lana would sit in the hotel and write postcards to P.C. Pendleton and to Julius Bernard. Lana took day trips to the Bois de Boulogne and Montmartre. And Ellen did visit the Bibliothèque Nationale to peruse the psychology periodicals. In the evening, they would dine together and not discuss food.

On the day they departed Paris, Ellen Rovner was stunned to realize that she actually missed Chicago, that she missed work, and that she even missed her home on Sacramento, even her husband. She wondered what he had done while she was out of town, if he and Steve Ross had consummated that which she had suspected all along. And though she found the image of the two men—all soaped up in the JCC showers after a tennis match—amusing, she was surprised to discover that she rather hoped it hadn't happened. She wondered if he'd be at O'Hare with roses and found something charming about his pathetic predictability. She knew this moment would pass, that all too soon she would be plotting her escape. But for the first time in ages, she was looking forward to spending the night in Michael's bed, and she was even considering not faking not having an orgasm.

Lana Rovner, on the other hand, as she sat in the departure lounge of Charles de Gaulle Airport, was—for the first time—imagining her parents' divorce, something she had always feared, and was surprised to discover that she liked the idea. Weekdays during the school year with Mom and weekends and summers with Dad didn't seem like the worst possible plan. It might be best for both of them—her mother needed her space and her father needed someone to take care of him, someone sweet and nice and bubbly, like that girl Laura Kim who'd been sitting at the table with the Rosses at her Bat Mitzvah.

So it was with a fair amount of inner turmoil that Lana experienced her parents' reunion as her mother lugged all of their bags out of the customs hall and ran into the arms of her husband, who presented her with the bouquet of red roses that Lana had immediately assumed were for her. She had never seen them kiss before and when they did, she thought it looked low-class. On the ride home, Ellen told Michael all about Paris. And Michael told Ellen how he'd let Deirdre Wills go; he'd caught her drinking their Kahlúa. He had called up a cleaning service to see if they had any French housekeepers available—he thought it would be a good way for Lana to practice her French—but he hadn't heard back. Ellen told Michael she liked his new mustache.

That night at dinner, the table was set for three—Larry had left a note saying that he had to practice with Rovner! because he thought they might have a chance to meet with someone from a major label about their music. Michael had picked up dinner from the Parthenon on Devon. But Lana didn't eat much of the food, even though her mother and father said that they'd thought Greek food was her favorite. During a quiet moment, Michael said he was sorry he hadn't been able to come along for the trip; the next time, he'd make sure that the four of them went together. Michael said maybe they could all take a road trip to Waltham, Massachusetts, to drop Larry off at college. They could buy an old station wagon, load it up, drive it east, and leave it with Larry. When Ellen said that they should seriously plan for it, Lana suddenly stood up and skittered upstairs, saying she had to get something, after which she ran to the bathroom and threw up. And that night, after they had all gone up to bed at eight "because of the jet lag," Ellen had said, Lana heard squeaking bedsprings in her parents' bedroom. At which point, she threw up again.

WILLS / SILVERMAN

Deirdre & Carl

Though Michael Rovner's lewd proposition had led Deirdre Wills to quit her part-time job cleaning the Rovners' house, it was not what made her start packing her and Muley's things in preparation to move from Chicago to her brother's house in Atlanta. What had happened with Michael had disgusted and angered her, but she had endured such advances and humiliations before and found it unlikely that any place existed where she could avoid them. Nor was her decision a result of the fact that she was only one chapter away from having accomplished her goal of reading every book in the Nortown Library's modest literature collection. The thing that did in fact lead her to start packing was, instead, a surprise phone call from Carl Slappit Silverman. He was in Chicago. He said he wanted to "rap" with her. And he said he wanted to do it "in person."

Ever since he had left Chicago for L.A., Carl had respected Deirdre's wishes to be left alone. It had made it easier for him to tirelessly pursue his business career. That December, however, two events occurred in such close proximity to each other that Carl was unable to dismiss them as coincidental. In thirteen years, Carl had not heard the voice of his son speak one word. For all he knew, the boy might have been mute. But then early one Saturday morning, he was driving his white Rambler on the 405 from Beverly Hills to Malibu after another forty-eight-hour stint at the studio. His eardrums were so shot that he couldn't listen to anything but public radio. He'd been hoping for a morning blues show, one that might play some old Champion Jack Dupree, but instead found himself listening to a show called *Young Town* where some kid was telling a fairly amusing, if somewhat implausible, story about a cousin named Peachy Moskowitz. Carl thought the show suffered from all the usual liabilities of children's programming—overdirected, overzealous pubescent voices and the patronizingly enthusiastic voice of the main adult actor, presumably the host, who had the same breathless cadences of one of his old producers, whom he'd last seen making balloon animals in front of the Pickle Barrel on Howard and Western. Still, the Moskowitz story had been cute and diverting; it almost made him sorry that he didn't know any children. But then Carl nearly drove off the freeway as he heard that Pickle Barrel voice once again, this time saying, "You've been listening to *Young Town,* featuring your friends Vicky Blackwell, Pablo De La Fuente, Muley Scott Wills, Lisa-Anne Williams, Julie Ying, and me, your *Young Town* tour guide Lennieeeeeeeee Kidd."

Then, two days later, just one day before Christmas, a letter arrived in the mail. The envelope, a bit heavier than a standard letter—it seemed to contain a cassette—had been pristinely typed, addressed to Carl Slappit Silverman at Slappit Records. "PERSONAL" was written in red marker in the lower right-hand corner of the envelope, and though there was no return address, in the upper left-hand corner was written "Muley Scott Wills-Silverman." Seeing the name filled Carl with a strange combination of pride and fear. After staring at the envelope, flapping it about, trying to determine what was inside, contemplating whether or not to leave it for one of his unpaid interns, he ripped it open. There was a tape inside it, but he looked at the letter first.

"Dear Dad," it began. "I know it's been a long time since you've heard from me. But since it's the holiday season, I thought I'd write. Things are good here in Chicago. Mother is well, as am I, and I hope all is well for you also. I would like you to know that although you don't hear from me often, I do think about you and have followed your career closely. And whenever I see a Slappit record, I feel proud to be your son. This brings me to why I'm writing. I know you're very busy and I shouldn't bother you. I also know you are very serious about your business and very good at what you do. There is not a single artist on your label who is not incredibly talented. So I thought I might direct your attention to another artist I know who, like me, is very young, and, like your artists, also very talented. His name is Lawrence Elliot Rovner. Mom works for his family. He gave me a copy of the cassette for his band Rovner! and asked me to listen to it. He does not know that you are my father. Though I am no professional judge of music, he really has some talent and some of the songs (particularly "Six Days" and "Soar") are as good as anything I've heard on radio in a long time. Anyway, here's the tape. I hope you enjoy it and, if you do, that you might consider signing Larry with or without the members of his band Rovner! to a record deal. If you would like to get in touch, you can use Larry to get a message to me. He's a great friend and an even greater songwriter."

The letter was signed "Your son, Muley" and included Larry's phone number. The letter's true author had figured this was a long shot, that, most likely, Silverman would understand it was a forgery, that the letter might not even get to him. But it didn't for a moment occur to Carl, who was now certain he had heard his son's voice on the radio, that the letter could be fake. He got on the phone immediately, booked a plane reservation, and set up a meeting with Lawrence Rovner.

After he got the call, Larry Rovner—terrified now that his ploy had actually succeeded—scrambled to retroactively introduce an element of truth to the letter he had written. When his calls to Michelle Wasserstrom went unanswered, he tried to enlist his sister, who went to Hebrew school with Muley Wills's friend Jill Wasserstrom, to set up a meeting between Muley and himself. But Lana—who didn't like how Jill spoke out against Zionism in class, and was irked by the fact that Rabbi Meltzer had said Jill was a shoo-in for valedictorian and would receive a full scholarship to Ida Crown even though Jill said she didn't want it—told Larry she'd tried to call Jill but she was "at church." Later, Larry—having listened to the second episode of *Young Town* even after Lana had run out of the room shouting "Shut it off shut it off shut it off"—attempted to contact Muley through the radio station, but was informed by a man who identified himself as the station manager, "I know the brother, but I'm not gonna get you in *touch* with the brother. That's how it is, brother."

Larry decided the best approach was to play dumb, to proclaim no knowledge of how his music might have gotten into Muley Scott Wills's hands. It was funny, he told Carl as they dined together at It's in the Pot!, but he honestly didn't know how Muley had heard the tape. He'd only made three or four copies. He guessed there must have been something in the music that really moved Muley; his music tended to have that effect on people. It was at about this point in the conversation that Carl realized that this Orthodox kid with his Foghat T-shirt and his yarmulke wasn't going to be much help. He glanced down at his watch and started eating more quickly, shoveling down his slimy salami omelet. A deli like this couldn't stay in business in New York or L.A., he thought, only in the Midwest where there weren't enough Jews to know what Jewish food was supposed to taste like.

Larry asked Carl what he thought of the tape. In truth, Carl hadn't listened to it for more than a half-minute. What he heard sounded like a bunch of kids hammering on Sears instruments in somebody's basement while some kid mumbled in a vague imitation of Bob Dylan. To shut the kid up, Carl told Larry the same thing he usually told talentless musicians who wanted him to sign them. He said he heard a lot of promise in Larry's music, but Larry had to be certain he was committed to being a performer if he wanted to succeed; it wasn't something you could do part-time. If he wanted to do it, he'd have to quit everything else—school, girls, sleep—and focus only on being the best possible performer he could be. He also told him to lose the yarmulke, change the name of the band, and stop trying to imitate Bob Dylan. Even Dylan was sick of listening to Dylan, he said; that's why he'd found Jesus. He said that Larry should get comfortable performing in front of an audience. Larry said he had a gig at the Purim Carnival. Carl said that was a good start; he could even wear his yarmulke for that one. Larry said that he and the band had a rehearsal that night and maybe Carl could check it out and give them some pointers. Carl asked if Muley would be there. Larry said he would. Carl said he'd stop by, then told Larry that since the bill at It's in the Pot! came to $15, Larry could just put in $8 and he'd cover the rest and the tip.

Muley didn't come to the Rovner! rehearsal, though. And neither did Larry, as it turned out. Larry had desperately tried to get the band together for an unscheduled rehearsal. But Randy was going to Nassau with his family and had to stay home to pack. Ben had just gotten an Intellivision video game set and had already asked people over to play; Larry was welcome to join. Arik Levine said that he might be able to make it, but Larry had been unable to impress upon any of them the importance of coming to his basement just for an hour or two that night, that their futures could all be secured. The only audience members he'd been able to scare up consisted of his sister, Missy Eisenstaedt, and Rabbi Meltzer from K.I.N.S., who had asked if he could sing lead on a couple of tunes. But when it became obvious there would be no rehearsal, he called them back to cancel. Just before Carl was scheduled to arrive, unable to face the embarrassment, Larry dashed across the street to Chippewa and shot free throws on the icy court until he saw Silverman's rented, sky-blue Mercury Bobcat approach his house, at which point he slipped into the warm fieldhouse and played one-on-two with a pair of Cub Scouts, to whom he showed little mercy, skying over them until they quit with the score 20–2. He stayed in the fieldhouse playing basketball by himself until he was sure Carl was gone, thinking that his New Year's Resolutions would include learning how to play guitar.

Carl arrived at the Rovner house bearing a greasy white paper bag filled with *kichels* from Knopov's Bakery. Ellen Rovner, who was tossing the remainder of her daughter's dinner into the trash while her husband washed dishes, invited Carl to sit in the living room and wait for Larry. She offered him a plate for his *kichels,* but he said no, the bag was fine. He said he actually wasn't here to see Larry; he'd been told his son Muley would be here. Oh, Ellen said, Deirdre's son. That was right, he said. Ellen said Deirdre didn't work for them anymore. Carl asked if she had a phone number and an address—he said he'd mislaid them. Ellen wrote them down. Then Carl asked if he could borrow some change for a pay phone. She gave him fifteen cents, and when Carl was on his way out, Ellen asked if he had any message for Larry.

"Yeah," Carl said. "Tell him to lose the yarmulke and find himself a new guitar player." With that, he exited the house, got into his car, and drove east on Pratt until he got to California. He parked in Gunther's Shell service station and made a call from the pay phone.

D eirdre Wills had a bad feeling when she heard the phone ringing, but she picked it up anyway. And the moment she heard the voice on the other end, she knew why. She hadn't heard Carl's voice in more than twelve years, but she instantly recognized it. The voice had a clipped expectancy to it that seemed to give out orders even when just supplying basic information. When he was on the phone, his voice suggested that there was another call on hold and a third one coming in.

"Deirdre?" Carl asked.

She had just finished the second-to-last chapter in Joseph Conrad's *Chance* and was going to the freezer to get another scoop of Neapolitan ice cream. Had the call come a moment later or earlier, when she was in the middle of Chapter 12 or just starting Chapter 13, she would not have picked up the phone. But as it happened, she had just finished reading the words "Presently a bell rang for the officers' supper" when the phone rang.

"Yes, Carl?" she asked.

Carl never prolonged conversations with preamble or pleasantries. He said he was in town and he wanted to see Muley; he had to talk to him. Deirdre said he had to be out of his mind. They had come to an agreement a dozen years ago, and unless she had missed something, Muley was not an adult yet, she was his mother and, she added, his legal guardian, and she had long ago decided that his father would not be playing an active role in his life, or in hers. Carl said yes, he "dug" that, but this was different, because he had heard from Muley; that's why he was in town. He asked if he could see him tonight. Deirdre said that was out of the question. Carl said he didn't want to make this difficult, but it would be easy to do so. He said he wanted to "rap" with his son, he wanted to figure out what was "shaking," why he had written him, and he wasn't going to "book out of town" until he had. Deirdre quickly said that tonight was no good and neither was the next; they were taking the train down to her brother's house in Atlanta. Carl asked when they were coming back. Sunday, she improvised. Carl said all right, he'd be at their crib on Sunday at four. Then he hung up as he always had—without saying good-bye.

When Muley Wills arrived home that night from a *Young Town* appearance, he noticed boxes in the living room. But before he could ask why they were there, his mother slapped him hard across the face. She regretted it the moment after she had done it, but she didn't apologize—she figured he knew her well enough to understand that she was sorry. What was he doing, she asked, sneaking around, writing letters to his father? Muley said he had no idea what she was talking about. Well, she asked, then why would he just pop out of nowhere, call their unlisted number, and say that Muley had written him a letter if it wasn't true? Muley said he had no idea why; he didn't even know his father's address, what the hell was this all about? What it was about, Deirdre told her son after she had censured him for swearing, was that they were leaving Saturday night, he should pack whatever he wanted and get ready to go to Atlanta.

"I'm not going anywhere," Muley said, and he walked past her into his room and shut the door. Deirdre continued packing. She'd talk to him later and explain the situation better when both of them had calmed down. Carl's call wasn't the only reason she had decided to move; it was just the catalyst. There was nothing quite like a voice from the past to demonstrate that you hadn't moved beyond it. So few things seemed to change in this city. Shops went in, shops went out, people moved in, people moved out, but for her everything felt the same as in 1967. Nothing good had happened to her since then, nothing that she could recall. Muley's arrival had been the last good thing. She had wanted to study, she had wanted to teach, she had wanted to write, she had wanted to do so many things, but for some reason, all that desire had bled slowly out of her. The entire decade of the 1970s had passed by in one long, evil mood. She knew that Muley thought she might be suicidal, that he had to look out for her, and she, to her great shame, had done nothing to dissuade him of those notions. Now she was done letting her son fret about her welfare. From now on, she would take charge, try to alleviate Muley's worries, assure him she would be there for him; she could teach, she could study, she didn't have to vacuum the rooms of naked radiologists to make ends meet. But she couldn't be in Chicago; they had to start over somewhere and there was a room waiting for them in Atlanta.

When Deirdre had packed everything she thought they needed for their journey and thrown out all of her ice cream and other assorted sweets, she knocked on Muley's door. He had set up his hockey net and was firing the orange plastic puck into it as he rehearsed lines for his next *Young Town* episode. Muley stopped shooting the puck when his mother entered the room. He leaned up against his desk, resting his hands on top of the hockey stick, twirling it from time to time. She asked if he wanted to talk. What about? he asked. Moving, she said. Muley said if that's what she felt like talking about, he didn't feel up to it. He asked if she had finished her novel and if she wanted to tell him the story. She said she wasn't done yet; she was on the last chapter. Muley said maybe they should talk when she was done, then she could tell him the whole story. Deirdre said it was an adult story, maybe she had spent too much time telling him adult stories, maybe she had made him miss out on a lot of the great stories she should have been telling him.

She told Muley she was tired. She hadn't realized it, but she thought she'd been tired forever. She didn't want to have to work the same mindless, demeaning jobs. She needed to go somewhere else where they could both do what they wanted. Muley said she didn't have to worry about that. He was getting the money she needed. He was making $200 a week now, plus whatever else he could scrape together through "contests and things." He had most of it in a Lincoln Federal account, but a fair amount in spare cash. He showed her a glass fishbowl on his desk filled with dollar bills. Deirdre tried not to register what Muley said about the money; yes, it was impressive, but it was also humiliating and worrisome—when she wasn't blaming herself for her father's death, she was blaming Carl Slappit Silverman and, to her, Carl was synonymous with money. She told Muley that he was too young to be worrying about money; the idea was ridiculous, a grown woman being supported by a thirteen-year-old. Muley said he didn't mind. Deirdre said if he didn't mind so much, what was he doing writing letters to his father. Muley repeated that he didn't know what she was talking about. He was happy living with her. He wanted to work so she could go back to school and teach. Deirdre said yes, she would go back to school, yes, she would teach, but not with her son supporting her. They were going to Atlanta; that was the only thing that made sense. Friday, she wanted him ready to go. Muley asked, as she was leaving the room, if she'd come back to tell him the story of the novel she was reading. Deirdre said she didn't think she had enough energy. Maybe tomorrow, she said.

But when that tomorrow arrived and Deirdre came home from the Nortown Library where she had calmly resigned her job after having finished the last chapter of *Chance,* Muley was not there. His room was exactly as it had been the previous night. He had packed nothing. The hockey net was still out. There were books scattered all over, blocks of wood and crystal diodes, marbles from a gravity demonstration kit, his Radio Shack computer, the bookcase and the books she had given him. Deirdre hoped they wouldn't have to have the same argument again. But when midnight came and Muley still hadn't come home, she became concerned. An hour later, after she had fallen asleep and woken up, she went back into Muley's bedroom. He still wasn't there. There was a possibility that he was sleeping over at a friend's house, but then something she saw made her fearful, then livid. On the desk, there was an empty fishbowl, one that had been filled with cash the night before. There was also a legal pad on which was written "Sunday: Los Angeles." Underneath, a list of flight numbers and prices.

Until that moment, Deirdre had not thought her disdain for Carl Slappit Silverman could get any deeper. She had never allowed herself to hate him. She knew that Muley thought she hated everybody, had heard him say that once to his little friend Jill when he was explaining to her why he tried not to hate anyone at all. But what was the point of telling Muley that the hatred she sometimes felt was as much for herself as it was for those around her; let him think she was full of hatred if that was what helped to make him so improbably full of kindness. Still, though what Deirdre was feeling didn't quite descend to the level of hatred, it was getting awfully close. It would be so typical of Carl; when she was finally taking control of her life, he would return to destroy everything.

The next evening, after she had packed most of Muley's belongings and he still hadn't returned, Deirdre became more concerned, not with the fate of the moving plan, which was hardly an issue, since they had very little to move, and not with the welfare of her son, who was known to wander, then return home safely long after she had imagined the worst had befallen him. The one thing that was truly disturbing was how little Deirdre knew about Muley; if she wanted to find him, she had no idea where to begin. She knew he spent a lot of time with that pale little girl, Jill, who was always walking around in a dark mood, but she didn't know her last name. She didn't know any of his teachers; the idea of going to parent-teacher conferences had always seemed embarrassing to her—what did she have to say to those teachers, knowing she wanted jobs like theirs but had never finished college herself? She was aware that Muley had won some debate about Iran and the hostages recently, but she knew none of the details. She knew Muley was on some radio program, but he had been cagey about it; the one time she'd expressed interest in learning more, he'd seemed to find it strange that she was asking him at all, and had told her she wouldn't be interested.

She hadn't pursued the matter further. She didn't nag. It had never been that sort of relationship. In truth, Deirdre had never treated Muley like her son. He was her roommate, her confidant. They shared household chores. He didn't speak for the first two years of his life, but then suddenly he came out with a full sentence ("I'm still looking, Ma," he'd said when she'd tried to pull him away from the Christmas windows at Marshall Field's). The only other person Muley knew who had started speaking in full sentences was Jill Wasserstrom, who'd told her mother, "Turn that off," when she was playing a recording of the actor Danny Kaye reading the story of the Brementown musicians. To Deirdre, Muley had never really been a child; he was an adult who didn't know anything yet, and the fastest way to get him to know things was to treat him as if he already did. Once Deirdre knew Muley could speak and could understand sentences, she never once talked down to him. She asked his advice about whether to quit this or that job, consulted him on all financial matters. She read him the stories by the authors she liked. On the first day of kindergarten at Boone Elementary, he had been the only kid whose mother didn't walk him to class ("Take a map out of the drawer," she'd told him. "You don't need me to figure that out for you").

Deirdre's brother Victor, who had been asking her for years to move in with him and his wife and their daughters to finally figure out what she was doing with her life, told her she should contact the police. But she said she wasn't going to call them; a smart young black kid was safer on his own than in the hands of the Chicago police. Victor offered to come to Chicago, but she said no, she had to find him herself. If she wasn't capable of finding Muley, the one person in her life who mattered to her, what good was she? She contacted airlines to see if Muley was scheduled on any of the flights he had listed for Sunday evening. No, they all said, no one was listed under that name.

Early Friday morning, she began her search in earnest, walking into every shop and restaurant on Devon Avenue. She had brought a picture with her—one from a magazine in which Muley had won a trick photography contest; it depicted him and Jill standing atop the two spires of the Hancock Center. But she didn't need the picture; everyone she asked said they knew Muley, but no, they hadn't seen him lately. By Friday evening, she had interviewed most of Devon; many shops were closing for Shabbos, and though Deirdre had learned a great deal about her son that she hadn't known—that he was a fan of spicy bean curd, that he enjoyed *kichels* from Knopov's, that he could make a crystal radio in ten minutes flat, that he was one of the best floor hockey players in West Rogers Park—she knew nothing more about where he might be.

By Saturday evening, when the shuls had started releasing their congregants, she had become desperate. She went back to every store and restaurant, asked everyone the same questions, and got the same responses. She became resigned to the fact that she would not be going to Atlanta. She would not return to school, she would not get a teaching job, she would go back to the Rovners', she would endure the naked radiologist's propositions, clean the young drummer's semen-stained sheets, return to the Nortown Library, reshelve the books she'd already read, never read anything more, since there was nothing left for her to read. She would make any promise, perform any demeaning chore, as long as she could find Muley.

Late that night, she began calling airlines again to see if Muley was on one of their flights. He wasn't. Then on a hunch, while she was on the phone with Continental, she asked if there was a reservation for a Carl Silverman. Yes, the ticket agent said, on the 9 P.M. Sunday flight, there was a reservation for two under that name. So that was Carl's idea? That he and Muley would travel to L.A. together? She felt a generalized ache growing throughout her entire body. *That's what Carl thought?* she wondered.

Deirdre had once vowed she would never again call Carl Slappit Silverman for any reason. But after she had talked to Continental, she pulled out the Yellow Pages and sat on the floor leaning up against a stack of cardboard boxes while she called virtually every hotel and motel in the city to see if Carl was staying there and if he had Muley with him. Once she had called everyone from the Allerton to the Zanzibar Motel, she flung the phone book against the wall and curled up in a heap surrounded by the boxes. She never once cried, though. That was not something she would let herself do. She picked up *Chance* and began to read. She stayed up all night reading, waiting for Sunday evening, when she would go to the airport to track down Carl and Muley.

B ut Muley was not with Carl. And Carl was not at any hotel listed in the phone book. He had chosen to stay at the New Hi-Life Motel on West Madison Street, which only advertised late nights on "the all-day all-night bluesman" Pervis Spann's radio show. Spann spoke highly of the New Hi-Life, which featured "a color TV in every room, a water bed at your request, and free X-rated movies." Carl, who relished squalid surroundings, particularly if they were redolent of what he considered authentic black culture, had chosen the motel for its price and its proximity to South and West Side blues clubs, where he enjoyed listening to the music and slapping his table with every beat, although his record label no longer handled blues artists because there was very little money in it.

In the days before Sunday, when he said he would meet Muley and Deirdre, Carl devoted himself indefatigably to his label. He stormed into record stores and demanded to know why certain artists got better positioning in the stores than his. He barged into the offices of radio station managers, demanding why "Do Ya Think I'm Sexy" was still in heavy rotation, even though it had dropped off the charts months earlier. He showed his Slappit ID to get into rock and folk clubs, often leaving in the first half minute if the band wasn't worth signing.

On Sunday, he ate breakfast early at It's in the Pot!, got into an argument with the owner about the freshness of the bialys, bitched out a few more record store owners, dropped off stacks of 45s to bars with jukeboxes, then drove down Devon, parked across the street from Laundrytown, and, at 4 P.M. on the dot, rang the doorbell marked "Wills." Deirdre came downstairs and opened the door a crack. "Who do I pay the ransom to?" she asked. Carl tried to laugh it off, but Deirdre said it wasn't funny, she wanted to know where her son was and she didn't want to hear any bull about it, and if he gave her any bull about it, she would call up her brother Victor. Carl remembered Victor. He'd never liked Carl much, was always polite, but looked upon him self-righteously with both pity and scorn, as if Carl was a lost member of a lost race. Victor was going to call up a private detective, Deirdre said, he was going to initiate legal action, and if he didn't take legal action, then Deirdre was going to get a broomstick and "knock the stuff" out of him.

Carl asked if he could come in. No, Deirdre said. No, he couldn't come in. This was no time for coming in, she didn't have any stinking coffee, she didn't have any stinking cinnamon rolls, and if she did have cinnamon rolls, she wouldn't give them to him anyway, because he'd crumb up the whole apartment and get his hands all sticky and who wanted to look at a grown man with sticky hands and cinnamon in his beard. She said she'd ask one more time and then she was done being civil: Where was her son? But after Carl said he had no idea where Muley was, Deirdre stopped accusing him. She knew that Carl was the only person more honest and direct than she was; she now guessed that, slob that Carl was, he had reserved two tickets so he could spread himself out over two seats and crumb up the plane. Carl told Deirdre she looked the same, that she hadn't changed in twelve years—and though she said he was full of it, he wasn't lying. He had never taken much note of her appearance and didn't see that she was twenty pounds heavier now and her hair was already graying. Deirdre told Carl that he looked the same too, and she wasn't lying either. Even as a freshman at the U of C, he looked older than his professors. He was only now beginning to look his age.

Deirdre sat down on the pale-green carpeted steps, exhausted beyond words.

She felt an odd, numbing sensation in her head akin to being shell-shocked. She told Carl she'd been all over the neighborhood, she'd talked to everybody, she had no idea where Muley had gone, he'd been away for three days now, but somehow deep down she knew he was okay, he was only doing this because he was trying to tell her something, something that she wished he could just come back and tell her right now. But if she didn't find him soon, she'd have to call the police. Carl said he didn't trust the Chicago police; he asked if she'd been to see Lawrence Rovner. Deirdre said no, she never wanted to set foot in that house full of psychotics and perverts ever again, what would they know about it? Carl showed her the letter from Muley. Deirdre scanned it briefly and snorted. He'd actually fallen for that? she asked. She said it was obvious Larry Rovner had forged it.

"Wow," Carl said. "That kid's got nuts." He made a mental note to listen more carefully to the Rovner! tape. Carl said maybe they should go over to the Rovners' house and see what Lawrence knew. Deirdre said she'd go; she'd run out of ideas. But she added that when they got to the Rovners', she'd stay in the car; she said she didn't want to see anybody naked again.

Once Carl and Deirdre arrived at the Rovners' house—Deirdre had changed her mind and decided to walk to the front door with Carl because the car smelled like lox spread—Lana answered the door. Seeing Deirdre, she asked if she had come by to fetch more Kahlúa. Carl asked if Larry was home. No, Lana said, he was out with Randi Nathan, they were at the Devon Theater seeing the movie *10*, which was rated R. Since he'd turned seventeen, Lana said, Larry had seen every movie that was rated R. She said her parents were upstairs taking a nap and she didn't want to wake them—could she help them with anything? Deirdre, in as polite a manner as her trembling voice could muster, said they were trying to find her son; did she have any idea where he was? Lana said she hadn't talked to Muley since second grade, when she had transferred to a private school, but she knew he spent a lot of time with Jill Wasserstrom. They lived *east* of California, she said triumphantly, on Campbell.

Jill wasn't any help, though. She answered the door, leaving the table where she'd been dining with her father and Gail Schiffler-Bass—Michelle had canceled at the last minute, citing plans with Myra Tuchbaum, even though lately Myra had been too busy to hang out. Jill said she actually hadn't seen Muley in almost a week; the last time had been when she'd gone to see the *Young Town* cast perform at the Pickle Barrel. She had endured the live performance, a five-minute version of a thirty-minute radio show with everything excised except the theme song, the intro, Lennie Kidd's comedy bits, and the conclusion, in which Muley got to say his only line—"And I'm Muley Wills . . . and we would like to thank you for having come on down to *Young Town*." After which, the *Young Town* kids signed autographs while Lennie made balloon animals and terrified children.

The autograph session was scheduled to last until five, but when 3:30 rolled around, the audience had dispersed. Muley asked Jill to meet the cast and Julie Ying had invited her to sit down, whereupon Donna Mayne walked sternly over to Jill and informed her "This area's for *Young Town* kids only." Muley pointed out that everyone had gone home, but Donna was firm; that area was for *Young Town* kids only. Jill said she'd see Muley later. Muley asked what she'd be doing that night. Working on her Bat Mitzvah speech, Jill said. She hadn't seen or talked to him since.

From the Shell station pay phone, Carl made another call to WBOE and was told the same thing he'd heard once before—"I know the brother to whom you are referring, but I don't know where that brother is," Mel Coleman lied. As Carl drove back toward Deirdre's apartment, Deirdre said that she had been every-where she could think of and now, much as she despised the idea, she would have to call the police. She asked if Carl had time to go with her to the police station before his flight. Carl said sure, he had time; his flight wasn't leaving until Monday. Deirdre said she had called up Continental and they had him booked for two seats on tonight's nine o'clock flight. Carl said he never flew Continental, and what would he be doing with two seats? A short silence followed. Then Carl turned the car around and started heading west toward O'Hare.

December 31, 1979

————

We can solve any problem if we only stop wringing our hands about the problems of the past, and look forward to the eighties.

—GEORGE HERBERT WALKER BUSH,

REPUBLICAN PRESIDENTIAL CANDIDATE, 1979

Deirdre & Carl

On December 31, 1979, while the U.N. Security Council debated a resolution demanding the immediate release of the hostages in Iran, Deirdre Wills left Los Angeles, boarding a Continental Airlines DC-10 bound for Chicago O'Hare. Two tickets had been booked for the Chicago-to-L.A. leg of the trip, but only one for the way back. When Deirdre and Carl had arrived in L.A., Carl had assumed they would find Muley, if not on the airplane itself, then either at the airport waiting for them or, perhaps, standing in front of Slappit Studios. But there'd been no sign of Muley save for a telegram in which Muley thanked Carl for listening to Rovner!'s tape. He said he understood that Larry was learning to play guitar. He encouraged his father to listen once more to the cassette.

"That kid's got nuts, big round ones," Carl said, then he asked Deirdre if they should call the police. No, Deirdre said, they didn't have to now. She said she knew how it would all play out. When she got back to Chicago, Muley would be waiting for her at the airport. She was so calm, so sure of herself, when she said this that Carl did not question her.

Carl and Deirdre had been civil to each other on the way to the airport and on the plane before takeoff. Carl had been timidly polite, and Deirdre, disarmed by Carl's consideration, found little to despise in his manner. During the flight, Carl slept and snored while Deirdre read *Two Prisoners,* by Lajos Zilahy. During her two days in L.A., she stayed in Carl's shimmering white Malibu mansion while Carl worked feverishly in his upstairs office. But when 6 o'clock came, he would come down, order barbecue in for the two of them, eat with impeccable table manners, and discuss in great detail various theories regarding Muley's disappearance and carefully broach the topic of reconciliation between himself and

Deirdre. And Deirdre rarely raised a dissenting voice. She still thought Carl was perhaps the most solipsistic individual she had ever encountered, but now found him piteous, not worth the consideration implied by argument. She was tired of despising him, hadn't realized until then how exhausting disdain could be. When Carl said he knew that legally he was responsible for some sort of child support and would it be okay to give her $5,000 and call it square, Deirdre didn't lambaste his avarice, his lack of perspective. She merely thought that $5,000 was a good amount of money; she would take it and call it square.

From the moment they had arrived at the O'Hare ticket counter and learned of the two seats on the outbound flight and the single seat on the inbound, and Deirdre had seen Muley's name as the purchaser of the tickets, she understood what it meant. It may have appeared that Muley had orchestrated his parents' reunion to avoid moving to Atlanta to a house lorded over by an uncle who made shallow, patronizing statements about school ("Hit those books, son; that's how a boy grows into a man") and regularly sent him scriptural passages signed "Yours in Faith, the Wills Family." But Deirdre understood that Muley had other motives for having her reestablish contact with Carl, chief among which was to demonstrate the fallacy of clear breaks, of definitive starts and endings. He was asking through his actions that Deirdre acknowledge Carl's existence, accept responsibility for her plight, live in the present moment, anticipate what was possible as opposed to fearing and resenting what wasn't. At least that was what Deirdre suspected her son was attempting to tell her by having her chase him all the way from West Rogers Park to Malibu and back; at least, that's what became most useful for her to believe. As she expected, when she arrived at O'Hare, Muley was waiting for her, accompanied by a man in a fake fur overcoat who greeted her as "Sister Wills."

When Deirdre saw her son, she did not burst into tears, nor did she embrace him. She gave a slight smile, trying to conceal the larger one she felt, and said, "How are you, Muley Scott Wills?"

"Fine," Muley said. "How are you, Ma?"

"Tired," said Deirdre. She couldn't take her eyes off of her son; she stared at him as if seeing him for the first time.

There would be no talk now of the long journey on which Muley had sent his mother, none of Carl Silverman, none of the son Deirdre did not know she had, the one who was friend to the shopkeepers and restaurateurs of Devon Avenue.

For now, all Muley said was, "I'm not going to Atlanta, Ma," to which she replied, "I know you're not." As they walked toward the parking garage, Muley asked his mother if she'd read anything on the plane. Yes, Deirdre said, she'd read *Almayer's Folly*. Muley asked if she would tell him the story. Yes, she said, if he wanted to hear it, she would. Then Muley asked her if she would call Carl to tell him that everything was okay. Deirdre said yes, she would do that too, but she hoped that Muley wouldn't ask anything more. Talking to Carl Slappit Silverman once every dozen years was plenty for her.

ROVNER

Ellen & Michael

Once they had dropped Lana off at Julie Ying's house for what had been billed as a girls' sleepover, Michael and Ellen Rovner headed northwest to Monastero's Banquet Hall where they were to meet the Rosses for New Year's Eve dinner. Monastero's, located on Devon in Lincolnwood, had a special New Year's dinner featuring singing waiters, a prix fixe menu, and a grab bag of noise-makers, streamers, and confetti. Afterward, the Rovners and the Rosses would go downtown and have drinks at Images, a bar on the 96th floor of the John Hancock Center.

Whenever Michael and Steve were together, they could talk endlessly about sports and sex, topics that were off-limits when their wives were present. There was considerably less for them to discuss at dinner except for work-related gossip, which alienated Steve's wife, Mandy, and bored Ellen. Ellen and Mandy had even less to talk about; Ellen couldn't begin to respond to Mandy's effusive statements and questions ("Aren't kids just the greatest?" "Your work must be so interesting," "Isn't this pasta just out of this world?"). Mandy found Ellen intimidating, rude, and just a bit mean, opinions she was too polite to share with even her husband. The result of which was that when the Rovners and Rosses had "couples' dinners," all they discussed were places they'd been together or places they might go together; thus, evenings were spent avoiding acknowledgment of the rather stiff time they were having by planning other stiff times they would have in the future.

It was Mandy who suggested at Monastero's that it might be "great fun" for the four of them plus their kids to spend a weekend together. Michael said the Rovners' house in Lake Geneva was available anytime. And it was Mandy who also suggested that maybe "that sweet girl Laura Kim" could babysit, the task she also happened to be performing this New Year's Eve—"She just loves kids," Mandy said. Steve joked to Michael that he hoped the shower in Lake Geneva was working now. Ellen asked what he meant; the shower had never been broken. Steve said he'd been under the impression that the shower had been broken. Ellen said no, never. Steve said he must have confused their house with somebody else's, at which point the entrees, carried by a waiter singing "La donna é mobile," thankfully arrived.

Midway through the meal, a waiter arrived to tell Steve he was wanted on the phone. Steve said it was probably the hospital and followed the waiter. Once it was just the three of them, Mandy told Michael and Ellen she was really glad they had chosen this restaurant. The service was excellent and so was the food. The only problem was the bread basket—she would have preferred that it contain a larger selection of snacks. It was a better choice than that weird Japanese place they'd tried the previous New Year's, where they'd had to take off their shoes and sit on the floor. It was funny, she said, her parents had just returned from a trip to Rome, and they had said that the pasta was nowhere near as good as it was at Monastero's. That's generally how things turned out, she said. When she and Steve had gone with her parents to China, only one restaurant served egg rolls as good as the ones from Shanghai Lil's. Ellen asked if she really thought that. Mandy said yes, that's why she said it. Michael asked how the food in Paris compared to the fancy French place they'd all tried in Wheeling, Illinois. Ellen said that the topic was boring, and the three ate in silence until Steve returned, carrying his coat. Mandy asked what the matter was.

Steve said it was nothing. That had been Laura on the phone. Steve Junior had been throwing up and she couldn't find any Pepto-Bismol. She wanted to run out and get some at the drugstore but didn't want to leave the kids alone. Mandy's eyes watered. "Dang it," she said, and apologized. That was the thing about having kids, she said; they always interrupted a really good time. She was sorry they had to go home now. Steve said there was no reason for both of them to go home, why didn't the three of them stay there. Michael, who suspected an ulterior motive for Laura's phone call, said why didn't he come with and keep Steve company. Steve—who saw in Michael a possibility to bolster his alibi—said yes, why didn't he come along; two doctors were better than one. The four of them could meet up at Images. Mandy, who approved of the two-doctors approach but less so of driving with Ellen, said that maybe all four of them should go. Steve said that was ridiculous—four people going—besides, then they'd never get a table. He told Michael to get his jacket and said they'd probably be at the Hancock before "the gals" got there. Ellen remained silent, stewing over what she understood to be a scheme but unsure of the nature of said scheme. She wondered at Michael's sudden eagerness to drive with Steve. And while she was driving with Mandy in the passenger seat, trying to find something good on the radio, finally settling on Chicago's "If You Leave Me Now," Ellen thought once again about the times her husband and Steve spent in the showers after tennis. Just before midnight, when Steve strolled into Images smelling strongly of shampoo and explaining that Steve Junior had thrown up on him and he'd had to take a shower, Ellen felt a quiet fury taking hold inside of her. Michael, noticing her pinched, monosyllabic responses to whatever he happened to say and the uncharacteristically sympathetic discussion she was having with Mandy when he and Steve had walked in, asked what was wrong. Ellen said they would discuss it later, not in front of people.

Michael had gone along for the ride with the intention of talking Steve out of his liaison with Laura Kim, but Steve had interpreted Michael's offer to join him as an expression of male solidarity. Before Michael could launch into the noble speech he had been planning, Steve told him that when they got to his house, he would run inside and Michael could pick him up in a half hour. He told Michael he was his best friend and thanked him for always being there. He told Michael that he was the only one who could possibly understand that what he was doing wasn't being unfaithful; in fact, his relationship with Laura was saving his marriage, for being with Laura prevented him from making unreasonable demands on Mandy, asking her to be the sort of person she wasn't. He told Michael it was true what they said about Oriental women, but did not elaborate. And when they got to Steve's house, he told Michael to go to Walgreen's and pick up some Pepto-Bismol.

Michael tried to explain all this to his wife on the drive home shortly before one in the morning after she had accused him of having an affair with Steve Ross. Michael, flustered and humiliated by the implication, insisted that she didn't understand the intricacies of male friendships, probably because she didn't have any relationships with women that were as close as the one he had with Steve, and, further, if he were having an affair with anyone, it would far more likely be with Laura Kim. Ellen said the idea that someone young, intelligent, and attractive like Laura would desire Steve Ross was pathetic; the idea that she would desire Michael was implausible. Michael said well, no, it wasn't all that implausible, considering that she rubbed his shoulders every day, called him "Doc," and had invited him out drinking with her while Ellen had been out of town and that he had, in fact, declined an invitation to have a nightcap at her apartment. Ellen said that he was either a liar or a coward and she didn't relish the idea of living with either.

WASSERSTROM

Charlie

Although she could have gotten in free to any of the New Year's Eve bashes being thrown that night in West Rogers Park, Gail Schiffler-Bass had turned down every offer, including the JCC's annual Latkafest, which promised "noshing, mingling, and dancing to every hit song of the year, except 'Y.M.C.A.'" She had recently purchased a Sony Betamax videocassette player and recorder and had asked Charlie Wasserstrom if he and his daughters wanted to join her for "coffee and." They would have champagne and Marshall Field's crumble cake and, Charlie explained to Jill and Michelle, they could watch one of three movies Gail had purchased—*Jaws, The Sting,* or *"Taxicab Driver."* To his surprise, Jill had said yes, while Michelle said she was sorry but she had "Tuchbaumian plans."

Jill was somewhat miffed that Michelle had said no, because that meant she had to accompany her father for at least part of the evening. She didn't want him to think she was protesting his new relationship with the woman he referred to as a "real nice friend." She knew Michelle was less than excited about the idea of their father having a girlfriend. Jill, however, did not object to the concept of her father having coffee, dinner, or wild, passionate sex with Gail, although she preferred to remain ignorant of the specifics. The truth was that there had been, during the course of the three dinners Charlie and Gail had consumed together, no wild, passionate sex whatsoever, and only three hugs. Nevertheless, Jill—who'd been inculcated into Michelle's view of the world—assumed that whenever adults were together and not eating, drinking, or driving, they were having wild, passionate sex.

Jill joined her father for crumble cake and milk at Gail's, but left early, right before *Taxi Driver,* saying she was going home to work.

"Work?" Gail asked. "On New Year's Eve?"

"Work," Jill repeated.

"She likes to do work," Charlie explained cheerfully after Jill left. "She gets enjoyment out of it."

Which was more than Charlie could have said for the movie. He tried to feign enthusiasm for it. During some of the more profane scenes, he hummed quietly to himself and muttered a few "oy vey"s, thinking Gail wouldn't hear. Several times, he rose from Gail's couch, ostensibly to refill his water glass or get more crumble cake. The third time Gail noticed Charlie squirm, she asked if he'd prefer shutting the film off. Charlie said no, it was okay, the picture was "a bit rougher" than those he usually saw, but the worst was probably over anyway, right? Gail said no, actually the vulgarity had really just begun, and she hoped that he had the stomach for the "rough stuff" that was yet to come. Charlie mulled this over for a moment or two, then finally said, well, maybe it would be better if they just shut it off, it wasn't his kind of picture.

After she had shut off the film, Gail asked him what sort of movies he liked to watch. Charlie said he didn't see a lot of pictures. When he'd been growing up on the West Side, he'd liked John Wayne pictures and Jimmy Stewart pictures. When Becky was alive, she'd taken him to see lots of pictures with subtitles, which he had enjoyed a lot more than he'd expected. But lately he just tended to see whatever his kids wanted to see. Gail asked what sorts of films his daughters liked and, to Gail's surprise, Charlie enumerated them quite specifically. Jill liked black-and-white pictures, he said, generally movies made before even he had been born; she liked silent pictures, although she preferred Harold Lloyd to Charlie Chaplin; she liked old comedies, but enjoyed the Marx Brothers more than Abbott and Costello and Buster Keaton more than any of them. Her favorite movie was Keaton's *Sherlock Jr.* Michelle, on the other hand, liked modern pictures, particularly horror movies, musicals, and concert movies. She liked Judy Garland and Barbara Stanwyck movies, but she also liked Steve McQueen, Peter O'Toole, and Richard Burton. Her favorite movie was *Woodstock,* Charlie said.

Charlie was wrong about some small matters regarding his daughters' likes and dislikes—for example, his impression that Michelle's favorite movie was *Woodstock.* She liked it fine but had gone to see it at the Parkway six Saturday nights in a row because one of the concession workers was giving free joints to anyone who purchased a large popcorn and a medium drink. Still, despite Charlie's errors in recounting Jill and Michelle's tastes, when he started discussing them, in Gail's eyes, he transformed from being refreshingly unpretentious to being improbably charismatic and, though she would not have used the exact term, since her first marriage, to Lennie Bass, had been such a disaster, *husband material.* He knew the title of every play Michelle had acted in, could quote from memory a handful of her lines, and could even, though he promised Gail he wouldn't, sing some of the songs she had sung in musicals. He knew about the political groups Jill favored, remembered the candidates she'd told him to vote for—since 1976, he had let Jill fill out sample ballots for him. When Charlie said if it hadn't been for his daughters, he probably wouldn't have even voted in the last mayoral election or known the words to "Supercalifragilisticexpialidocious," from *Mary Poppins,* Gail had a sudden urge to kiss Charlie Wasserstrom. But she resisted that urge, at least until it was 1980 and each of them had had two glasses of champagne.

Peachy Moskowitz

Comedian, radio host, balloon animal sculptor, magician, bird trainer, and, briefly, husband to Gail Schiffler, Lennie Kidd was driving from the Latkafest at the JCC to Zanies, a comedy club in Old Town, a large cage with six twittering parakeets resting precariously on the backseat of his rumbling 1974 Ford Country Squire station wagon, when his mind suddenly settled on the topic of Peachy Moskowitz. At the JCC, Lennie's parakeet routine had gone poorly; his act had followed Josh the Jewish Pantomime, who muttered in Yiddish while performing standard pantomimes ("*Oy gevalt,*" he would groan while walking against the wind; "*Oy, vot's* the schmuck doing inside a glass box?" he'd say while pretending he was encased in a glass box). During Lennie's routine, Pinchas the Parakeet had not followed the other parakeets through the flaming rings Lennie juggled, alighting and refusing to descend from Lennie's head. The audience had laughed uproariously, infuriating Lennie, who was deadly serious about his budgie act. The biggest laugh of the routine came when Josh the Jewish Pantomime reentered to coax Pinchas off of Lennie's head, yelling, "Get off his *kopf,* you putz." Lennie had departed to thunderous applause, but he felt enraged.

Lennie had arranged his New Year's Eve schedule so he would be inside his car at midnight. For someone whose livelihood was based on entertaining people, he was surprisingly cowed by almost all situations that required social interaction. Even though he performed practically every night of the year, he still was unable to shake the crippling stage fright that had only gotten worse in recent years. Whenever he had to make a gig, he drove slowly, hoping to get there too late. Whenever a show was canceled, he'd throw a tantrum, but would secretly be relieved.

This night, he took side streets all the way from West Rogers Park to Old Town. He had stalled briefly, then driven slowly past the funny-looking house on North Shore that he had once shared with Gail Schiffler during the only period of his life where his stage fright was, if not nonexistent, certainly less debilitating. It had been nearly five years since Gail had insisted he move out and four years since she had gotten an unlisted number. There was a blue glow that framed the lowered shade in the picture window of the Funny House. Lennie wondered who was living there now and what they were watching on TV. He contemplated checking the name on the mailbox, but it was cold outside and he didn't want to get out of his car, so he turned left on Richmond and headed south to Zanies.

Since the no-fault divorce—neither had wanted to wage a protracted legal battle, Gail because she thought such a battle would humiliate Lennie, Lennie because he didn't want to be humiliated—Lennie Bass, who legally changed his name to Kidd after Gail changed her phone number, had been romantically involved with numerous women, most of whom were either younger than he was or foreign. Lennie's ideal woman was a combination of both. He liked women who spoke enough English to understand his jokes but not a whole lot more. None of his relationships lasted particularly long, largely because none of the women with whom he'd been involved since the divorce had won the approval of his mother, who had sided with Gail during the divorce, and frequently asked him during Shabbos dinners if he had heard from her. When he would say no, Dorothy Bass would tell him, "You really blew that one, Lennie."

Lennie was certain that neither the French au pair working for the family who lived across the hall from his apartment nor the Greek waitress at the gyros joint he frequented would pass muster with his mother. And then, as he was driving nineteen miles per hour north on Kimball Avenue—the street with the lowest speed limit in the city—trying desperately to hit every traffic light, Lennie wondered if there was any woman who could please his mother. He knew Dorothy Bass would like a woman who was attractive but not intimidatingly so. She would have to be intelligent but not arrogant, polite but not officious, Jewish but not too Jewish ("Those Orthodox are all creeps," she frequently said. "They should put them all in the Middle East where they belong"). In short, she would have to be someone like Peachy Moskowitz. The tantalizingly beautiful cousin Muley Wills frequently described was exactly the girl he could bring home. She was young and Russian, which was perfect for Lennie. She was smart, attractive, and Jewish, which was perfect for Dorothy. At the next *Young Town* taping, Lennie would ask Muley if he could invite his cousin to a taping. He could interview her about one of her "Lessons from Life."

Lennie was so excited by this idea that he started driving the speed limit en route to his 1 A.M. set at Zanies. When he stepped out onstage, he was brimming over with energy. As he stood before the audience, he decided to stop seeing his therapist Dr. Rovner; he felt too good now. The stage felt too small; he wanted to be in an arena performing in front of twenty thousand instead of the hundred or so Zanies held; his characterizations were broader than ever, his accents dead-on; he wished there was a *Tonight Show* scout in the audience to hear him singing "Miss Riordan's on the Rag," to see him pirouetting and somersaulting for his finale, in which he imitated every single member of Lech Walesa's Solidarity party performing *Swan Lake,* a routine he had just invented. It was only when he'd finished that routine that Lennie noticed the red light blinking, the light that had been blinking on and off for the past fifteen minutes, the light that was telling him that he was well over the time limit for his thirty-minute set.

R O V N E R

Larry

Shortly after he arrived at the JCC, Larry Rovner realized he was not the right age for either the Latkafest or the Junior Latkafest. The Latkafest, held on the first floor in the JCC auditorium, was attended by men and women between the ages of twenty-eight and forty-nine, most of them divorced. Their children, few of them over the age of seventeen, were downstairs either in the game room or the gym. Larry had considered sleeping over at Ben Jacobs's house, but since it had only been two days since he'd informed the members of Rovner! that, based on Carl Silverman's advice, he was disbanding the group and re-forming it as a solo project, he didn't feel he would be welcome there.

There had been some resistance to the breakup, most notably from Arik Levine, who said that this was a band and a band was a democratic unit and that the three other band members had the power to vote him out, but he didn't have the authority to do that to them. Larry had said no, a band wasn't a democracy;

that was the whole point of a band, that there was a charismatic leader with a vi-sion and everything had to be designed to fulfill that vision. Arik said fine, he could keep his shitty songs, but it was *him* leaving the group. Larry said okay, but he was keeping the gig at the Purim carnival for himself and if they kept the band going, they couldn't call it Rovner! No one seemed to have a problem with that.

For a short while, Larry reminisced with his bandmates about their inauspi-cious beginnings, how they'd started out jamming in one another's basements and garages, how each member had found his way into the group. Someday, Larry said, maybe he'd bring them all back for a reunion concert, perhaps a ben-efit for the Walk for Israel. Arik Levine told Larry he could fuck off—maybe he ought to perform live once before he started planning reunion tours. Randy Weinstock said hey hey hey hey, the idea when they'd started was to be friends; they could still be friends now whether they were part of the same band or not. Arik said yeah, whatever, grudgingly shook Larry's hand, and said he didn't mean to be rude but there was a band rehearsal going on now, man, and whoever wasn't in the band couldn't be part of it. Larry said he'd see them around.

Missy Eisenstaedt had called Larry to suggest they go to the Latkafest, and since all the former members of Rovner! were going over to Ben's, there was no chance they would see him and mock him for being with Missy. Sure, he said, he'd go. He thought there was the possibility she'd be so grateful he accepted her invitation that she would have sex with him, but when he met her in front of her house in the company of her younger sister Bibi, the possibility was reduced to a slim chance. And when, on the walk over, she mentioned that her cousin had gone out with a Hasidic boy and on their second date he'd tried to stick his tongue inside her mouth and wasn't that just sick, Larry was already manufac-turing ways to extricate himself from a chaste evening in the company of a girl with whom he was embarrassed to be seen. The best way would have been for him to meet another girl at the Latkafest, start making out with her, and have Missy leave in a jealous huff. But that proposition seemed unlikely. He decided that after an appropriate amount of time, he would feign a headache and say he was going home. Then he would drive over to Warren Park and climb Mt. War-ren, where he would, in accordance with one of his New Year's resolutions, mas-turbate for the last time, take a piss and spell his name in the snow, then sing "Soar" as loud as he could.

After Larry, Missy, and Bibi had sat through the Latkafest performance by

Josh the Jewish Pantomime but not Lennie Kidd—Missy had requested they leave after Josh had called Lennie a "putz," the language was just a bit much for her, she said—they went downstairs to the Junior Latkafest. A circle of adolescents in their stocking feet were dancing the hora to "Hava Nagilah." As the circle transformed itself into a hokey-pokey line, Missy and Bibi dashed to the back of the line, Missy waving to Larry that he should join in. But rock stars didn't do the hokey-pokey, and Larry sullenly went off in search of a basketball. There were none in the gym, so Larry went out into the hallway and tried doors, hoping one of them would yield a supply closet with at least a medium-sized red rubber bombardment ball inside. But most of the doors were locked; a couple opened onto classrooms, and one into a closet filled with paper towels and detergent. One door was marked "MEN'S LOCKER ROOM." Larry pushed it open.

When Larry opened the locker room door, it was dark inside, and a gust of warm, acrid air enveloped his body. He found a light switch and flipped it. Fluorescents flickered lavender, then burst on full white, illuminating rows of steel-gray lockers and dull wooden benches. The last time Larry had been in a pool he had been a fearful boy of ten, feebly trying to swim with Ellie Sherman's "Porpoise" class. Now he walked through the locker room, remarking to himself how small the lockers seemed, how low the urinals were, how short the distance was from the locker room to the showers, where he had never once removed his swimming trunks, preferring to leave them on wet when he put on his pants.

Opposite a row of eight showerheads, there was a white door marked "POOL." When he opened it and breathed in the warm, slightly sharp odor of chlorine, he felt calm, confident, and energized, like a star professional athlete returning to the site of his high school glory. But unlike the locker room, the pool area wasn't dark when Larry entered it. And unlike the locker room, it wasn't empty. There, atop the diving board, was a slim, naked, bearded man slowdancing with a plump, naked, familiar-looking girl.

As Larry stood there gaping, a strong, sweet scent of marijuana mingled with that of the chlorine. *Shiffra Tuchbaum*, Larry said incredulously. His eyes briefly met those of the dancing naked girl on the diving board. "Happy New Year, Yehuda," Myra cackled as she broke free of the man's arms and dashed full speed over the diving board, landing with a resounding *splooosh* while the man applauded and shouted, imitating an Olympics TV commentator, "A perfect ten for Shirley Babashoff!" And Larry, feeling ashamed for being clothed, ashamed for being a domestic virgin if not an international one, ashamed for attending the Latkafest in the company of Missy Eisenstaedt and her little sister Bibi while people his age were having sex to ring in the New Year, ran back into the locker room, out into the hallway, past the gym where Missy and Bibi were running in a three-legged race, up the stairs and past the auditorium where couples were dancing to a disco version of "Yiddle Mit Ein Fiddle," out into the parking lot and onto Touhy, where he ran east to Sacramento, until he got to his mother's Volvo, which started with a cough. He shifted into gear and pulled into traffic, heading straight for Warren Park.

The fog outside was dense, and snow was coming down hard, which meant that the view from the top of Mt. Warren was confined to a mere few blocks in either direction. Larry could see Hank Schiffler Ford but only one block west of it. He couldn't see north of Pratt or south of Devon. And when he looked east, he couldn't see anything beyond the park; it was a dark abyss that dissolved into an impenetrable wall of fog. On the one hand, the obscured view detracted from the majesty of the moment. On the other, it meant that it would be difficult for any passerby to see him jerking off. But as Larry stood atop Mt. Warren, the original order—to masturbate, then spell his name in the snow, then sing—seemed exactly wrong. What he wanted to do was sing his anthem first, then spell his name with piss to relieve the pressure on his bladder, thus magnifying the intensity of the orgasm he would experience at the exact onset of the New Year.

As he sang "Soar," realizing that when he recorded it for real, he might have to do it up here with the sounds of wind and blowing snow giving his words extra emphasis, Larry felt completely in tune with the wind rustling through the branches. "I wanna soar," he shouted. "But I feel so sore." "I wanna soar soar soar soar soarsoarsoar," he repeated, riffing on his own lyrics. "But I feel so so so goddamn sore." More wind blew, branches snapped, more wind, more snapping. Until Larry became aware that the sounds he was hearing belonged neither to the wind nor the branches. The wind was somebody whistling. And the snapping was the sound of applause. At the end of the song, Larry began unzipping his fly, but then he stopped, certain there was someone else atop Mt. Warren.

"Sing it, yeshiva boy," Michelle Wasserstrom said.

Michelle

For the first time since her mother had died, Michelle Wasserstrom was without a date on New Year's Eve and she was perversely thrilled by the prospect of entering 1980 alone. Millard Schwartz's bait-and-switch Who concert antics had only been one of the recent proofs of her hypothesis that dating was stupid, a pathetic effort to distract lonely people from their lack of self-confidence. She enjoyed sex, but it was overrated; the emphasis people put on it was completely out of proportion. The way people complimented others' sexual prowess was comical. It was the performance of an instinctive animal need; saying how good someone was at it was like saying they were good at eating.

A further proof of dating's folly had presented itself the previous day at the back booth of Wolfy's with Myra Tuchbaum, who had all along been evasive about her New Year's plans. But when pressed by Gareth Overgaard on the topic ("Just say what you're doing, Tuchbaum. No one gives that much of a shit"), she admitted that no, she wouldn't be doing anything with them; she had a *date.* Neither Michelle nor Gareth bothered to ask who her date was with, but Myra said she would tell them if they swore to keep it a secret. "I'm not promising shit, Tuchbaum," Gareth said.

"Okay," Myra said, as if divulging crucial information under duress. "But you're not going to believe it; it's Mr. Sternberg."

"Sterndick?" Michelle asked, revolted.

"But you can't tell anybody," Myra insisted. She said that, like everybody else, she had at first had a negative reaction to Doug—now she was calling him *Doug*—but he was really an interesting *man,* he knew so much, he had taken her to this opera about Einstein and she thought she would hate it, but she loved it, plus he was a great kisser and his come tasted great.

"I don't want to fucking *hear* about it, Tuchbaum," Gareth said, while Michelle offered that everybody's come tasted the same and nobody's tasted great. But Myra, not used to being the center of attention, insisted it was true: "Kind of like spearmint." She said she felt she'd really grown as a performer since she'd met Doug and that was why he was using her to "workshop" the role of "Mary Hyman," a new character he had invented for *The Burden of Biff*, a musical version of *Death of a Salesman* that Sternberg had written from the perspective of Willy Loman's son, the football star who had never been able to equal his high school glory. Myra began to regale her dining partners with songs from the musical, including "Say Hi to the New Mrs. Loman," "Happy Ain't Happy No More," and "Hyman's Lament." "What's the matter with your daad, Biff?" Myra warbled. "Why does he always seem so saad, Biff? / You say he had guts / But I think he's just nuts / Yes, he's just a little bit maaad, Biff."

"I'm eatin' here, Tuchbaum," Gareth said.

"Isn't it awesome?" Myra giggled proudly, and went on to discuss her plans to sneak into the JCC pool with Sternberg.

Well, Michelle thought, so that was what all that BS with Mr. Linton had been about. She had found it slightly odd that Linton had been so solicitous toward her after the closing performance of *H.M.S. Pinafore,* telling her he would allow her to choose whichever role she wanted in a list of plays they were considering for the first drama club spring production. Michelle had skimmed the list of predictable shows where she could play one of a few predictable roles—ingénue, slut, or old maid—and asked Linton if she really could choose any role. He said yes, he didn't break promises. All right, Michelle said, then she wanted to play Hamlet. Mr. Linton said she could certainly play Ophelia. But Michelle didn't want to play that whiny little psycho bitch; if she couldn't play Hamlet, she didn't want to be in the spring show. But now, knowing that if she did get the part it would be because Mr. Linton felt guilty that she wouldn't be able to star in some *Death of a Salesman* musical directed by a past-his-prime perv with Wrigley's Spearmint come, she felt that victory would seem that much cheaper. As far as she was concerned, Myra was free to frolic naked with Douglas Sterndick in the JCC pool during the Junior Latkafest; Michelle would be spending New Year's alone.

Once Jill had declined the opportunity to accompany her to the Junior Latkafest—normally Michelle was insulted when her sister told her she didn't want to go out with her, but this time she was thankful she didn't have to entertain her—Michelle made plans for her solo New Year's Eve date. With the little money she had saved from her small allowance and her occasional crappy jobs, she would treat herself to dinner, a good dinner with a bottle of wine. Then she would go to a movie, and afterward she would ascend Mt. Warren. As 1979 turned to 1980, she would contemplate how she would pursue her acting career. And then, she had told Gareth—because she felt bad that *he* was spending New Year's Eve without a date—he could join her atop the hill and they could set off the Roman candles he'd purchased that summer in Kenosha. She brought a copy of *Hamlet* with her to Fondue Stube on Peterson Avenue. It was the most romantic restaurant she could think of within walking distance of her apartment, and she was the only person dining by herself. She tried to stop the waiter from hitting on her by feigning a limited knowledge of English and speaking in a vaguely Eastern European accent. When he asked where that "interesting accent" came from, she told him, "*frum yer muzzer*" and told him to put the wine in a doggie bag.

Michelle enjoyed her own company. There was no meaningless conversation, no worrying about who would pay for the bill. The jokes she told herself were funnier than those her dates usually tried. She could read a play and drink a glass of wine and dip an apple chunk into melted cheese without either hoping she was impressing somebody or, more often, hoping she wasn't. In the movie theater, she didn't have to debate where to sit. She could walk right to the front row with a medium buttered popcorn and watch *The Black Hole,* glugging the wine she hadn't finished at the restaurant.

Michelle was the last person to leave the theater. Someday she was going to be one of those names on the credits, and she wanted people to wait to see her name too. As she exited the theater and walked north toward Warren Park, her mouth open to catch the snowflakes, Michelle was sorry she hadn't seen anyone she knew inside or outside the theater. She wanted someone to see her alone and happy about it.

Never mind, then. She would climb Mt. Warren with her bottle of wine and her copy of *Hamlet;* she'd drink and recite Shakespeare until Gareth arrived, and they'd set off Roman candles to cap off the best New Year's celebration she'd ever had, or at least the best one in the past five years. She wanted to spend all of her New Year's Eves exactly as she had spent this one—with the sweet buzz of wine making both her body and the world around her seem lighter, with the snow falling on Western and beyond the fog where she could not see. With the sound of wild, hungry animals baying in the park, crying out for food.

But those weren't wild animals; that was Larry Rovner. *Oh fuck,* Michelle thought, was this what she had to look forward to in the New Year?

WILLS / SILVERMAN

Muley

After his mother had told him the story of *Almayer's Folly,* left a perfunctory message for Carl Silverman, and gone to bed, Muley Wills met Mel Coleman, with whom he'd been staying while his mother had searched for him. Mel had initially resisted the idea of Muley staying with him, saying, "Once my old lady comes, you go." The way Mel had said it made it seem as though he had a girlfriend living with him, but in fact "old lady" referred to his mother, who lived upstairs and had a tendency to sleepwalk. Muley only encountered her once during his stay, and though she kept calling Muley "Mel," all Muley could discern from talking to her was that either she had a vivid imagination or Mel was less than candid when he discussed his life. She asked Muley if *Mel's Manual for Men* was still a bestseller, how he enjoyed hosting a radio show, and when he was going to marry that nice girl from the radio station he kept talking about. In response, Muley told her that yes, the manual was still selling well, the radio show was going fine, and that he liked that "nice girl" well enough, but he wouldn't marry her until he was sure she was the right one. Mel said, "Damn, I never answer her questions so well."

In truth, Mel was barely scraping by. When he wasn't working weekends for public radio, he sold stereos at Pacific Stereo in Lincolnwood, a job that left him too tired to write more than a page or two at night. And though Mel spoke frequently of a girlfriend, the sentences he employed to refer to her were cast in the past tense; instead of saying, "My lady can't keep her damn legs closed," as he once had, on this night, Mel said, almost wistfully, "My lady never could keep her damn legs closed."

That night in Mel's car, Muley had mentioned something about wanting to dedicate his life to helping out people in need. Mel suggested, "How 'bout you start by helping out Mel Coleman?" Muley said he'd do what he could; Mel had helped him out the past week and he hoped he could return the favor. He said he had once gotten encouraging letters from a game manufacturer and maybe they could turn *Mel's Manual for Men* into a board game. It wasn't a bad idea, Mel said, but he wanted to complete his novel, too, because it would make a great flick. Muley said his father had show business connections; though he didn't want to talk to him, maybe Mel could write to him and drop Muley's name. Mel said he liked Muley's can-do attitude and proposed discussing the future over a couple of "pops" at the Double Bubble.

After the past week, in which Muley had helped to radically alter the course of his and his mother's life, stepping in to help out Mel seemed comparatively easy, as if he were an architect who had just completed a skyscraper and was now being called in to supervise a modest condo rehab. The odd thing was that though recently Muley had been able to realize many of his most profound wishes, he felt little satisfaction. He had long wanted a girlfriend and had not considered it more than a remote possibility since Jill Wasserstrom had rebuffed his advance on the jungle gym in sixth grade. And now, even though Jill said he couldn't refer to her as his girlfriend (she didn't like the possessiveness of the term) and even though she had said they couldn't kiss or hold hands whenever he wanted (sometimes they could, but not in front of other people, because that was exhibitionistic) and even though they had only slowdanced together once since the first time in her apartment (Jill said if they did it too often, it would get repetitive) and even though Jill said she was busy for New Year's, still he had someone who was, for all intents and purposes, his girlfriend, even if he couldn't say it out loud. But having a girlfriend was not as satisfying as Muley had thought it would be.

Muley felt similarly let down by *Young Town*. He had been truly excited by the idea of a show that he would help write, produce, and direct. But except for the two-minute Peachy Moskowitz scripts that Donna Mayne gushed over every week, the show was entirely scripted by adults. The applause was dubbed in; the laughter was canned; the interviews were all fake. At least the money was good, though, more than he'd ever made with any of his other creative projects. But now that his mother had said on the drive from the airport that she was taking charge of her destiny, that she would actually complete her missing credits at Circle and try to get a job substitute-teaching before she got her certification, Muley didn't know what to do with that money. Deirdre Wills had initially refused to take anything whatsoever from Muley. But Muley, who, notwithstanding his mother's deep depression, had somewhat enjoyed their previous relationship, in which he felt responsible for her well-being, said he wanted to contribute to the household. Since his age was 39.3 percent of hers, he wanted to pay 39.3 percent of the rent, do 39.3 percent of the laundry and 39.3 percent of the cleaning, and if not cook 39.3 percent of the food, at least pick it up from some of his favorite neighborhood vendors. After some objections, Deirdre consented, but said she would be diligent about checking his math.

For the first time in ages, Muley had no clear vision of his future. Just the day before, Muley had been planning on at least trying to take care of 100 percent of household expenses while his mother went back to school, and other than buy a Bat Mitzvah gift for Jill, he had little idea what to do with the remaining 60.7 percent. He no longer needed to find a girlfriend, no longer needed a job, no longer needed money, no longer needed to flee exile in Atlanta. He should have felt contented, but instead he felt aimless. He wished there was some occupation, some goal that could consume him as much as his games and inventions once had.

When midnight struck and the regulars in the Double Bubble halfheartedly cheered the TV as the great ball dropped in Times Square, Muley wondered if he'd lived through his most creative years in the 1970s. For him, that decade had been about ingenious solutions to insurmountable problems. The 1980s beckoned, and judging from the great progress he had made in such a short time, they seemed to represent a period of ease and boredom, of domesticity and routine, of financial reward at the expense of creativity—above all, a period of that until-now-unfamiliar feeling of discontent, where you got everything you desired and it turned out you really didn't want it at all.

After three beers, Mel was full of plans, full of schemes, full of questions and pleas for counsel. He wanted to work on a demo for a radio show they would host together called "Mel and Son," he wanted to take Muley up on his suggestion of a *Mel's Manual* board game, he wanted to finish his novel and take it to Hollywood. After four beers, Mel said he was certain the New Year would be a good one. But after four ginger ales, Muley Wills was not so sure.

Later that night, Muley walked along Devon toward home, rejecting Mel's suggestion that they wake up Muley's mother to see if she wanted to play quarters or go out for pancakes. The snow had slowed to a flurry, and on the streets of Chicago, New Year's Eve revelry was already transforming into New Year's Day silence. Only an occasional, lonely pop of a firecracker or the sounds of laughter or car brakes a long way off gave any hint that this night was different from any other. Muley had planned to walk straight home, but when he got to his apartment, he kept walking west. He thought he might walk by the Wasserstroms' apartment to see if Jill was still awake, working on her Bat Mitzvah speech, but he stopped when he got to the west side of Western Avenue. In the window of General Camera, there was a treasure trove of cameras, tripods, projectors, and telescopes. "It almost feels like we're inside of a movie," Jill had told him a little more than a month earlier, and now the words returned to him. With the money he now had at his disposal, Muley could afford more of these toys in the window than he had ever thought possible. But buying things was nowhere near as interesting as finding them, and since the store was closed anyway, Muley went into the alley to see what was there.

R O V N E R

Lana

Lana Rovner had been permitted to attend a New Year's party at P.C. Pendleton's house on the condition that she receive counseling for what her parents referred to as her "eating disorder." She agreed quickly, knowing she'd be able to get out of the therapy session later. She had told her mother when she was ten and had stopped eating for nearly a week that she didn't need therapy; if her brother wanted to go, that was fine for him, but as far as she was concerned, she was *normal,* and she thought that had been the end of it. But now that her mother had returned from Paris and had spent every evening in her father's bedroom, the two of them had formed a consolidated front in opposition to her. They had even made her get on a scale the day after the Paris trip. She knew how much she weighed: eighty-nine pounds in gym shoes. That was *not* abnormal for her height. She didn't want to weigh *ninety.* It wasn't as if she didn't eat; she ate plenty, not as much as her parents perhaps, but they ate crap. Was that what she was supposed to do, she asked them—eat crap? Her father, the traitor, had told her, "I understand there's something you really want to do, but there's also something *we* really want you to do," meaning that if she wanted to go to P.C.'s party, she would have to consent to see some perverted doctor who'd ask her all kinds of perverted questions about her sex life. She didn't *have* a sex life; she'd played Spin the Bottle once, she'd never gone *exploring,* nobody'd ever gone up her shirt. But maybe that's what she'd do tonight, she thought, maybe she'd go exploring if P.C. let her, maybe she'd give P.C. a big, nasty hickey, maybe she'd let P.C. go up her shirt, just so she'd have something to tell the creep obsessed with getting her to eat crap, if she was going to actually go through with the appointment once she'd gotten what she wanted. Which she wasn't.

What was worse, after she'd agreed to waste her parents' money on psychoanalysis, was that they changed the rules on her. She had *told* them that P.C.'s party was a sleepover—why did they think she was packing *pajamas,* why did they think she asked if they had extra toothpaste and *ChapStick?*—and now after telling them she'd see Dr. Mandell, here was her father up in her bedroom, telling her, "Your mother and I don't think it's right for you to sleep over at a boy's house." What was she supposed to tell P.C. after she'd already agreed to be his partner in the "orgy." Of course he didn't mean there was going to be a real *orgy,* that's just how classy people referred to fun parties with lots of dancing and good conversation.

Getting angrier and angrier with her mother—her father was the one telling her, but she was sure her mother was behind it—and angrier and angrier with the girl who would wind up being P.C.'s date for the orgy, what a *bitch,* excuse her French, what a *sale putain*—Lana called Julie Ying. She hadn't really enjoyed herself when she'd gone with Julie to *Ice Follies.* When Lana's parents picked her up at Julie's house, they seemed to like her more than Lana did, especially her father, who kept saying, "Doesn't she kind of remind you of a younger Laura Kim?" Julie was nice enough. Too nice. The few times Lana pointed at somebody in the audience and said that they were really fat or really ugly or that they didn't look at all like their children and who did Julie think the father *really* was, Julie said, "I don't think it's right to judge people. It's okay if you do it. But I don't like to." When they went out for Italian food with Julie's parents, Julie refused to criticize the waiters or agree that the food tasted like Chef Boyardee. And her parents were so serious—wanting to know where she went to school, where she was going to high school, where her parents were from, where they had gone to school. They liked that she was Jewish. Jews were smart, her father had said; they gave their children good educations. Still, what was most important was that Julie lived within a mile of P.C. Pendleton. Lana asked Julie what she was doing for New Year's. Julie said that she and her sisters were cooking dinner for their parents and then they would play Charades, followed by an impromptu recital. Lana was welcome to come over and bring an instrument.

Lana figured it wouldn't be hard to talk Julie into leaving before Charades began when there was an opportunity to attend a high-class orgy at the Pendletons'. But after Ellen and Michael Rovner had dropped their daughter off at the Yings' house, Lana was crestfallen to discover that Julie actually wanted to help her sisters cook dinner, that she was truly happy Lana was going to play Charades with them, that she was excited about the recital—she was going to play a bourrée by Bach. Julie said P.C.'s party sounded fun, she had never been to an "orgy" before and it sounded interesting, but she had already made a commitment to her parents.

Lana asked if it would be okay if she walked over to the Pendletons' house herself—she, too, had made a commitment, to P.C., and would feel bad about breaking it. Julie said she'd have to check with her parents to make sure. Julie's mother said it would be okay, as long as it was okay with Lana's parents. Lana said of course—her parents were hoping both she and Julie could go to the orgy. Julie's mother said they should call Lana's parents just to make sure. Lana said her parents weren't home; they were at Monastero's. Julie's mother said she was sorry; they couldn't do it without the Rovners' permission. Lana burst into tears. Julie brought Lana a Kleenex, then put a hand on her shoulder and said it would be okay, there would be other orgies; Charades would be fun. Lana said she hated Charades, it was the easiest game she'd ever played, she didn't want to eat whatever funny food the Yings were cooking, and she didn't want to listen to Bach bourrées unless the Chicago Symphony, conducted by Sir Georg Solti, was playing them. Julie said she was sorry Lana felt that way; she was probably just tired and missed her parents. She could still join them for dinner and the recital and Charades, but if she didn't want to, she could just stay up in her bedroom and Julie would come up to check on her later. Lana said no, she'd be all right; she just had to use the phone. Julie told Lana to come downstairs whenever she felt ready.

It took Lana five minutes to invent a reason why she could not attend P.C.'s party. During that time, she rummaged through Julie's belongings, searching for Christian propaganda to explain why Julie was so irritatingly nice. But though Lana found a science lab book, for which Julie had gotten an "Excellent," a series of letters from a pen pal from camp, a photo album with pictures of the Yings' trip to San Francisco to visit what looked like relatives, and drawers filled with underwear and socks, the only evidence she could find of Julie's fanaticism was a copy of the Bible. But there was a bookmark in it, one that said "Love Your Neighbor." This was evidence enough; Julie Ying was one of those people who read the Bible; Julie Ying was creepy and Lana was going to have her revenge. When they played Charades, Lana would act out nothing but Jewish musicals and Jewish celebrities, and during the recital, she would play songs from *Fiddler on the Roof.*

Lana told P.C. she'd gone to a barbecue restaurant with her parents and had been throwing up ever since. She said she was sorry to miss the orgy but hoped they could get together soon. She was thinking of having a couples-only party and maybe they could have an orgy there. P.C. told her not to concern herself; he would be delighted to attend her orgy. After she hung up, Lana skipped downstairs to the dinner table and took small bites of the meal the Ying sisters had cooked, and said "Mmm, delicious" the moment before she demonstratively pushed her plate away. But when it came time for Charades, she was unprepared for her competition, as Mr. and Mrs. Ying and their other daughters Grace, Ethel, and Hazel had no trouble acting out *The Chosen, The Apprenticeship of Duddy Kravitz,* Leonard Bernstein, Moshe Dayan, and *The Golem,* while Lana did not know one single title she was supposed to act out and had to endure Julie whispering hints to her when she tried to pantomime *Portnoy's Complaint.* And after Lana had played "Sunrise, Sunset," and Mrs. Ying crooned "Is this the little girl I carried?" and all the Yings joined Lana for the chorus of "If I Were a Rich Man," Lana wanted nothing more than to go to bed and cry. Which was just as well, because at 12:01 on January 1, 1980, Mr. Ying pointed to his watch and the Yings dispersed to their respective bedrooms.

That night, when they were both in their beds in Julie's room, Julie whispered, "Happy New Year," but Lana didn't respond. She wasn't really asleep, though; she was already planning her couples-only orgy and hoping that Julie wouldn't find a date.

WASSERSTROM

Jill

W hen Jill Wasserstrom agreed to accompany her father for "coffee and" at Gail's house, she knew that Gail lived west of California. But Charlie had neglected to mention that Gail lived in the Funny House. And the moment he stopped the car in front of that house, Jill became quiet. Charlie hoped she might have forgotten how he and Becky used to talk about moving into the Funny House. But both the Wasserstrom girls had encyclopedic memories. And though Jill now had difficulty recalling what her mother looked like and how her mother's voice sounded, she could remember word for word conversations her parents had had: "One day we'll move into the Funny House," "When you get better, we'll move into the Funny House," and, worst of all, the words her mother spoke during the final week of her life when every sentence she uttered seemed designed to survive long after she had passed away: "I guess we'll never get to live in that Funny House."

Avoiding the Funny House had been one of the last remaining rituals from the year after her mother's death. During that period, Jill had devised numerous methods by which she tried to cheat death—she never walked west of California, she skipped over cracks in the sidewalk, she held her breath when she passed cemeteries, and she tried her best to avoid the number 37, her mother's age when she died. She would make certain not to sit in row 37 of movie theaters, shut her eyes tight when her father drove past 37th Street. She was certain she would die on the seventh of March, that like her mother she would be buried against her wishes in Waldheim Cemetery, even though she had requested that her ashes be scattered at the lake. But a year later, when that didn't happen, Jill began to curtail these obsessive and above-all private practices—to have acknowledged them out loud would have been to deprive them of their power and strike her dead on the spot—and became obsessed instead with the futility of existence; she stepped on cracks, counted her steps up to 37, then started back from one. She spent hours walking through cemeteries, carving her initials into headstones with her keys. She crossed California as many times as she could.

She never walked by the Funny House, though. And now, as if in a dream where the boogeyman you thought you'd escaped is standing before you in a room you thought was locked, she was walking to the front door of the Funny House, and what could she say? To admit she was afraid of the house was to either render herself powerless against it or reveal herself as irrational, neurotic. She felt the same emptiness that she felt in her stomach at night when she was in bed alone and everyone else was asleep, when she couldn't turn on the light and read or write because it would wake Michelle, when she couldn't just laugh off statements like "We'll all be dead by then," and write off the creation of the universe as mere stellar accident, and dismiss the *Adon Olam* as a meaningless chant. It was all returning to her now, and somehow she was convinced that the moment she entered the Funny House, the floor would open up and she would tumble into a great, endless abyss and the rest of her life—the little that remained—would be just one long sensation of falling.

But when what stood behind the door on North Shore was not a deep black hole or a disintegrating skeleton but a zaftig woman in a navy-blue flightsuit who offered to take their coats and asked if Jill liked crumble cake and Robert De Niro, Jill didn't feel relieved. Instead, all she felt was that this was proof of the insignificance of things, of the randomness of events. Everything happened by accident. The number 37 was the same as any other. Stepping on a crack was no different from skipping over it. The Funny House looked different from the other houses in West Rogers Park, but that was where the differences ended. One day you lived in a house; the next day someone else lived in it. One day you were here; a hundred years later you wouldn't be. All you could do was take advantage of the time you had and make each moment as significant as you possibly could before it, too, disappeared.

Which was why she was glad she hadn't heard from Muley Wills, wherever he may have been. For though she enjoyed Muley's company when he wasn't being overly possessive, though she enjoyed slowdancing with him and hoped she'd be able to do it again sometime soon—though, please, God, not at the Bat Mitzvah or, rather, please, *whoever,* not at the Bat Mitzvah—such hedonism paled considerably when compared with the prospect of writing a Bat Mitzvah speech that would actually have an impact on her audience. She would spend her New Year's Eve writing a speech that would stir Aunt Peppy and Uncle Dave to the soul, that would make Rabbis Meltzer and Shmulevits realize the fundamental error of their blind support of Zionism, that would make Hillel Levy see that he should be worshiping Julius Nyerere instead of Gene Simmons, that would make Lana Rovner shut up for once and pay attention to something besides herself. If her speech could move one person to donate to a cause they hadn't considered before, make Uncle Dave or Artie Schumer stop saying *schwarz* and give to Operation PUSH, then someplace in private after the Bat Mitzvah she could make out with Muley Wills, as long as he didn't start falling in love with her. For Jill didn't really believe in love; it was all attraction and repulsion, all protons, neutrons, and electrons.

When her father and Gail started watching *Taxi Driver*—Jill had no idea why Gail had chosen a movie that would frighten her father—Jill was able to thank Gail for the crumble cake, get her coat, say Happy New Year, endure her father's embrace and Gail's well-meaning but somehow inappropriate kiss on the cheek, and exit the Funny House as quickly as possible and head home.

No one was driving on California when Jill crossed the street, walking eastward, paying no attention to the cracks in the street or the number of steps she was taking. She was focused entirely on the speech she would give at the Bat Mitzvah; she knew it was the only way she could change people's hearts and minds, the only way she could survive Rabbi Shmulevits's sermon. And though she felt no fear as she walked along the dark, icy sidewalks, she started walking more quickly, and when she got to Maplewood, she ran without stopping until she got to the apartment.

She threw her coat on the floor as she entered her bedroom, grabbed a fistful of paper, and rolled a sheet into her typewriter. She began typing her speech and didn't stop until 11:59. And then, because she thought she should do something festive for the New Year, she went to the refrigerator and took out a can of orange pop. She put on her coat and her shoes and walked out of the apartment, downstairs, and then outside. As 1979 became 1980, Jill shook the can of soda pop furiously up and down, up and down, then ripped off the pop top and watched a powerful stream of orange liquid shoot up in the air over the cars and out onto Campbell Avenue. As the orange pop flowed, she could see past the orange rain and the snow, past the tops of houses. The sky over Warren Park was suddenly illuminated with a shocking burst of shimmering green and white lights. Someone was setting off fireworks atop Mt. Warren as Jill went back inside her apartment to work on her Bat Mitzvah speech.

1980

— — — —

"I had a teacher once who told me that I'd have to learn that there was more to life than hockey. Looking back, I figure, 'What did she know?'"

—MIKE ERUZIONE, CAPTAIN OF THE

1980 U.S. OLYMPIC HOCKEY TEAM

Jill

W hen Jill Wasserstrom told her father that she didn't want a lot of relatives at her Bat Mitzvah, when she told him that she really didn't want
a band, when she told him that she didn't want to invite everyone—or really
anyone—from Hebrew school, when she told him that she didn't want prime rib,
when she told him that she didn't want a sweet table, when she told him that she
didn't want a Bat Mitzvah at all, really, Charlie Wasserstrom assumed it was because she was shy and that she actually wanted all of those things.

In truth, if her mother had been alive, Jill most probably wouldn't have been
having a Bat Mitzvah. She would have left Hebrew school in *Gimel,* right after
Mrs. Veizor told Moshe Cardash no, he couldn't wear a costume on Halloween,
since it was a Christian holiday named after "Saint Halloween." Or if not then,
perhaps in *Dalet,* after Rabbi Grossman whipped a full *tzedakah* box at Hillel
Levy's head, spraying change across the room. And if not then, perhaps in *Heh,*
when Shmuel Weinberg experienced a spiritual crisis during rehearsal for the
Sukkos play, in which Jill had been tapped to play the role of grand inquisitor
Torquemada—Shmuel had accidentally extinguished the synagogue's eternal
light. "What's the big deal?" she'd said when Rabbi Meltzer had tried to comfort
Shmuel. "Nothing's eternal, especially not electricity in this wasteful society."
And if she hadn't dropped out at any of those points, she certainly would
have done so at the Sunday Bat Mitzvah practice in which Rabbi Shmulevits
had handed her the speech she was to deliver. It began with the words "On this
day, as in olden days, it is said that boys became men." The word "boys" had
been crossed out and replaced with "girls." The word "people" was scribbled
above "men."

But since her sister Michelle's Bat Mitzvah had been a rushed affair done on the cheap in Uncle Dave and Aunt Peppy's basement with takeout food on card tables and Blood, Sweat & Tears records on the hi-fi just a few weeks after Becky Wasserstrom died, there was added pressure on Jill to do the Bat Mitzvah the way Charlie Wasserstrom kept saying her mother would have wanted it. Becky Wasserstrom might indeed have wanted the Bat Mitzvah that way—she'd always liked a good party—but if she'd been alive, Jill would have been able to argue with her, to explain that there was no point in this outdated, chauvinistic ritual that was more about status than religion. Since Becky's death, however, her presence had become somehow indelible, her opinions intractable. With all of Charlie Wasserstrom's talk of "what your mother would have wanted," Jill felt obligated to endure the humiliation of a "real classy" Bat Mitzvah and all that entailed, never mind that when it came to Jewish ceremonies, Charlie Wasserstrom had hardly been faithful to Becky's wishes.

In *Dalet* and *Heh* at K.I.N.S., virtually every member of Jill's class was Bar or Bat Mitzvahed. And Jill, because her father had taken so long to put down a deposit, was one of the last. Whenever she returned from one of her classmates' Bar Mitzvahs, her father would ask her how the service had been, what the sermon was like, how the food was at the synagogue, then how the band was at the reception, what sort of music they played, if there was a champagne snowball, what the food was like. Jill's answers were always so similar that Michelle began to exasperatedly supply her sister's responses herself: "The service was long, she didn't listen to the sermon, they served sheet cake and Canadian Club." Then "The band was fine, they played 'Bad, Bad Leroy Brown,' yes, Dad, there's always a champagne snowball, and they served some kind of chicken." The exceptions were Hillel Levy's Bar Mitzvah, held at the Skatium in Skokie, where, after she lost out early in the roller-skating limbo competition, Jill sat in the bleachers reading *A Wrinkle in Time* while Shmuel Weinberg, who claimed he had a sprained ankle but was just afraid of roller-skating, quizzed her about eternity; and Lana Rovner's, where beef tenderloin was served instead of chicken. For most K.I.N.S. students, all the Bar and Bat Mitzvahs blended into one another except for Lana's, which had the best food, and Hillel's, which was the most fun.

Jill was convinced that her Bat Mitzvah wouldn't be any fun. The only chances she would have to survive the event would be to quaff as much grape wine at the synagogue as she could, to make sure she and Muley Wills were out of the ballroom the moment the champagne snowball began, and to substitute the speech she was writing for the boilerplate one Rabbi Mortimer Shmulevits, whom she had nicknamed Rabbi Filibuster, had provided. Over the course of Bat Mitzvah planning, Jill had made several suggestions that she thought would make the experience more palatable—screening Akira Kurosawa's *Throne of Blood*, not inviting any guests. But Charlie, who had never been Bar Mitzvahed—his parents hadn't had the money for that luxury—wouldn't budge. "That sounds nice," he said repeatedly. "But not for a Bat Mitzvah. We can do that for your wedding."

The guest list had quickly mushroomed to eighty people. And worse, seventy-two of them were coming. The only people who Jill didn't mind being on the list were her sister Michelle (who could be condescending, but generally meant well), her father, of course (why else would she be getting Bat Mitzvahed if it wasn't for him?), Gail Schiffler-Bass (who was overbearing but certainly not the "boorish wench" her sister described), Gareth Overgaard (who treated Jill like an adult, talked to her about socialism, and called her "Wasserstrom"), Myra Tuchbaum (who used to babysit Jill and let her stay up late watching black-and-white movies), her kindergarten teacher, Miss Molly O'Meara, and her friend and constant companion Mary Mitchum (who worked as an internist at Holy Covenant), Mel Coleman (who said he hoped there would be some single ladies in attendance), and Muley Wills.

There were a few guests Jill truly despised: Uncle Dave's buddy Artie Schumer, who used to tickle Jill mercilessly and repeatedly cackle "I'm gonna take out your clavicle; this is your clavicle; I'm gonna take it right out," Artie's revolting wife Bess, whom everybody called "Shorty," and their four mean children. Most of the rest of the guests Jill could either take or leave. Those who had RSVP'd included Uncle Dave, Aunt Peppy, and their sons Manny and Arthur, who was already engaged to Debby, a dental hygienist. There were cousins from her father's side of the family whom Jill hadn't seen since her sister's Bat Mitzvah: unscrupulous used-car salesmen like Al Minkoff, Solly Meyer, and their wives and children; somewhat more scrupulous new-car salesmen like Irv Stein and Seymour Bernstein and their wives and their children. Jill never could figure out exactly how they were related to her, or why their wives' occupations were never discussed. Ditto for her great-aunt Beileh, who was exceedingly wealthy for reasons her father never explained. She lived in a gorgeous condominium on Lake

Shore Drive and every Sunday morning would call up the Wasserstrom apartment and ask Jill, "Do you know who this is?" To which Jill would always respond, "I haven't the foggiest, Aunt Beileh." Aunt Beileh never got the joke and always said, "Tell your father it's his aunt Beileh." She would be coming with her son Teddy, who was a writer, which, according to Uncle Dave, made him a *faygeleh*.

And with the exception of Aaron Mermelstein, who hadn't been the same since he'd slammed his head against a desk to see if it would hurt, the entire *Heh* class of K.I.N.S. would be there—dour, mopey Shmuel Weinberg; Lana Rovner, who had told her therapist she found it "chintzy" that Jill hadn't permitted her classmates to bring dates; Dvorah Kerbis, who was as tall as her mother and always wore her outfits; Shoshana Levine, whose brother had recently left a band called Rovner! to join one called Weinstock!; David Singer, a kleptomaniac who swiped chocolate bars and *Playboy* magazines from Sun Drugs; Simon Small, who was addicted to Space Invaders; Bibi Eisenstaedt, who wanted to be a ballerina and whose sister Missy attended Ida Crown; Connie Sherman, who often showed up at Hebrew school wearing suggestive T-shirts that said things like "Mm Mm Good" or "Yes, But Are They Real?" and was routinely sent home to change, as well as Hillel Levy and Moshe Cardash, who planned to leave the Bat Mitzvah early to sneak into a matinee at the Nortown of the movie that Hillel said concerned his future occupation: *American Gigolo*. Some of Dave Wasserstrom's old Jewish West Side buddies would be coming, as would some of Charlie Wasserstrom's new friends from Schiffler Newspapers; several relatives from Jill's late mother's side of the family, most of whom lived in Poughkeepsie, had been invited, but they had written back to say they wouldn't be coming. Jill had also sent invitations to President Carter and Mayor Byrne, figuring that with the former's inept handling of the stalemated Iranian hostage crisis and the latter's increasingly corrupt administration, either could use the PR boost from attending a noncontroversial event such as a Bat Mitzvah. But neither had responded.

On the night before the Bat Mitzvah, Charlie asked nine separate times if he could hear Jill's speech because he wanted to tape-record it, and she knew he wouldn't let up until she had delivered it. But rather than recite the speech she intended to perform in the synagogue, she let him hear the one that Rabbi Shmulevits had provided. Her father loved it. He liked the formality of the introduction—"Ladies and gentlemen, members of the congregation, friends, relatives, and honored guests," even when Jill pointed out to him that there really wouldn't be any honored guests. He liked how Jill stretched her hands out in front of her, exactly as Rabbi Shmulevits had instructed, when she spoke of "entering a community that opens up before me like a great umbrella," an umbrella that was, in fact, *"beeegger"* than the synagogue—she couldn't resist imitating Rabbi Shmulevits's vaguely Yiddish inflection—*beeegger* than our Jewish community, as *beeg* as the history of Judaism itself.

Charlie liked how Jill paused before important questions—"What *ees* a Jew?" "What *ees* a *Baht Meetz-VAH?*" And he was nearly moved to tears when Jill concluded, thanking her parents, her rabbis, her teachers, her family, and her friends, "without whom I would not be here before you, inviting you to join me for sheet cake and Canadian Club." Jill told her father she might add some quotes from Antonio Gramsci, but the speech would be fairly similar. Charlie said she shouldn't add a thing. He asked if she would mind repeating it so he could tape another version. But Michelle, who had wandered in midway through the speech, said grouchily, "You're not gonna make her say that shit again, are you?" Charlie said he supposed not and said Jill should go to bed—she had a big day ahead of her. Michelle, whose moods had been rather foul lately, muttered something about tomorrow being the day when Jill would get both a Torah and a tampon. When Charlie opined that what Michelle had said hadn't sounded very friendly, Michelle suggested he take the matter up with his "girlfriend" and went off to her and Jill's bedroom to smoke.

Since Jill didn't feel like listening to one of Michelle's once-amusing but lately-just-bitter tirades about either Myra's sluttishness, the Mather drama club's intransigence, or the Shiva family's unscrupulousness, she called up Muley to see if he wanted to watch movies or listen to records. But Muley said he was making secret preparations for the Bat Mitzvah and wouldn't be able to see her before the service. Jill said she hoped he wasn't planning to get her an elaborate gift— that would be "weird and uncomfy." Muley quickly said he had to go—he and his mother still had some unpacking and cleaning to do in their new apartment.

It was a slushy Saturday morning when Jill and Charlie arrived at the synagogue. Michelle had said she would meet them there once she'd figured out "which ugly dress" to wear to the "grave ritual." Actually, she had already decided on a shimmering gold sweater dress considerably shorter than those generally worn by members of the K.I.N.S. sisterhood, but she didn't want her father's nervous comments on the appropriateness of the outfit to take away from the enjoyment of titillating Rabbis Shmulevits and Meltzer, making Cantor Fishman—who used to *koochkie* her during *haftorah* practice—feel guilty, and making Gail Schiffler-Bass feel fat.

Behind the glass window of the K.I.N.S. announcement board, the order of the day's events was listed: "Bat Mitzvah: Jill Wasserstrom." Above it, "Sermon, Rabbi Shmulevits: 'I Buried Paul.'" Charlie insisted Jill pose for a picture in front of the announcement board in the black dress she had picked out for the occasion; her navy-blue topcoat covered up the "Better Red Than Dead" button she had pinned over her heart. Already, cars were circling the block in search of parking spaces. Uncle Dave, Aunt Peppy, and their sons were getting out of their Oldsmobile. Lana and Larry Rovner were walking toward them. On the east side of California, Hillel Levy and Moshe Cardash were throwing snowballs at each other, their parkas open, three-piece suits underneath. A Checker taxicab, its flashers on, was double-parked in front of the synagogue, and Jill's cousin Teddy was helping his mother, Jill's great-aunt Beileh, out of it. Charlie, noticing Aunt Beileh and Teddy after he had snapped about half a roll of photographs, said he was going to help Beileh out of the car; Jill said she had to go meet with the rabbi and scurried into the synagogue, just in time to miss having her cheek sloppily kissed by Aunt Peppy, who would call her *"mummeleh,"* just in time to miss having her cheek pinched by Great-aunt Beileh, who would tell her she had a *"shayna punim"* and engage her in conversation about one of her favorite topics—brassieres or TV game shows or Lawrence Welk.

As she entered the synagogue, halfway down the hall, Jill could see Muley Wills—in a light-blue three-piece suit that was just a bit too short for him—gazing at the Tree of Life, whose branches blossomed into tiny white lightbulbs indicating donations in memory of one individual or another. Jill turned hard left toward the washrooms, just across the hall from Rabbi Shmulevits's private chambers, darted into a stall, closed the toilet cover, and sat down on it. The bathroom door opened. Through the space between the stall's wall and the door, Jill could see two of her classmates, Dvorah Kerbis and Connie Sherman, head for the mirror, where they checked their makeup and spritzed themselves with hairspray, Dvorah giggling about an eighth-grader from Jamieson Elementary who had "curly locks," which gave her "chills," while Connie said that any boy who didn't know how to tie his shoes wouldn't be much of a kisser, and didn't she think Muley Wills was H-O-T?

When the bathroom was empty, Jill dashed out of it, practically colliding with Rabbi Shmulevits, who squeezed her shoulder and asked if she was ready for her big day. Jill said she thought so. If she wasn't, it would all be over soon anyway. Shmulevits told Jill that she was one of the most mature Bat Mitzvah girls he'd ever had; he hoped she would make him proud. Jill felt slightly guilty, but less so once she had decided to delete the reference in her speech to the "petrified leaders of this faith," replacing it with an inoffensive statement about alternative fuel sources, such as gasohol. A moment later, she decided to reintroduce the phrase—this after Cantor Fishman emerged from the men's room, sighing loudly with boorish satisfaction, remarking that he felt ten pounds lighter, then asking Jill if she was ready to read her *haftorah* portion; he quipped that it was much easier to memorize than the *whole Torah*. This was it, Jill thought: her moment. After her speech, when Solly Meyer would ask her if she knew of a good bookstore that sold Gramsci's *Prison Notebooks,* when Artie Schumer would say he didn't like *schwarzers* much but that Frantz Fanon was okay by him, when Aunt Peppy would say, "*Mummeleh,* I always thought Emma Goldman was *meshuggeh* until I heard your speech," Jill would know that her entire Hebrew school education would have been worth it.

The service proceeded slowly. Harry Wein, the synagogue president—better known as the "Heysiddownda"—asked everyone in the congregation to "heysiddown." Charlie and Dave Wasserstrom opened the ark and took out the Torah. Jill read her *haftorah* portion in the cantillating, singsong style Cantor Fishman had taught her. Rabbi Shmulevits used a pointer to guide her through the text. Charlie and Dave returned the Torah to the ark. All the while Rabbi Meltzer, who had been awaiting Rabbi Shmulevits's retirement for the past seven years, sat onstage reading a copy of *Rolling Stone,* while Lana Rovner, seated next to her brother, wondered how Jill managed to be so small when her father and her uncle were so big. The congregation said the *Shehecheyanu* as Larry told Lana that he'd be back in a minute, then went over to sit down behind Gareth Overgaard and Michelle Wasserstrom, and asked Michelle how it was going. He said that even though he hadn't been invited to the Bat Mitzvah, he thought it important that all members of the community show their support when someone took the life-changing step of making herself subject to the Ten Commandments. The congregation said the *Ashrai,* and Michelle said she was going outside to smoke. Larry said he would join her, but Michelle refused, saying she couldn't live with herself if she managed to turn a real yeshiva boy away from his faith. The congregation said the *kaddish,* while Larry approached Charlie and Gail and asked if they were enjoying the service. The congregation said the *Adon Olam* with its creepy passage about *"and in the end, when all will cease to be,"* while Jill stared at her shoes, knowing that now the only other part of the service that remained aside from her speech was Rabbi Shmulevits's sermon.

But Jill had nicknamed Shmulevits "Rabbi Filibuster" for a reason, and depending on his mood, which current event had been in the news, or which celebrity had recently died, his sermon could last anywhere from thirty minutes to an hour. And in the previous weeks, not only had vaudevillian Jimmy Durante died—"the only thing bigger than his nose was his heart," Shmulevits opined—but also Paul McCartney had been deported from Japan for marijuana possession.

"I read the news today—oh boy," Shmulevits said, leading into one of the rabbi's typically roller-coastering sermons, which always seemed like some hopped-up beatnik writer's cut-and-paste poetry. Shmulevits used McCartney's lyrics to introduce the topics he wanted to address. "Won't you listen to what the man said?" led to a discussion of young people's failure to adhere to the commandments, "you'd think that people would have had enough of silly love songs" to a passage from the Song of Songs, "take me down to Junior's farm," to a paean to life on a kibbutz.

Forty minutes later, as the speech reached its conclusion, Jill was still looking at her shoes. She did not notice that Hillel Levy and Moshe Cardash had already crept out of the synagogue, en route to the movies; she did not notice that Uncle Dave, Aunt Peppy, and their children were already sampling the ruggelach at the Oneg Shabbat, that Shorty Schumer was pumping change into the hallway pay phone as she talked with her sister in Philadelphia, that David Singer was flooding the Hebrew school toilets with gefilte fish, that Shmuel Weinberg had left the service during the *Adon Olam* because it frightened him, that Larry Rovner— who didn't really view the sermon as a legitimate part of the Sabbath service— had gone to Sun Drugs to buy cigarettes in the hopes that Michelle Wasserstrom might ask if she could bum one.

Only after she had stepped to the podium and thanked the rabbis (one of whom was still reading *Rolling Stone*) and her cantor (who was digging into his ear with a paper clip) did Jill notice that her voice was echoing. And shielding her eyes with her right hand, she could now see that Shmulevits's sermon had just about cleared the synagogue. Charlie and Gail were still listening attentively, as was Muley. Gareth Overgaard seemed dead asleep. Aunt Beileh was still seated, but only because the chairs were comfortable. Jill's kindergarten teacher Miss O'Meara was still there, though her friend Mary Mitchum had fled. Lana Rovner—who knew how rude it was to leave during the service and was terrified someone might see her depart—sat frozen, thinking how much better her Bat Mitzvah had been, how many more people had stayed to listen to her, how many more would come to her couples-only party, how she might let P.C. Pendleton go up her shirt.

And now, as Jill stood there—silent for a few uncomfortable moments—she was unsure whether to admit defeat, scrap the speech she had so assiduously pre-pared, and race through the drivel that Shmulevits had written, or to march for-ward and commit fully to yet another of the acts of futility that defined her existence. Knowing that many great revolutionaries had begun their careers with no organization, speaking to just a few dedicated followers in echoing commu-nity halls, she proceeded.

"On this day, as in olden days," Jill began, "it is said that boys became men, that girls became adult people. Now I stand before you on a threshold." Charlie Wasserstrom nodded. It was the speech he had heard, the one he had taped in his kitchen. Rabbi Shmulevits smiled. It was the speech he had written, the one Lana Rovner had said months before, the one Yehuda Rovner, Chaya Wasserstrom, and Shiffra Tuchbaum had recited several years earlier. Rabbi Meltzer studied the record reviews and tried to find a band he had heard of; it was the same speech he heard every Saturday, butchered by one pubescent after another. Mu-ley Wills sighed. It was the same speech Jill had mocked for months, said she would have shot herself before delivering; he didn't know what great defeat had led Jill to recite it. For some reason, he felt like crying. "I stand before you," Jill said, "on the shoulders of the ancestors who came before me, those brave men and women who allowed me to stand up here and mindlessly parrot a speech that, as far as I can tell, makes no sense whatsoever."

Lana snapped to attention. That wasn't the speech *she* had given; that wasn't the way *she* had said it. Muley grinned, a chill of satisfaction and relief quickly ascending his spine. He loved Jill, loved her passion, her courage, and her guile. She was giving the speech she wanted to give, nobody was noticing, and still she persisted. He wished he could tell her exactly how he felt at this moment, but his gift would speak for him. Charlie Wasserstrom was still nodding; the speech sounded much like the one he'd heard in his kitchen. Rabbi Shmulevits kept smiling. Cantor Fishman kept cleaning his ears. Rabbi Meltzer kept reading his magazine. Nobody except Lana and Muley, and perhaps Gareth Overgaard, noticed anything was amiss when Jill spoke of a community "opening up before [her] like a great umbrella," one that was *"beeg"* enough to encompass more ideas than those contained within an "outdated, mythological document."

"A people united shall never be defeated," Jill declared, pounding the podium with her palm, then added, "I thank you for your attention, I thank Mr. and Mrs. Sweig for the beautiful floral bouquet that decorates our *bima,* I thank Cantor Fishman, Rabbi Shmulevits, the sisterhood, and the men's club, and I look forward to seeing you all at the Oneg Shabbat. Ho Ho Ho Chi Minh." Rabbi Shmulevits shook Jill's hand and thanked her for her "stirring speech." He led the congregation in the *Alenu,* said *amen,* then invited everyone to join the Bat Mitzvah and her family in the next room, where all who hadn't escaped were gathered, pretending they had made it through the entire service.

They were noshing on sheet cake, sipping thimbles of Canadian Club, piling dusty pink and pale green cookies shaped like elm leaves onto paper plates. They were standing in small groups—high school buddies with high school buddies, relatives with relatives, kids with kids. Al Minkoff and Solly Meyer were discussing how to push back odometers on used cars; Danny and Mickey Marks were reminiscing with Sammy Eisen about Eddie Pinsky, who'd been the star of the Manley High School baseball team and had once signed a minor league contract with the White Sox; they were wondering what had happened to him when Hy Saperstein of Saperstein's Caskets broke into the conversation to tell them that he was dead. TB. Shmuel Weinberg was sipping a thimble of grape juice, trying to make it last long enough to determine exactly how he might approach Lana and talk to her. But before Shmuel could invent a suitable pretense, Lana saw her brother Larry enter and bounded over to him.

Larry said he was sorry he'd had to take off—he'd had to get cigarettes. Lana said she thought it was Shabbos. Larry said yeah, but he was out of cigarettes.

Lana said she didn't realize he smoked. Sure, he smoked, he said. Usually not cigarettes, but sometimes, sure. Lana wondered if she should smoke cigarettes. Suddenly, it hit her that in half a year, Larry would be in college and there would be no one left in Chicago whom she could trust. She wondered whether she should spend as many moments as she could with her brother or if she should avoid him and get used to the idea of him not being around. Lana told Larry she wanted to leave, but she first had to congratulate Jill. Larry said he'd wait for her outside. Lana asked if he'd be smoking. "Could be," Larry said.

Jill was standing in a corner of the room, a few paces to the left of her father and Gail, who were snacking on cookies, a few paces to the right of Michelle and Myra, who were pretending that thimbles of grape wine were "double shots" of whiskey as they ordered each other to "cannonball it, cannonball it." She was standing next to Muley, who was telling her that he had dropped his gift off at her apartment but would prefer her not to look at it until after the Bat Mitzvah. But Jill, somehow emboldened by the speech she had given, paid scant attention to Muley. As relatives, classmates, and family friends offered their congratulations, Jill contemplated various subversive acts she could perform at the Bat Mitzvah reception. "Such a beautiful singing voice, *mummeleh,*" Peppy Wasserstrom said. "You and your sister should be on Broadway." Jill smiled painfully, told her thanks very much, all the while wondering what she could do that would be truly subversive. She kept grimacing and smiling as Shorty Schumer smeared her cheek with coral-red lipstick and told her she was "a knockout, a real knockout, kid." Jill weakly accepted an equally weak hug from Lana.

Lana remarked that she and Jill had been the only ones in their class who hadn't "made one screwup" in their *haftorah* portions and said she found it "really interesting" that Jill had veered from the script. Jill said she admired a lot of African and Latin American revolutionaries and wanted to honor their accomplishments. Lana pointed out that she was good friends with an African intellectual who would be serving in the Ivory Coast government. Jill said, "Thank you for coming," then smiled painfully as she endured the congratulations of Shmuel Weinberg, who said, "Nice job," then stood by her for thirty seconds before leaving, unable to say anything more. She continued smiling as Tuffy Sachs asked her if she had any idea how much this spread had cost her dad, smiling as Al Minkoff and Solly Meyer approached her and Solly said when you turn sixteen, make sure your dad doesn't buy you a car from this guy, and Al Minkoff said no, make sure your dad doesn't get you one from this guy, smiling as Hy Saperstein told her he hadn't seen her sister since her mother's funeral and she had sure grown since then.

Jill did smile genuinely when a bleary Gareth Overgaard told her it was a "pretty cool speech, Wasserstrom, but you lost me with that Nkrumah reference," but when she saw Artie Schumer approaching, Jill's mind whirled back to the times he'd tickled her mercilessly and said that because she was laughing she must have been enjoying it, so she dashed in the opposite direction and smacked into her great-aunt Beileh, who asked her if she remembered who she was and when Jill said yes, Aunt Beileh, I do, Aunt Beileh told her she was her great-aunt Beileh. Then Aunt Beileh reminded her that at the reception that night, she would give her more money than any other guest and asked Jill if she was a fan of the game show *Jokers Wild* and what her brassiere size was. And it was at this point that Jill realized exactly what she had to do. For Act II of her Bat Mitzvah subversion, she would take the money she'd receive at her reception and donate it to causes that would horrify those giving it to her. Uncle Dave and Aunt Peppy's money would be signed over to the United Negro College Fund; her car salesmen relatives' money would go to Ralph Nader's consumer watchdog group; Hy Saperstein's money would be donated to a society that supported Jewish cremation. She would have given the money to her father, but she knew he would never accept it, and this was a more meaningful way to part with money from people whose gifts she would have preferred not to accept. She was so enthusiastic about the idea that she asked Gareth for his opinion. He told her the idea was "righteous." But Myra Tuchbaum had a different opinion. "Fuck that," she said. "Buy pot."

Once the crowd had cleared out of the synagogue, Jill thought she might have a few hours to herself before the reception. But Charlie had invited some family and friends over to their apartment for cold cuts. Charlie said it wasn't going to be anything fancy, Jill could wear her overalls if she wanted. Jill would really have preferred reading a book, but then that would mean everyone coming into her room and asking what was wrong, why was she reading, this party was for *her,* this was *her* day, maybe she should have something to eat, maybe that would make her feel better, why didn't she have some cold cuts, maybe some Romanian pastrami, none of them realizing that maybe reading was what she *enjoyed* doing, maybe she felt *uncomfortable* chattering with relatives with whom she had nothing in common. And then, as she exited the synagogue with Muley, expecting to see the synagogue steps empty—but no, all the Manley High buddies and relatives were still out there, reminiscing, commiserating—the question arose as to whether she should insist that Muley accompany her or brave her fate alone. Selflessly, she chose the latter. She asked Muley if he would need a ride to the reception. Muley said no, he'd be coming with Mel. Jill said fine, then she'd see him over there. Muley reminded her again not to look at the gift he had gotten her; he wanted them to open it together. Jill said okay, she'd see him at the hotel.

But after a half hour had passed at the Wasserstrom apartment and Jill had run out of things to tell Rabbi Meltzer—who had informed Jill that he was really hoping to devote more time to his music—and when shocking Aunt Peppy by telling her that she thought she would join the Socialist Party ceased being amusing, Jill found herself sneaking down the hall to her room, where she closed the door so she could privately inspect Muley's Bat Mitzvah gift.

The gift came in two cardboard boxes: one about two feet high and wrapped in cellophane tape; the other, similarly wrapped but smaller—it looked as if it might contain a stack of record albums. Muley had asked her not to open the gift, but she was curious. As a general rule, she didn't like gifts—if she didn't like what she received, she felt guilty for being selfish or rude; if she did like something, she felt guilty that a material object could make her happy. Always, she felt guilty that someone had spent their time and money on someone who didn't like gifts.

She started with the larger box first. She tried to lift it onto her bed, but it was too heavy; the bottom started to rip the moment she grabbed it. Instead, she used a key to cut through the tape and ripped open the top flaps of the box. Inside, there was an aquamarine movie projector, its arm sticking out of a white plastic shopping bag. She reached inside the box and lifted the projector, stumbling slightly under its weight as she placed it atop her desk. She uncoiled the power cord and plugged it into a socket. She lowered the pickup arm of the projector and fished the pickup reel out of the box and affixed it. She twisted the knob to its Forward position and the machine hummed to life, the lamp of the projector illuminating a rectangle of light on her wall below the picture of Ayatollah Khomeini, a slight scent of burnt dust rising from the lamp's housing, the pickup reel twirling like a propeller. She twisted the knob back to Off.

Jill turned her attention to the second package and heard a tin clank as she sat down on her bed with it, placing it atop her knees. Opening that box, she found three metal film canisters. The first two were labeled in black marker *"Sherlock Jr.,"* her favorite film. The third was labeled "To Jill." Jill made sure her bedroom door was shut tightly, that her shutters were drawn, that the room was as black as it could be in the bright winter afternoon.

She opened the canister and removed a fairly light reel—the film was only about an inch and a half thick on it. She attached it to the projector, twisted the knob to Forward, and threaded it through. There was a flickering and a clattering that transformed into a soothing whir as the pickup reel grabbed the film, jittering slightly, then smoothing out. A bright white rectangle on the wall was interrupted by a vertical orange-red stripe that shimmied upon it and was then replaced by a ten, a nine, an eight, down to a three. Two short beeps were heard and then words appeared on the screen, white type on a black background: *"'It almost feels like we're in a movie,'* Jill Wasserstrom, 1979," and then the title, again plain white on black:

TO JILL

A film

by

Muley Scott Wills

The title faded to black, and music faded in slowly—Billy Joel: "The Stranger." And from out of the black appeared an image of wet dirt, nothing more than that for a moment or two, then an iridescent green sprout pushing slowly through the dirt—a bud appearing at the top, then blossoming into a pink rose opening and filling the screen. Then the rose sprang loose from the dirt, into the air, rising, rising above a model of a city—cars zipping back and forth on its streets, night, then day, night, then day, yellow streetlights turning on, then off, on, then off, then the rose rising against a background of blue sky and white cottonball clouds, the rose turning ninety degrees, flying on its side, its leaves flapping like wings. The rose growing larger, larger, the leaves becoming wings now, the stalk of the rose growing fat, slowly turning into the body of a green airplane zooming through clouds, rosebuds for wheels, a flower for its nose, and then white smoke trailing out of the back of the rose airplane, first just puffs. Then the airplane turning and dipping, doing loop-de-loops, threading itself through the white puffy smoke that was now beginning to spell something out, an "I," then an "L," then an "O," then a "V." Jill knew what it was spelling but she remained transfixed, a strange vibration resounding over her heart as the plane kept twisting and turning, zigzagging against the beautiful blue sky. An "E," then a "Y," then an "O," then a "U."

"I LOVE YOU," the rose plane spelled out—"I LOVE YOU, JILL WASSERSTROM." Then, the plane picked up speed and flashed across the screen leaving nothing but blue sky and a trail of white letters fading slowly into blue, then into black, Billy Joel still singing as the words "written, produced, and directed by Muley Scott Wills" appeared on the screen. The song faded out and the screen faded to black. And for some reason she could not identify, Jill felt a gulp in her stomach that she wanted to push back down. She inhaled sharply, shut her eyes tightly, and twisted the projector knob quickly from Forward to Reverse so she could watch those words sucked back into the tail of the airplane, so she could watch the plane fly backwards through a sky devoid of letters, then the plane shrink into a stalk, transform itself back into a rose dropping downward until it was nothing but a sprig of green hiding back down below the earth. And soon the image on the wall was nothing more than a white rectangle, and there was no music anymore, just the *fft fft fft* of the film reel whipping around and around. And around and around.

The Bat Mitzvah reception was held in the ballroom on the second floor of the Sovereign Hotel. There were nine tables, between seven and nine chairs around each of them—white tablecloths, white napkins, and breadbaskets on each table. Four tables were on one side of a rectangular dance floor, five tables on the other. At the top of the dance floor, the Brenner Brothers five-piece band. It was thought that there were five Brenners and that they all played together. In truth, there were only three—Morrie, Fred, and Stu—and each fronted a different band composed of four other musicians who went by the name of Brenner, so that on one night during a particularly busy Bar and Bat Mitzvah season, fifteen Brenners could be playing "Hava Nagilah" simultaneously in three different places. Nobody particularly enjoyed the Brenners' music. But few West Rogers Parkers—with the exception of the Rovners, who had hired the Lindsay Brothers (which was actually just Morrie Brenner using a different surname to play *goyishe* weddings, where he charged more)—would have chosen a different band. Their limping rendition of "Spanish Eyes" was as much a part of West Rogers Park Bat Mitzvah tradition as a drunk uncle saying the *hamotzi* over the challah.

Before she had watched Muley's short film, Jill had been thankful that Muley would be at the reception to protect her from the cheek pinching and congratulations of relatives and family friends. Now, as she rode the Sovereign elevator to the top floor, hoping that she might get stuck along the way, she was dreading Muley's arrival at the reception as much as anybody else's. Perhaps even more. Because although 49 percent of her thought Muley's movie was more beautiful than anything anyone had ever given her, the images more beautiful than any she had ever seen, so much so that when she saw the rose airplane flying before her, she had felt like falling into Muley's eyes and flooding him with her tears, 51 percent of her was disturbed by the film, frightened by it, and even a bit angry, for implicit in the generous gift seemed to be an equally selfish demand.

Muley was in love with her—she had known that already, really. But saying it ruined everything. She thought as she rode the elevator down, stopping on every floor—for she had pushed every button—that they could have gone on for years just as they had, if he had just kept those feelings to himself, saved them for the day when they would both be going to different colleges and it wouldn't matter anymore. More than ever, Jill wanted to be alone, but when the elevator doors opened on the second floor and she walked out, she found herself standing in a crowd of guests converging on the ballroom.

Perhaps the worst thing was that because she was feeling lonely and miserable, sadder than she'd felt in years, Jill felt obligated to feign happiness. It was all well and good to sit off in a corner with a Jane Austen paperback and tell all those shallow people who didn't understand the difference between being alone and being solitary that no, she wasn't sad, no, she didn't need any company, thank you very much. But when she was actually feeling sad and alone, she knew the words would come out differently, because she would be lying. And she hated the idea that people would see her sad, on the verge of inexplicable tears, and have all their clichéd notions of her confirmed. What she wanted to do right now more than anything was to find Muley and stay close by him for the entire evening; the discussion of that beautiful-awful lovely-miserable film could wait for another time. But Muley, who was walking up the Sovereign's dirty red carpeted steps with Mel Coleman, had already caught a glimpse of Jill's face, and in that glimpse he had seen that she had changed somehow that day, as if she had been defeated, her eyes unnaturally large as if trying to keep herself from blinking, a half-smile on her face like a mask. And in that glimpse he knew that Jill had already seen his film, became angry with her for watching it, angry with himself for having made the film at all, angry that he hadn't made a better film, a smarter film. He barely registered when Mel, at the top of the steps, told him, "Single ladies—twenty-one to thirty-five. Be on the lookout, son."

As Jill entered the ballroom, Morrie Brenner was singing "Back Door Man," and already Mickey Marks, Solly Meyer, Al Minkoff, and Tuffy Sachs had descended upon her to give her envelopes, Mickey Marks saying, "Use it in good health, dear," and Solly Meyer pointing to Al Minkoff, saying, "Open his up right now; make sure he put somethin' in it," and Solly thumbing back to Al, saying, "Cash that before this schmuck goes broke," and Jill saying, "Thanks, thanks; glad you could make it" more times now than she ever had. She was only slightly cheered by the fact that the money she was receiving would soon be in more worthy hands.

Charlie and Gail had spent many difficult hours determining seating arrangements. Jill would sit with the two of them at Table 1, along with Dave and Peppy, Aunt Beileh and her son Teddy, and Artie and Shorty Schumer. Michelle would sit with Myra and Gareth at the "young singles' table"—Table 2. Muley and Mel were also assigned to this table. There was a table of Manley High buddies, a table of car salesmen and spouses, a table of synagogue clergy and their families, a table of Hebrew school students, and several tables of mismatched guests.

During the band's first set, Uncle Dave's rushed *hamotzi,* the serving of the three-bean salad, and Charlie's toast, Jill did not once lay eyes on Muley, and she realized that what she had usually found to be a chaotic, jam-packed schedule of events at every other Bar and Bat Mitzvah she had attended actually served a higher purpose—the idea seemed to be to keep people constantly moving, getting up, sitting down, going to the dance floor, getting off of the dance floor, so that they wouldn't have time to argue. Or at least that's how it worked up until Morrie Brenner hollered, "And now the moment we've all been waiting for: The Bat Mitzvah girl will have the first dance with her father."

Until that moment, events had progressed with sufficient speed to keep Jill's mind off of her inner turmoil. There had been more congratulations, more envelopes. Jill's father had clinked his glass and stood up, his cheeks flushed and his belly swelling more with pride than with recently ingested carbohydrates. He said that he wanted to be the last member of his family to have come of age without having been Bar Mitzvahed and invited everyone to join him at the Bar and Bat Mitzvahs of Jill's children. Jill wondered if her father really expected her to have children and to raise them up indoctrinated in any religion. And if through some crazed circumstance she did do all that, did he really expect she'd invite these people? Still, she clapped for her father, though she didn't give him a sloppy kiss on the cheek as Gail did.

But then came the daddy-daughter dance. Jill submitted to this humiliating, vaguely creepy ritual, waltzing with her father as Morrie Brenner sang, "Isn't it rich? Isn't it queer?" Charlie had always been quite a dancer, and even though Jill didn't know any dance other than the rocking-boat she and Muley had performed in her bedroom to "The Stranger," following his steps was remarkably easy, like swimming through the ocean on the back of a dolphin. Charlie told her she'd been the most beautiful girl in the synagogue and that she had made her mother proud. Then the music switched, the drums kicked in stronger and faster, Morrie Brenner sang "Makin' *Vhoopie* Every Night," and Charlie boogied over to Table 2, extended his hand to Michelle, and led her out onto the dance floor. Jill knew she was supposed to pick another partner, but she walked right past Muley's table to the Hebrew school table and asked Shmuel Weinberg to dance. Shmuel blushed, stood up, made a step toward her, then ran for the doors, saying he'd forgotten something at home and had to make a phone call. Hillel Levy said Moshe Cardash would dance with her. Moshe said *what*? Jill tried not to cringe. Hillel said what was wrong with Moshe didn't Jill like dancing with short people, was she prejudiced or something? There was no way to refuse, so Jill walked to the dance floor with Moshe as Lana Rovner wondered why Jill wasn't dancing with Muley and was Jill about to become a slut like her sister, who was gleefully dancing with her father, Charlie spinning her around, dipping her, Michelle laughing as Mel Coleman, back at Table 2, observed Jill dancing with Moshe and asked Muley if he was "gonna take that shit." Muley said it was a free country, people could do what they wanted. He fiddled with his salad. Mel said Muley had better either get up and dance with his old lady or find another lady to make his old lady jealous, like that Connie girl who had been eyeing him all night. Muley said he wouldn't do anything of the sort. Mel asked Muley if he wanted him to slap him around. Muley said fine, he'd go up to the dance floor, but if Jill didn't want to dance with him, Mel would have to leave him alone.

Muley reached the dance floor just in time to see Jill dancing with Moshe Cardash with all the enthusiasm of a dime-a-dance girl near the end of her shift at a USO hall and just in time to see Charlie doing the Tango Hustle with Michelle as Gail Schiffler-Bass stepped onto the dance floor, tapped Michelle on the shoulder, and asked if she could cut in.

"What?" Michelle asked.

Gail asked again if she could cut in—Michelle and her father had been dancing for a while and maybe she wanted to take a break. Michelle stopped dancing and stared contemptuously at Gail. No, she said, she didn't want to take a fucking break, how long had she been dancing anyway? Ten minutes? How old did Gail think she was? Forty-five? "Can you cut in?" Michelle scoffed. She'd cut into their entire fucking lives; now she wanted to cut in on the dance floor too? Charlie told her to take it easy. No, she wouldn't take it easy, Michelle said. Why did everyone always tell her to take it easy? Fat people could take it easy; why did she have to? Gail said maybe she should calm down. Jill stopped dancing with Moshe and went over to try to break up the argument, but her words were powerless. "Look," she said as Charlie told Michelle that she should apologize to Gail. "Listen," Jill said as Michelle said she wouldn't apologize to that cow cunt. "Come on," Jill said as Gail reminded Michelle that she wasn't one of her little high school girlfriends, she could stick up for herself and Michelle wasn't going to bully her out of having a relationship with her father because she was too caught up with being "Daddy's little girl" to see that maybe her father had needs too. "Stop this," Jill said as Michelle told Gail that her sister's Bat Mitzvah was no place to start discussing her father's *sexual needs,* that was just fucking disgusting. Lana came over to watch, always enjoying arguments that her family wasn't part of. Charlie told Michelle it was enough, he'd had enough, as Morrie Brenner instructed his band to up the volume and started crooning "Raisins and Almonds," and Gail told Michelle that if she wasn't mature enough to listen, then maybe she should leave. Charlie said it was enough, as Michelle told Gail she wouldn't do anything Gail said, so if she told her to leave, then she'd stay. Gail said fine, then why didn't she stay? All right, Michelle said, she was leaving. Jill said fuck this and stormed off past Muley, not even noticing him standing there as she went to the bar and ordered a whiskey sour. Muley followed slowly behind her.

"Michelle," Charlie called after his daughter. "Michelle!" Gail told him to let her go. Teenagers were like that. He had to let her be that way; she'd come around. Come on, she said, why didn't they dance? Charlie said he didn't feel like dancing; he wanted to see how his daughter was. Gail said she was sure she was fine, why didn't they dance? With the whole *mishpacha* looking at them, Charlie said okay. Morrie Brenner yelled into the microphone that he wanted to see all the kids on the dance floor, all the kids; it was time for the champagne snowball.

Michelle had already gotten her coat. She was standing at her table, her entire body pulsating with ferocious energy. She had her hand on the back of Mel Coleman's chair. She asked what he was doing the rest of the evening. Mel said he thought he was attending a Bat Mitzvah. Michelle said yeah, he could do that, or they could go get a room and screw. Mel said he didn't think they'd been formally introduced. Michelle said her name was Michelle Wasserstrom; now did he want to go get a room and screw? Mel said his name was Melvin and he usually liked to begin his dates with a bit of polite conversation before he got down to business. Michelle said she wasn't in the mood for polite conversation. Mel asked how old Michelle was. She said she was thirty-two. Mel laughed as Myra Tuchbaum said no, actually Michelle was almost seventeen. Michelle told Myra she could go fuck herself—she was the last person who should have been talking about people's ages, screwing Sterndick every night in the JCC pool. Myra said that was different, she was in love with Dougie. Michelle said she'd never realized Myra was so fond of animals. Gareth said Michelle should calm down and stop being a bitch. Michelle said she was sick of everybody telling her to calm down, she wasn't being a bitch, and she'd be happy to screw Gareth if he hadn't already told her he was gay; Gareth said he'd never said he was gay, just that he didn't know deep down if he was or he wasn't and that he really didn't think that deep down anyone knew one way or the other—gender preference was just a societal construct. Jesus Christ, Michelle said, why did everything have to turn into a fucking political discussion; all she wanted to do was get laid and all she wanted to know was if Mel was going to join her or not. Mel said maybe she should give him a call in four or five years. "JESUS CHRIST," Michelle shouted. "DOESN'T ANYBODY WANT TO GET LAID ANYMORE?" Morrie Brenner repeated that he wanted all the kids on the dance floor for the snowball. Come on, Michelle said to Gareth and Myra, she was going to smoke pot, were they coming or not? Mel said if they were smoking reefer, he'd join them. No, Michelle said, reefer was only for people who wanted to get laid.

Jill was at the bar, downing a whiskey sour. She wondered why people liked drinking so much; it just gave her a headache. Lana asked her if anything was wrong, if there was anything she could do. Jill told Lana to mind her own business and not to revel in others' misfortunes. Lana said she was just trying to help but if Jill didn't want her help, that was fine and didn't she know she was too young to be drinking alcohol? Jill ordered another drink as Lana scurried off to tell her table of Jill's rudeness as Muley hesitantly approached Jill, wondering if he should speak to her or whether it would be better to just leave her be.

The sour mix had collected at the bottom of Jill's glass and was slithering down her throat like sweet, wet dirt when Morrie Brenner repeated that he wanted all the kids on the dance floor. Muley stood behind Jill and asked if she was okay. Jill said she guessed so. She didn't turn around at first, but then she slowly faced him. The look in Jill's eyes suggested she'd been betrayed—by him or someone else, Muley was uncertain. Muley said he was sorry he'd given her his film. Jill said he shouldn't be sorry; she was sorry she'd watched it. Muley said he hoped they could still be friends. Jill said she was sorry, she just didn't feel like talking right now. Muley said that was okay, he understood, he'd leave her alone. Jill asked if he was mad at her. Muley said no. He asked if she was mad at him. Jill said no, just confused. Muley said okay, maybe they'd talk some other time. Jill said yeah, maybe they would.

Which, Muley thought as he edged slowly away from her, was the worst thing she could have said; maybe they would also meant maybe they wouldn't. So Muley said all right, he'd talk to her whenever, and walked across the dance floor and out toward the coat check, not even noticing as a young girl's voice—definitely not Jill's—called after him. He did not even deign to look at the circle of kids in the center of the ballroom, as Jill was being summoned to pick a partner, a *partner,* to dance with and kiss when Morrie Brenner unctuously intoned the words "champagne snowball."

It was like being forced to choose your method of execution: death by Moshe Cardash, death by Hillel Levy, death by Shmuel Weinberg, or death by David Singer. This would be her future—a world full of choices, all of them wrong. She looked for Muley to see if he might still dance with her. But he was already gone.

Just blocks from the hotel, Muley was walking along the beach where the wind, the lake, and the snow had formed miniature ice caves, stalactites dripping down on the sand from their roofs. He was thinking of a movie he might make, a movie that would be far better than the last one. It would begin with a stone thrown into water, but the water would turn out to be ice and when it hit the ice, the stone would shatter into a hundred fragments that would ascend into the sky like rain falling backwards into clouds, and the clouds would spin around so fast that a hole would form in their center and it would suck up everything in its midst—flowers, trees, plants, people, all spinning around inside of the cloud, all of them looking down and seeing the earth below them. Then the earth being sucked up by the cloud as if it were nothing more than a marble, the earth spinning around in the cloud. But he wouldn't be able to watch that movie after he'd made it. The projector he'd salvaged for Jill was at her apartment, and the only thing that would be worse than not having that projector would be her giving it back to him. He'd send the film to her, then, he thought. And if there were others he wanted to make, he'd send those to her too.

He was thinking about what would happen to the earth once it was sucked up into the spinning white cloud when someone called out, "Hey, Wills." Gareth Overgaard, bundled up in a black ski cap and a black down coat worn over his suit was sitting on a rock, nursing a bottle in a paper bag while Myra Tuchbaum, leaning against the rock, passed a joint to Michelle Wasserstrom.

"Bat Mitzvahs suck," Michelle said. She took a hit, then asked Muley if her sister was giving him a hard time. Muley said nothing. Michelle said she liked her sister, but dating her would always be a pain in the ass. She advised Muley to date exclusively sluts; virginal girls were far less fun.

"Amen, you little bitch," Myra said.

"You said it, you big fat cunt," said Michelle. The two of them laughed and embraced.

"Pass that joint over to Wills, either one of you bitches," Gareth said.

After the reception—after Jill had let Shmuel kiss her cheek during the champagne snowball and Lana had said, "Gross. I bet she likes giving hickeys and letting guys go up her shirt," and Connie Sherman said, "Yeah, who doesn't?"; after Morrie Brenner stopped singing "Squeeze Box" at exactly 11 P.M. and hotel employees began removing tablecloths and stacking chairs; after Charlie had dropped Gail off at her house and went out driving to see if he could find Michelle—Jill Wasserstrom sat alone at her kitchen table with a stack of envelopes.

She ripped one open—the return address was marked "Eisen." A piece of typing paper had been folded twice. On it was written "Happy Bat Mitzvah, Jill. Love, Sammy and Carol Eisen." Inside, to Jill's dismay, there was a $50 State of Israel savings bond. Suddenly panicked, she opened another envelope—"Happy Bat Mitzvah, Jill. Love, Danny and Mickey Marks"—with another $50 bond. She opened another envelope—another bond. Another envelope—another bond. And another. When she had opened every single envelope, she had only come up with $100 cash, all in wrinkled $10 bills from K.I.N.S. classmates, two tickets to a science fiction play called *WARP!* and a playing card with a joker on it and an I.O.U. from Aunt Beileh. The remaining approximately $3,000 was all in bonds that would not mature for five years, and it seemed wasteful and irresponsible to Jill to cash them in now. Whatever organizations would have been the beneficiaries of Jill's charity would have to wait until at least 1985.

R O V N E R

Lana

A fter she had finally consented to see Dr. Cheryl Mandell, the therapist who worked across the hall from Ellen Rovner, Lana was chagrined to realize that Mandell had little interest in any of the issues she wanted to discuss. Lana had tried to talk to her about P.C. Pendleton, about the classmates who resented her, about the orgy she wanted to host. But all Dr. Mandell wanted to do every Friday after school was to put Lana on a scale, then show her pictures of women in fashion magazines and ask her if she thought they looked fat. After which she would press Lana for details about what she characterized as Lana's parents' "imminent divorce." Lana wasn't particularly interested in this topic, but since Dr. Mandell asked her about it incessantly, Lana began providing details about the end of Michael and Ellen Rovner's short-lived reconciliation and ever-more-frequent arguments, not knowing that Cheryl Mandell's interest was based on the fact that Ellen had once shown her a picture of her husband and she had found him quite sexy.

Lana's bedroom was located directly above the kitchen, and as she told a riveted Dr. Mandell on one particular Friday in January, if she put one ear to the carpet and covered her other ear with her hand, she could hear just about every word of her parents' arguments. Recently, Lana had overheard her father apologize to her mother, saying he was sorry he hadn't taken an equal part in bringing up the children, and that if her mother ever thought he wasn't doing his fair share, she should tell him. Her mother responded that she didn't think it was her responsibility to tell him what was and what wasn't his fair share, and if he had to be told, maybe that was part of the problem. He apologized again, said he wasn't perfect; there were bound to be times when he failed and he wanted to be made aware of them. Lana's mother said she wasn't paid to be his therapist, that if she were, she didn't know how many sessions and how many thousands of dollars it would take to bring every single one of his failings to his attention. Lana's father said well, they had time; they had all the time in the world to fix things and why didn't they start now? Lana's mother said it was too late for that; their marriage was "finite." Lana's father said all things were finite; their lives were finite too. Yes, Lana's mother said, but not as finite as their marriage. Her father asked her where she was going. To get the *Nortown Leader* real estate section, she said; she wanted to get a sense of what one-bedroom apartments cost. This was the sort of thing that Lana spent her nights listening to, she told her psychologist, wishing the divorce would finally happen so she could get some sleep.

At school, the lack of sleep had begun catching up to Lana. She routinely fell asleep while futilely attempting to make her way through *The Chronicles of Narnia* during Sustained Silent Reading (SSR) in Ms. Powis's homeroom. During a unit on gases in Science class, her hair caught fire in a Bunsen burner and she didn't notice until Mr. Maki danced and jumped around the room like a foiled Rumpelstiltskin, shouting, "I smell burning hair! I smell burning hair!" before swatting her with rags. The only classes where Lana maintained her previous level of performance were Tallying (Ms. Powis thought it would be instructive for students to discover how big the number one million was by having them make tally marks for forty-five minutes each day and see how many they could make by the end of the semester) and French. As for gym, swimming, and recess, Lana would often feign headaches and go to the nurse's office to lie down.

Going to the nurse's office, though, was often as much a form of self-preservation as it was a method of catching up on her rest. Miss Kryskow, the school nurse, told her it was "hormones, only hormones" when she would complain, but to Lana, recess was still mortifying. During the winter months, recess meant ducking out of the way of dodge balls that Jamie Henderson and some of the tall, scary eighth-podders whipped across the gym. Recess meant Jonathan Wolk and the rest of the sweaty, basketball-dribbling boys playing four-on-four, shirts versus skins, bumping into anyone who got in their way. Recess meant Earl Weith, Todd Taylor, and Megan Knox taking Earl's three-foot bong, nicknamed Big Red, and firing it up underneath the bleachers. Recess invariably culminated with a chant of "Fight, fight, fight, fight," as when Greg Sonada threw chemicals he had stolen from the science lab onto Edgar Barnes and Edgar gave Greg a grundy, then beat him over the head with a yardstick. In the sixth pod, Lana might have gone to the principal's office to tell on Earl Weith and Todd Taylor for smoking pot or Greg Sonada for stealing chemicals. In the fifth pod, she had grown her fingernails long to scratch boys when they tried to grab at her breasts and Jamie Henderson chanted at her, "Sprout and blossom, Lana. Sprout and blossom!" But now everyone had gotten too big to scratch and she didn't want to have acid thrown on her, so she would visit Miss Kryskow in the nurse's office. She preferred to spend as much time as she could with adults who were obligated to talk to her, as opposed to kids her age who weren't and, often, didn't. Earlier in the year, Mary Beth Wales had issued a "silent treatment" order toward Lana after Lana had told Ms. Powis that Mary Beth hadn't been studying times tables in the quiet study room but had actually been reading aloud from a book about a boy who named his penis. The order was suspended when Lana gave Mary Beth $3 in quarters, but the suspension of the order didn't mean that anyone talked to Lana, just that they weren't forbidden from doing so.

Lana figured all that would change with the party she was planning to throw at her parents' house—The Not Valentine's Day Couples-Only Orgy: The Official Orgy of the 1980 Olympics. Not that she necessarily wanted her classmates' approval or affection. She thought that Earl Weith, Megan Knox, and Todd Taylor were burnouts, that Greg Sonada was a crazy freak, that Mary Beth Wales was a bitch, that Jamie Henderson was a cackling idiot, that Steve Orenstein and Alice Benske were dorks, that Jonathan Wolk was a dumb jock, that Roz Vernon and Edgar Barnes were only at Baker because they were on scholarship. Once, Lana had actually had close friends at Baker, but one had moved to North Carolina, one had transferred to the Latin School, and Abby Fishman, who had been Lana's best friend for three short months during the third pod—they had worn the same outfits, played Chase before school, and slept over at each other's houses every other weekend until Abby told Lana that her mom found it "weird you're always copying me," after which the two barely spoke to each other again—moved at the end of her one year at Baker to Phoenix with her family.

Four and a half years later, almost everybody who was still at the school had grown tired of one another. There were school assemblies every other month and every assembly provided the same entertainment. Greg Sonada would play Scott Joplin's "Maple Leaf Rag" on the piano. Lana would play "Nadia's Song." Miss Koroll, the Math teacher, would lead a singalong of "Don't Stop Thinking About Tomorrow." Mary Beth Wales would show slides of her horse, Mr. Blackie. The first- and second-pod kids would sing "Hey, Ho, Nobody Home"; the third- and fourth-podders would sing "Come Saturday Morning"; the fifth- and sixth-podders would sing the theme to *Billy Jack* ("One Tin Soldier"); and the seventh and eighth pods would sing "Top of the World." There was some excitement when it was discovered that the recently arrived Megan Knox was taking modern dance classes, but the third time she had danced solo to "Lorelei" by Styx, even the boys most challenged by puberty had lost interest.

But if the Couples-Only orgy wouldn't allow Lana to see her classmates with new perspective, at least it could change her image in their eyes. If everyone saw her with handsome, smart, wealthy, and sort-of-famous P.C. Pendleton, they'd give her the respect she deserved and Mary Beth would stop telling her she was a loser because she hadn't had sex. After all, she knew perfectly well that twelve- and thirteen-year-olds didn't have sex; they were just boasting.

Lana figured she wouldn't have sex until she was at least twenty-one, she was a senior at Dartmouth, and was engaged either to P.C.—who was planning to go either there or Princeton—or someone who had all of P.C.'s attributes but happened to be Jewish too. It was not the mechanics of sex that repulsed her the most. Nor was it the idea of someone touching her body, although she was certainly self-conscious about it and had been appalled when she had first menstruated the previous year and Edgar Barnes had pointed to the stains on her white painter's pants, laughed loudly, and shouted, "That's blooded; that is *blooded.*" No, the main difficulty she had with sexual congress before the age and circumstances prescribed was that it was low-class. Sex in high school was for hillbillies, it was for people who smoked pot, it was for people who lived east of California, east of Western, especially. Jewish people didn't do it; people who lived in houses didn't do it, unless those houses happened to be bungalows; for a Jewish girl who never smoked pot and lived in a house west of California, it was out of the question. And she knew that for P.C., it would be out of the question too, which was why she was glad he would be her date for her orgy.

The problem, as Lana had told Dr. Mandell, was that her mother had declared that she could not have the Couples-Only orgy at all. And further, Ellen Rovner—who Lana had assumed would rubber-stamp her proposal—gave no reason for her refusal. When Lana had introduced the topic at one of the family's twelve-minute sit-down dinners, her mother had just said "No, nothing doing" and stood up to take the remaining pizza off the table and hurl it into a trash bag. Lana tried all her usual techniques: a fit, a pathetic pouting demonstration, bargaining, bribery, and outright lies. None proved effective. Even when Lana asked if her mother would let her have the party if she gained five pounds, Ellen Rovner said no, absolutely not. At the end of one of Lana and Dr. Mandell's sessions, Dr. Mandell asked her if she thought the reason her mother wouldn't let her have the party was that she thought that P.C. didn't care about Lana, that he was just using her and would make her do things, maybe sexual things, she'd later regret. Lana said that was ridiculous; she and P.C. had only Frenched once and that had been for five seconds and both of them had agreed it was icky. Which showed a certain lack of perception on Lana's part, since that had been exactly Ellen Rovner's reasoning when she and Dr. Mandell had discussed the matter over lunch.

Lana's luck changed, however, one Wednesday when her mother called to say she would be out looking at real estate. That night over dinner picked up from the new Brown's Chicken on Devon, Lana remarked that her father had purchased dark instead of white meat, a symbol of the fact that she never got what she wanted anymore. Her father said that was a terrible thing to say; as far as he was concerned, she could have anything. Then why, Lana asked, after doing everything asked of her, was she still not allowed to have her party? Lana's father said she should really take that matter up with her mother. Lana said she'd done that, but now she wondered if the reason her mother didn't want her to have the party was that she was afraid she'd wind up having sex with P.C., even though they had only Frenched twice and both had agreed it was icky.

Michael Rovner practically spat up his potato salad. He had never discussed sex with his daughter, didn't even want to fold her underwear, didn't want to look at it, really. So rather than confront the issue, he said that her mother didn't think anything of the sort, which was why he would give his permission for Lana to have the party on two conditions: one, that he and Ellen chaperone the event; and two, that Lana get a 20 on her final creative report. Lana thanked her father, asked if he needed help throwing out plates, then went up to her room to start work on her invitations.

Lana was almost done using a burnishing instrument and a plastic sheet of rub-off letters to write "You and a guest are cordially invited to attend the official couples-only party of the 1980 Olympics"—P.C. had advised her not to use the word "orgy" on the invitation—when she heard the argument downstairs. At first, all she could hear were muffled voices, but then she put her ear to the carpet. Her father said he didn't want to deprive his daughter of her right to enjoy herself, particularly with all the pressure she'd been under lately; besides, he had suggested the two of them chaperone the event. "Chaperone?" her mother asked. She wasn't going to chaperone; did he want to be responsible when somebody's mother called the next day and asked why her son's clothes smelled like smoke and beer? Michael said he trusted his daughter; it wasn't going to be pot and beer, for Christ's sake, she was twelve—everyone was just going to dance and play Charades. *"Charades?"* Ellen asked. Well, if that's all it was going to be, then he certainly wouldn't need help chaperoning; she would go to Lake Geneva for the weekend with a carload of books, and if anything went wrong, he could deal with it himself. Lana heard footsteps coming up the stairs, her mother's door opening, then slamming shut. Then her father turned on the radio ("It's Day 96," a reporter said before Michael switched the station). Lana returned to her invitation, carefully rubbing off the letters that spelled out "The favour of a reply is requested."

The next day, when she had finished the invitation, fished a handful of change out of her mother's and father's pants pockets, and put on her coat en route to the Nortown Library, where she planned to Xerox the invitation, Lana stopped at the kitchen counter and glanced through a stack of unopened mail. In it was a copy of the *Young Town Newsletter,* a glossy, eight-page, black-and-white bro-chure stapled together; on the cover, a picture of Vicky Blackwell, Pablo De La Fuente, Muley Wills, Lisa-Anne Williams, and Julie Ying standing on the rocks by Lake Michigan, the downtown skyline of Chicago behind them. The caption read "*Young Town* Kids Win Over the Big Town." Lana's first impulse was to throw up; her second was to pitch the offending document into the trash. Instead, she took it to the library and leafed through it once she was done copying her invitations.

On the second page, there was an open letter from producer Donna Mayne— her picture in a small square in the left-hand corner of the page—and printed next to it, "The Mayne Thing." In the letter, Donna discussed how thrilled she was about the show. Then she thanked all the generous contributors who had made the show possible and explained how others could contribute. On the op-posite page, Lennie Kidd's black-and-white photo was in a small square. His col-umn, "Just Kiddin'," said how thrilled he was to be on the show, how thankful he was to those who had contributed, and how grateful he would be if others did too. Each of the remaining five pages was devoted to one of the *Young Town* kids. Vicky Blackwell's was called "All's Well That's Blackwell" and contained recipes and dieting tips. Pablo De La Fuente's ("The Pablo Papers") had puzzles, jokes, and a maze. On Lisa-Anne Williams's page ("L.A.W.'s Laws"), Lisa thanked the Good Lord Jesus Christ for providing her with talent, and offered lessons her fa-ther had learned during his football career. Julie Ying's page was called "Yings and Yangs" and was set up as a chart with two columns, which separated wrong ways of thinking ("Yangs") from right ways of thinking ("Yings"). "This home-work is too darn hard!" was a Yang way of thinking; "I can do it if I put my mind to it!" was the Ying way.

Muley Wills's page ("Wills's Ways") featured a transcript of the first mono-logue he had written about his cousin Peachy Moskowitz, where he described how she had come to North America in the melee that erupted following Mikhail Baryshnikov's defection. The story was fascinating, and Lana felt intense envy for anyone who had come in such close contact with Baryshnikov—whose picture was taped up inside her school locker and who was to be the subject of her final creative report. She was even tempted to plagiarize a great deal of it, since she had hardly done any research. But when she checked the *Reader's Guide to Periodical Literature* at the library, she discovered no references to Peachy or her daring escape; she found nothing in the card catalog, nothing in the *Tribune* or *Sun Times*'s indexes, nothing in any article about Baryshnikov, ballet, or Soviet defections.

When she called up P.C. that night to discuss the party, she mentioned Muley's story. P.C. said they should both write to WBOE immediately. Sooner or later, the truth would come out, Wills would be discredited for inventing his story, and someone would have to replace him. P.C. even suggested that she might get him to confess the truth himself; she could invite him to her party. Lana said she was planning on inviting Jill Wasserstrom, who she assumed would be coming, since she was no doubt looking for entertainment after her wretched Bat Mitzvah. She figured that Jill would bring Muley along. That was excellent, P.C. said; now he was really looking forward to the party. He asked if he needed to bring a toothbrush.

All that was left for Lana was to forge the 20 for her creative report, something she was so confident she could do that she chose not to prepare further. For the report, she put her hair up in a bun, threw on a ballerina's outfit, and executed a few pirouettes for her attention-getter, before rambling on with anything she could remember about Baryshnikov. For the interaction portion of her report, she returned to something that one of her classmates—Jamie Henderson— had said when she had announced that Baryshnikov would be her topic: "He's not real masculine." With that in mind, Lana turned the classroom into an obstacle course and hosted a game show entitled "Are You as Masculine as Mikhail Baryshnikov?" in which every student had to stand in front of the class and see if they could leap as high as Baryshnikov, if they could stand on point, if they could lift Ms. Powis's desk—which was, Lana said, far lighter than what Baryshnikov could bench-press. Whenever someone tried and failed, Lana would say, "You lose; you're not as masculine as Baryshnikov!"

It was a weak report and Lana knew it. She was, therefore, floored when Ms. Powis gave her a "20. Great job, Lana." She tried to figure it out for the rest of the class—maybe it was pity; maybe Ms. Powis saw the bags under her eyes; maybe it was guilt; maybe Ms. Powis knew that Lana had deserved a 20 on her last report and was making up for it. It made more sense at the end of the class, though. For when Jamie Henderson was graded for his Led Zeppelin report ("Led Zeppelin is, uh, basically, uh, John Bonham, Jimmy Page, Robert Plant, and, uh, John Paul Jones"), he got a 20 too, as did Alice Benske, who barely raised her voice above a whisper while reporting on the TV show *Star Trek*. And though Ms. Powis's policy was to keep the creative report grades a secret, at the end of the period, she got up before the class and said she had given everybody the same grade.

"It's been a long day," she said. "I think we all deserve a 20."

On Saturday, the day of the Not Valentine's Day Couples-Only Party: The Official Party of the 1980 Olympics, it had started snowing early in the morning and by evening, it hadn't let up. There were six inches on the ground and the weather reports were calling for six more. But that wasn't why so few people were coming. The main reason was that upon hearing that Lana was throwing a party, Mary Beth Wales, who had rescinded her silent treatment order against Lana but still harbored resentments toward the girl she viewed as a snitch, had decided to throw her own party. And since Mary Beth lived in north Evanston, where her father collected suits of armor and chess sets forged from precious metals, and since Mary Beth's parents had two show-quality Swiss mountain dogs named Tristan and Isolde, and since she didn't require her guests to bring dates, most Baker students—except for Alice Benske and Steve Orenstein, who weren't invited to Mary Beth's party—opted to go to Mary Beth's instead. Still, some of Mary Beth's guests said they might have older siblings drive them to Lana's afterward, just to see if anyone showed up. Jill Wasserstrom had declined Lana's invitation, citing too much homework.

A major problem with Lana's party was that few took the Couples-Only stipulation seriously. Julie Ying called to say she was looking forward to the party and was bringing her cousin, Lambert. Hillel Levy said he was coming with Moshe Cardash, and when Lana explained that he couldn't come if he didn't have a date, he asked her what her problem was, did she have something against gay people? Who was she, Anita Bryant? What was she, *Iranian*? Which meant that there would only be three other couples at the party aside from Lana and P.C.— Dvorah Kerbis and Connie Sherman were bringing two eighth-grade boys from Jamieson Elementary School: Denny O'Toole, whose curly black locks gave Dvorah chills, and Britt Hurd, who had just turned fourteen and had already grown a thin mustache. Steve Orenstein and Alice Benske were coming too, though to Lana they hardly counted. Todd Taylor said he and Earl Weith might show up late with Megan Knox if they could skitch to Chicago. Lana said her party was for couples only and there were going to be couples-only activities at the party. Todd said that was okay; they were having a threesome.

Though the comparatively low turnout meant that Lana had to reassess her party plan, she ultimately did not alter it much. There would still be Charades until her father was satisfied that nothing mischievous was going on and he had gone off to bed. Then the racier games would start, the couples' competitions. The climax would be a game Lana invented called Didja? One couple would go upstairs for fifteen minutes and while they were gone, everyone would answer questions on a score sheet guessing what the couple was doing during the intervening time period. The party would end with a slowdance marathon; whoever stopped dancing would have to go home.

P.C. Pendleton arrived promptly at 8 P.M. bearing a bottle of red wine and a plastic container of salted nutmeats. Lana had just put the finishing touches on the house. In the kitchen, there were bowls of Jay's potato chips, containers of onion dip, big glass bottles of Canfield's pop, stacks of Dixie riddle cups, and an open can of Poppycock caramel popcorn. She had made three tapes of mood music and was playing the first one, which began with "Annie's Song" by John Denver. In the den, which adjoined the kitchen, Lana had set up a blackboard on which was written "C'mon Everybody! Let's Play Charades!" On the flipside of the blackboard, Lana had written, "It's Orgy Time!" Lana's father was asking if there was anything he could do when the doorbell chimed, announcing P.C.'s arrival.

"Yes, Dad," Lana had said, dashing upstairs to check her mascara. "You can get the door."

Michael Rovner had been prepared to despise P.C., but Prescott Connor Pendleton's warm handshake, his gifts, and his obsequious "It's a pleasure to meet you, sir" were completely disarming. Michael could easily recognize when people had money and he admired them for having it. He offered to take P.C.'s coat, which P.C. relieved himself of quickly as if the house valet had greeted him. P.C. said he was glad his driver had made it through the snow. "It's nasty out there," he said. Michael asked P.C. if he wanted some of the wine he had brought; it looked like a good year. No, P.C. said, that was a gift. He would just have a glass of Honee orange soda pop, please, no ice.

By a quarter to nine, all the guests had arrived and had gathered in the den for Charades. Everyone had been informed in advance that the tone of the evening would change as soon as Lana's father had gone upstairs, but Michael Rovner was enjoying the energy of all the young people in his house. He kept score for

Charades, amazed that with just Dvorah Kerbis's few small pantomimed gestures, Connie Sherman could guess she was acting out *Charlie's Angels.* Moshe Cardash acted out a movie and Hillel Levy called out titles of X-rated films (*I Am Curious (Yellow), Behind the Green Door,* and others he had seen broadcast on YOUR-TV), with which Michael pretended to be unfamiliar ("What *are* those movies?" he asked as Hillel sniggered loudly. "I've never heard of any of those"). But then the phone rang and Michael ran to answer it.

Lana had been acting out a film and Julie Ying had correctly shouted, "*The Mad Adventures of Rabbi Jacob!*" when Lana's father reentered the den and told Lana that he had to talk to her; there was a problem. The hospital had just called; he had to go in to read X-rays. He wouldn't be gone more than an hour. He had tried to reach Larry, who was jamming at Rabbi Meltzer's, but no one had answered. He left a message on the machine telling Larry to come back as quickly as he could, but he trusted that Lana could take care of herself. Oh, that's such a shame, Lana told her father—everyone seemed to be enjoying his company so much. He would be back within an hour, Michael said, and with that, he grabbed his coat, jogged out the front door, got in his car, and drove over to Laura Kim's apartment. Steve Ross had just broken up with her.

After her father's car pulled away, Lana changed the tape from the slow love mix she'd been playing to something considerably louder and nastier. And with Al Stewart's "On the Border" turned off and Rod Stewart's "Do Ya Think I'm Sexy?" cranked up, Lana interrupted Hillel Levy right in the middle of shouting "*Deep Throat!*" and informed her guests it was time to play a different sort of game. She brought out a shoebox filled with plastic medals upon which she had written such phrases as "Best Frencher" or "Sexiest Slowdancer." The first game would be the Frenching competition. Lana said she was sorry that everyone in the party couldn't participate, but she had stressed that this was a Couples-Only event and those who were feeling alone and "down in the dumps" had only themselves to blame. Julie asked if she and Lambert could play piano duets during the Frenching. Lana said she was sorry, but the music had been chosen especially for the event. Julie and Lambert could go downstairs and play air hockey, though. Which they did.

Hillel Levy said he would have liked to make out with Moshe Cardash, but Moshe's lips were still chapped from playing the shofar on Rosh Hashanah and he would have to pass up the opportunity. He offered to serve as referee. Lana consented. Hillel said, "Gentlemen, start yer lickin'." Four couples began to kiss as Debbie Harry sang "Call Me." Dvorah Kerbis and Denny O'Toole were professional about their kissing, with a gas station competence and weariness to their technique; Britt Hurd was tight-lipped about his Frenching, despite Connie Sherman's well-practiced moves—taking her gum out of her mouth and placing it on an index finger, flicking her hair out of her eyes ("We have a disqualification here, ladies and gentlemen," Hillel said. "No tongue. You can't win a Frenching competition without tongue"); Alice Benske and Steve Orenstein seemed untutored though exuberant, less competent professionals than eager amateurs thrilled to be playing in the big leagues. Meanwhile, Moshe Cardash meandered about the den, studying the contents of various dusty cookbooks.

Lana, for her part, despite boasting to her therapist and her father that she and P.C. had Frenched before, had really never kissed him at all. But when she had said that French-kissing P.C. had been "icky," she had unconsciously hit upon a larger and prophetic truth. It *was* icky. *Quite* icky. She thought it would be like kissing a frog, but that was only half-right. It wasn't like kissing a stationary frog, as Lana had thought it would be; it was like kissing a frog that was constantly sticking its tongue out to catch flies. She wondered if she was doing something wrong, whether she should open her mouth wider, flick her tongue, wag it side to side, whether her nose was too big, if that's why it got in the way; why, she wondered, did it all feel vaguely like drooling?

"I think we got a winner here, ladies and gentlemen," Hillel Levy said. "Yes, definitely a winner. They've got the moves, they've got the grooves, they know the tricks, they know the licks. It's Laaaaana Rovner and her *gooooooyishe* boyfriend, P.C. Pendlestick."

After placing one "Best Frencher" gold medal on P.C. and one on herself, Lana said it was time for the "Sexy Slowdance" competition. Four pairs of dancers rocked and swayed to the music as Hillel danced with a chair. "We want a clean dance, boys and girls," he said. "That means no touching below the belt." He twirled with the chair, circling each couple, saying, "Nice, nice, very nice, very good technique" as he ogled Dvorah Kerbis, her hands doing the "itsy-bitsy spider" up and down Denny's back. "Good, good, let's see some energy, though; it's a party, not a funeral," he told Britt Hurd. "We want a clean dance, a clean dance," he scolded Alice Benske, whose hand was cupping Steve Orenstein's buttocks.

Lana had her hands clasped together behind P.C.'s neck just as she had learned in her JCC dance lessons. But P.C.'s hands weren't holding her waist gently, as Sandi Hirsch had instructed. He was holding her tightly, too tightly, there was something imprisoning about his grip. "Loosen up a little," she told him, and he let up a bit, but then he grabbed tighter as if he were trying to see how much fat he could find. "Not sexy," Hillel said. "It's not a wrestling match. You guys are ejaculated from the competition!" Hillel called the Sexy Slowdance competition a draw and asked Dvorah and Denny to share their medals with Connie and Britt. "How long's this bullshit gonna go on?" Britt wanted to know. Connie told him to take his medal and shut up—having a big dick was cute; having a big mouth wasn't. Then Lana explained the rules of Didja? to the group. She had called downstairs to Julie and Lambert to see if they wanted to join in the judging. Julie said no, thank you; they were playing a best-of-seven air hockey playoff series and they were locked up two games to two.

Lana distributed questionnaires to everyone except Britt Hurd, who said he didn't want one because he "didn't feel like it." But when Lana told him that if he didn't cooperate, his couple wouldn't be allowed to have fifteen minutes in private and have the others guess what they were doing together, Connie elbowed him in the ribs and he said, "Fine. Give me the fucking thing." Through a lottery, it was determined that Alice and Steve would go first. Once they had gone upstairs and everyone else in the den had filled out a questionnaire, Dvorah Kerbis asked if anyone had any hash—her sister had told her that just two years earlier, hash had been really easy to come by, but lately she hadn't found any. P.C. said he knew where to get some and he'd sell her some if she wanted. Lana laughed and said that P.C. was funny. Denny O'Toole returned to Dvorah's remark and agreed that hash was tough to find and that the problem was that when you found it, it was weak and people charged you up the ass for it. He turned to Britt and wistfully recalled seventh grade, when they had gotten stoned all the time. "It was like a permanent high," Denny said, and he slapped five with Britt. "You coulda got a contact high from just smelling the air around us." Lana asked if anyone wanted punch or juice. "I got some juice," Hillel Levy said, and everybody laughed.

Shortly after Alice and Steve had returned and responded to their questioners, Hillel disqualified them for lying. They had answered yes to every question: "Did you hold hands?" "Did you kiss on the cheek?" "Did you get to first base?"

"Did you kiss with your mouths open?" "Did you use your tongue?" "Did you get to second base?" "Did you get to third?" "Did you score?" Everyone assembled agreed that they were full of it and anyway there was a horn honking, which meant that Mrs. Orenstein's BMW was outside and it was time for them to go. That left three couples for Didja? and it was Lana and P.C.'s turn to go upstairs.

After they had gone to her bedroom and shut the door, Lana sat beside P.C. and revealed her strategy: She told him that what they should do was agree on the most appropriate answers for the Didja? questions, fill those in on their questionnaire, but not really do any of them. There was no need to hold hands or to kiss on the cheek, on the lips, or with the tongue. They'd already done that anyway. And as for those second-base, third-base, and scoring questions, she figured they could just say no—well, maybe they could say yes to the second-base question, but definitely not to third base or scoring.

P.C. shuddered. He said he didn't like lying. His father had served in the military and had told him that it was one of the worst sins a man could commit. It wasn't a big lie, Lana said. Nobody would be hurt by it and nobody would know. *I'd* know, P.C. said. All right, Lana said, then what did he think they should do? P.C. asked if she cared about being as experienced as everyone else at the party. No, Lana said. Well, yes, well, maybe, she didn't know; it depended. P.C. asked if most of the people at the party were over twelve. Yes, Lana said, she thought so. Because, P.C. continued, everyone that age had already had sex. No way, Lana said, he was lying, he was joking, he was sick, he was funny, no way had everybody there had sex. Well, perhaps not sex, P.C. said, perhaps not all of them, but they all certainly had gotten to third base. No way, Lana said, he was joking, he was weird, how did he know anything, he didn't know. Well, perhaps not third base, he said—though he said that he certainly had—but definitely second base. Everybody got to second base.

Lana was less sure of her response to this hypothesis, for she was fairly certain that P.C. was right, that everyone at the party had either gone up a shirt or had their shirt gone up. The problem was that having someone go up her shirt seemed a lot different when it was an abstract concept. Now it all seemed so clinical. There was nothing romantic about this—romance was a Broadway show, it was Ginger Rogers and Fred Astaire. Mikhail Baryshnikov loved Fred Astaire. Romance was the way it happened in old movie musicals with a close-up on a kiss and then the scene switching to the next morning. There was no icky tongue action, no hickeys, and certainly no removing of shirts—who would want to see Ginger Rogers and Fred Astaire without shirts? Who would want to see Fred Astaire pawing Ginger Rogers's boobs? It struck Lana that sex must have been a modern invention, that there was no way Fred Astaire had ever taken off his tuxedo trousers and his underpants, God, *yuck,* no way. Well, fine, whatever, she told P.C., they'd do everything on the checklist, including second base, but they'd do it all quickly.

They held hands. Lana wrote down "yes." She kissed his cheek. Lana wrote "yes." They kissed with mouths open. She wrote "yes." They touched tongues. Lana wrote "yes." Okay, Lana said; she began unbuttoning her blouse. P.C. gazed blankly at fingers and buttons. He held his hands out in front of him, as if performing an up-tempo number in a minstrel show, and when she was done he jerked his hands forward, hooking a thumb behind a brassiere strap, then moving it over her shoulder. Then the bedroom door swung open and Larry Rovner—yarmulke nesting, almost hovering halo-like, over his head—asked what in the name of *Hashem* was going on here.

For a split second, there was silence, a gulp in time. Lana, caught between cowed shame and defiant pride, debated which of those emotions should guide the excuse she would devise. Larry's sentiments were divided between outrage and shock, outrage that some Aryan cretin was touching his sister, shock because when he'd been Lana's age, he'd never even touched himself, let alone anyone else, while P.C. considered whether anyone in a yarmulke who wasn't a member of the Israeli army or Mossad—both of which he admired greatly—could be all that tough. But Larry *was* tough. He was a self-declared Jerusarock-jock, a ferocious point guard who could drain a jumper from the top of the key. Back in 1978, when some Nazis were threatening to march in Skokie, he had gone out looking for Nazis with Ben Jacobs and Randy Weinstock with baseball bats in the trunk of Randy's mother's car. And when they hadn't been able to find any, they took the bats and smashed two windows of a hot dog joint whose owner, according to the *Nortown Leader,* had used disparaging terms to refer to his Jewish tailor.

Larry grabbed P.C.'s tie with one hand and the back of the collar of his blazer with the other and started dragging him out of Lana's bedroom as the other party guests began racing upstairs to see what the ruckus was. P.C. flailed his arms wildly, a puppet without its stuffing doing the backstroke. Larry asked P.C. if he wanted a "piece of this." If he wanted a "piece of this," then he'd be happy to "dance," did he want to dance? Lana screamed to Larry that he should let P.C. go; she had seen Larry mad before—back when he was in seventh grade and he had seen Bob Dylan in the film *Don't Look Back* and had decided that the way to get girlfriends was to be surly and belligerent.

Larry yelled at Lana to go back into her room, damn it, he wasn't through with her yet. He dragged P.C. toward the stairway. P.C. slackened as if surrendering, then flailed again. Moshe, Hillel, and Dvorah were down the hall, transfixed by the scene, Hillel saying, "Did you see that tittie?" Larry told everybody to go back downstairs, there was nothing to look at here, this wasn't a show. Lana yelled, "Larry!" Larry said he thought he'd told her to get back into her room.

P.C. said fine, he was going, leave him alone, he was going. Larry let up his grip as they got to the stairs, but then P.C. whipped back toward Larry, charging at full speed, headfirst into Larry's stomach, driving him back into the linen closet. *All right, you fucker,* Larry said as he landed on the floor, *if that's how you want to play, we can play that way.* P.C. lay atop him as Britt and Denny ran upstairs, Britt climbing two steps at a time, remarking that it wasn't a party until somebody got into a fight or something got broken. P.C. pummeled fists into Larry's flanks. Larry asked if that was all he had while Hillel shouted the play-by-play—". . . and a right and a left and another left, that had to hurt, ladies and gentlemen." Britt grabbed P.C. by the shoulders, lifted him off of Larry. Larry said no, it was all him, he didn't need anyone's help; it was *all him.* Britt told Denny to get P.C.'s feet; Lana stepped out of her bedroom; Larry said, *Get back in there*; Lana ran back to her room, then slammed the door. Britt and Denny maneuvered the spasmodic thirteen-year-old down the stairs, asking if he liked fighting. "You like fighting, little dude?" Britt asked threateningly, while Denny offered the information that he was made of "TNT and dyn-o-mite" and he was "just looking for a fight."

When they got to the bottom of the stairs, Britt told Denny to open the door, at which point P.C. said all right, he was going, let him alone, he said he was going. Britt said that P.C. didn't understand something, he didn't get to choose when he left; he would leave when they decided it was time. All right, P.C. wanted to know, when would they decide? *Now,* Britt said, driving P.C. full force out the door, P.C. tripping over the stairs, tumbling knees-first into a snow-covered rhododendron bush. Then, as Hillel Levy yelled that it was *over,* that this fight was *all over,* Larry Rovner leaned outside, wind smacking his cheeks with wet snow. "That's what you get, you *goyishe* motherfucker," he yelled, "that's what you get." As a triumphant Denny O'Toole strutted around the Rovner house, asking where the "free shit" was, and Britt Hurd opined that there was nothing free in this world except for ass-kicking, Larry climbed back upstairs and went to Lana's room. But when Larry walked in, Lana was gone and the door to her porch was unlocked.

By the time Larry had cased the entire house, interrupting Julie and Lambert's air hockey game to inform them that it was a grown-up's game and they shouldn't be playing, because if someone got injured, it would be his legal liability, Lana had just found P.C. She had thrown on two sweaters, slipped onto her bedroom porch, shinnied down a drainpipe, landed softly in a snowdrift, and run through her backyard and out into the alley. She had run north through the alley until she got to Pratt. P.C. was two blocks east at Francisco, stomping his way toward California through the snow. The streets had not been plowed; cars skidded and fishtailed as they drove with hazard lights on. Lana caught up to P.C. at Mozart Street. Come on, she said, they had to hurry; her brother would be looking for them. They turned south at the alley behind Gunther's Shell station.

As they stood in the alley, Lana said it looked like P.C.'s lip was bleeding. P.C. said it was all right; it didn't hurt. Lana kissed his lip. To make it feel better, she said. She told him it tasted like metal. She liked it when they had kissed before, she lied. P.C. said he'd liked it too. Lana asked if he'd kissed lots of girls before. Not a lot, P.C. said. Maybe only seven or eight. How about her? Not as many, she said, five or six. She asked if he'd gone up lots of girls' shirts before. Not a lot, he said, only four or five, how about her? That sounded about right to her, she said, four or five. She asked if he'd ever really gotten past second base. P.C. suggested that they go into that place to the left, maybe they could sneak in through a window, she must be cold. He asked if she knew what the place was; no, Lana lied, she had no idea.

They had been walking through the alley behind K.I.N.S. P.C. entered the little cement playground with its snow-covered seesaw and its icy jungle gym. He tried to force a classroom window. They were frozen shut. Up a few steps, a heavy brown door led into the Hebrew school. Lana said he couldn't go in there; it wasn't allowed. But P.C. pulled hard and the door gave way. Come on, he said, no one would know. In the alley, as Lana followed P.C. into the darkened Hebrew school, Muley Wills was walking slowly with his movie camera, photographing the swirling snow, while a splotchy white dog followed about ten yards behind him.

There was only one flickering pink light in the Hebrew school hallway vaguely illuminating Rabbi Meltzer's office, the bathrooms, and the door to the basement. Beyond the light, a door led to the synagogue and the Tree of Life memorial donation board. Lana said they should go, she didn't like this place; P.C. said no, it was fascinating. He walked straight for the door, but Lana said why didn't they turn left—she certainly didn't want him to go into the synagogue without a yarmulke; she thought they might both go to hell.

Their wet shoes squeaked against the floor as they walked past the classrooms. P.C. asked why didn't they go in here; he pointed to the *Dalet* classroom, the one where Rabbi Grossman used to slam the *tzedakah* box against the table and insist that this *tzedakah* was "not a joke," where Grossman had held a competition for the best menorah and Lana had come in second to Bibi Eisenstaedt, and Jill Wasserstrom had been the only kid who hadn't bothered to bring in any menorah at all. In the *Dalet* classroom, there were four rows of wooden desks, twenty desks altogether. There was a blackboard on which someone had written "I must not make fun of Maimonides" twenty-five times.

P.C. sat down on Rabbi Grossman's desk and invited Lana to sit beside him. Lana said they should go. P.C. said her brother was still probably looking for them, so why didn't they take up where they had left off in her bedroom. Lana asked what he meant. P.C. kissed her. Lana said she didn't feel like kissing right now. P.C. tried to burrow underneath her sweaters. Lana said she didn't feel like going up shirts right now. Jesus, P.C. said, she really knew how to be cruel. *Cruel?* Lana asked. Well, P.C. wanted to know, what did she call inviting him to a party as a date, taking him up to her room, and planning to have her brother interrupt them and beat him up? What was he talking about? Lana asked, she hadn't planned that. Well, P.C. said, it seemed awfully convenient. Probably she'd invited him just to reject him and have her brother beat him up. Well, if that's what she wanted to do, fine. He wished her luck with the rest of her life. Wait, Lana said. She touched his neck lightly and kissed him, then began removing her sweaters. No, forget it, P.C. said—he didn't need her charity. Lana pulled him closer and kissed him again; P.C.'s hands fumbled with the buttons on her blouse.

When P.C. had undone the last button, he reached a hand underneath Lana's brassiere. She tensed, but said nothing, fearing he would say something mean to her, something about how mean she was, so she let his hands creep around beneath her brassiere like a cold, wet insect; his tongue flicked around, probing her gums and the roof of her mouth, while his pelvis, pointy and warm, poked her kneecap. She was hoping he would say something nice to her, something romantic like you smell good or you taste good or this feels good, but he didn't say anything; he just slobbered, grabbed, and shoved as the desk rocked and clunked underneath them. And when P.C. did finally speak, it was not to tell her that she smelled good or that he loved her; he wanted to know how many times she'd grabbed a cock. *What?* Lana asked pushing him away from her. He'd had four girls grab his cock, P.C. said; how many times had she grabbed a cock? *Never,* Lana said. She had to be joking, P.C. said, by their age, everybody had grabbed two or three cocks. He unzipped his pants and pulled out his penis. Lana wanted to laugh, to run, to throw up, all at the same time. She told him to put that thing back; it was disgusting. Come on, P.C. said, it was no big deal. No, Lana said, she wouldn't grab his cock, that was final. She told P.C. her last name was Rovner, not Wasserstrom. Well, she could at least have the courtesy of going to the bathroom and getting him a stack of paper towels, P.C. said.

On her way to the bathroom, Lana briefly wondered if she should go back and grab P.C.'s cock as he had asked her. She didn't want to, but still, she liked having a boyfriend, liked the idea of talking on the phone to her boyfriend, liked the idea of coming to school and telling Mary Beth Wales what she had done with her boyfriend. But then there was something even better than telling people that she was dating P.C. Pendleton, she realized gleefully, and that was telling people that she had broken up with him. No, she could tell everyone, she wasn't dating P.C. anymore; he kissed like a goy. In fact, he didn't kiss at all; he slobbered. He didn't even know how to go up her shirt; her boobs weren't volume knobs, she'd told him—a phrase she'd heard Megan Knox use. When she got back to the classroom, P.C. was in a corner, pants around his ankles, industriously rubbing his penis.

"I'm breaking up with you," Lana shouted. She slapped the paper towels down on the desk. "Don't call me." As she exited the Hebrew school, she heard a loud, distant groaning noise. "Like a goat," she would tell everyone. "He grunted just like a goat."

When Lana got home, her mother was cleaning the kitchen. In the den, Lana's guests had been joined by Earl Weith, Todd Taylor, and Megan Knox.

They were playing a spirited game of Led Zeppelin Charades; all the clues were for Zeppelin albums or songs. Todd pantomimed spray-painting on a wall and Julie shouted, "Physical Graffiti." Earl said damn, this girl knew her Zeppelin, he wanted to party with her.

Lana's mother said she'd come back early from Lake Geneva because of the weather. When Lana joined her in the kitchen, she asked Lana where she'd been. Lana said she'd been out with P.C. Oh, Lana's mother said very calmly, did she know where her brother was? Lana said he was probably out looking for her; they'd gotten into a fight when Larry had seen her and P.C. making out. Oh, Lana's mother said, again very calmly, did she know where her father was? Yes, Lana said, at the hospital; there'd been an emergency. Oh, Lana's mother said, that was interesting; was anything else new? Yes, a couple of things, Lana said. She had good news and bad news, she said. The good news was that she thought she might have a chance to make it into the cast of *Young Town* after all; she was sure that the black kid Muley had made up his story and would probably get kicked off the show. Oh, Ellen said, what was the bad news? Lana said the bad news wasn't really bad news; she hoped her mother wouldn't be upset, but it was for the best. What was that? Ellen asked.

"I had to break up with P.C.," Lana said. "He was just too immature."

Ellen said she thought Lana had liked P.C.

"Yes," Lana said. "But the world moves on." She grabbed a bowl of chips and began snacking on them. Then she went to join the others in the den, thrilled that Mary Beth's party was probably over by now and hers was still going strong. She hoped her mother would go to bed soon, so she could tell everybody what had just happened.

Muley

After three months, Muley Scott Wills had gotten more or less used to the relative luxury of living in a new two-bedroom apartment with his mother on the east side of California Avenue. Deirdre Wills had used a chunk of Carl Slappit Silverman's $5,000 check to furnish the place. There was a dining room with matching chairs and a lacquered oak table. There was a living room with a leather couch, a TV, and a stereo. There was a big kitchen with appliances, kitchen stools, a small breakfast nook, a refrigerator that was always full, and two dozen bookcases.

By most measures, Muley's life would seem to have improved. In a neighborhood where progress was judged by whether one had moved east or west or stood still, Muley was a mile farther west than he had been in December 1979. His mother was finishing up her credits at Circle; she was substituting in the Chicago public schools, tutoring, and teaching college test prep classes, and though Muley saw her a good deal less than before, at least she seemed happier when he did. *Young Town* had been picked up by four other public radio stations nationwide and Donna Mayne said it would surely sweep the Jack Benny radio awards. And Muley's mother had allowed him to sell every gift his father had ever given him, and he'd sold all of them—save for his hockey net, sticks, and puck—to buy the film editors he kept atop his desk. Muley had taken an entrance exam for Lane Tech, the magnet high school nearest his apartment, and though he'd arrived late and left early to get to a *Young Town* taping, he ranked a respectable 218 out of more than 900. It was not as impressive a score as Jill Wasserstrom's—Jill had ranked eighth overall—but it was more than sufficient to ensure his admission.

Muley was also enjoying an unprecedented popularity among his peers. With the exception of Jill, he had always found his most rewarding friendships with adults—listening to Knopov's Bakery manager Bess Vaysberg take on the Iranian situation, drinking ginger ales and, once in a while, beers with Mel Coleman at the Double Bubble. But now girls were calling him—every week or so, Connie Sherman would call just to say, "Hey, Mules" and "see what was going on." Lisa-Anne Williams had invited him to go with her family to church and then to a Bulls game (he had declined, citing little interest in sports aside from hockey). And often on weekends, Gareth Overgaard would drop by with Michelle Was-serstrom and/or Myra Tuchbaum to see if Muley wanted to smoke a doob on Mt. Warren, grab a grilled cheese at Gulliver's, or have what Gareth termed a Wau-kegan Night, which involved buying 32-ounce pops at a 7-Eleven and consuming them in a parking lot. Sometimes Gareth would come on his own to see if Muley wanted to go driving.

About every other time, Muley would say yes and spend his evening listening politely to Michelle's relationship advice or Gareth's political opinions or Myra's lurid tales of swimming pool antics with Douglas Sternberg. But invariably, an hour or two into the evening, he would regret having come along and wish he was back home working on his films. In cinema, Muley seemed to have found his true métier. It was art and it was science, and unlike acting on radio, it was creative. He loved the process, watching how images cut together. It almost didn't matter that all three short films he had made since he had become obsessed with the medium were now at Jill's apartment; he had no real interest in watching them once he was done. And even though she had barely spoken to him since her Bat Mitzvah, he knew Jill was the only person who could truly appreciate his films. Those two obsessions—cinema and Jill Wasserstrom—had begun causing Muley enough difficulty at Boone Elementary that he called up Gareth to discuss it.

It had been several years since Muley had been particularly interested in school. Science and Math were easy. Of the books covered in Reading, he had ei-ther read them before or heard his mother describe them in detail. When he hadn't read a story, it was usually because it was something didactic and dull, something with a message so blatant that Deirdre Wills would never have pa-tronized her son with it, something replete with labored symbolism—something, say, about a world full of green people who shun a purple person within their midst. Muley spent almost every one of his classes dutifully storyboarding so he wouldn't have to make eye contact with Jill. Most teachers were too concerned about the boys carving smiling penis faces into their desks to worry too much about a smart, underachieving kid doing well enough to get by.

But then there had been the U.S. Constitution test, administered by Mrs. Korab. Taking and passing The Constitution was Illinois's only solid requirement for passing eighth grade. Students memorized the preamble and were required to answer a series of multiple-choice questions about the articles of the Constitution and their amendments. It was a test everybody feared, everybody studied for, and, as a rule, everybody passed. Muley had little interest in memorization and none in politics. When Mrs. Korab had conducted a mock presidential primary and had already censured Jill for choosing Barry Commoner of the Citizens' Party ("Democrats and Republicans, Jill," Mrs. Korab had said, wagging a finger, "we're only interested in Democrats and Republicans"), Muley said he didn't know who was running. Mrs. Korab had tried to help—she said that Howard Baker was running in the Republican primary. Howard was a nice name, maybe Muley wanted to vote for him. "I'll abstain," Muley said, quoting from an old movie he had once watched with Jill, *"courteously."* The night before the test, everything tempted him. He chatted on the phone to Connie Sherman and listened to her talk endlessly about the singer Rex Smith, whom she'd seen perform at the amusement park, Old Chicago; he stayed out late at a Waukegan Night with Gareth; when he got home, he didn't even open his Constitution sample test booklet. Instead, he spent hours drawing a flying trout for a stop-motion animation film he thought he might make. When he finally went to sleep, he assumed that he could pass the test by figuring out the right answers from context.

The following day, Muley found himself staring blankly at a booklet filled with indecipherable questions. He didn't know what the items in the Bill of Rights might have been, had no idea what Section I, Article II, might have consisted of, certainly hadn't memorized the preamble, had forgotten he was supposed to. When Mrs. Korab came to class the next day with the results, she beamed, effusing that the class had performed far better than expected. Only two people had failed. "Muley and Jill, see me after class," Mrs. Korab said.

Muley had successfully avoided Jill up until that point. She always sat up front while Muley sat in the back. Jill was first to arrive and first to leave, while Muley would saunter into class just after the bell and take a long time packing up his bag when class was over. Whenever he saw Jill in the hallway, he would look down at the floor. By this point, the only contact they had with each other was the films he sent to her and the critiques of each that she sent to him through the mail, in which she skillfully avoided acknowledging the films' emotional subtexts, concentrating instead on lapses in logic—"Penguins are monogamous so it seems unlikely that the penguin would leave her mate for the skunk," she wrote. "I understand this is a cartoon, but it still has to be consistent."

But when the bell sounded and the other students joyously bounded for the door, thrilled that they had passed The Constitution, Muley felt a sudden panic plunge through him. Trapped. There was Jill, sitting cross-legged in the front row, tapping her eraser against her desk—*tap tap tap, tap tap tap;* she was clearly aware that he was still in the room, but she didn't turn around; obviously, she didn't want to talk to him. But still he had to talk to her, it was ridiculous—it had gone far enough. He stood up, but Mrs. Korab told him to sit back down. This wasn't a social club, she said.

As far as The Constitution was concerned, Korab said she was most disappointed with Muley. He had received the lowest score—was there some personal situation she should be made aware of? No, Muley said quietly. Jill stared straight ahead. As for her, Mrs. Korab said, she thought she had been more than tolerant of Jill's tendency to spout political opinions that were not favored by the majority and had even done Jill a service by not tacking her essays to the classroom bulletin board, where they would incur the wrath of her peers. But now Mrs. Korab had to say that she really didn't understand how someone could get every question right, yet leave the entire section on the Bill of Rights blank, thus ensuring her failure. Jill said that the test hadn't asked her about the Bill of Rights; it had specifically asked her "What ten rights do *you* enjoy as an American citizen?" And since she prided herself on being truthful, the answer, she said, was none. She hadn't been allowed to vote for the candidate of her choice in the school primary; in her apartment, all of her belongings could be subject to unreasonable search and seizure; her Bat Mitzvah had proved the absurdity of free speech; she may have had the right to bear arms but certainly didn't *enjoy* it; and she was most certainly subject to cruel and unusual punishment—being forced to memorize all Constitutional amendments was a prime example. Mrs. Korab said that she didn't want to discuss this "foolishness" any further. She told Muley and Jill that they would have to make up their Constitution tests the next Friday after school, and if they didn't pass, they'd have to keep taking it until they did. The bell rang and Mrs. Korab wrote out late passes for PE.

As Mrs. Korab made out the passes, Muley knew this was as good a time as any to approach Jill; if he didn't do it now, then they'd both be back in the classroom next Friday after school and they would both know that they'd been here today and neither had said anything to the other and it would be that much easier to not say anything ever again. But just saying her name was difficult, just getting out the "J," so much so that Muley wanted to dash out of the classroom as quickly as possible, wondering what would happen if he dropped out of school, if it would have been better for him and his mother to move to Atlanta to Uncle Victor's.

"J-Jill," Muley said. Her head snapped quickly toward him, ponytail swishing. She didn't say anything, just stared expectantly and raised her eyebrows slightly.

"Can I talk to you for a minute?" he asked.

Jill rolled her eyes. As she responded, her voice had a snap to it, a hint of an exasperated sneer. "Sure you can talk to me," she said quickly. "Who's stopping you?"

She knew it sounded harsh and abrupt. But she couldn't stand the timidity of the request, the self-effacement and the expectation inherent within it. Having someone in love with you was wonderful in theory; in practice, it was just plain irritating. Not that anybody had ever been in love with her, not as far as she knew anyway—maybe Shmuel Weinberg, who fell in love with any girl who said hi to him. But she didn't want Muley to be in love with her. She didn't want to be in love with Muley. If it was going to be all about expectations, all about being afraid to face her, all about "Jill, can I talk to you for a minute?" what good was it? Being in love was all about letting people down and being let down by them. It was about being lifted up too high, then dragged down too low. It was better to be alone, she thought; at least that was easy and even.

"Sure you can talk to me. Who's stopping you?" To Muley, hearing the words felt like being dunked in ice-cold water. That was it, then, he thought. He'd expressed the depth of his feelings and what good had it done? He thought all he had to do was be honest and Jill would understand. This was the end of love, as far as Muley was concerned. Being in love was all about telling the truth and wishing you'd lied. It was about being lifted up too high, then dragged down too low. It was better to be alone; at least that was easy and even.

When Muley got home from school, he couldn't even look at his Constitution study packet. And even more worrisome, he found himself unable to write or draw. He'd jot down ideas for sequences of images, then stop suddenly and stare into space, wondering who would see them and what difference any of it made. He called Gareth's house and left a message with his father—a professor of Religion and Ethics at Northeastern Illinois. Gareth called back around midnight and asked if Muley was up for a Waukegan Night.

In Gareth's car in the parking lot of Poppin Fresh pies, Muley felt better. In response to Muley's concerns about Jill, Gareth said he had just been reading Ayn Rand's *The Fountainhead* in preparation for an Objectivist Party meeting the following night—Muley was welcome to come. He said he'd found most of Rand weird, creepy, and vaguely fascist, but there was something worthwhile to be found in almost every philosophy and Rand's was no exception, particularly its espousal of individualism. People working at the height of their abilities to serve themselves best served mankind, Gareth observed. Altruism was a trap. "Don't be a humanitarian, Wills; be an artist," he said. "Do something for yourself; everyone will come running to you. Do something for someone else; that's when they'll start running away. That's the best advice I can offer." As for the rest of *The Fountainhead,* Gareth said that Ayn Rand could suck his dick.

As far as Jill was concerned, Gareth said, the moment Muley stopped thinking about her and started thinking about himself was when she would come back to him. Muley didn't know if it was comforting or frightening that Mel Coleman had told him the exact same thing. But at least when he got home, he could look at his Constitution study packet. And he realized that once he had figured out how to pass the exam, he could stop studying and start penciling ideas for a new film, one that would finally break through to Jill or put her out of his mind.

When he had dropped Muley off at his apartment, Gareth told Muley to call him if he wanted to attend the Objectivists' meeting. Muley told Gareth that he had to go to *Young Town,* then study for The Constitution ("They still make you take that?" Gareth asked. "That's so frickin' previous") and work on his next film concept; it was unlikely he'd have time. But the next day, the minute Muley got home from the *Young Town* taping, he found himself dialing Gareth's phone number and leaving a message with his mother—a public policy professor at Circle. Something had happened before the taping and Muley didn't know anyone else with whom he could discuss the matter.

The *Young Town* taping had begun as every previous one had—with Muley, Vicky Blackwell, Lisa-Anne Williams, Pablo De La Fuente, and Julie Ying arriving promptly at 9 A.M. and then waiting an hour in the studio for the grown-ups to arrive while Mel Coleman set up mikes and checked levels. Pablo entertained the other *Young Town* kids by performing the Foreigner song "Head Games" while standing on his head, which precipitated a gymnastics demonstration, in which Julie giddily turned cartwheels and tried to get a reluctant Muley to try one; he did a half-cartwheel, then landed hard on the ground. "It's hard when you're learning without mats," Julie said apologetically, and Muley wondered why he couldn't have a crush on a nice girl like Julie, who, as Lennie Kidd had recently observed, would someday make somebody "a helluva wife."

At 10 A.M., Donna Mayne walked briskly into the studio and tapped an index finger in Muley's direction, pointed it back at herself, and told Muley she had to talk to him in private.

"Don't let her make you tote any bales," Mel said as Muley followed her out.

Once they had entered Donna's grim little office, she closed the door and indicated a shaky swivel chair for Muley to sit in. She told him that a "situation" had developed, one she hoped he might be able to "shed light upon." She said she had received two letters from two different sources suggesting that Muley's Peachy Moskowitz essays, which she felt were the strongest part of the show and which would be nominated for numerous Jack Benny radio awards, were fabricated. She had done some investigation and had been unable to find any record of a Peachy Moskowitz who'd worked in any of the professions Muley had attributed to her.

Well, that made sense, Muley said quickly. His cousin's first name wasn't Peachy; it was Clara. Yes, Donna said, she knew that, but she hadn't found Clara Moskowitz either. She said Peachy was getting more and more popular. People were more interested in Russia since the U.S. hockey team had defeated the Russians during the previous month's Olympic games. Now Lennie was constantly suggesting that Peachy appear as a special in-studio guest, and Donna wanted to be certain that this cousin truly existed. *Does she or doesn't she?* Donna asked. Not knowing how to respond, Muley quickly said yes, of course she did, and not only that, she'd be more than happy to appear on the show whenever Donna wanted. He had not anticipated Donna's curt reply. "Good," she said. "Let's make it next week."

That night in Gareth's car, when Muley presented his dilemma, Gareth said, somewhat testily, "I thought you were going to ask me something hard, Wills." It wasn't hard, Muley said; it was impossible. "Bullshit it is," said Gareth. "Have Wasserstrom do it."

Michelle Wasserstrom had always been good at accents, Gareth said, particularly when she was high. Plus, he was worried about her. She hadn't had a date since the 1970s. She was arguing constantly with her father about his new girlfriend. There were now two signs on Jill and Michelle's bedroom door. On the top one, Jill had written, "This Is a Nuclear Weapons–Free Zone." On the one below it, Michelle had written, "This Is a Gail Schiffler-Bass–Free Zone." Lately, Gareth said, Myra Tuchbaum was being condescending to Michelle now that she'd started getting laid. Michelle had been screwed over by the Mather Drama Club, which had offered her and then, after a furious internal debate, retracted the title role in *Hamlet,* subsequently casting her as Ophelia, a role she refused. Furthermore, she had shown up hungover for her Preparatory Scholastic Aptitude Test (PSAT) and because she thought it would be funny, had misspelled her name on the exam and listed her race as "Pacific Islander." Gareth thought she could use something to take her mind off all that. Muley stammered something about Jill. "That moment's gone, Wills," Gareth said. "Deal with it."

Later that night, when she joined them in the car for a Waukegan Night, Michelle said sure, she'd do it, what the fuck. Muley had begun to long-windedly explain the situation, but Gareth interrupted. "Look, Wasserstrom," he said. "It's not that hard. All you gotta do is pretend you're some Russian chick and make a call." Once they agreed that, at the next taping, Muley would tell Donna that Peachy would be calling her and that they would set up a weekday evening for Michelle to phone in, Gareth tried to move on to other topics, but Michelle, who had not performed in public since *H.M.S. Pinafore* and was looking for an opportunity to feed her addiction, kept bringing the conversation back to Peachy. She wanted to know everything about this bitch, she said, what she looked like, how old she was, what cigarettes she smoked, whether she was a virgin. "Stop grinning, Overgaard," she said. "This shit's important." But the more information Muley provided (Peachy was twenty; she smoked Marlboros; she had many boyfriends but was saving herself for her marriage—"Bullshit," Michelle interjected. "That's just what she *tells* people"), the less satisfied Michelle was. No, she finally said. She couldn't do things this way; it was too half-assed. She wanted to know when they were rehearsing. She figured they needed

at least three rehearsals to do this right, otherwise they could find some other little slut to do it; if they wanted a professional, they'd have to do things professionally, and that meant getting paid, too, by the way.

Michelle added that she herself didn't care about getting paid, but Peachy
would want to get paid and she wanted to be paid what Peachy would want to be
paid and that meant, she said, "you pay me up front, two cartons American *see-
garettes.*" Muley said Peachy wasn't like that; she would never accept money.
"Two cartons American *see-garettes* or else I *vill valk,*" Michelle said. "Do not try
to *deek* me around." Muley said all right, he'd get the cigarettes, but he wasn't
sure if he had time for rehearsals; he had to study for The Constitution. "Peachy
Moskowitz say that Constitution test *ees bowlsheet,*" Michelle said. "Now, do *vee*
rehearse or do you *vant* I should *valk?*" All right, Muley said, they'd rehearse.
"*Thees ees vot* I *vanted* to hear," Peachy said. "Now, tell your *fett,* gay friend
to unlock *hees* glove compartment; Peachy Moskowitz should like to *schmoke*
a bowl."

On Wednesday evening, Deirdre Wills knocked on her son's bedroom door
and said with a perplexed smile, "There's some girl with a Yiddish accent here to
see you." Still, though Michelle's accent was not perfect, it was not for lack of trying. As she explained to Muley while sitting at his editing table, she'd taken her
inspiration from Dennis Christopher's performance as an Indiana townie who
passes himself off as an Italian bike racer in the film *Breaking Away,* and had been
speaking in this accent all week. She had also added blond highlights to her hair
and started wearing *"a sheetload"* of blue eye shadow. "*Ees veddy* Eastern European," she observed. The only downside of it, she said, was that in school, more
guys were hitting on her, more girls were treating her like a psycho bitch, and
creepy Mr. Hull had told her right in the middle of Trig, "Hey, Michelle, niiice
haiiir!" In class, she had exhausted her teachers with her "Peachy-esque" questions. "What *ees* con-DOME?" she asked Rob "Straight Arrow" Farrow. "*Ees
somesing* you *vear?* Or *somesing* you *eet?*" In History, when Millard Schwartz was
faking his way through a question about the Industrial Revolution, she'd interrupted, saying, "Here *ees menn weeth schmall* penis. Here *ees menn* who *kennot
admeet* he does *nyet* know *sheet.*"

With Muley, she was less confrontational, and also less gregarious. She
brought a pen and a pad to his apartment so she could take notes to understand
her character's motivation. Muley answered her questions as best he could, and

then "Peachy" helped him study for The Constitution. At one point, Muley asked about Jill.

"Who *ees zees Jeel?*" Peachy asked. "I do *nyet* know *zees* person."

"Your sister," Muley prodded.

"I *heff nyet seester,*" Peachy said. "Once I *heff* three *seester,* but *zhey* all die in *eexplosion* at *wodka deesteelery vhen* some jerkoff light *metch.*"

"I was just wondering how she was," Muley said.

"Do not *sink* so much about *zees Jeel,*" said Peachy. "*Zhere* are *plenchy* more *feesh* who *sweem een* Volga."

"I don't want any other fish," Muley said.

"*Zhat* makes me *veddy* sad, *Meester* Mules," said Peachy. "I go cry me *beeg reever* now." Peachy Moskowitz touched his arm. "Play *eet* cool, *Meester* Mules," she said. "Stay cold and dry, and she *veel* get hot and *zhen vet. Zees ees* Peachy's next lesson from life."

At Friday's Constitution makeup test, Muley sat at the back of the classroom and studied his notebook, in which he had started storyboarding a short film that would be half animation, half live action. In it, a cartoon character would fall in love with a real girl. But in order to win the girl, either the cartoon character would have to become human, or the human would have to become a cartoon character. He was sketching out a concept for a dividing line over which the cartoon world would begin blending into the real world when he noticed Jill standing over his desk.

"If you want to know how I am, you can ask me. You don't have to ask my sister," she said.

Muley smiled at her, but she didn't smile back. "All right," Muley said, "how are you?"

"Too late," Jill said, and took her seat.

He was going to follow her, but then Mrs. Korab handed out the tests. Two hours later, when Mrs. Korab said "Stop. Put your pencils down and close your test booklets," he was checking his answers one final time and hadn't even noticed that Jill had already left the room.

Before Saturday's *Young Town* taping, Donna Mayne, who was doing double duty as producer and engineer, since Mel Coleman had taken the day off for unspecified reasons, was quite enthusiastic when Muley said that Peachy would be calling in on Tuesday, and Lennie was elated. "Peachy's coming to town!" he kept shouting. "Peachy is coming to town!" He said he'd make sure to be at the station for the call. Donna asked Muley if he would come to the station that evening. Muley told Donna he was sorry, but he had to babysit his girlfriend's sister.

On the night of the call, Muley gave Ajay Patel from Radio Shack $10 and asked if he would buy him two cartons of Marlboro Lights. *Vhat vas thees sheet,* Michelle wanted to know when she arrived at Muley's apartment with Gareth, and Muley gave her the cigarettes. *Poossies schmoke* these, she said. Michelle had painted on new coats of blue eye shadow and red lipstick, and her yellow-blond hair had been newly feathered. Her high heels matched her lipstick. The three of them went to Muley's room and Michelle began her vocal exercises—*mee-may-mi-moe-moo; the tip of the tongue, the lips, the teeth, and those tantalizing testicles.* Muley had replaced his phone with a salvaged Illinois Bell; he had unscrewed the mouthpiece of the receiver and stuffed it with tissue paper to make it sound as if Peachy were calling from out of town. At their last rehearsal, Muley had typed up a list of possible questions and a series of answers from which Michelle could respond, but Michelle refused. Stay out of her way and let her do what she did best, she said.

Muley had already resigned himself to the certainty that his lie would be discovered, that he would be relegated to the status of a neighborhood joke, that Bess Vaysberg would no longer give him free *kichels.* He told Michelle and Gareth he would be in the living room with his mother and when they were done, they should tell him how it had gone and whether they would all be arrested or not. But Michelle protested: "No, no. Peachy need audience. Peachy *kenn* only perform *weeth* audience." Muley paced the room, eyes gazing down at the floor as Michelle dialed the number. "Sit your ass down, Wills," Gareth hissed, then dutifully rolled himself a joint while Muley regarded him disapprovingly. "I'm not smoking it, Wills. I'm just rolling it," Gareth said.

"I *emm searchink* for a *Meesus* Donna Mayne," Michelle said into the phone.

"Miss Moskowitz?" Donna asked.

"*Ees* correct," said Michelle.

Donna thanked her for calling and said she had some questions and thought Lennie might have some too. Michelle said she hoped *zey vould* be brief, because she *vas vorking* on a new *translession* of *Zee Cherry Orchard* for a *seater* company in *Menhetten* that had *eppedently* hired some *pud-puller* by the name of Douglas

Sternberg to do the job and it had been an *ebbsolute* mess. "So," Michelle asked, "*vot ees eet* I *kenn* do for you?"

"Lay off that 'pud-puller' stuff, Wasserstrom," Gareth whispered. Michelle waved him off.

"Ignore *thees* voice in *bekground,*" she said, "I *emm beink* harassed by some *fett,* gay *menn* who's *giffink* me *advise* on how I should *spikk* to *reddio.*" Gareth gave her the finger, pointed to the joint, and whispered, "Ten bucks if you want any of this shit, Streep." He dropped the joint in a bag and extracted another rolling paper from his wallet as Donna and Lennie peppered Peachy with questions.

"Do you think there will ever be a nuclear war between America and the Soviet Union?" Donna asked Peachy.

"*Zhe* Russian *pipple* are not a fighting *pipple,*" Michelle responded. "*Vee* are poets; *vee* are *drimmers; vee* do *everysink pessionately,* but nuclear *var ees nyet pessionate think; ees pooshink bottons. Zhe* Russian *pipple, vee* do *nyet poosh bottons.*"

"Have you ever dated a stand-up comedian?" Lennie wanted to know.

"*Zhere ees nussink* more *pessionate zhen mekkink luff* to a *shtend-oop comiddien,*" Michelle said. She had kicked off her shoes and her bare heels were against the wall as she leaned back in Muley's swivel chair.

Donna asked why Peachy's exploits hadn't been better publicized in the U.S. media.

"Because *journaleests* are all *fett mozzers* of *fokkers,*" Peachy said. "*Zhey sink* KGB *vill kesstrate zhem.*"

Donna asked Peachy if she would be interested in phoning in again and making her contributions a regular segment.

Lennie suggested that the next time she was in town, they could even invite her into the studio.

"*Deepends,*" Peachy said.

"On what?" Donna wanted to know.

"*Ees keppitaleestic* society," Peachy said. *Eet vas* like her friend Svetlana Tuchbaum used to say: "*Ess, gess, or gress; no vun* rides for free."

Donna said she and Lennie would discuss it and get back to her.

"*Nyet,*" Michelle said. "I get *bekk* to *you.*"

After she hung up, Michelle stood up on Muley's table and, fists in the air, did an impromptu barefoot dance, kicking as she shouted, "*Keek-ess, mozzerfokker;*

keek-ess, mozzerfokker. Geef me *wodka. Geef* me *seegarettes."* She jumped down to the floor, slapped five with Gareth, and shouted, "Ho yeah! Ho yeah!" then detailed the highlights of her performance, while also critiquing her missteps ("I don't think the accent's all the way there yet," she said). She lit a cigarette, sat cross-legged on the floor, contemplated her toes, and asked Muley if he had an ashtray. No, he didn't have a fucking ashtray, Gareth answered for him. He stood up. You didn't just go lighting up in people's rooms; that wasn't cool. Sorry, Michelle said. She gestured with the cigarette, looked for a place to put it out, didn't find one, then said that she and Gareth were going to find someplace to smoke. No they weren't, Gareth said, he had a test in frickin' AP English class at 9:30 the next morning. Well, why didn't he just bullshit it, Michelle wanted to know; he'd already been accepted by the U of C—who gave a shit whether he got an "A" or a "D" on that test; she wanted to "debrief." No, Gareth said, he didn't bullshit about literature; that's why he was going to the U of C, because he didn't bullshit about literature, and that's why she'd wind up going downstate, because she did. Going downstate? Michelle asked, why didn't he go down *this*. She played off his remark as if it was part of their usual banter, but the memory of that hungover PSAT exam she'd taken soured her mood. Pretending to be Peachy was one thing; being Michelle Wasserstrom was something else entirely. Fine, she said, dejected, they were going home, thanks for the cigarettes, maybe she and Muley could rehearse again on the weekend before she called up Donna to negotiate the terms of her weekly contributions to *Young Town*.

At the front door of the apartment, Michelle, cigarette in her hand, gave Muley a hug and a kiss on the cheek. "You go wash off that *leepsteeck* now, *Meester Mules*," she said. Muley and Gareth shook hands. "Waukegan Night, Friday?" Gareth asked. Sure, maybe, Muley said, thanks for everything. "Don't thank me till it's over, Wills," Gareth said.

"*Anythink* I can tell to *Meeshell's seester Jeel*?" Michelle asked.

"Yeah," Muley said, "Tell her I didn't ask about her. Tell her you asked me if I had anything to tell her and I said no."

"*Ees goot* idea," Michelle said. "I tell *thees* to the *leetle beetch.*"

The next day at the end of class, after Mrs. Korab told Muley, "Great job on the Constitution test, Muley," and Jill, "See me after class," Jill went straight up to Muley and said, "So, did you not ask about me or did you tell my sister to say you didn't?" But before he could respond, Mrs. Korab was tapping Jill on the shoulder, saying, "Jill, this minute." And it wasn't until the next week—when Mrs. Korab had agreed to change the question on the Constitution exam from "What ten rights do YOU enjoy as an American citizen?" to "What are the amendments of the Bill of Rights?"— that Jill finally passed. She approached Muley before PE and said it had been a couple of weeks since she'd gotten Muley's last film. Yeah, Muley said, he'd been working on one, but it was going to take a lot longer than his previous ones.

When they got to the locker rooms, Jill asked Muley what he was doing over the weekend. "Going to a funeral," he said. "Wanna come?" Jill stopped short of the locker room door. Her face turned suddenly fierce. She said that wasn't funny—Muley must have known, she thought, that she didn't like being reminded of funerals; it was a bad joke, malevolent. He knew she hadn't gone to her mother's funeral, that her father had disobeyed her mother's wishes, that she had stayed home alone in protest that day, then walked all by herself to the lake. It wasn't funny, Jill repeated, and smacked open the door to the girls' locker room.

But it wasn't a joke, he wanted to tell her during PE; he was, in fact, going to a funeral. But getting to Jill proved impossible. The new teacher, Ms. Aviva Bernstein, formerly the recess monitor, wouldn't let Muley talk to Jill. Bernstein, who called everybody "Mister" or "Miss," took her new responsibilities seriously, especially with regard to the required "gym suit"—white T-shirt and dark pants. She had the students stand in line, shortest to tallest, and then she made them march, following the rhythm she beat out against the gymnasium floor with a warped pool cue. While the students marched, Ms. Bernstein grabbed and repositioned those who were either too tall or too short to be in the places they had chosen, which meant that Jill (one of the shorter students) and Muley (the second tallest) marched on opposite sides of the line and Muley couldn't explain to her what he had meant. He tried to break out of the line to tell her, but Ms. Bernstein snapped, "Inspection, Mr. Wills." No one was allowed to stop marching; otherwise, he or she would be sent to the principal's office.

"Remember our white shirts and dark pants," Bernstein said. "Dark pants, Miss Wasserstrom, dark pants," she said, sneering at Jill's white painter's pants. "That's the third time this week." She promptly sent Jill to the principal's office. Muley broke from the line to follow Jill, but Ms. Bernstein's voice stopped him. "Don't borrow trouble, Mr. Wills," she said.

"White shirt, Mr. Weinberg. White shirt," Ms. Bernstein said, pausing at

Shmuel Weinberg. He wore a white T-shirt, but it displayed a blue press-on logo of the White Sox "South Side Hitmen." Shmuel, too, was sent to the principal's office. Forty-five minutes' worth of shuttle races, forty-yard dashes, jumping jacks, burpees, and dribbling exercises later, the bell trilled and a mass of white T-shirts and dark pants blurred on the way out the gymnasium door. But Ms. Bernstein's "Mister Wiiiiills?" stopped Muley again. She told him he'd broken from the line twice, and now he had to help put away the balls and the cones. By the time he had changed out of his "gym suit," Muley assumed that Jill was probably almost all the way home. In fact, she was walking east on North Shore toward the beach and the lake, because thoughts of funerals and death and the *Adon Olam* always led her there, far away from anyone she knew. Soon she would run into Shmuel Weinberg, who would just happen to be walking toward the lake too. Muley was too late to find Jill and explain that the following morning he would be at a funeral for Mel Coleman's mother.

W hat impressed Muley most about the funeral service for Mrs. Oneida Coleman, held at Church of Our Savior in Evanston, where she had worked as a secretary and where her husband had served as deacon, was not so much the solemnity of the occasion or the profundity of the eulogies as the sheer number of people who had turned out. It seemed as though all the pews were filled. Each time Muley counted, he got a different number, but it was always somewhere around 150. He thought about his mother and about how few people would attend a funeral when she died, and though he was heartened that his mother's doom no longer seemed to be an imminent concern, still this gnawed at him, at least until he considered how little things like that would matter to his mother. Then he remembered Jill's mother's funeral. He hadn't gone, but he recalled their teacher Miss Strimling saying how sorry she was to hear about Jill's mom. And then she had asked Jill how the funeral was and if she'd gotten through it okay and Jill had said she supposed so. What do you mean *supposed,* Miss Strimling had asked. She hadn't gone, Jill said, but offered nothing more. Later, Muley had asked her why. Jill had told him but asked that he never mention it again.

At the church service, Muley sat in one of the rearmost pews. And at the burial in Calvary Cemetery at the Chicago-Evanston border, Muley stayed a good distance away as well, watching light flakes of snow melting the moment they landed on the dirt, letting the words of the preacher pass by his ears like so much wind and snow. By the grave, he saw Julie Ying, Lisa-Anne Williams, and their parents—he had not asked his mother to join him, for he knew how much she despised all religious rituals—but he did not approach them. Nor did he respond in kind when Ajay Patel waved. It seemed disrespectful to acknowledge friends in a time of someone else's loss. When the graveside service was over and the hundred or so people, all in black hats and overcoats, began walking over the slushy mud and grass, Muley approached Mel Coleman.

Mel was lagging behind the others, hands stuffed in the pockets of his overcoat, a tweed cap on his head. He seemed not to be looking at the grave or the cemetery but past it, at the gray waves of Lake Michigan. Muley offered his hand to shake, but Mel put his arms around him instead, clasping the young man strongly, patting his back twice. Mel asked Muley if he was all right; funerals could be rough on a kid. Muley said he was sorry for Mel's loss. He figured Mel would want to be alone now; they could talk after Mel had had time to work through everything. No, no, Mel said, don't worry about that. He'd loved his mother; she had been a good woman, but now she was "in the ground," and he wanted to discuss the future over a beer. Didn't he have to spend time with his family? Muley asked. Yeah, Mel said, but he needed a beer first.

As they sat at the Double Bubble, both of them still in their black suits, Mel told Muley he was going to quit the radio station; the job was all right but it wasn't leading anywhere. His mother had left him some cash, enough to live on for a little while and maybe make a small investment; he said he wanted to start a recording studio and film company. He would call it 3M—Mel's Music and Movies.

Mel said he knew *Godfathers of Soul* wasn't progressing as quickly as he'd anticipated because it was, at heart, a movie, not a book. He said he already had an idea for the film promotion campaign; the tag line would be "Never Take Sides Against the Brothers." He also had conceived the opening shot. The screen would be black, and then in white the words "Chicago, 1929" would appear. Then some introductory text, as seen in the old gangster pictures he liked watching: "A dude named Al Capone runs the white underworld downtown. But one mile south, on 35th and State, there's another underworld. They call it Bronzeville. And the man who runs it is Tiny Walker." The text would fade into black and Tiny Walker would appear in a cream-colored suit, spats, and a Panama hat in front of the Domino Club. He would light a cigarette and throw down a match. The match, still lit, would hit a pool of gasoline. The gas would ignite and the flame would slither underneath the door. Then *"Bam,"* Mel said, the Domino Club would explode.

Mel figured he could do the scene mostly with miniatures and models, didn't Muley think that would work? Muley said sure, it might, but he wasn't listening carefully. He was thinking of his own short film, the one about the cartoon boy who falls in love with a real girl, the one that he was now thinking might finally break through to Jill. The other films had been sketches, crudely realized. For a film to truly have an impact, it would have to be more complex. Muley had wanted the film to have a happy ending, with the cartoon boy stepping over a threshold, becoming real, and then embracing and kissing the girl. But now he thought it would have to work the other way, with the real girl stepping over a threshold and becoming a cartoon. They would embrace, but then a hand would reach in and erase the cartoon boy and the cartoon girl and their entire cartoon world as they kissed, oblivious. The film would begin with the following title: "I LOVE YOU, JILL WASSERSTROM," but then a hand holding a pencil would reach in and erase all the letters except the "L" and the "O" in "LOVE" and the "S" and the "T" in "WASSERSTROM." *"Lost,"* the title would then read, "A film by Muley Wills." That night, Muley told his mother to take a message if any phone calls came for him. He was drawing cartoon characters and could not be disturbed.

WASSERSTROM

Michelle

M ichelle Wasserstrom was feeling unusually magnanimous on the March afternoon when she asked Jill if she could take her to the Purim Carnival at K.I.N.S. Jill had seemed droopy of late—she'd barely talked to Muley since her Bat Mitzvah nearly two months earlier and Michelle had heard that she had recently been seen spending time with some kid named Shmuel. Michelle had never met Shmuel, but Muley was the coolest eighth-grader she'd ever met and there was no such thing as a cool person named Shmuel. Obviously, Jill needed cheering up.

Until recently, Michelle had also needed cheering up, but over the past week, things had changed drastically. She had been feuding with almost everybody in her life, particularly her father and Gail. Every night she talked with her father, she tried to work Gail's name into the conversation—"Oh, but I guess I wouldn't know how to wash dishes right, because my name isn't Gail Schiffler-Bass," "Hmm, this is a difficult math problem. How would Jesus approach it, or Gail Schiffler-Bass?" Anytime her father suggested an activity, Michelle would snarl, "Gail coming?" She worked hard to avoid seeing Gail, sequestering herself in her bedroom whenever she heard Large Mouth Bass lumbering up the stairway, staying in there with the door closed until she heard the woman waddling out. Gail had come to represent all the frustrations besetting Michelle. Since she had vetoed the role of Ophelia and then refused to audition for *Arsenic and Old Lace,* she had turned her back on the one vocation that could have rescued her from her despair; now her only respite was pretending to be Muley's cousin Peachy once a week on WBOE.

Her lowest point had arrived one night when she went to a Blackhawks game, something she had done with Myra frequently the previous year. They would buy tickets in the standing-room section and find guys to buy them beer. And when the guys would ask them to go drinking after the game at McCuddy's, they would say yeah, sure, why not, then say they had to use the powder room and run like hell down the stairs and out of the stadium. Or if the guys were cute, they would accompany them to the bar and get dropped off at the bus stop when the guys found out they were Jewish (whenever their dates were getting boring or it was getting late, Michelle would say, "I hope this doesn't bother you, but our names aren't really Heather and April; they're Shiffra and Chaya").

This time, Myra showed up late at the Wasserstrom apartment; she said she was sorry, but Douglas had taken a while to get dressed and it had taken even longer to convince Gareth to attend the game. Michelle said she thought it was just going to be the two of them and Myra said yeah, she knew, but she thought it would be fun to double-date. *Double-date?* Michelle asked. Since when was she dating Gareth? Well, Myra said, it was not as if she had been dating anybody else lately, who else did she have in mind? Michelle was going to say forget it, she'd stay home, but then she remembered that Gail was coming over for dinner.

While Gareth read next to her in the backseat of Douglas's Jaguar, Michelle spent the ride to the game trying to suck in as much pot and throw back as much Old Style (a product that she referred to as "Dog Style") as she could so that she might find Douglas and Myra's antics—making out at every traffic light, Myra's eyes closed, Douglas's gazing back jubilantly at Michelle—amusing instead of nauseating. But by the time they had gotten as far south as the Oak Theater, Western Avenue was spinning and Michelle was asking to stop the car so she could get out at the corner, where she threw up near a parked gold Avanti. And though at first she had found funny Gareth's book choice of Nabokov's *Lolita,* when he kept reading it aloud, it just gave her a headache.

The game had been miserable. The guys sitting nearby—a flock of Red Wings fans chanting "U.S.A.! U.S.A.!" when the PA announcer dedicated the game to the U.S. hostages, bellowing, "It's a puck, not a pussy," then "Put some hair around it" during the first period, throwing octopi down to the ice when Mike Ogrodnick scored a hat trick—were repulsive. Gareth, who hadn't gotten into a fight since fourth grade, when Avi Sherman had told him he wasn't all that smart and Gareth had punched him out, almost got into three different brawls with some Detroit fans who referred to him as "Doughboy." At the end of the second period, when the interior of the stadium was enveloped in cigarette smoke, the whole place smelled like stale beer and piss, and some fox in high heels and a miniskirt was headed out to center ice for a slapshot competition, Michelle had had enough and asked Gareth if he wanted to go. "Come on," she said, "you're my date. Take me home; you might get lucky."

It was a slow bus ride home all the way up Western past vacant lots and burnt-out storefronts, past Logan Square, where street gangs battled over turf, on into West Rogers Park, where it seemed as if there were nothing but car dealerships stretching all the way north toward Evanston. When Michelle got home earlier than expected, declining Gareth's offer to "head over to Wills's house and see what he was doing," the apartment was dark except for a small band of light at the bottom of her and Jill's bedroom door. From the living room were the unmistakable sounds of sex—she could suddenly picture her father on top of Gail Schiffler-Bass or under Gail Shiva-Bass, Gail Shiva-Basshole grinding on top of his crotch. What the fuck were they doing? That's why there were *motels with hourly rates on Lincoln Avenue.* Is that how she sounded when she was fucking? It sounded disgusting, like when she would sit at Aunt Peppy and Uncle Dave's table on Parmesan Sundays; when everyone had stopped imitating Negro accents, there would be silence except for the sounds of slurping, smacking, chewing, and crunching, and she would realize that she was with a pack of beasts, lions delighting in the kill, ripping apart the flesh of still-quivering zebras, blood dribbling down their chins—*pass the salt, pass the margarine, pass the Diet Rite, snort snort, grunt, slobber.* It was fucking disgusting.

Michelle made a beeline for her bedroom door, threw it open loudly, then slammed it shut behind her. She didn't attempt to engage her sister in conversation—Jill was seated at the desk, designing a pamphlet for Art class calling for the San Salvadoran killers of Oscar Arnulfo Romero to be brought to justice. Michelle snatched a marker and several sheets of paper out of the desk drawer, sat on her bed, and created a brand new "Edict." "BE IT RESOLVED," she wrote, "THAT THE FOLLOWING ACTIVITIES WILL FROM THIS POINT FORWARD BE OUTLAWED ON 6519 NORTH CAMPBELL AVENUE, CHICAGO, ILL.: COITUS, CUNNILINGUS, FELLATIO, AS WELL AS ANY AND ALL OTHER ACTIVITIES WHICH COULD RESULT IN SUCH. VIOLATIONS OF THE AFOREMENTIONED EDICT WILL RESULT EITHER IN EVICTION OR PAYMENT OF TWENTY DOLLARS PER VIOLATION, PLUS ALL APPLICABLE LAUNDERING FEES. THE SUM WILL BE PAYABLE IN CASH TO MICHELLE AND JILL WASSERSTROM." She signed "The Management" at the bottom of the edict.

The next day when she got home, she took the mail out of the box and replaced it with two copies of the edict addressed to her father and Gail. Amid bills and fund-raising letters from various nonprofit organizations for Jill, there was a thin envelope addressed to Michelle "Waterstrum": the results of her PSAT exam. She was going to pitch the envelope, then stopped—it was just a practice exam anyway, she had misspelled her name and listed her race as Pacific Islander, who gave a shit what it said. She ripped open the envelope, looked at her score, and laughed—the moment she saw it, she called Gareth to tell him how bad it was. And when Gareth answered, she told him she hoped she could marry him so that they could have kids with his brains and her body. How bad did she score? Gareth asked. Oh, not too bad, she laughed, she was in the 98th percentile, which meant that at least 2 percent of the population was dumber than she was.

"Hey, dumbshit," Gareth said, "98th percentile means *98* percent of the population is dumber than you." He asked her what her raw score was. She said she had received a 71 on the verbal portion and a 68 on math, which sounded sucky to her. Gareth asked her if she really was as stupid as she was pretending to be—the scores were out of 80, not out of 100, you fucking moron, he said; she'd scored higher than he had and she was sure to be a National Merit semifinalist. What the fuck was that? Michelle wanted to know. Gareth said it meant you got honored in a ceremony and got your picture on the wall of the school, plus you got piles of mail from crap colleges asking you to apply.

When Michelle got off the phone with Gareth—after they agreed to celebrate at Wolfy's that night—she felt as if she had undergone a strange, instant transformation. Though just the night before, she had been livid at her father and Large Mouth Bass, had wanted to throttle Douglas Sternberg, now none of that mattered. She was filled with the desire to take her PSAT score sheet and mount it on a sheet of posterboard so she could wear it around all day; she wanted to turn it into an iron-on for a T-shirt, to use it as a design for place mats and distribute them in the cafeteria. It was one of the first times in years that she had received independent confirmation of her intelligence. What she wanted now more than anything was to call somebody up and boast, but she had no idea who that person would be. Her father would have the same reaction no matter how well or poorly she'd done; he'd smile vacantly and say, "Terrific; that's just terrific." There was no point in calling up Myra—she'd gotten crap ACT scores and was wait-listed at Southern Illinois. She could tell her sister she was in the 98th percentile, but that too was pointless; when Jill would be her age, she'd undoubtedly be in the 99th.

Late that night, when Michelle came home with a stack of books Gareth had lent her—suddenly she was interested in fitting in a schedule of reading between bong hits—her father was seated at the kitchen table, two crushed cans of Miller beer and a full glass of it in front of him. He was staring at the edict Michelle had issued. "I got your note," he said.

For a moment, Michelle didn't even know to which note he was referring. And when it occurred to her, it seemed like something she had written months as opposed to hours earlier. What went on between her father and Gail no longer made any difference to her—well, that wasn't entirely true; she still found it disgusting, but she didn't care about it particularly. Look, she said, don't worry about the note, she wrote it when she was angry, she hadn't been thinking, she would prefer to just forget about it. She hoped that would be enough to table the issue, but her father asked her to come back. Sit down a second, he said.

Uh-oh, she thought. She hoped this wasn't a serious sex talk; the last thing in the world she wanted to do, other than see Douglas Sternberg naked, was to have a serious sex talk with her father. Luckily, her mother had survived long enough to give her the basics—she'd been totally cool about it, handing her a copy of *The Joy of Sex* when she turned twelve and telling her to come to her if she had any questions. Michelle had only two questions—why did the book use sketches of ugly people to depict sexual techniques and why were the pages in the masturbation section stuck together? Responding to the first question, Becky Wasserstrom said that, in general, people were a lot uglier naked than you might ever suspect. And as for the second question, she said she'd have to ask her PTA friend Ellen Rovner, from whom she'd borrowed the book, for an explanation.

Charlie turned the edict facedown on the kitchen table and took a sip of beer. He didn't want to discuss the note in detail, he said—there were a lot of words in there he didn't understand, and after he'd looked one up in the dictionary, he'd decided he didn't want to know what the others meant. The one thing he wanted to tell Michelle—that he wanted to tell both her and Jill when Jill got home from playing Scrabble over at Shmuel Weinberg's house ("That little twerp?" Michelle interjected)—was that he was sorry. He knew he'd been thinking of himself more than of his children and that was "cruddy" of him. It had just been a long time since he'd had "someone his age" he could "be friends with" and the excitement of being able to be friends with someone his age had made him overlook more important matters. It had been wrong of Gail to suggest she stay over at their apartment and he'd been wrong to say yes—she was a very persuasive woman, he said (*Ick,* thought Michelle), but he wasn't about to make excuses. He'd told Gail that they could still go out to movies and have dinner, but as far as all that "staying-over jazz" was concerned, that would have to wait either until they were married or his girls were grown up and out of the house. He knew that might sound old-fashioned, but he couldn't help it; that's the way he was. He wanted to set good examples for his daughters, he'd told Gail. He couldn't expect them to live up to expectations to which he didn't himself conform. And what did Gail say? Michelle asked. Charlie reported that Gail had said that his daughters probably understood a lot more than he realized. Charlie said maybe that was true, but still there was no reason for him to behave in a way of which he would absolutely disapprove were his daughters involved.

Michelle thought of herself lying on top of Millard Schwartz in the backseat of his Opel shouting "Yabbadabba-do me!" at the moment of climax. She contrasted that moment with a walk she and her father had once taken to Lunt Avenue Beach, where she'd spent an entire afternoon shoveling sand into a little windmill to make it spin. For a moment, she was depressed, thinking about the innocence of childhood and the defilement of puberty. But then she recalled that afternoon with her father more clearly and realized she'd never cared much for the smell of alewives on the beach and that she had found the windmill toy boring but kept playing with it because her father had been so excited about buying it for her. And then she thought of her Flintstone-esque yodeling in Millard's car and realized that though Millard had turned out to be a Who ticket–cheating scumbag, that evening had actually been a hell of a lot of fun. And now here was her father making her feel like some whore, because he was stuck in the 1950s when, most probably, everybody had been getting laid except him. She knew— didn't guess, *knew*—that she had already notched more sexual partners than he ever had, and though, for a while, keeping her father ignorant of that fact seemed best for everybody, the tactic now seemed to have outlived its usefulness. If he was going to start developing unreasonable expectations about her behavior, if he was going to start setting curfews and scheduling serious sex talks, then some misconceptions had to be cleared up right away.

Oh, by the way, she said, she'd had sex with five guys since she'd turned fourteen and she usually used protection and, anyway, she wasn't dating anybody right now, so there was really nothing to worry about, because reading gave her a better high than pot and alcohol and pot and alcohol gave her a better high than sex. So what she guessed she was saying was that if he was going to change the nature of his relationship with Gail on her account, he really didn't need to. So, she said, she was glad to have that all on the table, and now she was going to bed. "Good night, Dad," she said as Charlie Wasserstrom contemplated his beer.

The next weeks in school had the quality and impact of a revelation for Michelle, beginning with the announcement that she had been named one of seven National Merit semifinalists, along with Matthias Kimmel and five other dweebs she didn't know. On the day the pictures went up in the hallway with "Mather Salutes Our National Merit Semifinalists" cut out in orange construction paper on a teal construction paper wall, she giddily loitered near Vice Principal Ralph Mulvey's office as Sarah Silver complained loudly that she thought it was "beyond unfair" that students who got straight A's never got their pictures on a construction paper wall, while people who either "got lucky," she said loudly, or "happened to be good at tests," she said even louder, wound up with this "completely disproportionate" honor.

Unlike the thrill Michelle got from performing, which began to dissipate the moment the applause stopped and the set was struck, leaving her desperately scrambling for another fix, another role, the excitement she experienced from her PSAT score did not wear off. She no longer felt self-conscious, clumsy, and slow around her precocious sister—let Jill see if she could do a dimebag, cannonball a forty-ounce, do her homework with Lynyrd Skynyrd blasting, and still pull a 3.0 grade point average. As most people saw it, she knew how to party and her sister knew how to excel in school, but now it was her duty to teach Jill that it was possible to do both. Neither Jill nor she had a mother anymore, and she could either brood about that fact—which she did occasionally when she was alone with Gareth and had drunk too much of his parents' Framberry Dolfi liqueur—or, she thought, she could be a good, responsible maternal figure for Jill.

The Purim Carnival was held every Sunday in March and it was one of the most popular events the synagogue sponsored, though it took in significantly less cash than the monthly Las Vegas Nights. The carnival took place on both the main floor and in the basement of the synagogue. Events changed weekly. One week, there would be an auction, another week a costume contest. The carnival always ended with musical entertainment and dancing. In the basement, there were games and juice and hamantaschen. All week long, Rabbi Meltzer would drive his beat-up Datsun with a roof-mounted speaker, announcing "Purim Carnival, this Sunday at one. Come for the games, come for the music, come for the parade. Only $2 to get in and only $1 a ticket."

Michelle had fond memories of the Purim Carnival. She remembered it as the occasion on which she had first discovered the power of her stage presence, playing Queen Esther in *Einmal in a Purim,* a rock opera written and directed by Rabbi Meltzer. Michelle had more lines than anybody and stopped the show with her three solos (the only solos in the show other than Larry Rovner's, which had to be cut because his voice was changing). She sang "I Got Such *Tsuris,* Ahasuerus," "Don't Ask Me Why, Mordecai," and "It's a Shame about Haman," and led the whole cast in the final chorus of the title song: "Everybody, get your *groggers,* / it's time to make some noise. / That old Haman was a *khazer,* / just like all the other *goys . . .*"

When Michelle asked Jill if she wanted to attend the carnival, Jill said she'd rather be throttled. When Michelle asked Jill a second time, Jill said she'd rather be hanged. The third time Michelle asked, she said Jill had two choices—go with her to the carnival or with their father to Parmesan Sunday at Uncle Dave and Aunt Peppy's—Charlie had recently declared Sundays were family days and his daughters could not spend them alone. And that meant spending the evening listening to Artie Schumer's abominable imitations of Negro accents, which had grown even worse since he had discovered that Jill would be attending high school at Lane Tech, which had a sizable black population. The last Parmesan Sunday, Artie Schumer had spent the time after dinner (when the women cleaned off the table) and before dessert (when the women brought in new paper napkins, plastic forks, and Marshall Field's fudge cake) imitating "Lucius Jefferson," a character he invented to be Jill's prom date. *"Yes suh, Mistuh Wassuhstrum, suh,"* Artie said, *"Ah'd sho' 'nuff lahk to take yo faahhn daughtuh to duh prom, Mistuh Wassuhstrum, suh."* Better to be subjected to a thousand Purim Carnivals than one more Parmesan Sunday.

That Sunday afternoon, before Jill and Michelle went to the carnival, they walked all the way west down Devon to the Schwartz-Rosenblum Judaica Bookstore and picked out two masks—a cat mask for Michelle; a Richard Nixon mask for Jill. The sidewalks were mostly unremarkable—people waiting in the checkout line at the North Water Market with bags full of vegetables, snacking on fried perch sandwiches in front of Robert's Fish Market, browsing through paperbacks in revolving wire racks at Rosen's Drugs. But every so often, a shock of Purim would burst through the quotidian—at Jerusalem Pizza, men with black overcoats, fedoras, and *payess* were shooting each other with squirt guns, five Queen Esthers and three Mordecais were waiting for their mothers to finish their loads at the Laundromat on California, and in front of Burghard's Egg Factory, boys in army fatigues, dressed up like Israeli commandos, played Hide-and-Seek.

At Devon and Albany, Michelle asked Jill how Muley was. Jill said that Michelle had probably talked to him more recently than she had. At Devon and Sacramento, Michelle asked Jill what the deal was with this Shmuel guy—she wasn't really dating him, was she? Jill said nothing was going on. He wanted to hang around her and sometimes she didn't say no. Near Devon and Richmond, Michelle asked Jill how school was going. Jill said fine. Near Francisco, Michelle asked Jill if she was looking forward to high school. Jill said she guessed so. At Mozart Street, Michelle asked Jill if she was considering participating in any extracurricular activities once she got to high school. Jill said she didn't know, maybe something involving politics. Once they turned onto California, Michelle, trying to contain her pride, revealed that she had scored in the 98th percentile on her PSAT and she was now about to be flooded with mailings from crap colleges. "Oh, that's pretty good," Jill said. The two masked girls walked in silence the rest of the way to the synagogue.

The K.I.N.S. announcement board said "Purim Carnival." Below it, the title of Rabbi Shmulevits's most recent sermon—"Reagan is Haman." On the front steps of the synagogue, Hillel Levy—dressed as a gorilla ("It *is too* a Purim costume; it's Megillah Gorilla," he told anyone who challenged him)—was trying to get Moshe Cardash (dressed as Mordecai in sackcloth) to mount his shoulders to challenge Connie Sherman and Dvorah Kerbis (who wore heels and miniskirts and tube tops under denim jackets, calling their costumes "Queen Esther for the '80s") to a chicken fight. All the while, Rabbi Meltzer's Datsun, parked with its flashers on in a loading zone, blared its tape-recorded message: "Only $2 to get in and only $1 a ticket. We've got rock 'n' roll, *groggers,* Megillahs, and more."

Inside the synagogue, Rabbi Jeff Meltzer in tennis shoes, a tie-dyed shirt, and blue jeans, *tsitsis* dangling out of the faded Levi's, was lugging an amplifier into the auditorium. Rabbi Shmulevits was standing near the yarmulke bin, chuckling politely as Cantor Fishman told him about a hotel he had discovered in the northwest suburbs called the Sybaris, which catered solely to couples and had revolving beds and mirrors on the ceiling. A half dozen kids from the *Aleph* and *Beth* classes in shimmering gold Esther outfits and pointy-hatted Haman costumes were walking past the carpeted Tree of Life memorial hallway and into the Hebrew school. On the wall opposite the basement door, there were framed pictures of each Hebrew school graduating class since 1953—pale boys in pressed white shirts and skinny black ties, their hair short and slick or trimmed into crew cuts, two girls in the class, hair dark and shiny, starched white blouses buttoned up to the neck, black skirts; one of the girls wore pearls. In 1967, the photos turned from black-and-white to color. In that year's picture, there were thirty-one students, a number that edged slowly but unmistakably downward with nearly each passing year.

Michelle Wasserstrom, Jill tailing grudgingly behind her, found herself in the 1975–76 picture, hair down to her waist. She had deep shadows under her eyes that contrasted starkly with her white spaceman-style pantsuit that zipped up the front. It was only four years since she had graduated from K.I.N.S., and of the twenty people in the picture, she only could say for sure what six were doing. There was Yehuda Rovner, their *Heb* class valedictorian —an honor that resulted largely from the fact that he was the only one who really wanted the scholarship to Hebrew high school—in a white ruffle shirt with a black bow tie. That boy in the tan corduroy sport coat was Millard Schwartz. She had seen Missy Eisenstaedt, Ben Jacobs, and Randy Weinstock around the neighborhood, Missy shopping with her mom at Dominick's, Ben and Randy with basketballs, dribbling them down North Shore. As for the others—the girls with their horsetail hair and their knee-length patterned dresses, Rivka Fishman with her pale-orange pantsuit, the boys with their sideburns and their salmon, powder-blue, or dark-brown sportcoats, Avi Sherman with his stoned blue eyes that matched his suit— Michelle had no idea what had happened to them. They were at Lane Tech, Ida Crown, or private schools in the northern suburbs; their parents had moved either north to Evanston or Skokie, or south to condos on the Magnificent Mile; or else, they had moved out of state altogether—to Las Vegas, Phoenix, Miami. The great Diaspora continued.

Behind a small, wobbly wooden desk placed in front of the basement door, Lana Rovner was seated, taking $2 entrance fees and selling strips of $1 tickets. She had a plastic tiara in her hair and glitter on her cheeks. She had recently been appointed class treasurer, an honor that resulted from her attention to detail and propriety. And she had, over the past two Sundays, only embezzled a total of $17, far less, she reasoned, than what any of her classmates would have taken. Charlie Wasserstrom had given Michelle a $20 bill and, with it, she paid for admission and ten carnival tickets. She and Jill walked downstairs, the sounds of Jewish comedy disco and rock 'n' roll records ("Take a Walk on the Kosher Side," by Gefilte Joe and the Fish, "Shul's Out for Summer," by K.C. and the Shabbos Band) becoming louder as they descended.

In the dank, low-ceilinged basement festooned with already-faded and dusty streamers, there were tables with cups of Kool-Aid and hamantaschen. The walls were covered with floor-to-ceiling Purim murals created by each of the classes from nursery school to *Dalet.* They began with scribbly, Crayola depictions of Queen Esther and led all the way up to magnificent, illustrated comics in which a snake-wielding Mordecai felled a phalanx of soldiers, saying, "Take That, You Persian," while a voluptuous Queen Esther in a slit skirt beckoned King Ahasuerus—"Come into my casbah, big boy." There was a pyramid of borscht jars you could try to knock over with a Wiffle ball; a strongman contraption that called out different phrases depending on how hard you hit it with a mallet ("Oh, big shot, *vot* a *mensch,*" "All right, so you're strong—*vot* do you *vant,* a medal?"). There was a Purim quiz game—get four questions right and you'd win a plastic bag with a pair of goldfish in it. Hillel Levy had been working the Haman dunking booth, until Rabbi Meltzer had informed him that his Haman had been too abusive to the *Aleph* students ("You Jews are all pussies," he had declared, adding Yiddish slurs his father had taught him—"Go get killed by a Chinaman," "Be a chandelier—hang by day, burn by night," and "Grow like an onion with your head in the ground"). In the Queen Esther kissing booth, Connie Sherman had also been relieved of her duties when it was discovered she was taking extra money for frenching. At the hockey net, Muley Wills—who was taking a break from editing his film, *Lost*—fired shot after shot past the outstretched arms of Shmuel Weinberg.

Michelle had not recalled the basement being so small; she had remembered it as a dark, labyrinthine hideaway where she had smoked her first, unremarkable joint with Avi Sherman and made out with him while everyone else was outside enjoying pound cake and grape juice in the yellow canvas sukkah. Jill found the carnival dull, so Michelle took an overly interested attitude in everything around her. She insisted they spend all of their tickets. They were wearing masks, she reasoned; no one knew who they were.

Thus, they bought hamantaschen and drank cherry Kool-Aid. They whipped Wiffle balls at borscht jars, listened to the strongman machine mock their efforts: "*Vot,* you got a *hoinia?*" Jill got four Purim questions right and won a pair of goldfish, which she vowed to set free in Lake Michigan. Jill told Michelle the answers to four other questions and asked Michelle if she'd give her her pair of goldfish, so she could set them free too. Behind her Richard Nixon mask, Jill was smiling just a bit—this was altogether better than veal Parmesan in Elmhurst. And then Michelle said oh, there's Muley Wills over by the hockey net, why don't we just go say hi. Jill asked where. Michelle said over there, shooting the puck at that troll in the hockey net. Jill said that Muley was Michelle's friend, why didn't she say hi if it was so important to her. Michelle said that Muley was Jill's boyfriend, not hers. Jill said Muley was not her boyfriend. Michelle asked who was, that troll in the hockey net? Jill said no, nobody was her boyfriend, she didn't want a boyfriend, why was it so important for her to have a boyfriend, why couldn't people just hang out and be friends and not be girlfriend and boyfriend? Michelle said there was no need for Jill to bottle everything inside her, she'd wind up with an ulcer before she was twenty-one. Jill said when she was twenty-one, she hoped she'd be a lesbian. Michelle asked why she wanted to be a lesbian. Jill said it was because lesbians were cool and nobody bothered them if they didn't have boyfriends. Michelle said that if Jill had a boyfriend, nobody would bother her about getting one. *Come on,* she said, grabbing Jill by the arm and pulling her past the kissing booth, where Hillel Levy was standing in line with three tickets asking whether he could get to third base if he used all three tickets at once. Come on, she repeated, we're going to say hi to Muley.

"Leave me alone!" shouted the girl in the Nixon mask, a bag of goldfish in each hand, fish sloshing against the sides of the bags as she broke free of her sister's grip and ran past the Queen Esther kissing booth and the Haman dunking tank to the stairway, which she scampered up, upsetting Lana's cash box when she got to the top, scattering quarters and crumpled $1 and $5 bills. "Hey," Lana shouted after her. "You have to register your prizes before you can take them out." The girl in the Nixon mask didn't respond, didn't turn around, just threw open the door and ran past the Tree of Life memorial board, down the synagogue hallway where Rabbi Meltzer was carrying a guitar case into the auditorium, out the front door of the synagogue, and down the stairs where the Datsun was still blaring "rock 'n' roll, *groggers, Megillahs, and more*" as, goldfish bags in hand, she crossed California heading east for Lake Michigan.

When the girl in the cat mask reached the top of the stairs, she saw Lana on her hands and knees picking up coins and dollar bills and returning some of them to the cash box. She asked Lana if she had seen a girl in a Nixon mask run by. Yes, Lana sniffed, she had just been knocked over by such a girl and she might have dislocated her elbow. Michelle said she was sure Lana's elbow was fine and if not, her father could take some X-rays. She asked if Lana had seen in which direction the girl in the Nixon mask had gone. Lana pointed to the synagogue door. Michelle began walking toward that door but then stopped when she heard someone walking behind her—Muley Wills, hockey stick in one hand, $5 bill in the other, ready to buy more tickets to shoot more goals.

"*Meester Mules, ees* pleasure to see you *vunce* again; I *emm fessinated* by Purim *reetual,*" Michelle said, extending her hand. Lana was getting up from the floor and setting her cash box back on the table when she saw Muley shaking hands with the girl in the cat mask, who was now speaking in a voice that sounded different from the one she had just heard. Muley asked Michelle how she was doing. Michelle said she was *teep-top,* but she had come with a *leetle beetch* named *Jeel,* who had run out *weeth* two *beggs* full of *feesh*; she wondered if Muley would help *trekk* her *ess* down. Lana stared at the two of them; there was something peculiar about the cat girl's accent.

Michelle told Muley she thought her sister had left, but suggested they check the auditorium. Muley said he wasn't sure Jill would want to see him at all; she was a complicated girl. "*Cumplicating garrull?*" Michelle asked. "*Bowlsheet.*" Muley asked Michelle if she wouldn't prefer speaking in her normal voice. "*Ebbsolutely nyet,*" Michelle said. "Oh, by *zee* way, *Meester* Mules, *deed* I tell you I score in 98th percentile *een* college *ixemm*? Bet you *deedn't* realize I *emm setch* smart *leetle beetch.*" Muley said Gareth had already told him. "*Jesus fucking Christ,*" Michelle said, dropping her accent entirely, couldn't anyone act like they were surprised? She opened the auditorium door in disgust.

It was dark in the auditorium except for two baby-blue spotlights crisscrossing each other on the stage where Michelle had once performed the role of Queen Esther and decided to become a star. There was a black backdrop behind two amps, a guitar, a bass guitar, and two microphones on stands in front and one bent at a 90-degree angle, hanging over a drum kit. There was a hushed, expectant murmur in the auditorium, the squeak of metal chairs against the floor, Rabbi Meltzer at one mike saying, "Check, check," going to the next mike— "Check, check"—then to the mike over the drum kit.

Jill didn't appear to be in the auditorium. Muley asked Michelle if she wanted to leave; he had to get back to work on his film anyway. Michelle said she wanted to wait a minute to see if Rabbi Meltzer would play "Runaround Sue" again or if he'd updated his repertoire since the Bicentennial. She had always liked him; the fact that even her father thought his rock opera was awful only made him more endearing. She always felt sorry he had gotten stuck waiting for Rabbi Shmulevits to retire and being disappointed every year, though he had always said that when the rabbi retired and he took over the shul, he would have to give up rock 'n' roll.

The blue spotlights went down, a yellow-white spotlight switched on, and Rabbi Meltzer stepped into it as a drummer and a bassist crept onstage from behind the black backdrop. Rabbi Meltzer said he had a question to ask the congregation: He wanted to know if they were ready to rock. A few people shouted *yeah*. Meltzer said that wasn't good enough; he wanted to know if they were ready to *rock*. *Yeah,* a few more people shouted. Were they ready to *roll*? *Yeah,* said perhaps fifteen people, Michelle shouting along with them, embarrassed for the man. Were they ready to *rock and roll*, Rabbi Meltzer wanted to know. *Yeah,* said twenty people plus Rabbi Shmulevits, who said, "Yes, so get on *mith* it, already." "We call ourselves Rovner!" Rabbi Meltzer said, strapping on his guitar. "And this one's called 'Soar.'"

The two blue spotlights swept the stage, the first one picking out Gabe Goldstein, a man with long, stringy hair and a heavy beard, wearing a flannel shirt, jeans, and cowboy boots with spurs. Meltzer had known Goldstein since the two of them had been camp counselors and played folk duets at campfires. Goldstein now taught guitar at the Old Town School of Folk Music and had released an album of solo material, *Bridge Over a Troubled Goldstein,* and a live cassette, *Solid Goldstein,* on a local label called Slapthis Records, which was currently involved in a trademark dispute. The second spotlight landed on Larry Rovner, who wore an Israeli flag as a cape over jeans and a black T-shirt, on which Rovner! was spelled out in a semicircle.

"A'right, a'right," Larry bellowed, and he counted out four. He slapped his drumsticks together over his head. Meltzer hit a power chord and Goldstein thumped out a bass line as Larry sang, grimacing with his eyes closed and squinting, "Sooore. I feel so sooore," Goldstein and Meltzer singing harmony on the last "soooore" while Meltzer hit another power chord and the drums kicked in.

When Michelle saw the fierce expression on Larry's face as he beat out the basic rhythm, his five o'clock shadow, the Israeli flag cape, and the blue-and-white disk of a yarmulke that matched it, she almost burst out laughing. But by the third measure of the song, when the lyrics began, the laugh caught in her throat. Rabbi Meltzer, teeth biting his lower lip, seesawing the neck of his guitar up and down, was a competent musician but trying far too hard. Goldstein, hair hanging down in his eyes, never once smiling as he tapped his boot to the rhythm, was,

Michelle thought, a rock 'n' roll bass-playing cliché. But the hard-driving beat was undeniably infectious, and there was something oddly captivating about the way Larry attacked his drum kit, the beads of sweat dripping down on his cape, the sweet falsetto that dropped down to a gruff, growling baritone and back up again. Larry Rovner was ridiculous, his song was stupid, and yet, by the second verse, Michelle was singing along and thinking yes, this song was stupid but then there were few songs she liked that weren't stupid if you thought about them too carefully, and maybe just maybe this one was a little less stupid than most. If Larry had had one visible shred of doubt or lack of conviction about him, it would have completely given him away, but the way he threw his soul into every single syllable he shrieked canceled out any criticism. In a way, he was like her, Michelle thought—born to perform. The band galloped into "Six Days" as Michelle made her way to the front, where about twelve people—boys in yarmulkes and girls in skirts—were clapping along, the girls dancing on the heels of their tennis shoes as if at a sock hop, Michelle not noticing that Muley Wills had already slipped out of the auditorium.

The girl in the cat mask shouted "Whoooo" when Larry introduced "My Milk, Your Honey" by saying that this was a song about sex, "You know what I mean, fellas." When they were through with that number, Larry stepped down from the drum kit. Rabbi Meltzer handed him an acoustic guitar, and he and Gabe Goldstein went backstage. Larry strapped on the instrument. He stood in the spotlight. He didn't say "Thanks for coming," because Bob Dylan didn't say that at his shows. He said he had a brand-new song about a girl he knew—it went something like this. All through that song, the one called "Synagogue Girl" ("I like your button; now it's time to press it / Meet me in the back of the *Beth Ha'knesset*"), Michelle wondered what it would be like to have sex with Larry Rovner. It was at first an appalling notion, but one that only became stronger as she watched how he fingered his notes and slashed out his chords. She wondered if the way he contorted his face as he sang was the way he would look at the moment of orgasm, all sweaty and desperate, unspeakably ugly and at the same time indescribably handsome. Then she wondered as Rabbi Meltzer returned to the stage with his doubleneck acoustic guitar to accompany Larry on "(I'm a) Man of Faith" and "(My Lovin' Ain't) Always Orthodox" what the rabbi would be like in bed—an eager performer, she was sure, always happy to try cunnilingus yet not particularly skilled at it. And when Goldstein came out with a third guitar to join an acoustic reprise of "Soar," she wondered with a shudder what he would be like as a sexual partner—furry and smelly, she figured, a decided lack of deodorant and the pervasive odor of crotch.

Rovner! closed out its set with the premiere of "No Sukkah Tonight," which stole its bass line from the band The Guess Who, and a rollicking rendition of "Runaround Sue," Rabbi Meltzer on lead vocals, Gabe and Larry on backup. The three band members grasped hands, held them over their heads, then bowed as applause rippled faintly through the auditorium, Michelle's ferocious clapping and whistling only serving to underscore the relative silence of those around her. Rabbi Meltzer said thanks very much, they were called Rovner!; he said to look for them at the After-Seder party and maybe that summer at Chicagofest on Navy Pier. The girl in the cat mask fished a lighter out of her denim jacket, flicked it, and raised it just over her head as Larry grabbed his sweat-drenched Israeli flag cape and spread it behind him, arms reaching straight out from his sides, like a damp, pale white butterfly with a blue Star of David on its wings. When he saw the girl in the cat mask with her lighter raised, he reached into the front pocket of his jeans and took out a set of house keys. He flung them toward the girl, who caught them. Larry leaned into a mike, said the *Shehecheyanu* prayer, then said "Good evening" even though it was only about four in the afternoon. Then he stretched his cape and walked backstage, the Star of David disappearing behind the black backdrop as what audience remained began to disperse.

The set of house keys Larry had thrown was the only one he had, which meant that since most of the families on Sacramento Avenue had begun locking their doors after an incident of vandalism at K.I.N.S. (someone had scrawled "Jewish Girls Are Easy" in the *Dalet* classroom), and since his father wasn't home and his mother was either at the house in Lake Geneva or at the new "studio" she had just rented on Fairfield Avenue, he would have to borrow a set from his sister, who would be working the carnival cash box until the costume contest at eight, which he had promised to attend. He had also neglected to throw his address to the girl in the cat costume; if she didn't know where he lived, she would have to spend the rest of the afternoon trying doors all through West Rogers Park, unless she would be hanging around waiting for him when he was lugging his gear out to Rabbi Meltzer's Datsun, asking him to autograph her breast or toss her his sweaty Israeli flag.

But when Larry emerged, trailing behind Rabbi Meltzer and Gabe Goldstein with an amp in each hand, the only people in front of the synagogue were Missy Eisenstaedt with her sister Bibi (the music was a little too loud, but there were some "real toe-tappers," Missy said), and Arik Levine, who said that the band sounded a lot more "stripped down" than he had expected. He invited Larry to check out Weinstock!'s first gig at Randy Weinstock's eighteenth birthday party at Lou Malnati's pizzeria in Lincolnwood. Larry said maybe he'd come, maybe he wouldn't—he had a lot going on—then he asked if Arik had seen a girl in a cat mask walk by. No, Arik lied, he hadn't.

When Michelle got home, she called out her sister's name, but Jill wasn't there; Jill was walking east toward the lake, a bag of goldfish in each hand, Muley Wills about a half-block behind her with his movie camera. Michelle had Larry Rovner's keys in her jeans pocket and there was little doubt in her mind that she would go to his house, have sex, or at least make out with him to see what it would be like, then go home and do homework. She liked the fact that she had seemed to be the only audience member who had enjoyed the performance, that his talent was her personal discovery. She liked the idea that Larry, valedictorian of her Hebrew school class, was smart; even though he seemed a good deal slower than any of the guys she had dated before, she was sure he did better in school, and part of being smart in school, it seemed to her, was being stupid in almost everything else. Now that she was smart in school as well, she wondered if that meant it was time for her to become dumber in other matters as well, such as sleeping with Larry Rovner.

Plus, she hadn't had sex in nearly four months, hadn't even made out with anybody, had begun referring to her plight in the same way *Nightline* talk show host Ted Koppel had begun referring to the Iranian hostage crisis—"It's Day One-forty without a date," she would tell Gareth. That was fine for now, but, she thought, what if this went on for a year, what if when she got to Yale, she hadn't had sex since Millard Schwartz? That seemed pathetic. It was one thing to arrive at college as a virgin or having only had sex with that one special guy who was now away in the Marines; but having been sexually active up to the age of seventeen and then suddenly stopping would make her a suspicious character. People would wonder if she had joined AA. People would wonder if she had been briefly institutionalized. People would wonder if she had found God.

After she quickly worked a brush through her hair, she went to her bedroom, got Larry's keys, and placed them in a small cloth purse where she kept her perfume, her wallet, her cigarettes, her lip balm, her tampons, and her pipe. She wondered, as she exited the apartment and half ran, half skipped down the stairs, which Larry would answer the door when she reached his house—the Ida Crown Academy dweeb whose calls she never returned or the rock star she had just seen onstage. As she walked west on North Shore, and the apartments on Campbell gave way to bungalows on Washtenaw and Fairfield and then, past California, pristine houses with front yards, backyards, patios, porches, and maple trees with yellow ribbons tied around them, she realized that she'd never had sex in a house. She had had sex on a bench in Warren Park, behind a mausoleum at Graceland Cemetery, in the backseat of an Opel Manta. Never in a house, though. Walking past the Funny House, she thought briefly that it would be nice to have her own room in a house where she could fuck or smoke or listen to records or read. And then her thoughts moved in tense from future to past. It *would have* been nice to *have had* her own room, she thought, but now it was too late. Her youth would run its course in apartments and dorm rooms; houses would come only with adulthood. Or maybe not even then.

Michelle arrived at the Rovners' house at half past six in the evening with a rack of her father's Miller High Life. When no one answered the door, Michelle let herself in. There was an odd odor, like day-old fried food. Everything was in its place—but somehow not quite right. The chairs around the kitchen table were pulled out slightly at odd angles; there were bits of lint, fuzz, and string on the living room carpet; there were scuff marks, scratches, and footprints on the floor of the front hallway, duct tape holding together rips in the stair carpet. A sign on a door leading down to the basement read "Larry's Space-Age Bachelor Pad This Way."

When Larry, who had borrowed his sister's keys, heard footsteps coming down the stairs, he thought it might be his mother. But she had said she wouldn't be coming around this weekend. It couldn't be his father—he was barely home at all lately. It had to be either a burglar or the girl in the cat mask. He wondered who that girl was, holding up her lighter, singing along with his lyrics. It could have been any girl from Ida Crown, maybe a freshman who idolized him, somebody's sister maybe—Ben Jacobs's sister used to babysit for him, maybe she was home for spring break, maybe she wanted to see how he had turned out and, after seeing him onstage, she just couldn't help herself. Or maybe it was Hannah Goodman, maybe she had been reading his postcards and had flown in secretly from New York.

He had had crushes on more than ten girls in the past year—he kept index cards where he rated practically every girl he knew in categories including Face, Body, Sense of Humor ("laughs at my jokes"), Breasts, Butt, Overall Sexiness, Musical Taste, and Compatibility ("likelihood she'll say yes"). He'd plotted the scores in his lab book on graph paper, which had one dot at the top marked HG for Hannah Goodman, who, since she had such a high Compatibility score, represented the standard by which all others were measured, and one dot at the bottom marked MW for Michelle Wasserstrom, whose score had declined with each unreturned phone call, and a slew of dots bunched around the middle.

After showering, he had taken out the lab book, which he frequently studied during Chemistry class, having once explained to his teacher, Rabbi Hiram Scheinbaum, that HG (Hannah Goodman) was the periodic table symbol for Mercury, MW (Michelle Wasserstrom) stood for molecular weight, while ME (Missy Eisenstaedt, who scored fives in every one-to-ten category) represented the median of his graph. And now one of those dots would soon be pushing open the door, eagerly awaiting sex. He was ready. He had washed and rinsed twice with Agree, lathered up his entire body, and foamed up his pubic hair. He had liberally applied Mennen Speed Stick under his arms and in his crotch, shaved with lemon-lime Barbisol, and slapped his cheeks with Aqua Velva. His shirt was open two buttons to show his mezuzah. He had dimmed the lights in his room and put Marvin Gaye on the stereo. He took three condoms—he referred to them as *"kippot"*— and threw them into the trash, so that it would look as if the contents of his 64-Trojan box, displayed prominently on his night table, had gotten some use. When the door to his room opened, he was on his bed, leaning against his wall, a foot propped on his knee, guitar against his chest as he strummed.

"Hey, yeshiva boy," Michelle said as she stood in his doorway, purse strap over her shoulder, paper bag in her hand. "You got something to smoke or are we gonna smoke mine?"

When Larry saw the lowest dot on his graph standing before him, he felt an intense pressure in his groin. Not an erection—an unbearable urge to urinate. His voice quavered as he asked if she wanted something to drink or eat. She said that was okay, she'd brought beer—she handed the bag to him. She asked if he had any pot. Uh, no, Larry improvised, he'd had a dimebag, but he and his guitar player had smoked it all before the show. *Rabbi Meltzer?* Michelle asked. Yeah, Larry said, Jeff liked to party. All right, she said, they'd use her pipe and her stash. Why didn't he throw her a beer. She sat cross-legged on the floor, lit her pipe, inhaled, and handed it to Larry, who sat down next to her.

Larry smoked, observing that Michelle's "stash" was "some pretty fine stuff." He asked if it was from Colombia. No, she told him; it was from Skokie. "That's pretty kick-ass," Larry said. He passed the pipe back to Michelle, then asked if listening to Marvin Gaye was all right. Michelle said she generally didn't like making out to traditional make-out music—it was more fun to make out to AC/DC than to Marvin Gaye. Larry jumped up, ripped the needle across his record, grabbed Led Zeppelin's *Physical Graffiti,* and threw it on the turntable. Yeah, that was better, Michelle said, she could make out to that. Larry asked if she meant now. No, Michelle said, not *now;* they were *smoking* now. She asked him to turn the lights down a bit more, but when Larry turned them off completely she said no, she didn't mean *off,* she meant *down,* after which Larry turned the lights back up slightly.

Michelle figured that the more Larry spoke, the less chance she would have of remaining aroused, so she said she really liked this album and maybe they should just smoke and listen to it. Larry pantomimed drumming along with John Bonham as Michelle stared straight ahead, trying her best not to look at his pantomime. When the second record on the album dropped down, the needle hit it, and "In the Light" began to play, Michelle told Larry to uncross his legs and relax, she wasn't going to hurt him. She then unlaced her tennis shoes, took them off, rolled down her tights, heaped them beside her, unhooked her bra underneath her T-shirt and slipped it out through her sleeve. She got into Larry's bed, pulled his quilt over her knees, sat with her back up against the wall, and sang along with the music. Larry said he'd be right back.

Larry ran up to the second-floor bathroom and urinated so forcefully that he was convinced she would hear him, be disgusted, and leave. When he came back down, having chosen not to flush for fear that she would hear the toilet, be disgusted, and leave, Michelle's balled-up T-shirt was on the floor and she was lying on her stomach under the covers. Larry knew that he was a senior and she was a junior, and he wondered if he wasn't taking advantage of her; she might, after all, be a virgin. Maybe they should go slow, he said as he sat down next to her. Slow didn't matter, Michelle said, just so long as they went at some speed. She pressed her lips to his and began undoing the buttons of his shirt, then stopped when she noticed the mezuzah hanging on a chain around his neck. Did he ever take this off? she asked. Only for one thing, he said. He undid the clasp, kissed the mezuzah, and laid it down on the night table. Michelle said she bet he said that to all the yeshiva girls.

Once Larry's shirt was off and Michelle had tugged off his pants, Larry said again that he'd be back in a second. Larry had three major sexual fears—premature ejaculation, impotence, and being unmasked as a rank sexual amateur. And those last two fears sent him skittering toward the washer-drier, his hand in his briefs, trying desperately to coax his penis into some semblance of stiffness. In Israel with Hannah, there'd been no pressure—everything had been too quick for him to experience a more reasonable sense of terror. He wished Missy Eisenstaedt were in his bed, someone mousy and unintimidating, he thought as he relentlessly tugged away. Then he resolved to blame his impotence on Michelle. Clearly she was doing something wrong, he'd tell her; he'd never had this problem, not even in Israel. Michelle sat in bed wondering how long it would take Larry to either give himself an erection, admit he couldn't get one, or come back and blame his impotence on her.

Larry returned, looking skinny, hairy, and pale in his lumpless white briefs. As Michelle lay in bed curled up in the covers, Larry took his guitar out of its case. He nudged Michelle aside and sat beside her. He always liked to play before he "made love," he said. He didn't call it "having sex," he said; he called it "making love." He asked Michelle what she called it. "Fucking," she said. Larry strummed a chord and began to sing "Soar." At first, he was tentative, but then he began to strum harder, sing louder, and as Michelle sang harmony with him on the chorus, he felt his groin awakening. He sang "Six Days" and "Synagogue Girl" and "My Milk, Your Honey," and by the time he was through, he had an erection straining against his underwear. He plunked the guitar down beside the bed and ripped off his briefs. He slid an arm under Michelle's neck, placed a knee between hers, and kissed her, wanting desperately to use this erection before it disappeared. No, Michelle said, why didn't he play some more—she liked how he played. He picked the guitar up and played "Man of Faith" quickly, as if it were an encore of a hit single of whose surprise success he'd always been embarrassed. "I'm a man of faith / I believe in you / I believe on the eighth day / He created you," he sang. When he was through, he put his guitar down, jumped back between her knees, and placed his lips to a breast. Didn't he know any other songs? Michelle asked—she thought it would be great to sing a duet. He picked the guitar back up and hit the opening chords for "Runaround Sue." Not that one, Michelle said. All he knew were folk songs, he said. Michelle said that was fine. They sang together on "Wade in the Water," they switched off verses on "This Land Is Your Land," and Michelle sang while Larry strummed on "I'm a Woman (W-O-M-A-N)." As he played "Soar" and let Michelle sing as much of it as she remembered, feeding her lines when she laughingly forgot them, Larry thought that what Rovner! needed were fewer surly bass players and rabbis and more foxy backup singers, maybe three of them wearing tight, revealing outfits, singing harmony and banging tambourines. Michelle thought there would be nothing more fun than fronting a band. She wished there could be some way for Larry to play and for them to sing together while they were having sex, or better, for him to sing and play while she was having sex with someone else.

After they'd gone through Rovner!'s entire song catalog again, plus all of the folk songs, Larry said he was hoarse and couldn't sing anymore and Michelle said that was all right, she figured they should probably have sex before she fell asleep. But the moment the head of his penis clad in a hastily unrolled condom or *"kippah"* had disappeared between her legs, Michelle said wait a minute, was that the doorbell? No, Larry said, his rear end suspended momentarily in midair, his body supported by his fists, he didn't think so. They both listened for a moment, heard nothing, resumed for a split second, then stopped. That sure sounded like the doorbell, Michelle said. Yeah, maybe it was, Larry said, it didn't matter, probably someone collecting for the Walk for Israel. When it rang again, Michelle asked if he was expecting anybody. Larry said no, then looked at the clock. *Oh shit,* he said. He threw on his clothes, ran upstairs, and opened the door. Lana was standing in her soaking wet Queen Esther costume as rain fell upon her.

Tears and raindrops were streaming down Lana's cheeks as she stood on the front stoop, swearing at Larry, asking where the f-u-c-k he'd been and why the f-u-c-k hadn't he been at the costume contest, and now that Mom was in f-u-c-k-i-n-g Lake Geneva and Dad was God-knows-f-u-c-k-i-n-g-where, was he going to betray her too? By the time he'd managed to get her inside, help her dry off, calm her down a bit, and return to his bachelor pad, Michelle was fast asleep. When she awoke at four in the morning, her mouth feeling furry and tasting somewhat like a barnyard, she asked Larry—who hadn't really been sleeping at all, just dozing until his erection went limp, then working to bring it back up in case it would be called into service—if he could get her something to drink. Larry leaned over the side of the bed, grabbed one of the remaining cans of warm Miller, and handed it to her. She popped open the beer, took a swig, swallowed, made a face, and told Larry he really knew how to treat a lady. Larry asked her if she felt like having sex now. Michelle said not really, her mouth tasted disgusting, she was exhausted, and she had a history test in the morning. Larry said they could have sex quickly. All right, Michelle said, but he'd have to do some work to get her in the mood. Larry said it was too late to play guitar. All right, Michelle said, why didn't he hand over her pipe.

As Michelle lit up, she asked Larry about his plans for the summer. Larry said he would be making a demo tape and starting to shop it to labels—Slappit Records, for example. He wanted to get his musical career going as quickly as possible; that way he could justify deferring college admission at least a semester and maybe live in L.A. or Nashville. The idea hadn't seemed real when he had first thought of it, but now that he had seen Michelle's reaction to his music, he was starting to wonder if he might be able to do it after all. What college was he going to? Michelle asked. Brandeis, he said, taking Michelle's pipe and inhaling; it was kind of like Harvard for Jews. Michelle nodded. She had to get her grades up in her last three semesters, she said, but she was hoping to go to Yale. Larry said yeah, a lot of people wanted to go there, but first you had to get in. Michelle said that she had scored in the 98th percentile on the PSATs and figured she might have a shot. Yeah, Larry said, chuckling dubiously, sure. Michelle asked what the fuck he was chuckling about. Nothing, Larry said, just if she got into Yale that would be pretty impressive.

Look, Michelle said, she didn't need his smug attitude; when he said he was going to cut albums in Nashville and go to Harvard for Jews, she hadn't made any sarcastic remarks. Larry told her she had beautiful eyes. Michelle told him not to change the subject. Larry said he wasn't changing the subject, just that he had never really taken the time to look at them before; also, she had a beautiful smile. Maybe, Michelle said, but she wasn't smiling now. Larry offered to go down on her—maybe that would put her in a better mood? he said. What in the world made him think that would put her in a better mood? she asked. She wouldn't know until she tried, Larry said. Michelle, weary of boys with eager mouths and unskilled tongues, said she'd never tried sticking her head in a toaster either, maybe she'd like that too. Larry said he'd never had any complaints from any of the girls he'd gone down on. Oh Jesus Christ, Michelle said, if they had sex, would he fucking shut up and let her sleep? Okay, Larry said, but he didn't have an erection anymore. Michelle said fuck, then told Larry to "hand over a con-DOME." He gave one to her. She brushed her hand against his testicles, touched a finger to his penis, which sprang to life. She unwrapped the condom, rolled it down, and said all right, why didn't they do this and get it over with, all the while thinking that it would just be this one time and only for research, so that when she was cast in a movie where she was supposed to be enjoying sex with Woody Allen or Elliot Gould, she would already know what it was supposed to be like.

About ten minutes later when they were done, Larry asked her if she could pass him her lighter and her pipe. And then he asked her to pass him a beer. He was going to say the *Shehecheyanu* prayer for new things, but stopped, realizing that he'd had sex once before, so instead he said the prayer for wine *(Baruch atah adonai elohenu melech haolam boray pre hagafen)* over the Miller Beer and the prayer for things of the Earth *(Baruch atah adonai elohenu melech haolam boray pre haadamah)* over the marijuana, then smoked and drank. And then he asked Michelle if she would be his date to his senior prom. Michelle said proms had to be the queerest thing in the history of the universe. Larry went to sleep heartened that Michelle hadn't said no.

It was nearly six in the morning when Michelle got dressed and left Larry sleeping in his bed, wishing that she felt shamed or satisfied or humiliated or ecstatic, instead of just tired and puky. As she approached Campbell walking east on North Shore, nobody driving on the streets except the *Sun Times* and *Tribune* deliverymen, she caught sight of Muley Wills walking west on the other side of the street. He was looking through the viewfinder of a movie camera that was pointed south toward the Wasserstrom apartment. Michelle thought of greeting him but was too exhausted to attempt a Russian accent. She turned south on Campbell. Jill was walking about a half-block in front of her. Michelle sped into a light jog but didn't catch up until they were at the front door of their apartment building and Jill was fitting her key in the lock.

Hey, Michelle said. Hey, Jill responded, unfazed. As they walked upstairs, Michelle asked Jill where she'd been. At the beach, Jill said. She had put the goldfish back into the lake and then she'd wanted to watch the sunrise, so she'd stayed there all night. Michelle asked if that was safe. Jill said she guessed so; nobody had bothered her. Michelle asked how Muley was. Jill said she didn't know; she hadn't seen him since the carnival. Michelle asked Jill if she hadn't noticed Muley on the sidewalk less than a block away from her. No, Jill said, she had noticed a stray dog on the beach; other than that, she hadn't noticed anything at all. When Jill and Michelle entered their apartment, their father was sleeping on the couch. The lights and the TV were still on.

Larry

In late April, about the time that an aborted hostage rescue attempt left eight Americans dead in the Iranian desert, Ellen Rovner announced that she and Michael were officially separating. For Larry, the announcement was poorly timed, given that he had just been planning to ask if he could borrow $1,000 to cut a demo for his band. That practical matter aside, his reaction was fairly subdued. After the family meeting in which his mother made the announcement, Larry had tried to focus intently on the impending separation, hoping that it might inspire a profound song evoking the dissolution of the American family. But he ultimately discarded all of the songs initially inspired by the separation, including "It's About Time," "Gotta Get a Job," and "Touch Myself (Whenever I Want)." The only tangible use he was able to make of the news was to get Michelle to commit to being his date for the senior prom ("It would mean a lot to me," he said. "My folks just split up, I'm hurtin' pretty bad"), and even she couldn't bring herself to say no.

Ellen Rovner had wanted to separate from her husband at numerous times over the course of the past five years but had resolved to keep the marriage together for the sake of Larry and especially Lana, whose weight loss had made separation seem impossible. However, as she monitored Lana's weight fluctuations during February, March, and the beginning of April, she made a stunning discovery: During the week, Lana would usually lose between a pound and a pound and a half. But after Ellen would come back from a weekend in Lake Geneva, Lana would have gained a pound. When Ellen took an extralong weekend, Lana gained two pounds. Two days after Ellen returned, Lana's weight went down a half-pound. Keeping the family together was clearly having a deleterious effect on Lana's health, Ellen reasoned; there was no longer any need to slow down the separation. The proof was right there during the family meeting. Lana had picked at her food all through dinner, but not ten minutes after Ellen had said, "Your father and I think it's best that we spend some time apart" and Lana had cried, she polished off not only her entire corned beef sandwich but also her coleslaw, dill pickle, and potato chips.

Larry, for his part, did not cry at all. Once he had established that for the foreseeable future he would maintain his bachelor pad on Sacramento, he would not be responsible for any additional babysitting chores, he would get frequent use of both of his parents' cars, and his parents would still be able to afford Brandeis—if he didn't get discovered first—he asked if he could go over to Rabbi Meltzer's; he had to work on some new material. There had been a time when Larry had felt a deep emotional attachment to his parents, particularly his mother, but that had dissipated shortly after his thirteenth birthday. Until then, almost every night Ellen would take the bottom bunk in Larry's bed and lie there chatting with him and singing along with the songs he made up until either he fell asleep or Michael told them to "knock it off." All this changed abruptly a few days after Becky Wasserstrom's funeral, when Ellen had seen the devastating effect a mother's death could have on a family and resolved to distance herself from her children, lest they come to think they needed her too much. Instead of crawling into the lower bunk in Larry's bedroom, she would merely stand outside his room and say good night, and later, not even that. Shortly thereafter, Larry broke down the bunk bed, lugged one of the beds downstairs, and officially "Jewished" his "space-age bachelor pad."

If he had stopped to think about it for more than a moment or two, Larry might have felt regret or guilt about his parents' separation. But his main concern was the minimum $1,000 Gabe Goldstein said he would need if he wanted to record a demo that sounded "professional" as opposed to what Goldstein termed as "recording some crappy songs in your garage for your friends and your deaf grandma." Goldstein had further added that his $1,000 quote would not include the cost of "session musicians," a category in which he included himself.

With the exception of Bar Mitzvah money that he had spent on his drum kit, Zeppelin tickets, and tefillin, Larry had never possessed more than $100 in his life—and that he had earned from Boone Elementary bake sales and paper drives. He had never worked a summer job, had never had an allowance. Lana had always taken greater advantage of Ellen Rovner's open-wallet policy than Larry had; he'd take a $10 bill for a movie or a record but never had any great sense of how much things cost or how much money he was entitled to and invariably spent most of what he took within a day.

After Larry had guilt-tripped her into agreeing to attend his prom, Michelle said that $1,000 sounded a bit rich and that she knew a friend of a friend who might be able to cut Larry a deal. On the corner of Devon and Western, across the street from Hobby Models, stood the Devon Building, which housed Adelphi Liquors, as well as the offices of the few dentists, podiatrists, and family doctors who hadn't already moved out of West Rogers Park, either to slicker, strip-mall quarters in the suburbs or to positions in hospitals just west of downtown. The building had the seedy, forlorn atmosphere of a 1940s film noir: warped stairways, long, dark hallways with flickering fluorescents, hand-lettered signs on frosted glass doors, one of which on the top floor read "3M—Mel's Music and Movies" and below it "Mel Coleman—Everything's on the Record."

With the inheritance he had received from his mother, Mel had rented a 1,500-square-foot space. He had initially sought to rent space in Streeterville on what was known as Studio Row, but instead cut his rent in half by choosing a neighborhood where the only music studio was the tiny Make-Your-Own-Record, where Bar and Bat Mitzvah boys and girls came to record their *haftorah* portions for practice and posterity. Mel spent the money he saved on equipment. There was a waiting room with couches from his mother's apartment, and two studios, one with a 64-track console, the other with a 32. There was a third area, "the film suite," with a rudimentary editing system, which, Mel told Larry and Michelle when they came by, was operated by one of his "freelance associates." The idea was to produce records, ad jingles, and radio spots, then branch out into video and films, including *Godfathers of Soul,* which, he said, was in "pre-production."

Mel's $700 estimate, which included recording, production, and mixdown, plus twenty cassettes, was the cheapest price that Larry had been quoted. And though he had only five dollars left over from the last $10 bill he had filched from his mother's wallet for falafel sandwiches, when Mel blocked out three days of studio time, Larry said he'd come up with the cash; recording the demo was vital.

It had always been vital, but it had become more so over the past few weeks. Michelle's enthusiasm for his music and a recent letter from Carl Slappit Silverman's office ("Mr. Silverman says he can't find your tape and asks you to send another copy") were only two of the most important factors. Another was the after-Seder party at K.I.N.S. Rabbi Meltzer had booked Rovner! for the gig, but had neglected to inform Larry that they would be playing with another new band called Weinstock! made up, he said, of some of Larry's "buddies." Larry said they weren't his buddies; they'd been in a band and had split up "acrimoniously." But that wasn't the point. If he thought it was a good "band decision" to play the event, he wouldn't let personality issues get in the way of business. But he didn't want to be ghettoized playing alongside another band of Ida Crown Academy teens. He declined the gig, more than happy to let the boys from Weinstock! fall on their faces without his music there to prop them up.

Alas, Weinstock! hadn't fallen on their faces. Larry—who was curious about whether Weinstock! might play some old Rovner! tunes and whether he would have to slap them with a cease-and-desist order—attended their debut incognito, wearing sunglasses, a turned-around Cubs hat, and ripped jeans. He found their material uninspired and sophomoric, replete with derivative lyrics, but the crowd that gathered to watch them at K.I.N.S. danced all through their forty-minute set, laughing gleefully at Ben Jacobs's lewd stage antics and off-color songs, such as "Everything's Comin' Up Rosenberg" and "It's Not the Meat, It's the Moshe." After the show, they gave away free cassettes professionally produced at Chicago Trax Recording on Studio Row. The members of Weinstock! had no doubt pooled money from their parents, all of whom were still married to each other and lived in nice houses north of West Rogers Park, while all Larry had was a pair of parents for whom it seemed to be the exact wrong time to ask for money.

After he had given Michelle and Larry the tour of 3M, Mel Coleman told them he wouldn't need a deposit; he'd just take a check for the full amount on the first day of recording. Larry said that sounded fair and tried to give him a soul handshake. Mel told Larry with a slight smile that if he tried to act "down with the brothers" one more time, he'd have to kill him. If Larry attempted what Mel termed a "brotherly handshake," if he asked him anything about basketball or good barbecue restaurants, if he came into the studio with "three sisters singing backup" and "no sisters singing solo," he'd have to kill him too. Larry said he dug what Mel was saying. Mel said no, he didn't *dig* it; he *understood* it. Now, did he understand? Larry said sure, right on. Mel said he liked this brother's sense of humor and he looked forward to recording the first demo for Rosenstein! *Rovner!,* Larry corrected him. *Right on,* said Mel.

As they exited the building, Larry remarked to Michelle that in the grand scheme of things, $700 was not much money. In just a few years, $7,000 wouldn't be much either. There would come a time when the question would be which house he wanted to buy and which solid gold menorah he wanted to adorn his mantelpiece, not whether he'd have to pass up buying the Rolling Stones' *Hot Rocks* LP at Dog Ear Records, where double albums cost $8.49. Michelle's employment experience consisted of assistant-directing Fables in the Park for the JCC ($200 for an entire summer), bagging groceries at Dominick's on Pratt and Kedzie ($3.35 an hour), and spending all of two miserable weeks sealed inside a red-and-white polyester suit at Lippy's Red Hot Ranch, where she was routinely chastised for giving extra ketchups to customers without being asked (total take: $0). Michelle suggested that $700 was, in fact, a lot of money. Her father wasn't poor, she said, but he had just been filling out his tax returns and agonizing over where he'd find $900. And unlike Larry, Michelle pointed out, her father had a job.

Larry told Michelle he'd worked a number of jobs previously—he'd tutored kids in Hebrew, he'd refereed basketball, he'd worked for a pollster, going door to door in the neighborhood to see who they'd be voting for in the 1979 mayoral election. All this was true with one notable omission: He hadn't been paid for any it. The refereeing had been at Chippewa. The student he'd tutored was his sister. And the door-to-door polling had been part of a Social Studies project whose results he had faked after everyone on Sacramento had either slammed the door on him or refused to answer his questions, still fearing the power of Richard J. Daley's machine even after the mayor's death. Larry's half-truth was only one of many he had told Michelle after she had recently informed him of her predilection for dumping boyfriends not for vague generalities but for specific "instances of malfeasance." Larry had a sense that not having worked for money in all of his eighteen years and having taken some slight advantage of his mother's open-wallet policy might have been just the sort of instance to which Michelle had been referring.

The next meeting of Rovner! was held in a practice room at the Old Town School of Folk Music. Neither Gabe Goldstein nor Rabbi Jeffrey Meltzer was helpful in Larry's search for cash. Meltzer didn't have any, and Goldstein wouldn't provide any. The one concession made by Goldstein—who insisted he not be referred to as a member of Rovner! and that he only be listed on the demo with the credit line, "Mr. Goldstein appears courtesy of Slapthis Records"—was that he would take "deferred payment." Rather than taking $20 an hour up front, he would take $40 an hour to be paid within six months of completion, or "2 percent of gross album sales and proceeds should such album ever be realized," whichever was greater. Larry quickly though dubiously signed the piece of paper Goldstein had typed up—Larry felt that when he got to the point that 2 percent of gross album sales and proceeds, whatever the hell proceeds might have been, was a somewhat significant number, he could be generous, and that when he got to the point where 2 percent was truly significant, it would be no trick to hire a lawyer to squash Goldstein for the parasite he was.

Larry went to the library to find books about raising cash quickly. He only managed to find one: *How to Get Money When You Don't Have Any,* by Dr. H. C. Pendleton. The slim book's cover promised "*real* tips for getting *real* cash *real* fast." The inside of the book was less heartening. The first chapter was called "How to Spot a Rich Person." The second chapter was full of anecdotal rags-to-riches stories. The last section featured "no-nonsense tips" on how to get money from people who were "just waiting to give it to you . . . or somebody else—if you don't ask fast enough." The book advised readers to make a list of potential donors who might fork over $100 to "that best of all causes: YOU!" Larry only needed $700, which meant that he would need seven people to give him $100 each. Perhaps he could wangle that much out of his mother's wallet and perhaps he could get another $100 from his father, particularly if he could come up with a ruse that would impress the man, such as telling him he had knocked up a girl and had to pay for half of the abortion. That still left $500, and though the book left pages of blank lines in which to fill in more donors, Larry had maxed out at two. At which point Larry began to consider the radical and unpleasant move of soliciting his surviving grandparents, even though he hadn't seen his mother's father and his wife in more than a decade, and even though he knew Grandma Rose didn't have any money to speak of.

Though Dr. Max Leventhal was eighty-one, and his sixty-eight-year-old wife Essie Mallen-Leventhal had difficulty climbing stairs, they refused to move out of their Hyde Park mansion. When they were not vacationing in Europe, they rarely traveled outside of their neighborhood. Though they were hardly more than a thirty-minute drive from West Rogers Park, the only times they contacted the Rovners were on their grandchildren's birthdays—on Larry and Lana's first birthday, they received $1 gifts; on their second birthday $2, and so on to the present. For a time after her father remarried in 1973—just a bit over a decade after Ellen's mother's death, which she had always blamed partly on the domineering Max—Ellen would occasionally call home. But her father would always ask if she needed cash and then, after she'd said no, would tell her, "talk to Essie." Now Ellen only called on their birthdays, and Lana and Larry didn't talk to them at all.

Nevertheless, on a cool Sunday morning in May, Larry found himself driving south on Lake Shore Drive in his mother's Volvo. He had asked his mother if she'd needed any help setting up her apartment. No, she said—what did he really want, money or the car? Uncomfortable with saying "both," he had settled for the Volvo. During the ride, the time Larry didn't spend improvising songs with titles like "(Just to See You) One More Time" and "(Your Gelt Makes Me) Guilty," he tried to invent a reason why he might have "just happened" to be driving through Hyde Park to the house of his grandparents, whom he had visited twice in his life. He half-wished his sister had joined him—she was far better at ruses and schemes. But she had said she would be shopping with her new best friend, Mary Beth Wales.

Essie Mallen-Leventhal, who had been married twice before to men even more successful than her current husband, answered her door with a faint and vaguely displeased sense of recognition, as if Larry were the paperboy come round to complain about his Christmas bonus. She let him stand explaining and muttering for quite some time in the arched doorway of the dim, sarcophagal dwelling redolent of a university library, then took a step to the side, granting him admittance. Larry's officious remarks about how great it was to see her and what a happy coincidence it was that he had been visiting a girlfriend at the U of C— Michelle Wasserstrom of the Nantucket Wasserstroms—did not register. Essie turned her back on him and hobbled ahead, her cane smacking against the floor as she gave him a brief, unilluminating tour of the dwelling. She didn't say that the house had once been owned by a former trustee of the U of C who had made his money in coal or that it boasted the country's largest collection of first-edition art books. Instead she said, "This is our dining room," "This is our kitchen," "That's the upstairs where we sleep," and "These are our books." Larry asked where his grandfather was. Essie said he was upstairs reading. Larry asked if "the doctor" might come down at some point. "Perhaps," Essie said. Larry sat down in a pale-green armchair in the library where he determined that selling three or four of Essie and Max's first editions might get him the money he needed. But Essie, eyeing her husband's grandson cautiously, told Larry he could only look at the spines of the books; if he wanted to take any out, she would need to fetch him a pair of cloth gloves.

Larry asked Essie how she had been. Fine, she told him. And Max? He was fine too. Larry offered that he was also fine, though the question had not been posed. He asked Essie if she would sit down. No, she said, an arm leaning against a rung of a library ladder; once she sat down, she generally found it difficult to get up and she preferred to stand if she wasn't going to be in a room for any great length of time.

Larry said he was embarking on a musical career—he said he recalled that his grandfather had subscribed to the Chicago Symphony. Yes, Essie said, they still had a series, but they only used their tickets when Sir Georg Solti was conducting, which was once per series, and not when he was conducting Wagner. Larry said what he himself composed wasn't really classical, but he liked to think of his songs as miniature symphonies—with overtures, codas, variations, and themes. Yes, Essie said, music was hard. Hard, yes, Larry said, and expensive too. He was trying to make a demo for record labels that had expressed interest in his "song stylings," and it was going to cost him $700. Yes, Essie said; music was hard and there wasn't much money in it. She said that she had recently fielded a call from the Lyric Opera asking her to donate; when you reached a certain age and comfort level, people assumed you had nothing better to do than to pay them. For a time, she had found it sad, but lately it just angered her. Once, they had donated to many organizations; now, they just donated $5,000 a year to the Jewish United Fund and wrote it off on their taxes. Larry said that he assumed she didn't make any donations over and above that amount. No, Essie said, she was sorry to disappoint him. Oh, Larry said, he wasn't talking about himself—he was just speaking in general. No, Essie said again; she knew how disappointed he must be.

There were few things more frustrating than being told you were asking for something before you had asked for it, Larry thought. He had merely come over to say hello and now he felt filthy and small. Not only was he not going to get the money, he would have to spend at least a half hour pretending he hadn't come to ask for it. He talked about art books, how fascinating he found the collection, how well his sister and their parents were, how they all should get together sometime, no *really* they should—it had been too long. A surly voice descended from the second floor to the living room, demanding that Essie come upstairs. "Hiya, Grandpa," Larry called out as Essie went to see Max. There was no response. When Larry stood, his mind already concocting schemes to separate Grandma Rose from $500, Essie returned downstairs with an envelope with $19 in it and handed it to Larry. She told him that she and Dr. Max would skip next year's birthday.

R ose Rovner had lived on the sixth floor of the Winston Towers condo complex ever since her husband had passed away, and she had sold their small house in Albany Park, which had already begun to "change shades," as she put it, from a Jewish neighborhood to a Korean one. Winston Towers, located at the western edge of West Rogers Park, was technically in Chicago, but in spirit it was far more closely linked to the neighboring suburbs of Skokie and Lincolnwood. A series of five tan brick buildings, reminiscent of a housing project but with unnaturally blue fountains out front and wading pools in back, the complex created a cheap version of Miami time shares for those who couldn't afford to move to Florida, or those who chose not to live there all year round.

Rose lived mostly on Social Security, supplemented by investments that her daughter-in-law Ellen had made for her. The immense love she felt for her son and her grandchildren, as well as her other children and grandchildren who lived in Montreal and Seattle, was more than offset by the great disdain she felt for almost everything else, Ellen Rovner included. Her apartment was a small one-bedroom with a view that looked west onto Kedzie Avenue and the canal. Three times a week, she would push her grocery cart south to Dominick's with a purse full of coupons cut out of the *Nortown Leader.* On Tuesday and Friday mornings, she played bridge at the JCC. On Saturday nights, she took the Pratt bus east to Western and gambled at Bingo City.

Winston Towers was less than a mile from the Rovners' house, but Larry didn't visit Rose frequently. When Grandpa Al had been alive, Larry had enjoyed going to their house for dinner and listening to Al tell stories about selling suits on Roosevelt Road. But then Al had died, and Rose had had the first of two strokes. Whenever Larry saw her veined, slightly shaky hands, heard her breathing heavily as she walked, he wondered if she might die in his presence, and what he would do if she did.

Larry gave his name to the doorman, who called up to Rose's apartment, then told Larry he could go up. When Larry exited an elevator on the sixth floor, he was greeted with the usual omnipresent food odor—beef in some sort of thick sauce. He rang Rose's doorbell, and when she opened the door and saw Larry, her eyes suddenly watered and she told him how beautiful it was that he had come to visit her, what a beautiful *boychik* he was to visit a little old yenta like herself. She offered him a dietetic chocolate candy.

Larry sat down on the couch—black with a pattern of orange and pink irises and snapdragons. He nibbled a chocolate while Rose went to her bedroom to get the photo albums. Photos dominated the small apartment. They were on a side table in the front hallway, on an end table between the couch and the far wall, on the low, brass-rimmed glass table in front of the couch, on the top of the TV, and on the walls. There were photos of her parents that resembled charcoal sketches, photos of her and Grandpa Al and all of their relatives at their wedding, photos of Michael Rovner as a boy in a Pony League uniform, photos of Larry and Lana as babies, of Larry collecting leaves in Caldwell Woods, of Lana in a yellow slicker on the way to her first day at Boone Elementary, of Larry as a patrol boy on the corner of Fairfield and North Shore, of him in a powder-blue suit at his Bar Mitzvah, of Larry's cousins, his uncles, his aunts. And when Grandma Rose returned with an ancient, gold-trimmed photo album with pictures slipping out of it, there were more photographs to inspect. And even though Larry had seen all of them every time he had been over at Rose's, he sat next to her on the couch as she looked over every single one and said, "Doesn't he look so handsome" when she pointed out Grandpa Al and "Didn't I look young once" and "What was your mother wearing in that picture—it looks so Polish."

Nearly an hour later, when they had studied every picture and Grandma Rose had plied Larry with three dietetic chocolate cherries and a pair of dietetic grape-fruit sucking candies, she put the photo albums away and came back to sit beside Larry. She thanked him for indulging her—he had always been a sweet *boychik*. But she knew he hadn't come to look at pictures—what was it she could do for him? Nothing really, Larry said, he had just wanted to say hello. He told her about college and he told her about music. Rose said it sounded like he'd need an awful lot of money to do the things he wanted to do. She went into her bedroom. Larry heard her opening and closing drawers.

She returned with a small, dark-green box from Joseph's Shoes. It jangled as she walked slowly back to the couch. She was an old woman, Rose told him, and she didn't have much. But she wanted him to know that everything she had was his, if he wanted it. All she needed were her pictures and her memories. She re-moved the top of the box. Inside were dozens of silver dollars. She picked one up and handed it to Larry; it was dull and gray, dated 1878. It was solid silver, she said, and she told him to keep it. If he wanted more, he could take those too. Larry stared at the shoebox of silver dollars; he guessed each one was worth $25, maybe $50. He could take them to Smilin' Seymour's Coins on Devon—they wouldn't give him a fair price, he was sure of that, but they certainly would give him enough to pay Mel Coleman. He reached a hand into the shoebox, felt the coins' dull, grimy surfaces. Rose had saved them ever since she was a girl, she said, and she'd be happy if he took them—she didn't need them anymore.

But Larry said no. That was sweet of her, but he hadn't come over for money—he had all that he needed; he had only wanted to see her. He put the cover back on the shoebox and brought it back into the bedroom. He placed it on her dresser. He couldn't bear for Rose to think he had only come to take her money. And so when he left Grandma Rose's apartment, hugging her and telling her he loved her and that he would come over more often, he didn't tell her that he had taken five silver dollars out of the shoebox. He figured she had no idea how many coins there were. She had said he could take them and didn't need them anyway. As long as she believed that he had come there to see her and as long as he had been able to amass some of the money he needed, everybody would be happy. Besides, "Special Thanks to Grandma Rose" would be near the top of his album's liner notes. Larry only felt a slight twinge of guilt as he drove the Volvo east toward his mother's apartment, but that soon was transformed into fear and confusion as he stopped at the Sacramento traffic light and saw two Skokie Police Department squad cars double-parked outside his house.

When Larry reached his house, he saw two uniformed officers on his front landing; one was pressing the doorbell. Larry asked what was the matter. The younger policeman—earnest, blow-dried, pie-faced, and goyish—asked if Larry was the man of the house. No, Larry said, Dr. Rovner was at the hospital—what did they need? The cop—"Basnett" was printed on his brass nameplate—said they had picked up a girl by the name of Lana Rovner for shoplifting at Bonwit's. The store didn't want to press charges; he just wanted to know somebody was home to make sure the young lady didn't get into any more trouble. Larry said it was okay; he'd take care of his sister.

Another cop, blond with a ponytail, led Lana—in a short black leather jacket, jeans, and dark blue shin-high boots—out of the first squad car and led her to the house. Lana's face bore an expression of suppressed anger and superiority—a princess mistaken for a pauper. She apologized for having "inconvenienced" the officers but did not admit to the crimes of which they accused her. She said she knew it was wrong to steal; it was against the Commandments.

At the same time as she spoke, seeming to convince the officers of her scrupulous nature, Larry was equally convinced of his sister's guilt. And after the officers had left and Lana had indignantly explained the injustices to which she had been subjected, Larry was even more convinced. He was convinced because he had done it himself. Not always wanting to reach into his mother's wallet and pull out a twenty or a ten, in eighth grade he had gone to Roband's Drug Store and stolen CliffsNotes for the Christian novels he didn't think it was right for him to read: Flannery O'Connor's *Wise Blood* and Walker Percy's *The Moviegoer.* And he had stolen a pack of condoms on the day he had returned from Israel. He'd justified it to himself, saying it was no different from what his parents did—taking towels from the Fairmont Hotel in San Francisco, martini glasses from the Cape Cod Room in Chicago, an ashtray from the Berghoff downtown. He remembered when he had just turned seven and his sister was still in a stroller and the family had gone to the toy department of Marshall Field's—back when his parents still shopped together and didn't just check off clothing items from catalogs and send back the ones that didn't fit. Lana had pointed and squealed, demanding a yellow duck pull toy with wheels and a string. They searched for a salesperson, but then, since Michael knew the meter was running out on their parking space, they pulled the duck out of the toy department, onto an escalator, and out the Randolph Street exit, Larry and Lana's parents laughing that no one had stopped them. Larry hadn't stolen anything in 1980 yet, not really, and as he listened to his sister, he vowed never to do it again. It was like pornography, masturbation, and infidelity, something his parents engaged in of which he disapproved. He would not buy *Oui* magazine; he would not cheat on Michelle Wasserstrom or Hannah Goodman; he would not steal.

As Lana stood in the kitchen, making herself a sundae, she said that she and Mary Beth had seen some cute skirts with the wrong prices on them and that they had been trying to put the right price stickers back when some mean, burly man who smelled like Chee•tos grabbed them and dragged them into an ugly room with no windows and accused them of stealing. *Jewish girls shouldn't steal,* Larry opined. Mary Beth wasn't Jewish, Lana said; no one in her school was Jewish, she said—Steve Orenstein's father was Jewish, but they colored Easter eggs, bought German products, and ate *chametz* on Passover. Jewish girls shouldn't steal, Larry repeated. They shouldn't make out with goyish boys, not with any boys until they were at least sixteen, they shouldn't wear makeup or black leather jackets, and they shouldn't steal. What was he talking about? Lana wanted to know; she didn't steal. Don't steal, Larry told her, let shiksas and goyim steal. And with that, he was out the door and off to Smilin' Seymour's to see how much he could get for the silver dollars.

The coins fetched $45 each, which meant that after he had pooled Essie Mallen-Leventhal's $19 and added it to a twenty he lifted from his mother's purse once he had returned her car keys and helped her unload two boxes of books, he was still more than $400 short of his goal. Michelle suggested, when he called her asking for advice, that he sell his body. He said he had thought about it, but that it was forbidden in the Tanakh. Michelle laughed. She was actually beginning to like Larry; he said funny things that were even funnier since he didn't realize they were funny. Larry was resourceful, Michelle said; she was sure he'd think of something.

But none of the ideas he pursued in the five days before the first scheduled Rovner! recording session succeeded. He went to the presidential campaign offices for Jimmy Carter and Ted Kennedy, but all he was offered was a $3.35-an-hour after-school gig stuffing envelopes for Carter. He drew a label and affixed it to a can, but only collected $4.36 for a Walk for Rovner! One night at dinner, Larry mentioned to his father that he knew some kids with trust funds; he wondered if he had one. Michael said he had no idea; he should ask his mother. Larry said, after Lana had left the table, that his father was lucky he hadn't started shoplifting—it was easy to do and lucrative; his sister had done it and even though she had been caught, she hadn't been punished. He told the story of the Bonwit's incident. But Michael Rovner only laughed. "Those girls," he chuckled. "Girls, girls, girls."

As of Friday, Larry had scraped together $271.36, but he had not yet called 3M Studios to cancel. He still hoped for a miracle; it had happened for Noah, for Moses, why not him? But all he found in the gutter as he walked east on Pratt toward Western after school was a quarter. The sun was just about down; it was technically the Sabbath and picking up money was forbidden. But for Larry, music was just as much a religion as Judaism now, and even the most devout Jews were allowed to break the Sabbath in the case of emergencies, such as driving one's pregnant wife to the hospital, going to the Knesset to vote on a declaration of war, or presenting Mel Coleman with $271.61 and trying to talk him into letting one's band record its demo anyway.

"You wanna do what?" Mel asked. The era of the plantation was over, Mel said. He wanted to know if Larry saw a sign anywhere in his studio that said this brother charged $700, but really only meant $250. He wanted to know if Larry thought that the studio came with a free bowl of soup and a shoeshine, if Larry wanted him to pour down some sand on the floor, do a soft-shoe, and sing "Mr. Bojangles" too. He asked Larry if collecting 30 percent of the price they'd agreed to sounded like something a smart businessman would do.

Larry said he intended to pay the full amount; he just didn't have all the money yet. Well, Mel said, once he had the money, they could proceed. Larry said he could pay in installments, and Mel could take anything of his he wanted as collateral. Mel asked if Larry knew any ladies between the ages of twenty-five to forty with long legs and a nice-sized chest looking to marry an audiovisual entrepreneur. Larry said he didn't. Well, Mel told him, then he didn't have anything he wanted. Larry asked Mel if he'd ever had a dream, something he believed in. Yeah, Mel said, but he'd gotten over it. Well, Larry said, he hadn't gotten over his; he kept it deep within his soul and he knew there would always be people who doubted him, but that was part of being an artist and he was willing to accept that, because what he had to say was stronger than that, it was stronger than he was; he wasn't making the music himself—he was just its messenger. Mel told Larry to hold on one second. He asked how much more of this bullshit he'd have to listen to if he didn't give him the answer he wanted. A lot, Larry said, he had a lot more to say. Well, then, Mel said, why didn't he shut the hell up, give him the $271.61, and pay him $20 a week until he'd paid off the balance. Larry told him he'd give him a percentage of "gross album sales and proceeds" as well. Mel said Larry could keep the percentage of "gross album sales and proceeds"; the cash would be fine.

Larry had hoped to record all his songs in one take to give his demo a live, improvisational, and immediate feel. But it only took two takes of "Soar" to realize that Gabe Goldstein and Rabbi Meltzer just didn't have the chops. At one point, when Larry told him that he'd thought he was a professional and why didn't he start playing like one, Goldstein had threatened to walk, but Meltzer calmed him down, telling him that Larry just "ran hot" and hadn't meant anything personal. At first, Michelle, who was providing "backing vocals and additional percussion," found the arguments entertaining, but after the umpteenth time that Larry said "We're on the clock here" or "Let's get back on the stick," if she didn't have a vocal to contribute, she excused herself and went to read, practice various accents, or eat fries in the small adjoining studio where Muley Wills was editing a film, one he said he wouldn't show anyone until he was done.

Near midnight on the last night of Rovner!'s recording session, Larry listened to the playback of the twelfth take of "Stain on My Tallis" and said yeah, that was probably the best they could get it. He shook Gabe Goldstein's hand and said he was sorry he'd ridden him so hard, but he thought the results spoke for themselves. Then he cupped Jeffrey Meltzer's shoulder and said, "Great work, Rabbi; that was the stuff." As Goldstein and Meltzer left the studio, saying they were going to go get falafels at the Jerusalem, Larry thanked them again and gave them a thumbs-up sign, all the while thinking that what he really wanted to do was to go back into the studio and rerecord both of their parts. He asked Mel if he wanted to grab a quick bite and celebrate. Hell no, Mel said. That's right, Larry said, they had a big week of mixing ahead of them.

That week passed at two speeds—quickly for Larry; slowly for Mel. Mel was a talented but not yet seasoned producer, only interested in working as hard as his underpaying client was willing to push him. But the more persnickety Larry was, the more respect Mel gave him, and the more he tried to get the mix just right. Every once in a while during their long sessions, for which Larry would cut classes—having secured admission to Brandeis, he no longer had much interest in putting in the work to maintain his grade point average—Mel would ask Muley Wills to emerge from his dark editing broom closet and listen. And though Muley would usually say it sounded pretty good, he would always make a small suggestion—a machine-gun sound effect on "Six Days," an AM radio station broadcasting news of Secretary of State Cyrus Vance's resignation in the background of "Man of Faith," a deep, reverberating echo on the chorus of "Take Me to Your Promised Land"—and return to his sanctum. Muley had some idea of how Larry had used his name to attract his father's attention, but he didn't hold grudges. Larry, for his part, was thrilled by the prospect of being able to write "additional production by Muley Wills" on the credits of the demo he'd send to Carl Silverman.

Once they had mixed down all ten of the songs, Larry insisted they add an echoing intro with a booming voice punctuated by crackling thunder. It declaimed "In the beginning, all was unformed and void with darkness over the surface of the deep and a wind from God sweeping over the water, and God said"—here there were two clashes of cymbals—"'LET THERE BE ROVNER!'" And at the end of the tape, in a barely audible whisper, the echoing voice returned with *"And there was Rovner! And it was good."* Yes, it was bombastic; yes, it was pretentious. But it was confident. It was brash, it was courageous, and it didn't give a damn what people thought of it. Or, as a less confident Mel Coleman said, "Well, it is what it is."

On the day before the senior prom at the Lincolnwood Hyatt House, Larry had talked to Carl, who said he'd be in town on business soon and wanted to know if Larry would be able to talk. Larry asked if he'd listened to the new tape he'd sent him. Carl said yeah, he'd heard it through once; he wanted to know how much Larry had made it for. Larry said about $250. Carl said they definitely had to talk. Why didn't they meet for lunch at It's in the Pot! when he was in

Chicago? Enthused by Carl's reaction to his music, Larry borrowed $190 from his mother—"borrow," not "take," he insisted. He explained that he needed $70 for the tuxedo rental at Gingiss Formalwear, $20 for the shoes, $10 for champagne, $50 for dinner at Arnie's Restaurant, $10 for the corsage, $20 for his weekly payment to 3M Studios, and $10 for "incidentals." Ellen told him not to worry about repaying her, but that if condoms cost less than $10, he should bring her back the change.

Michelle Wasserstrom's horror at the prospect of prom night was more than compensated for by her delight in the absurdity of its trappings. She decided to have the ultimate prom experience, never mind that it was with Larry Rovner. She would wear the sluttiest prom dress she could track down at the Salvation Army, and tuck a hip flask of Wild Turkey into one garter and a joint in the other. She would order filet mignon and champagne at Arnie's. She would wear eye shadow and rouge and lipstick and mascara and her most ridiculous pair of high heels. She wanted to slowdance to every dreadful Journey and Billy Joel song, get all teary, and tell Larry, "This should be our song." She wanted to have sex in the backseat of a car and say, "Please, be gentle with me." She wanted to go skinny-dipping in Lake Michigan, then get dressed and go to the IHOP in her beer-stained evening gown and eat waffles with too much syrup, go to bed at 8 A.M., and wake up with a hangover.

Larry picked her up at 7 on the dot, shook hands with Mr. Wasserstrom, and told him he'd take good care of his daughter. Michelle had stifled a giggle at the tuxedo, the cummerbund, the cuff links, the red bow tie, and the matching red yarmulke, and just said, "That outfit is so *you.*" She told Larry to kiss her on the cheek; she didn't want him to smudge her lipstick, honey. Michelle was so enthusiastic during the first part of the evening that Larry was almost frightened. She said his cologne was just "delish," did he like her perfume?—she thought maybe she had dabbed on too much. At the restaurant, she said she just didn't know what she wanted—could he be "the man" and order? And when the steak came, she said she thought it was just too hard to cut—could he slice it for her? She told him she didn't want to eat dessert; patting his belly lightly, she said they should both watch their figures. And in the car ride from Arnie's to the Hyatt House, she turned on LITE-100, cranked it up, and sang along with Barbra Streisand.

When they got to the hotel, Larry stopped thinking she was mocking the whole event and thought that maybe she was really in love with him. He nodded, smiled, and said "Yeah" when Michelle said that this was the best hotel; Hyatts were absolutely the best. When they walked into the basement of the hotel toward the ballroom, joining the swarm of awkward, tuxedoed boys and evening-gowned girls, Larry agreed with Michelle when she said that everybody looked so handsome and that the décor was "just darling," that the streamers were such pretty colors, and who was that—was that Ben Jacobs? He had filled out, hadn't he—he looked so much better than he had in Hebrew school. And who was that over there—was that Missy Eisenstaedt? Oh, she had to talk to her; that is such a pretty dress, Michelle told Missy; where had she gotten it, Saks? It really suited her, she said, then added, "Wear it well, dear. Wear it well." And who was that creep at the reception desk, making balloon animals? Why didn't they get away from him as soon as possible, Michelle told Larry.

The band started playing "Le Freak (C'est Chic)" and Michelle grabbed Larry's hand, exclaiming that this was the best dancing song—*the best ever!*—then tore toward the ballroom. But just when they were about to disappear into the crowd, a body blocked their way. A hand that had been clutching the neck of a balloon giraffe dropped the article and reached out for Michelle's wrist instead.

"Peachy Moskowitz," Lennie Kidd said blearily. "What are you doing here?"

WILLS / SILVERMAN

Peachy Moskowitz

Amazingly, the Peachy Moskowitz Debacle, as Michelle Wasserstrom would later refer to it, did not occur on the night of the senior prom. It would occur exactly two weeks later at her sister's graduation from K.I.N.S. The Senior Prom Incident had been alarming, but yielded no damaging, long-term consequences. She had slipped effortlessly into character when accosted by a haggard Lennie Kidd with bruises on his wrists and dark shadows under his eyes, telling him, "*Ees* long story," and when Larry had asked her how she knew the balloon guy, Michelle merely said, "It's amazing the creeps you meet when you're an actress."

The rest of the evening had been an odd game of keep-away, with Michelle leading Larry onto the dance floor to do the bump to "Is She Really Going Out with Him," over to the buffet table to snack on lox and bagels, out into the parking lot to smoke, always making sure that Lennie, who seemed to be drugged or sleepwalking, was just out of earshot. Larry said if Michelle wanted that guy to stop bothering her, he'd take care of him quick. Michelle said that was all right—she'd tell him the whole story later; she didn't want to ruin their "special night."

In truth, Michelle had only herself to blame for both the Senior Prom Incident and the Peachy Moskowitz Debacle. She could have just kept calling WBOE once a week and offering her wry ruminations about Iranian politics ("Hostage *seetuation ees bowlsheet. Jeemy* Carter should bomb *zemm eento shtone* age") and the American boycott of the Summer Olympics ("*Mekks* no *deef'rence* to me; *Oleempics borink* as *hale weeth* or *weethout Ameddican ethleets*"). But the fact that she hadn't been on stage since *H.M.S. Pinafore* had become increasingly frustrating and she craved a greater challenge. So when Lennie told her, as he always did after they were done taping her *Young Town* segment, that it sure would be swell to meet her if she ever visited Muley, Michelle didn't say "*Ees veddy deefeecult* for me to *leef* my *creppy* job," as she usually did. This time she said, "Yes, I *weel* be *een* town *bott* only for a *copple* of *dezz, end* I *weel* be *veddy beezy.*" After which, Lennie would not let her off the phone until she had committed to tape their show in person, then go out for dinner to Pizzeria Due.

Michelle called Muley to ask if he wanted to rehearse with her to make sure everything would go smoothly, but he said he was too busy editing. Instead, she rehearsed atop Mt. Warren in front of an uninterested Gareth and a distraught Myra, who had been dumped by Douglas Sternberg after an associate artistic director at the New Iroquois Theater had read his musical *The Burden of Biff* and offered to produce it if she could play Mary Hyman herself, an offer that took Douglas Sternberg all of two seconds to accept; he had told Myra he was sorry to replace her, but the truth was that she was neither slim enough nor talented enough for the role. Michelle worked a long time on her walk—was it Russian enough? she asked Myra and Gareth—and on her smoking technique. Russians *schmoked* a lot; she had to look like she *schmoked* every day. Then she decided no, she wouldn't *schmoke* at all—*Ameddicans* don't *schmoke ett* all, she said; *effer seence* she *hed* "set feet" on *Ameddican* soil, she *hed geefen op schmoking.* That's what she would say, she told Gareth.

"Who gives a shit what you say, Wasserstrom?" Gareth asked, adding that she sounded more Albanian than Russian. And, he said, if she screwed things up at the radio station for his little buddy Muley, he'd be forced to kick her ass. Michelle asked Gareth why he was so defensive about Muley—did he have a secret crush on him or what? Gareth said first of all that was bullshit; second of all, just because he'd protested the exploitative Al Pacino leather-bar movie *Cruising* didn't mean he was gay; and further, that gay people were perfectly capable of having normal relationships with people of the same sex without having crushes on them. Michelle said she had no problem with Gareth being gay just so long as he wasn't a hypocrite about it. Gareth said he didn't think he was gay, but he found heterosexuals boring. "Particularly you, Wasserstrom," he said. Michelle asked if she'd be more interesting if she started "lezzing off" with Myra. Myra said that was *so sick;* she couldn't believe Michelle would say that. Michelle and Gareth looked at each other, then at Myra. "Lesbian," they said in unison. "Definitely a lesbian."

For the Saturday taping of *Young Town,* which Muley chose not to attend, Donna Mayne and Lennie Kidd had written a script in which the *Young Town* kids take the wrong airplane and crash-land in Red Square. They are questioned by a KGB officer named Boris (Lennie Kidd), then held hostage. While in prison, they strike up a conversation with their warden, Alexandra (Peachy Moskowitz), who asks them about America. They tell her about a land full of wonders—hamburgers, baseball, Disney World, rock 'n' roll, and a document called the Constitution. Alexandra gets a special audience with Soviet premier Leonid Brezhnev (Lennie, again) and argues the case of the *Young Town* kids. Brezhnev agrees to release them on one condition—that they all get to go to America together. In the final scenes, Brezhnev, Alexandra, and the *Young Town* kids arrive in D.C., where they are met by President Carter (Lennie yet again), who presents them with a key to the city. "Now that y'awl are in America," Carter says, "what do y'awl wanna do first?" Brezhnev responds, "Get a hamburger," and all the kids shout, "YAY!"

Michelle Wasserstrom found the script ridiculous, but Peachy Moskowitz found it sweet. And while Peachy found the *Young Town* kids adorable, Michelle found most of them insufferable, particularly Pablo, who kept asking her questions: "Do they have ice cream like we do in America?" "Yes," Peachy said. "*Bot only one flevver*—coconut." "Do they play baseball like we do in America?" "Yes, *bot eef* you drop ball, they send you to gulag." "Do you think they'll drop a nuclear bomb on America?" "Yes, *bot* only on boys who *esk* too *menny kvestchens.*"

During the taping and afterward, Michelle had to struggle between what *Michelle* would do and think and what *Peachy* would do and think. Michelle liked being the center of attention, testing microphone levels, listening to herself in headphones, but Peachy was shy, embarrassed. Michelle was an instinctive, confident actress, but Peachy was self-conscious and sounded as if she was reading directly from a script. This disparity between what was Michelle and what was Peachy was directly responsible for her decision to dine with Lennie and go back to his place. Michelle found Lennie pathetic and lecherous. But Peachy was far more naïve.

After dinner at Due's, Lennie asked Peachy if he could show her some magic tricks at his apartment. Michelle wanted to laugh in his face or say, "Sure, I like magic tricks; have you ever seen The Disappearing Date?" But Peachy had little experience with men; she had been too busy with matters of international significance. While she had been researching a book about the phallic subtext of the space race, she had had a few passionate evenings with a Soviet cosmonaut. She had let Henry Kissinger get to second base with her, had necked in the backseat of a Citroën with Valéry Giscard d'Estaing, and had refused West German chancellor Helmut Schmidt's offer to "eat her out." She had only been in love once, but that had been when she was a mere slip of a girl and Mikhail Baryshnikov had broken her heart. These days, she would let men get close to her, but only for an evening or two and only when she knew she wouldn't see them again.

Lennie's apartment was a wretched little place located at the easternmost edge of West Rogers Park on the third floor of a small cluster of three flats with cement patios and rusted charcoal grills out back. Lennie boasted that corner apartments like his were the most desirable in America, though his only afforded him views of the S & C Electric Company and the Chicago Health and Tennis Club on Ridge and the steeple of Angel Guardian Church on Devon. Upon entering the dismal apartment, one heard a fluttering and a chorus of squawking from the caged budgies in Lennie's bedroom. "I could *nyet shleep* in *setch* a room," Michelle said. "I *vould fill zat* all *zee* birds *vere vawtching* me."

On the early June evening that Michelle would later identify as The Evening of the Unfortunate Oedipal Budgie Incident, Lennie began by demonstrating how to make a penny disappear; he later pulled a budgie out of a hat, then went to the bedroom, opened the birdcages, and directed a phalanx of birds to fly back and forth through a set of rings as he juggled them. Michelle delayed the inevitable moment of attempted seduction, always demanding *"anozzer treek"* the moment Lennie started to put away his magic set. All the while as he barked at his birds, which he had named after famous classical musicians—"Fly Pinchas, move it Itzhak, upside-down Jascha, up and over Luciano"—Michelle contemplated the best way to depart in such a way that would allow her to keep her *Young Town* gig but give Lennie no hope of ever seeing her again: There was something scary about Lennie, reminiscent of serial killer John Wayne Gacy. There was laundry all over his floor, bird shit smeared on the TV screen, stray pubic hairs twisted around the buttons of his dark-brown couch. Michelle sensed that if she said the wrong thing, she would end the evening hacked up or stuffed into a crawl space.

She was almost out the door when the phone rang and Lennie went into his bedroom, where he had a heated telephone conversation. "I'm on a date, Mother," he hissed. "No, I don't know when I'll be coming by." "Yes, I will ask her if she wants to come to dinner," then "Yes, Ma, yes, Ma, yes, Ma, okay, Ma, okay, Ma, okay, all right, all right, bye." After Lennie hung up, Peachy asked who had called. "An old gal pal," he said, then brought out two sets of handcuffs and a blindfold. Michelle had a sudden urge to kick him in the nuts. But Peachy only said, *"Vot* do you *plenn* on *doink veeth zeese?"* Lennie said he was going to show her his most miraculous trick. He asked her to handcuff him behind his back, then cuff his ankles. *"Ees* like *bekk een gulag,"* Peachy said as she complied. Then he asked her to blindfold him. Peachy said she'd seen this trick before. Not like this, Lennie told her. Because he wasn't going to escape on his own; his parakeets were going to pick the locks and free him.

For Michelle, this would have seemed the ideal time to leave. But Peachy wanted to see the trick. She stood by the door, her hand on the knob as the odd little bearded man called out, "Open sesame, Yehudi, work it, Vladimir, and move it, goddamn it, Pinchas." The birds encircled him, then pecked away, two at each ankle, two at each wrist. Peachy thought it was sad that a man who obviously had at least some talent could be reduced to this—alone, middle-aged, tied to his chair, birds hopping up and down upon him, shitting and twittering as he tried desperately to impress an audience of one. It was a *deefeecult* society for an artist to survive, Peachy thought. The older he got, the less *peety Ameddika vould* show *heem; eef* you *deedn't mekk eet een* your chosen *filld, thees vas vot* you *vould* become. She watched as Lennie kicked one foot free from the chair and shouted, "That's the way, Vladimir. Attaboy! Now work it, Pinchas. Work it, you fucking piece of shit bird!" But as he kicked his other foot free, shouting "You're a slow-ass bastard, Pinchas!" Michelle told Peachy that she admired her sense of charity, but there was absolutely no way she would fuck the Pickle Barrel balloon man, and yes, it was sad that society would have less room for artists and iconoclasts, but that's the way it was, and the fewer successful performers there were, the greater her own chances of succeeding would be.

"So *goot* to *heff* met you *een* person, toots; you are *vun* sexy *babushka,*" she said. "But I *heff* plane to *ketch.*" With the birds fluttering and twittering by his ears, Lennie did not hear Peachy's farewell, the sound of the door quietly opening and closing, or footsteps on the stairs.

As Michelle emerged onto Ridge, quickly turned the corner, and started walking west, she thought she heard a parakeet flying just over her head, but when she looked up, she saw nothing. She half-expected that Lennie would fire her the next time she called for her *Young Town* segment, but when she did call, Donna Mayne told her that Lennie was taking a leave of absence for "health reasons," and that she would be hosting until he returned. Meanwhile, she said, the show would take on "a different configuration." There would be less about time travel and outer space. She would treat such topics as "Your Own Backyard," about how kids could get involved in community activism, or "What's So Bad About Prejudice?" and there would be a new, weekly "Ask the Alderman" feature.

The truth of the situation was that after the Unfortunate Oedipal Budgie Incident, Lennie, convinced that Peachy hadn't left but had been rendered invisible by his least-favorite parakeet—Pinchas—had emptied all of his closets and his desks, his dresser and his magic cases, looking for her. He took out his frustration on Pinchas, whom he grabbed and hurled out his window; the creature traced the entire perimeter of West Rogers Park before alighting upon the jungle gym of Boone Elementary's playground, where Muley Wills, camera in hand, captured its flight path. At dawn, Lennie drove to Old Orchard to see if he could meet his therapist before her first appointment.

Lennie had vowed to stop treatment with Dr. Rovner, whom he had been seeing ever since the breakup of his marriage. For $60 a week, she tended to give him the same insulting input that his mother did. But the session following the budgie incident didn't even last the full fifty minutes. Disarmed by a new hairdo (short and becoming as opposed to long and hangy), a new outfit (formfitting and tapered instead of worn and schlumpy), and a new facial appearance (Was she wearing makeup? Had she lost weight?), Lennie made the error of suggesting that Ellen Rovner's new appearance might have been adopted for his benefit. Dr. Rovner called the session to an early close. "Find yourself a male therapist," she said.

Lennie had planned to drive back to West Rogers Park to pick up his vampire costume from the dry cleaners but instead drove to his mother's house in Morton Grove, where he had lived until he was married, where he had holed up for three and a half years after his divorce, and where his bedroom had not changed in more than twenty years. There were old magic sets on his desk, a collection of Golden Book encyclopedias and *National Geographic School Bulletin*s in the bookcase, a metal case filled with baseball cards in the closet, model racing cars on the night table, cap guns in leather holsters in the dresser. After the panic over Peachy Moskowitz's disappearance slowly gave way to an unspoken acknowledgment that she had, like so many women before, walked out when he produced his handcuff trick, Lennie could not muster the energy to emerge from his room.

Lennie did not call any of his employers to let them know where he was or when he was planning to resume his duties. He pissed into a juice jar and hurled the contents out the window. He locked the door whenever his mother's friends came over to play gin rummy or watch *M*A*S*H*. Each night he would resolve to emerge from the bedroom, but each morning his mother would sit by his bedside and say something that would make him want to draw up the covers and hide for the rest of his life. "Maybe I did something wrong in the way I brought you up," Dorothy Bass told him the first morning. "Maybe you just weren't born for this world." On the fifth morning, she informed her son that she had called up his ex-wife.

Lennie had always resented that his mother had taken Gail's side during their divorce and still occasionally lunched with her. But this invocation of Gail's name at one of Lennie's most vulnerable moments sent the radio host and balloon sculptor into a frenzy, angrily cursing his mother as he sprang out of bed and followed her downstairs. Why did she always have to bring Gail into it? he wanted to know. Why did she always idealize Gail and infantilize him when the truth was that Gail had been a rotten girlfriend, a rotten wife, and rotten in bed? If his mother wanted to marry Gail, well, that was just dandy, but he never wanted to hear that bitch's name again. That was too bad, his mother told him, because Gail was in the kitchen and she'd brought a crumble cake.

Lennie stopped dead at the bottom of the stairs. He used a thumb and forefinger to sculpt his lips into a polite grin. Gail was sitting at the kitchen table. She wore a navy-blue jogging suit with white piping. Lennie offered Gail his hand, said it was nice to see her again; she looked well. Still smiling, he went over to the kitchen counter and cut himself a slice of crumble cake and went to the refrigerator for a glass of milk. He sat across from her at the table, took a forkful of cake, brought it to his lips, tasted a morsel, said it was good. Then his entire body went slack.

After a week of bed rest, Lennie was informed by his doctors that he could begin work again but only a little at a time. Doped up with Valium, he performed at Zanies and won new fans with his unblinking, deadpan, monotone style. He made good on a commitment to sculpt balloon animals at the Ida Crown senior prom, where he had seen Peachy Moskowitz. And two weeks after what had been labeled a breakdown had seemingly subsided, Lennie was feeling a good deal less manic. He had lunch twice with Gail, and they had their first reasonable conversations since the first year of their marriage. Gail told him about Charlie—how old-fashioned he was and yet how charming just the same. Even though he had given her the classic "Let's be friends" speech, she knew he would come around soon. In turn, Lennie told her about Peachy Moskowitz—he knew that he might be too old for her, but he was truly in love. Gail said that age didn't matter when you were in love. She hoped that he would find her and that they would be very happy together. In the meantime, though, she thought it would be nice for Lennie to get out and meet people; friends were what one needed in life's most difficult moments. She was going to Charlie's daughter's graduation and then there would be a dinner afterward—why didn't he join her?

Throughout the graduation ceremony at K.I.N.S., Lennie had to grasp the arms of his chair hard, fearing he was experiencing vivid, terrifying delusions. He could have sworn that the girl at the podium, giving the class speech and declaiming, "Hey, hey, we made it through *Heh,*" was the same Rovner girl who had auditioned for *Young Town* and against whom he had lobbied strongly in favor of the kid with the Spanish-sounding name who reminded him of what he'd been like as a child. And he was fairly certain that his therapist was sitting five rows from the stage, one leg crossed over the other, her foot tapping agitatedly as it always had in his sessions when he was telling an anecdote she had heard before. He tried not to shiver during the presentation of the diplomas and Rabbi Shmulevits's speech eulogizing the recently passed Henry Miller, likening *Tropic of Cancer* to the Song of Songs.

At the end of the ceremony—after the members of the *Heh* class, accompanied by a sullen Rabbi Meltzer on acoustic guitar, had sung "Quando El Rey Nimrod," a Ladino song, in which Hillel Levy substituted the words "Avraham's a penis" for the real lyric *"Avraham Aveenoo"*—the graduates in dour suits and frumpy dresses, diplomas in hand, filed out of the auditorium followed by parents, siblings, and family friends in dourer suits and frumpier dresses. Lennie followed Gail's every movement, stopped applauding the moment she stopped, stood up the moment she did, and followed her into the hallway, where they admired the Tree of Life memorial display.

Gail asked Lennie if he would feel comfortable meeting some people. Lennie said sure; he was "feeling real chipper." From his face issued a frightening grin. Gail grabbed his elbow and moved him toward a large circle of people, where Rabbi Meltzer was explaining to Larry Rovner that the reason he liked playing music with Rovner! and not at K.I.N.S. was because he didn't get to "rock out" and "strut his stuff" here, and when were they going to get some gigs? Larry told him he'd had some "interesting meetings" recently and they had to get together, but this wasn't a good place to talk. Charlie Wasserstrom had taken off his gray suit jacket because he found it too hot in the synagogue—there were sweat stains under his arms. Jill—who carried not only her diploma but also her copy of the Tanakh and the Hebrew high school scholarship she had been awarded ("I hope this is transferable," she had said)—was discussing dinner plans with her father. Jill said it was fine if he wanted to have prime rib at Victoria Station, but she didn't think there was anything there for vegetarians to eat. Shmuel Weinberg, standing next to Jill, suggested they go out for cheese pizza, to which Jill said she was happy to go anywhere as long as it wasn't for pizza. Why did everyone think vegetarians should eat nothing but pizza? Shmuel agreed and said they should go out for steak.

Nearby, Dr. Ellen Rovner—Lennie was sure it was her—was standing by the yarmulke bin talking with that girl who'd given the "Hey Hey *Heh*" speech, saying that the girl had to come home with her, since her father hadn't shown up to the graduation; she didn't care if Lana thought her new apartment was "icky"— she wasn't an adult yet, and that was the end of it. Lennie thought this might be an appropriate time to insinuate himself into their conversation and ask if they wanted to join him for dinner. But before Lennie could approach Ellen and Lana, Gail began introducing him to Charlie, his daughter Jill, Rabbi Meltzer, Larry Rovner, Jill's friend Shmuel, and her sister, Michelle.

Lennie gasped. He didn't hear a single name Gail uttered. He couldn't avert his gaze from Peachy Moskowitz—it couldn't be her; it *had* to be her, that was the same skinny teenager with an Isro he'd seen her with before, so who else could it be. What could he say? He couldn't say anything, he had to say something, something suave, something that acknowledged he knew her but nothing more, nothing to attract attention and make people know there was something wrong with him, because there was nothing wrong with him, it's just that he knew her, that was all.

"Peachy," he grinned, smooth and nonchalant. "Good to see you again."

If Michelle Wasserstrom had thought the situation through, she would have ignored the greeting completely. If she had known something of Lennie's recent mental state, she would have dropped the accent and said something to throw him off the scent, something on the order of "Buzz off, buster; my name's Michelle." But because she thought the surest way to achieve any desired result was to deliver an impassioned performance, she threw up her arms and shouted, "*Vhy* does *thees menn nyet leef* me *een* peace? All I *vant ees* to be *lift* alone, but all *zee* time he *ees fullowink* me; *ees vurse den* KGB."

This remark may have passed unnoticed, a teenager acting like a teenager, as Gail thought, a joke that made about as much sense to Charlie as any of

Michelle's other jokes did. But in speaking as loudly and as dramatically as Michelle did, she attracted the attention of Lana Rovner, who broke away from her conversation with her mother, approached the circle, and poked Lennie on the shoulder. Who was that? she whispered loudly, pointing a finger toward Michelle. Her name was Peachy Moskowitz, Lennie said, she was a very famous woman from Russia. No, she was not, Lana said. Her name was Michelle Wasserstrom, she was her brother's girlfriend, and she attended "public high school" at Mather. What was *thees leetle beetch sayink?* Michelle asked. Larry flinched. What was Michelle saying to his sister, he wanted to know? Jill said she was leaving and stormed down the hall. She couldn't tolerate arguments; why couldn't people argue when she wasn't around? Lana reiterated her initial statement: This girl was not Peachy Moskowitz. "I *vill nyet shtand hyere* and be *shlandered,*" Michelle said as her father crinkled his forehead.

"Why are you talking that way, honey?" Charlie asked Michelle. *Yeah, honey,* Larry wanted to know. *Why was she talking like that?*

"Oh, now *eet ees* 'honey,'" Michelle responded, indignant. "*Allvays mit dees* 'honey.'"

Lennie told Lana she was wrong; he knew this woman. They had gone out for pizza together and she had come back to his apartment. Gail said wait a minute—who'd been to whose apartment?

"*Ees* my body; I do *weeth eet vot* I *em choosink,*" said Michelle.

Larry wanted to know who the hell this guy was, wasn't he the same creep from the prom? *Thees vas* complete *bowlsheet,* Michelle said. Lana asked Michelle to say out loud what her name was. Michelle said she *vould nyet shtoop* to *enswer setch* a *kvestchen.*

"What's her name?" Lana asked her brother.

Michelle told him not to answer: Lana was just jealous. "*Effrybody een zee vorld ees* jealous of us," she said. "*Effrybody ees* jealous of our *luff.*"

"What's her name?" Lana repeated.

"You know her name," Larry said.

"What is it?" Lana asked.

"Michelle Wasserstrom," Larry said.

"What?" Lennie Kidd asked.

"Who went over to whose house?" asked Gail.

Michelle's face flushed. She turned fiercely to Larry. "You fucking suck," she said. She had no accent now. She reiterated that Larry fucking sucked. He had no concept of what an artist did, had no place telling anybody who she was—her identity was something she decided, she alone, she didn't need some piece of shit making choices for her. She swatted open the front door of the synagogue as Larry, torn for only a second between loyalty to his sister and lust for the one girl who would sleep with him, followed Michelle, practically colliding with his father, who was entering at the same time Michelle was leaving, a lab coat folded under one arm and, in his hand, a small wrapped present from C. D. Peacock Jewelers, which he had taken an hour and a half to pick out, thus making him miss the graduation ceremony entirely. "Hey, Larr," Michael Rovner said, adjusting his tie. He said he hoped he wasn't too late.

Larry caught up with Michelle at North Shore and Washtenaw. He asked her to slow down; he wanted to tell her he was sorry. Sorry for what? Michelle wanted to know. She maintained her pace. For everything, Larry said. Oh, Michelle said, then he didn't even know what he was apologizing for. No, he said, but he knew she was angry with him so he thought he should apologize for something. Well, Michelle said, an apology wasn't worth much if the person apologizing didn't even know what the fuck they were apologizing for. Larry said he was sure they both had things to apologize for. Michelle said she wasn't sure about that at all—what exactly did he have in mind that she should apologize for? Well, swearing, for example, Larry said. *Swearing?* Michelle asked. She suggested that Larry suck her dick. Larry said she didn't have a dick. Michelle told Larry to stop swearing; it offended her "virgin ears." She said if he couldn't handle her, he should go to the yeshiva and study Talmud and marry a nice, mousy Jewish girl who would cut off her hair for him and sit on the other side of the synagogue with the kids and fuck him once a week through a bedsheet. Larry said he wasn't like that; he loved studying the Mishnah, but he loved playing music too. Well, Michelle said, then he had to choose; he couldn't be a rock 'n' roller and a yeshiva boy. Yeah, Larry said, he *could;* that's what *she* didn't understand.

Larry asked Michelle to stop as they reached Campbell Avenue. He said he had to tell her something important. He said he had sent his tape to Carl Slappit Silverman. They'd talked on the phone and Carl said he had really liked what he'd heard. He just thought Larry needed seasoning, and that he needed to learn a lot about the industry before he was ready to break out on his own. Carl had offered him a job that would start in July in L.A.; that would mean that he could conceivably defer his Brandeis admission and see whether he had what it took. But he didn't know anyone out in L.A.; if he had someone to go with, that would be absolutely "awesome." Just think about it, Larry said—Michelle could audition for films; he could play gigs. Michelle asked what the fuck he was thinking about. She wasn't going to be some two-dollar whore in L.A.; she was going to finish high school, then go to Yale. Well, Larry said, then maybe they could just try it for the summer; if it didn't work, Mather and Yale would always be there.

Michelle asked Larry if he was high. Larry said yeah, he was, high on life. Michelle smirked; had he really just said that? she asked. Yeah, Larry said, he had. He said all he wanted Michelle to do was to think about it—not give him a definite answer now. He wasn't sure that he wanted to do it himself—he was looking forward to college, looking forward to coming home and visiting her on Simchas Torah. But he was eighteen years old, man, and he loved the idea of being independent. Sometimes, man, he felt like Moses. The Promised Land was out there, but he couldn't get in—he had to stay here in the fucking desert. That's what Chicago was—it was a fucking desert, man.

Larry wasn't going to let her break up with him here; if he could get away from her without having her break up with him, it would be a major victory. He knew this was a lot to think about; he had hoped to spring it on her when they were in a quieter mood, maybe in his basement after some weed, when they both were naked and listening to Aerosmith, but he couldn't let her run away now not knowing his plans, what they could do if they just had "some imagination and some nuts." He told her once again to think about it—whatever she decided, he'd understand. Michelle said nothing. She just watched him as he turned and jogged away as fast as possible and headed back west, ecstatic that she hadn't said no yet, ecstatic that she hadn't broken up with him. As he neared the Boone playground, he was thinking about drinks with umbrellas and the beach in Malibu.

Michelle was headed the other way, east toward Warren Park. As she crossed Western, she realized she didn't have cigarettes. She hoped Myra or Gareth or some other random burnout might be on top of Mt. Warren and she could bum a square. But as she walked south on the east side of Western, she noticed a shoulder-high wooden fence encircling Mt. Warren. At the base of the hill, there were two earthmovers. On the fence, there was an official sign from the City of Chicago. "Another project with YOU in mind. Jane M. Byrne, Mayor." A small map depicted the "New Warren Park." The map promised that construction would be completed by October 1980. Well, this was great, Michelle thought. Where could she smoke weed until then?

The celebratory dinner at Victoria Station for Jill's *Heb* graduation was a rather muted affair. Only Gail, Charlie, Shmuel, and Jill wound up going, and Shmuel spent the whole time staring at his prime rib, uneasy about eating meat in the presence of a vegetarian. At the end of the meal, in the parking lot, Gail asked Jill if she would mind if she spent some time alone with Charlie after they had dropped Jill and Shmuel off at the apartment; there were some important matters she wanted to discuss privately with Charlie. Jill said that was fine with her and asked Shmuel if he wanted to go home or come over to watch the film of Ingmar Bergman's *The Seventh Seal* that she had taken out of the library. Shmuel said he loved movies and would be happy to join Jill, but he ended up hurrying home before the film was over because he found it creepy and Jill refused to stop it.

That night over highballs at the Mark II Lounge, Gail apologized for Lennie Kidd's behavior—she took full responsibility for his outbursts, she said. Charlie said that it wasn't her fault. Gail thanked him for saying that, but added that that wasn't really what she wanted to discuss anyway. She told Charlie that she respected that he had been trying to stay away from her, but if this night proved anything, it was that bringing up two girls was a lot of work. She said she thought that he had done a great job with Michelle and Jill, but maybe they needed a woman around the house, someone who could be a mother to them, a big sister, or a friend. Maybe if she'd been around for them, Michelle wouldn't have gone off "looking for love" at Lennie's apartment. All she was saying, she said, was that Charlie might need a little more help than he cared to admit. After Charlie had ordered a second highball, he admitted to Gail that she was probably right.

News regarding Peachy Moskowitz's identity reached Donna Mayne quickly, but when Lennie Kidd recommended Michelle and Muley's immediate ouster and suggested legal action, Donna was uncertain. Dismissing the two of them would be a public admission that she and the station had been duped. Though *Young Town* was one of only two children's newsmagazine programs in the U.S., the other being an amateurish Boston show called *Young City*, her program would probably not even receive a Jack Benny nomination. As she suggested to Michelle after spending twenty minutes reprimanding her, however, if she submitted one of the Peachy Moskowitz scripts in several *fiction* categories, she would be able to own up to the lie, claim credit for it if anyone questioned her, and receive several awards as well. She now foresaw at least a "Triple Crown" in the Jack Bennies. What she further suggested to Michelle was that in the half hour that preceded *Young Town*—a no-man's-land between 8:30 and 9 occupied by *Fishin' with Fred*—Muley and Peachy could host a new thirty-minute talk show called *Chi-Town Chatterbox,* in which they would interview Chicago personalities about subjects of interest to kids. For example, they would talk to the curator of exhibits for the Art Institute about how to get the most out of a museum. She asked Michelle to suggest the program to Muley, who hadn't been returning phone calls.

Muley wasn't home when Michelle called. His mother said crisply that she didn't know where he was. She asked if this was the "Connie person" who kept calling. No, it was Michelle Wasserstrom, Michelle said. Oh, Deirdre Wills said, her voice softening, was she the girl who had scored so well on her PSATs? Yes, Michelle said. Deirdre said she could find her son at 3M Studios.

When Michelle tracked Muley down at 3M, he was standing by the console in Studio A, where Mel was reading aloud from the current draft of *Godfathers of Soul.* "The camera settles on Al Capone's mistress Jasmine Huggins, tall, long legs, medium-sized breasts," Mel said, reading out camera directions and dialogue. "She is wearing a sheer kimono, through which her nipples are visible. In the background, Tiny Walker is lying on the bed in a black robe. He carries a gun." Michelle asked if she was interrupting. Mel said she was, but if she wanted to listen, she could pull up a chair. Muley said she wasn't interrupting anything; they could talk in the other room.

As they sat in the tiny film-editing suite, Michelle told Muley that she assumed he'd heard about the Peachy Moskowitz Debacle. Muley said no, he hadn't heard much of anything lately, but after Michelle explained the situation, Muley said the whole thing came as a relief; he'd grown tired of *Young Town.* Maybe he'd gotten everything out of it that he could. But when Michelle mentioned the possibility of a new half-hour talk show—"*Chi-Town Chicken Shit* or something"—Muley became more interested. He said it would be great if they could have a half hour to really experiment with. They could do site-specific programs utilizing sound effects on the streets, in the sewers, underwater—they could do new scripts, old radio dramas. There were so many different things you could do with radio, and people only used it for music and talk shows. Well, Michelle said, that's what Donna wanted to do—a talk show; they'd be interviewing museum curators, shit like that. Muley said no offense, but he really wasn't interested.

When Muley explained this over the phone to Donna Mayne, she shouted angrily at him that he could not refuse to do *Chi-Town Chatterbox;* if he did this to her, his future in public radio would be ruined. Muley told Donna that he understood her position, he appreciated what she had to say, he didn't mean to offend or insult her. Donna asked if he understood that if he did this, she would have no choice but to replace him. Muley said he understood that too. He said that Lana Rovner and P.C. Pendleton would both be excellent replacements.

After that phone conversation, Michelle asked what Muley was working on—another movie for her sister? Muley said he hadn't talked to Jill recently. Michelle said that was because she was fucked up. Muley said he didn't know about that; they'd been good friends, but now she was better friends with Shmuel, and that was all right with him. Michelle asked if Muley meant that dork who hung around Jill, wanted to kiss her, and still hadn't gotten up the nerve to try. Muley held back a smile and said he had nothing against Shmuel; he seemed nice. Michelle said there was a difference between being nice and being too much of a dork to be anything else. She asked if she could see a bit of the film he was working on. Muley said there wasn't much to see; he'd been working on it for months, but only had about ninety seconds done. Michelle said she'd like to see anyway.

Muley told Michelle that in his film, he was trying to create two separate and distinct worlds—one West Rogers Park in the present day, the other an exaggerated, animated version of it. Creating those two worlds wasn't hard per se, though each element of the animated world, from the lush pear trees to the crystal castle, required hours of tracing and copying from encyclopedias and illustrated children's books. The true difficulty came in moving back and forth between the two worlds. Numerous frames took place simultaneously in West Rogers Park and Muley's fantasy version of it, and creating transitions had proved exceedingly time-consuming.

The glimpse Muley showed Michelle began with a shooting star streaking across the night sky, growing, then transforming itself into the body of a flying parakeet. The camera traced the parakeet's path, then stopped as the bird flew from the left side of the frame toward the right side. As it crossed the centerline, the parakeet suddenly acquired a deep golden hue and turned into a cartoon bird and the right side of the frame faded into a muted watercolor world. The bird passed by the walls of Boone Elementary, which resembled a crystal-blue castle, before alighting near the top of a violet jungle gym. Then the image faded to black.

A suitably impressed Michelle—who told Muley that whenever he wanted to make a movie with people in it instead of cartoons, she'd be more than happy to star—left 3M Studios certain that one day in the future, if her sister continued acting foolishly, she (Michelle) would wind up dating Muley, if Gareth didn't get to him first. She discarded that thought and moved on, wondering what heinous prepubescent boy Peachy Moskowitz would be paired with for *Chi-Town Shitbox* now that Muley had taken himself out of consideration. She sincerely hoped it wouldn't be that insufferable Pablo creature. In fact, later in the week, Donna told her that Pablo was one of three finalists being considered for *Box*. The other two—Michelle was horrified to discover—included Lana Rovner, as well as someone she would refer to in discussions with Myra as "P.C. Pencildick." The prospect of having to spend Saturdays doing some queer show with a spoiled bitch, a spastic retard, or some other thirteen-year-old cretin was terrifying enough. But it was not what ultimately made her more seriously consider the move to L.A. that Larry had proposed.

That momentous decision came on a June evening when she had already resolved to spend her summer taking History in summer school at Mather, doing *Chi-Town Chatterbox*, working part-time at the North Shore Bakery, hanging out with Larry once in a while and boning him when she felt like it, and leading JCC drama camp. But plans for that idyllic last summer were soon crushed at the Campbell Avenue dinner table when Charlie Wasserstrom announced that he wanted to have a "serious family talk." He said it wasn't about "bad stuff"; actually, it was about some "really pretty neat stuff." At the moment Charlie said "neat stuff," Michelle dropped her spoon. There had been something oddly ceremonial about the dinner her father had prepared that night—he had broiled whitefish and boiled green beans. He had made his special "buhp" salad dressing—Thousand Island to which he added chopped olives and bits of hard-boiled egg. When she was a little girl, Jill had said that eating it made her go "buhp," hence the name. He had poured wine for himself and seltzer for the girls. He was wearing a pressed white shirt and a red tie with gold diagonal stripes.

Charlie said that he wanted Michelle and Jill to "hear him out" before they made any snap judgments. He wanted their opinions, but after they thought through what he was about to tell them, he was fairly certain they would approve of his decision. The fact was he loved his daughters very much—he wanted them to know that—but sometimes he thought that being a parent was more than he could handle. Not that they'd ever been a burden to him—he loved reading Jill's report cards and listening to her speeches; he loved watching Michelle in her plays. But the fact was, Michelle would soon be going to college—"someplace real good if she can get in," he said—and Jill would be in high school. And doggone it, sometimes he felt real lonely. He had spent a good deal of time away from Gail, and the more time he spent away from her, the more he realized that maybe they were really right for each other. Of course she'd never replace their mother—no one could do that—but he felt a real sense of friendship with her. Which was why he had offered to marry her, and she had said yes—provided, he emphasized, that his daughters agreed to the match.

Michelle had bought several books in preparation for her History class—its focus was Chicago politics. She had already started reading the first book—*Boss,* by Mike Royko. And the only remark she felt was suited to eloquently yet directly express her opinions was one she paraphrased from a statement made by an assistant to black powerbroker Congressman William Dawson, who had objected to the renomination of then-mayor Kelly. "The candidate," she said as she rose from the table and brought her plate to the sink, "is unacceptable to Congressman Dawson."

As she left the apartment, while Jill was telling her father that families really weren't democracies, and ultimately, in the benevolent dictatorship under which they were living, she was bound to whatever choice he made, Michelle had little doubt where she was headed—the Rovners' house. She needed to discuss L.A. Her mother hadn't been able to make a go of it there; maybe fate was leading her to succeed where Becky Wasserstrom had failed. When she got to the Rovner house, Larry's father—adjusting the umpire's suit he was wearing—answered the door with officious self-assurance. "Big man's downstairs," he said. "Which one of the lady friends are you?" "The good-looking one," Michelle said, and she walked past him, not acknowledging—in fact, pretending she hadn't noticed— Lana at the kitchen table rehearsing a *Chi-Town Chatterbox* audition script by announcing, "That's right, Peachy, and we have a very special guest this morning—Lester Fisher, director of the Lincoln Park Zoo" into a tape recorder.

Larry was on his bed in his bachelor pad, barefoot and shirtless. He wore denim cutoffs and a matching denim yarmulke held in place with a silver clip. He was strumming chords with an expression of intense concentration, working on a song tentatively titled "The Ballad of Chaya and Yehuda." He acknowledged Michelle coolly with a tight reverse nod, chin out. "Hey, baby," he said, "it's been a while," though it had only been a little over a week since he had proposed the L.A. journey. Yeah, Michelle admitted, sitting at the foot of his bed and lighting a cigarette, there'd been some crazy shit going on; it looked as if she would be moving with her father and sister to "The Shiva-Asshouse" on North Shore. That sounded cool, Larry said, it would be good for her to live west of California for once; he knew some nice families on North Shore—doctors, lawyers, teachers, the "good Jews," Larry said. Maybe he and Michelle could hang out at Chippewa sometimes and play H-O-R-S-E or play tunes and party bongs or something, he proposed. He kept strumming chords and softly singing "la-la-la's" just out of his register.

Michelle was waiting for him to say something about L.A.—to bring it up herself would have meant completely violating the rules under which their relationship, such as it was, operated. Under their unspoken arrangement, Larry proposed things and she either accepted or rejected them. She wasn't sure she wanted to go to L.A. There were other options to consider: the Tuchbaums' couch on Bell Street, the Overgaards' guest room, the dreaded Asshouse, running away. She wasn't sure she wanted to go with Larry at all; the main appeal of that arrangement was that Larry had the fewest expectations. If she wanted to have sex, they had sex; if she wanted to smoke, they smoked; if she wanted him to shut up, leave her alone, and let her read, he did that too.

When Michelle finally broke down and asked Larry what the L.A. deal was, he asked if he could take a drag on her cigarette. When he handed it back to her, he said yeah, he'd been meaning to talk to her about that. He'd decided he couldn't go to L.A., not right away anyway. He'd had a long conversation with Slappit and the two of them hadn't been able to come to an agreement over money. Silverman had, in fact, not offered him any, and suggested that Larry work as an unpaid intern for two months. If that worked out, then they could discuss salary. And the more Larry thought about it, the more suspicious he had become about Silverman's motives; he seemed far more interested in how much Larry had spent on his demo tape than in what was on the tape itself. He had said nothing about the chord progressions, nothing about the song order, only that it would be tough to get teenagers excited about the "electric *brachas*" Larry promised to intersperse between songs on the next album. And besides, Larry didn't see a lot of opportunity to "play out" if he had to spend two months learning "the ropes of the music business." What he really needed to do this summer was get his performing chops—he'd already sent out tapes and started booking gigs at summer city festivals and rock clubs.

Yeah, well, that was cool, Michelle said—disappointed that the L.A. experience was no longer something she could accept or reject. She said she was okay with the idea of working at the "J," the radio station, and the bakery, and taking summer school. The only wild card was where she would be living. She said she would be doing the "World Tour of Couches" and would probably have a change of clothes, a toothbrush, and a pipe at every house in West Rogers Park. Larry said if she needed a place to stay, Jeff Meltzer and his wife were short on cash and might be willing to rent out their basement. He wished he could help her out himself, but he was going to be busy with his music.

Wait a minute, Michelle snapped, was he sending her to Davy Jones's locker? Larry said he didn't understand her lingo. Michelle asked again if he thought he was sending her to Davy Jones's locker, for it was her understanding that they hadn't even been officially dating yet. Oh, Larry said, finally understanding, was he "dumping" her? No, he said, not really. He would be busy, but they could still hang out some, maybe have sex sometimes, plus she could bang a tambourine at the Rovner! gigs in July and August. All he was telling her was that he was going to be pretty busy for the next two months, but she could always call if she wanted to hang.

Torn between feeling the humiliation of being dumped for the first time in her life and the absurdity of the fact that it was Larry doing it, Michelle was briefly rendered speechless. "All right, that's cool," she said after a moment. "Let's hear some of these shit songs you're working on." Larry played her five new songs, finishing up with the latest ballad. "It's kind of about us," he told her as he sang, "Once there was this girl named Cha-yaaa /And she could put a man through fi-yaaa /And then she met this boy Yehu-daa /And they made love like two barracu-daaas." On her way out, Michelle said she liked all the songs except for that last one. "The lyrics need work," she said.

She let herself out of Larry's bachelor pad, walked up the stairs, and headed straight for the front door, trying her best to ignore the precise, perfectly enunciating voice in the kitchen saying, "That's so interesting, Dr. Fisher. Thank you for being on our show today." She walked back slowly toward her apartment, heading east on North Shore. She paused for a minute in front of the Funny House. Tears welled up in her eyes, slid down her cheeks, then dried up as she swallowed hard. This part of West Rogers Park seemed so boring, so middle-class, so pristine, so white. Where were the pot smokers driving Plymouth Dusters, the T-shirt–clad gang members beating the shit out of kids with two-by-fours? This was only a mile away from where she lived now, but she could see her life transforming from working-class striving to an almost-suburban, middle-class angst. She liked the idea of being the one girl east of California being a National Merit semifinalist and going to Yale; doing it from the West Side seemed typical, obvious. She picked up her pace and walked toward California. Whatever, Michelle thought, maybe the worst wouldn't happen, maybe "Large Mouth" Bass would stand Charlie up at the altar, maybe she'd find a new boyfriend at the Weight Watchers clinic, maybe she'd have enough money to send her through Yale.

As Michelle crossed California, Larry Rovner put down his guitar and reached under his mattress to pick up the letter he'd received from Hannah Goodman and reread it yet again. No, he hadn't dreamed it. Hannah, that luscious vixen of the King David Hotel, would be attending Brandeis. She wanted to know what dorm he would be living in, what his major would be, if he was still as cute as she remembered. The letter was signed "With much love, your Hannah." Larry put the letter aside and reached inside his denim cutoffs; masturbation in service of a likely reality rather than a dubious fantasy was, in the formerly self-abnegating Larry Rovner's mind, perfectly acceptable.

Charlie

C harlie Wasserstrom was happily surprised by the sudden turnaround in his oldest daughter's attitude toward his proposed marriage to Gail Schiffler-Bass. Less than a week after he had first presented the idea, Michelle approached him while he was eating his eggs. And though he had no idea who the "Congressman Dawson" was to whom she referred, he was fairly certain that the "candidate" she found "acceptable" was Gail. And so when Michelle left the house to "teach rugrats to butcher Shakespeare" at the JCC, Charlie immediately called Gail to tell her the match was on.

Michelle's decision had been influenced, not only by her growing realization that she had few other realistic options, but also by a remark Gareth had made one night when they had been smoking on Lunt Avenue Beach. Earlier, Michelle had been reading in her bedroom, trying to drown out Newsradio 78, when she heard a reporter describe the general malaise of the U.S., now in the eighth month of the hostage crisis. The reporter used a phrase that, she felt, accurately depicted her own predicament. "Michelle Wasserstrom," she told Gareth, "is experiencing a crisis in confidence." When Michelle had complained once again about the prospect of waking up in the middle of the night and hearing her father's grunts or walking into the bathroom and smelling Gail's "musky odor," Gareth impatiently told her that if she wanted to be both famous and interesting at the same time, she had to distinguish between what was "good for her *personally*" and what was "good for her *biography.*" She could, say, marry Larry Rovner and move to Skokie. This would, perhaps, be good for her personally, but completely uninteresting for biographical purposes. Or she could shoot heroin and be the first woman to deliver Yale's valedictory address strung out on horse; that would make for a great chapter in a biography. Gareth added that he himself didn't read biographies and found them boring, but other people read them, and he wanted to be sure that those people would buy hers. It was in this way that

Michelle decided that while arguing with, avoiding, or pretending to tolerate Gail would be personally excruciating, it would be good for her biography.

The wedding of Charles Wasserstrom and Gail Schiffler-Bass was held on July 17, 1980, across the hall from the main auditorium of K.I.N.S. in the small Beth Ha'Knesset, which charged a significantly reduced room rental. It was a small affair officiated by Rabbi Jeffrey Meltzer, who charged less than Rabbi Shmulevits. The ceremony was attended only by a dozen relatives and a few friends from the Schiffler papers. Though Gail had told Michelle and Jill they could each invite three friends, neither did—Michelle because she chose not to subject anyone to what promised to be an "ugly, ugly scene," Jill because the only person whom she might have invited, Shmuel Weinberg, had tried to kiss her when he met her after the summer school First Aid course she was taking for credit at Lane Tech, and she had responded coolly, saying she was not a CPR dummy.

Afterward, Uncle Dave and Aunt Peppy sponsored dinner at Moscow at Night, a Russian restaurant and banquet hall. After consuming borscht, blini, and chicken Kiev, and enduring a couple of crude toasts, one of which was from Hank Shiva—"He may be related to me now, but I'm still not gonna cut him a deal on a car"—Charlie and Gail danced to "You're in My Heart" and "Angie." By midnight, they were headed back to the Campbell Avenue apartment to get some sleep before the next day's move west to the Funny House, while Michelle— desperate to avoid any wedding-night shenanigans at home—dragged Jill to the Thirsty Whale to catch Rovner!'s late set, but left shortly after Larry dedicated his latest song, "Sad Eyed Lady of the Sinai," to her.

Initially, Gail and Charlie had planned to honeymoon in Las Vegas, but Jill had objected to being carted off to summer camp—"Once was enough," she had said, recalling a mosquito-filled six weeks shortly after her mother's death, in which she was supposed to participate in sports activities and sing-alongs led by counselors Gabe Goldstein and Jeffrey Meltzer, who repeatedly asked her what was wrong, didn't she like singing "Hatikvah," didn't she like horseback riding? "Not when I'm in mourning," she had said repeatedly. Gail and Charlie decided instead to take a week off from work to settle into the Funny House. Moving, Gail said, would be a good family bonding experience.

Charlie had talked about having an apartment sale, but most of his worldly belongings fit easily into six large cardboard boxes, plus three other dusty boxes marked "Memories and Such" held shut with green duct tape. Gail had asked what was in those boxes. "Nothing important," he'd said. "Just pictures of the kids and baby shoes and stuff." He actually hadn't opened those boxes since Becky's funeral, not since he had stuffed them with as many of her belongings as he could find—and taped them shut. He knew the boxes contained *Playbills* from musicals they had seen together, a tin filled with matchbooks from restaurants they had frequented, Regular 8 movies of their Niagara Falls honeymoon. He never wanted to open the boxes again, but he never wanted to be rid of them either.

In their bedroom, the two girls had what Michelle termed a "purging party." But Jill did most of the purging—she kept nothing except her clothes, her books, Muley's movies, and her projector. All of the old board games, puzzles, paperweights, and dolls went into boxes, each marked with the name of a different charity, while Michelle carefully hid her pipes and her bong in a shoebox and taped it shut. As for the toys, games, old school papers, lab books, and other assorted *khazerai* Michelle had accumulated over the years, she stuffed most of it into boxes marked "For the Biography."

From a distance of two alley blocks away, Muley Scott Wills, camera in hand, watched as the Wasserstroms took the last armloads of boxes down the back steps into the alley. He began filming as Charlie brought down the rear door of a rented van, got into the front seat, started the motor, shifted into drive, and signaled a right, westward turn. He kept the camera running until the van made the turn and moved out of frame.

While Jill sat sullenly but quietly in the backseat as the Wasserstroms drove west on Devon, Michelle leaned out a rear window and reprised her role as Emily Gibbs returning resignedly to the valley of death in Thornton Wilder's *Our Town*. "Good-bye, Grover's Corners," she crowed lugubriously. "Good-bye to sleeping and to waking up. Good-bye, Campbell Avenue walk-up. Good-bye, Parthenon Gyros; good-bye, Crawford's department store; good-bye, Bud Schaibly Bowling Alley; good-bye, Dog Ear Records and Miller's Meat Market. Good-bye, Gigio's Pizzeria. Oh, Gitel's Bakery, you're too wonderful for anybody to realize you." By the time they crossed California, Michelle had switched from Emily in *Our Town* to George Bailey arriving home in Bedford Falls in *It's a Wonderful Life*. "Hello, Kosher Karry," she trilled gleefully. "Hello, Knopov's Bakery; hello, Manzelman's Hardware Store; hello, Minky's Bicycle Shop; hello, you old Schwartz-Rosenblum Judaica Bookstore." It was really accurate and wonderful, Gail said of Michelle's imitation. Michelle kept silent for the rest of the ride to the Funny House.

Once the boxes had been moved into the house and the garage, Gail asked if the girls wanted to see their rooms. Charlie said he wanted to come too, but Gail said no; she had designed them herself and wanted to show them off herself: Why didn't he go to the kitchen and grab an ice-cold beer. Though Charlie had initially wanted the girls to design their own rooms, he had warmed to Gail's suggestion that she design the rooms and have the girls make alterations, if they so chose. Gail led the girls along a latticework fence that hid the backyard from the street toward the back entrance of the house, navigating a small cement pathway between rows of hot peppers and tomatoes. They entered through the glass rear door. Gail asked who wanted to see their room first. Michelle pointed at Jill. "*She* does," Michelle said.

Inside, the Funny House was laid out like many of the other houses west of California, the key difference being that the house was sunk deep into the ground. So that, though it resembled a ranch house, there were actually three floors, two below the main level. Gail said that the girls were on the "Lunch Meat Level"—the house was built like a sandwich and the top level and the basement were the slices of bread above and below them. As Gail led the girls downstairs and into Jill's new room, Jill thought that any bedroom design scheme would be flawed. After all, her idea of the perfect room consisted of white walls, unfinished bookshelves, and an enormous desk; anything else was consumeristic and, consequently, wasteful. But the room Jill entered was relatively tasteful; the walls were a bluish green that matched the blue carpet; there was a reading lamp on a night table beside the bed; there was a dresser, a generous closet, a wall of bookcases, and room for her desk once it was lugged in from the garage. Tucked in a corner by the closet, there was a collapsible movie screen. The posters Gail had chosen to decorate the room—a Black Power fist, "Free the Chicago Seven," "Save the Whales"—might not have been Jill's choices, but they were reasonably close. Gail asked Jill if she liked her bedroom. Jill said yes, she thought she'd be able to get a lot of work done here.

Michelle's bedroom was just down the hall—their own private girls' bathroom ("That's important for girls to have," Gail said) was across the way. When Michelle pushed open the door, she braced herself for the worst, thinking that there was no way Gail could have any idea of her tastes, that she was undoubtedly out of touch with anybody her age. Even if they were the same age, they would never have been friends; she and Gareth and Myra would have hung out at the Superdawg hot dog stand in 1956 listening to Bill Haley and the Comets on the car radio and made fun of Gail's Sinatra records. Michelle was, as it turned out, correct, but so correct that the room thrilled her. It was so tasteless, so grotesque, so insulting to her intellect that she loved it, loved the hot pink walls and the leopard quilt cover on the bed, found it hilarious that Gail had spray-painted a cannabis leaf and the phrase "Legalize It" beside it on the wall. She loved the room in the same way she loved ordering Salisbury steak at greasy diners and going to laser light shows, the same way she loved Elvis movies and snooping through porn magazines, the way she loved things that she couldn't for a moment believe anyone else took seriously. "It's everything I thought it would be," she told Gail. The room made her happy; there was no way she could be in it and not laugh the whole time. That night, as Michelle and Jill slept in their rooms—Jill with her night-light on—they were well insulated from the sounds of Gail and Charlie's energetic lovemaking. Though at three in the morning, when Michelle heard two sets of feet tiptoeing down the hallway, then the sink going for quite some time, she did have the wherewithal to moan "Gross!" and bury her head in her leopard-skin pillow.

That first week in the Funny House was one of the happiest in Charlie's memory. He was thrilled by the spaciousness, the luxury of being able to take a beer out of a refrigerator in one room, transport it through another, and sit down with the same beer to watch TV in yet another. He was both amazed and delighted by how well his daughters and Gail seemed to get along, how Gail seemed always to know the right thing to say, how even when Michelle seemed upset or Jill seemed depressed, Gail could suggest something like "Maybe we should all play a board game," or "Who feels like working a puzzle?" and the girls would immediately start giggling. He felt a strong sense of pride when one of his older daughter's friends—a portly young man in a German army jacket—came over, surveyed the surroundings, and told Michelle, "Well, you've done it now, Wasserstrom; you've joined the bourgeoisie." Yes, Charlie Wasserstrom thought. Yes, he had.

It had been a wonderful week. Even when he had been dating Gail, Charlie still had been convinced that he would live out his middle years alone, eating meals by himself, going to movies by himself, certainly going to bed by himself.

The most difficult part had been convincing his daughters that he didn't mind, that he didn't mind Jill and Michelle eating their dinners quickly or not at all, going out and coming back long after he had pretended to go to sleep, just so they wouldn't know he had stayed up waiting for them. Now, as he frequently told Gail, lying next to her in his pajamas, he felt luckier than he had any right to feel. It was only during the next week, when he and Gail returned to work, that his glee began to ebb.

At 7 Monday morning, Gail, while standing at the bedroom mirror hiking up her panty hose, informed Charlie that, since they were married, they should have distinct boundaries between work time and home time. They should arrive at work separately, leave separately, have lunch separately; any other arrangement would be bad for office morale, especially since Howard Schiffler would be stepping down as publisher at the end of the year. When she took over, her employees would need to know that she did not play favorites. Charlie raised no objection, only saying that the lunches were the highlight of his day, but he was a big boy and didn't mind eating alone.

On the masthead of Schiffler Newspapers, Charlie was listed as sales associate (restaurants/food service). And though some of his colleagues had worked at Schiffler for decades while he had been selling ad space for less than a year, his name was often atop the sales board. Virtually every restaurant owner and manager in West Rogers Park and its surrounding neighborhoods knew him and almost all, except Alan Farbman of It's in the Pot!, liked him. He never pushed anybody to buy; he came in for a cup of coffee or a sweet roll, and tipped generously. He talked to people, and he listened to their stories. One time he spent a whole day listening to Raymond Shen at the House of Canton tell him about his son who'd dropped out of college because he thought he could make a living playing billiards. At the end of the discussion, Charlie thanked Shen for the tea and the almond cookies and said he'd be back later in the week to see how he was doing. "Aren't you supposed to sell me an ad now?" Shen asked. No, Charlie said, not today; being a salesman was about more than selling ads.

Charlie's approach served him well. In previous years, the papers' restaurant calls had been handled by both Howard and Gail Schiffler, but neither had sufficient time to devote to them. Marty Eisenstaedt only handled the retail sales display ads, Mike Romano did real estate, and Bev Pohlen was responsible for classifieds. Anything that didn't fit into those categories was usually handled by

Howard or Gail. Since Charlie's arrival, Schiffler Newspapers had seen its gross retail bar and restaurant ad sales nearly double.

For Charlie, this all seemed like good news. The Schiffler "Good Employee" plaque was a delightful surprise when he received it at the company luncheon at the Fin 'n' Claw. And even in early August, he had his eye on the Salesman of the Year trophy, which Marty Einsenstaedt had won every one of the past ten years except in 1976, when he was out with gallstones for part of the year. Charlie didn't necessarily want to beat out Marty, whom he liked, and whom he remembered from birthday parties where he would pick up his daughters, Bibi and Missy, in his gleaming, punch-red Lincoln Continental. But he did like the idea of winning the trophy, of being the best at something.

The Thursday sales meeting was held, as always, around a table in the commissary at 3 P.M. just before the week's papers would be coming out. ("Citywide Music Festivals Have a Rogers Park Flavor" was the front-page headline. Below it was a triptych—one picture of a rock singer in an Israeli flag cape, one of a little girl eating corn on the cob, another of a band on an outdoor stage. On the bass drum, Weinstock! was printed.) Normally, Gail introduced the week's sales reports by saying, "How's business, Charlie?" But this time, she said curtly, "Let's start with you, Marty." It was at this point that Charlie noticed that his week's total on the sales board had been erased and replaced with a question mark. He assumed that this was what Gail meant when she told him she didn't want to show favoritism. The meeting proceeded as Marty listed his numbers and his new display clients.

Charlie made as if to speak a half-dozen times, opening his mouth, then closing it, inhaling deeply and grimacing, not knowing if he should correct Gail's oversight or if he should mention it afterward. Luckily, Bev, peering at the board over her half-glasses, asked the question for him: "What about Chuck's numbers?" Well, Gail said, she wasn't going to put Wasserstrom's numbers up anymore until she was sure they were "reliable." She would discuss them with "Wasserstrom" privately after the meeting. Howard Schiffler said he didn't understand—family was family, but business was business and he wanted to know what was going on.

What she meant, Gail explained, was that Charlie's sales figures were misleading. On the one hand, he had racked up more restaurant and bar contracts than anyone ever had. But that didn't mean that the papers were collecting as much money as Charlie's contracts indicated; nearly a quarter of his advertisements weren't being paid within the required thirty-day period. Charlie said he could vouch for everyone with whom he had signed a contract—they were all good people and they were all good for the money. Gail asked if everyone he had signed a contract with was good for the money within thirty days of their having signed. Charlie said well, obviously not, because apparently they hadn't paid yet. Marty thought this was funny and laughed, but Gail did not. She looked down at her clipboard and cited $1,350 worth of unpaid bills from Ravi Khan at the Family Pizzeria. Charlie said Ravi's rent had recently doubled and he was in the process of securing a loan from the bank. Gail mentioned the House of Canton's $1,260 deficit. Charlie said that there was a difficult situation with Raymond's billiard-playing son. Gail said she didn't care about any of this, didn't care that Bess Vaysberg had glaucoma, and furthermore, it was not Charlie's job or anyone else's to care either. No doubt there was a place for people who cared deeply about the welfare and financial hardships of people, but the ad sales department wasn't it.

That night at dinner, Charlie apologized for his poor ad sales performance. Gail said they shouldn't discuss it; she only wanted to discuss work at the office. At work, she would be pissed off about every ad he didn't collect on; at home, she didn't give a damn if he ever sold another. Over the weekend, they caught both ends of a twi-night doubleheader at Comiskey Park, and had sex a total of five times. On Sunday night with Michelle in the bedroom below blasting Led Zeppelin's latest album, *In Through the Out Door,* as loud as it could go, Gail called her husband "Charlie." But Monday at the office, he was "Wasserstrom" again. When he arrived in the morning and took carbons of the previous week's contracts out of his file cabinet, Gail told him, "Don't sell anything today; just try and collect."

During times of stress, there was an odd sensation Charlie felt in his chest. It was midway between a gulp and an ache and it asserted itself whenever he thought about whatever was disturbing him. He referred to it as his "little friend." Oh, don't worry about it, he would tell his first wife Becky when they were working at the Candlelight and a customer had really laid into him; don't worry about it, he would say as he grimaced—it was just his "little friend" coming to visit. Oddly, it tended not to affect him in extreme situations, so that when his mother was in the hospital and kept confusing him with his brother, even though Dave had never come to visit her, or when Becky was confined to their bedroom for the last month of her life, he never encountered his "little friend" at all. Now that he was driving north on Western bound for Ravi Khan's Family Pizzeria, his "little friend" was knocking hard, eager to burst out. It was okay, he thought, there was nothing to get excited about, this was part of the job. He would explain that if it were up to him, he would let people pay whenever they could. They were businessmen too. They would understand. They would pay him.

But for the most part, they didn't. Ravi Khan, who incessantly called Charlie "my friend," told Charlie that he was truly truly sorry, my friend, that of course Charlie knew that if he had the money in the bank, he would pay it, my friend, but he would need at least another week. Raymond Shen was more than accommodating—he went into the back office of the restaurant for the money—but then returned and muttered that he should never have brought his checkbook to work because it was missing along with his credit cards; he didn't know what to do because if he called the cops, they'd surely arrest his son. Bess Vaysberg, on the other hand, told Charlie he was a "very rude man"—she had taken out an ad to help him, and now here he was harassing her. Here, she said, take your *vershtinkeneh* gelt and she'd find a way to pay her ophthalmologist. Charlie did not have the heart to tell her that she still owed $100 more. The customers with their accounts in arrears followed a pattern—the more they owed, the more polite they were, but the more likely they were to pay, the less likely they were to be pleasant about it. Boaz Levy at Nagilah Israel was the only person to pay in full; he made Charlie wait while he walked over to Lincoln Federal and returned with the entire $375 in tens, fives, and crumpled ones that he counted very slowly before he shoved the pile of cash across the counter and told Charlie, "Now go and get killed."

On Tuesday, Charlie had nine sales calls to make, but Gail told him not to make new sales calls until he'd collected on the ones he'd already made. Charlie said he'd seen everyone who had outstanding bills and he had received either payments or reassurances. Gail told him to go back and replace the reassurances with cash or checks. Charlie asked what he was supposed to do—keep going back until all the bills were paid? Yes, Gail said. Charlie said he didn't know, maybe he wasn't cut out for this job, maybe he needed a job that wasn't so intense, one that didn't send his "little friend" pounding against his rib cage so hard that he had to pop Rolaid after Rolaid. Gail said there was no reason he should feel any pressure at all. He was too nice, she said. Nice might have worked in business at one time, but now less and less; now whenever people saw "nice," what they really saw was the weakness underneath.

Gail was right, Charlie thought, maybe he was too nice, maybe he was no different from the way he had been in eighth grade when Coach Minkoff had told him that he could be a great first baseman, and he had told the coach that he didn't like playing sports because he couldn't live with himself when he saw the sadness on the pitcher's face after he had knocked a homer, because he felt just an itty-bitty gulp when he stepped on first base and forced a runner out. Okay, he told Gail, she was right—he would collect the money; he didn't like people taking advantage of him. That was the spirit, Gail said, maybe he should give these people a piece of his mind—maybe it might make him feel better.

But it didn't make him feel any better and it didn't get him the money. When Charlie told Raymond Shen that he was taking advantage of his friendliness, that he didn't come into his restaurant, order egg rolls, and leave without paying, Raymond said the two situations were not remotely comparable; he wanted to know if Charlie was feeling all right—he wasn't being himself—maybe he would like some tea; he was breathing heavily and didn't look at all well. Ravi Khan said he knew he owed $1,350, but he just didn't have it, my friend. If Charlie wanted to take $1,350 worth of cooking equipment and silverware, he was welcome to it. He asked if Charlie wanted a glass of water.

Normally after he finished his sales calls, Charlie returned to the office, assessed his day, and planned the next one. But he knew how his day had gone and how he had to spend the next, so he returned home immediately, back to the house where his wife kissed him hello and said how good his cooking was, where his universe was filled with fresh laundry and cold beer in the fridge, where his little man left him alone until Newsradio 78 woke him in the morning.

That Wednesday, Charlie swallowed a fistful of Rolaids as he circled the block around Lincoln Federal looking for a parking place. The Thursday sales meeting was approaching and he was still $3,700 below the minimum threshold he needed. He was certain the next day he would be at the bottom of the sales board; he hadn't gone on a call in nearly a week, how was he supposed to make a living? It didn't matter that his wife outearned him nearly three-to-one, he had to make his own money, he couldn't be a loafer all his life. Taking $3,700 out of his savings account, where he kept $10,000 for emergencies, seemed like the only logical solution. He would withdraw it in cash, say that Ravi Khan, Raymond Shen, et al had paid such-and-such amount, and then have each of them pay him on their own schedule. There was nothing else to do; he had to tap his account or quit his job.

Charlie was sweating hard and patting his thumb methodically against his chest at the same rate as his heart was beating; on his tongue was a sticky pepsin paste of antacid tablet residue. He was craving a cigarette and thinking about the time when he had quit smoking. Jill had been five at the time; the plan had been for the family to go to Disney World for Memorial Day vacation, but as the day to purchase the tickets approached, Becky and Charlie determined they couldn't afford the trip; the best they could do was drive to the Wisconsin Dells, they said, whereupon a petulant Jill did some quick math and determined that Charlie—a pack-a-day smoker back then—had "smoked up all of our vacation money." If he had quit smoking one year earlier, they could have gone anywhere in America. Charlie was thinking about the fact that within a year, his oldest daughter would be going to college, maybe Yale, and he was sure that those sorts of schools cost $10,000 a year. It was okay, it was all right; he would tell everybody that he had spent his own money. Once they understood, they would pay him back promptly, he reasoned, as he reached the front of the line at the bank.

When he reached the teller, Nellie Kerbis, he told her the management should consider turning on the air conditioner—it was boiling outside. She said that the air conditioner was on full blast; that's why she was wearing a sweater. Charlie said he guessed he wasn't used to wearing a coat and tie in the summer. As she began counting out $3,700, Charlie said he'd changed his mind; he didn't want $3,700—really all he needed was $3,500; it wasn't that much of a difference, but it sounded like a lot less. He slipped off his suit jacket and wiped his forehead with the back of his hand. As the teller put the bills in an envelope, Charlie thought maybe he should forget the whole thing, maybe what he should do was to tell Gail and Howard that they should get someone else to close and collect on his deals and the two of them could split the commissions. But he was certain they wouldn't go for it; why would they bother to have him make half a sale if someone could make the whole one? The economy was rough; good people were out of work—nearly 8 percent of the population was unemployed, that's what John Cody had said on Newsradio 78. No, this was the only solution, he thought as he approached the front door of the bank, head down, counting his bills and walking smack dab into Gail.

"Charlie," she said cheerfully. It was lunch hour and she was making a deposit. What was he doing here? she asked. Nothing, he said, just taking some money out of the bank. Yeah, she smiled, there was a lot of money in that envelope, what was he doing—buying a new car? No, no, he said. Actually it wasn't all that much money, he just needed to buy some gifts for the girls. Gail asked him if he was okay; he looked tired. Did he want to get some lunch? No, he was fine, just hot, he said. He said he'd see her at home.

And now that Gail had seen him with the cash, there was no way he could divvy it up among the contracts and say that Ravi had paid this much and Raymond had paid that much. And not only that, now he had to buy gifts for the girls so that Gail wouldn't get suspicious. He drove quickly over to Dog Ear Records to get an LP for Michelle. He asked a salesman what was good, what people were listening to. The man pointed to *Sandinista!* by The Clash. Charlie said fine, paid for it, took it, and left. He spent even less time at General Camera, purchasing an Instamatic camera, three rolls of film, and two packs of flashbulbs for Jill, stuffing the change in the front pocket of his jacket.

Charlie thought he could walk home from General Camera and drop off the gifts, but as he tried his key in the lock and couldn't force the door open, he realized that he didn't live on Campbell anymore. Stupid, he said to himself. *Stupid.* He knew he didn't live here, what had he been thinking? He was smarter than that. You fucked up—that's what his father would tell him—you *fucked up,* every time at the pop factory that he or Lloyd had filled twenty-five orders but neglected the twenty-sixth, every time he broke a bottle full of sarsaparilla pop. He walked back south, crossed Devon, and heard a horn honking at him. *Jesus Christ,* the owner of a dirty white van shouted, why didn't he look where he was going, *you tubba shit?* Charlie hadn't even seen the van coming. He needed to lie down. Just for a little bit. It was hot outside, how hot was it? he wanted to know as he flipped on the car radio and pulled into traffic. Newsradio 78 would tell him how hot it was. He fumbled with the radio knob as he hooked a left onto Western and drove north, not noticing the light was red.

The meteorologist said it was eighty-two degrees at O'Hare, but that couldn't have been right. Maybe he was getting sick. Maybe he had a fever. He just needed to get home, turn up the air conditioner as high as it went, lie down, take a few deep breaths, and close his eyes—then the little friend would stop his thumping, his head would cool off, the tilting would stop too, because things were tilting when he looked at them. He would stare at something and it would tilt, not all the way, just a bit to one side—the sign for Sun Drugs, the lampposts in front of the Shang Chai Kosher Restaurant. And the more he stared, the farther things would tilt, just a little more this way, as his heart beat faster and the little friend kept gulping and gulping away until it felt just like one giant gulp, one unrelenting hiccup right in the middle of his chest. But no, he couldn't nap just yet, he had to get something for Gail, because maybe she would be jealous if he just got presents for the girls. So he turned west onto North Shore and drove past the Funny House as Jill crouched in the backyard picking tomatoes, Muley Wills just a half-block away on Richmond with a stop-action clicker on top of his camera, focusing in on dandelions.

When Charlie got to the parking lot of Dominick's, he left the motor running and the car in park in the fire zone. He headed straight for the flower section, everything tilting at 45 degrees. He grabbed the first bouquet he could find. He went into the Ten Items or Less aisle, paid $10, didn't even wait for the change or his receipt, just went back out the automatic door and jumped back in his car wondering why he'd left the door open, the keys in the ignition, the motor running—how could he be that stupid?

Sleep, sleep, sleep, all he needed was a little sleep and a lot of air-conditioning. But by the time he slammed on the brakes in front of Gail's house—*his* house, *their* house, was it their house now, could he call it *their* house?—everything was tilting even farther to the left, soon the entire world would be upside-down. The North Shore Avenue sign was tilting so far to the left that it looked as though it would crash through the asphalt, tilting so far to the left that as he approached the front door of her house, *their house,* Charlie Wasserstrom—his hands full of flowers and bags—had to tilt his head that far to the right so that everything would return to its proper place. He walked unsteadily, a few steps quickly, then stopping, a few steps more quickly, then stopping, so that he could shut his eyes tightly and right himself for a moment or two before everything started leaning again—squinting stepping stopping, squinting stepping stopping, his little friend slamming against his chest, the front door of the house just ahead of him now but the distance between him and it almost insurmountable as the sidewalk suddenly felt as though it were being ripped out from under him as fast as a magician's tablecloth from a fully set table.

The sidewalk slipped away quickly, but Charlie fell slowly as North Shore Avenue and the front door of his house stood straight up in front of him just for a moment before it all came crashing down—flowers, flashbulbs, record album, front stoop, street signs, cars, an envelope full of cash and Charlie Wasserstrom, who stared straight up at the hot blue sky. *"Oy,"* he said. *"Gott im himmel."* His eyelids fluttered before they gently shut. Off in the distance, a dog barked three times.

Jill Wasserstrom was in the back garden grasping a poison-red tomato when she heard a thud, a moan, three barks, and the pop and crackle of flashbulbs. And though she immediately sensed danger—she could almost feel her body temperature drop twenty degrees—she walked slowly to the front of the house, fearing that each step she took was a step toward something awful, frightening, deadly. And when she reached the front yard, she was met with a vision that, though horrifying, was almost exactly the one she had pictured: her father lying faceup on the sidewalk, eyes closed, his white shirt drenched with sweat, around his head roses and carnations arranged almost like a halo or crown. Lying in the grass beside him, *Sandinista!* still in its cellophane, a broken camera, shattered flashbulbs, and a pile of $50 bills slipping out of an envelope.

Though the first instruction Jill's First Aid teacher had given was to call the fire department, Jill didn't think she had the time—when the ambulance came, her father would be dead. Jesus, she couldn't have her father be dead, couldn't deal with somebody else being dead; if that happened, she would never trust another person in her life. And maybe that would be all right, she thought, maybe that would be the best way to live, to go through life always knowing that this person beside you one moment was just as likely to not be there the next, that the only person you could count on to be there for you was yourself until you weren't there either—and then it wouldn't matter anyway, at the end *when all would cease to be.* Still, she undid her father's tie, unbuttoned his shirt, and opened his mouth, taking a breath and exhaling, then pressing down on his chest, breathing then pressing, breathing, then pressing, not even paying attention to whether he was breathing or not, whether his heart was beating or not, because of course he wasn't breathing, of course his heart wasn't beating, of course he was dead, because that's the way it would turn out for her because that's the way it had turned out before when she had believed in praying to God, when she had believed in trusting the doctors. Though she wondered what the point was of doing anything when she knew quite well how it would end, she persisted, pressing, then breathing, pressing, then breathing, until she became aware of a figure standing above her, casting a shadow over her father's body.

"He just fainted," Muley Scott Wills said.

D r. Mary Mitchum of Swedish Covenant Hospital had consulted with the hospital's new radiologist, Dr. Michael Rovner; he had read Charlie Wasserstrom's chest X-rays and found nothing remarkable. Still, it was her recommendation that Charlie stay overnight for observation. His blood pressure was a good bit above normal, and though Charlie said that nothing was tilting anymore, it would probably be best, Mitchum said, if he took a week off from work.

"Or more," Gail said. She was sitting at Charlie's bedside in a hospital room that looked out onto a tiny grocery store across Foster Avenue where it intersected with California. Jill and Michelle had just left to drop Muley off at his apartment, where he said he had "editing to do," before they went to see a movie. Days of family crisis were good days to see movies, particularly shitty ones, Michelle had said.

Charlie was wearing a hospital gown and sitting up in bed. He apologized to Gail for the "fuss and ruckus" he had caused. He'd been doing a lot of thinking, he said. Ever since he'd awoken in the back of the ambulance, he'd been thinking there was either something wrong with him or with the rest of the world and he'd have to change either one or the other if he wanted to survive. Since there was no way to change the world, he'd have to change himself. Somehow, he'd been conditioned to care about people, but he could just as easily have been trained to care about himself, the way his brother did. It was a new decade now, he had a new family, maybe he would behave in a whole new way. From now on, he would choose whom he cared about—his family and his close friends—and that would be it.

Gail asked if he really thought he could live like that. Why not? he asked. Other people did; didn't she think he could too? He didn't want the paper to lose money. Gail told him not to worry about the paper or about money. Charlie said he had to worry about that; if he didn't, then he couldn't keep his job. Or—he felt his little friend tapping lightly against his sternum—maybe that's what she had been thinking about all this time, that he really couldn't have that job anymore. Well, he understood, he said, there was no sense in keeping somebody around when they were only doing half the job. He felt his voice crack and his eyes burn. He was sorry, it had been a long day, he was tired, he'd been scared, he was angry—not with her, with himself.

Gail handed Charlie a Kleenex and told him to blow his nose. She took back the tissue and tossed it in the wastebasket. She said he shouldn't worry about collecting the money; that had been dealt with, and not in the crazy way he'd been planning—she said she knew all about his "cockamamie scheme." When she had called the newsroom with word of Charlie's collapse, her father had been able to use the news of his health in order to collect most of the money Schiffler was owed. A few people—Raymond Shen, for example—had been moved by guilt to pay up. And those who didn't feel responsible for helping to precipitate what Howard Schiffler had referred to first as "chest pains" and later as a "massive coronary" were threatened with legal action and bad press. Still, Gail said she didn't really think Charlie's talents were best suited to ad sales. There were far better uses for someone who always tried to see the best in people, who was so enthusiastic about small things. Charlie asked where he could find a job where these were considered assets instead of liabilities.

Gail said he should write reviews for the paper—restaurants, theater, movies. Charlie said he thought that was Gail's job. Yes, Gail said, but when she became publisher, she wouldn't be able to do it as much. Plus, the fact that Charlie actually liked restaurants and shows would make businesses more enthusiastic about advertising. Charlie said he hadn't written anything since high school. Gail said that was okay—writing well was only required if you were giving a negative review; if you were saying someone's food was great, they didn't care how eloquent you were.

The day after he was released from the hospital, Gail treated the entire family to dinner at Myron and Phil's. "If Dante were Jewish, this place would be in the last ring of his Inferno," Michelle said while inspecting a relish tray laden with three giant scoops of chopped liver. But there was no way either she or Jill could have avoided the evening, particularly since Jill—during the ambulance ride to the hospital when she had thought about asking to hold Muley's hand but decided not to—had spoken a quiet prayer promising that even though she didn't believe in God, if her father survived she would give Him thanks and try her best to observe His commandments, even though she didn't believe He had really written them anyway.

At dinner, the Wasserstroms first discussed *The Blues Brothers,* the movie Jill and Michelle had gone to see in Skokie ("Heinous," was Jill's review), the quality of medical care at Swedish Covenant ("That Dr. Rovner would be happier if he could find himself a nice girl," Charlie opined), and the new Hasidic neighbors moving in across the way. But their conversation almost always returned to the food they were eating. And Charlie, thrilled to have survived the scare he'd had the day before, thrilled to be seated with his wife and two children, thrilled to be eating the steamed vegetable platter and a tossed salad with cream garlic dressing, couldn't say enough about the décor (how "swell" it was that there were signed photographs from so many actors and entertainers, such as Joey Bishop and Paul Anka), the friendliness of the waitstaff (how they really "worked their tails off"), and the quality of the cuisine (how the carrots and squash were "perfectly succulent").

When the Wasserstroms left Myron and Phil's and waited for the valet to bring them their car, Gail said that all Charlie had to do was write down everything he'd said at the restaurant and he could write for the Schiffler Newspapers. Charlie said he was sure there was more to the job than that.

No, Dad, Jill Wasserstrom said, really there wasn't.

ROVNER

Ellen & Michael

I n August, not long after Massachusetts senator Ted Kennedy declared that he would no longer challenge Jimmy Carter for the Democratic presidential nomination, since the U.S. hostage crisis had distracted attention from his own candidacy, and shortly before Ellen Rovner would buy a ticket to Paris with an open return date, Michael Rovner was driving Larry east to Brandeis in a station wagon full of boxes, suitcases, crates, an amp, two guitars, and a drum kit, plus an unopened pack of ribbed condoms. The vehicle had been purchased for $400 from a comedian who said he was leaving Chicago to "start a new life." Except for the cleaning costs incurred by having to pay a car wash to remove every last feather and drop of bird shit, the car had been a steal.

As Michael signaled a turn off the highway, he began looking for a place to have lunch. Somewhere on I-80, he and Larry had run out of conversation topics. After a long silence, Larry had pulled his acoustic guitar out of the back and had tried strumming some of his songs, but when his father tried to sing along, he stopped playing; he said his father's off-key singing was distracting. Michael tried to keep the conversation going by discussing sports, but except for basketball, which mystified Michael, Larry was indifferent to the topic. Thus, the car game that Michael and Steve Ross had invented, in which they called out every numeral from 1 to 99 and named the Chicago athletes who had worn that particular uniform number, stalled out at number 14 (former Blackhawk center Ralph Backstrom) with Michael leading 14 to 0.

Even in the first hours of the trip, conversations had been punctuated by long pauses and quick flurries of misunderstanding followed by longer silences. Past the Chicago Skyway, when only Newsradio 78 was audible, broadcasting something about the Polish labor movement, Michael said if Larry had any questions—about money, about marriage, about how he and Larry's mother had met—Larry could feel free to ask. Larry said thanks; if he thought of anything, he would. Near Hobart, Michael joked that now that he was a single man, maybe Larry could teach him some dating techniques, but Larry—who had lived so long fearing that he would never again receive so much as a good-night kiss—took the remark as sarcasm and informed his father tersely that he *did* have a girlfriend, that for a few days over the summer until he'd "dumped Chaya Wasserstrom," technically he'd had two. Not far from South Bend, Michael asked Larry what he thought was the key to a good relationship. Larry said not sticking with any one thing too long. That's why he'd pursued Michelle when he was still with Randi Nathan, why he'd wooed Hannah Goodman while he was still with Michelle. Just out of Angola, Michael asked if Larry thought people who got divorced were losers. Larry said it depended on the person. Michael asked if Larry was hungry and wanted to find something to eat.

The temptation might have been to stay on the road, drive as fast as possible, not stop other than for gas and fast food ("I'm not eating McDonald's, Dad; we shouldn't eat *traif,*" Larry had told his father). But the dorms didn't open until Friday, and Michael had taken an entire week off. And though the men's trip Michael had envisioned—the two of them going to clubs, drinking beers, and staying up late in the Travelodge discussing sports, women, and the meaning of life—seemed unlikely to materialize, it was not as if the alternatives were any more attractive. Thank God for his daughter, Michael thought, thank God for Lana, for she seemed to be the one person in the world who still deigned to talk to him, deigned to tell him things. In whom else could he confide now that he had fucked up his relationship with Steve Ross, now that he could no longer call Laura Kim?

That evening six months earlier, when he had left his daughter's Not-Valentine's Day party unchaperoned and had stolen away to Laura's apartment, had been the most satisfying and passionate of Michael's life, more so even than the hummer he'd received from the Marine through the glory hole at Little Bo's Peep Show. But the fallout from it had been so devastating that there was virtually no pleasure whatsoever in recalling the moment Laura had told him he was a nice man and he replied that he wished he could show her just how nice he could be. Laura had said she would be happy to let him show her as long as he promised not to leave her alone that night. And as she led him back to her glowing, orange, lava-lit bedroom, circular mattress on the floor, she told him to "take it easy" with her; she hadn't "had it in five weeks."

When they made love for the second time, Michael felt a surge in confidence. He was talented at this activity. He knew how to give women pleasure if only they would let him. He wondered why he hadn't dallied with infidelity before. Cheating on one's spouse was what kept a marriage alive. He liked the idea of being a swinger. He loved the thought of someone at the hospital asking him if he was faithful and being able to say, "Oh no; I swing." And the next evening when Ellen asked him where he had gone during Lana's party and why Laura Kim was leaving messages for him at home, he was so proud of himself that he chose not to lie and instead said that they'd been spending a lot of time together. And when Ellen probed further, he was naïve and hopeful enough to guess that Ellen was subtly trying to suggest a threesome. Shortly before packing a suitcase, Ellen told Michael that if Laura Kim was that attractive resident she had first met at a Chicago-Lutheran Christmas party, she might indeed be interested in a threesome, as long as Michael wasn't the third party involved.

When Ellen left that night for Lake Geneva with her diaphragm and a copy of the *Tribune* real estate section, Michael said that if she wanted to reach him that night, she could try calling him at Laura's. As it turned out, though, he would be at home and not with Laura, though he did keep calling her every hour on the hour until 11 P.M. He got her on the line the following morning, but she said she was on her way out. He said he was sorry and asked if she was perhaps on her way to church. No, she said, she was an atheist; she would be having brunch with some of her girlfriends—she'd try to call him when she got back. He asked what time. She said she didn't know, maybe two o'clock. He said then he'd make sure to be home and by the phone at two. She said she wasn't sure she'd be calling at two; it might be at three—depending on how many Bloody Marys she drank. Michael said no problem; he'd be home between two and three so they could discuss their relationship. Laura laughed and said sorry, she hadn't heard what he'd said—her girlfriend had been "making funny faces" at her; she'd try to call him back that afternoon. But Michael didn't reach her until that night. Her tone was short. She was busy, she said. Doing what? he asked. *Talking,* she said. No problem, he said, she should just call him back when she was done.

He looked for her the next day at the cafeteria, but instead found Steve Ross at the coffee machine. His eyes had shadows under them and his earlobes were scarlet. He told Michael he'd been looking for him. He wanted to know what the fuck Michael was doing, and *don't say you don't know what I'm talking about.* Michael asked if this was about Laura. Steve said fuckin' right it was, what the hell was Michael doing sticking his dick where it didn't belong—that was the worst form of "cockblock." Michael said he thought that Steve and Laura had broken up. Steve said that was complete bullshit—all he'd said was that they were going to be taking it easy for a while. Michael said Steve shouldn't be treating his wife the way he did. Steve said that Michael was an asshole and that he was better off keeping his sage opinions to himself, given that he'd been cheating on his own wife forty-eight hours earlier. Michael said all right, why didn't he get it all out of his system, and then after work they'd get a beer. No, Steve said, Michael didn't understand—once he called somebody an asshole, that meant they were an asshole forever, and if Michael even thought of talking to Laura again, he'd kick his ass. Michael said it was up to Laura to make up her mind. Steve said she'd already made up her mind—who the hell did he think she was talking to the day before when he'd called? Michael said he hoped this wouldn't affect their working relationship. Steve called Michael a pathetic, low-class jitbag and stormed out of the cafeteria.

Michael went straight to Tammy Silver, the Radiology Department secretary, and asked if Laura had come in yet. No, Tammy said, she had called in sick. Michael said he was taking the rest of the day off too; he had personal business. He drove to Laura's apartment, and after she didn't answer the door, he wrote her a love note on hospital letterhead and wedged it into her mailbox. Afterward, when he was driving north, he wasn't sure where he was going, but when he turned west at the Evanston border, the idea—only half-formed before—crystallized. He was going to see Mandy Ross. Someone had to be man enough to tell her the truth.

When he got to the house, Mandy answered the door. What was he doing here, she asked, surprised and delighted, why didn't he come in? God, she was beautiful in that powder-blue sweatsuit, Michael thought, almost moved to tears by the sight of all that beauty wasting away in this hideous suburban home, Mandy spending her days scouring pans, reading stories to her kids, helping them color, race Hot Wheels, play Zim Zam, all the while her husband was trying to stave off middle age by pursuing a girl whom he could never hope to satisfy. Michael didn't for a moment believe Steve's assertion that Mandy was cold in bed, that all she did was lie there. People were only as good in bed as their partners allowed them to be. Maybe Steve needed to read a few more manuals, maybe he needed to read a few more magazines.

Mandy took Michael's jacket and asked if he wanted anything—she could make him a tuna salad sandwich or a PB and J. No, thanks, Michael said. He wasn't hungry. How about some juice or some punch? Mandy asked. Michael said he'd take some punch. She poured him a tall glass of Very Berry and they sat together in the toy-littered playroom. They had to talk quietly, Mandy said, the kiddies were napping upstairs. She asked Michael how Ellen was. Ellen was fine, he said—Ellen was Ellen. Mandy said she really liked Ellen; she was challenging, but that's what she liked about her. Michael asked how Steve had been lately. Fine, Mandy said, but she barely saw him these days. He was working so hard to make sure they'd have enough money to move to Buffalo Grove when the kids reached school age. Michael asked if Steve had been acting at all differently lately. Not really, Mandy said, oh maybe a little more tired; he had a lot on his plate.

Michael said he had a confession to make. He hadn't come by because he'd been in the neighborhood; he had wanted to talk to her when her husband wasn't around. Oh, Mandy smiled, that was so thoughtful of him—she liked having friends; she liked when they stopped by just to talk. Michael said sure, but what he had to tell her wasn't all that nice. He suppressed a sudden urge to surprise her with a passionate kiss. Mandy asked if everything was okay at work, if Steve was all right. Sure, Michael said, Steve was all right—at least as far as his physical health was concerned, but with respect to his mental health, Michael said he just didn't know. He said he was just going to come out and say it—Steve had been cheating on her. He had urged Steve to either break it off or tell Mandy, but he had refused, and now Michael thought she had a right to know. He said he didn't understand how anyone could cheat on someone so beautiful and devoted—he was hoping she'd kiss him now, that's the way it would happen on TV and he thought that Mandy was the type of woman who watched a lot of TV.

But she did not kiss him. She placed her hand over his and smiled sadly. Yes, she said, she thought something like that was going on and she had a pretty good idea who with. She was certain Steve was just going through a phase and soon enough he would realize what was important. Michael said he didn't understand why she wasn't angry. Mandy said she believed in treating everyone with love and good faith. If you did that, most of them would treat you with love and good faith. Michael told Mandy that Steve didn't deserve her. Mandy asked if he wanted more punch.

It took more than three months, but Michael finally found a new job at Swedish Covenant. It didn't pay as well, but at least it saved him the humiliation of enduring Steve Ross repeatedly entering the Chicago-Lutheran Radiology offices, throwing down a large manila envelope filled with pelvic X-rays, and saying loud enough for everyone to hear, "Why don't you read those, Rovner? You like looking at pelvises." At least he wouldn't have to listen to Laura Kim's pitying apologies anymore. At least the Swedish Covenant job came with a lighter workload and was closer to his house, especially since, given the fact that Ellen had moved east of California, he had resolved to be home for his daughter more often. At least now he had more free time.

He had far too much free time, though. There was no one with whom he could socialize at Swedish Covenant; most of the radiologists were twenty years older than he was, and practically every female doctor or nurse that he didn't find ugly was married or, in the case of Dr. Mary Mitchum, a lesbian. He finally purchased a YOUR-TV decoder device so that he could watch unscrambled late-night adult films broadcast on Channel 46, but found himself unable to watch a single one, since he had told Lana that he had purchased it so she could watch musicals. Instead of watching *Taboo* at eleven, he would either watch *Brigadoon* with his daughter at eight, or listen to Lana and Mary Beth Wales on weekends as they watched *Godspell* and talked about the "lonely perverts in trailer parks and bungalows" who just subscribed to YOUR-TV for the dirty movies. During one of his lowest moments, he entered a booth at Little Bo's Peep Show, and shoved his penis through the glory hole, hoping the mustache of a marine wouldn't feel too scratchy against his shaft. But after thirty minutes, no one arrived in the neighboring cabin and the stripper behind the glass said it was a slow night and he'd be best off taking care of business by himself.

It was shortly after this incident that Michael decided to change his approach. While in college, he had read a novel that became his absolute favorite. Now he didn't recall either the title of the book or the name of the author—something goyish, he thought—but there was one line that kept going through his mind, something to the effect of how if you had the guts to be yourself, there would always be people willing to pay your price. Michael took this to mean that if he proceeded with self-confidence, sooner or later people—particularly women— would flock to him. Though he had no real hobbies, he invented some. He bought a set of golf clubs and practiced his swing at the Stop-and-Sock in Morton Grove, he joined the board of the JCC and sat on the Singles Events planning committee, he jogged every evening after work along the canal. He let his mustache grow into a Fu Manchu. In the summer, when Lana and Mary Beth signed up for the YMCA softball league, he umpired games and stayed on, even after the embarrassment associated with his participation had made Lana quit her team. "Umpires aren't supposed to cheer," Lana had told him tearfully. Some nights, he went out for beers at the Round-Up Tavern on Western and watched sports, trading wisecracks about the sad state of the White Sox uniforms with Schiffler Newspapers' gossip columnist, J. Leslie Peterson, who said he liked Michael's mustache, gave him his business card, told him "You look like a guy who plays on my team," and suggested that someday they get together for a beer at Stallion's Pub. Michael said it sounded like fun, and he'd be sure to give him a call. But Michael Rovner didn't call people anymore.

Stopping by Ellen's apartment on Fairfield one early August night went counter to his new life's philosophy, but the idea hadn't been his. He had gone to Chicagofest—a food and music festival held on the lake at Navy Pier, later dubbed Honkeyfest by Reverend Jesse Jackson—to see Rovner! perform. They were scheduled to play on the "Rock Around the Dock" stage from 1 to 1:45 P.M., sandwiched between Poison Squirrel and Bad Boy, whose lead guitarist tried to rev up the unresponsive crowd with the exhortation "Hey, Chicago, let's see some hands," whereupon a number of denim-clad men in attendance gave him the finger. Michael had driven with Lana and Mary Beth, both of whom had giggled all the way down Lake Shore Drive as Mary Beth taught Lana the hand gestures for "Peace," "Love," "Drugs," and "Sex." As instructed by his daughter, Michael sat in the bleachers as far away as possible from the girls, and drank flat $3 Budweisers in souvenir cups. Larry had warned his father beforehand that the crowd might get rough, and if anybody shouted anything anti-Semitic not to come to his defense, because he wanted the music to speak louder than any words. But with the muddled, feedback-heavy sound, it was difficult for anyone to be moved by even Larry's most ardently Zionist Jerusarock songs, though during a Jeff Meltzer guitar solo, a spectator in a Harley jacket said, "Cool. An Amish rock band."

After the aggressive "Hatikvah" opener, which Larry introduced with "This one goes out to the Shah," who had died the previous week in Cairo, Michael's attention was distracted by a woman in a yellow halter top and tight blue jeans who asked if the spot next to him was taken and if he was "Ellen's ex-husband." She offered her hand, introduced herself as "Cheryl," and said she "worked with Ellen," who had told her about the concert. This was, in fact, untrue. Ellen Rovner had made no mention whatsoever of the Rovner! performance, but Cheryl Mandell had not forgotten the picture of Michael that Ellen had once shown her, and when Lana had mentioned the concert in therapy and the fact that her father would be going, Cheryl could not pass up the chance to see in person the man Ellen referred to at their lunches as "the closeted husband." Cheryl frequently found herself quite jealous of Ellen. While she herself was approaching forty, unmarried, childless, and not at all happy about the prospect of entering middle age alone, there was Ellen talking every day at lunch about how much she enjoyed her solitude, how much she wanted to send her daughter off to a "boarding school for privileged girls of overburdened parents," how much she envied Cheryl's lonely life. Which was why, during the third song of Rovner!'s set ("The Dybbuk in Me"), Cheryl told Michael to "stop by some night. She talks about you all the time. I think she really misses you." The lie served two purposes. If it succeeded in bringing Michael and Ellen back together, then she would no longer have to endure Ellen's paeans to her "independent lifestyle." If it failed, there was a good chance that Michael—who didn't seem all that gay to her—might call her to commiserate. "Call me up and tell me how it goes," she urged him.

It went poorly. During the course of Rovner!'s set, Michael drank three Budweisers. After the set, Lana, horrified by the sight of Dr. Mandell spilling out of her halter top and flirting with her father, desperate to avoid encountering Mandell and letting Mary Beth know that she saw a therapist, hurriedly told her father that she and Mary Beth didn't need a ride home, thus subjecting herself and her friend to the terrors of integrated public transportation. And Larry, notepad in hand, said he'd be spending the rest of his evening studying the moves of other musicians—Chuck Berry would be performing with his daughter Ingrid on the mainstage at 7 and Larry wanted to learn Berry's duck walk. So Michael wandered around Navy Pier for the rest of the afternoon, eating greasy street fair food, and chasing it with flat beer—by sundown, he had stacked nine plastic souvenir cups—and Cheryl, who trailed him for most of the day and had started calling him "Michael-san" because she said she was fascinated by Asian culture, had matched him beer for beer. "You're such a gentleman, Michael-san," she told him when he walked her to her car and assured her he would call her after he had stopped by at Ellen's to tell her "how it went." He felt sorry she was such a good friend of Ellen's; if she hadn't been, he might have considered asking her out.

Instead, he wound up standing waveringly in the dimly lit, restaurant flyer–strewn vestibule of Ellen's building, blearily scanning mailboxes and buzzers, trying to determine why Ellen's name wasn't listed. It was only when he picked up a piece of junk mail from Crawford's department store that he understood. The name Rovner had been struck out with black pen. Above it in Ellen's handwriting was written "No Rovner here! LEVENTHAL!" He pressed the "Leventhal" buzzer.

Ellen, with her hair cut short and held back with a headband, looked severe and muscular, far less girlish than she usually did in Michael's fantasies of their purportedly romantic past. She displayed little if any surprise when she opened the door a quarter of the way and asked what Michael wanted. Michael said he had just had a sudden vision—for Cheryl had made him promise not to tell Ellen what she had said to him—that maybe she might have missed him. It would have been humiliating enough if Ellen had just told him she had no interest whatsoever in returning to the claustrophobia of married life. But instead of mocking Michael's presumption, she regarded him sadly, asked if he wanted to get a cup of coffee and talk, said he looked bloated and smelled of beer—she hoped he was taking care of himself—all of which was a dozen times worse than a door slammed in the face.

They walked over to Western and bought coffees at Dunkin' Donuts, Ellen saying how much she loved their house in Lake Geneva, reminiscing about how they had gone snowmobiling and Michael had almost crashed into a wolverine. They brought their coffees to a bench on Devon and Washtenaw and talked about Larry—how funny it was that he thought he could be a musician. They both agreed that he'd be married as soon as he got out of law school. And Lana, how she was destined to be rich and famous. Once Ellen's coffee was gone and Michael's was cold, they walked back to her apartment. At the door, she said it was good to see him again and told him to take care of himself, then shook his hand. She was feeling so cordial and generous that she didn't even remind him to sign the divorce papers. She trusted he would find all the details in the papers to his benefit. All she wanted was the house in Lake Geneva; the rest was his.

Though he had told Dr. Cheryl Mandell that he would call her to tell her how things turned out, Michael did not, in fact, do so. The next day when Cheryl called, he had only the slightest recollection of who she was or what she looked like. When Cheryl asked him how things had gone the previous night, he said, "Oh fine, fine." Good, Cheryl said, then he and Ellen were back together? No, Michael said, their status hadn't changed. Oh, Cheryl said, *poor you.* No, it was okay, Michael said. He had a lot of things going on and wasn't ready to commit to anything or anybody right now. Cheryl's tone became noticeably curt. She said she had to go.

About a week later, Cheryl called again "just to say hey" and see if he felt like driving to County Stadium to see a Milwaukee Brewers game. She figured he might be a "beer-and-brats kind of guy." No, Michael said, fearing she meant he was overweight. He insisted he was a healthy eater. Cheryl waited another week before she called again. This time she said she was really worried about him—it was really strange that such a handsome man was home every time she called. She said she was going to the Thirsty Whale to see a band. Michael—who recalled that Laura Kim hung out at that club and couldn't remember whether Cheryl was good-looking enough to make Laura jealous—said he wished he could go but he had promised his daughter he would take her and her friends to a laser light show. Cheryl said okay, but he was being a mope and she wouldn't let him be a mope; she would make him pick a time, a date, and a place, and they would go out—her treat. Michael suggested that they go out the Saturday he returned from driving his son to college ("You're such a devoted dad; that's so admirable," Cheryl told him). But the Saturday evening after he got back from Waltham, he had forgotten that he had even made the appointment. He told her he was sorry, but he had to pick Lana up at eleven from the Skatium's "Moonlight Roller Night." Cheryl said that would give them plenty of time to have coffee and dessert and chat beforehand. She would meet him in a half hour at Poppin Fresh Pies.

Now it was happening, he thought; now that he was alone in a house that felt more quiet than empty, now that he wasn't calling a soul, his phone was starting to ring. The moment he became completely uninterested in sex, he thought, would be his best chance to start having it.

I n the Shoney's off I-80 in Angola, after Michael and Larry had finished off their eggs and french toast, Larry broke the silence. "Dad, don't worry, I love you and everything," he said. "It's just that I have nothing to say to your ass." Michael smiled grimly and clapped Larry twice on the shoulder. This heartfelt endorsement of his eighteen years as Larry's father would be one of two highlights of Michael's road trip with Larry. The other would come two days later on the campus of Brandeis, where Larry would introduce him to Hannah Goodman—when they would start to unload the station wagon, Michael would be able to get a quick peek at her chest.

After the road trip, when Michael picked up Lana in front of her mother's apartment, he told her wearily that he was happy to see her. She said she was happy too, but avoided his kiss as she strapped on her seat belt, insisting he do the same. He asked Lana if her mother would be coming downstairs to say hello. No, Lana said, she was upstairs reading some book in French; she said she thought her mother was copying her, because only when she had started doing her French homework had her mother started reading. Michael asked how her mother was as he lazily turned his car onto Devon, heading west for California. Weird, Lana said. What did she mean, "weird"? Michael wanted to know. Lana said she meant that her mother had been being nice. Then she asked if Michael would be able to drop her off and pick her up at least a block away from the Skatium that night.

By "being nice," what Lana meant was that Ellen had been buying her things, and openly giving her money instead of just leaving her wallet lying around for her to rifle through. It was less an expression of Ellen's newfound generosity than a tactic of self-defense. She had recently ordered a pair of new charge plates and was certain that if she maintained her open-wallet policy that the cash might remain, but the plates would soon be gone, put into service to buy items that were too risky to shoplift. Thus, Ellen kept her wallet on or near her person at all times and attempted to stem her daughter's material lust by presenting her with a $20 bill the day Michael and Larry went on their road trip, and $10 each subsequent day. She also purchased a number of items to preempt the unreasonable requests Lana would no doubt make. For instance, Ellen noticed that Lana's jacket smelled vaguely of smoke. Therefore, she made a quick run over to Woolworth's and picked up a carton of Kents for Lana; she figured that demystifying cigarettes by making them available was as good a method as any to ultimately make them unappealing. Also, a little bit of nicotine was a small price to pay to reduce her daughter's tight-assedness—on their first night together in the apartment, Lana had insisted on vacuuming the entire place and spraying Raid along every inch of baseboard.

Over the first part of their week together, Ellen and Lana only interacted at the very beginning of the day and in the evenings when they weren't in their rooms working or reading. Lana no longer wanted to be driven to or from school—though taking the bus to the Loyola El stop, switching trains at Howard, and taking the northbound Linden-Howard El train all the way to the end of the line turned a twenty-minute drive into a seventy-five-minute odyssey, and though Lana said she had to breathe through her mouth, close her eyes tightly, and whisper the *Sh'ma Yisroel* whenever a scary black person got into her car, all that was worth it to avoid the humiliation she experienced when Mary Beth said, "God, you still get rides to and from school?"

On Wednesday evening after she had agreed to pick her daughter up from school the next day and drive her and Mary Beth to Old Orchard, Ellen retired to her room with a half-finished copy of Jean-Paul Sartre's *Nausée.* She was sitting in her bed, back against the wall, covers up to her waist, her reading glasses on. She had a sudden urge to masturbate—an activity in which she had rarely engaged on Sacramento and one that had become one of the joys of living alone. She took the book to the bathroom, closed the door and locked it, dimmed the lights, ran a warm bath, and emptied a packet of lilac bubble bath into the tub. When the tub was not quite half full and a layer of foam had formed on top of it, she stepped inside and let the warmth envelop her body, bringing with it a sense of utter calm and contentment. But the sensation was short-lived, for the moment she put her book aside and soaped up a foot and a calf, she heard her daughter's voice trumpeting away in her guest bedroom and echoing off the walls of the bathroom. At first, it was an unintelligible muffle, but when Ellen put her soap back in its dish and brought her hand underneath the surface of the water, she could identify one sentence that Lana kept repeating. "It is time," Lana said as Ellen stopped caressing her breast, "for a change." "It's time for a change," Lana said as Ellen stopped stroking her pubis. "It's time," Lana said as Ellen removed her middle finger from her clitoris, "for a change."

Well, there was no use attempting to read, masturbate, or even bathe, Ellen thought, not with that racket going on. She grabbed the white terry-cloth Washington Hilton bathrobe that she and Michael had stolen from that hotel during happier times, and stepped out of the tub. She walked barefoot and fairly sopping over to the guest bedroom door and knocked on it. She asked Lana what was going on in there. Lana said she was rehearsing. Ellen opened the door.

Lana was standing by the window with a piece of paper in one hand and a microphone in the other. She said she was rehearsing her "Lana's Perspective" for WBOE. Lana had just begun her first week in the eighth pod at Baker and her second week as commentator on *Chi-Town Chatterbox,* hosted by Peachy Moskowitz and Pablo De La Fuente. Lana had once again lost out in the final rounds of auditions, beating out P.C. Pendleton, who had whispered "Bitch bitch little virgin bitch" two seconds before her audition and one month before he was shipped off to boarding school, but ultimately losing to Pablo. But Lana had been so eloquent and passionate in defense of her own audition and so politic in her criticism of Pablo ("My concern isn't his capabilities; it's his maturity," she'd said) that Donna rewarded her with a two-minute editorial to run in the middle of each show, thus allowing the station to enter yet another Jack Benny awards category, this time for Youth Opinion-Based Programming.

Ellen had listened to the show once but hadn't been able to get past the prepubescent squealings and outlandish accent of the show's two cohosts to listen to her daughter's brief contribution. Lana asked Ellen if she wanted to hear her Perspective. The answer was, of course, no. Ellen didn't want to hear her daughter's Perspective—she wanted to read, she wanted to have an orgasm, she wanted to take a bath, she wanted to go to bed. Ellen said she would be happy to listen.

After Ellen had gotten dressed, Lana told her that the title of the Perspective was "It's Time for a Change." Because, Lana declaimed, it was, in fact, time for a change. Inflation was on the rise, and so was unemployment. The hostages had been in Iran for almost a year and America—"once a superpower"—was now a "laughingstock." Four years earlier, Jimmy Carter—a *"peanut* farmer," a man who thought the word "nuclear" was pronounced "nuke-a-ler"—had debated President Ford and invented a new statistic to measure the state of the country's economy. Carter had called it the Misery Index, which added the percentage of unemployment to that of inflation. Four years ago, Carter had said it was too high. Now it was even higher, and this *"peanut farmer"* was asking us to give him four more years. It was time for a change, Lana said. It was time for new leadership. It was time, Lana said, for Ronald Reagan, a "bold new leader for a bold new decade."

Once Lana was done reading the editorial, she asked her mother what she thought of it, how it had made her feel. "It makes me want to move out of the country," Ellen sighed. The remark was not necessarily a comment on Lana's politics—it was hardly surprising that Lana would cast her lot with the Republicans. Lana was, after all, the one who had argued in *Gimel* with some girl named Jill about health care and declared that because her father was a doctor and made a good salary, she had the right to see better doctors. What truly chilled Ellen's blood, though, was Lana's response to a question she posed: "So do you think that Reagan will make a better president?" Lana did not say—as Ellen had expected her to—that yes, she did like Reagan for such-and-so reason. Instead she admitted that she didn't know that much about Reagan or any of the other candidates. The fact was, she'd seen enough magazine articles to know that Reagan would win easily, and, she said, she wanted "always to be for the winner."

Ellen had remembered hearing Lana say things much like this at birthday parties. When there were games or relay races, she would often shout, "I'm for winner!" The statement now struck Ellen not merely as one self-centered thirteen-year-old's desperate plea for acceptance. Instead, it seemed an all-too-fitting credo for that society at large. "I'm for *winner.*" It was a bumper sticker to affix to ostentatious, gas-guzzling automobiles, a billboard to place atop grotesque steel-and-glass skyscrapers, a commercial slogan to flash on and off between soporific TV sitcoms and game shows, a button to stick onto the purse of practically every patient who came to her sessions and whined about this overprotective parent, that philandering spouse, this fear of aging, of death. "I'm for winner." I'm for *winner.* After Lana had asked how the speech had made her feel and Ellen had responded that it made her want to move out of the country, Lana had asked her where she would want to go. "I don't know," Ellen said. "I just don't know." But in fact she knew perfectly well.

The next day, Ellen Leventhal was standing in a Skokie American Express office looking through Paris travel brochures after having dropped off Lana and Mary Beth in front of Best & Company in Old Orchard. They were having a really big sale, Mary Beth had said. The woman behind the American Express counter had asked Ellen for her departure and return dates. Ellen had said the second Wednesday of November would be her departure date, largely because she wanted to leave before having to endure her patients' inevitable monologues about the impending misery of the holiday season. But when the travel agent asked when she wanted to return, Ellen did not immediately respond. Her initial thought had been to take a good long vacation, longer than any she had ever taken. She would return, she thought, the first week of January, thus maximizing the opportunity to spend time with Julius Bernard, who had written to say that he would be in Paris over the holidays.

But the moment Ellen's lips began to form the "J" for January, she stopped. What reason, she thought, did she have for returning the first week of January or any other month for that matter? The question, at first, seemed absurd. Of course she had dozens of reasons to return within a *week*'s time, let alone six. She had her patients, a son in college, a daughter in the eighth pod; she had to make a living. But Lana would be adequately taken care of by her negligent father and whatever slut babysitter he would no doubt hire. He could eventually find a wife. Someone like Cheryl Mandell would be perfect for him; she liked kids, she was lonely, she probably enjoyed watching pornography. But surely her patients needed her, she thought. Or maybe they didn't either, she decided. That many of her patients had been seeing her for nearly ten years could have been viewed as testimony to Ellen's skills as a psychologist, but it could just as easily have been seen as evidence of how little progress patients made under her treatment.

As Ellen stood at the counter, there was little sadness in the acknowledgment that her presence was no longer vital, that perhaps it had never been, that Lana could find her own way to school, Larry could muddle through college, her patients could find someone else in whom to invest their salaries and sorrows. Nothing bad would happen if she didn't go to another parent-teacher conference or PTA meeting, and whether her patient Myra Tuchbaum threw herself out a window or came to terms with the fact that she'd lost her virginity to a cretin had little to do with whether or not she showed up to her next session. People had such an inflated sense of their own importance, Ellen thought. It was difficult enough to make a positive impact upon one's own life let alone someone else's. The fact that the older her children became, the less attached they would feel to her was something they might someday thank her for, she thought now, just as in some small way she was thanking her gruff, distant father for making her feel no guilt about telling the travel agent to leave open the return portion of her plane ticket.

When she picked up Mary Beth and Lana at the shopping mall, their arms full of booty, their cheeks flushed with the thrill of undetected theft, their voices squealing at an unnaturally high pitch, delighting in their unlikely stories of closeout sales, overstocked items, and mismarked prices, Ellen felt even more confident in her decision. The mantra of her daughter, the mantra of a new decade and a new generation, would become her own—"I'm for winner," she said to herself. "The winner will be me." The next day when she called up Julius to inform him that she would be in Paris for a few days in November or December, he asked her why only a few days—why not a week or a month or more? She said she'd consider it. When he asked if her "very beautiful daughter who speaks such beautiful French" would be accompanying her, Ellen said no. It was better that way, Julius told her. One could behave with more candor outside of the presence of children.

Ellen told no one of her decision. Once she had decided something—either as banal as refusing to dye her silvering hair or as significant as moving out of the Sacramento house for good—she never backtracked. Telling people only served to give them a momentary illusion of influence. She would make her preparations quietly. She would keep her appointments. She would be particularly brutal in her assessment of her patients' neuroses in the hopes that they would be relieved when they found out she would be canceling all future sessions. In November, on the weekend of her fortieth birthday, she would take a final trip to the house on Lake Geneva, the only physical remnant of her marriage still worth calling hers. She would spend that weekend grilling fish in the backyard, rowing around the not-yet-frozen lake, reading outside in the hammock bundled up in a blanket until it got too dark. She would buy a bottle of wine at the liquor store, find a pothead working in one of the fudge or taffy shops who would sell her a bag of dope, and sit out on the patio by the lake, smoke, and watch the stars. And then on Monday morning, she would drive back to the city to pack.

She assumed that after a month or two she would return home. But she didn't have to. She could live forever in France. Or on the Ivory Coast with Julius, but hopefully not. The idea of establishing her independence on another continent and immediately allying herself to another man was depressing. She would want a decidedly nonexclusive relationship—the sort she had enjoyed in college before she had gotten pregnant, the sort her patients always said they desired until the moment it actually happened. She wanted to have affairs with Ivory Coast cocoa planters, with Sorbonne students, with Nouvelle Vague film directors, cigarette girls, and Lido dancers.

She tried to put herself in the calm, contented mindset in which she would find herself the day she left, so that all the preceding days would have the sensation of a long yet ultimately irrelevant prologue—something to be sped through or skipped altogether. Thus, it hardly mattered when Lana called the same day Michael returned from his men's road trip with Larry, asking Ellen to please pick her up a block away from the Skatium—her father had once again forgotten about her. Ellen acquiesced to Lana's demands, not even phoning to berate Michael—who she assumed was either in a tittie bar or summoning up the courage to enter one, but was in fact closing down Poppin Fresh Pies with Cheryl and, as he would explain later to his tearful daughter, had lost track of time.

The intervening time passed quickly with even the most seemingly significant incidents hardly registering. Ellen's apartment was burglarized and she didn't file a police report; she had little interest in ever again wearing any of her jewelry and further assumed that one day she might well see her thieving daughter—in an unself-conscious moment—wearing it. When Lennie Kidd's mother arrived distraught at Ellen's office one morning, Ellen calmly but completely violated patient-client confidentiality and informed the woman that the last time she had seen Lennie, she had advised him to leave town and tell no one where he was going, especially not his mother. She even considered—though ultimately rejected— the possibility of attending the Brandeis parents' weekend, having expressed enthusiasm for the idea until Larry informed her that he would be performing that weekend at Bonzofest!, a concert memorializing recently deceased Led Zeppelin drummer John Bonham, but that he would try to block out an hour or two for her so that they could have lunch.

The weekend of her fortieth birthday went just as planned, perhaps better. For not only did she swim naked in ice-cold water and warm herself up with hot cocoa and cigarettes, not only did she row around Lake Geneva with only the waxing gibbous moon to light her way, not only did she read mysteries at night and philosophy texts in the morning, but the stoned nineteen-year-old soda jerk at the Fudge Shoppe who sold her four joints told her she "looked awful nice" and said maybe they could go smoke together. Ellen normally wasn't taken in by such compliments; still, she enjoyed the flattery, though not enough to take the young man—"You can call me Millard," he said—up on his offer. You must be kidding, she told him, shortly before calling him a burnout and a freak.

She returned to Chicago late that Wednesday—the day after Election Day, on which Ronald Reagan carried 51 percent of the national vote—feeling refreshed and energized. She felt a powerful urge to do something physically taxing— jogging or weight lifting or having sex with a partner more challenging than her ex-husband, whom she had once admonished for "treating intercourse as a spectator sport." She had flung her overnight bag onto her bed and had begun cleaning, organizing, and, most important, throwing things out. She turned the radio to a random FM station that was playing "Miracles" by Jefferson Starship;

she generally didn't like any music other than folk, but still she turned it up loud. Just then, the telephone rang.

"Ellen, who is that? I hear noise, what's that music?" the voice on the other end said after Ellen picked up the phone. Ellen recognized the voice—her evil stepmother, Essie Mallen-Leventhal. Ellen, wanting to be rid of her quickly, thanked her for the annual birthday call but informed her she was three days late, so she would look forward to hearing from her in 362 days. Essie said that she had in fact called on the birthday, she had called the day after too, and why hadn't Ellen purchased an answering machine. What if there was an emergency? Essie asked. If there was an emergency, Ellen said, then it probably would be best to call somebody else—what was the use of talking to a machine during an emergency? Why, Ellen asked, was there an emergency? Yes, Essie said, there was. What was it? Ellen asked. Essie said Ellen's father had had a stroke.

It had happened at Orchestra Hall during Mahler's Symphony No. 9. Around five minutes before the end of the final movement, Max had gotten up to go to the Grant Park Garage to get his car before the inevitable traffic jam at the end of the concert. There had been a "new couple" sitting next to them, and the man, a high school music and drama teacher whom Essie called "young, rude, and pretentious," had told Max that the concert was almost over; why didn't he sit back down? Max said like hell he would. And the rude, pretentious man said that he wouldn't move his knees and told the skinny girl accompanying him not to move hers either; Max would have to climb over them. An usher arrived to tell Max to stay in his seat; they were filming the evening's concert for PBS. Max said he didn't give a damn; he was getting his car so he could beat traffic. He stumbled over the man's knees, and that's when he fell, Essie said. Then there were ambulances and paramedics and Chicago Lutheran Hospital—"an absolute pit; you could die in such a place," she said.

Ellen asked if she could talk to her father. That wasn't a good idea, Essie said. He was sleeping for the first time since he had returned from the hospital. Ellen asked if he was lucid. Yes and no, Essie said. Ellen said she didn't need any more preamble; she wanted to know specifically why she was being called, what the situation was. "The situation," Essie Mallen-Leventhal said, "is that he keeps asking for you."

Oh Jesus, Ellen thought. She was uncertain whether Essie was lying or telling the truth and she wasn't sure which would be worse. There would be something utterly reprehensible, though not the least implausible, about Essie concocting a scheme to get the one Leventhal child who hadn't been moved beyond state borders by the callousness, indifference, and generally antisocial nature of the Leventhal family's patriarch to save them the money it would cost to hire a professional to do nursing and custodial work for them. At the same time, there was something even more horrifying about the image Essie presented: that the once-formidable Max Leventhal—feared by many a waiter in the city as the physician who would sample his dinner and send it back with a simple "This slop's no damn good"—was now reduced to a hobbled, impotent figure, once King Lear, now his fool waking up in the middle of the night, asking was Ellen here, when was she coming home, had Essie heard from her, did Essie think she might be calling soon?

Ellen got off the phone, telling Essie she'd "think about it." What was she supposed to do? she wondered. Return to see the great man humbled? Play witness to a deathbed conversion? Grant absolution? Ellen Leventhal did not believe in deathbed conversions; she did not believe in absolution. Once—one moment in an entire history of neglect and emotional detachment—Max had saved her life. She had been three years old and the family had gone to the Museum of Science and Industry. In the Hall of Math, there was a giant abacus upon which a mathematician in a white lab coat was flicking the counters from left to right. During the demonstration, one of the counters, a shiny metallic sphere the size of a golfball, came loose from its unhinged rod and rolled across the floor. Ellen remembered the ball coming toward her and she remembered thinking that it looked like food. She picked it up, put it in her mouth, and attempted to swallow it. She remembered nothing after that moment, but what happened had been told to her so often that she could picture the incident. She had choked on the ball, she had turned red, then blue; her father had seen her choking; he grabbed her, shook her, flipped her upside down, shaking her by the ankles until the counter popped out and rolled across the floor and into the Hall of Chemistry. Her father had saved her life. She had heard that often enough—her father had *saved her life*. But what did she owe him for that now?

Perhaps she owed him a trip to his bedside, but no more, she decided as she whipped a pair of panty hose into the trash. She would see him and Essie, help to address any practical matters they might have. But there would be no attempt to resolve their relationship—there would be no bedside vigil, no nursing the old man back to health. For what would "healthy" truly mean for her father? Healthy would mean refusing to put down his newspaper when she entered the house; healthy would mean hollering at Essie, asking her to do his bidding just as he had done with Ellen's mother, sending her to an early grave; healthy would mean asking her why wasn't she married—a woman couldn't make a living on her own, particularly not her; healthy would mean asking her why she was still hanging around, was she waiting for money? Let the old man say what he wanted and then it would be time for her to get on with her life. On the drive to Hyde Park, Ellen turned on the car radio, which was tuned to WBOE. A familiarly confident, insistent, and expectant voice said that it was "time for a change." Ellen flipped off the radio. Whatever happened, she told herself, she was going to France.

WILLS / SILVERMAN

Deirdre & Carl

W hen Ira Mallen, attorney for Mallen and McKenzie, called, saying he was pursuing civil litigation against Carl Slappit Silverman for un-scrupulous business practices and that he wanted her to provide evidence, Deirdre Wills told him the offer was tempting but that she had neither the time nor the inclination. Mallen told her he was representing a number of musicians, and in some cases their estates, and he had begun to build a fairly significant case against Silverman, who, he said, had built his "recording empire" on the backs of struggling performers who had been coerced to sign away their song catalogs for "rent and wine money." But though Deirdre had found Carl's past conduct against her father despicable, she had never considered it illegal, and at this point, she almost pitied the man. Still, that pity was hardly enough to move her when a plaintive Carl—who even as he beseeched her to assist him sounded as if he were chewing on day-old bread—told her that if she would serve as a witness in his defense, he would cut her in on a percentage of Slappit Records' net profits ("Sorry it can't be gross; I just can't justify it"). He didn't need her, Deirdre told him, he'd come up with an angle; he always did. No, Carl said, she didn't get it; she was the last angle he had.

Deirdre told him she was sorry—even if she'd wanted to, she couldn't help him. She was substitute teaching regularly during the day, taking two classes at night at Circle, and on weekends she was proofreading and editing for Mel Coleman, who had needed someone to help structure his script for *Godfathers of Soul* before he started submitting it to agents, producers, and studios. Mel had initially asked Muley, who demurred, saying he had difficulty working on two creative projects at once but his mother might be able to help for a small fee.

During some weekdays, it was not unusual for Deirdre to spend four hours in her car, driving back and forth between Circle and wherever the public school system assigned her to substitute. Sometimes she would teach in North Side schools, such as Mather or Von Steuben, but often she would have to drive all the way south to Kenwood, Orr, or Marshall, once the epicenter of Jewish culture during the 1930s and '40s, now a focal point for the gang activity of the Vice Lords, one member of which stood up to Deirdre when she passed out exams and asked her what the fuck she was gonna do if he didn't take the test. "Call your mother and tell her you're illiterate," Deirdre said shortly before he sat back down.

On a Wednesday morning in November, Deirdre arrived at Mather to substitute and entered the offices of Vice Principal Ralph Mulvey, a pale man in a tan suit who reminded her of sack lunches and life insurance policies. He seemed to like her, smiled at her whenever he caught her glance. He informed Deirdre that she would be assigned to the classroom of Mr. Sternberg—"one of our youngest, most energetic teachers"—who had permanently replaced Henry Linton. Linton had retired following the turmoil surrounding the previous spring's faculty-student production of *Hamlet,* in which he played Polonius to Douglas Sternberg's Hamlet—there had been some brouhaha over a girl being considered for the title role, which had led Sternberg to take the part to avert further controversy. Though funding for Sternberg's *Burden of Biff* musical never materialized, the cancellation of its premiere paved the way for Mather to hire him for the fall as drama club director and instructor for Intro to Theater and Public Speaking, the latter of which was taught during first period.

Michelle Wasserstrom, who was already sitting front row center with a denim three-ring binder open in front of her when Deirdre entered the classroom, was taking the class even though Sternberg had told her she wouldn't do well in it. Michelle told him that she would be a professional and "put the past behind her" and forget how shabbily he had treated her friend Myra, now struggling in her first semester at SIU. She fought him every time she received C's and D's for speeches and class assignments, insisting that he was out to ruin her academic career and that she would file a grievance with Vice Principal Mulvey. The joke, however, seemed to be on Sternberg, for Michelle was taking the course pass-fail.

Michelle greeted Ms. Wills as she entered the classroom. She asked why "Douglas" was out and if he was finally getting the help he needed for his hemorrhoids. Deirdre, stifling a smile, told "Ms. Wasserstrom" that the medical conditions of her fellow instructors were not within her purview. Michelle said she was just wondering, because he usually smelled of cod liver oil and always seemed to be trying to discreetly scratch himself with the eraser end of a pencil. She asked Ms. Wills how Muley was—if he was still "working on *Citizen Kane,*" and if she was helping Mel Coleman on his "*crapamundo* script." Deirdre said she would thank Michelle not to discuss personal matters in the classroom; she did not believe in favoritism or fraternization between teachers and students inside the school building.

Public Speaking was divided equally between lecture and classroom participation. Sternberg would lecture at the beginning of class about a particular topic—eye contact, speaking from the diaphragm, vocal warm-ups—and then students would give speeches, which the class would critique for the rest of the period. Homely and hardworking girls fared best in Sternberg's class; he didn't want them visiting him to dispute their grades. The ones he found more attractive were routinely given C's and D's in the hopes they would visit him to talk and bargain. He was bored by boys and gave most of them B's, except for Noel Jefferson, a tall, heavy black student who frightened Douglas and consequently received straight A's.

Michelle had little interest in honing her public speaking techniques—she did that every Saturday with a Russian accent at WBOE and on Wednesday evenings at the professional monologue class she was taking at the Body Politic Theater. The only reason she was taking Sternberg's class was to humiliate him, in part to retaliate for how he had treated Myra, in part for a perverse pleasure all her own. One of her weekly speeches concerned pornography addiction; another

concerned onanism among high school theater directors. When she wasn't reciting invented statistics to bolster her claims ("High school speech instructors,
according to the August 16, 1978, edition of *U.S. News & World Report,* masturbate 9.8 times per week on average"), she would relate lurid anecdotes
involving "an acquaintance of mine whom I'll call 'D.'" Today, she was scheduled
to give a speech that she titled, "Those Who Can't Do Teach, and Those Who
Can't Teach Try to Have Sex with Their Students," between Sarah Silver's on
anorexia ("The Skinny on Eating Disorders") and Matthias Kimmel's on the
merits of supply-side economics ("The Upside of Trickling Down"). She had offered to postpone her speech until "Douglas" was back, but Deirdre told a somewhat disappointed Michelle that Mr. Sternberg had left instructions for her to
adhere to his schedule.

Deirdre took a seat in the back of the classroom and listened to the speeches.
She was a fair grader and an attentive listener, and thought it her duty to always
supply critical but constructive remarks. She gave Sarah Silver good marks for
her dutiful approach, but took points off for her overabundance of clichés ("In
America, people who are starving for attention are literally being eaten alive").
When it was Michelle's turn, an excited murmur coursed through the classroom
and even Barry Tewlow, who had spent the entirety of Sarah's speech sketching a
picture of the Trans Am he wanted to buy, stopped writing "Trans Ams Rule" in
block letters and closed his notebok, gleeful at the prospect of a typically irrever-
ent Wasserstrom speech, as opposed to the earnest claptrap the class usually endured.

Ms. Wasserstrom was asked to take her place. And in the few steps it took her
to get to the front of the class, she completely transformed from a smart-
mouthed, tousled-haired high school student into the invincible professional actress she was certain she'd become once she graduated from Yale (she was certain
her 1420 combined SAT score and her dramatically improved grade point average were her tickets to the Ivy League). The speech, she told Deirdre, was Rated
"R," adding that Mr. Sternberg encouraged students to use profanity if it made
their speeches sound more natural. That was right, Barry Tewlow piped up, bol-
stering Michelle's invention, Mr. Sternberg was "real cool" about that. Many
others—Sarah Silver excluded—voiced their agreement.

"Picture this," Michelle began. "Two people—let's call them 'D' and 'M'—
are engaged in coitus on the diving board of the JCC swimming pool. His penis

is small, but it does the job. After he ejaculates, D tells M to keep what happened absolutely private. Why? Because she is a senior and he teaches Public Speaking. Unlikely scenario? Not entirely. According to a recent study by the Educational Research Service, 68.9 percent of high school teachers admit to having sexual fantasies about their students. The same survey reports that 90.2 percent of students find the idea of sex with their teachers 'disgusting'—a number surpassed only by the percentage who are repulsed by the idea of sex with Public Speaking teachers (94.7 percent)."

Though Sarah Silver walked out in a huff during the speech, it was Deirdre Wills's steadfast policy as both parent and teacher not to dignify profanity or sexual discourse with any overly disapproving remarks. The only time Muley had ever sworn in her presence was in fifth grade, when he asked her what his friend Jill meant when she said "Fuck the world and everybody in it." Deirdre had merely asked what illiterate had taught him such foolishness and he had never used the word again.

Michelle continued in this manner, consulting note cards when she cited statistics ("88.9 percent of high school instructors find 'woman-on-top' sex 'intimidating'") or quoted bogus authorities ("Dr. Michael Rovner, an expert on perversion, has coined the term 'Sternberglary' to refer to this nationwide surge"). But Deirdre said nothing during Michelle's speech. She did not even grant Michelle a smirk or a disapproving glance at the speech's conclusion: "So next time you're in a dark room with your legs spread and your feet by your ears, just remember that the guy huffing and puffing above you just might be your Public Speaking teacher." Deirdre did, however, tell Michelle that she wanted to talk to her privately.

After class, Michelle told Ms. Wills she couldn't stay long; she was on her way to Chemistry. Deirdre said she would only take a moment. Michelle clutched her three-ring binder to her chest and stood pivoting back and forth on the heel of a sneaker as Deirdre told her that she didn't want to discuss the appropriateness of Michelle's speech; that was a matter for her and her instructor. There was something, however, she said, that disturbed her about the speech, and that was the fact that behind the "statistics and sources you made up," there seemed to be a larger truth. She wanted to know if Michelle's speech was based on a specific individual or if she was just "titillating her peers and wasting everyone's time."

Michelle was intrigued by the possibility of repaying Douglas Sternberg for all of the dull, self-pitying monologues she had endured courtesy of Myra Tuchbaum. She enjoyed the idea of Sternberg getting booted from Mather, made to pay his debt to society, not for seducing innocents or corrupting America's youth or anything ridiculous like that but simply for being a prick. At the same time, though, she thought Myra—though she was her friend and though she felt sorry for her—was responsible, as everybody was when it came right down to it, for her own predicament. And though it had been great fun to stare at Sternberg during a speech on impotence ("Colloquially, according to Anita Wiener, PR director of the AARP, it is referred to most often as 'limp dick'"), actually accusing him seemed like wasted energy. She told Ms. Wills that she had just been titillating her peers and wasting everybody's time, then said she looked forward to seeing Deirdre over at the Wills's residence next time she and Gareth were taking Muley to a movie. She said she hoped that someday her sister would come to her senses and realize that Muley was the coolest kid in West Rogers Park. And though Michelle's statement did make Deirdre a bit proud, she said she would not discuss such things within the confines of the school building. Not during the school day.

Two weeks later, Deirdre returned to Mather, this time to sub in Ms. Rota's U.S. History classroom. At 3:40, shortly after the final bell, she happened to pass by the auditorium. She was walking quickly, hoping she would have enough time to pick up groceries and sit down for a quick dinner with Muley—something she tried to do with her son at least four times a week now—before her 7 o'clock Rhetoric class. On her way out, she paused at the auditorium door, where a piece of notebook paper was sticky-taped—"Costume Day for *Guys and Dolls*" was written on it. She looked in and saw a young man in a flannel shirt and blue jeans kneeling on the stage in front of a girl while a group of students sat in the first few rows and watched. He had a tape measure and was measuring her inseam. "Thirty-one," he called out, and a girl with a clipboard wrote something down. The young man stood up, motioned for the girl to put her arms out at her sides, and proceeded to measure her chest. "Thirty-four," he announced. He then moved on to the waist. An officious boy in a black T-shirt that read "Stage Crew" on the front and "Weinberg" on the back was carrying a mug of steaming coffee into the auditorium. Deirdre asked the boy who that was on the stage. That was

Sarah Silver, the boy said, she was playing one of the "Hotbox Girls." And who was the young man on the stage and what was he doing? Deirdre wanted to know. That was Mr. Sternberg, the boy said, he was measuring for costumes. Mr. Sternberg—now measuring Sarah's hips and calling out "Thirty-two"—wouldn't let anyone else do the measurements, the boy explained; he wanted to see if he could "get an hourglass." Deirdre said she didn't understand. "An hourglass figure," the boy said. "Thirty-six, twenty-four, thirty-six. He wants to know if any of the girls have an hourglass."

"And what are you doing here?" Deirdre asked.

"Getting Mr. Sternberg his coffee," Shmuel Weinberg said.

Shmuel walked briskly down the auditorium aisle and brought the coffee to Sternberg, who was now measuring another girl's inseam. He whispered something to Sternberg, who suddenly stood and turned to see Deirdre in the doorway. Sternberg, who had recently recovered from hemorrhoidal surgery, said that this was a private rehearsal. He told Shmuel to shut the auditorium doors.

This incident, though infuriating enough, did not provide sufficient cause for Deirdre to lodge a complaint against Sternberg. Grounds for that decision were established a few nights later, when she was looking for a place to park. A light snow was falling. Deirdre had been in bed reading Thackeray when she heard the air-raid siren, which meant that all cars had to be moved off California so that the plows could clear the streets. All the parking places were taken on Mozart Street, but about three-quarters of the way down the block, a black Jaguar was stalled with its flashers on. Deirdre was about to lay on the horn, but then the driver's-side door opened and Douglas Sternberg—in a belted, slate overcoat—emerged and shuffled around the back of the car to the passenger side. He motioned for the person in the car to roll down the window.

When the window was down, Sternberg leaned his head in the car and told the person sitting inside that he wouldn't let her out until she gave him a kiss. A head poked out of the window and the girl kissed him on the cheek. Sternberg laughed and shook his head. He put a finger to his lips, indicating where he wanted the kiss to be placed. Once the request was granted, he opened the door and bowed theatrically to the girl—she was too bundled up for Deirdre to identify her as anything other than a teenager. At this point, Deirdre laid on the horn hard. As the girl galloped full speed toward her house, Sternberg—fuming at the indignity of being honked at—trudged angrily over to the driver's side of

Deirdre's Mazda. But when he saw that the driver was black, he became frightened, apologized, and ran back to his car.

The next day, Deirdre was assigned to substitute at Von Steuben, but she left early enough to make a quick stop at Mather Vice Principal Mulvey's office. He had just been preparing to dispatch the morning's substitutes to their classrooms when Deirdre asked if she could speak with him. Mulvey told her that his time was her time. Deirdre asked Mulvey if he shared her opinion that a teacher pursuing a relationship with a student was among the worst violations of trust someone in her profession could perpetrate. He agreed; the "teacher-student compact" was inviolable. That was good, Deirdre said. She mentioned that a certain student—she would not abuse the student's trust by identifying him or her—had alerted her to certain improper acts being performed by a certain teacher. She had conducted her own investigation and had found evidence that this teacher was, in fact, violating the compact that both she and Mulvey "held dear."

Vice Principal Mulvey rolled the matter around in his mouth. This was a serious charge, he said, and asked which student was making it. Deirdre said she didn't think it was appropriate to reveal the student's identity. Mulvey said he was troubled by anonymous accusations; if someone were to come forward and accuse a teacher of such a grievous offense, the least they could do was to identify themselves. He muttered something about the Salem witch trials. Deirdre asked why he was so curious about the student's identity but had not asked her to identify the accused party. He said he assumed they were talking about Mr. Sternberg, then went on to say that the previous year there had been a controversy when "some gal" wanted to play *Hamlet* and he thought that matter had been settled. He hoped these charges were not related to that incident.

Deirdre said that if Mulvey was looking for someone to accuse Mr. Sternberg, she would be happy to do so herself; she mentioned the inseam measurements, Sternberg's search for an hourglass figure, the scene on Mozart. Mulvey looked concerned. Oh, then this was a more serious matter, he said. He wanted to "level" with her: If what she said turned out to be true, then he couldn't forgive "that boy," no matter how much he cared for Douglas personally. He thanked Deirdre for her bravery, then asked if she wanted some coffee. Deirdre said no, she was on her way to Von Steuben. Mulvey told her to call him Ralph. He asked how far she was along in her studies. Deirdre said she would finish her coursework in the spring and would be ready to teach full-time the following September. Mulvey told her that when she was looking for work, she should talk to him; she reminded him of the civil rights activist Angela Davis. Mather needed more people like her.

Deirdre was not naïve enough to think that her accusation would cost Mr. Sternberg his job. She had an innate distrust of people in authority; they generally protected their own. Nonetheless, she hadn't anticipated that drawing attention to Douglas Sternberg's foibles would jeopardize her career in the public school system. At first, she made no connection between her tête-à-tête with Mulvey and the fact that early-morning calls asking her to substitute ceased. The week after that meeting, she had worked all five days and was so exhausted that she was relieved when no call came to wake her on Monday morning. When no calls came Tuesday or Wednesday, she figured it was a slow week. But when the next Monday morning came and went without a phone call, she grew suspicious. She called the Board of Education and asked whether there was any reason why she wasn't receiving assignments. The woman who answered the phone said Deirdre's card was in the file box, but they hadn't gotten that far back yet.

Vice Principal Mulvey beamed the next time he saw Deirdre at his office door. He took her hand in both of his and patted it lightly. He said he was going to the faculty cafeteria to get himself a hot cocoa; why didn't she walk with him and he would treat her to a beverage of her choice. As she walked alongside him to the cafeteria, she said this wasn't a social call. She asked if he knew any reason why it had been nearly two weeks since she'd received a substituting assignment. As he pushed the Hot Cocoa button on the beverage dispenser and brown liquid streamed into the paper cup behind an opaque plastic window, he told her he had no idea—he'd heard nothing, but he didn't make the substituting assignments; those were all made from Board headquarters.

Mel Coleman—who when he had worked as a weekend engineer for WBOE had been an official employee of the Board of Ed—blamed Deirdre's predicament on a conspiracy perpetrated by The Man. He offered this opinion while Deirdre was helping him rewrite *Godfathers of Soul*. It had seemed to Deirdre when Mel had first discussed hiring her as his "script doctor" that she would work for one weekend at most. And it probably wouldn't have taken very long if they'd stuck to the work. Deirdre had arrived on the first day with several pages of edits and suggestions ("Capone's neighborhood was called 'Levee District,' not 'Mr. Levy's District,'" "Anachronism no. 37—No one in 1929 would say, 'Hey, babe—why don't you come over to my pad and we'll groove to some records'"). Occasionally, Mel would argue with Deirdre's suggestions on the grounds that his anachronisms were intentional so that "today's brother" could relate to his "picture"—he loved the idea of a 1920s gangster driving a cream-colored Lincoln with a sweet sound system—at which point Deirdre would laud him for his use of pastiche. "Sounds like art shit," Mel would say. "We'd better change it."

This would last for a half hour, after which Mel would become discouraged or distracted and ask Deirdre if she wanted to go for a drive up Sheridan Road to look at the big houses he would buy when he sold his script, or just walk over to Tel Aviv Kosher Pizza and get falafel sandwiches; he'd pay her for her time and they could discuss the script. True to his word, Mel did pay Deirdre, but they rarely discussed the script. Mostly Mel would discuss the difficulties he had meeting a "smart, educated sister such as yourself," while Deirdre would usually try to switch the topic.

Which was how discussion of Deirdre's predicament began. She was drinking an ice water and Mel was enjoying a falafel at the Tel Aviv. Once again, Mel had bemoaned his single status. Back when he'd been at Roosevelt with no money and no prospects, he'd been able to "hit it" any time he wanted with anyone he liked; now that he was a successful entrepreneur, he was being treated "like a goddamn eunuch." Deirdre said she wasn't in the mood for this conversation; there was more to life than his woman troubles. "Tell me what's wrong, baby," Mel said.

As she described her interactions with Vice Principal Mulvey, the behavior of Douglas Sternberg, the deafening silence at the Board of Ed, Deirdre felt herself growing angrier, and that anger expressed itself in seemingly ceaseless run-on sentences, her voice and hands trembling while Mel tried to placate her by offering her sips of his iced tea, a bite of his falafel, and ultimately a pile of napkins with which to blow her nose. Before Deirdre unleashed her fury, Mel had thought he might find the appropriate moment to reveal his infatuation with her. But this hardly seemed like the evening to make such a bold declaration. Instead of telling Deirdre he knew how to make her feel good—he'd been waiting for her to pause so he could say just that—he told her he thought she was a victim of The Man.

Deirdre told Mel she didn't believe in conspiracies, racial or otherwise. People acted in their own self-interest. It wasn't about race; it was about power. Mel asked her who had the power. Deirdre said it seemed to her that if anybody had the power, it was men, not white men per se. Mel said he didn't want to get into that. Look at him, he said, he was a man; did he have any power? Why did she think WBOE wouldn't give him his own talk show—same reason the Board of Ed wouldn't call her. What would his parents think—dead in their graves—about where both of them were? Why had they marched from Selma to Montgomery? What had Mel been doing in college on his own radio show ("All Power to the Music," which he hosted using his then-deejay moniker, Mel Cooley) if he had known all the power would wind up in the hands of some crackers? Don't get him wrong, there were a few black crackers too, but they were just the exceptions to the rule. Pretty soon the world would be run by the Japanese, and then he'd be taking guff from Japanese crackers. The world he had once known was over, Mel said. Even Muhammad Ali had tried a comeback but now he was done, and soon they would see everything they had marched for reversed; soon everything would be exactly the way it used to be.

Like Mel's late parents, Deirdre had marched in Alabama, had taken a Greyhound with her brother Victor from Chicago to Atlanta when she was a teenager, had met up with her brother's pious and lecherous church friend, Nolan Walsh, and the three of them had driven to Alabama. But now she no longer had much interest in political discussions. She needed money to support herself and her son, she needed to teach regardless of who was in charge of the system, and, she told Mel, if that made her a "black cracker," so be it. Mel said she shouldn't get him wrong—first and foremost, he was out for Mel Coleman. But if the system was stacked against Mel Coleman, then he wanted to change the system. The system was responsible for her predicament, he said. And that's why he was going to help her find a way out of it. Deirdre asked what he had in mind.

Mel said he still had a lot of friends who worked at the Board of Ed, and a few of them held a grudge against the Board in general and the radio station in particular over the shabby treatment to which he had been subjected there. Lloyd Cubbins, the security guard who had once worked in the soda pop industry and now worked the front kiosk on weekends, was especially sympathetic. Cubbins's son Tiny was a little messed up, Mel said, but Lloyd was a good man.

On the Saturday evening he was driving with Deirdre Wills down to the Board of Ed, Mel thought out a number of stories he could tell Lloyd to convince him to lend him his master key. But the moment he saw Lloyd seated on his black, vinyl-cushioned stool, sullen, bored, and alone at the kiosk in his navy blue uniform, a yellow "Cubbins" sewn above the fraying breast pocket of the jacket, Mel understood that the truth would yield the quickest, most favorable result. "There's the boy," Cubbins shouted joyfully when Mel walked in. "There is my *boy.*" Mel asked Lloyd if he wanted to help "a sister with a problem." Anything for Mel's old lady, Lloyd said, though he couldn't get them into the party upstairs. What party? Deirdre asked. Mel said it was probably the Jack Bennys, the public radio awards, though he thought those were held in D.C. Yeah, Lloyd said, but they were broadcasting the show live in the Donors' Lounge.

Mel told Lloyd about Deirdre's situation ("Unbelievable," Lloyd kept saying. "Unbe*liev*able!") and said that he wanted to get into the office where the substitute teaching assignments were made to see if he could find some document to explain why Ms. Wills had been discriminated against. He asked Lloyd if there was a directory of offices. From a cubbyhole behind his kiosk, Lloyd produced a dozen wrinkled sheets of mimeographed paper held together in a clear plastic binder, but added that most of the information was outdated. The Board was in utter disarray, many of the offices in the building were vacant while others were overcrowded; the Board's two thousand–plus employees had been without an official leader for approximately a year, since the superintendent had left during the financial crisis that still embroiled the school system. Lloyd suggested that Mel take his place at the security kiosk and he could escort Deirdre around the building until they found what she was looking for. If anyone asked why he was sitting there, Mel was instructed by Lloyd to say that he was the "new man" and that "Ol' Man Cubbins"—as Lloyd liked to refer to himself—was "on his rounds."

"You're ruining my image here, Pops," Mel said as he grudgingly took Lloyd's stool.

Deirdre and Lloyd were looking for the personnel offices. They started on the top floor and worked their way down. Each floor was cast in a harsh, white fluorescent glow, motes of dust suspended in the air, each office a series of variations on the themes of gray and green: wobbly steel desks and file cabinets, faded family pictures and manual typewriters, the few electric Smith-Coronas reserved for the secretaries of the executives on the top floors. Within an hour, they had worked their way down to the sixth floor, which housed the studios of WBOE. On each previous floor, as Deirdre and Lloyd walked from office to office, Deirdre slipped quickly into each one that seemed promising, and spent just enough time to convince herself that she was in the wrong place. Each time she emerged, Lloyd would ask if she had found what she was looking for, and when Deirdre would say no, he'd say "We'd best move on." Deirdre felt an immediate affection for Lloyd, a man who surely should have achieved a higher station in life, yet held no grudges. He was, most probably, born only a few years after her father, which was part of the reason she felt an immediate desire to protect him.

From the 28th floor on downward, Lloyd narrated his life story—the time he'd served in Okinawa, the time he'd worked in the pop factory on 45th and Lenox, how he'd met his wife at the Club De Lisa, where he'd stolen her from a bouncer named Cisco, how he had two boys, one of them in the "*in*surance business," the other of whom was still trying to learn to be an "*ad*ult." He had a penchant for describing his past in terms of addresses—"Back then I was living on 3504 West Jackson," "My boy Samuel lives on 3535 South Indiana Avenue, and Tiny, he's got a beautiful place on 7024 South Shore Drive." Though, Lloyd said, he didn't much like what Tiny had done to be able to afford that house. He proceeded to narrate one of Tiny's exploits, which, to Deirdre, bore more than a passing resemblance to a key scene in *Godfathers of Soul.* But before she could ask Lloyd whether he had ever told Mel this story, the elevator doors opened on 6.

In fact, Lloyd had pushed "5"—he said there was no point in investigating the 6th floor; Deirdre wouldn't find what she was looking for, plus there was the awards party and he didn't want to rouse the suspicions of anyone "there celebrating." But behind the doors to WBOE, there was little celebration. Donna Mayne had planned for a sweep of all the children's awards categories and had gone overbudget planning the evening's event. Most of the station's hierarchy, their spouses, and a good deal of the "talent" were in attendance, and all of them were enjoying canapés, champagne, and kiddie cocktails as Boston station WBPR's *Young City* claimed the award for "Best Children's Newsmagazine" and the Best Children's Fictional Series prize went to KCPR's saccharine radio adaptation of Shel Silverstein's *The Giving Tree.* In the categories for which

WBOE had no competition, *Chi-Town Chatterbox* still won nothing. The only award for the Chicago station was presented for Creativity in Children's Program Production; Muley Wills was not present to hear of his victory for his contribution, "Peachy Moskowitz, Episode No. 4: The Softer Things Are, The Harder They Get."

Had Deirdre and Lloyd arrived on the 6th floor five minutes earlier, they would have encountered *Young Town* actress Lisa-Anne Williams and her parents leaving so that they could be in bed by ten and thus sufficiently rested for the drive to Wheaton for a church service the following morning. Had they arrived five minutes later, the door would have opened onto a distraught yet indignant Lana Rovner accompanied by her father, who would try to explain to her that awards were meaningless. But since the elevator door opened when it did, Deirdre and Lloyd came face-to-face with Michelle Wasserstrom in the company of Gareth Overgaard. Michelle told Ms. Wills she hoped she hadn't come to accept her son's award, because neither the food nor the company was worth the price of admission.

There was silence as the elevator doors closed and both Lloyd and Gareth reached to press the 5th-floor button. Deirdre wondered aloud why they were going to the 5th floor. Just to look around, Michelle said. She asked Ms. Wills why she was going. The same reason, Deirdre said. The elevator doors opened on 5. The four of them got out and the doors closed behind them, Gareth and Michelle searching for a more satisfactory explanation of what they were doing other than looking for a quiet, private place to smoke pot—a "nostalgia toke," Michelle had called it, because neither smoked much anymore, Deirdre trying to invent justifications for breaking and entering. Michelle asked Ms. Wills if she was dropping off grades for a class she'd been teaching. No, she said, she hadn't been asked to teach much lately. That was odd, Michelle said—Ms. Wills was the only competent substitute she'd had, the only one who wasn't either an alcoholic with a comb-over or a convict on a work release program. Why hadn't she been teaching? At this point, Lloyd spoke for the first time. "That's what I'm trying to explain to her," he said.

Lloyd said that this "talented and attractive young lady" had been troubled by the fact that the Board of Ed was no longer calling her and wanted to find out why. And he was giving her a tour of the building to show just how disordered and beleaguered the Board was and to make her understand that her situation wasn't the result of any particular personal vendetta. Michelle said that seemed fine and good, but wouldn't it make more sense to break into the personnel office, find Ms. Wills's file, and see if there was a reason why she wasn't being called? She suspected that Ms. Wills had probably said something disparaging to or about Douglas Sternberg, which had caught the attention of his buddy, Vice Principal Mulvey.

Deirdre insisted there was no way she would do something so blatantly illegal as breaking into an office to look through papers that were none of her business. She sternly asked Ms. Wasserstrom and Mr. Overgaard why they were snooping around the building unsupervised after hours. Michelle told her not to worry—they weren't looking for a place to make out, Gareth was gay anyway. Gareth said he wasn't sure he was gay; he just didn't enjoy the company of heterosexual men. Lloyd said he didn't much care for this conversation and suggested that they continue their tour.

They found the newly named Department of Human Resources on the second floor. It was a carpetless office with primer white walls, metal file cabinets and desks, and a fire escape–obstructed view of the back alley. Beyond the reception area, three doors led to the offices of administrators, their names and titles painted in black on frosted glass: a Superintendent of Human Resources and two deputies. "It's got to be one of the deputies," Gareth told Michelle. "Superintendents don't do dick." After much debate, Deirdre had allowed Gareth and Michelle to root around in the office while she and Lloyd waited outside. She had expressed such strong opposition to entering the office herself that when Gareth proposed, "Why don't me and Wasserstrom just go in; in the time it's taken to debate this, we could have been frickin' out of there already," she had little choice but to accept.

Deirdre had never engaged in any remotely criminal activity and kept looking up and down the hallways to see if someone was coming to arrest them, while Lloyd sat on a bucket chair and spoke more of the trials of his son Tiny—again the stories sounded much like those in *Godfathers of Soul.* Meanwhile, Michelle and Gareth rummaged inside and on top of desks—each taking one of the deputies' offices, which were gun-metal-gray mirror images of each other. They could have completed the process far more quickly had Gareth not emerged from Deputy Superintendent Ed Jarrett's office and burst into Deputy Superintendent Martha Pappin's office every two minutes or so, clutching one mimeographed document or another, decrying its bureaucratic jargon. "Listen to this shit, Wasserstrom," he would say, then turn philosophical, remarking that if the people in charge of education were such "dumb-asses," then kids really had no chance. He said he would consider going into education but for the fact that every day he would have to "contend with this shit."

The fourth time he entered Deputy Pappin's office, this time waving a "Blue Memo," one typed on blue paper with the legend "Blue Memo" upon it ("Tautological, Wasserstrom," Gareth announced. "A needless repetition of the obvious"), Michelle was sitting cross-legged on a desk, looking through the cards in a small metal box. Gareth read aloud from the memo, which concerned the "regularization of telephone response." But Michelle did not register what he was saying; she had found Deirdre Wills's file card.

On a white card, Deirdre's name was typed along with her address, phone number, social security number, and when she had begun service—"Spring 1980." The cards were organized alphabetically, and Michelle had also found the cards of other substitutes who had taught her during her high school career. There was Ms. Ethel Dietz, who had told Michelle she would be voted "Most Likely to Become a Whore." And there was Bud Tevins, who had answered every one of her wise-ass remarks with "Don't be jocular." Tevins had taught Michelle three times and each time had written "jocular" on the board. The only difference between Deirdre's card and the two others was that there was a yellow mark in the upper-right-hand corner of hers.

Mel Coleman, who had sat in the lobby while a humbled and award-less Donna Mayne had nonetheless condescended to him ("If you're looking for some better night watchman work, I might be able to help," she said), told Gareth, Michelle, Lloyd, and Deirdre when they returned downstairs that he knew what the yellow mark meant. "It means you're a sister," he said. He said that auto dealerships, Hank Shiva's in particular, used the infamous yellow mark to identify "shufflin' nigroes" whom they could easily cheat. Michelle said she didn't think it was a racial issue in this case, but she agreed that the yellow marks were meant to single out "rabble-rousers." In this city, "rabble-rouser" meant "brother," Mel observed. Michelle remarked that there were many people with "Afro-American–sounding surnames" who didn't have yellow marks on their cards. Mel said he wanted to know what an "Afro-American–sounding surname" was. Well, Coleman, for example, Michelle said. Oh, Mel said sarcastically, he got it, everybody named Coleman was a brother. Gareth suggested that everybody shut the fuck up. Deirdre said that this was the first sensible thing anyone had said. Then Gareth said he had another sensible suggestion: Why didn't they fill out another file card for "Ms. Wills here," this time without a yellow mark, and see what would happen. Michelle said that she approved of Gareth's idea—just as long as they could put a yellow mark on Ms. Ethel Dietz's card. Deirdre said that Gareth's proposal was illegal and she "could not sanction" anyone perform- ing this action in her name. But it was, she allowed with an appreciative chuckle, a "fine idea," and if Lloyd handed her the key, she'd go up and do it herself. While Deirdre went to Deputy Superintendent Pappin's office, Mel apologized to Michelle for "getting a little hot." He hoped she understood he'd just been "bulljiving" her. He said he respected a woman who could go toe-to-toe with him. He asked how old she was again. Michelle said she was fifty-seven.

Come Friday, Deirdre—who had been miraculously reinstated as a substi- tute—saw fit to celebrate her triumph. She planned an elaborate dinner to which she invited Michelle, Gareth, Lloyd Cubbins, and Mel Coleman. Muley had just recently finished his latest film and said he had to deliver it to a certain person, which meant that he missed Jill Wasserstrom, who accompanied Michelle and Gareth. Lloyd, the one guest whose company Deirdre actually sought, was warned off attending by Mel, who assumed the dinner was really being held to celebrate the imminent completion of the latest iteration of *Godfathers of Soul* and was Deirdre's subtle way of asking him out.

By 9 that night, the plates had been cleared away; Mel and Deirdre had fin- ished their wine and everyone else had drunk the sparkling grape juice Deirdre had poured for them; Gareth had washed the dishes ("Do that woman's work, Overgaard!" Michelle had crowed); Deirdre had served fruit for dessert; and Jill had politely excused herself for the evening, citing a "Freshman's View" column she was writing for the school newspaper at Lane Tech shortly after Deirdre had informed her that Muley probably wouldn't be back until late. After Gareth and Michelle had left—off to Gareth's house to make fun of his hopelessly dorky par- ents smoking pot and listening to Tom Paxton folk records, Michelle said—Mel said it seemed like it was just the two of them now, and they needed to find some- thing to occupy their time. After Deirdre had made a pot of tea, Mel suggested that they retire to the living room because he needed to "stretch out some." Once there, Mel told Deirdre he was impressed by her dedication to teaching. He wished he'd had a teacher like her when he'd been a student at Evanston and Roosevelt. Why didn't she teach him something now? Deirdre laughed and asked what he wanted her to teach him. Anything, Mel said.

Deirdre asked Mel if he wanted her to tell him a story. Mel said sure, ladies who told good stories were sexy. Deirdre told Mel she'd recently been reading a lot of nineteenth-century authors—Thackeray and George Meredith and Dr. Lewis Ridle, a little-known writer about whom she'd almost forgotten but who had written what had once been one of Muley's favorite stories, "The Talented Assistant." The story concerned an incompetent English country doctor (based loosely on the author himself) who had a remarkable record of curing his ailing patients, thanks to the storytelling talents of his nurse, Eleanor Hargraves. *Damn,* Mel said after Deirdre had described the intricacies of the plot, that story sounded "on time." He undid a few of his shirt buttons and asked if that story was the subject of her thesis. No, Deirdre said, she was writing about Joseph Conrad.

Oh yeah, Mel said, he'd read a lot of shit by that brother. Really, Deirdre said. Yeah, Mel said. He knew a lot of people talked about *The Secret Agent* and *Lord Jim,* but *Under Western Eyes* was the one that had blown him away, particularly that scene near the end of the novel where the shunned Razumov is forced out into the rain-soaked night and run over by a tram car. That was the one Mel said had inspired him to write the scene in *Godfathers of Soul* where Tiny gets run down by a Mazda, and dies saying, "Piece o' shit Japanese car."

There were many reasons why Deirdre had not taken Mel seriously before. But once he began revealing his familiarity with literature—his disdain for Nabokov ("Stop the art shit, brother, and tell me a story," Mel said), his admiration for Faulkner ("Those Compsons were fucked up in a major way"), and his ambivalence regarding Sinclair Lewis ("I just don't give a shit about his people, nothing against how he writes")—Deirdre began reassessing him. As she sat next to him on her couch, debating the quality of Conrad's *Chance*—"his most underrated novel," Deirdre said; "some bullshit he turned out to pay the bills," Mel countered as he slipped off his loafers—she wondered, perhaps it was the effect of the wine, if they had more in common than she had imagined.

Ever since the dissolution of her entanglement with Carl, Deirdre had been too busy raising her son, making a living, and schooling herself in literature to worry about serious relationships. Men were frightened of her, and those who

weren't generally didn't seem worth her time. But now Mel's unassuming com-
mand of literature combined with his dimpled smile, his endearing chuckle, and
the wine, of course the wine, was making her feel a rush, one she might have said
she hadn't felt since her first dates with Carl, except for the fact that the warmth
and contentment she was experiencing now were sensations she had never really
felt with him at all. Why didn't Mel ever consider being a teacher? she asked with
a sly smile—she was sure he could teach her something too. She wondered if
there were any other literary references in his script that she had overlooked.
Maybe, Mel said. He thought there was some shit from Dickens in there, a little
bit of bullshit from James Baldwin, but he didn't really want to talk about that.
He tried to stay as far away from literature as possible when he was writing; that
was the only way to sell a script. Deirdre said the only thing she had recognized
in Mel's script was Tiny's story—many of the episodes Mel described seemed remarkably similar to stories she had heard Lloyd tell about his wayward son.

Aww shit, Mel replied. He told Deirdre she had found out his "deep, dark,
dirty secret." Yeah, he said, Lloyd had told him a whole lot of stories about Tiny
and they had been so good that he had incorporated some into his plot. Deirdre
began to smile, but the smile stopped halfway. She asked Mel if Lloyd knew
about the script. Not yet, Mel said, it hadn't come up. Deirdre, feeling an ever-
so-slight quickening of her breath, asked if Mel intended to tell Lloyd he was using his son's stories. Mel said he hadn't thought about it, but he was certain Lloyd
wouldn't be upset. Besides, it wasn't like anyone had any right to their own
stories—stories were stories, and people could use them as they saw fit; that's what
artists did. The most important thing for Mel was to finish the script so he could
attract someone with money, someone in the entertainment business, someone
who could "talk his talk."

Deirdre sat still, but she felt as if everything in the room was slowly yet inex-
orably moving away from her. Though there was less than a foot between her and
Mel, it now felt as if there was a distance far too great for her to cross. A moment
before, she had felt a flush in her cheeks and a delightfully clumsy ease of motion,
but now the only sensation she could identify was a dull pressure against her tem-
ples. She quietly told Mel yes, she certainly did know someone with money,
someone in the entertainment business, someone who could "talk his talk." She
stood up and said she was going to get a pen. Mel touched her waist and asked
her to sit back down. No, Deirdre said, she was getting a pen and some paper.

When she returned to Mel, who had put his feet up on her ottoman and unbuttoned his shirt another button, she didn't even look at him. She merely scribbled down an address and a phone number for Carl Slappit Silverman.

"You two are kindred spirits," she told Mel. Then she asked him to leave her apartment.

The grim morning that Mel Coleman's letter arrived at the home office of Carl Slappit Silverman and presented him with the first of two brilliant solutions to his plight, Carl was suffering the indignity of opening his own mail. Laying off his secretary was only the most recent cost-cutting measure Carl had implemented once his recording empire had started to collapse. The lawsuit brought against him had, in fact, not made it to court—his conduct in securing the song catalogs of down-on-their-luck musicians may have been morally problematic but was legally sound. Still, the suit damaged his reputation to such an extent ("Slappit Gets a Good Slapp!" screamed a headline in *Variety,* while the *LA Reader* published a 9,000-word exposé entitled "The Sound of One Hand Slapping") that nearly all of his label's major acts shunned him and either balked at their contractual obligations or fulfilled them perfunctorily with greatest-hits records, live albums, collections of B-sides, or, in one case, a Spoken Word LP, in which the artists wailed on their instruments and caterwauled "Silverman's a ganif" over and over. Ultimately, Carl's lawyer, Lou Eisenstaedt, advised him that the most prudent course of action would be to declare bankruptcy, find God, and convert to Christianity, whereupon he could make a much-publicized statement of his newfound faith. Then he could start up his business again. Carl said he'd think about it when he went for his nightly walk along the ocean to the fried-shrimp shack.

The conversion idea had a certain appeal. From an anthropological standpoint, Carl found religion intriguing—he enjoyed taking Sunday morning trips into South Central L.A. churches and saying "Mm-hm" and "Tell it, Preacher" until ushers told him to hold it down. He liked gospel music, a genre he thought had not been sufficiently commercialized. The rock 'n' roll business was consistently cutthroat—its musicians were becoming financially savvy; now they had managers who were actually businessmen and lawyers, not lunkheaded hangers-on from the old neighborhood who could be bought off with cash and cocaine.

But if he could figure out a marketing strategy to mainstream gospel music, he could own that genre. The songs were cheap; most were in the public domain. His star performers could appear on Christian TV shows with faith-healing evangelists. He'd gaped at some of those shows and was stunned by how many people sang along with those blond families—the feathered-hair girls, the pie-faced boys, the mustached fathers, all with their vacant expressions as they stood in their royal-blue outfits mindlessly keening to an out-of-tune piano. This was virgin territory, ripe for plundering.

As he turned back toward home with a bag full of shrimp, Carl enthusiastically contemplated becoming an impresario of gospel and Christian rock. His acts wouldn't perform "concerts"; they'd present "revivals." There'd be jerseys and T-shirts with pictures of Christ on the cross on the front and "SOLD OUT" on the back. The bands on his label (Sayit! Records) would play Bangladesh, Budokan, and Bethlehem. They'd have tour buses with the Sistine Chapel ceiling painted on their sides. They'd keep track of their sales and attendance figures, publicize them like McDonald's hamburgers, but instead of "40 billion hamburgers sold," they'd say "40 billion souls saved." He'd move to Nashville, befriend political leaders, football coaches. The country's mood was becoming both more religious and more capitalistic—an explosion of million-selling Christian records was an idea whose time had come. The only problem, he thought as he walked up the steps to the veranda of his Malibu home, was that his parents were still alive. And he knew all too well that if he wanted to convert to Christianity, even to save his career, even if he donated every cent he made to the JUF, he would still have to wait until they were dead.

He entertained the idea of hiring a front man, but there were few people left in L.A. who still spoke to him. Before dismissing the notion entirely, he called once more upon "the Rovner kid"—the one who'd been the first with the balls to turn down the opportunity to become one of the endlessly hopeful interns who came to L.A. with dreams of making it big on Slappit Records and almost always left after three months of addressing envelopes, calling radio stations and record stores, and, once in a lucky while, traveling in advance of bands' tours to inspect accommodations and sample food. Larry had been the first to not only turn down that offer, but also to refuse the contract Carl had offered him for Rovner!'s first album, because he was unwilling to guarantee that he would actually release it. And recalling how Larry had used Muley's name to try to further his career,

Carl thought Larry might be the only kid he knew with enough chutzpah to implement his scheme.

When Carl got Larry on the phone this time, the Brandeis freshman told him with a laugh that he hoped he wasn't calling to ask him to reconsider the contract offer; he had his future fairly well figured out. After he and Hannah got married, she would study entertainment law at either UCLA or NYU and she would handle all of his contracts. He asked "Slappit" what was "shaking" with him. Carl spoke in vague terms about his plans for Sayit! Records and a possible move to Nashville. But Larry quickly cut him off. "Don't sell your soul to the goyim, Silverman," he said. He added that Hannah's father was a prominent international lawyer with connections in Hollywood, and if Carl needed a good lawyer, he might be able to help out. The moment before Larry said *"Shalom"* and hung up, he asked Carl if he needed any money, if he was doing okay. Then Carl heard Larry whisper to somebody in his room, "I'm getting off the phone; I'll go down on you in a second."

The conversion and subsequent Christian rock plan was thus dead, and as Carl lay on his sheetless mattress on his bedroom floor, he was kept awake by the unusual silence. There were now no raucous cocaine parties on the first floor, no groupies or actresses, no inarticulate drummers, sullen bassists, or once-earnest, now-conceited pretty-boy lead singers. For the first time since he had been in undergraduate Philosophy seminars, Carl felt utter futility. All his life he had merely tried to do what he loved and make some money at it, sure, maybe too much money in some people's eyes, but he had never coerced anybody, never forced anybody to sign anything, just tried to get the best deal he could. And now what did he have to show for it other than a massive checking account, and the animosity of everyone whose career he'd launched or saved. He had been in love once—or at least he thought the satisfaction he felt from a beautiful woman listening to what he had to say must have been love. He had a son whom he did not see, who did not care to see him. But he also knew that lives were never matters of simple rises and falls; all he had to do was withstand enough abuse, and soon enough his career would rebound. Endurance was ultimately all that mattered; even the biggest schmucks received lifetime achievement awards if they survived long enough.

Still, as Carl lay in bed that realization was more troubling than comforting. He had no control. He was, like everyone else, barely keeping up with the current in the eternal flow of events. Frightening images pirouetted across his mind's eye—nooses mostly, but also long walks into deep oceans, great falls from high windows, aimless walks down the center of the 405 freeway. He decided to sleep on the beach in his jeans and his shoes, hoping that if he wasn't able to rest peacefully, at least the ocean would be good enough to carry him away.

But Carl survived that night, and in fact slept soundly enough to wake up believing that everything was as it had once been. That thought evaporated, however, the moment he trudged over a week's worth of worn tube socks and white Jockey briefs flung haphazardly about his echoing mansion. There was still nobody here, nobody to answer the phones, not even an intern to open his mail, most of which was still in a dirty gray U.S. postal sack, which he turned upsidedown, shaking the contents out onto the floor. He dumped almost everything into a garbage bag. Bills weren't worth his time—after the final notice, there were always two or three more. Ditto for fan mail—none of it was addressed to him anyway. The heavy manila envelope from Melvin Coleman of 3M Studios was the only thing that caught Carl's eye: "To Brother Slappit Silverman," it read.

Carl liked being called "brother"—it reminded him of the times he spent on the streets, or rather, of the times he would have liked to have spent on the streets. Few of the people he met spoke in his jazz-inflected, hipster, pseudoghetto slang, the way he called everybody either "brother" or "sister," the way he liberally used the word "freak," said "Don't jive me, man" or "Don't do me like that, bro" in contract negotiations, the way he never said he liked or didn't like something, just that he was or wasn't "down" with that. Even though he generally received blank stares when he spoke in this manner, particularly from the occasional black people he encountered, it felt authentic to him.

The fact that Coleman said in his letter that he was writing upon the recommendation of "Sister Deirdre Wills" made Carl think this was some sort of hoax. But when Carl noticed the phrase indicating that Deirdre thought he and Mel were "kindred spirits," he immediately thought he understood—clearly, he reasoned, this was some other victim of Deirdre's unwarranted wrath, someone whom she wanted to mock by leading him to Carl. Most probably, a young musician had written the letter, someone forthright but arrogant, someone with an ego with which Deirdre could not contend. She was no doubt hoping that Carl would ignore the letter entirely or, better, sign the young man up and take advantage of him, buy his song catalog and his first album for bubkis. Well, if that's what she thought, he would do the exact opposite—sign the brother to a recording contract, overpay him, give him the percentages that established artists dreamed of.

Carl was so caught up in this plan, rummaging around in file cabinets for boilerplate contracts, ones that didn't have coffee or pineapple soda stains on them, that he did not immediately realize that Coleman's letter didn't refer to music of any sort, but to "an epic film in the tradition of *The Godfather, Bonnie and Clyde,* and *Superfly,*" for which Coleman was seeking financing. Carl didn't like movies, not since James Dean had died, not since Marlon Brando had started making flicks in color. He didn't like film people. They were too scrubbed—they lacked the jagged edges of musicians. He didn't understand the idea of a nonparticipatory art form, one to which you couldn't sing along, clap your hands, or get up and dance. Nevertheless, because he was sure Deirdre wanted him to either ignore or cheat Melvin Coleman, he read on.

Carl liked Coleman's decided lack of pretension, the way he introduced his pitch by telling him that if he was "looking for art shit," then he was "looking at the wrong brother," but if he was looking for some "real goddamn entertainment," something with humor that wasn't "white people funny" but instead was "black people laugh-out-loud funny," then by all means, he should check out the script. Carl rarely read anymore. He had no time to read novels and had never read a film script. At first he found the style off-putting—the Fade Ins and Fade Outs, the "Tight Shot on Tiny," the "Circle Wipe on Tiny's Cigar." But after reading a few pages on the john, Carl flushed the toilet and brought the script out onto the veranda, where he drank cold coffee, ate Apple Jacks out of the box, and became captivated by the story. To him, it read like a 120-page-long blues song, filled with swagger and braggadocio, tainted women and cheating men. The riffing, back-and-forth dialogue sounded like schoolyard kids playing the dozens.

Carl considered Hollywood the ugliest part of L.A. But even before he was half-through with *Godfathers,* he knew he wanted to make it. He wondered where people got the kind of money you needed to make movies. Maybe he could sell his song catalog, he thought, sell the contracts of his artists, sell his house and his studio, start anew. But no, that didn't make sense, because he would need all that music, all those facilities, because the script was all right—he liked it fine—but the way he would really make money was with the soundtrack.

This was how the Slappit empire could continue to thrive, he realized; he could make slews of cheap movies—gangster flicks and teenage romances and coming-of-age films, low-budget horror and exploitation movies. His music was what would make the movies popular. Each time he made a movie, he would release a soundtrack, and all that recycled music would seem absolutely fresh and it would sell all over again. When he ran out of songs, he could reuse the music for more movies he could make in Germany or France; anything with shots of American highways with blues, R & B, or American rock 'n' roll soundtracks would succeed overseas. Even if no artist wanted to work with him again, he could save his career.

On the night in December before Mel Coleman was scheduled to meet with Carl Slappit Silverman in Chicago, Mel called up Muley Wills to see if he wanted to join him for the meeting, and whether Muley wanted a job on the film he was sure he would be making with Carl. Muley thanked him but said no, he was busy filming most every night now and didn't have time. He warned Mel not to get taken advantage of by his father. Mel laughed at Muley's concern—"No one ever takes advantage of Mel Coleman," Mel said. Then Mel asked Muley whatever happened to that last film he'd been working on. Muley said he'd given it to someone and apparently that person hadn't liked it much because he hadn't heard back from her—but that was okay, since he wasn't sure whether it was any good or not. So now he was making a film that was more ambitious; filming it was occupying nearly all of his time now. Mel said maybe they should get together for some beers and pops soon—he missed seeing Muley around the studio. Muley said sure, he'd come by sometime, but his mother was on his case about first-semester finals, and besides, he wasn't ready to edit yet; he had to keep filming. Then he said he had to go. Mel asked him if he could put his mother on the line. He thanked Deirdre for suggesting that he write to Carl; he was coming into town and he thought they would be cutting a deal. He asked if he could cook her his famous, soon-to-be-patented "Chicken à la Coleman." Deirdre said she'd think it over, but in the moments before she hung up, Mel could hear her laughing.

In the time between reading Mel's letter and arriving in Chicago at the Sovereign Hotel with an attaché case that contained, among other things, a Ziploc bag filled with laundry detergent so he could wash his clothes in the hotel sink, Carl had seen two more artists leave Slappit Records. One left Carl a list written on notebook paper of the desired order of songs for a greatest-hits record; the other provided a crude recording of a recent performance to be used as a double-live album, accompanied by a note: "Contract Fulfilled, Now Fuck Off." In those ten days, Carl slept more than he had in the past six months, as if cocooning himself before shedding the skin of the older Carl. The hours he did not sleep he spent either in the Watts public library reading up on the history of the motion picture industry or in the UCLA law library studying movie contracts.

On the flight from LAX to Chicago-Midway, Carl began to plan out exactly how the film would look and where he would introduce particular songs. He had a sense of the visual style—tinted and somewhat opaque, as if viewed through stained glass. He wanted to see zoot suits and wide-brimmed hats; he could hear saxophones and gravelly vocals. He didn't like the idea of beginning the film with an exterior shot of the Domino Club. He wanted to start inside, onstage, with a big-hipped woman in a crimson dress with lipstick to match singing "Trouble in Mind." Then the camera would pull back to reveal the dance floor—men and women dressed to the nines in their Cotton Club duds, dancing close and nasty, gyrating their hips and buttocks. Throughout the plane ride, Carl made furious pencil marks on his script, which became a jumble of scribbles, X-outs, and notes.

From Midway, Carl drove his rental car north on Cicero, past airport motels, past the strip clubs and the liquor stores in the near south suburb where Capone's gang once ruled, and into Chicago's old West Side, whose streets had not been paved since the Jews, Carl's parents included, had fled all the way north to West Rogers Park and beyond, where the charred remnants of buildings fire-bombed during the 1968 riots following the assassination of Martin Luther King still had not been cleared. It was the sort of neighborhood, neglected for decades by the Democratic machine, that white people built highways to avoid, where honkeys drove with their windows rolled up, ignoring traffic signals, assuming that being stopped by the police was one of the best possible things that could happen.

But even though the temperature was near freezing, Carl drove with his driver's-side window rolled down. He left the motor running when he stopped at Dock's for fried catfish and hot sauce. He waved out the window at a pair of old men passing a forty-ounce bottle of Schlitz Malt Liquor back and forth in front of a shuttered cocktail lounge. When he saw a morose drug dealer in a black down vest standing expectantly at the corner of Cicero and Jackson, where Carl had played as a kid, Carl saluted him with a black power fist. And when a man with a squeegee offered to wash his windows, Carl handed him a five and told him to keep the change—he knew just how bad things were around this 'hood, brother.

Carl considered just how much good a man like him could do in a neighborhood like this. In L.A., he was just another record mogul, but if he moved his studios here, brought motion picture production back to Chicago where it had begun, he could run this town. They'd rename Cicero Avenue "Slappit Street." Everyone in every Harold's Chicken Shack would know his name—they'd say they didn't like crackers much, but that brother Silverman, he was all right. He was still thinking about remaking the city in his own image as the old West Side disappeared and was replaced by the warehouses, factories, and shot-and-a-beer joints of the near South Side, then by the Kennedy Expressway, which bordered the avenue, angling out to Skokie, Wilmette, and Touhy Avenues, which led straight into West Rogers Park.

As far as Mel Coleman was concerned, Carl's plan to revitalize the West Side was absurd. Not so much because of its racial presumption—such arrogance was to be expected—but more because Mel didn't feel any greater comfort there than most garden-variety honkeys. West Side cats were crazy, Mel told Carl over beers and peanuts at the Double Bubble; they'd cut his tires, then his throat. As a rule, when Carl discussed contracts, he made sure that conversation happened in a swanky establishment to create a certain discomfort in his foe. Mel, however, had brushed aside Carl's suggestion of the Pump Room, saying he had no interest in dining at "someplace where they'll be looking at me like I'm their car jockey." Instead, Mel offered to cook up fried chicken, greens, and a batch of his mama's special okra recipe. Though Carl had a rule against negotiating on his foe's turf, the offer sounded too mouthwateringly delicious to pass up. But Mel informed Carl that he was just joking—he didn't eat that "nigro heart-attack food," though he allowed that Carl could certainly run over to the Chicken Unlimited and pick himself up a bucket, and maybe a bag of Funyuns at the gas station.

Over the first two pitchers of Falstaff beer, Carl and Mel talked in general terms about movies, gangsters, and blaxploitation films—none of which had been good in years, Mel said; they were all some cracker vision of the streets, thought up by some brother named Rosenstein. No offense, Mel said, he knew Carl was different; Carl understood where a brother was coming from—he had a white man's skin but a black man's soul. Carl usually had a sixth sense for bull-shit, but was too flattered to notice. He knew perfectly well that in L.A., the white rock 'n' rollers viewed him as comic relief, some stooge with whom they dealt only because he had money. He knew the moment he left the studio, the members of the R & B and funk acts on his label were commenting on his sloppy dress, his eating habits—that when he turned his back they were calling him Smearit instead of Slappit. No one talked to him the way Mel did. No one had ever told him, as Mel had, that if every cracker had been like him, there would have been no need for anyone to have marched in Alabama. Mel waved to the bartender for a third pitcher, whereupon Carl told Mel how much he admired his script, how authentic he thought it was. He told Mel that he had never liked the film business, but *Godfathers* was a different kind of movie, more like a song, the language was musical, he really liked the rhythm of it.

Yeah, Mel snarled—it *did* have a really good rhythm; you could really *dance* to it. At which point, Carl—thrown off-kilter by concern that he might have offended Mel—said he wanted to see this picture get made and he wanted to be the one who got it done. Well, then, Mel said with a smile, why didn't he say what sort of deal he had in mind. Carl asked Mel what he thought was fair. Mel said he wasn't that concerned about percentages on the movie or upfront money—he trusted that he and Carl could agree on those numbers—what he was most interested in was having complete creative control over the project and in having a piece of the soundtrack, which was where he thought some real money could be made. Carl was rendered momentarily speechless as Mel poured him another beer and, in Carl's silence, Mel remarked that he knew he was asking a lot, he knew most white men wouldn't think of entrusting a black man—particularly one as untested as he was—with so much control. That was why Doug Williams and Vince Evans were the only black quarterbacks starting in the NFL, that was why the most powerful black men in Chicago politics were the hacks who had said "yassuh, boss" to Richard J. Daley, that was why they called it the *"White House."* Carl—suddenly wondering if someone sharp enough to demand creative control and a percentage of the soundtrack was smart enough to deserve it—said of course he didn't see things that way, he thought Mel understood that. Mel said he did understand that, but maybe they should put it down on paper. Carl said he'd brought along a contract. Mel said he had too.

Carl had never been so thoroughly overwhelmed and defeated in a contract negotiation but at the same time had never felt so elated after signing. Usually when he signed, there was a nagging sense of winning in a game where one hasn't played by the rules. This time, even after conceding to every single demand Mel made, he was giddy. He insisted on ordering still more pitchers of beer, on pumping the jukebox full of quarters and selecting every Ray Charles and Muddy Waters song he could find, on declaiming at length about every soul food delicacy he enjoyed, every blues performer he had ever met. At last call, he suggested they take the party back to his hotel room. Mel told Carl he liked him, but not that much; he suggested they talk on Monday when Carl was heading back to L.A.

And even after the alcohol had worn off, even after he had taken the plane with the intention of returning to Malibu to pack up his house and move at least part of his operation back to Chicago, Carl didn't regret what he and Mel had agreed to. Yes, he did regret that after they had parted for the evening, he went directly to Deirdre's apartment and kept ringing the doorbell until she came to the door. He regretted that she said he was a drunken fool. He regretted that he had told her—tears streaming down his cheeks—that he still loved her, that he had done everything wrong, that he wanted to start over, that he was moving back to Chicago and he wouldn't leave her alone until he had won her back. He regretted that his son had come down—the boy he hadn't seen since he'd been an infant—that his son, a tall, beautiful, and gangly young man with a kindly gaze and an almost mystical demeanor, had asked who that man was, and Deirdre had responded with pity in her eyes that she had no idea, just some poor lost soul who had no business coming by. He regretted that he had agreed with his ex-wife and said yes, he was just some poor lost soul who had rung the wrong doorbell. He regretted that Muley Scott Wills saw through him immediately yet still showed no sign of emotion—not anger, not love, not even exasperation—as he told him, "Go home, Dad." He regretted all that. But he did not regret signing a contract with Melvin Coleman. That made him happier than anything had in years.

Mel and Carl had agreed that filming would not begin for at least a year. In the meantime, Carl would get the money together and Mel would learn the basics of filmmaking (he didn't say that he would prevail upon Muley to teach him as much as he could) and Mel would keep refining the script until it was ready to shoot (he didn't say that he hoped he could convince Deirdre to work with him again). And after he took the Monday evening flight back to L.A., Carl was still so elated that he didn't care—or almost didn't care—whether *Godfathers of Soul* and its soundtrack would be successful. On the way from L.A. to Chicago, he thought he had discovered the solution to what he saw as his impending ruin. But on that second Monday in December, when he arrived back in L.A., that solution hardly mattered, in part because he was going to be doing something in which he truly believed, and in part because when he passed by the airport bar and learned the reason why people were gathering around televisions, shell-shocked expressions on their faces, he had found, perhaps, the second brilliant solution to his financial dilemma.

January 20, 1981

— — — —

"I guess I can go back to California now . . ."

—RONALD REAGAN, JANUARY 20, 1981

Deirdre & Carl

T he day Ronald Wilson Reagan took the oath of office to become the fortieth president of the United States and the fifty-two remaining hostages
were released from the U.S. embassy in Tehran marked the second time in less
than two months that Deirdre Wills requested a TV for the Mather room in
which she was substituting. The first time was on December 9, when Michelle
Wasserstrom insisted that her Public Speaking class honor a moment of silence
for John Lennon, slain in New York the night before. Michelle had stated that
the way in which she had learned of Lennon's death—in the TV room of Gareth
Overgaard's U of C dorm, where the news was announced during Monday Night
Football watched by a dozen pale, overweight young men with stubble and tube
socks—had been disrespectful to the man's memory, and she insisted on a more
proper remembrance.

On January 20, 1981, however, Matthias Kimmel, founder of the Mather
Young Republicans Club, suggested the TV be brought into the study hall
Deirdre was monitoring. Deirdre had become ever more popular among school
administrators here since she had been secretly blacklisted, then secretly reinstated, leading Vice Principal Mulvey to assume that she had an influential ally at
the Board of Ed. Though there were only three TVs in the Mather A/V department, Deirdre's request for the one color TV was granted without question. A
TV broadcast was a rare treat, reserved only for events of grave importance: the
first lunar landing, the declaration of cease-fire in the Vietnam War, Richard J.
Daley's funeral, Cubs' opening day. And as such, it attracted the attention of several other classes.

Michelle Wasserstrom had recently devised a game entitled Which, and suggested to Barry Tewlow that they play it in study hall during Reagan's speech. The game had been invented during a school assembly, one that featured a presentation by a manufacturer of class rings. The assembly had been absolutely excruciating until the moment that the company rep said he wanted to "put a jewel on every one of your fingers." Michelle had muttered, *"Which is what I was doing last night."* And when that same rep introduced Vice Principal Mulvey by saying, "Put your hands together for someone really special," Barry Tewlow interjected, *"Which is what I was doing in the john this morning."* For Michelle and Barry, this was an amazing discovery: Even the most boring lectures were rife with hilarity if one could discover the masturbatory references within them. So that when her AP History teacher discussed "disciplining Galileo" or her English teacher characterized criticism as "a mental push-and-pull exercise," or Ronald Reagan spoke of "piling deficit upon deficit," Michelle and Barry and whoever else could bark out *"Which is what I'll be doing when I get home tonight,"* or the more economical abbreviation of said phrase: the exclamation "Which!"

During the inauguration broadcast, Michelle began by shouting "Which!" when Reagan spoke of a "solemn and momentous occasion." Tewlow countered by barking "Which!" when the president spoke of "mortgaging our future." Michelle cried "Which!" when Reagan said the country should be "managed by self-rule." A trio of voices responded with "Whiches" to Reagan's call to "unleash the energy and individual genius of man." And nearly a quarter exclaimed "Which!" when Reagan decried "limiting ourselves to small dreams."

All the while, as Deirdre stood at the back of this unruly study hall, Matthias Kimmel was fuming. When a third of those present cried out "Which!" in response to "measuring progress in inches and feet," "reawakening this industrial giant," and finally, "acting worthy of yourself," Kimmel stood, red-faced, short of breath, his hands balled up into fists. "Ignorant," he said quietly, then said it louder. "Ignorant. You're all ignorant." The world was moving on, he said. Times were changing. Accountability was coming. The end of government handouts and welfare queens was imminent. He would not stand for people pillorying what they didn't understand. *Then sit down,* someone shouted. No, Matthias said, he wouldn't sit down. In fact, he was going to stand on his desk to be heard. Sit down before you *fall* down, Barry Tewlow called out as Kimmel mounted his desk, just as Ronald Reagan's proclamation that he would endure, fight cheerfully, "and do my utmost, as if the issue of the whole struggle depended on me alone" triggered bellicose roars of "Which!" Barry whipped a paperback *Julius Caesar* at Matthias, who blocked the book with a quick forearm.

At that moment, it seemed as if all pandemonium was breaking loose; students were rummaging through bookbags for paperbacks to hurl; Ed Ruggierio was waving around a flask of whiskey and shouting "Party with Jack! Who wants to party with Jack?" Michelle was yelling for everyone to stop it—this was no way for people to conduct themselves; they were missing tons of good "Whiches." Vice Principal Mulvey had entered to shout at the students, threatening suspensions, detentions, and parental notifications as a copy of *Babbitt* whizzed over his head.

But a split second later, the chaos suddenly stopped dead; the study hall turned silent, and all eyes were fixed on Ms. Wills. She did not avert her gaze from the students until every single one of them had returned to his or her books. Vice Principal Mulvey stared at her, dumbfounded, awestruck. What had happened, he wanted to know, what had she done? How had she commanded such respect? "I turned off the TV," Deirdre Wills said. At the end of the study period, Mulvey told Deirdre that, come September, there would be a position opening up in Mather's English department and he couldn't imagine a better-qualified candidate. He asked if she'd have time to discuss it over dinner. Deirdre thanked him for the offer but told him she wanted to see what other jobs might be available before she made any commitment. And besides, she was busy that evening anyway, cooking dinner for a "special friend."

That night, Deirdre cooked dinner for three, but Muley was already out filming when Lloyd Cubbins arrived. When Lloyd had told Deirdre that he did not see either of his sons more than a few times a year, she had suggested they dine together on a weekly basis. This was the third time Lloyd had been over in as many weeks, even though Lloyd said he got along fine on his own and she didn't have to worry about him. And on this occasion, as on the two previous ones, Lloyd asked Deirdre whether "my boy Melvin" would be coming by. Deirdre did not ignore the question as she had the two times it had previously been posed. This time, as she told Lloyd to sit down—she didn't need his help clearing the plates—she said that she was no longer talking to Mel, not since he had done something she could not forgive. After Lloyd pressed her, she gave him the

details—how Mel had used Lloyd's stories, how he had wanted to turn Tiny Cubbins's tragedy into entertainment.

After he made a move to take his plate to the sink, then thought better of it,
Lloyd asked her if that was all she was angry about. Yes, Deirdre said, wasn't that
enough? Lloyd said it didn't sound all that bad to him; no one had a right to his
own story. Once someone heard a story, it became their story too. He told
Deirdre that she should call Mel, maybe even that night. Deirdre said she certainly would not be calling Mel that night, she had better and more important
things to do.

After Lloyd had gone home and had told Deirdre that it would be nice to see
Melvin at their dinner the next week, Deirdre went to her bookshelf and pulled
out a worn, handwritten original manuscript, one that she hadn't read in years:
"The Talented Assistant," by Dr. Lewis Ridle. Just a little before midnight, after
she had finished reading it, she held it in her hands for more than a minute before she brought it to Muley's bedroom. He was still out filming, so she left it on
his pillow and wrote a short note, which she placed beside it. In it, she said that
she knew that Muley had always liked games, anagrams, and puzzles. She suggested he rearrange the letters of the story's author to see what it might spell. For
a moment, she felt a slight, soft dampness in her left eye, which she blinked away
before she closed the door to Muley's bedroom. Then she got a pen and a pad
of paper out of a drawer and sat up in bed writing as she waited for her son to
come home.

M eanwhile, that same day in Malibu, Carl Silverman was supervising a
recording session for a John Lennon tribute album produced by the
Slappit Penny Lane Foundation. The foundation had been incorporated as a
not-for-profit the day after Silverman had learned at LAX of Lennon's assassination. Carl held the positions of foundation president, vice president, and treasurer. The corporation's mission, Carl had written, was to preserve the music of
the Beatles in general and Lennon in particular.

For Carl, it had proved substantially easier to approach musicians about
a charity project as opposed to a new album. In most negotiations, he found
himself haggling over $200 on a $50,000 deal; in the case of the tribute album,
he offered each artist one shiny new penny for their contributions while all

"proceeds"—that is, all monies not earmarked to pay the foundation's president, vice president, and treasurer—would be donated to charity. Nearly every artist in the Slappit catalog signed on to the project and posed for publicity shots, smiling and holding their pennies for the cameras. Disbanded groups with careers cut short by acrimonious splits regrouped not only for the double album but also for the foundation's anticipated all-day tribute concert to be held at the Hollywood Bowl. The media, which in late 1980 had lambasted Silverman, now in 1981 lauded his efforts in an endless procession of puff pieces.

On January 20, an all-star band calling themselves the Penny Dreadfuls gathered in Carl's home to record the album. And every star performer arrived on time. Carl had hoped that the album would allow him to pay some bills and counteract the ill will that had been dogging him, so that he might approach investors for the *Godfathers* film project. But the cooperation the project engendered was beyond any he could have conceived. What he had considered a one-shot deal presented itself as a viable alternative career. The morbidity rate in the music business, particularly rock 'n' roll, was depressingly high. Several times a year, there would be an opportunity for another tribute album, another charity concert for a dead artist who would inspire a whole series of tributes by Slappit Artists, all of whom would sign on for a penny apiece. Airlines would sponsor the tours, fast-food restaurants would cater them, beer distributors would pay for the venues, any superstars in need of repairing an image without resorting to an overpublicized religious conversion would donate their talent and their time.

At the end of the day, when the limousines had lined up in Carl's driveway, when a who's who of the L.A. music scene had begun exiting the mansion, the feisty, short, and ill-tempered lead singer of a certain UK band, whose first hit had been a blues number entitled "Don't You Do That Thang," approached Carl and offered his hand and an apology. He said he was sorry for having called Carl a "tosser," he was sorry for having rubbed his Slappit contract against his groin before returning it to Carl with his "crotch residue" on it, he was sorry for having "hurled" in Carl's hot tub. And he further apologized for having signed with a rival record company. But that didn't matter, he said, for he was willing to re-sign with Slappit now. All Carl had to do was say yes and not only would *he* return, he was certain that nearly everyone else who had abandoned Slappit would come back too. So, he asked Carl, half a smile forming on his reptilian face as he cupped Carl's shoulder, "*Wot* do ya *sigh* to *thaht,* mate?"

The response seemed a foregone conclusion. Carl never said no to financial arrangements that could benefit him. But on that day, when Carl should have been thinking of the next charity project, he was actually thinking about *Godfathers of Soul,* and just a little bit about Deirdre and Muley Wills; mostly about *Godfathers of Soul,* it was true, but still a little bit about Deirdre and Muley, too.

"I'd love to, but I can't, brother," Carl said. "I gotta move my white ass back to Chicago."

ROVNER

Ellen Leventhal & Michael

Though no one in her family knew, Ellen Leventhal had already been back in Chicago for a week and a half when she drove to the house in Lake Geneva, the only possession she retained from her nearly twenty-year marriage to Michael Rovner. She had stayed in Paris for more than six weeks, and though she first thought of leaving after a claustrophobic New Year's Eve melee on the traffic-choked Champs-Élysées, she remained there well into January.

After two weeks at Julius Bernard's apartment, she had begun to feel vaguely like a prostitute. Not because she'd had sex with Julius; rather because she hadn't. The entire time in Paris, he only showed up twice, with the perfunctory and proprietary air of a landlord checking up to surprise a tenant late with the rent. He spent all but the first evening elsewhere, and that particular evening had been so awkward that, at separate points, both parties offered to spend it in a hotel. Ellen had assumed the overly formal demeanor Julius had exhibited in Paris the previous year had been designed to maintain the illusion of platonic intentions in front of her daughter, and once they reunited in Paris, all pretense would be removed and with it, thankfully, all sense of decency.

But as Ellen knew, events rarely occurred in the manner described in her patients' narratives. She would have liked to experience something approaching one of Nola Mulvey's sordid accounts of anonymous sex, to be able to say, as Edwina Benske frequently did, "I couldn't wait for it anymore; my panties were just sopping." Ellen's "panties" had never been "sopping." Once in a very long while, maybe a teaspoon, but sopping? Alas, alone in the presence of Julius Bernard, no clothing item needed changing, particularly not "panties." His conduct was stiff, clumsy. He grabbed her shoulders too hard when he greeted her, kissed the air so far away from her cheek that she did not even hear a sound, offered compliments that would have sounded more appropriate from her great-uncle Sholem: that she was "a handsome woman" and "quite, quite learned." He spent much of the time standing uncomfortably; when he finally sat down, it was at the very edge of an ottoman, where he rested an ankle upon a knee, clutching the knee with both hands.

Ellen's efforts to loosen up the atmosphere were fruitless. He continually misinterpreted her sexually frank discussion as referencing some other man not present. When she remarked that his bed was tremendously comfortable but too large to sleep in alone, Julius said the apartment was hers; he didn't mind if she had visitors. When Ellen said she enjoyed her solitude but was thankful someone had arrived to add some romance to her stay, Julius asked whether this "someone" might be coming by later. And because she was irritated with Julius's thickheadedness, she invented a romance with Raoul, the humpbacked waiter at the Café De La Paix. After which Julius further distanced himself, not wanting to interfere with the budding romance between Ellen and Raoul. And after Ellen became so frustrated that she just came out and said that there was, in fact, no Raoul, that she'd tried her best to be subtle and now she wasn't sure whether Julius's inability to read a hint was pathetic or insulting, it was too late. Julius remarked that she had "wonderfully buoyant" breasts and he enjoyed watching how they "swung." Ellen told him she would sleep on the sofa.

The decision to leave France and move back to Lake Geneva, where she would set up a modest psychology practice that could double as a bed-and-breakfast for those in need of extensive treatment, came on January 1, but Ellen wanted to wait at least ten more days to return in case there was a funeral for her father that she would rather miss. The last time she had seen Max Leventhal, he had been so uncharacteristically kind that she assumed he had only a few weeks left. Still, as he clasped her hand and told her how well she looked, she remained unmoved. For Ellen valued consistency more than kindness. Which was why she resisted the temptation to write postcards to either of her children, for fear of presenting to them an inconsistent image of herself, and why she sought at all costs to avoid any of the funereal niceties she would have to exchange with the bereaved—Michael's concerned gazes, the *brachas* Larry would solemnly intone, the slim, black dress Lana would charge especially for the occasion. People often said funerals weren't for the departed; they were for the living, and Ellen had little desire to spend any time with them.

She let no one know of her return to Chicago or of her departure. She closed out her Lincoln Federal account, didn't reconnect her phone, didn't collect her mail from the post office until the day she was leaving for Wisconsin. She made only one potentially risky move and that was on the day she left. She was taking Devon west toward McCormick Boulevard, but when she crossed California, she was moved by both nostalgia and morbid curiosity to see the Sacramento house, the one where she thought she might live forever, or at least where it seemed as if she might have thought that once. The risk was not great—Larry was in Massachusetts, Lana was in school, and Michael was either at the hospital or in the shower with Steve Ross. Yet her heartbeat quickened when she turned onto Sacramento. At Chippewa Park, she tapped the brakes lightly and turned toward the old house, wanting to see and feel the smallness of the world she'd left behind. But if she thought she was leaving it, it was leaving her too. There was a "For Sale" sign planted in the front lawn and new Astroturf carpeting on the front steps.

She was curious about the sign, curious about where Michael might be moving—perhaps to some swinging bachelor pad on the Magnificent Mile as he always wanted, perhaps to Steve Ross's house where the men could take out the kiddy pool and install a Jacuzzi. She was curious, but not curious enough to take down the real estate agent's number. She was curious, but not as curious as she was when she arrived in Lake Geneva and found the bedroom's beautiful, unfinished wooden walls plastered over with ghastly wallpaper—hospital white with a fruit bowl pattern.

The wallpaper was in the cupboards and in all three upstairs bedrooms. On the walls, there were posters she didn't recognize—Monets, Renoirs, and Kliban cats. There was a rocking chair on the screened-in front porch and beside it, a magazine rack with copies of *Better Homes and Gardens*. The couches were covered with plastic. On the rear porch, the lake view was now obscured by a stereo inside a tall, lacquered wooden housing, which contained easy-listening records beginning with Herb Alpert and concluding with Bobby Vinton. From the attic, there came odd mewing and fluttering sounds. She wondered if Michael had sold the place, or if he had already moved in and redecorated in that nouveau immigrant style she had consistently overruled, leading her to rip off all the plastic he had wanted to keep on the furniture, to apply paint thinner to the dining room table to remove the clear plastic Contac paper he had affixed to it, to forbid Astroturf on the outside steps.

Unable to decide on a course of action, Ellen walked out into the backyard to look at Lake Geneva, a giant snow-dusted ice rink. She wondered how long the temperature had been below freezing, if it would be all right to skate, if her skates were still in the basement. She reentered the house to look for them and had just opened the basement door when she heard a key in the front lock.

Ellen stopped dead. Outrage slowly filled her from stomach to throat. She half-expected Michael to appear in the doorway with a slack-jawed "Honey, what's wrong?" expression on his face. She half-expected to see some pantsuited real estate agent, blow-dried and curling-ironed within an inch of her life. What she did not expect was to see Lennie Kidd in a safari jacket and pith helmet rubbing his frozen hands together and stamping his combat boots, crystals of ice in his unkempt black beard.

"Dr. Rovner," he said, momentarily surprised, then confused as if he had misunderstood something, as if the past months of his life had been an illusion dreamed up during his weekly session. Ellen asked softly, as if scolding a well-meaning child, what he was doing here. Lennie said he had been under the impression she wasn't returning. Who had given him that impression, she wondered, *Michael?* Oh, that would have been rich, for Steve Ross to have turned down Michael's advances and for him to have taken up with this first available male. A series of images of copulating balloon animals played out before her. No, Lennie said, Dr. Mandell had told him. *Cheryl?* Ellen asked. She told Lennie to take off his boots and coat and sit with her in the front room. Lennie asked if there would be an hourly charge. No, Ellen said, she trusted the explanation wouldn't take that long.

The explanation Lennie provided was, by turns, appalling and hilarious. Lennie, against Ellen's advice, had returned to Chicago to take over at WBOE for Donna Mayne, who'd been relieved of her duties. Still, he hadn't wanted to inform his mother he was coming home. He'd tried to track down Dr. Rovner and had learned that Cheryl had taken over her practice. In their first session, Lennie told Cheryl that he had no place to live except his mother's house and wouldn't be getting his first check from the radio station for at least another week. Cheryl suggested that he borrow her car and stay at her "lover's" house in Lake Geneva, which she was redecorating. Ellen asked Lennie if he was aware that this was her house, that in the divorce papers, the house was the only item to which she had laid claim. Lennie said Cheryl had mentioned something about that, but said she was fairly sure Ellen wasn't coming back—there had been a funeral for her father and she hadn't even managed to attend—and in the unlikely scenario that Ellen did return, "she'd be cool with it." Ellen asked if he had any idea where Cheryl was. Lennie said she was in Maui with "her lover."

W hen the phone rang in Room 3737 of the Maui Sheraton, Michael Rovner was lying on his back, dead asleep on the king-sized bed, a filled condom dangling off of his penis as Dr. Cheryl Mandell, dripping wet, wrapped herself in a heavy, white Sheraton towel and picked up the receiver. The trip to Maui had been her idea, intended to test whether they were truly compatible, whether they could truly be "lovers." Ellen had always cringed at the word "lover," but Cheryl used it constantly, greeted "Michael-san" with it when he picked up the phone the morning after their first sexual experience together (in an empty room in the geriatric ward of Swedish Covenant). An entire row and a half of her bedroom bookshelf was devoted to books with "Love," "Lover," or "Loving" in the title—half of them had photos and diagrams, which was Michael's first inkling that he had found a soulmate, someone who enjoyed pornography almost as much as he did. It was Cheryl who convinced Michael that it would be okay to let Lana stay with a friend's family for a week—she thought that it would be good for Lana.

Before Cheryl picked up the phone and withstood Ellen's verbal assault, she and Michael had just completed their third night together and their seventh time having sex in the position she mistakenly called "Congress with a Crow." Michael, exhausted but content beyond words, slept through the entire phone call. Cheryl—first defensive, then accusing—explained to Ellen that Michael had planned on selling the Sacramento house, splitting the profits with Ellen, and using his half to purchase a Gold Coast condo so that Lana could attend a good public high school near the prestigious private ones that had rejected her. She told Ellen that the sale of the Sacramento house would generate enough cash to buy a house nicer than the one in Lake Geneva. A short time later, she berated Ellen for treating a "terrific man and a terrific lover" so poorly. The last thing Cheryl—finally resigned—said to Ellen was, "Well, then, that's the way it will have to be." The remark came in response to Ellen's assertion that she would never move out of the Lake Geneva house, that she planned to live, work, and die there, and that if either she or her "lover" trespassed on her property, Lars, her "lumberjack lover," would shoot them on sight. "Isn't that right, Lars?" she said. "Damn right," Lennie barked back. Then Cheryl, the phone conversation concluded, lovingly snapped off the condom adorning her sleeping lover, carried it to the toilet, and flushed it down.

When Ellen hung up, she sighed and closed her eyes. When she opened them, Lennie was slinking upstairs. He stopped halfway up and told Ellen not to worry, he was leaving. There just were some belongings he needed to retrieve. Ellen said she thought he didn't have any place to sleep. That was true, Lennie said, but he knew Ellen was angry and he assumed she wanted to be alone. Actually, Ellen said, she did want to be alone, but if he didn't have anywhere to go, she wouldn't kick him out. Lennie asked if that meant he could stay with her until he got his first check. Ellen told him he'd be paying to stay at her house, but not with his check; she didn't really need the money. Instead, she would put him to work. He would remove all the horrid wallpaper, rip off the plastic covers that had been placed over the furniture—in short, return the house to the same condition in which she had left it. In exchange, Ellen said, she'd allow him to sleep in her basement. Okay, Lennie said, but would it be all right if he took care of something personal first? Ellen asked if there was any reason it couldn't wait until later. Lennie said he supposed not.

Late that night, after Lennie had installed new locks, Ellen Leventhal, newly orphaned, sat on her screened-in back porch with an afghan over her feet, a mug of hot cocoa in her hands, her ice skates beside her. Upon occasion, she thought about her father, but mostly she thought about the view. She loved gazing at the bare maples, their branches arching over the snowy pathway that led down to the frozen lake. For a brief moment, an image of Lana floated before her. She wondered if what Cheryl Mandell had told her—that everything was fine and that Lana was staying with a friend—was true. She thought maybe she should call to make sure. But when she phoned the Sacramento house and no one answered, she assumed Cheryl had been telling her the truth and that she herself had been right all along. Her children, after all, were better off without her.

Ellen Rovner finished her cocoa. She put on her skates and walked gingerly over the crackling snow and ice to the lake. The only sound she could hear at first as she glided, then twirled, past the backs of Wisconsin mansions, their TVs tuned to news of the hostage release and the inauguration, was that of her own skates slicing and scraping the lake. But then that sound was joined by a fluttering and a twittering, then a flapping of wings, and Ellen looked up to see a half-dozen parakeets silhouetted against the night sky. In her backyard, which seemed to fairly pulse with light, Lennie was standing and smiling. He held an empty cage.

WASSERSTROM

Charlie

A t the beginning of Charlie Wasserstrom's stint as critic for the Schiffler Newspapers, his column, "The Wasserstrom Watch," was limited to his restaurant recommendations. The column was popular, particularly with restaurateurs who favored Charlie's policy to not write about any establishment whose cuisine he did not favor and to give every restaurant a second chance. The mail, largely planted by family members of restaurant owners, was overwhelmingly positive. And in a marked change from Gail Schiffler-Bass's reign, there had not been a single death threat. The worst criticism came from a miffed Alan Farbman, who blamed the closing of It's in the Pot! on lack of coverage in "Chuck's column."

But one week when Charlie was suffering from food poisoning and had consumed only Coke, Mister Salty pretzels, and plain rye toast, he suggested to Gail that he skip his column for the week. That was impossible, she said, people had come to expect the column and, more important, ad space had been sold against it. Charlie protested that he had nothing food-related to write about. Gail said that was all right, but he'd have to write about something else.

The day his column was due, his tongue pink from Pepto-Bismol, Charlie racked his brain for things worth writing about, but he led, in his estimation, a very uneventful life. He woke up and made breakfast for his wife and his daughters, he puttered around the house, he fielded phone calls from restaurant owners who pled for coverage. And he struggled to write his column, first longhand on legal paper, then typed with two fingers at a rate of one key every two seconds—700 words a week that Gail invariably sent back marked up with red pencil. At a loss for how to complete this week's column, he instead wrote a laundry list of the previous day's events: his older daughter was interviewing for colleges, and though he hoped the interviews would go well, he would be happy if she got into college anywhere, because he regretted that he had never gone. He had had a long conversation with his younger daughter, who, though it was winter break, was already researching a report for Humanities class about South Africa's apartheid regime. He had gone grocery shopping at Dominick's and decided against buying his favorite raspberry coffee cake because his doctor had warned him to eat only foods that didn't put a strain on his heart. He had watched TV and couldn't believe how much "off-color humor" was on during prime time.

When Charlie had filled up four pages with these and other, similar entries, he walked into Gail's offices and presented them to her. He hadn't even bothered typing them up, just placed them in front of her as if to say, "That's my life, I have nothing worth writing about." He hoped she'd understand but feared she'd be angry. Instead, she said that this was by far the best thing he'd written, that he shouldn't change a word, that it would be the one part of the paper everyone would read. She blocked out additional space for "The Wasserstrom Watch" and relabeled it "Life of Charlie." Charlie thought it was a joke, but it wasn't. Letters soon arrived, praising "Life of Charlie" as a "breath of fresh air," and "the side of the American man that we don't normally see; what a shame he's married."

The only dissenting voice came from Charlie's younger daughter, who, though she didn't want to hurt his feelings, said as the family sat around the dinner table the day the first column came out that she didn't think it was right for him to use her and her sister's names in print. Michelle said she liked seeing her name in print and hoped that "whichever prep school prick" would be interviewing her for Yale would see the article. Charlie said he didn't really see any problem with writing about his children—he would always write "about good things" that made him happy or proud. Michelle said he could write about her "bad shit" too—he could write about her weekend evenings and win a Pulitzer for exposing "the depravity of contemporary youth." Jill said she understood that she didn't have the legal right to her own story, but still, professional journalists had to check quotes with their sources. Charlie asked if it would be all right if he showed her what he wrote before it was printed in the paper. Jill said that only half-addressed her concerns, but he could do as he chose. Charlie said all right, that's what he'd do. And maybe sometime, she and Michelle could contribute to his column. Gail said that was a great idea; people would really eat it up.

When Charlie decided that the presidential inauguration could be a worthwhile topic to explore in "Life of Charlie," he thought (or at least Gail thought and he wholeheartedly agreed) that the occasion would be one worth honoring by including the thoughts of his daughters—the next American generation. Michelle demurred when Charlie asked her to write a page of her thoughts on the inauguration, citing "interview crap" for which she had to prepare. She sensed that Gail, not her father, was behind the idea, and though she had told Gareth that she and Gail had "deescalated" their conflict and arrived at a "shaky détente" (the Bulletin of the Atomic Scientists had pushed the Atomic Schiffler Clock back to fourteen minutes before midnight, she said), she was still uninterested in contributing. Before locking herself in her room with the Yale college catalog, which she hoped to memorize before her interview, she told her father to invent her quotes and make her "sound smart." Jill, on the other hand, typed up three pages along with specific instructions indicating that Charlie was welcome to make edits but that she hoped he would clear them with her. Charlie requested and received extra space so that he could incorporate as many of Jill's observations as possible. Although he did not agree with much of what she wrote, did not support the position that sometimes the best way to reform a political system was to overthrow it completely, did not admire Fidel Castro, and had no idea who Antonio Gramsci was, he still thought it important for her to express her views. Charlie had not voted for Reagan, but he did not share Jill's animosity for the man. He felt comfortable and confident when he saw Reagan speak. He was also looking forward to reduced inflation and lower taxes, which were among the reasons Reagan had received the endorsement of the Schiffler Newspapers.

To his surprise, on the Tuesday Charlie arrived at his office, he found a copy of his column filled with more red marks than he had received since he had started writing "Life of Charlie." Every sentence of Jill's had been crossed out; in its place, Gail had substituted the following sentences: "My youngest daughter, Jill, was dissatisfied with the November election. She called it a 'travesty' and thinks we not only need a new president but a new government. But then again, she's not even fourteen yet; she doesn't really know what inflation is, and she has never filled out a tax return."

Charlie always deferred to Gail's judgment. He thought she was his protection against being revealed as the fraud he usually thought himself to be. But in this instance, he went down the hall to her office. Gail told Charlie she knew exactly why he had come to see her, that as a "parent," she understood why he would want to let Jill publish her "inflammatory prose." But she also had to think like a newspaper publisher, and she encouraged Charlie to think like the husband of a newspaper publisher. For it was likely, she said, that if Jill's remarks were published, many local businesses, car dealerships in particular, would pull their advertising. She wanted to know if Charlie thought it was worth the lost ad revenue to publish the ravings of a thirteen-year-old who would probably retract them if she ever found a boyfriend. Charlie told Gail she was right; he would leave in all the changes. He would try to explain them to Jill when she got home from school.

To Charlie, Jill seemed surprisingly understanding when he explained those changes that night. After Charlie walked into her room, where she'd been dusting off the movie projector she had taken out of her closet, he showed her the galley copy with the red lines through her words and the new sentences Gail had added. Jill merely nodded, made a doodle in the margin, and said she had expected as much. Charlie touched a hand to Jill's suddenly tense shoulder and made some remarks about life being a great series of compromises and that he wished someone had told him that when he'd been younger and saved him from a great many disappointments. Jill told her father she realized that compromises needed to be made, that money and comfort were more important than principles, that if people were paying you, it was best to believe what those people wanted you to believe. "That's the way it is, Charlie," she said as she threaded a length of film through her projector. She asked him to hit the lights on his way out.

Charlie smiled. He was surprised by how much his daughter had understood, how quickly she had grown. He told her he was going up to get a Popsicle and he asked if she wanted one. No, Jill said, she had work to do. Charlie patted her head and told her that was all right; she should just know that there were Popsicles in the freezer if she wanted any. As Charlie closed the door to his daughter's room and headed upstairs to bed, he had no idea that the doodle his daughter had made in the margin of the galley was the word "stet," an editing term she'd learned at school, meaning ignore all edit marks and leave everything as previously written. He would come to understand that fact when the paper came out on Thursday and the first calls from the car dealers and the members of the Chicago Republican Party would flood the Schiffler editorial offices. But for this moment, all he felt was happiness and pride.

WILLS / SILVERMAN

Peachy Moskowitz

Donna Mayne, formerly children's programming director at WBOE, had not yet found an apartment in Milwaukee when she arrived for the second day of her new job at WMPR, the local public radio station. She had eschewed staying with either of her brothers in Racine and instead chose the Pfister Hotel, a luxury she could in no way afford yet felt she deserved after the fiasco that followed the Jack Benny Awards shutout. It would have been better if she had been told directly that her job was only secure insofar as Washington continued to fund her programs and that that funding was dependent primarily on awards. But the constant reassurances she received—even after the cancellations of *Young Town* and *Chi-Town Chatterbox*—up until the day she was dismissed had left her with few options outside of Milwaukee, where she had started her career fifteen years earlier.

Still, change was welcome. Donna had grown weary of working twelve-hour days for $20,000 a year. She was eager to work with adults, thus avoiding the time wasted by telling Pablo De La Fuente to stop swearing ("But I'm only saying 'Fudgestick Dam,'" he would always insist), cautioning Lisa-Anne Williams to refrain from fingering the cross around her neck because the microphone picked up the sound, or insisting that Lana Rovner put back those pencils unless she was planning to pay for them. Even Michelle Wasserstrom grated on her, always arriving in character: "*Eexcyuse, plizz,* so *soddy* I arrive *een shtudio retarded;* my Volga *steel een* shop. Must *tekk sheet-ess pyooblic trenshportayshun.*" When Lennie Kidd took his "leave of absence," Donna was thrilled to finally be able to put her stamp on the station's children's programming and was flabbergasted when Scott Blackwell of WBOE told her one month later that he wanted "to go in a new direction," that the station had never recovered from Lennie's departure. That someone in Blackwell's position could so easily be duped by a neurotic fraud with whom she had only slept twice was sufficient reason for her to be glad to return to Milwaukee.

What she liked most about the Milwaukee station was that it was not as well funded as its Chicago counterpart, and consequently couldn't afford anything approximating *Young Town.* All there was money for was her salary, a half-time assistant, and an engineer (she had left a message for Mel Coleman, but he had not returned her calls). And that meant that she would have to rely solely on what she had always thought made the best, most economical radio: talk. The shows she would produce, *Storytime* and *Teens Talk to Teens,* she explained to program director Lance Busby, could be produced quickly and affordably, which would be crucial in light of what would probably be a new climate in the nation's capital, far less appreciative of public radio.

Busby, whom she had not met on her first day but had only seen zipping up and down the hallway, a pair of headphones around his neck, looked nearly young enough to be her son. And the reason she had neglected to introduce herself Monday was that she had assumed him to be a college intern, the position he had held four and a half years earlier. He was tall, lanky, and eager, with dangly limbs, as if his body was not through adjusting to his most recent growth spurt. As they sat in his office, he apologized for not having had a chance to talk with her or introduce her to anyone. He said half the staff was out in Washington dealing with the inauguration, and many tasks, such as reading the news and announcing the names of those who had won WMPR tote bags, now fell to him. He told her he admired her work and thought it was a coup that the station had been able to lure her out of Chicago. He said that he'd been on the executive committee for the Jack Benny Awards for the past four years, and though he hadn't cast a ballot for *Young Town,* he deeply admired what that show was "trying to do." The one award he had voted to give one of her shows was the Creativity in Children's Programming honor, which the Peachy Moskowitz segment had won. He said that the executive committee was sorry that they couldn't have given more awards to Moskowitz and her cousin Muley, but they had only been nominated in the fiction categories, which he said must have been a clerical error: Clearly Moskowitz was a real person. For, he said, why would a fictional character host a talk show? Donna said evasively that there had been a lot of debate on the question of how to handle the Moskowitz character. She hoped the subject would end there. It didn't. Busby noddingly acknowledged Donna's programming ideas but kept steering her back to Moskowitz—with her own show, what a model she could be for listeners young and old.

Donna had no interest in pursuing this line of thought. Yes, it would be great, she said. Unfortunately, Peachy was no longer in the country; hadn't he heard the last episode? No, Busby said, he hadn't. Although Donna had cringed throughout the long good-bye Michelle had given to "all my *byooteefull,* loyal *leesuners*" the day *Chi-Town Chatterbox* was canceled, not to mention the shudders she felt when a tearful Lana Rovner instructed listeners to send letters of protest, Michelle's histrionic performance now served Donna well. She repeated as much as she could remember of Michelle's monologue about how her *"darlink fahther"* had *"wreeten"* her a letter asking her to return to see him "one *lest* time before they *tekk* me to Siberia," where he had been sentenced for protesting the war in Afghanistan.

Busby turned serious. Well, that was a problem, he said. Donna said she didn't really see it as a problem. Right, Busby said, he knew she didn't, but he did. You see, he said, he'd justified to his boss the financing for her position on the basis of bringing the same kind of programming both of them had admired. Donna said that of course she would bring the same *kind* of programming, just not the exact same program, because, she repeated, that program's star was already in Siberia. Busby said he wished they'd had this conversation earlier, but there hadn't been time and he'd been so excited to get someone from Chicago— that was a feather in his cap and, he said darkly, his best argument for keeping her around.

Donna inhaled deeply. For years, she had known that anytime she took a job outside of radio, she would never return to the medium. Programmers' jobs were dwindling; so were independent stations. When WBOE had let her go, Donna had sent her résumé and demo cassettes to every public station. Busby was the only person who had answered, and now it was clear that it was only because of a misunderstanding. Maybe she should just leave right now, she thought, find a profession more lucrative than radio—most all of them were. And yet every other option seemed so much like defeat.

Donna said it was a shame about Peachy; she assumed he had already known. "No, sir," he said, "no, sir." Donna said Peachy had exhibited great bravery in returning to Russia, a beautiful selflessness in choosing to sacrifice fame for family duty. It was a great loss for the country and for radio as well. Yeah, said Lance. Donna said she assumed Lance wouldn't be interested in a talk show hosted by Peachy Moskowitz's sister Bunny. Lance said he didn't remember any of the Moskowitz shows mentioning Bunny. That's right, Donna said, Peachy had never discussed her on the air. Lance paused for a moment. How old was this Bunny Moskowitz? he wanted to know.

R O V N E R

Larry

E ven before the January 20, 1981, Anti-Inauguration party was held at The Castle at Brandeis, Larry Rovner was already wondering if the period of wild sexual experimentation that had characterized his first semester was reaching a premature close. It had only been October when he had visited the campus health center because the rim of his penis was chapped from excessive friction.

The doctor had given him a tube of cream to apply three times daily to the affected area and told him to "ease up for a week." But Larry found the process of applying the cream so arousing that it led to a seemingly endless cycle of chafing, either self- or Hannah Goodman–induced, followed by excessive cream application.

The only relief came over Thanksgiving weekend, which Larry spent in Manhattan with the Goodman family at their Upper East Side apartment. Hannah's parents gave Larry and Hannah their bed while they slept in Hannah's younger sister Liesel's room and Liesel slept over at her boyfriend's house. Sex, to Larry, was most appealing when it was forbidden, and the idea of parent-sanctioned sex—especially when accompanied by Mrs. Goodman's instructions as to where extra sheets and washcloths were located and Mr. Goodman's winking admonition to "try to keep it down in there, kids"—left Larry not so much impotent as uninterested. Throughout the weekend, Hannah kept saying how "cool" her parents were. Weren't they *cool* for letting her and Larry have sex whenever they wanted, weren't they cool for putting her on the pill when she was fourteen, weren't they cool for hiring a limo so she and her sister could see Neil Diamond last year? Larry shrugged. He was similarly unimpressed that Saturday when Hannah announced that her father had given them his Bloomingdale's charge plate so that they could pick out a new bed for her dorm room. Larry had sat there in the bedding department feeling a bit guilty that he wasn't in shul but mostly just bored. He'd been perfectly happy sleeping on his used dorm room mattress with the yellow-brown stains that looked like countries on a map. And now here he was, asked to discuss whether the Serta Perfect Sleeper, whose foxy spokesmodel Joey Heatherton had once inspired his masturbatory fantasies, was worth $100 extra. He thought of how much money Hannah's father had authorized her to spend, thought of what he could buy with that money—a Stratocaster, a Les Paul—and became disgusted. Beds were for people who no longer had sex at all; the more money you spent, the less sex you had. As he sat on the edge of a department store mattress while Hannah quizzed the salesman, he could see her plotting, see the whole Goodman family plotting, luring him in with sexual favors and the promise of expensive goods. Then, when he least expected it, they'd ask him when he was taking his LSATs, wasn't it time to get started on a family, shouldn't he put the music aside? He began composing a song about Hannah's father, one called "Mr. Richman." ("Hey, Mr. Rich-man / I won't ever be your bitch, man"). He would premiere the song at the Anti-Inauguration party along with his other recent opuses, "Too Much Sex" and the reggae cover "Exodus (Movement of Jew People)."

Except Hannah said she wouldn't be at the party. There was a meeting of the spring formal committee, and if she missed it, she was certain they would scrap her idea for a classy Barbra Streisand tribute and adopt Sharon Wishner's vulgar "Fiddlin' on the Roof" theme instead. Hannah had informed Larry of her prior engagement in an offhand "Didn't I tell you?" sort of way at dinner. They had arrived at the cafeteria at five, right when it opened, along with the premeds and the international students. And in the spaghetti line, when Larry asked her if she would be able to help him with his gear, she said she thought she had told him about the meeting. Larry said no, she hadn't told him, but then muttered that he assumed if it wasn't that, it would be something else. Hannah asked what he meant—she could show him the minutes of the last meeting if he didn't believe her. No, he believed her, Larry said, just wasn't it funny that whenever he had a gig, she had something else to do. Well, she *had* had things to do, she said. Sure, Larry said, he'd had things to do too when he'd gone to her grandparents' fiftieth wedding anniversary party in Westport, Connecticut; he'd blown off studying for his Econ midterm when she'd wanted to see *The King and I* ("which sucked my circumcised dick, by the way," he said); he'd missed his grandpa's funeral because he had promised Hannah he'd go to Mexico with her family. Hannah said she didn't understand what he was talking about; he'd said his grandfather was an asshole—even his mother didn't show up for the funeral. That wasn't the point, Larry said. Well, what was the point? Hannah asked.

The point, Larry said, was that he was available for whatever bullshit she wanted to do, while when his father and sister had visited on parents' weekend, all she had done was say "Good to meet you" to Lana and didn't so much as greet his dad. Hannah said that was because his father kept looking at her breasts. Larry said so what, his father looked at everybody's breasts; he wouldn't have given a shit if her mother had looked at his dick in Mexico. Hannah told him to move—he was holding up the spaghetti line and he was being weird. After Larry asked for some Parmesan cheese to sprinkle on his meatballs, he said he thought lots of things were weird, particularly the fact that she had never seen him perform live.

It was true, and Larry had numerous theories about Hannah's nonattendance. Jealousy, for one. Or perhaps she was still upset that when she had told him she wrote poetry, he had said he wouldn't read it—a poem without music was just an unfinished song. Or perhaps she didn't want to know the effect the music would have on her, because then she'd always wonder about the effect it had on other girls. Perhaps she knew he didn't really care what she thought of his music. Here was a girl who had every album ever recorded by Dan Fogelberg, who owned everything on the Top 40. Larry couldn't give two shits about the Top 40. The day he made the Top 40 would be the day he had sold out and he looked to that day with a mixture of pride and regret. He wondered what he'd do with the money from his first gold album. Not buy a bed, he thought; even when he became a millionaire, he'd still keep his mattresses on the floor. He figured he'd donate the money to K.I.N.S., so they could build a state-of-the-art concert facility, that he'd do exactly what Paul McCartney had done when he'd formed Wings. McCartney had gone back to playing small clubs to recapture the excitement of the Beatles' early days in Hamburg and Liverpool. Larry would play Comiskey Park and Poplar Creek, but he'd also play intimate gatherings at K.I.N.S., Ida Crown, and Ezras Israel to remain true to his roots. As they sat down for spaghetti, Larry told Hannah he might stay late at the gig and not to wait up for him.

The trouble was that Hannah did show up at the Anti-Inauguration party after all, though Larry remained completely ignorant of her presence until he hit the stage. Before the show he sat in an empty hallway and went over song lists with his roommate, Nate Yau, a lightning-fast guitarist with a taste for Manchester punk and garage rock. Nate's talent had made Larry embarrassed for ever having relied upon the likes of Gabe Goldstein and Jeff Meltzer—who had sent Larry a postcard telling him he had quit the shul to pursue music and they should really get together and talk. Ever since freshman orientation, Larry and Nate had been best friends. They spent most of their time when they weren't trading chords and songs or going out with their girlfriends—Nate claimed to be dating a girl from his neighborhood in Jackson Heights, Queens, who was still a senior at Stuyvesant High School—discussing the unreasonable sexual demands those girlfriends placed upon them.

Nate would express dismay with Judy Tallon (the name he bestowed upon his mythical girlfriend) for wanting to experiment with anal sex in the backseat of his canary yellow Firebird ("She says it will take three weeks of prep time to get her ready," Nate complained. "Man, I got better things to do with my time"), while

Larry objected to Hannah's checklist approach to sex. He said he longed for his old girlfriend, Michelle, who had been more interested in him for his musical talent than his sexual prowess. Why didn't he just call her up, Nate once asked. Because her father couldn't afford to help them cut an album, Larry said.

Larry and Nate's music was an extension of their friendly-yet-competitive sexual banter—Larry's drum solos besting Nate's boastful guitar licks, which, in turn, shouted down Larry's ever-more-aggressive vocals. When they played guitar together, fingers gripping the frets, heads bobbing back and forth in unison, Larry's Isro and Nate's thin ponytail flapping up and down, Larry wished that sex with Hannah could be as satisfying and spontaneous. Lying underneath Hannah, he would strain to hold in his ejaculate as she provided a Mission Control–like countdown to orgasm. Whereas everything with Nate happened simultaneously and they didn't even have to try.

At least it felt that way to Larry, although Hannah's review of his performance would later suggest otherwise. After her Barbra Streisand theme concept had been voted down, she had scooted tearfully out of her meeting, didn't even stay for the ruggelach, the halvah, or the Hi-C. She went directly to The Castle and sat through every act preceding Rovner!'s. She clapped politely for folksinger Shoshana Brown, a Brandeis senior who dedicated her performance to the Navajo Indians, "the first American hostages." She yelled out the suggestions "aroused" for an emotion and "synagogue" for a place when a Brandeis comedy troupe, the Fourteenth Tribe, requested audience participation. But the moment after Rovner! hit the stage and Nate grabbed the mike and said, "You've heard the crap; now here's the real shit," Hannah pulled out a notepad.

Larry, stunned to see Hannah in the audience with her pad and her pen and livid with her almost contemptuous unresponsiveness to his music, blew the lyrics three times in the opening song, "Don't You Ever Leave Her"—a tough warning to the new president to maintain U.S. support for Israel. He tripped over his Israeli flag cape during the jig he attempted while telling the crowd to "put [their] hands together for Mr. Nate Yau." Later, he accidentally flung a drumstick into the crowd and it beaned Rhonda Meltzer, who was reviewing the show for the *Brandeis Judge.* Larry and Nate nearly came to blows while tuning their instruments for the acoustic portion of the show. Nate asked Larry what the hell was the matter with him, and if "that ugly bitch with the big tits" was distracting him. Larry channeled the anger he felt toward Nate into a searing performance of "Mr. Richman," contorting his mouth into alternating expressions of nausea and fury as he lingered over the words "Rich" and "Bitch." But by then it was too late. There were classes in the morning. Shoshana Brown's small fan club, composed of earnest young women and ever-hopeful boys, had stopped mocking Larry's bumbling rock star antics and went off to her exquisitely appointed off-campus apartment to roll cigarettes, talk politics, and watch TV.

The majority of the people who remained, aside from Hannah Goodman and Rhonda Meltzer, were Nate's acquaintances, whom he'd met during the only meeting of B.A.S.S. (Brandeis Asian Student Society) he had attended. They hadn't left him alone since. They were a clannish bunch, the Asian equivalent of the Hillel Society, continually badgering Nate to join their flag football games and potluck dinners. When he'd turn them down, a few—most notably, B.A.S.S. president Hank Lee—would ask him what he would be doing instead, would he be hanging out with "that American guy"?—meaning Larry. What the fuck did they mean, Nate would ask; they were all American, weren't they? Now they were near the front of the stage at the Anti-Inauguration Party, even though most of their parents had voted for Reagan. They were nursing bottles of Carlsberg and cheering Nate, shouting, "All right, Nate!" and "Come on, Nate!" and "Let Nate sing one already," then chanting, "Nate, Nate, Nate, Nate!" Finally, when Larry unstrapped his guitar, stared darkly at Nate, and told him, "They're your crowd, man; it's all you," a roar of approval rose up from the B.A.S.S. contingent. They woofed and hooted until Nate left the stage to make way for student president Neil Eisen, who led a lackluster chant of "Mondale in '84."

When Larry had envisioned this evening, he had seen it concluding as his performances usually did—on a note of triumph, sharing a plate of fries and gravy with Nate at the Waltham Diner before driving around in Nate's yellow Firebird, trading rhyming couplets and sex stories. But though they shook hands at the end of the set and they both ended up at the diner, they sat at different tables. Nate sat with Hank Lee and his cronies, all of whom were discussing how to rescue Betty Hong—a former B.A.S.S. member who was now dating "some American guy named Gianni Palatucci." Larry, meanwhile, was in a back booth with Hannah.

Hannah told Larry his songs were much better than she had imagined they would be. She liked most of the melodies and some of the lyrics. But she didn't think they sounded right as rock songs. She knew that what she was saying might seem biased because she had never been a big hard-rock fan, but she wondered what would happen if Larry rethought his songs as part of a Broadway show. Maybe he could write a story about a guy, maybe a Jewish guy from Chicago, maybe an Orthodox Jewish guy whose father is a rabbi, who longs to be on Broadway and turns his back on his roots to follow his dream. "Soar" would close the first act when the main character stands before an empty Broadway stage where someday he'll be a star; the song would be reprised at the end of the second act sung by the rabbi when he leaves shul to see his son perform on opening night.

This was quite possibly the most retarded idea Larry had ever heard. The only other thing that came close was when Ben Jacobs, during the first meeting of Rovner!, suggested they all wear matching togas and sandals and call themselves the Crucifiers. But Larry would not say anything to jeopardize this relationship, not when he still needed money to record his next demo, not when there was the possibility that nobody else on campus would want to sleep with him. Later that night, Hannah consulted her diary and determined that she and Larry had not had oral sex in more than a week. And during the moments when the lights were out and Larry Rovner wasn't imagining he was lying naked next to Michelle Wasserstrom, he was thinking long and hard about the sacrifices he would always have to make for his art.

WASSERSTROM

Michelle

Before that Tuesday when Gareth Overgaard drove her downtown to the Garland Building for her Yale interview, Michelle Wasserstrom had already completed five other college interviews, and had been demoralized by how poorly all five had gone. With the exception of Weezie Berkman, a 1956 graduate of Sarah Lawrence, who had put Michelle to work fixing her coffeemaker, all of the interviewers had been stuffy, humorless men. Two were corporate lawyers, one was a surgeon, and the other was the chairman of Midwest fund-raising for Penn, who'd asked her a lot about football. They asked her about her class rank, they asked her about her SAT scores, they asked what her father did for a living, and to what sorts of institutions he donated. Harvard interviewer Mason Gaffney asked how it would feel to be the first member of her family to attend college. Michelle said it had always been hard cooking lard and gruel every night for a family of three, teaching her father English while speaking to him in her rudimentary Yiddish. When Michelle said the word "Yiddish," Gaffney made a brief note.

Throughout the interviews, when it seemed, as it often did, that her responses were failing to impress her interlocutors, she invariably fell back on improbable stories and amateur theatrics. She told Wilbur Ying of Duke that she'd run out of room on her application and thus hadn't made mention of the fact that she spoke fluent Swahili. She explained to Georgetown's Stephen Angotti that the reason her grades were somewhat lower than the university expected for its prospective students was that she had always thought that getting straight A's was a sign of arrogance. None of it seemed to make any impression, not even after Weezie Berkman had complimented her SAT scores and Michelle had responded, "Yeah, they're pretty good, considering I was raised by wolves."

Gareth had said he couldn't make a late night of it—he had an Anthropology class the next morning. Still, he said he was happy to be off campus to avoid both the celebrations and protests of the inauguration—he didn't know whose simplistic, bigoted slogans would infuriate him more. Michelle said that was all right—she just wanted company in case she bungled this interview too, in case she would need to run screaming because her Yale interviewer, Bruce Sternberg, would turn out to be the dastardly Douglas Sternberg's uncle or twin brother or something.

Ever since the euphoric hilarity of the day's study hall and the all-time-best game ever of "Which," Michelle's mood had steadily declined. During her last interview, she had been told that candidates from urban public schools were not as highly regarded as those from private or prep schools, and that it was important for her to "have a Plan B." And now as they merged onto Lake Shore Drive from the Bryn Mawr entrance, Michelle said there was little point in going through with the interview anyway, since her father's name wasn't Walpole, and she had no interest in making small talk with losers who had nothing better to do than volunteer for their alma maters twenty years after graduation. She was certain she would wind up in Bumblefuck, Illinois, where she would have to endure the self-righteous monologues of Myra Tuchbaum, who, since overcoming her depression, had become a sexually abstemious, proselytizing teetotaler who called Michelle frequently to boast about how much weight she had lost or how much fruit juice she had just consumed ("I can't even handle talking to that Jesus freak anymore," Gareth had said). For Michelle, New Haven now seemed out of the question, and she wondered if the evening might be better spent having a Waukegan Night in the Adler Planetarium parking lot, where she said Gareth enjoyed taking his boyfriends. "Fuck you, Wasserstrom," Gareth said; he hadn't been out for a Waukegan Night in months, not since Muley Wills had stopped returning his calls. Michelle asked what had happened—had Gareth been "a naughty, naughty man?" Gareth gave her the finger.

Just before 7 P.M., the Garland Building was already deserted. Michelle had told Gareth to keep a lookout for "drifters" while he waited for her—she had said that Loop office buildings were the sorts of places where people were routinely assaulted at night by individuals who would later be referred to in newspapers as "drifters," "handymen," or men "active in their church." The offices of Mecklenburg, Stamos and Sternberg, attorneys-at-law, had a stale, gritty feel to them, suggestive of the least glamorous aspects of the legal profession—entertainment lawyers for clowns or court-appointed attorneys for traffic court were Michelle's immediate associations.

A receptionist directed Michelle to Bruce Sternberg's corner office, and once Michelle entered and saw the man seated behind his desk, she felt every one of her worst premonitions suddenly being confirmed. The man might have been a cousin, he might have been a fairly young father, but there was little doubt that Bruce Sternberg was forged out of the same genetic material as Douglas Sternberg. The unwavering, rodent-like gaze, the head of tight curls—gray in this instance—the dry, pursed lips that always seemed to be detecting some unexpectedly fishy flavor were all depressingly familiar. She wondered what character she should play, which emotions she should emphasize. She hurriedly rummaged through her mental file drawer, settling on the role of prim, virginal intellectual.

For the first minutes of the interview, after Bruce Sternberg had asked her to sit down and offered her a cup of coffee, Michelle daintily answered all the de rigueur questions about her test scores, her extracurricular activities, her markedly improved grades over the past year. Then, when it seemed as if the greatest danger had passed and Michelle would be able to impress the man with her intimate knowledge of Yale's theater program, Bruce Sternberg—a shiny black shoe atop his desk, an inch of hairy pale skin showing above a droopy black sock—said he noticed Michelle was attending Mather. He wondered if she knew his nephew Douglas.

Michelle bit the inside of her lip hard. She reached instinctively for a cigarette she did not have. The best approach seemed to be to remain innocuous, inoffensive, then quickly move on. Oh, Douglas, sure, she said with the faintest hint of an English accent, she'd worked with him and learned a lot. That's what she liked about Mather: There were so many different teachers, and each could teach you so many different things. Bruce Sternberg said he supposed so. Then he asked Michelle what sort of impression she had of his nephew. Michelle said she tried her best not to be judgmental—her accent was now vaguely Southern—she understood that you could learn something valuable from every single person in the world. Bruce asked what she had learned from his nephew. A lot about life, Michelle said. What did she mean by that? Bruce asked. Oh my dear, Michelle said, laughing, adding that she imagined Bruce was a very good lawyer. Bruce said he didn't spend much time in court anymore. Michelle said that was a shame; someday his nephew would need a good trial lawyer.

The phrase had just slipped out. Michelle instantly felt her throat go dry; she wished this were a courtroom so she could shout "Objection: relevance" or "Objection: asked and answered" or "You're out of order; this whole goddamn court is out of order." And to think that all the past year's struggles had been in vain, that she had dutifully studied every night, curtailed her pot smoking, lowered her alcohol intake, endlessly practiced Amanda's "Watch the parades go by" speech from *The Glass Menagerie* for her monologue class, worked at the North Shore Kosher Bakery and endured the condescending looks of her Pakistani coworkers as they corrected her pronunciation of the word *babka* so she could pay for an SAT prep class. And all for what? So she could endure the pesky questions of some pervert's uncle who would single-handedly destroy her fantasy of systematically crushing every single member of Yale's drama department, of fulfilling the dreams of thespian glory that her mother did not live to see realized? If only

Henry Linton hadn't retired; if only Sterndick hadn't replaced him; if only she'd just gone to his stupid-ass opera and blown off the closed-circuit Who concert, if only if only if only. She was dead; Yale was dead; she knew it. She could say anything now; it wouldn't matter.

Bruce asked what Michelle meant by saying that Douglas might need a good lawyer. He took his foot off the desk and swiveled his chair toward her. Michelle shook her head and smiled ruefully. Well, if she was going to go, there was no need to go quietly. There was a coming attraction she had seen recently—"You may love him, you may hate him, but you will never forget *The Great Santini,*" it declared. Bruce Sternberg might hate her before she left, but he would never forget her once she had played the character whom she understood most thoroughly: herself. The reason why Douglas would need a good lawyer, Michelle snapped, was because he didn't know how to keep his dick in his pants, because he was a pathetic creep who overcompensated for his lack of talent by treating some high school drama club as his personal fiefdom, because his musicals were so dreadful that his audience would someday file a class action lawsuit against him, because soon Douglas would be asking for damages after she'd smacked the crap out of him.

Bruce Sternberg stared at Michelle blankly. Then a small smile formed upon his lips. The smile resolved itself into a grin, and then the grin became a chuckle—a chuckle, then a laugh, then a hysterical, high-pitched giggle as he breathlessly told Michelle to stop, not to say anything more or else he was going to pee. Yes, he said, that sure sounded like Dougie, completely irresponsible and immature—did Michelle know he still lived at home? No, Michelle said, she didn't know that. Oh, it was a scandal, Bruce said, Dougie was the oldest and he was the only one still living on Sacramento. "Sacramento?" Michelle asked. God, that was "creeporific." "Creeporific?" Bruce asked—he had never heard the word. Michelle said that was because she had just made it up. Bruce said that Michelle was obviously a very creative thinker.

It was astonishing; it had been perhaps her most effective performance ever and she'd done nothing but say exactly how she felt—this must be what Method acting is all about, she thought. She felt that somewhere up there in *himmel,* Becky Wasserstrom was smiling down at her as Bruce posed further questions about his nephew. Did he still wear those awful brown cords and those Hush

Puppies, had she met that fat girl he had dated and tried to pass off as an Israeli Olympic swimmer, had she seen *H.M.S. Pinafore*—wasn't that the worst thing ever?

By the end of it, Michelle wasn't sure whom she loathed more: lecherous Douglas Sternberg or his gossiping uncle Bruce. And when she looked at the digital clock on Bruce's desk and saw that it was 8:19, Michelle, for perhaps the first time in the history of Yale—and this would be a good thing to include in her biography—told her interviewer she was sorry, but she had to cut this short; her ride was waiting outside. Sternberg said he was sorry he had kept her so long—it was just that he had enjoyed their talk so much. He shook Michelle's hand, said it had been a pleasure, then asked who was waiting for her—her father or her boyfriend. Neither, Michelle said, just some guy she'd picked up in the gutter. Because, Bruce said, if she was going north, he could drop her at a convenient el stop. No, that was all right, Michelle said, "the ride department" was "under control." Well, then, maybe some other time, Bruce said. Then maybe some other time *what*? Michelle asked. Maybe some other time coffee, Bruce said. Oh God, Michelle thought, did it always have to come down to this, that men would always have to ask her for something hellish that they would refer to as "coffee"? If ever a man would show absolutely no interest in her, she would marry him on the spot—cheat on him, probably, tire of him, certainly, but marry him nonetheless and stay with him forever.

But there was no need to change the way the world worked, at least not until she got into Yale. Coffee, she said, that sounded so fleeting; she only liked coffee when dinner and dessert preceded it. She batted her eyelashes at him and asked when Yale made its decisions, was it the twelfth of April? Something like that, Bruce said. Well, then, why didn't they have dinner on the thirteenth, Michelle asked, thinking there was no need to see him before that date and certainly no need to see him afterward. Bruce marked down the date, then asked if they could meet sometime before April too.

"See ya later, Sternberg," Michelle Wasserstrom said.

Several hours later, before Gareth drove back to the U of C, he and Michelle stood eating Dunkin' Munchkins atop the new Mt. Warren—a construction team had built a new toboggan hill several hundred yards east of the former one, where a parking lot now stood. Michelle gazed west through the swirling snow at the car dealerships of Western Avenue and the city and the suburbs that lay beyond. She'd always remember this spot, she thought. When she was accepting her Oscar for Best Actress, she'd say that it had all begun here, on top of this hill. "What are you thinking about, Wasserstrom? Your Oscar speech?" Gareth asked. Michelle looked at him quizzically. Actors don't care about awards, she said, they just care about doing good work. She looked down at the foot of Mt. Warren and noticed two figures walking through the park. Hey, she said, wasn't that Muley down there with a dog, didn't that look like his walk? She shouted down, "Hey, Muley." *Keep it the fuck down, Wasserstrom,* Gareth said, she must need glasses, or better, a lorgnette; Wills didn't have a dog. A short while later, a white Cadillac DeVille with a moon roof and a red, white, and blue Reagan-Bush bumper sticker came barreling down Western. Gareth and Michelle both instinctively reached for Munchkins but the car was going too fast and the new Mt. Warren was too far east; their projectiles reached no farther than the parking lot. Shortly before they descended, Michelle asked Gareth why he had never asked her to have sex with him. Gareth gave her the finger. No, Michelle asked, seriously, why had he never asked?

"Because I'm not into that shit, Wasserstrom," Gareth Overgaard said.

WILLS / SILVERMAN

Muley

That January evening, when Muley Scott Wills went out with the intention of filming West Rogers Park from the top of the Angel Guardian bell tower, was only a week after he had gone into General Camera on Western and asked Norm Weinberg how much he would pay for his movie camera. Muley had never thought he would sell the camera, but the fact was he needed money. Ever since he had quit WBOE, his share of the rent for the California Avenue apartment had become more and more difficult to come by. Though he could have told his mother he wanted to restructure their financial arrangement, he found himself unable to do so. And though Deirdre Wills had, in recent months, become much more solicitous toward Muley and interested in both his schoolwork and his extracurricular projects, asking her for money would have been an admission of defeat, necessitating a reversal in their roles that Muley found unacceptable.

But other than his camera, his editors, and the film he kept in the vegetable drawer of the refrigerator, he owned little of value, and his knack for scraping together as much money as he needed at any given time had begun to elude him. The market for crystal radios had dried up, and now that he was fourteen, Muley was too old for a great many contests he could have entered and easily won. Of course, he could have lied about his age for the Dominick's coloring contests, but he would have been too proud to accept either the $50 gift certificate or the collection of encyclopedias. He was still waiting to hear back from one contest, but there was no money in it—just a trip down to Cape Canaveral to see the first space shuttle launch and watch a TV monitor to see the astronauts perform his experiment in space.

Norm Weinberg, however, wouldn't take Muley's camera. How could he know Muley hadn't stolen it if he couldn't produce a receipt? he asked. Muley explained he didn't have a receipt because he hadn't purchased it; he'd salvaged and refurbished it. That was no way to do business, Weinberg said. What was strange was that though Muley had approached selling the camera with resignation, he was disappointed when Weinberg refused. And rather than take Weinberg's reluctance as a sign indicating that he should never be so foolish as to part with the camera, he became all the more convinced that he had to sell it, that it was what was holding him back. It was the reason he had wasted so much time pining away for Jill, who still hadn't said a word about the last film he had made for her. It was the reason he couldn't say yes to Connie Sherman's increasingly direct advances in Woodshop. It was the reason he hadn't done the one thing at Lane Tech he had wanted to do more than anything else, even though he figured his mother would have grounded him for life if he had told her he wanted to play on the floor hockey team. It was the reason he hadn't called Gareth back after they'd had their last Waukegan Night at Rainbow Beach and Gareth had told him, "You're just like me, Wills; you're cerebral, you're antisocial, the only things you can love are the ones that can't love you back, and the only things you want are the ones you know you'll never have."

Muley was pretty sure Gareth was right. But he didn't want to be cerebral, he didn't want to long only for that which he could never possess. He wanted to make out with Connie, wanted to taste cigarettes and Dr Pepper on her breath. He wanted to go over to people's houses and study all night for Geometry quizzes because they were so hard. He wanted to work mindless jobs and ride bikes with his coworkers because they weren't old enough to drive cars. He wanted to bag groceries, he wanted to spoon relish and spatula mustard onto Vienna hot dogs, to take tickets at the Nortown. He wanted to play floor hockey, no matter how pointless it might seem; he felt more satisfaction whizzing a slapshot past the outstretched arm of a goaltender than he had ever felt hearing his voice on radio. Nothing could compare with the sight of that orange puck lifting off the ground, whooshing through the air, and hitting the back of the net.

But he couldn't do any of that, because every night when he had finished his homework, he had to go out to film. He had become obsessed with a project that was even more difficult than *Lost,* one for which he was trying to film every inch of West Rogers Park, all the way from the canal at the western border to the cemetery at the east. The houses, apartments, and stores would all be real, but the characters Muley would superimpose upon them would create a new animated world, one that would illustrate all the invisible borders that existed between them. He didn't know what he would call it, but it would be feature-length, perhaps even longer. If only he could sell the camera, he thought, he wouldn't have to finish it.

But every camera store gave Muley the same answer Norm Weinberg had given him—that without any receipt or proof of ownership they wouldn't take it. He brought the camera to a pawnshop in the Loop one night, but was only offered $125, hardly what the camera was worth and not quite enough to cover his share of the rent for more than a month anyway. He made fliers and Scotch-taped them on every corner lamppost from Kedzie to Ridge ("Want to make your own film? Arriflex available in great condition! $500 or best offer"). Only one call came. And that one was from Norm Weinberg, who said he'd be happy to look at it if there was a receipt. So every night after homework, he went out with his camera and a powerful bulb strapped to the top of it to film the streets one at a time—one night Fairfield, one night Richmond, one night California. He captured street signs, storefronts, and illuminated windows, the empty Boone schoolyard, the last patrons exiting the Sabra restaurant. By week's end he had amassed an additional eighty minutes of footage, increasing his total to seven hours of as-yet-undeveloped film, all of which would have to be edited together before he could animate the characters he wanted to create.

On January 20, 1981, Muley decided he could no longer keep the camera, regardless of whether anyone would ever buy it from him. Every day he kept it represented another day the world remained at a distance, another day without floor hockey, another day without knowing the scent of Connie Sherman's menthol and Dr Pepper breath, another day of Wasserstromian silence. When he left his apartment, apologizing to his mother that he would be too busy that night to have dinner with her and Lloyd Cubbins, Muley imagined the last shot he would take. He would spend the night documenting as much of West Rogers Park as he could. When he reached Angel Guardian, he would find a way into the church and climb up to the bell tower, and then when dawn was breaking, with the camera running, he would hold it in both of his hands and spin it as hard as he could, and the camera would capture the images of the neighborhood spiraling away while it corkscrewed down to the ground.

Muley traveled from west to east, beginning at the stagnant drainage canal and proceeding past the signs of suburbia that were spilling over the border of West Rogers Park: a Go-Tane gas station, Brown's Chicken, its asphalt parking lot dusted with a thin layer of snow. As Muley walked east, he filmed the boarded-up windows of Smilin' Seymour's, now closed after the owner was slain in an armed robbery. Across the street, Kornick Monuments, which sold headstones for Jewish cemeteries. There was the 7-Eleven in a small shopping mall on Albany and Devon; Professional Hair Designers for Men stood beside it. Ravi Khan's Family Pizzeria had a Sold sign in its icy window, and across the street, Osco Drugs had replaced Manzelman's Hardware Store. Knopov's Bakery was gone as well, and its *delcos, kichels,* and kosher red-tinted, cream-filled chocolate cupcakes along with it. In its place was a tiny ice cream parlor called Nutcracker Sweet, which made most of its money on the pinball machines still aglow in its foggy windows.

Across California, the turnover continued. Gitel's Kosher Bakery and Lazar's Juvenile Furniture remained, but Bella Roma and the Parthenon had moved— the former to Little Italy, the latter to Greektown. In their places stood two Indian restaurants. At the corner of Devon and Western, a Dollar Store had taken the place of Woolworth's. East of Western, however, where Muley had once lived, little had changed: the gang graffiti in the alleys, the Blue Peacock and Pekin House Chinese restaurants, Hobby Models, Adelphi Liquors, now with 3M Studios above it, the bars, Laundrytown, Burger King. Muley stopped when he reached his old apartment building. He stepped into the vestibule and checked the name on the buzzer. Blank. Still not rented. Then he walked east faster, past Burger King, past the Seconds to Go Thrift Shop until he got to the fence surrounding the cemetery behind Angel Guardian.

Scaling the fence was easy. Once he reached the top, he dropped the camera into a snowy mound atop the grass. Then he jumped down after it. Putting it back on his shoulder, he switched on the bulb at the top of the camera and aimed the lens at the gravestones, the pinkish light from the streetlamps further illuminating the names of those who now rested in the one small quadrant at the edge of West Rogers Park where the Indians, the blacks, the Jews, and the Russians had still not made any inroads. Muley tried to film the names of the deceased— he thought they might make for an interesting collage at the beginning of his film. But his attention was distracted by one particular gravestone. Underneath a thin layer of snow, it appeared that someone had scratched his or her initials into it. Muley reached his hand out to dust off the letters that came after the "J," but as he did, he felt the ice crunching under his boot, his boot sinking down in mud, his ankle twisting underneath him, then his body doing a half-spin as he fell backwards onto the ice, the camera slipping out of his grip as his head caught the top of the headstone. His head throbbed as he lay flat on his back, staring up at streetlights and the snow falling down at a sharp angle past the church steeple, the highest point in all of West Rogers Park. The camera and its bulb—still shining—were now encased in the snow.

As he lay on the grass, the gravestone just behind him, Muley felt a sudden dampness against his forehead and a shadow passing over his eyes. He touched the tips of his fingers to his forehead to see if there was blood, but as he reached his hand back, it too became coated with the same sudden warm wetness. He expected there to be blood on his hands, but there was none. Then, when he put his hand back down at his side, he felt that wetness too—now hot and just a bit rough—up against his cheek. And as Muley used his palms to sit up, his back now resting against the cold, hard gravestone, he suddenly became aware of the source of all that moisture. His eyes locked on those of a dog staring straight back at him.

It was a smallish dog and fairly skinny, its white fur dirty with large brown splotches; it shivered slightly in the cold. Muley reached a hand out to the animal. The animal licked Muley's hand enthusiastically and wagged. The dog had no tags, no collar. Muley petted the dog's head. He had always liked animals but had never thought of bringing one home; he could only imagine his mother's tirade. Muley quickly fashioned a leash out of a length of film and tied it loosely around the animal's neck. The animal accepted the leash stoically and complied when Muley gave the leash a slight tug. After they had walked along a good portion of the cemetery's perimeter, they found a hole cut into the fence and the two of them, first the dog, then Muley, squirmed through it back onto Devon, then walked side by side along the snowy sidewalk, the steeple behind them, snow falling down upon the glowing bulb of the camera. Muley had already forgotten about the gravestone, the one Jill Wasserstrom had once defaced, back when she used to walk through graveyards, back when she used to count up to 37, then carve her initials into the stones. Instead, he was thinking about what to do with the dog. He thought he might bring it to Mel—Mel would no doubt protest but would secretly be pleased by a creature who could provide unconditional affection. That wasn't a bad idea, but it was not as good as bringing the dog to Connie Sherman's apartment.

Connie lived in one of a series of new, speedily built town houses on Touhy west of California, but so far west that the neighborhood seemed more like Lincolnwood than Chicago. Connie had always told Muley to stop by whenever he wanted—her mom and stepdad, Ellie and Dave, were rarely home, and when they were, they were usually passed out drunk. But he had never been able to bring himself to do it. The dog now provided a convenient excuse and it added a level of urgency. Plus, Connie had told him she loved "playing with furry things." He figured she'd like a dog.

Muley and the animal crossed Warren Park. At one point, he thought he heard somebody calling "Hey, Muley" after him, but he kept walking. He took a shortcut through the parking lot past the new field house with construction paper signs in the window: "Sign Up Early for Summer Day Camp," "Warren Park Community Players Audition for *The Burden of Biff*." He and the dog emerged from the park at the corner of Western and North Shore. And it was only when they crossed Western that Muley became fully conscious of the fact that he had left the camera on the cemetery ground. He could have turned around, he supposed, but he wanted to get the dog to Connie's house before midnight. He wondered what would happen when he was in Connie's house and the dog was asleep; he wondered if they'd kiss right away or if she'd first want to slowdance to Billy Joel. He picked up his pace, tugging the film every time the dog lagged behind. As he reached Fairfield, he became convinced that forgetting the camera had been the absolute right thing to do. True, he might have missed out on the opportunity to film that ultimate shot, that image seen through the camera falling from the bell tower, but what good were movies compared with the pleasures that no doubt lay behind the door to Connie's apartment? As he stood at the corner of North Shore and California, air-raid sirens were sounding loudly, reminding residents that this was a snow route and their cars would be towed. Muley didn't notice Jill Wasserstrom walking toward him from the other side of California until he had stepped onto the street. And that sight was so disturbing to him that he did not have time to see the gleaming white Cadillac DeVille speeding toward both of them.

ROVNER

Lana

I f it was true, as Lana Rovner would claim later, that by yelling "Stop, let me out here!" to Mrs. Ernestine Wales she had saved the lives of Muley Scott Wills, Jill Wasserstrom, and some mangy white dog, then it was also true that if Mary Beth Wales hadn't accused Lana of stealing several pieces from her father's solid silver and gold chess set, Mrs. Wales wouldn't have had to take her home and therefore wouldn't have had to slam the brakes of her Cadillac and come to a screeching halt on California. To Lana, the fact that she had actually taken the gold and silver kings and queens was only a minor detail. The real issue was that

Mary Beth had accused her of doing it, which was traitorous considering that it had only been two nights since they had taken an oath that they would remain best friends forever, or at least until one of them became famous.

They had spent every second together from Friday after school to Tuesday evening, when Mr. Wales took Mary Beth and her mother to dinner at the Union Club, which Lana presumed didn't allow Jews. Up until that moment, everything had gone swimmingly, just after Lana had stopped crying in the school bathroom and Mary Beth had come in to tell her that her mom was waiting outside and to hurry up or they would miss the 5 o'clock show of *Ordinary People,* the first R-rated movie that Lana would ever see. The plan was for Mary Beth's brother Greg—who was sixteen but looked older—to say he was their uncle and buy them the tickets if they gave him money to buy beer for the Northwestern frat party he and his water polo buddies were going to crash. Lana's tears had come from the realization that while she was going to spend the next eight days at the Wales house, her father was going to Hawaii with her stupid stupid stupid former psychologist. He'd said he was going for a medical conference, but she had broken into his desk with a butter knife and found both plane tickets. She was certain they would be fornicating with each other. The only thing worse would have been if she had found out that her father was taking her mother and fornicating with her—but luckily her mother had left town and was probably fornicating with somebody else. She was alone, Lana thought as she cried in the bathroom, there was no one to trust. Everyone was mean. Everyone was a traitor. Everyone was a dirty fornicator.

But when Mary Beth came to get her, Lana's misery passed in seconds; she was practically an adult now, she realized. Adults didn't cry in bathrooms; adults watched movies with people fornicating in them and bought each other beer, even though Greg got carded at both the Old Orchard Theater and Buy-Low Liquors, so that he and the rest of the water polo team spent the evening riding bikes up and down the icy streets of North Evanston, while Lana and Mary Beth locked themselves in Mary Beth's bedroom and made "phony phone calls" to guys from their class saying they were "red hot" for them and why didn't they meet them at midnight in the parking lot by Dyche Stadium and they'd show them "a real good time," until Mrs. Wales slapped loudly on the bedroom door and told them to get their mouths shut.

The best part of that first night had come shortly thereafter, when Mary Beth had started crying because her parents were arguing about a broken cuckoo clock and she feared they might get divorced soon. Lana wasn't happy that Mary Beth was crying per se, but she was happy that Mary Beth trusted her enough to cry in her presence. She was also happy that, for once, she wasn't the one crying. She climbed into Mary Beth's bed, said "There, there," and gave her a Kleenex, which was what people did in movies when their friends started crying, even though few people had ever done it for her.

On Saturday, they had gone out for breakfast at IHOP with Mrs. Wales, who had nothing but black coffee and ordered the Hispanic busboy—whom she referred to as "Sanchez"—to keep pouring her more. Later, they again tried to see *Ordinary People,* got carded, and saw *Song of the South* instead—Mary Beth for the third time, Lana for the fifth. Afterward, they went to a party at Megan Knox's mansion on Sheridan Road, where Lana drank a glass of cherry cordial while the others smoked hash and drank beer, and they all played Truth or Dare. And because Lana had dared Mary Beth to touch Earl Weith's "thing," Mary Beth paid Lana back by daring her to make out with Todd Taylor and use her tongue. Which Lana did. But after Todd had blushed, broken away from the kiss, and exclaimed "Damn, that was good," Megan got angry and said that the party was over and everyone should go home. Lana and Mary Beth had walked home two miles through the snow and stayed up *past midnight* drawing pictures of boys from their class with funny thought bubbles above their heads. Mary Beth drew a picture of Todd naked, thinking, *I wanna go around the bases with Lana Rovner,* but Lana made her cross it out. The next day, Mr. Wales drove the girls to the stables so they could see Mr. Blackie.

On Sunday and Monday nights, Lana and Mary Beth did homework, or rather, Lana did her homework and then allowed Mary Beth to copy hers, because Mary Beth didn't like doing homework. She knew she was going to be a veterinarian when she grew up and her father had told her that all she needed to do to become one was to not be able to get into medical school. On Tuesday night, they intended to work on their skits for Music class; everyone in the class was supposed to pick a partner and act out a favorite song. Most students were treating the assignment as a joke (Todd Taylor and Earl Weith said they would mime passing a joint back and forth for the entire nine minutes of Led Zeppelin's

"Kashmir"), but Lana and Mary Beth were planning to dress up as Elton John and Kiki Dee and create an entire miniature musical based on "Don't Go Breakin' My Heart." Lana had just begun describing the costumes to Mary Beth when Mr. Wales knocked on the bedroom door and said he was taking his daughter and his wife out to the Union Club to celebrate something that had happened during the day, something that Lana and her "people" were "probably not real happy about." No, Lana had told Mr. Wales, he was wrong, she had delivered her Perspective on WBOE supporting Ronald Reagan. Well, that was swell, Mr. Wales said, but somebody had to feed Tristan and Isolde and take them out for their walks. There was some ham in the refrigerator if Lana got hungry, he said.

Like many of Lana's forays into criminal behavior, the idea to snatch the kings and queens from Mr. Wales's chess set was not necessarily based on a desire for personal enrichment. The theft was an effort to even out the disparities that existed in the world, to punish those who planned dinners at tony professional clubs with the sole purpose of excluding others. For no good reason that she could discern, she had had a truly bad run of luck lately: *Chi-Town Chatterbox* had been canceled, her mother had skipped town, her father was in Hawaii with some hag, and she hadn't scored well on any private school placement exam. The next year she would either be at a public school, at Ida Crown (where you had to pray every morning), at Regina (where you had to pray Catholic every morning), or at Roycemore, where all the scary burnouts and Mary Beth would be going. The whole situation was dreadfully unfair, and remedy was called for. If someone took something from you, Lana reasoned, you had the right to take something from somebody else. When Lana was certain that Mr. Wales's white Mercedes had pulled out of the driveway, she darted into the front room, flipped up the Lucite cover of the chess set, took the four heaviest pieces, and stuffed them into the front pockets of her trousers.

When Lana heard someone at the front door, she dashed, terrified, up the stairs to Mary Beth's bedroom. But when she determined it was not Mary Beth and her parents returning but Mary Beth's brother Greg and his girlfriend, Jolene Hey (he called her "Hey HEY Hey," imitating a character from the TV show *What's Happening*), Lana immediately hid the chess pieces in her luggage. She wondered if Mr. Wales would find out, or rather, *when* he would find out—she was certain he was the sort of person who kept a detailed inventory of every one of his belongings. Therefore, after a half hour of working on her French homework, which she no longer enjoyed now that Julius Bernard had stopped returning her letters, then another half hour trying to block out the sounds of smacking lips, squeaking bedsprings, and Fleetwood Mac music emanating from Greg's bedroom, she devised another plan. Rather than keep all four chess pieces in her luggage, she removed two of them, put one in each pants pocket, and sneaked past Greg's closed bedroom door. And because Greg and Jolene weren't supposed to be fornicating when the Waleses were out having dinner and because it would distract attention from her own crime, she opened Jolene's book bag, which she found at the bottom of the stairs, and put the two silver pieces in it. Then she went back upstairs and drew a few anatomically correct pictures of Todd Taylor.

After an hour had passed, Lana remembered that she had to walk Tristan and Isolde. When Mr. Wales had first told her of this chore, she figured she would just say she had done it—she wasn't the serving wench and so what if the dogs pooped in the house, Sanchez would take care of it. But since Lana wanted to appear honest and responsible, which she felt she would have been if she lived in a more equitable world, she decided to walk the dogs. She wouldn't bring a bag to pick up their poo, though. That was disgusting.

Evanston was nice, Lana thought as she walked north on Sheridan Road toward the Baha'i temple, which resembled a miniature Taj Mahal fashioned out of spun sugar. Wilmette was even nicer. All the houses were big. Everybody was rich. Everybody was white, or if they weren't, then they were Japanese, Chinese, Indian, or Korean. The lake was just a block away, and even though Lana was afraid of swimming and got nauseous on boats, she still liked the idea of living near it. For the past month, she had been telling her father that they should move into a Michigan Avenue high-rise, but now she thought she should try to convince him to move into a house around here. Until this moment, she had only thought of her status in terms of east and west. She had always been glad to live west of California, thrilled to live west of Western, thrilled that her father didn't drive a truck like all those people who lived in the east. But the truth was, Lana thought, if you really wanted people to respect you, then you had to live north. She remembered a line from *The Sneetches,* a Dr. Seuss book she'd enjoyed when her mother used to take her to Story Hour at the Nortown Library—"I'm a

North-Going Zax and I always go north." That's what she would tell her father, Lana thought as she turned back at the Baha'i temple, the dogs having crapped in the snow out in front of it: "Always Go North."

When Lana returned with the snow-flecked dogs, Mary Beth was in the front hallway, hands on her hips, eyes squinting dubiously, her tongue poking the inside of her cheek. Well, Mary Beth said caustically, at least she hadn't stolen the dogs too. Mr. Wales was standing with his back to her. He was staring down at the chessboard, slowly shaking his head. Hey, Lana said, unleashing Tristan and Isolde, who bounded for the kitchen. Lana shimmied off her parka and tried to walk past Mary Beth toward the hall closet. Where were they? Mary Beth wanted to know. Where were who? Lana asked, pretending to only half pay attention as she got a hanger out of the closet and poked one end into a sleeve. Mary Beth said she didn't want any shit—if Lana gave the chess pieces back, they wouldn't call the police; her father didn't want to call the police, he didn't want his insurance rates going up. Lana asked what chess pieces; why would she be interested in chess pieces? Because, Mary Beth said—so angry that she wasn't even raising her voice—each piece in her father's set cost $500.

"For these?" Lana asked, walking over to the chess set, flipping up the cover on its hinges, and holding one of the pieces in her hand—she had heard Mary Beth mention the police and wanted to make sure that if anyone questioned her, there would be a reason why her fingerprints were all over it. "For *these*?" Lana said she couldn't believe it; she thought the chess set looked *Polish*. Mr. Wales, quiet and menacing as he stood less than a foot away from Lana, said he did not like to yell, but if Lana knew what was good for her, she would hand over those chess pieces immediately. Mary Beth added that Lana wouldn't like to see her father mad. Well, Lana asked, why was he the only one allowed to get mad? If anyone had the right to be mad, it was she herself. What if she hadn't taken the pieces? she asked. What if that Appalachian hussy Jolene Hey had, in fact, been the culprit?

As she stood in the Waleses' hallway, Mary Beth in front of her, Mr. Wales behind her, Lana let the outrage of the accusations build up within her until she felt her cheeks flush. "How dare you?" she asked Mary Beth, almost whispering. What did she take her for? Some common thief? She quickly moved on to the topic of Jolene and wasn't it funny that as soon as they had all left to go for dinner that Greg and Jolene had shown up and gone upstairs and started listening to

Fleetwood Mac and making lip-smacking noises, and wasn't it funny that between the time she had left and the time she had returned, Greg and Jolene Hey HEY Hey were gone and so were the chess pieces, and wasn't it funny that her father was a doctor and she lived in a nice house in West Rogers Park while Jolene lived in a Mafia suburb out by the *airport,* but she was the only one being interrogated. When she felt the tears coming, she ran upstairs whimpering, "I thought you were my friend." As she reached the top of the stairs, she heard Mr. Wales ask Mary Beth if that was true, what Lana had said about Greg and Jolene. Mary Beth said she didn't know. Then, a moment after Mr. Wales loudly called out his wife's name, Ernestine, Mary Beth went upstairs where Lana was already packing her suitcase.

What did she want? Lana asked her. Did she want to look through her luggage? She stood back from the suitcase. Go ahead, she said, look all you want. No, Mary Beth said, she just wanted to know if Greg and Jolene had been there while she and her parents had been out. Why did she want to know, Lana asked, so she could accuse them too? She wasn't a snitch; she didn't go around telling on people. If Mary Beth was so interested, why didn't she go into Greg's bedroom and figure it out for herself. She wasn't saying anything; she wasn't a *Communist.*

It didn't take Mary Beth long to enter her brother's bedroom and find the gold queen Lana had placed on the night table in the seconds she had had between the time when she had gone upstairs and when Mary Beth had followed her up. But when Mary Beth came back to apologize, Lana had already zipped up her suitcase and was lugging it toward the stairs. She was going home, she said; she didn't like being in a place where people accused her of things. Mary Beth said she wasn't accusing Lana of anything anymore; she had just found the gold queen on Greg's night table. Lana said she couldn't believe Mary Beth was touching it; that was totally disgusting—Greg and Jolene had probably been using it as a "marital aid." That was sick, Mary Beth said. No, Lana said, she was the one who was sick. She asked if Mary Beth would call her a cab or if she had to do it herself.

Downstairs, an argument had erupted between Mr. and Mrs. Wales concerning their son's relationship with Jolene Hey ("I don't mind him running around with girls; I mind him running around with a white trash thief," Mr. Wales said. Mrs. Wales had responded that he had been every bit as much white trash as the

Heys until he had married into her family), after which Mrs. Wales said she was going out for a drive. Not when she was drunk she wasn't, Mr. Wales said. Absolutely when she was drunk, Mrs. Wales said; she was more relaxed behind the wheel after she'd had a few drinks. Lana asked if she could get a ride home. Absolutely, Mrs. Wales said as Mary Beth pleaded for Lana to stay, didn't she accept her apology? Lana didn't respond; she had resolved to give Mary Beth the silent treatment at least until the next day at school. She hoped no one would notice the head of the solid gold king poking against the side of her suitcase.

On the drive south from Evanston to Chicago, Mrs. Wales listened to Tommy Dorsey big band music and chain-smoked Pall Malls. She asked Lana if her parents were divorced, and when Lana said yes, Mrs. Wales told her she was lucky. She said she was glad that Jolene had stolen those "Polacky chess pieces"—she wished that she had stolen the "whole damned Polacky set" from her "damned Polacky husband." She was driving fast, her left hand flicking ashes out the window, her right palm just touching the top of the steering wheel as they motored through the snow, past Warren Park, where two small shadowed figures were vaguely visible atop Mt. Warren. But Lana did not notice them, nor did she notice the fact that the speedometer was creeping up toward 45 as Mrs. Wales turned west onto Devon. What she was desperately trying to determine was how she could tell Mrs. Wales they had to turn back because she'd forgotten her housekeys and she didn't know how she would get in. But then again, going back to the Waleses' house would mean having to face Greg, who would say that no, he didn't know how the chess piece had gotten into his bedroom, and no, he hadn't used it as a marital aid. Then it would be his word against hers. But then again, she couldn't just have Mrs. Wales drop her off in front of the house on Sacramento, because what was she supposed to do—just sit there until she froze to death? Her father wouldn't be coming back until Saturday.

Seeing Muley and Jill walking toward each other from either side of California seemed almost like a mirage to Lana as Mrs. Wales sped north, Lana breathing harder and heavier, feeling penned in by the tale she had told. At any given moment, she seemed to want two things, each of which contradicted the other. She wanted to turn the clock back to the moment before Mr. Wales came home and said he was taking his family out to the Union Club, or better, turn it forward to Saturday, when her father would be home; or turn it back even further to the time—years ago now—when her mother and father were still together and

the thought of it made her feel safe instead of nauseated; or forward much further to sometime in 1984, when she would be majoring in Communications and
preparing for a career as a TV journalist; or all the way back to August 1972, before she'd started school and her world consisted of nothing more than her seemingly enormous house and the Juvenile section of the Nortown Library, where
she could spend all day reading *Puck's Peculiar Pet Shop*. The past was not the
problem for Lana, really, nor was the future. The only difficulties lay in the precise moment of the present, which seemed completely insoluble. If she could find
a way out of this predicament, the rest of her life would be easy.

"Stop," Lana cried as the faces of Muley, Jill, and a dog suddenly appeared in
the flash of the Cadillac's headlights. "Let me out here."

WASSERSTROM

Jill

S ince Jill Wasserstrom had gone out on the evening of January 20 looking for
Muley Wills, the moment she saw him she was certain he hadn't been looking for her. There was something so suffused with destiny in that instant that it
had to have been a dreadful mistake. If you planned for something to happen, or,
worse, prayed for it to happen—whatever it was, your mother pulling through
her illness, John Anderson winning the presidential election—there was absolutely no way it ever would. When she had seen her father lying motionless on
the sidewalk, she had prayed for his recovery and it had worked. But that had
been only that one time. Once was coincidence; twice was impossible. When she
stood at the intersection of North Shore and California and saw Muley approaching her, the blinding flash of headlights, the piercing sound of brakes, and
the even more piercing sound of Lana Rovner exclaiming, "This is so lucky, running into you guys" became little more than sad, frustrating proof of her own fa-
talistic doctrine. She'd wished that she would be wrong, that the future would
play out exactly as she had imagined it. But it never did and never would.

The three of them stood in the intersection, the three of them and the dog, as Mrs. Wales's Cadillac swerved around, then past them, its red-white-and-blue bumper sticker fading into the distance. And as the three of them stood there, not knowing to which side of California they should cross, each thought he or she was the one who was not supposed to be there. Muley assumed that Lana was there to meet Jill, perhaps for a sleepover—that's why she was lugging the suitcase. Lana assumed that Jill and Muley were meeting to continue their perverse agenda of miscegenation. And Jill assumed that Muley was now dating Lana as part of yet another ploy to get her attention—she would be so infuriated he had chosen Lana that she would come rushing back, pleading for him to choose her instead. Didn't he realize that all she wanted was for him to act normal? Not to pine away for her, not to turn away the moment he saw her, not to make films that he thought would make her fall in love with him. The most recent film had nearly done that, as she had feared it might, which was why she had waited so long to watch it. She had decided to wait a good long while to watch Muley's film, to wait until she felt so desperate or irritated with the world and her insignificant role in it that she would welcome the momentary illusion of her importance in the fantasy worlds Muley created.

That moment did not result from the day's inauguration—which, if anything, energized her with the knowledge that, for four years, she would have a focus for her political rage: an imminent nuclear exchange between the U.S. and the U.S.S.R. that she would have to try futilely through her essays and activism to combat, for she knew it was coming; she was dreaming almost every night about mushroom clouds and nuclear fallout. Nor was the decision to watch Muley's film a result of her frustration with the euphoria in the press regarding the release of the fifty-two remaining American hostages in Iran, even though that release had indeed troubled her, for it suggested—she was positive of this—some underhanded deal between the Iranian government and the new U.S. administration.

Actually, Jill had not been sure when she would ever watch Muley's film until the moment she found the marked-up galley of her father's "Life of Charlie" column, which had reduced all of her diligent reporting to a joke at her expense. She had seen the offending document tucked underneath the large blue "key bowl" that Gail had bought Charlie for his birthday so that he would stop searching for his keys every morning. Jill had scanned the edited copy briefly and replaced it under the key bowl and waited to see if her father would have the nerve to tell her about it. And then, when he brought the article into her room, she wound up pretending that she wasn't offended by the butchery, because he still made her feel guilty whenever she tried to confront him.

It would have been one thing, Jill thought as she searched in her closet for the box that contained her movie projector, if her father had decided just to eliminate her observations from the column entirely; that would have been pathetic, but understandable given her father's limited worldview and the sad fact that the man was always on the verge of being fired. But to have written or have let someone write *"But then again, she's not even fourteen yet; she doesn't really know what inflation is"* was so insulting, dismissive, and, Jill had to add, *unsophisticated* that it was beyond comprehension. Jill was certain her sister would have blamed it all on Gail—"This reeks of Bass," Michelle frequently said. But Jill was far more sympathetic to Gail's insensitivity than to her father's acquiescence. Jill found many of Gail's opinions morally reprehensible but respected the directness with which she stated them. No, this was all the work of *Charlie,* Jill thought as she lugged the film projector box and clunked it on top of her desk—big, lumbering Charlie who was so frightened of offending anyone that he tried to hold all opinions at once; plodding, well-meaning *Charlie,* who had never matured to the point where anyone could take him seriously enough to call him Charles.

It was the second time he had betrayed her. The first had been the occasion of her mother's funeral—ignoring Becky Wasserstrom's clearly stated wishes, blaming his cowardice on Jewish law and what other people might think. And now, when he entered her room, that big, worried smile on his face, those big, sweaty hands in his pockets, she wanted nothing more than to dispatch him as quickly as possible. She nodded, glanced at the text, surreptitiously wrote "stet" on it, and, concealing her anger, made a few remarks about how she had expected as much. And then she delivered the greatest insult to her father she could imagine, one that completely dismissed his intelligence, his maturity, his humanity: She called him Charlie. "That's the way it is, Charlie," she said just before he left the room. And then she took the film Muley had given to her, the one marked "Lost." As she threaded the film through the projector, she asked Charlie to hit the lights.

During the opening credit sequence of the film, the words "I Love You, Jill Wasserstrom" appeared on the screen and then were transformed by means of an eraser into the word "Lost," a word that swirled into a vortex, the letters spinning around so quickly that they formed a centrifuge, into which the phrase "A Film by Muley Scott Wills" spilled, then disappeared. The screen faded to black and opened on an image of Jill walking along the east side of California, dressed in a red-and-white top, blue jeans, and navy blue sneakers. Then the east side's small tan brick houses and boxy apartment buildings slowly began mutating. The colors drained out of the images, and then even the black and white began to fade, so that soon there was nothing left of the street except the penciled outlines of the buildings that Jill—now the only figure in the neighborhood still in color— was passing.

On the screen, Jill walked past the pencil-line buildings—the phrase "Real Girl" written out in cartoonish block letters hovered momentarily above her head and then disappeared as a golden parakeet flew into view. Jill crossed the street and the houses and the apartments and the stores on the west side began to acquire new, bright, and unnatural shades—fluorescent pinks and phosphorescent purples, chartreuses and magentas. A violet cupola appeared on the top of Gunther's Shell station, the Shang Chai restaurant was now guarded by nine small pillars, each representing one of the Muses. Suddenly, there appeared a Cartoon Boy, a taller, gawkier version of Muley, who would fall in love with the Real Girl as they crossed back and forth from real world to cartoon world and back.

But though Muley's cartoon world was whimsical, replete with storybook inventions, as she watched the film, Jill found it deeply depressing. And it was the animated images that existed in this world—more than the cleverly rendered yet perhaps too-familiar story of impossible love between two individuals from conflicting backgrounds—that truly affected her. To Jill, they quite astutely demonstrated just what was missing from her neighborhood and, by extrapolation, her life. Where Muley's film showed children playing and couples walking hand in hand, cartoon hearts beating above their heads, Jill only saw the solitary and, at times, oppressively lonely nature of her self-sufficient existence. Where Muley's world was filled with glorious, misshapen castles and spaceship mansions, Jill saw only bleak apartments and tiny, irrelevant strip-mall businesses.

As she watched, Jill felt two damp trickles on her cheeks and the taste of salt upon her tongue. The film's coda—in which a hand reached into the frame and erased the Cartoon Boy and the Real Girl the moment they were about to kiss—

was the first since the opening credits in which Jill finally felt able to catch her breath, to wipe her cheeks and her burning eyes. She was thankful, so thankful, to see the words The End on the wall and then the static white square cast by the projector lamp.

The idea of trekking out into the snow to find Muley was first born of a simple and practical desire to return his films so that she would never have to watch them again. Ever. But then, after she had boxed up the films and started rummaging through her dresser for woolen socks, she wondered why she needed to make such a dramatic gesture. Wouldn't it just be better to drop them off at his locker with a brief note? She had all but decided to stay home, but then she heard a knock on her door, then Charlie asking if everything was all right in there, he'd been sleeping and thought he'd heard sniffling. Everything was fine, Jill said, go back to bed. After which Jill felt it absolutely necessary to leave the house that night, if only to avoid her father if she happened to feel like crying.

As she stepped out of the Funny House and shut the door quietly behind her that snowy January night, Jill decided she would walk east to Muley's apartment, ring his doorbell, and tell him she had watched his movie, that she had never seen anything as beautiful, that she was in love with him and had been hiding it all this while, and now she hoped they could be together forever and ever. She would tell him this with the sole desire to make sure that it didn't happen, because planning for something was the surest way to prevent it. But then, as she walked east on North Shore toward Francisco, she couldn't be certain if the statements she planned to make if and when she found Muley weren't deep, subconscious wishes. Maybe underneath all of her other desires was a deep longing to combat her loneliness, maybe she yearned for someone with whom she could discuss all her existential fears, with whom she could slowdance to Billy Joel when she was feeling scared and lonely. If only there was some way, Jill thought as she approached Mozart Street, some method by which she could dub Muley her boyfriend but see him only, say, twice a week and work the rest of the time on her U.S. History Fair project, the one that would create a detailed model of Chicago as a mass Native American graveyard. Maybe, she thought, she could tell Muley she loved him and loved his movie—she crossed Mozart and started walking past K.I.N.S. with the hopes that if she said that, Muley would say her emotions were a little too strong, that maybe they should take it easy and she would say yes, he was right, why didn't they see each other only on weekends and not associate with each other during school other than to say hi. But again, now that she had envisioned this ideal scenario, she knew it wouldn't be the one to actually happen either. She decided she would walk to the lake. The chances she would run into Muley were just about nil, and since she knew she wouldn't find him, she wanted to go to the place where she always went when she felt betrayed or alone.

Jill stood at North Shore and California, preparing to cross, when she suddenly noticed Muley and a smallish white dog with brown splotches on it standing on the other side of the street. Muley's and Jill's eyes found each other's at exactly the same moment. It was so close to a realization of a prophecy, so near a fulfillment of destiny, that Jill was convinced it had to mean something else, that their meeting was completely accidental, that Muley was merely outside walking his new dog. But still, she had no other choice but to follow that unlikely destiny, whatever it might be, to cross the street. She had nearly reached the center of the intersection when she noticed that she and Muley were standing in a halo of headlights, a white Cadillac stalled on the street to their immediate south, and that out of the car Lana was emerging with a hefty suitcase and telling them how lucky they were; if Lana hadn't yelled "Stop!" they would have been run over and left for dead.

Neither Jill nor Muley had said so much as hello to each other when the three of them and the dog reached the west side of California and Mrs. Wales's Cadillac sped north. Before they had a chance to speak, Lana was breathlessly telling both of them about the horrible ordeal she had just endured, how she had been booted from the house where she had been staying under bogus accusations of theft, how she wanted nothing more than to go home, but her mother had disappeared, her father was in Maui, and she didn't have a key to the house.

Lana had hoped that either Jill or Muley would ask her to stay with them (she was frankly hoping that Jill would, because she had never been in a black person's house and thought that, at worst, it would be fatally dangerous and, at best, it would smell strongly of cocoa butter and skin lotion and she would have to breathe through her mouth the whole time). But rather than state her desires outright, she said that if either Jill or Muley could help her get into her house, she would be eternally grateful and give them a reward. And before Jill could speak, Muley said he could help out, no problem; he was good at breaking into places.

And in those next moments, when all three of them were situated at that street corner on the west side of California, Jill had little opportunity to say any of the things she had planned. She'd only been able to tell Muley that she hadn't seen him around the neighborhood in a while, that she wanted to talk to him about his movie sometime, and that she didn't know he had gotten a dog. Muley stammered, then said yeah, actually he'd been out looking for Jill to see if she was interested in adopting the animal. And the only statement Jill could muster was that yes, she liked dogs, she thought her father might like one—she thought he might relate to dogs better than to people—and if Muley didn't have a place to put it, why didn't she take him home for a day or two and see how it went. Muley said that was fine; if it didn't work out, he'd take the dog back. Jill asked if the dog had a name. Muley said no, not yet. Lana said could they please go now; she thought she was getting frostbite. Muley said okay, he'd talk to Jill later. Jill smiled, said, "Thanks, Muley," took the leash, and began walking the dog south on California. Muley stared up the block as she walked, thinking about how long it had been since he had seen her smile, wanting to follow her but being tugged on the sleeve of his too-thin-for-the-weather army jacket as Lana said hurry up, it was freezing.

There were three other directions in which Muley could have walked and each seemed preferable to the westward trail he was being led on. East was home and farther east was the Angel Guardian cemetery, where he had left his camera. North was Connie Sherman's apartment; even though he didn't have a reason to visit her now, he trusted she would welcome him, assuming her parents had passed out. South were Jill and the as-yet-nameless dog. But instead, he was walking west, following Lana, who told him how he was "so so so so nice" for helping her, in contrast to the Waleses, who were "so so so so mean," even though they were rich. Lana filled the three-and-a-half-block walk from the corner of North Shore and California to the Rovner House with numerous complaints and boasts: how she was tiring of grade school cliques and was looking forward to the respect that would come with being in high school, how she might soon be moving to the northern suburbs, the denizens of which all got into good colleges, even if they "happened to be dumb." She was thankful that she would soon be leaving West Rogers Park; the neighborhood was just too small.

When they got to the house on Sacramento, Lana told Muley she was glad they had had this conversation; they were practically neighbors and they had never talked. Lana could hear the phone ringing inside her house, probably the Waleses calling to once again demand she return their chess piece, she thought, as they walked up the unshoveled front steps of her house ("We didn't always have Astroturf," Lana said). Muley eyed the lock and pulled out a Swiss Army knife from his jacket pocket. Lana remarked that the Rovners had only recently started locking their doors. Until a few recent break-ins and other assorted crimes, nobody west of California had ever thought to lock them. Muley extracted the file blade from the pocketknife. One smooth downward motion, three quick jerks of the blade, and the front door popped open. Lana gleefully asked where he had learned that technique; had he ever robbed houses? No, Muley said, he hadn't. Lana said "Oh," somewhat dejected—it would have been so interesting to be friends with someone who robbed houses. Inside, the phone had stopped ringing. Lana asked Muley if he wanted to come get his rewards.

"Rewards?" Muley asked.

Yes, Lana said, there were two. Once inside, she took off her coat and asked Muley to take his off too. She hung them both up, taking an extra long time to do so, knowing the moment Muley departed would be the moment she would be alone in the house and would continue to be alone until her father's return some ninety hours later. She told Muley to sit on the couch and then she lugged over her suitcase, sat down next to him, and popped it open. She removed the solid gold chess piece and handed it to Muley—it was worth at least $1,000, she told him, and when he tried to say something, she said she wouldn't let him protest. She was giving it to him because she had promised a reward; it had been given to her by someone she now hated and of whom she did not want to be reminded. Muley held the gaudy object in his hands, felt its weight. He thanked Lana and began to stand up. No, Lana said, he had another reward coming, and in one smooth motion she had learned from Olivia Newton-John in *Grease,* she stunned Muley by kissing him soft, wet, and full on the lips. And then she said he could stay over at her house if he wanted; she was sure the house was far more comfortable than his apartment on Devon—here, they didn't have bugs.

Muley told Lana he didn't live on Devon anymore; he lived on California. Lana said, "Same difference," did he want to stay over? It would be a slumber party with kissing. She had many different ChapSticks and they could try different flavors to see what they liked. Muley stood suddenly, nervously, said no, his mother was expecting him home. Okay, Lana said, but she wanted to make sure Muley knew that her father wasn't coming home at all this week, so if he wanted to come over, any night was fine; he could let himself in with his knife. They could kiss or go ice skating or just sit and do homework and watch musicals (they subscribed to YOUR-TV, she said proudly). She said it would be nice to have a friend in the neighborhood. That was the downside of having dropped out of Boone Elementary and transferred to the Baker Demonstration School: You didn't get to meet too many people who weren't from either the Gold Coast or the suburbs. Muley said thanks, that would be nice if he wasn't too busy. Lana asked if they could kiss a bit more before he left—the fact that Muley was black was no longer disturbing; now it made her feel safer in case any black hit man wanted to break in and murder her. Muley wasn't sure if he should say yes or no—he had liked the idea of being kissed more than the kiss itself, but he didn't want to be rude. He said okay, they could kiss awhile. When they were through, Lana asked him if she was as good a kisser as Jill Wasserstrom. Muley said nothing and Lana said that was all right, he didn't have to answer. Then Lana asked if it was really true, what Jill had told her that one time, that she had given him a hickey after PE. Muley said he was sorry, but now he really had to go.

His lips still moist from the last kiss, Muley walked down the front steps of the Rovner house and headed south toward North Shore. One week earlier, he had filmed this street, filmed each house on each side of it, filmed every street-lamp, every lawn, every inch of sidewalk, every inch of Astroturf. With each film he had thought he had to do something more ambitious, more creative, more impressive—not only for Jill but also for himself. But now he was wondering if there wasn't a simpler way to make a film: with houses instead of castles, with just a few characters instead of thousands, with people instead of animals and cartoons. Well, he thought as he turned east on North Shore, bound for Angel Guardian to retrieve his camera, there would have to be at least a few cartoon characters; making a movie would hardly seem as fun without them.

At the moment that Muley Wills began walking east on North Shore and Lana Rovner was systematically turning on every light in the house to make sure no burglars or hit men were hiding inside, Jill Wasserstrom had just exited Café Hanegev, a new restaurant on California and Devon, which was the only food establishment in all of West Rogers Park open past eleven on weekdays. The Greek fruit and vegetable markets and the Korean restaurants, Kosher Karry and Gigio's Pizzeria, Levinson's and Gitel's bakeries, the Hashalom, Moti Mahal, even Dunkin' Donuts and the 7-Eleven, were all dark now; a good four inches of clean, white snow had accumulated in front of their doorsteps. Jill was unsure if the shawarma that she had ordered and paid for while Muley had been in Lana's house was the healthiest thing for a dog, but the animal consumed it greedily. She liked this dog, had always liked animals; in her younger, more idealistic years, when she had cared more about protecting endangered species than fighting for human rights, she had imagined herself working for Greenpeace, steering the *Rainbow Warrior* between whaling ships and innocent humpbacks. And there was something about this dog—which she had already named Fidel—that made her feel a great deal more affection for Muley than she had since early 1980.

Shortly after her mother died, Jill had asked her father if the family could get a dog. Charlie Wasserstrom, his brow furrowed, his nervous, guilty smile on his face, told her they had two choices; either they could get a dog or go to Disney World on a family vacation, one they had originally planned to take with Becky. Jill said she didn't need much time to think about that; she wanted the dog. Charlie came back after work the next day with three plane tickets to Orlando, and when Jill protested, he said the tickets were nonrefundable and he guessed he'd misunderstood her and he was sorry. He told Jill that they'd discuss "the dog question" after they got back from Florida, but Charlie never brought it up again, and whenever Jill did, he looked so worried and depressed that Jill eventually stopped mentioning it.

In a way, Jill hoped that her meeting with Muley that night had been accidental, that he had had no intention of bringing her the dog. That would have made Muley's act seem so much more like destiny, something in which Jill was just beginning to believe—that on the day her father had betrayed her for the second time, Muley had emerged out of nowhere, through some act of fate, to compensate. But in neither scenario—intentional or accidental—could Jill imagine that she was not supposed to be with Muley Scott Wills forever and ever. Or at least until they graduated from high school. Or at least for a little while.

It may have been morning in America, but on the northwest side of Chicago, it was just a few seconds before midnight, and there was a true Chicago blizzard outside now, the kind that closed schools and destroyed the careers of mayors who were unable to keep the streets clean. Air-raid sirens were sounding, and the snowplows and salt trucks were out. Yes, snow was general all over Chicago. The snow was falling down past the hot pink lights of West Rogers Park as Jill walked north on the west side of California, Fidel trotting enthusiastically at her side. That terrifying Hebrew prayer *Adon Olam* was swirling through Jill's head as she walked—*"And in the end, when all shall cease to be, he will remain the eternal king"*—but this time she remembered the rest of it: *"And my soul shall remain with my body. Hashem is with me and I am not afraid."* Jill could now see Muley, who was already on the other side of the street, heading east on North Shore, bound for the very edge of West Rogers Park to retrieve his camera. But Muley was walking fast now on the slippery sidewalk and Jill would have to cross California quickly if she wanted to catch him.

Glossary of Selected Terms

Adon Olam. A Hebrew prayer. Literal meaning: "Master of the world."

Aerosmith. American rock band fronted by Steven Tyler.

aleph. First letter in the Hebrew alphabet; also, first grade in Hebrew school.

Alinsky, Saul. Chicago-based grassroots organizer.

Allen, Woody. Noted Jewish filmmaker and comedian.

American Gigolo. 1980 film starring Richard Gere.

Amin, Idi. Former Ugandan dictator.

Anderson, John B. Former congressman and 1980 independent candidate for U.S. presidency.

Annie. Broadway musical based on the *Little Orphan Annie* comic strip.

Arsenic and Old Lace. Creaky farce, written by Joseph Kesselring.

Astroturf. A form of synthetic grass popular on front porches of Chicago houses in the 1970s.

Avanti. Sporty automobile manufactured by Studebaker.

Avraham Aveenoo. Abraham our father (Ladino).

Babashoff, Shirley. U.S. Olympic swimmer.

Babbitt. A novel by Sinclair Lewis.

babka. A particularly tasty Jewish coffee cake.

Backstrom, Ralph. Former player for the Chicago Blackhawks.

"Bad, Bad Leroy Brown." Jim Croce song played by numerous Bar Mitzvah bands.

Baryshnikov, Mikhail. Latvian-born dancer, choreographer, and sort-of actor.

Behind the Green Door. Popular 1972 X-rated feature film, starring Marilyn Chambers.

beth. Second letter in the Hebrew alphabet; also, second grade in Hebrew School.

Belafonte, Harry. New York–born singer, actor, and social activist.

Benny, Jack. Waukegan-born comedian and radio pioneer.

Bilandic, Michael. Fortieth mayor of Chicago (1976–1979).

bima. Pulpit (Hebrew).

Blues Brothers, The. 1980 movie starring John Belushi and Dan Aykroyd, filmed largely in Chicago.

Boston. Rock group fronted by MIT graduate Tom Scholz.

boychik. Endearment for a young boy (Yiddish).

bracha. Prayer (Hebrew).

bro. A term of friendship (contraction of "brother").

bubkis. Nothing (informal).

Byrne, Jane M. First female mayor of Chicago (1979–1983).

Bye Bye Birdie. A 1960 Broadway musical and rock 'n' roll spoof.

Canadian Club. A whiskey popular among older Jewish men.

Capone, Al. Legendary Chicago mobster and underworld figure.

Captain Whammo. A Chicago disk jockey popular in the 1970s, presumably a pseudonym.

Carter, Jimmy. Thirty-ninth president of the United States.

Cauthen, Steve. A youthful jockey, circa 1970s.

challah. A Jewish white bread.

Chanukah. Eight-day Jewish celebration. Also known as "Feast of Lights."

Charles, Ray. Pianist and R & B performer of such songs as "Hit the Road Jack" and "Georgia on My Mind."

Cheap Trick. Rockford, Illinois–bred rock band.

Chef Boyardee. Popular producer of canned Italian food products.

champagne snowball. A partner-switching dance involving smooching. Popular at Bar and Bat Mitzvahs.

China Syndrome, The. Prophetic 1979 film about a nuclear accident, starring Jack Lemmon and Jane Fonda.

Chee•tos. Cheese-flavored snack product.

chametz. Food not kosher for Passover.

Chronicles of Narnia, The. Series of fantasy novels written by C. S. Lewis and layered with Christian symbolism.

Clash, The. Influential punk rock band, aka "the only band that matters."

Clancy Brothers. Irish musical group.

Clapton, Eric. Famous rock 'n' roll guitarist for the Yardbirds and Cream, who later, inexplicably, became a popular adult contemporary music performer.

cockblock. An attempt to prevent another from pursuing sexual congress with someone (vulgar).

Conrad, Joseph. Polish-born author of *Heart of Darkness* and *Lord Jim.*

Commoner, Barry. Presidential candidate in 1980 running on the Citizens' Party ticket.

Comaneci, Nadia. Romanian gold-medal–winning gymnast.

Cournoyer, Yvan. Montreal Canadiens' captain nicknamed "The Roadrunner."

cracker. Disparaging term for a white person.

Crosby, David. High-voiced, mustached singer for the Byrds and Crosby, Stills, Nash, and Young.

Cruising. Controversial film starring Al Pacino.

dalet. Fourth letter in the Hebrew alphabet; also, fourth grade in Hebrew school.

Daley, Richard J. Thirty-ninth mayor of Chicago (1955–1976).

Davis, Angela. Noted left-wing political activist.

Davy Jones's Locker. A grave at the bottom of the ocean.

Dawson, William L. Black congressman and political power broker.

Dayan, Moshe. Former Israeli defense minister.

delco. Jewish jam-filled pastry.

Deep Purple. Rock band founded in 1968 and led, at first, by guitarist Ritchie Blackmore.

Denver, John. Colorado pop singer.

Derek, Bo. Star of the film *10* and popularizer of cornrow hairstyle.

Diamond, Neil. Pop singer and star of the 1980 film *The Jazz Singer.*

Dire Straits. British rock band led by guitarist/songwriter Mark Knopfler.

Disco Sucks. Late-1970s slogan popularized by Chicago deejay Steve Dahl during "Disco Demolition Night" at Comiskey Park.

do bongs. Popular expression meaning "Enjoy marijuana while using paraphernalia."

dreck. Yiddish epithet, meaning excrement.

dreidel. Spinning four-sided top featuring Hebrew letters.

Durante, Jimmy. Vaudeville performer best known for the song "Inka Dinka Doo."

Dylan, Bob. Seminal songwriter and rock musician who underwent a controversial Christian conversion in the late 1970s.

Einstein on the Beach. Experimental, minimalist 1976 opera by Philip Glass.

Electric Light Orchestra. British rock band fronted by Jeff Lynne.

Falstaff. A popular Chicago beer, advertised by legendary radio and TV announcer Harry Caray during Chicago White Sox baseball games.

faygeleh. Disparaging term for homosexual (Yiddish). Literal translation: little bird.

Fleming, Peggy. U.S. Olympic skater, winner of the 1968 gold medal.

Fluky's. Famous Chicago hot dog restaurant.

Foghat. Rock band founded in 1971.

Ford, Gerald. Thirty-eighth president of the United States.

Franklin, Aretha. Rhythm-and-blues singer, best known for "Respect."

French Postcards. 1979 film directed by Willard Huyck.

Funny Girl. Biopic of Fanny Brice, starring Barbra Streisand.

Funyuns. Onion-flavored snack product.

ganif. Thief (Yiddish).

gelt. Money (Yiddish).

Gilmore, Artis. Former center for the Chicago Bulls.

gimel. Third letter in the Hebrew alphabet; also, third grade in Hebrew school.

Gott im Himmel. An expression of woe. Literally: God in Heaven.

Gould, Elliot. 1970s actor and Semitic sex symbol, former husband of Barbra Streisand.

goyim. Non-Jewish people.

goyishe nachas. Disparaging phrase indicating activities in which only non-Jewish individuals would participate. Literally: pleasure for gentiles.

Gramsci, Antonio. Early-twentieth-century Italian Marxist revolutionary.

grogger. A noisemaker.

Guess Who, The. Canadian rock group eventually led by Burton Cummings, best known for "American Woman" and "No Sugar Tonight."

Haggadah. Book for Jewish holiday of Passover.

halvah. Sweet Middle Eastern confection made with sesame seeds.

Harold's Chicken Shack. Popular Chicago eatery.

haftorah. A portion of the Torah.

Haman. Persian persecutor of Jewish people.

hamantaschen. Jewish jam-filled pastry. Triangular shape meant to signify hat worn by HAMAN.

hamotzi. A prayer said over bread.

Hamm's. A cheap beer best loved for its cartoon bear mascot.

Hanrahan, Ed. Former Cook County State's Attorney.

Hampton, Fred. Former leader of the Black Panthers, slain in ambush by Chicago police.

Hashem. Literally "the name." Used to signify God outside of prayer context.

"Hatikvah." The Israeli national anthem.

"Hava Nagilah." Popular Hebrew song.

Havlicek, John. Former captain of the Boston Celtics basketball team.

Heart. Rock group led by Ann and Nancy Wilson.

Heatherton, Joey. Actress and spokesmodel.

heh. Fifth letter in the Hebrew alphabet; also, fifth grade in Hebrew school.

Hi-C. A fruit drink.

H.M.S. Pinafore. Comic operetta by Gilbert and Sullivan.

honkey. See CRACKER.

hot shit. A respected individual (colloquial).

Houphouët-Boigny, Félix. Former president of the Ivory Coast.

hummer. Oral sexual gratification.

hurl. To vomit (colloquial).

I Am a Fugitive from a Chain Gang. 1932 film starring Paul Muni.

I Am Curious (Yellow). Popular 1967 Scandinavian adult feature film.

In Search of Historic Jesus. 1979 film based on popular religious leader.

Isro. Popular long, kinky hairstyle, also known as a Jew-fro.

Jagger, Mick. Diminutive lead singer of the Rolling Stones.

Jaws. Popular 1978 scare flick about a killer shark, directed by Steven Spielberg.

Jesus freak. An overzealous individual.

Joel, Billy. Bronx-born singer-songwriter.

Kahlúa. Coffee-flavored alcoholic beverage.

"Kashmir." A long and bombastic song by Led Zeppelin.

Kaye, Danny. Jewish actor and song-and-dance man, star of such films as *Up in Arms* and *The Court Jester.*

Kedem. A brand of Kosher wine.

Kenosha. Wisconsin town located over the northern border of Illinois.

khazer. Pig (Yiddish).

khazerai. Pig swill (Yiddish).

Khomeini, Ayatollah Ruhollah. Iranian religious leader. Returned to Iran from exile in 1979.

kichel. A Jewish cookie coated with sugar granules.

kick-ass. An expression of enthusiasm (exclamation or adjective).

King Richard's Faire. Popular Chicago-area medieval event featuring mud-eaters, lords, lasses, and wenches fond of asking, "Would ye like some more lemonade?"

kippah. Jewish head covering. Plural: *kippot.* See also: YARMULKE.

Kliban, B. Popular cartoonist famous for drawings of cats.

Kodály, Zoltán. Hungarian composer and thinker.

koochkie. To tickle (Yiddish).

kopf. Head (Yiddish).

Koufax, Sandy. Jewish hero and star pitcher for the Brooklyn and L.A. Dodgers.

kugel. A Jewish delicacy.

Kunta Kinte. Slave character from book and TV miniseries *Roots.*

"La donna é mobile." Aria from Verdi's *Rigoletto.* Literal translation: Woman is fickle.

latke. Potato pancake.

Led Zeppelin. Influential rock band that had the good taste to disband after the death of drummer John Bonham; penned anthems for entire generations of pot smokers.

Lenorman, Gérard. French pop singer.

Loman, Willy. Beleaguered salesman in Arthur Miller's play *Death of a Salesman.*

Lynyrd Skynyrd. Southern rock band, three members of which died in a 1977 plane crash.

Mad Adventures of Rabbi Jacob, The. 1973 French comedy.

Maimonides, Moses. Medieval Jewish scholar.

Makarova, Natalia. Leningrad-born ballerina.

make whoopee. To have sexual congress.

Mangione, Chuck. Popular 1970s trumpeter.

Marshall Field's. Legendary Chicago department store.

M*A*S*H. Long-running American TV series.

McCarthy, Eugene. Former Minnesota senator and unsuccessful presidential candidate in 1968 and 1976.

Megillah. The book of Purim.

menorah. Candelabrum used for Chanukah.

mezuzah. Parchment inscribed with scriptural passages.

Mikita, Stan. Star center for the Chicago Blackhawks.

Mishnah. Book of Jewish law.

mishpacha. Family (Hebrew).

mitzvah. Good deed (Hebrew).

Molly Hatchet. Southern rock band.

Morison, Samuel Eliot. Historian and author of *The European Discovery of America* and the *Oxford History of the American People.*

"Mr. Bojangles." Song written for legendary song-and-dance man Bill Robinson.

Mulligan Stew. Short-lived early-1970s educational TV series.

Munchkin. A doughnut hole produced by Dunkin' Donuts. Also, a diminutive person.

mummeleh. Term of endearment (Yiddish). Literal translation: little calf.

Muzak. A largely discredited musical style based on souping up pop tunes with orchestral arrangements for offices and elevators.

Myron and Phil's. Popular Jewish restaurant in Lincolnwood, Illinois, famous for its relish tray.

Nerf. Company known for producing soft, spongy balls.

Ner Tamid. West Rogers Park synagogue. Literal translation: Eternal Light.

Nixon, Richard. Crooked thirty-seventh president of the United States.

Nkrumah, Kwame. Former president of Ghana.

Oneg Shabbat. Celebration following Sabbath service. Literal translation: Sabbath Delights.

on the rag. In a particularly bad mood, perhaps as a result of menstrual cramps (vulgar).

Ordinary People. A film about family dysfunction shot in Chicago's north suburbs and based on the novel by Judith Guest.

Oui **magazine.** Periodical featuring women in various states of undress.

Oy Gevalt! Oh God (Yiddish).

Oy vey. Woe is me (Yiddish).

payess. Sidelocks.

Payton, Walter. Legendary Chicago Bears running back.

Pettit, Lloyd. Former radio announcer for the Chicago Blackhawks.

Petrouchka. A tragic story about puppets who come to life, set to music by Igor Stravinsky.

Pink Floyd. Art rock band that released *The Wall* in 1979.

Pippin. 1972 Broadway musical starring Ben Vereen.

Poitier, Sidney. Noted film actor, star of *In the Heat of the Night* and *Guess Who's Coming to Dinner.*

Pryor, Richard. Revolutionary comedian and star of unfortunate feature films, such as *Silver Streak* and *Stir Crazy.*

Puck's Peculiar Pet Shop. Children's pop-up book written by Dean Walley, illustrated by Roz Schanzer.

Purim. Jewish holiday commemorating the Jewish people's escape from likely extermination in Persia.

putz. A foolish individual. Literal translation: penis.

"Quando El Rey Nimrod." Ladino song. Literally: "When the King Nimrod."

Rand, Ayn. Author and founder of Objectivist philosophy; influential among certain high school students and rock musicians.

Reagan, Ronald. Former governor of California and 1980 Republican candidate for president.

Richler, Mordecai. Canadian author best known for *The Apprenticeship of Duddy Kravitz.*

Rolaid. An antacid tablet.

Rosencrantz and Guildenstern Are Dead. 1966 play by Tom Stoppard.

Roth, Philip. New Jersey–born Jewish author of *Portnoy's Complaint* and *Goodbye, Columbus.* Also, noted chronicler of masturbation.

"Runaround Sue." 1961 song by Dion and the Belmonts.

Rush. Canadian rock trio.

ruggelach. Jewish pastry.

sale putain. Dirty whore (disparaging French term).

schlumpy. Sloppy (adjective).

schmuck. See PUTZ.

schnook. See SCHMUCK.

schwarzers. Term for blacks, often used disparagingly (Yiddish). (Adjective: *schwarz.*)

Seeger, Pete. Folk singer and political activist.

Shehecheyanu. Prayer offered for new or unusual experiences.

Shabbos. The Sabbath.

shayna punim. What a sweet face.

shiksa. Disparaging term for a non-Jewish female.

shiva. A period of mourning.

Shubert, The. A downtown Chicago legitimate theater.

shul. Synagogue.

Silverstein, Shel. Popular playwright and children's book author.

Simchas Torah. Jewish holiday celebrating the annual completion of the Torah.

Simon, Yves. See GÉRARD LENORMAN.

Singer, Bill. Anti-Machine candidate for mayor defeated by Richard J. Daley in 1974.

Singer, Isaac Bashevis. Jewish author and winner of the 1978 Nobel Prize for literature.

"Slow Ride." Popular rock anthem by Foghat.

Smith, Jaclyn. Star of TV show *Charlie's Angels.*

Smith, Rex. Teen heartthrob and co-host of TV show *Solid Gold.*

Sneetch. An imaginary creature invented by children's author Dr. Seuss.

Song of the South. Controversial Walt Disney cartoon based on the stories of Joel Chandler Harris.

Solti, Sir Georg. Former conductor of the Chicago Symphony Orchestra.

Space Invaders. Early video game.

Spann, Pervis. Popular Chicago deejay, known as "the all-day, all-night bluesman."

"Squeeze Box." Suggestive 1975 song by The Who.

Steak Diane. A well-seasoned beefsteak.

stick it. To perform an activity infallibly; alternately, an epithet meaning "go away."

Streep, Meryl. American actress educated at Vassar College; star of such films as *Kramer vs. Kramer* and *The Deer Hunter.*

Styx. A river in Hell. Also, an appropriately named Chicago rock band, famous for the songs "Come Sail Away" and "Babe."

sukkah. A tent used in Sukkos celebrations (see below).

Sukkos. Jewish holiday. Also called "Feast of Tabernacles."

"Sunrise, Sunset." Lugubrious song from the musical *Fiddler on the Roof.*

supercalifragilisticexpialidocious. Excellent (adjective). Invented in film *Mary Poppins.*

tallis. Jewish prayer shawl.

Talmud. Encyclopedia of Jewish law and tradition.

Tanakh. The Hebrew Bible.

Tashlich. First day of Rosh Hashanah. Literal meaning: to cast away.

Taxi Driver. Martin Scorsese film about the titular character, played by

Robert De Niro; popularized the phrase "You talkin' to me?" and inspired a song by THE CLASH.

tefillin. Phylacteries.

Thousand Island. A pink, mayonnaise-based salad dressing.

Tiegs, Cheryl. Noted American fashion and poster model whose image adorned many a teen's bedroom in the 1970s and '80s.

tinkle. Disparaging term for blacks (Yiddish).

tosser. One who masturbates excessively (chiefly Brit. usage).

traif. Non-kosher food.

Trans-Am. A sporty Pontiac automobile.

tsitsis. Tassels located at the ends of a *TALLIS*.

tsuris. Troubles (Yiddish).

Tull, Jethro. Scottish folk-rock band, led by the flute-playing Ian Anderson.

tzedakah. Charity (Hebrew).

Vance, Cyrus. Secretary of state during the first years of the Carter administration.

Waters, Muddy. Legendary blues performer, born McKinley Morganfield.

Waukegan Night. An evening spent drinking beverages in an automobile.

Way We Were, The. Popular 1973 cinematic weepie starring Barbra Streisand and Robert Redford.

WBBM-AM. Chicago news radio station. Affiliate of CBS.

What's Happening. American TV series, which briefly popularized the greeting "Hey HEY Hey!"

Which. An exclamation calling attention to a masturbatory phrase (limited usage, contracted from "Which is what I was doing last night").

Who, The. Leading U.K. rock foursome fronted by ISRO-sporting singer Roger Daltrey.

Wings. Light rock band fronted by former Beatle Paul McCartney.

Wisconsin Dells. Cheesy vacation spot known for Tommy Bartlett's water show.

Wolfy's. See FLUKY'S.

Wood, Ron. Rolling Stones guitarist. Replacement for previous guitarist Mick Taylor.

Wrinkle in Time, A. Popular fantasy novel written by Madeleine L'Engle.

yarmulke. Jewish head covering.

yenta. A grandmother (Yiddish).

Yiddle Mit Ein Fiddle. Popular song and film starring Yiddish actress Molly Picon. Literally: Yiddle with a fiddle.

Yom Kippur. The Day of Atonement.

zaftig. Plump (Yiddish).

Zilahy, Lajos. Hungarian author of *Two Prisoners* and *The Deserter.*

Acknowledgments

Thanks to: Beate Sissenich, for enduring and, perhaps, enjoying countless readings of early drafts; Marly Rusoff, a rare agent who says what she means and means what she says; Cindy Spiegel, for her uncanny ability to make the editorial process pain-free; the Langer family, for obvious reasons; Paul Creamer, for a quarter-century of friendship; Jerome Kramer, for early encouragement, editorial guidance, and beverage consultation; Christopher Cartmill, Jane Gennaro, and Barbara Hammond, for participating in the first private reading of this book; Elizabeth Haas, for astounding knowledge of 1970s rock anthems; Señor Kazoo, for providing entertainment and relaxation during the author's most tortured hours; Mark Gleason, for a fortuitous introduction; and many thanks, for a wide variety of reasons, to Joan Afton, Preston Browning, Bess and Norman Budow, the *Chicago Reader,* Pat Clinton, Merrill Feitell, Alexander Fest, John Fink, Jessica Firger, Jennifer Gilmore, Doris Ingrosso, Belinda Lanks, Lali Morris, the National Arts Journalism Program, the Sissenich family, Colin Smith, Kate Steffes, Elaine Szewczyk, Amy Topel, Chip Wadsworth, Anna Weinberg, Eric Wetzel, and the staff of *Book* magazine; and finally, a special word of acknowledgment for Norman Herstein, who, during his life and during the writing of this book, stood out as an example of integrity, courage, and perseverance.